HANS CHRISTIAN ANDERSEN

CLASSIC FAIRY TALES

HANS CHRISTIAN ANDERSEN

CLASSIC FAIRY TALES

With Illustrations by
Dugald Stewart Walker and Hans Tegner

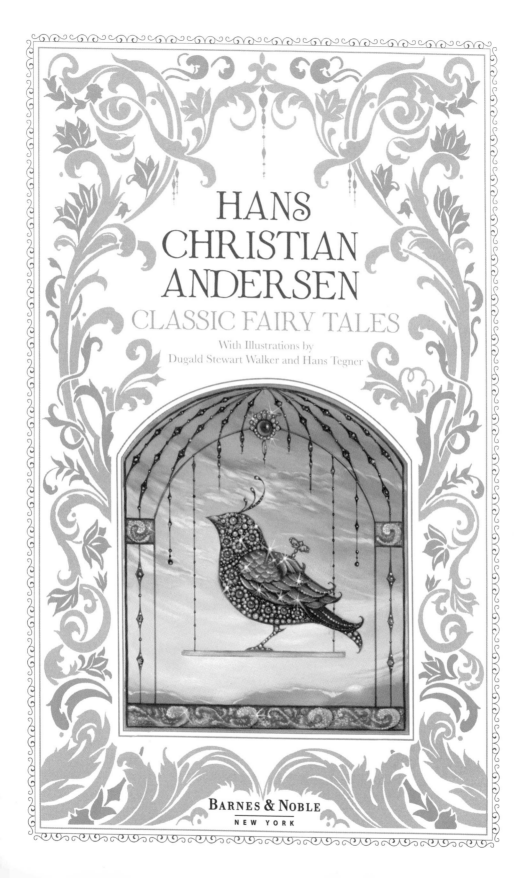

BARNES & NOBLE
NEW YORK

The stories in this edition are taken from Heinrich Oskar Sommer's translation
Stories & Fairy Tales by Hans Christian Andersen (London: George Allen, 1897).

This 2015 edition printed for Barnes & Noble by Sterling Publishing Co., Inc.

ISBN 978-1-4351-5812-2

Barnes & Noble, Inc.
122 Fifth Avenue
New York, NY 10011

Manufactured in China

2 4 6 8 10 9 7 5 3

www.sterlingpublishing.com

Cover art by Laurel Long
Cover design by Patrice Kaplan
Endpapers: *The Wild Swans* (watercolor) by Otto Svend/photo by Alfredo Dagli Orti/
The Art Archive at Art Resource, NY

Contents

Illustrations

BLACK-AND-WHITE ILLUSTRATIONS

COLOR PLATES

The Emperor's New Clothes

Many, many years ago lived an emperor, who thought so much of new clothes that he spent all his money in order to obtain them; his only ambition was to be always well dressed. He did not care for his soldiers, and the theater did not amuse him; the only thing, in fact, he thought anything of was to drive out and show a new suit of clothes. He had a coat for every hour of the day; and as one would say of a king "He is in his cabinet," so one could say of him, "The emperor is in his dressing-room."

The great city where he resided was very gay; every day many strangers from all parts of the globe arrived. One day two swindlers came to this city; they made people believe that they were weavers, and declared they could manufacture the finest cloth to be imagined. Their colors and patterns, they said, were not only exceptionally beautiful, but the clothes made of their material possessed the wonderful quality of being invisible to any man who was unfit for his office or unpardonably stupid.

"That must be wonderful cloth," thought the emperor. "If I were to be dressed in a suit made of this cloth I should be able to find out which men in my empire were unfit for their places, and I could distinguish the clever from the stupid. I must have this cloth woven for me without delay." And he gave a large sum of money to the swindlers, in advance, that they should set to work without any loss of time. They set up two looms, and pretended to be very hard at work, but they did nothing whatever on the looms. They asked for the finest silk and the most precious gold-cloth; all they got they did away with, and worked at the empty looms till late at night.

"I should very much like to know how they are getting on with the cloth," thought the emperor. But he felt rather uneasy when he remembered that he who was not fit for his office could not see it. Personally, he was of opinion that he had nothing to fear, yet he thought it advisable to send somebody else first to see how matters stood. Everybody in the town knew what a remarkable quality the stuff possessed, and all were anxious to see how bad or stupid their neighbors were.

"I shall send my honest old minister to the weavers," thought the emperor. "He can judge best how the stuff looks, for he is intelligent, and nobody understands his office better than he."

They asked for the finest silk and the most precious gold-cloth.

The good old minister went into the room where the swindlers sat before the empty looms. "Heaven preserve us!" he thought, and opened his eyes wide, "I cannot see anything at all," but he did not say so. Both swindlers requested him to come near, and asked him if he did not admire the exquisite pattern and the beautiful colors, pointing to the empty looms. The poor old minister tried his very best, but he could see nothing, for there was nothing to be seen. "Oh dear," he thought, "can I be so stupid? I should never have thought so, and nobody must know it! Is it possible that I am not fit for my office? No, no, I cannot say that I was unable to see the cloth."

"Now, have you got nothing to say?" said one of the swindlers, while he pretended to be busily weaving.

"Oh, it is very pretty, exceedingly beautiful," replied the old minister looking through his glasses. "What a beautiful pattern, what brilliant colors! I shall tell the emperor that I like the cloth very much."

"We are pleased to hear that," said the two weavers, and described to him the colors and explained the curious pattern. The old minister listened attentively, that he might relate to the emperor what they said; and so he did.

Now the swindlers asked for more money, silk and gold-cloth, which they required for weaving. They kept everything for themselves, and not a thread came near the loom, but they continued, as hitherto, to work at the empty looms.

Soon afterwards the emperor sent another honest courtier to the weavers to see how they were getting on, and if the cloth was nearly finished. Like the old minister, he looked and looked but could see nothing, as there was nothing to be seen.

"Is it not a beautiful piece of cloth?" asked the two swindlers, showing and explaining the magnificent pattern, which, however, did not exist.

"I am not stupid," said the man, "it is therefore my good appointment for which I am not fit. It is very strange, but I must not let any one know it"; and he praised the cloth, which he did not see, and expressed his joy at the beautiful colors and the fine pattern. "It is very excellent," he said to the emperor.

Everybody in the whole town talked about the precious cloth. At last the emperor wished to see it himself, while it was still on the loom. With a number of courtiers, including the two who had already been there, he went to the two clever swindlers, who now worked as hard as they could, but without using any thread.

"Is it not magnificent?" said the two old statesmen who had been there before. "Your Majesty must admire the colors and the pattern." And then they pointed to the empty looms, for they imagined the others could see the cloth.

"What is this?" thought the emperor, "I do not see anything at all. That is terrible! Am I stupid? Am I unfit to be emperor? That would indeed be the most dreadful thing that could happen to me."

"Really," he said, turning to the weavers, "your cloth has our most gracious approval"; and nodding contentedly he looked at the empty loom, for he did not like to say that he saw nothing. All his attendants, who were with him, looked and looked, and although they could not see anything more than the others, they said, like the emperor, "It is very beautiful." And all advised him to wear the new magnificent clothes at a great procession which was soon to take place. "It is magnificent, beautiful, excellent," one heard them say; everybody seemed to be delighted, and the emperor appointed the two swindlers "Imperial Court weavers."

The whole night previous to the day on which the procession was to take place the swindlers pretended to work, and burned more than sixteen candles. People should see that they were busy to finish the emperor's new suit. They pretended to take the cloth from the loom, and worked about in the air with big scissors, and sewed with needles without thread, and said at last: "The emperor's new suit is ready now."

The emperor and all his barons then came to the hall; the swindlers held their arms up as if they held something in their hands and said: "These are the trousers!" "This is the coat!" and "Here is the cloak!" and so on. "They are all as light as a cobweb, and one must feel as if one had nothing at all upon the body; but that is just the beauty of them."

"Indeed!" said all the courtiers; but they could not see anything, for there was nothing to be seen.

"The emperor's new suit is ready now."

"Does it please your Majesty now to graciously undress," said the swindlers, "that we may assist your Majesty in putting on the new suit before the large looking-glass?"

The emperor undressed, and the swindlers pretended to put the new suit upon him, one piece after another; and the emperor looked at himself in the glass from every side.

"How well they look! How well they fit!" said all. "What a beautiful pattern! What fine colors! That is a magnificent suit of clothes!"

The master of the ceremonies announced that the bearers of the canopy, which was to be carried in the procession, were ready.

"I am ready," said the emperor. "Does not my suit fit me marvelously?" Then he turned once more to the looking-glass, that people should think he admired his garments.

The chamberlains, who were to carry the train, stretched their hands to the ground as if they lifted up a train, and pretended to hold something in their hands; they did not like people to know that they could not see anything.

The emperor marched in the procession under the beautiful canopy, and all who saw him in the street and out of the windows exclaimed: "Indeed, the emperor's new clothes are incomparable! What a long train he has! How well it fits him!" Nobody wished to let others know that he saw nothing, for then he would have been unfit for his office or too stupid. Never an emperor's clothes were more admired.

"But he has nothing on at all," said a little child at last. "Good heavens! listen to the voice of an innocent child," said the father, and one whispered to the other what the child had said. "But he has nothing on at all," cried at last the whole people. That made a deep impression upon the emperor, for it seemed to him that they were right, but he thought to himself, "Now I must bear up to the end." And the chamberlains walked with still greater dignity, as if they carried the train which did not exist.

The Rose-Elf

In the midst of a garden grew a rose-tree; upon it were many, many roses; in one of them, the most beautiful of all, lived an elf. He was so very small that no human eye could perceive him. Behind every petal of the rose he had a bedroom. No child could have been more beautifully formed than he was; he had wings that reached from his shoulders down to his feet. All his rooms were so sweet and fragrant, the walls were so bright and beautiful, for they consisted of the pink rose-petals.

All day long the elf enjoyed himself in the warm sunshine, flying from flower to flower, and dancing on the wings of the fluttering butterfly. One day he measured how many steps he would have to take in order to pass through all the roads and paths which were on a single leaf of the lime-tree. These were what we call the veins of the leaf; to him they seemed to be endless roads. Before he had finished the sun set; he had begun his task too late. It became very cold, dew fell and the wind was blowing; at this time he would have been best at home. He hastened as much as he could, but his rose was closed up, he could not enter, and not a single rose was open. The poor little elf was very frightened. He had never before been out of doors at night; as he had always sweetly slumbered behind the warm rose-petals, this would mean certain death to him!

The elf knew that at the other end of the garden stood a summer-house, covered all over with beautiful honeysuckle; the blossoms looked like large painted horns; in one of them, he thought, he might enter and sleep until the next morning. Thither he flew.

But hush! Two people were sitting in the summer-house: a handsome young man and a beautiful girl. They sat side by side and wished that they need never part. They loved one another so much—much more indeed than the best child would love his father or mother.

"Alas! we must part," said the young man. "Your brother dislikes me, and that is why he sends me on an errand so far away over mountains and seas. Farewell, my own dear love, for that you will always be to me."

Then they kissed each other, and the girl cried and gave him a rose. But before she gave it to him she so ardently pressed it to her lips that the flower opened.

Now the little elf flew into it and rested his head against the fine fragrant walls; there he could hear very well how they bade farewell to each other! He felt that the young man placed the rose on his breast. Oh, how his heart was beating! The little elf could not fall asleep, it throbbed so much.

The rose did not long remain undisturbed on his breast. The young man, while walking alone through the dark forest, took it out, and kissed it so often and so passionately that the little elf was almost crushed. He could feel through the leaf how hot the young man's lips were; and the rose had opened its petals as if the strongest midday sun were shining upon it.

Then came another man, sullen and wicked; he was the malicious brother of the beautiful girl. He drew out a dagger, and while the other fondly kissed the rose, stabbed him to death; then he cut off the head from the body, and buried both in the soft ground under a lime-tree.

"Now he's gone and forgotten," thought the murderer; "he will never return again. He was to set out on a long journey, over mountains and across the sea; on such an expedition a man might easily lose his life, and he has lost it. He will never come back, and my sister dare not ask me what has become of him."

Thus thinking, he scraped dry leaves together with his foot, heaped them on the soft mold, and went home in the darkness of the night. But he was not alone, as he imagined, for the little elf was with him. He had seated himself in a dry, rolled-up leaf of the lime-tree, which had fallen on the wicked man's hair while he was digging the grave. He had put his hat on now; it was very dark inside the hat, and the elf was trembling with horror and indignation at the evil deed.

In the dawn of the morning the murderer reached home; he took off his hat, and entered his sister's bedroom. There the beautiful girl, with rosy cheeks, was sleeping and dreaming of him whom she loved so dearly, and whom she supposed now to travel over mountains and across the sea.

The unnatural brother bent over the girl, and laughed hideously, as only evil demons can laugh. The dry leaf dropped out of his hair on her counterpane, but he did not notice it, and went out of the room to have a little sleep in the early morning hours. The elf left his resting-place and slipped into the ear of the sleeping girl, and told her, as in a dream, the horrible deed; he described the spot where her lover was stabbed and where his body was interred; he told her of the blooming lime-tree standing close by, and said: "That you should not think all I told you is only a dream, you will find on your bed on awaking a dry leaf." And when she awoke she really found it. Then she cried bitterly. The window was open all day long; the little elf might easily have returned to the roses and to the other flowers in the garden, but he had not the heart to leave the unfortunate girl.

On the window-sill stood a little bunch of monthly roses in a flower-pot; in one of its blooms the elf sat down and looked at the poor girl. Her brother came several times into the room, and in spite of his crime seemed quite cheerful, and she had not the courage to say a word about her grief.

No sooner had the night come than she stole out of the house and went into the wood, to the spot where the lime-tree stood; she removed the dry leaves from the ground, turned the earth up and found her murdered sweetheart. And she wept bitterly. She prayed God that she might also die.

She would have gladly taken the body home with her, but that was impossible. So she took up the pale-faced head with the closed eyes, kissed the cold lips and shook the earth out of the beautiful curls. "I will at least keep this," she said. When she had replaced the mold and the dry leaves on the body, she took the head and a little bough of a jasmine-bush growing near the spot where the body was buried, and returned home. Upon reaching her room she took the largest flower-pot she could find, put the head into it, covered it over with mold, and planted therein the jasmine-bough.

"Farewell, farewell," whispered the little elf, being unable to witness any longer her grief and pain. He then returned to his rose in the garden; but the rose was faded, only a few withered petals were still clinging to the green stalk. "Oh, how soon all that is beautiful and good vanishes," sighed the little elf.

At last he found a new rose and made it his home; under the shelter of its tender and fragrant petals he could abide in safety. Every morning he flew to the window of the poor girl, and every morning he found her crying by the flower-pot. Her tears fell upon the jasmine-bough, and day by day, in the same measure as she grew paler, the bough became fresher and greener; one shoot after another sprang up; many little white buds burst forth, and she kissed them. The heartless brother scolded her and asked her if she had lost her senses; for he did not like to see her crying over the flower-pot, and he could not make out why she did it. He had no idea whose closed eyes, whose red lips were decaying in the flower-pot.

One day the little rose-elf found her slumbering and resting with her head on the flower-pot. He slipped again into her ear, and told her of the evening in the summer-house, of the sweet smell of the rose, and of the love of rose-elves. She dreamed so sweetly, and with her dream her life passed away; she died a calm and peaceful death. She had gone to Heaven to him whom she loved.

And the jasmine unfolded its buds into large white flowers, and filled the air with its peculiarly sweet fragrance, it could not otherwise give vent to its grief for the dead girl.

The wicked brother took the beautiful jasmine bush as his inheritance, carried it into his bedroom and placed it close by his bed; for it was delightful to look at, and its fragrance was very pleasant. The little rose-elf followed; he flew from flower to flower—for in each of them lived a little elf—and told them of the murdered young man whose head was decaying beneath the mold, and of the wicked brother and the poor sister.

"We know all about it," replied the little elves, "we know it, for have we not sprung forth from the eyes and lips of the dead man's face? We know," they repeated, nodding their heads in a strange manner.

The rose-elf could not understand why they remained so calm; he flew out to the bees, which were gathering honey, and told them the story of the wicked brother. The bees told their queen, and the queen ordered that they should all go on the next morning to kill the murderer. But when it was night—the first night after his sister's death—while the brother was sleeping close by the fragrant jasmine-bush in his bed, all its flowers opened and all the little invisible elves came out, armed with venomous spears, and seated themselves in his ears and told him terrible dreams; then they flew on to his lips and stabbed his tongue with their poisonous weapons. "Now we have avenged the dead," they said, and returned to their white flowers.

When, on the next morning, the window of the bedroom was opened, the rose-elf and the whole swarm of the bees with their queen entered to carry out their revenge. But he was already dead. People standing around the bed, said: "The smell of the jasmine has killed him."

The rose-elf understood the revenge of the flowers and told the queen of the bees about it, who with her whole swarm was humming round the flower-pot. The bees could not be driven away from it, and when at last a man took up the pot a bee stung him in the hand, so that he dropped it, and it broke to pieces. Then all saw the bleached skull and understood that the dead man in the bed was a murderer.

The queen of the bees hummed and sang of the revenge of the flowers and of the rose-elf, and said that behind the smallest leaf dwells one who can disclose evil deeds and revenge them.

The Storks

On the roof of the last house in a little village was a stork's nest; a mother-stork sat in it, and four young ones were stretching forth their little heads with the pointed black beaks, which had not yet turned red like those of the old birds. At a little distance the father-stork stood upright and almost immovable on the ridge of the roof; he had drawn up one leg, in order not to be quite idle, while he was watching over his nest like a sentry. He stood so still that one might have thought he was carved in wood. "Surely, it must look very important, that my wife has a sentry before her nest," he thought. "Nobody knows that I am her husband. People will think that I am commanded to stand here. That looks so distinguished." And he continued to stand on one leg.

A crowd of children were playing below in the street; no sooner had they noticed the storks than one of the pluckiest boys began to sing an old ditty to tease them; soon all his playmates joined in; but they only repeated what he could remember of it:

"Fly away, stork, fly away!
Stand not on one leg all day,
While your dear wife in the nest
Gently rocks her babes to rest.

"The first little stork they will hang,
The second will fry by the fire,
The third will be shot with a bang.
The fourth will be roast for the squire."

On the roof of the last house in a little village was a stork's nest.

"Do you hear what those boys are singing?" said the young storks, "they say we shall be hanged and roasted."

"Never mind what they say," replied the mother-stork; "if you do not listen to them, they can do you no harm."

The boys went on singing, and pointed at the storks with their fingers; only one of them, named Peter, said that it was wrong of them to tease the birds, and did not join them. The mother-stork comforted her children. "You must not pay attention to them; look at your father, how quietly he stands there on one leg!"

"Oh, we are so frightened," said the young ones, and then they hid their heads in the nest.

On the following day, when the children had come out to play and saw the storks, they sang again the song:

"The third will be shot with a bang.
The fourth will be roast for the squire."

"Shall we really be hanged and roasted?" asked the young storks.

"Certainly not," replied the mother, "you will learn how to fly; I shall teach you myself. Then we shall fly into the meadows and go to see the frogs, who will bow to us in the water and cry: 'Croak, croak'; and then we shall eat them up. That will be delightful."

"And then?" asked the young ones.

"Then," continued the mother-stork, "all the storks of this country will come together, and the great autumn maneuver will be gone through; every stork must be able to fly well, for that is of great importance. All those who cannot fly the general kills with his beak. Therefore you must take great pains to learn it well, when the drilling begins."

"Why, then we shall be stabbed after all as the boys sing; listen, they are singing it again."

"Only listen to me, and not to them," said the mother-stork.

"After the great autumn maneuver we shall fly away from here to warmer countries, far away over mountains and woods. We shall fly to Egypt, where you shall see three-cornered stone houses, the pointed tops of which almost touch the clouds; people call them pyramids, and they are much older than a stork can imagine. There is a river in that country which rises every year over its banks, covering the whole land with mud. We shall walk about in the mud and eat frogs."

"Oh, how charming," cried the young ones.

"Yes, indeed, that country is very pleasant; we shall do nothing there but eat all day long; and while we shall be so comfortable there, they will not have a single leaf on the trees in this country, and it will be so cold that the clouds will freeze, and fall down on the ground in little white rags." She meant, of course, the snow, but she could not otherwise explain it.

"Will the naughty boys also freeze to pieces?" asked the young storks.

"No," answered the mother, "they will not freeze to pieces, but they will not be very far from it. They will have to stay all day long in-doors, in the gloomy room; whereas you will fly about in foreign lands, where the warm sun shines and many flowers are blooming."

After some time the young ones had grown so tall that they could stand upright in the nest and look about into the neighborhood; the father-stork returned every day with frogs and little snakes and all sorts of stork-dainties which he had picked up. Oh, it was so funny to see him perform tricks for their amusement; he used to place his head quite back on his tail and clatter with his beak as if it had been a rattle; and then he used to tell them stories about the marsh-land.

"Come along," the stork-mother said one day, "now you must learn to fly." The four young storks had to come out of the nest on to the ridge of the roof. At first they tottered about a good deal, and although they balanced themselves with their wings, they nearly fell down.

"You have only to look at me," said the mother. "You must hold your heads like this, and place your feet thus: one, two, one, two—that's right; that is what will enable you to get on in the world." Then she flew a short distance away from them, and the young ones made a little jump, but they fell down with a thud, for their bodies were still too heavy. "I do not wish to fly," said one of the young ones, and crept back into the nest; "I do not care to go to warm countries."

"Now you must learn to fly."

"Would you prefer to freeze to death here, when the winter comes; or shall the boys come to hang and roast you? I will call them."

"Oh no, no, dear mother," said the young stork, hopping out on the roof again to the others. On the third day they could already fly a little, and now they thought they would be able to soar in the air like their parents. They tried to do so, but they tumbled down, and had quickly to move their wings again. The boys in the street began to sing again:

"Fly away, stork, fly away,
Stand not on one leg all day."

"Shall we fly down and pick their eyes out?" asked the young storks.

"No," said the mother; "do not mind them. Only listen to me, that is far more important. One, two, three, now we turn to the right; one, two, three, to the left; now round the chimney-top. That was very good indeed! The last clap with the wings was so correctly and well done that I shall let you come to-morrow with me to the marshes. There you will see several respectable storks with their families; you must let them see that my children are the prettiest and best-behaved. You must proudly stride about; that will look well, and by this you will gain respect."

"But shall we not punish those wicked boys?" asked the young storks.

"Let them cry as much as they like; you will rise high into the clouds and fly away to the country of the pyramids while they are freezing, and have not a single green leaf nor a sweet apple."

"We shall take our revenge upon them," whispered the little ones, and went on practicing.

Of all the boys in the street none was more bent upon singing the song than the one who had first started it, and he was quite a mite and not more than six years old. The young storks thought he was more than a hundred years old, because he was so much taller than their father and mother, and what did they know about the age of children and grown-up people? They made up their minds to take their revenge upon this boy, because he was the first to sing the song and was never tired of going on with it. The young storks were very angry with him, and the older they became the less they would suffer it; at last the mother had to give them the promise that they should be revenged, but not until the day before their departure.

"We must first see how you will behave at the great maneuver. If you do badly, so that the general has to thrust his beak through you, the boys will be right, at least in a way. But let us see."

"You shall see," said the young ones, and took still greater pains; they practiced every day, and soon they could fly so well that it was a pleasure to see them.

Autumn came at last: all the storks began to assemble and to set out for the warm countries, to pass the winter. That was a great maneuver! They had to fly over woods and villages, only to see what they could do, for their journey was a very long one. They acquitted themselves so well that they passed the review excellently, and received frogs and snakes as a reward. That was the best certificate, and they could eat the frogs and the snakes, which was better still.

"Now we shall take our revenge," they said.

"Certainly," cried the mother-stork. "I have already thought of the best way. I know where the pond is in which all the little children are lying until the storks come and take them to their parents. The pretty little babies sleep there and dream so sweetly, much more sweetly than they will dream ever after. All the parents wish for such a little child, and the children wish for a brother or a sister. Now we shall go to the pond and fetch one for every child who has not sung that wicked song to tease the storks."

"But what shall we do to the bad boy who began to sing the song?"

"In the pond lies a little dead baby that has dreamed itself to death, that we will take to him; then he will cry, because we have brought him a dead little brother. But the good boy—I hope you have not forgotten him, who said that it was wrong to tease animals—we will bring him a brother as well as a sister. And as this boy's name was Peter, you shall all henceforth be called Peter."

And so it was done, and all the storks are called Peter to the present day.

"I know where the pond is in which all the little children are lying until the storks come and take them to their parents."

The Daisy

Now listen! In the country, close by the high road, stood a farmhouse; perhaps you have passed by and seen it yourself. There was a little flower garden with painted wooden pickets in front of it; close by was a ditch, on its fresh green bank grew a little daisy; the sun shined as warmly and brightly upon it as on the magnificent garden flowers, and therefore it thrived well. One morning it had quite opened, and its little snow-white petals stood round the yellow center, like the rays of the sun. It did not mind that nobody saw it in the grass, and that it was a poor despised flower; on the contrary, it was quite happy, and turned towards the sun, looking upward and listening to the song of the lark high up in the air.

The little daisy was as happy as if the day had been a great holiday, but it was only Monday. All the children were at school, and while they were sitting on the forms and learning their lessons, it sat on its thin green stalk and learned from the sun and from its surroundings how kind God is, and it rejoiced that the song of the little lark expressed so sweetly and distinctly its own feelings. With a sort of reverence the daisy looked up to the bird that could fly and sing, but it did not feel envious. "I can see and hear," it thought; "the sun shines upon me, and the forest kisses me. How rich I am!"

In the garden close by grew many large and magnificent flowers, and, strange to say, the less fragrance they had the haughtier and prouder they were. The peonies puffed themselves up in order to be larger than the roses, but size is not everything! The tulips had the finest colors, and they knew it well, too, for they were standing bolt upright like candles, that one might see them the better. In their pride they did not see the little daisy, which looked over to them and thought, "How rich and beautiful they are! I am sure the pretty bird will fly down and call upon them. Thank God, that I stand so near and can at least see all the splendor." And while the daisy was still thinking, the lark came flying down, crying "Tweet," but not to the peonies and tulips—no, into the grass to the poor daisy. Its joy was so great that it did not know what to think. The little bird hopped round it and sang, "How beautifully soft the grass is, and what a lovely little flower with its golden heart and silver dress is growing here." The yellow center in the daisy did indeed look like gold, while the little petals shined as brightly as silver.

How happy the daisy was! No one has the least idea. The bird kissed it with its beak, sang to it, and then rose again up to the blue sky. It was certainly more than a quarter of an hour before the daisy recovered its senses. Half ashamed, yet glad at heart, it looked over to the other flowers in the garden; surely they had witnessed its pleasure and the honor that had been done to it; they understood its joy. But the tulips stood more stiffly than ever, their faces were pointed and red, because they were vexed. The peonies were sulky; it was well that they could not speak, otherwise they would have given the daisy a good lecture. The little flower could very well see that they were ill at ease, and pitied them sincerely.

Shortly after this a girl came into the garden, with a large sharp knife. She went to the tulips and began cutting them off, one after another. "Ugh!" sighed the daisy, "that is terrible; now they are done for."

The girl carried the tulips away. The daisy was glad that it was outside, and only a small flower—it felt very grateful. At sunset it folded its petals, and fell asleep, and dreamed all night of the sun and the little bird.

On the following morning, when the flower once more stretched forth its tender petals, like little arms, towards the air and light, the daisy recognized the bird's voice, but what it sang sounded so sad. Indeed the poor bird had good reason to be sad, for it had been caught and put into a cage close by the open window. It sang of the happy days when it could merrily fly about, of fresh green corn in the fields, and of the time when it could soar almost up to the clouds. The poor lark was most unhappy as a prisoner in a cage. The little daisy would have liked so much to help it, but what could be done? Indeed, that was very difficult for such a small flower to find out. It entirely forgot how beautiful everything around it was, how warmly the sun was shining, and how splendidly white its own petals were. It could only think of the poor captive bird, for which it could do nothing. Then two little boys came out of the garden; one of them had a large sharp knife, like that with which the girl had cut the tulips. They came straight towards the little daisy, which could not understand what they wanted.

"Here is a fine piece of turf for the lark," said one of the boys, and began to cut out a square round the daisy, so that it remained in the center of the grass.

"Pluck the flower off," said the other boy, and the daisy trembled for fear, for to be pulled off meant death to it; and it wished so much to live, as it was to go with the square of turf into the poor captive lark's cage.

"No, let it stay," said the other boy, "it looks so pretty."

And so it stayed, and was brought into the lark's cage. The poor bird was lamenting its lost liberty, and beating its wings against the wires; and the little daisy could not speak or utter a consoling word, much as it would have liked to do so. So the forenoon passed.

"I have no water," said the captive lark, "they have all gone out, and forgotten to give me anything to drink. My throat is dry and burning. I feel as if I had fire and ice within me, and the air is so oppressive. Alas! I must die, and part with the warm sunshine, the fresh green meadows, and all the beauty that God has created." And it thrust its beak into the piece of grass, to refresh itself a little. Then it noticed the little daisy, and nodded to it, and kissed it with its beak and said: "You must also fade in here, poor little flower. You and the piece of grass are all they have given me in exchange for the whole world, which I enjoyed outside. Each little blade of grass shall be a green tree for me, each of your white petals a fragrant flower. Alas! you only remind me of what I have lost."

"I wish I could console the poor lark," thought the daisy. It could not move one of its leaves, but the fragrance of its delicate petals streamed forth, and was much stronger than such flowers usually have: the bird noticed it, although it was dying with thirst, and in its pain tore up the green blades of grass, but did not touch the flower.

The evening came, and nobody appeared to bring the poor bird a drop of water; it opened its beautiful wings, and fluttered about in its anguish; a faint and mournful "Tweet, tweet," was all it could utter, then it bent its little head towards the flower, and its heart broke for want and longing. The flower could not, as on the previous evening, fold up its petals and sleep; it drooped sorrowfully. The boys only came the next morning; when they saw the dead bird, they began to cry bitterly, dug a nice grave for it, and adorned it with flowers. The bird's body was placed in a pretty red box; they wished to bury it with royal honors. While it was alive and sang they forgot it, and let it suffer want in the cage; now, they cried over it and covered it with flowers The piece of turf, with the little daisy in it, was thrown out on the dusty highway. Nobody thought of the flower which had felt so much for the bird and had so greatly desired to comfort it.

The Buckwheat

When you pass by a field of buckwheat after a thunderstorm you will often find it looking blackened and singed, as if a flame of fire had swept over it. Peasants say: "The lightning has caused this." But why did the lightning blacken the buckwheat? I will tell you what I heard from the sparrow, who was told by an old willow-tree standing near a field of buckwheat. It was a large imposing old willow-tree, although somewhat crippled by old age, and split in the middle; grass and a bramble-bush grew in the cleft; the tree was bending down its branches so that they nearly touched the ground, hanging down like long green hair. On all the neighboring fields grew corn, not only rye and barley, but also oats—splendid oats indeed, which look, when they are ripe, like many little yellow canary-birds on a branch. The corn was lovely to look at, and the fuller the ears were the lower they were hanging down, as if in godly humility. Close by, right opposite to the old willow-tree, was also a field of buckwheat. The buckwheat did not bend down like the other corn, but stood proudly and stiffly upright.

"I am certainly as well off as the corn," it said, "I am in addition to this much better-looking; my flowers are as beautiful as the blossoms of the apple-tree; it must be a pleasure to look at me and my companions. Do you know anything more magnificent than we are, old willow-tree?"

The willow-tree nodded its head, as if it wished to say: "Yes, certainly, I do." The buckwheat spread, full of pride, its leaves and said: "This stupid old tree! It is so old that grass is growing out of its trunk."

Soon a heavy thunder-storm arose; all the flowers in the field folded their leaves or bowed their little heads down, while the storm passed over them; but the buckwheat remained proudly standing upright.

"Bend your head, as we do," said the flowers.

"Why should I?" asked the buckwheat.

"Bend your head, as we do," said the corn. "The angel of the storm is approaching; his wings reach from the clouds down to the ground; he will cut you in two, ere you can cry for mercy."

"But I refuse to bend my head," said the buckwheat.

"Close up your flowers and bend down your leaves," cried the old willow-tree. "Do not look up at the lightning when it tears the clouds; even mankind can't do that, for while a flash of lightning lasts one can look into Heaven, and that dazzles even mankind; what would then happen to us, the plants of the earth, which are so greatly inferior to men, if we dared do so?"

"Why greatly inferior?" said the buckwheat. "If you cannot give a better reason, I will look up into Heaven." And in its boundless pride and presumption it did look up. Suddenly came a flash of lightning, that was so strong that it seemed for a moment as if the whole world was in flames.

When the storm had abated, the flowers and the corn stood refreshed by the rain in the pure, still air; but the buckwheat was burnt by the lightning, and had become a dead, useless weed.

The wind moved the branches of the old willow-tree, so that large drops of water fell down from its green leaves, as if the tree was weeping; and the sparrows asked it, "Why do you cry? Blessings are showered upon us all; look how the sun shines, and how the clouds sail on! Do you not smell the sweet fragrance of flowers and bushes? Why do you cry, old willow-tree?"

Then the willow-tree told them of the pride of the buckwheat, of its presumption, and of the punishment which it had to suffer. I who have told you this story have heard it from the sparrows; they related it to me one night when I had asked them for a tale.

The Nightingale

In China, as you know, the emperor is a Chinaman too. The following story happened many years ago, but that is just why it is worth hearing before it is forgotten. The emperor's castle was the most beautiful in the world and was entirely of fine porcelain; it was very costly, but so brittle and delicate to touch that one had to be very careful. In the garden were seen the most wonderful flowers, to the finest of which tinkling silver bells were tied, lest people should pass without noticing them. Indeed, everything in the emperor's garden was well thought out, and it was such a large one that the gardener himself did not know where it ended. If you kept on walking you came to a noble forest with high trees and deep lakes. The forest sloped straight down to the deep blue sea, and large ships could sail right up under the branches of the trees. In one of these trees there lived a nightingale who sang so beautifully that even the poor fishermen, who had plenty of other things to do, would stop and listen when, on going out at night to spread their nets, they heard it sing. "Heavens! how beautiful that is," they would say; but they had to attend to their work and forgot the bird. So if it sang again next night, and the fishermen came that way, they would again exclaim, "How beautifully that bird sings!"

Travelers came from every country in the world to the emperor's city, which they admired very much, as well as the castle and the garden. But when they heard the nightingale, they would exclaim, "That is the best of all!" And when the travelers returned home they told of these things, and the learned ones wrote many books about the town, the castle and the garden. Neither did they forget the nightingale: that was praised most of all,

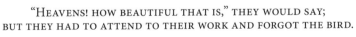

"Heavens! how beautiful that is," they would say;
but they had to attend to their work and forgot the bird.

and those who could write poetry wrote most beautiful poems about the nightingale in the wood by the deep sea.

These books traveled all over the world, and some of them came into the hands of the emperor. He sat in his golden chair reading and reading on; every moment he nodded his head, for it pleased him to find the beautiful descriptions of the city, the castle and the garden. Then he came to the words:

"But the nightingale is the best of all!"

"What is this?" said he. "I don't know the nightingale at all. Is there such a bird in my empire, and even in my garden? I have never heard of it. Fancy learning such a thing for the first time from a book!"

Hereupon he called his chamberlain, who was so important that when any one of lower rank than himself dared to speak to him or to ask him anything, he would only answer, "Pooh!" and that meant nothing.

"There is said to be a most remarkable bird here, called the nightingale," said the emperor. "They say it is the finest thing in my great empire. Why have I never been told about it?"

"I have never heard it mentioned before," said the chamberlain. "It has never been presented at court."

"I wish it to come and sing before me this evening," said the emperor. "The whole world knows what I possess, while I myself do not."

"I have never heard it mentioned before," said the chamberlain; "but I shall look for it and I shall find it."

But where was it to be found? The chamberlain ran up and down all the stairs, through halls and corridors, but not one of those whom he met had heard of the nightingale. So he ran back to the emperor, and said that it must certainly be an invention of those people who wrote books.

"Your Imperial Majesty will scarcely believe," said he, "what things are written in books. It is all fiction and something that is called the black art."

"But the book in which I have read this," said the emperor, "has been sent to me by the high and mighty Emperor of Japan, and there cannot therefore be anything untrue in it. I will hear the nightingale! It must be here this evening! It has my highest favor, and if it does not come, the whole court shall be trampled upon after supper."

"Tsing pe!" said the chamberlain, and ran up and down all the stairs again, and through all the halls and corridors and half the court ran with him, for they were not at all desirous of being trampled upon. Then there was a great inquiry after the remarkable nightingale which was known to all the world except to the people at court.

At last they came upon a poor little girl in the kitchen, who said, "Dear me, I know the nightingale well, and it can sing too! Every evening I have leave to take home to my poor sick mother the scraps from the table; she lives down by the seashore, and when I am tired I sit down to rest in the wood as I come back, and then I hear the nightingale sing. It makes the tears come into my eyes, and I feel just as if my mother were kissing me."

"Little maid," said the chamberlain, "I will get you an appointment in the kitchen, and permission to see the emperor dine, if you will lead us to the nightingale, for it has been commanded to appear this evening."

So they all went out into the wood, where the nightingale was wont to sing; half the court was there. When they were well on their way a cow began to low. "Oh," said the courtiers, "now we've got it! What wonderful power in such a small creature! I have certainly heard it before."

"No, those are cows lowing," said the little maid; "we are a long way from the place yet."

Some frogs then began to croak in the marsh.

"Beautiful!" said the Chinese court chaplain. "Now I hear it; it sounds exactly like little church bells."

"No," said the little maid, "those are frogs. But I think we shall soon hear it now." And then the nightingale began to sing.

"That's it!" said the little girl. "Hark, hark; there it sits!" And she pointed out a little gray bird up in the branches.

"Is it possible?" said the chamberlain "I should never have imagined it like that. How simple it looks! I suppose it has lost its color at seeing so many grand people around it."

"Little nightingale," the little maid called out in a loud tone, "our most gracious emperor wishes you to sing to him."

"With the greatest pleasure," said the nightingale, and sang so nicely that it was a pleasure to hear it.

"It sounds exactly like glass bells," said the chamberlain. "And look at its little throat, how it works. It is remarkable that we never heard it before; it will be a great success at court."

"Shall I sing before the emperor again?" asked the nightingale, believing that the emperor was also present.

"My excellent little nightingale," said the chamberlain, "I have great pleasure in inviting you to a court festival this evening, when you will bewitch His Imperial Majesty with your charming song."

"That is best heard in the woods," said the nightingale; but still it came willingly when it heard the emperor wished it.

"LITTLE NIGHTINGALE," THE LITTLE MAID CALLED OUT IN A LOUD TONE, "OUR MOST GRACIOUS EMPEROR WISHES YOU TO SING TO HIM."

The castle had been elegantly decorated. The walls and the floors, which were of porcelain, glittered in the light of many thousands of golden lamps; the most beautiful flowers, which tinkled merrily, stood in the corridors. In fact, what with the running to and fro and the draft, the bells tinkled so loudly that you could not hear yourself speak.

In the center of the great hall in which the emperor sat, a golden perch had been fixed for the nightingale. The whole court was present, and the little kitchen-maid, having now received the title of a real court cook, had obtained permission to stand behind the door. All were dressed in their very best, and all had their eyes on the little gray bird, to whom the emperor nodded.

The nightingale sang so beautifully that tears came into the emperor's eyes and ran down his cheeks, and when the bird sang still more beautifully it went straight to one's heart. The emperor was so pleased that he said the nightingale should have his golden slipper to wear round its neck. But the nightingale declined with thanks, saying that it had already received sufficient reward. "I have seen tears in the emperor's eyes, and that is the greatest treasure for me. An emperor's tears have a wonderful power. Heaven knows, I have been sufficiently rewarded." Thereupon she again sang in her beautiful, sweet voice.

"That is the sweetest coquetry that we know," said the ladies who were standing round, and then took water in their mouths to make them cluck when any one spoke to them. This made them think they were nightingales too. Even the footmen and the chambermaids allowed themselves to express their satisfaction—that is saying a good deal, for they are the hardest'to please. In a word, the nightingale was a great success.

The nightingale was a great success.

It was then accompanied by twelve servants, each of whom held it fast by a silken string attached to its leg.

It was now to remain at court, have its own cage, and liberty to go out twice a day and once during the night. It was then accompanied by twelve servants, each of whom held it fast by a silken string attached to its leg. There was by no means any pleasure in such flying.

The whole city talked about the wonderful bird, and if two people met, one would say to the other "Nightin," and the other would answer "gale." And then they sighed and understood each other. Eleven peddlers' children had even been named after the bird, though not one of them could sing a note.

One day the emperor received a large parcel, on which was written: "The nightingale."

"Here we have a new book about our celebrated bird," said the emperor. It was no book, however, but a small work of art, which lay in a casket: an artificial nightingale, supposed to look like the living one, but covered all over with diamonds, rubies and sapphires. As soon as the imitation bird had been wound up, it could sing one of the pieces that the real bird sang, and then it would move its tail up and down, all glittering with silver and gold. Round its neck hung a little ribbon on which was written: "The Emperor of Japan's nightingale is poor compared with that of the Emperor of China."

"How beautiful!" they all cried; and he who had brought the artificial bird immediately received the title of Imperial Nightingale-bringer-in-chief.

"Now they must sing together; what a lovely duet that will be!"

And so they had to sing together; but it did not go very well, for the real bird sang in its own way, and the imitation one sang only waltzes.

"That is not the new one's fault," said the music-master; "it sings in perfect time, and quite according to my method." So the imitation bird had to sing alone. It had quite as great a success as the real one; besides, it was much prettier to look at glittering like bracelets and breast-pins.

Thirty-three times it sang one and the same tune and still was not tired.

The courtiers would like to have heard it all over again, but the emperor thought that the live nightingale ought now to sing something as well. But where was it? No one had noticed it flying out of the window back to its green woods.

"But how is that?" said the emperor. And all the courtiers blamed the nightingale, and thought it a most ungrateful creature. "In any way, we have the best bird," they said; and so the imitation one had to sing again, which made the thirty-fourth time that they had heard the same tune. Even then they did not know it by heart, for it was much too difficult. The music-master praised the bird exceedingly; indeed, he assured them that it was better than a nightingale, not only in its dress and the number of beautiful diamonds, but also in its inside.

"For, see, your gracious majesty and my lords, with a real nightingale we never know what is coming next, but with the artificial one everything is arranged. You can open it, you can explain it, and make people understand how the waltzes lie, how they work, and why one note follows the other."

"That is just what we think too," they all said; and the music-master received permission to show the bird to the people on the following Sunday. The emperor commanded that they should also hear it sing. When they did so, they were as pleased as if they had all got drunk on tea, which is a Chinese fashion; and they all said "Oh!" and held up their first fingers and nodded. But the poor fishermen, who had heard the real nightingale, said, "It sounds pretty enough, the tunes are all alike too, but there is something wanting—I don't know what."

The real nightingale was banished from the country and the empire. The imitation bird had its place on a silk cushion close to the emperor's bed; and all the presents which it had received lay around it, and it had been promoted to the rank of Number One on the Left, with the title of Grand Imperial Toilet-Table Singer. The emperor considered the left side, on which the heart lies, as the most noble, and an emperor has his heart on the left just like other people. The music-master, too, wrote a work of twenty-five volumes about the artificial bird; it was so learned and so long, so full of the most difficult Chinese words, that all the people said they had read it and understood it, for otherwise they would have been thought stupid and had their bodies trampled upon.

For a whole year it went on like that. The emperor, the court, and all the other Chinamen knew every turn in the artificial bird's song by heart, and that was just why it pleased them now more than ever. They could sing with it, and often did so, too. The street boys sang "Tseetseetsee! Cluck, cluck, cluck!" and the emperor did just the same. It was really most beautiful.

One evening, when the artificial bird was singing its best and the emperor was lying in bed and listening to it, something inside the bird snapped with a bang. All the wheels ran round with a "whirr-r-r," and then the music stopped.

The emperor immediately jumped out of bed and sent for his physician; but what could he do? Then they fetched the watchmaker, and, after a good, deal of talking and examining, he got the bird into something like order; but he said that it must not be used too much, as the barrels were worn out, and it was impossible to put in new ones with any certainty of the music going right. Now there was great sorrow; the imitation bird could only be allowed to sing once a year, and even that was almost too much. On these occasions the music-master would make a little speech full of big words, and say that the singing was just as good as ever; and after that of course the court were as well pleased as before.

Five years had now passed, and a great sorrow fell upon the land. The Chinese were all really very fond of their emperor, and now he was ill and could not live long, they said. A new emperor had already been chosen, and the people stood out in the street and asked the chamberlain how their old emperor was.

"Pooh!" he said, and shook his head.

Cold and pale lay the emperor in his great, splendid bed; the whole court thought he was dead, and every one ran away to greet the new emperor. The pages ran out to gossip about it, and the maids-of-honor had a grand tea-party. Cloth had been laid down in all the halls and corridors, so that no foot-step should be heard, and it was therefore very, very quiet. But the emperor was not dead yet; stiff and pale he lay on the splendid bed with the long velvet curtains and the heavy gold tassels, and high up a window stood open, and the moon shined in upon him and the artificial bird.

The poor emperor could hardly breathe; he felt as though something were sitting on his chest. He opened his eyes and saw that it was Death who was sitting there; he had put on the emperor's golden crown, and held his golden sword in one hand, and his beautiful flag in the other.

All around, strange heads peeped out from the folds of the large velvet bed-curtains: some were hideous, others were sweet and gentle.

These were all the emperor's bad and good deeds, which were staring at him now that Death was sitting on his heart.

"Do you remember this?" they whispered one after another. "Do you recollect that?" And then they told him of so much that the perspiration ran down from his brow.

"That I did not know," cried the emperor. "Music! music! the great Chinese drum!" he shouted; "so that I may not have to hear what they say."

But they went on, and Death nodded like a Chinaman to all that was said.

"Music! music!" shrieked the emperor. "You precious little golden bird! Sing, do sing! I have given you gold and jewels, I have hung even my gold slipper round your neck. Sing, I say, sing!"

But the bird was silent; it could not sing without being wound up, and there was no one to do it. Death continued to stare at the emperor with his large, hollow eyes, and all was still, terribly still. Suddenly from the window came the sound of sweetest singing; it was the real little nightingale sitting on a bough outside. It had heard how the emperor was suffering, and had therefore come to console him and bring him hope by its singing. And as it sang, the ghostly heads grew paler and paler, the blood began to flow faster and faster through the emperor's weak limbs and even Death listened and said: "Go on, little nightingale, go on."

"Yes, but will you give me the beautiful golden sword? Will you give me the rich banner? Will you give me the emperor's rich crown?"

And Death gave up each of these treasures for a song, while the nightingale still went on singing. It sang of the quiet churchyard where the white roses grow, where the elder tree scents the air, and where the fresh grass is moistened by the tears of those who are left behind. Then Death longed to be in his garden, and floated out through the window like a cold white mist.

"Thanks, thanks," said the emperor. "You heavenly little bird! I know you well. It was you that I drove out of my country and my empire. And still you have charmed away the evil faces from my bed, and removed Death from my heart. How can I reward you?"

"You have rewarded me," said the nightingale. "I drew tears from your eyes when for the first time I sang to you; that I shall never forget. They are jewels that gladden the heart of a singer. But sleep now and get well and strong again. I will sing you something."

And as it sang the emperor fell into a sweet slumber. Oh, how mild and refreshing was that sleep! The sun shined in upon him through the window when he awoke strong and well. None of his servants had yet returned, for they believed he was dead; only the nightingale was still sitting by him singing.

"You must always stay with me," said the emperor. "You shall now sing only when you like, and I shall smash the imitation bird into a thousand pieces."

"Don't do that," said the nightingale. "It did its best, as long as it could. Keep it, as before. I cannot build my nest and live in the castle; but let me come just when I like. In the evening I will sit on that bough near your window and sing something to you, so that you shall be joyful and pensive at the same time. I will sing of those who are happy and of those who suffer. I will sing of the good and of the bad that are hidden all around you. The little singing bird flies far away, to the poor fisherman, to the peasant's cottage, to all who are far removed from you and your court. I love your heart more than your crown, and yet the crown has almost a halo of holiness around it. I will come and I will sing to you. But you must promise me one thing."

"Everything," said the emperor, and standing there in his imperial robes, which he had himself put on, he pressed his sword, all heavy with gold, to his heart.

When they saw him, they stood aghast,
and the emperor said, "Good morning!"

"I only ask one thing. Let no one know that you have a little bird that tells you everything; it will be for the best."

Saying this the nightingale flew away.

The servants came in to look after their dead emperor. When they saw him they stood aghast, and the emperor said, "Good morning!"

The Elfin Hill

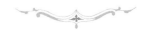

Some large lizards were nimbly running about in the clefts of an old tree; they understood one another very well, for they all spoke the lizard language.

"I wonder what is rumbling and rattling in yon old elfin hill," said the first lizard. "I have been unable to shut an eye for the last two nights, so great was the noise; it was just as bad as toothache, for that also prevents me from sleeping."

"I am sure there is something on," said another lizard; "they had the top of the hill propped up on four red pillars until the cock crowed this morning; it must be well aired; the elfin girls have also learned new dances. Surely, there is something on."

"Yes," said a third lizard, "I have seen an earthworm of my acquaintance, just when it came out of the hill where it had been groping about in the ground day and night. It has heard a good deal; the unfortunate animal cannot see, but knows well enough how to wriggle about and listen. They expect visitors in the elfin hill, and very distinguished ones too; but whom the earthworm was unwilling or unable to tell me. All the will-o'-the-wisps are ordered to take part in a torchlight procession, as it is called; the silver and gold, of which there is plenty in the hill, is polished and placed out in the moonlight."

"Who may these visitors be?" asked all the lizards. "What are they doing? Listen, how it hums and rumbles!" No sooner had they said this than the elfin hill opened and an old elfin girl, hollow at the back,* came tripping out; she was the housekeeper of the old elfin king, and being distantly connected with the family, she wore an amber heart on her forehead. Her feet moved so nimbly—trip, trip. Good gracious! how she could trip—she went straight down to the sea to the night-raven.†

"I have to invite you to the elfin hill for to-night," she said; "but you would do us a great favor if you would undertake the invitations. You ought to do something, as you do not entertain yourself. We expect some very distinguished friends, sorcerers, who can tell us something; that is why the old king of the elves wishes to show off."

"Who is to be invited?" asked the night-raven.

"All the world may attend the grand ball, even human beings, if they can talk in their sleep or know anything of the like which is according to our ways. But for the feast the company has to be strictly select: we only wish to have tiptop society. I have had an argument with the king, for in my opinion not even ghosts ought to be admitted. The merman and his daughters have to be invited first of all. Perhaps they may not like to come to the dry land, but we shall provide them with wet stones to sit on, or with something still better; and under these circumstances I think they will not refuse this time. All the old demons of the first class, with tails such as the goblins, we must invite, of course; further, I think, we must not forget the grave-pig,‡ the death-horse, nor the church dwarf; they belong, it is true, to the clergy, who are not of our class, but that is only their vocation; they are our near relatives, and frequently call upon us."

"Croak," said the night-raven, and flew off at once to invite the people.

---

* Elfin girls are, according to the popular superstition, to be looked at only from one side, as they are supposed to be hollow, like a mask.

† When in former days a ghost appeared the priest banished it into the earth; on the spot where this had happened they drove a stake into the ground. At midnight there was suddenly a cry heard: "Let me go." The stake was then removed, and the banished ghost escaped in the shape of a raven with a hole in his left wing. This ghostly bird was called the night-raven.

‡ In Denmark, superstitious people believe that under every church a living horse or pig is buried. It is supposed that the ghost of the horse limps on three legs every night to some house where somebody is going to die.

The elfin girls were already dancing on the hill, they were wrapped in shawls made of mist and moonshine, which look very pretty to people who like things of this kind. The large hall in the center of the elfin hill was beautifully adorned; the floor had been washed with moonshine, while the walls had been polished with a salve prepared by witches, so that they shined like tulip-leaves in the light. In the kitchen they were very busy; frogs were roasting on the spit, dishes of snail-skins with children's fingers and salads of mushroom-seed, hemlock and mouse noses were preparing; there was beer of the marshwoman's make, sparkling wine of saltpeter from the grave vaults: all was very substantial food; the dessert consisted of rusty nails and glass from church windows. The old king of the elves had his golden crown polished with crushed slate-pencil; it was the same as used by the first form, and indeed it is difficult for an elf king to obtain such slate-pencils. In the bedroom, curtains were hung up and fastened with snail-slime. There was a running, rumbling and jostling everywhere.

"Now let us perfume the place by burning horse-hair and pig's bristles, and then, I think, I have done all I can," said the old elfin girl.

"Father, dear," said the youngest daughter, "may I now know who our distinguished guests will be?"

"Well, I suppose I may tell you now," he said. "Two of my daughters must be prepared for marriage; for two will certainly be married. The old goblin of Norway, who lives in the old Dovre-mountains and possesses many strong castles built on the cliffs and a gold mine, which is much better than people think, will come down with his two sons, who are both looking out for a wife. The old goblin is as genuine and honest an old chap as Norway ever brought forth; he is merry and straightforward too. I have known him a very long time, we used to drink together to our good friendship; he was last here to fetch his wife, she is dead now; she was a daughter of the king of the chalk-hills near Moen. He took his wife on tick, as people say. Oh, how I am longing for the dear old goblin again! They say his sons are somewhat naughty and forward, but people may do them wrong by supposing that, and I think they will be all right when they grow older. Let me see that you can teach them good manners."

"When are they coming?" asked one of the daughters.

"That depends on wind and weather," replied the king of the elves. "They travel economically. They will come when they have the chance to go by ship. I wished them to come through Sweden, but that was not to the old man's liking. He does not advance with time, and I do not like that at all."

Just then two will-o'-the-wisps came leaping in, the one much quicker than the other, and therefore one arrived first.

"They are coming, they are coming," they cried.

"Give me my crown, and let me stand in the moonshine," said the elf king.

The daughters raised their shawls and bowed to the ground. There stood the old goblin from Dovre; he wore a crown of hardened ice and polished fir-cones; he was wrapped in a bear-skin and had large warm boots on; his sons, on the contrary, had nothing round their necks and no braces on their trousers, for they were strong men.

"Is that a hill?" asked the youngest of the boys, pointing to the elfin hill. "We should call it a hole, in Norway."

"Boys," said the old man, "you ought to know better, a hole goes in, a hill stands out; have you no eyes in your heads?"

The only thing that struck them, they said, was that they were able to understand the language without any difficulty.

"Don't be so foolish," said the old goblin; "people might think you are still unfledged."

Then they all went into the elfin hill, where, the distinguished visitors had assembled, and so quickly, that it seemed as if the wind had blown them together. But every one was nicely and well accommodated. The sea folks sat at dinner in big water-tubs; they said they felt quite at home. All showed very good breeding except the two young goblins of the north, who put their legs on the table, for they imagined that they might take such liberties.

"Take your feet off the table," said the old goblin; and they obeyed, though reluctantly. They tickled their fair neighbors at table with fir-cones which they brought in their pockets; they took their boots off, in order to be at ease, and gave them to the ladies to hold. But their father, the old Dovre goblin, was quite different; he talked so well about the stately Norwegian rocks, and of the waterfalls which rushed down with a noise like thunder and the sound of an organ, forming white foam; he told of the salmon which leap against the rushing water when the Reck begins to play on the golden harp; he spoke of the fine moonlight winter nights, when the sleigh-bells are ringing and the young men skate with burning torches in their hands over the ice, which is so clear and transparent that they frighten the fishes under their feet. He could talk so well that those who listened to him saw all in reality; it was just as if the sawmills were going, and as if servants and maids were singing and dancing; suddenly the old goblin gave the old elfin girl a kiss, and it was a real kiss, and yet they were almost strangers to each other.

After this the elfin girls had to perform their dances, first in the ordinary way, and then with stamping of their feet, and it looked very well; afterwards came the artistic and solo dance. Good gracious! how they threw their legs up; nobody knew where they began or where they ended, nor which were the legs and which the arms; all were flying about like sawdust, and they turned so quickly round that the death-horse and the grave-pig became unwell and had to leave the room.

"Hallo!" cried the old goblin, "that is a strange way of working about with the legs! But what do they know besides dancing, stretching the legs, and producing a whirlwind?"

"That you shall soon see," said the elf king, and called the youngest of his daughters. She was as nimble and bright as moonshine; she was indeed the finest-looking of all the sisters. She took a white chip of wood into her mouth, and disappeared instantly; that was her accomplishment. But the old goblin said he should not like his wife to possess such a power, and was sure his sons would be of the same opinion. The second could walk by her own side as if she had a shadow, while everybody knows that goblins never have a shadow. The third was quite different in her accomplishments; she had been apprenticed to the marshwoman in the brewery, and knew well how to lard elder-tree logs with glow-worms.

"She will make a good housekeeper," said the old goblin, drinking her health with his eyes, as he did not wish to take anything more.

Now came the fourth, with a large harp to play upon; no sooner had she struck the first chord than all lifted up the left leg—for the goblins are left-legged—and when she touched the strings again every one had to do what she wished.

"That is a dangerous person," said the old goblin; and his two sons went out of the hill, for now they had seen quite enough. "What does your next daughter know?" asked the old goblin.

"I have learned to admire all that is Norwegian, and I shall never marry unless I can go to Norway."

But the smallest of the sisters whispered into the old man's ear: "That is only because she has heard in a Norwegian song that when the world is destroyed through water the Norwegian cliffs will remain standing like monuments; therefore she wishes to go there, because she is so much afraid of being drowned."

"Ho, ho!" said the old goblin; "is that really what she meant? But tell me, what can the seventh and last do?"

"The sixth comes before the seventh," said the elf king, for he could count; but the sixth was rather timid.

"I can only tell people the truth," she said at last. "Nobody cares for me, and I am sufficiently occupied in making my shroud."

Now came the seventh and last; what could she do? Why, she could tell fairy tales, and as many as ever she wished.

"Here are my five fingers," said the old goblin; "tell me one for each of them."

And she took him by the wrist, and he laughed so much that he was nearly choked; when she came to the ring-finger, which had a golden ring upon it, as if it was aware that a betrothal should take place, the old goblin said, "Hold fast what you have; this hand is yours; I shall marry you myself."

Then the elfin girl said that the tales of the ring-finger and that of Peter Playman had yet to be told.

"Those we shall hear in the winter," said the old goblin, "and also those of the birch-tree, of the ghosts' presents, and of the creaking frost. You shall relate all your stories, for nobody up there can tell stories well; and then we shall sit in the rooms of stone where the pine logs are burning, and we shall drink mead out of the drinking-horns of the old Norwegian kings—Reck has made me a present of a couple of them—and when we are sitting there the mermaid will come to see us; she will sing to you all the songs of the shepherd-girls in the mountains. We shall enjoy it very much. The salmon will leap up in the waterfalls against the stone walls, but they cannot come in. Indeed, life is very pleasant in dear old Norway. But where are my boys?"

Where had they gone to? They were running about in the fields and blowing out the will-o'-the-wisps who had so kindly come to march in the torchlight procession.

"What have you been doing?" asked the old goblin. "I have taken a new mother for you; now you can each choose one of the aunts."

But the boys declared that they preferred to make speeches and drink; they had no wish to marry. And they began to make speeches, drank to other people's health, and emptied their glasses to the dregs. Afterwards they took off their coats and placed themselves on the tables to sleep, for they did not stand on ceremonies. But the old goblin danced with his young sweetheart about the room, and exchanged boots with her, for that is more fashionable than exchanging rings.

"The cock is crowing," cried the old elfin girl that did the housekeeping; "now we must close the shutters, lest the sun burn us."

Then the hill was closed up. But outside, the lizards were running about in the cleft tree, and one said to the other: "I like the old Norwegian goblin very much."

"I prefer the boys," said the earthworm; but the unfortunate animal could not see.

The Saucy Boy

Once upon a time there was an old poet, one of those right good old poets.

One evening, as he was sitting at home, there was a terrible storm going on outside; the rain was pouring down, but the old poet sat comfortably in his chimney-corner, where the fire was burning and the apples were masting.

"There will not be a dry thread left on the poor people who are out in this weather," he said.

"Oh, open the door! I am so cold and wet through," called a little child outside. It was crying and knocking at the door, while the rain was pouring down and the wind was rattling all the windows.

"Poor creature!" said the poet, and got up and opened the door. Before him stood a little boy; he was naked, and the water flowed from his long fair locks. He was shivering with cold; if he had not been let in, he would certainly have perished in the storm.

"Poor little thing!" said the poet, and took him by the hand. "Come to me; I will soon warm you. You shall have some wine and an apple, for you are such a pretty boy."

And he was, too. His eyes sparkled like two bright stars, and although the water flowed down from his fair locks, they still curled quite beautifully.

He looked like a little angel, but was pale with cold, and trembling all over. In his hand he held a splendid bow, but it had been entirely spoiled by the rain, and the colors of the pretty arrows had run into one another by getting wet.

The old man sat down by the fire, and taking the little boy on his knee, wrung the water out of his locks and warmed his hands in his own.

He then made him some hot spiced wine, which quickly revived him; so that, with reddening cheeks, he sprang upon the floor and danced around the old man.

"You are a merry boy," said the latter. "What is your name?"

"My name is Cupid," he answered. "Don't you know me? There lies my bow. I shoot with that, you know. Look, the weather is getting fine again—the moon is shining."

"But your bow is spoiled," said the old poet.

"That would be unfortunate," said the little boy, taking it up and looking at it. "Oh, it's quite dry and isn't damaged at all. The string is quite tight; I'll try it." So, drawing it back, he took an arrow, aimed, and shot the good old poet right in the heart. "Do you see now that my bow was not spoiled?" he said, and, loudly laughing, ran away. What a naughty boy to shoot the old poet like that, who had taken him into his warm room, had been so good to him, and had given him the nicest wine and the best apple!

The good old man lay upon the floor crying; he was really shot in the heart. "Oh!" he cried, "what a naughty boy this Cupid is! I shall tell all the good children about this, so that they take care never to play with him, lest he hurt them."

And all good children, both girls and boys, whom he told about this, were on their guard against wicked Cupid; but he deceives them all the same, for he is very deep. When the students come out of class, he walks beside them with a book under his arm, and wearing a black coat. They cannot recognize him. And then, if they take him by the arm, believing him to be a student too, he sticks an arrow into their chest. And when the girls go to church to be confirmed, he is amongst them too. In fact, he is always after people. He sits in the large chandelier in the theater and blazes away, so that people think it is a lamp; but they soon find out their mistake. He walks about in the castle garden and on the promenades. Yes, once he shot your father and your mother in the heart too. Just ask them, and you will hear what they say. Oh! he is a bad boy, this Cupid, and you must never have anything to do with him, for he is after every one. Just think, he even shot an arrow at old grandmother; but that was a long time ago. The wound has long been healed, but such things are never forgotten.

Now you know what a bad boy this wicked Cupid is.

The Steadfast Tin Soldier

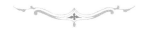

There were once twenty-five tin soldiers, who were all brothers, as they were cast from an old tin spoon. They all carried a gun in their left arm and looked straight forward; their uniform was red and blue. The first words which they heard upon seeing the light of day, when the lid was taken off the box in which they were packed, were, "Tin soldiers!" These words were uttered by a little boy who had received them as a birthday present, and clapped his hands for joy; he then put them in rank and file on the table. One soldier looked exactly like the other: only one, who had been cast last of all, when there was not enough tin, was not like his brothers, for he had only one leg; nevertheless, he stood just as firmly on his one leg as the others on two; and he was the one who became remarkable.

On the table on which they were placed were many other toys; but what caught the eye most of all was a pretty little castle of cardboard. Through its small windows one could look into the rooms. Before the castle stood little trees surrounding a clear lake, which was formed by a small looking-glass. Swans made of wax were swimming on it and were reflected by it. All this was very pretty, but the prettiest of all was a little lady who stood in the open door of the castle; she was cut out of paper, but she had a frock of the whitest muslin on, and a piece of narrow blue ribbon was fixed on her shoulders like a bodice, on it was fixed a glittering tinsel rose, as large as her whole face. The little lady stretched out both arms, for

All were brothers, as they were cast from an old tin spoon.

she was a dancer; and as she had lifted one leg high up, so that the tin soldier could not see it, he thought she had only one leg like himself.

"That is a wife for me," he thought; "but she is very grand; she lives in a castle, while I have only a box, which I share with twenty-four; that is not a place for her. But I must make her acquaintance." And then he laid himself at full length behind a snuff-box which was on the table; from his place he could see the little well-dressed lady, who continued to stand on one leg without losing her balance.

At night the tin soldiers were put back into their box and the people of the house went to bed. Now the toys began to play, to pay visits, to make war, and to go to balls. The tin soldiers rattled in their box, for they wished to take part in the games, but they could not raise the lid. The nutcrackers made somersaults, the slate-pencil enjoyed itself on the slate; they made so much noise that the canary woke up, and began to talk, and that in verse. The tin soldier and the dancer were the only ones who remained in their places. She was standing on tiptoe with her arm stretched out; he stood firmly on his one leg, never taking his eyes away from her for a moment. When the clock struck twelve, suddenly the lid of the snuff-box was flung open; there was no snuff in it, but a small black Jack-in-the-box, who had performed his trick.

One soldier looked exactly like the other.

"Tin soldier," said the Jack, "don't covet things that do not belong to you."

The tin soldier pretended not to hear anything.

"All right; wait till to-morrow," said the Jack.

When the morning had come and the children were up, the tin soldier was placed on the window-sill; all at once, whether through draft or through the Jack, the window flew open and the soldier fell headlong down into the street from the third story. That was a terrible fall! His one leg high up in the air, he stood on his helmet, while his bayonet entered into the ground between the paving stones. The servant and the little boy came at once down to look for him; but although they were so close to him that they almost trod upon him, they did not find him. If the tin soldier had cried: "Here I am," they would surely have found him; but he did not consider it proper to cry aloud, because he was in uniform.

Now it began to rain, first very little, but soon more, till it became a heavy shower. When the rain had ceased two boys passed by the soldier.

"Look, there is a tin soldier," said one of them, "let us make a boat for him."

They then made a boat out of a piece of newspaper, put the tin soldier in it, and let him float down the gutter; both ran by the side and clapped their hands for pleasure. Heaven preserve us! there were large waves in the gutter, and a strong current, too, for the rain had been pouring down in torrents. The paper boat was rocking up and down; sometimes it turned round so quickly that the tin soldier trembled; but he remained firm, he did not move a muscle, and looked straight forward, holding the gun in his arm. Suddenly the boat was driven under a large bridge which was over the gutter, and there it became as dark as in the tin soldier's box.

"Where am I going to?" he thought. "That is the fault of the black Jack-in-the-box. I wish the little lady were here with me in the boat, then I should not mind how dark it was."

Then came a big water-rat which lived under the bridge.

"Have you a passport?" asked the rat. "Give it up at once."

But the tin soldier was silent and held his gun tighter than before. The boat was rushing forward; the rat followed, gnashing its teeth, and crying out to the chips of wood and straws: "Stop him, stop him! He has paid no toll, and has not shown his passport!"

The current became stronger and stronger; the tin soldier could already see the light of day where the bridge ended; but he also heard a roaring noise, strong enough to frighten a brave man. Just think: the gutter ran there, where the bridge ended, into a canal, that was for him as dangerous as for us to cross a big waterfall. He was already so close to it that stopping was impossible. The boat drifted on, the poor tin soldier held himself as stiff as he could; nobody could say of him that he had blinked an eye. The boat rapidly whirled round three or four times, and was filled with water to the very brim; he must sink down. The tin soldier stood up to his neck in the water; deeper and deeper sank the boat, more and more the paper became wet and limp; then the water closed over his head. He thought of the sweet little dancer which he should never see again, and it sounded into his ear:

"Farewell, soldier, true and brave.
Nothing now thy life can save."

Then the paper-boat fell to pieces, and the tin soldier, sinking into the water, was swallowed up by a large fish.

It was indeed very dark inside the fish, much darker than under the bridge over the gutter, and, in addition, it was awfully narrow, but the tin soldier remained firm, and lay down at full length, holding his gun tightly in his arm. The fish was swimming about and made most extraordinary movements; at last it became quiet; it seemed as if a flash of lightning passed through it, the broad daylight appeared, and a voice said, "Hallo! there is the tin soldier." The fish had been caught and taken to market; there it had been sold and brought to the kitchen, where the cook was just cutting it open. With two fingers she took the tin soldier round the waist, carried him into the room, to show everybody the wonderful man who had been traveling about in a fish's stomach; but the tin soldier was not proud. They put him on the table, and there—what strange things occur in this world!—he was in the same place where he had been before; he saw the same children, and the same toys were on the table; there was also the pretty castle with the dear little dancer. She stood still on one leg and held the other high up in the air: she too was steadfast. The tin soldier was very much touched, and he nearly shed tin tears, but that was not becoming for a soldier. He looked at her but said nothing. Suddenly one of the little boys took up the tin soldier and threw him into the stove, without giving any reason for this strange conduct; surely it was again the fault of the Jack-in-the-box. The tin soldier stood there in the strong light and felt an unbearable heat, but whether this heat was caused by the real fire or by love, he did not know. His colors had vanished, but nobody could say if that happened during his journey, or if heart grief was the cause of it. He looked at the little lady and she looked at him, and he felt that he was melting, but still he stood upright with his gun in his arm. All at once a door flew

She flew like a sylph into the stove to the tin soldier.

open, the wind seized the dancer, she flew like a sylph into the stove to the tin soldier, where she was burnt and gone in a moment. The tin soldier melted down into a lump, and when the servant cleared out the cinders on the next morning, she found it in the shape of a little tin heart. Of the little dancer only the tinsel rose was left, which had become as black as coal.

The Flax

The flax was standing in full bloom; it had pretty blue flowers, as delicate as the wings of a moth, if not more so. The sun was warming it with his rays, the rain-clouds watered it; and that was as beneficial to the flax as it is to little children to be washed and afterwards kissed by their mothers. It makes them look much brighter. So it did the flax.

"People say I am standing very well," said the flax; "that I have a good length to make a piece of strong linen. Oh, I am so very happy! I am certainly the happiest of all plants! How well I am cared for! And I shall be useful! How much I enjoy the warm sun, how much the rain refreshes me. I am exceedingly happy—nay, I am the happiest of all plants."

"That is all very well," said a fence-post; "you do not know the world as well as I, for I have plenty of knots in me." And then it groaned quite piteously:

"Snip, snap, snurre—
Bassellurre:
Ended is the song."

"No, it is not ended," said the flax, "the sun will shine tomorrow, or the rain will refresh us. I feel how I am growing. I see that I am in full flower, I am the happiest of all plants."

One day people came, seized the flax and pulled it out by the roots; that was very painful! They placed it in water as if they intended to drown it, and afterwards hung it over a fire, as if they wished to fry it. It was dreadful!

"One cannot always be happy," said the flax; "one must also suffer in order to become experienced."

And things much worse happened to it. The flax was steeped, roasted, broken, and hackled. How could it possibly know the names of the various operations they performed upon it? Afterwards the flax was put on the spinning-wheel. "Whirr, whirr," the wheel turned so rapidly round that the flax was not able to gather its thoughts.

"How very happy I was," it thought, while it suffered agonies of pain; one must be contented with the good one has enjoyed in the past. Contented, contented!" Thus the flax still said, when it was put on the loom. A large piece of beautiful linen was woven from it, and all the flax, to the very last stalk, was used up for this one piece.

"But this is marvelous; I should never have thought it! Fortune favors me very much indeed. The fence-post knew something after all when it sang:

'Snip, snap, snurre—
Bassellurre.'

The song is by no means ended. No, on the contrary, now it only begins. That is very extraordinary. I have suffered a great deal, no doubt, but now I have turned out something useful I am the happiest of all plants! How strong and fine, how white and long I am. It is something very different from being only a plant, although it bears flowers; as a plant, one is not so much looked after, and gets water only when it rains. Now I am well cared for; the maid turns me over every morning, and at night she gives me a shower-bath with the watering-pot; the pastor's wife has even made a speech in praise of me; she said that I was the best piece of linen in the whole parish. I cannot possibly be happier than I am now!"

The linen was taken into the house and operated upon with scissors. How they cut and tore it, and pricked it with sewing-needles; it was by no means a pleasure! They made twelve garments of it of a kind which people do not like to mention, although nobody can get on without them; they made a whole dozen out of one piece of linen.

"Look at me now," said the flax, "only now I have become something really useful, and clearly understand what I am destined for in this world. What a blessing! Now I am useful, and so everybody ought to be, for that is the only true happiness in the world. Although they have cut twelve pieces of me, all the twelve are one and the same; we just make up the dozen. What an exceptional luck!"

Years and years passed: the garments were so much worn that they began to fall to pieces.

"There must be an end one day," said every piece. "I should have very much liked to last a little longer, but one must not expect more than is possible."

Then they were torn into rags and tatters. "It is all over now," they thought, when they were ground in a mill, soaked, and boiled, and went through various processes they were unable to remember. But they became beautiful white paper.

"That is a surprise indeed, and what a pleasant one," said the paper. "Now I am finer than before, and now they will write upon me. That is an extraordinary good fortune."

And really the most interesting stories and beautiful stanzas were written upon the paper, and there was only one ink-blot; of course this was quite an exceptional chance. And the people heard what was written upon it; it was good and clever, and made them better and enlightened them. Thus the words written on this paper produced a great blessing.

"That is more than I ever dreamed of, when I was a little blue flower in the field. How could it come into my mind that I should be destined to give mankind pleasure and knowledge? I can hardly believe it, and yet it is true. God knows that I have myself done nothing more with my feeble strength than what was necessary for my existence and growth, and yet He heaps honor after honor upon me. Whenever I think, 'Now the song is ended,' I pass into something better and higher. Now I shall probably travel about in the world, that all people may read what is written upon me. It can't be otherwise; it is most likely. I have so many great thoughts written upon me as I had formerly blue flowers. I am indeed the happiest of all plants."

The paper, however, was not sent on travels—nay, it was taken to the printer's, and there the whole manuscript was set up in type, and a book, or rather many hundreds of books were made of it, so that many more might have pleasure and profit from the writing than was possible if the paper on which it was written had been sent about in the world; no doubt it would have fallen to pieces before it had performed half its journey.

"Certainly, this is the wisest thing that could be done," thought the written paper, "although it never struck me. I remain at home, and am honored like an old grandfather, for that I am indeed to all new books. Thus some good can be done. I should not have been able to wander so much about. Only he who wrote the book has looked at me, for every one of his words run out of his pen straight upon me. I am the happiest of all!"

Then the paper was tied up in a bundle with other papers, and thrown into a cask which stood in the wash-house.

"When the work is done, it is pleasant to rest," said the paper. "It is wise to collect one's thoughts and to reflect on all that lives in one. It is only now that I thoroughly understand all that is written upon me. I wonder what will happen now? Surely there will be progress again; one always advances—that I know by my own experience."

One day all the paper was taken out of the cask and placed on the hearth; it was to be burned, for people said it must not be sold to tradesmen to wrap butter or sugar in it. All the children of the house were standing round the fireplace, for they wished to see the paper burning; it flamed up so beautifully, and afterwards one could see so many red sparks flying about in the ashes: one after another of the sparks disappeared as quickly as the wind. They called it "seeing the children coming out of school": the last spark was the schoolmaster. They thought they knew all about it, but that was a mistake. We, however, shall soon know.

All the old paper, the whole bundle of it, was put on the fire and was soon ablaze. "Ugh," it said, and flamed up high. "Ugh, that is not at all pleasant"; but when all was alight the bright flames reached much higher than the flax would ever have been able to stretch its little blue flowers, and the flames shined more brightly than the linen could ever have done. All the written letters turned red for a moment, and all the words and thoughts they expressed vanished in the flames. "Now I am flying straight up to the sun," said a voice in the flame; and it seemed as if a thousand voices repeated it, and the flames came out of the chimney-pot.

And finer than the flames, invisible to human eyes, there were rising up as many little beings as the flax had had flowers. They were still lighter than the flame that had borne them, and when it was extinguished and nothing left of the paper but black ashes, they danced once more over the ashes, and wherever they touched it red sparks leapt up. "The children came out of school, and the last was the schoolmaster." That was a pleasure! And the children sang:

"Snip, snap, snurre—
Bassellurre:
Ended is the song."

But all the little invisible beings said: "The song is never ended—that is the best of all; and therefore I am the happiest of all in the world."

Of course the children could neither hear nor understand it, and that was quite right, for children must not know everything.

The Swineherd

Once upon a time lived a poor prince; his kingdom was very small, but it was large enough to enable him to marry, and marry he would. It was rather bold of him that he went and asked the emperor's daughter: "Will you marry me?" but he ventured to do so, for his name was known far and wide, and there were hundreds of princesses who would have gladly accepted him, but would she do so? Now we shall see.

On the grave of the prince's father grew a rose-tree, the most beautiful of its kind. It bloomed only once in five years, and then it had only one single rose upon it, but what a rose! It had such a sweet scent that one instantly forgot all sorrow and grief when one smelled it. He had also a nightingale, which could sing as if every sweet melody was in its throat. This rose and the nightingale he wished to give to the princess; and therefore both were put into big silver cases and sent to her.

The emperor ordered them to be carried into the great hall where the princess was just playing "Visitors are coming" with her ladies-in-waiting; when she saw the large cases with the presents therein, she clapped her hands for joy.

"I wish it were a little pussy cat," she said. But then the rose-tree with the beautiful rose was unpacked. "Oh, how nicely it is made," exclaimed the ladies. "It is more than nice," said the emperor, "it is charming." The princess touched it and nearly began to cry. "For shame, pa," she said, "it is not artificial, it is natural!" "For shame, it is natural," repeated all her ladies. "Let us first see what the other case contains before we are angry," said the emperor; then the nightingale was taken out, and it sang so beautifully that no one could possibly say anything unkind about it.

"*Superbe, charmant,*" said the ladies of the court, for they all prattled French, one worse than the other.

"How much the bird reminds me of the musical box of the late lamented empress," said an old courtier, "it has exactly the same tone, the same execution."

"You are right," said the emperor, and began to cry like a little child.

"I hope it is not natural," said the princess.

"Yes, certainly it is natural," replied those who had brought the presents.

"Then let it fly," said the princess, and refused to see the prince.

The nightingale was taken out, and it sang so beautifully that no one could possibly say anything unkind about it.

But the prince was not discouraged. He painted his face, put on common clothes, pulled his cap over his forehead, and came back.

"Good day, emperor," he said, "could you not give me some employment at the court?"

"There are so many," replied the emperor, "who apply for places, that for the present I have no vacancy, but I will remember you. But wait a moment; it just comes into my mind, I require somebody to look after my pigs, for I have a great many."

Thus the prince was appointed Imperial Swineherd, and as such he lived in a wretchedly small room near the pigsty; there he worked all day long, and when it was night he had made a pretty little pot. There were little bells round the rim, and when the water began to boil in it, the bells began to play the old tune:

> *"A jolly old sow once lived in a sty.*
> *Three little piggies had she . . ."*

But what was more wonderful was that, when one put a finger into the steam rising from the pot, one could at once smell what meals they were preparing on every fire in the whole town. That was indeed much more remarkable than the rose. When the princess with her ladies passed by and heard the tune, she stopped and looked quite pleased, for she also could play it—in fact, it was the only tune she could play, and she played it with one finger.

"That is the tune I know," she exclaimed. "He must be a well educated swineherd. Go and ask him how much the instrument is."

One of the ladies had to go and ask; but she put on pattens.

"What will you take for your pot?" asked the lady.

"I will have ten kisses from the princess," said the swineherd.

"God forbid," said the lady.

"Well, I cannot sell it for less," replied the swineherd.

"What did he say?" said the princess.

"I really cannot tell you," replied the lady.

"You can whisper it into my ear."

"It is very naughty," said the princess, and walked off.

But when she had gone a little distance, the bells rang again so sweetly:

"A jolly old sow once lived in a sty.
Three little piggies had she . . ."

"Ask him," said the princess, "if he will be satisfied with ten kisses from one of my ladies."

"No, thank you," said the swineherd: "ten kisses from the princess, or I keep my pot."

"That is tiresome," said the princess. "But you must stand before me, so that nobody can see it."

The ladies placed themselves in front of her and spread out their dresses, and she gave the swineherd ten kisses and received the pot.

That was a pleasure! Day and night the water in the pot was boiling; there was not a single fire in the whole town of which they did not know what was preparing on it, the chamberlain's as well as the shoemaker's. The ladies danced and clapped their hands for joy.

He had made a pretty little pot. There were little bells round the rim, and when the water began to boil in it, the bells began to play the old tune.

"We know who will eat soup and pancakes; we know who will eat porridge and cutlets; oh, how interesting!"

"Very interesting, indeed," said the mistress of the household. "But you must not betray me, for I am the emperor's daughter.

"Of course not," they all said.

The swineherd—that is to say, the prince—but they did not know otherwise than that he was a real swineherd—did not waste a single day without doing something; he made a rattle, which, when turned quickly round, played all the waltzes, gallops, and polkas known since the creation of the world.

"But that is *superbe,*" said the princess passing by. "I have never heard a more beautiful composition. Go down and ask him what the instrument costs; but I shall not kiss him again."

"He will have a hundred kisses from the princess," said the lady, who had gone down to ask him.

"I believe he is mad," said the princess, and walked off, but soon she stopped. "One must encourage art," she said. "I am the emperor's daughter! Tell him I will give him ten kisses, as I did the other day; the remainder one of my ladies can give him."

"But we do not like to kiss him," said the ladies.

"That is nonsense," said the princess; "if I can kiss him, you can also do it. Remember that I give you food and employment." And the lady had to go down once more.

"A hundred kisses from the princess," said the swineherd, "or everybody keeps his own."

"Place yourselves before me," said the princess then. They did as they were bidden, and the princess kissed him.

"I wonder what that crowd near the pigsty means!" said the emperor, who had just come out on his balcony. He rubbed his eyes and put his spectacles on.

"The ladies of the court are up to some mischief, I think. I shall have to go down and see." He pulled up his shoes, for they were down at the heels, and he was very quick about it. When he had come down into the courtyard he walked quite softly, and the ladies were so busily engaged in counting the kisses, that all should be fair, that they did not notice the emperor. He raised himself on tiptoe.

"What does this mean?" he said, when he saw that his daughter was kissing the swineherd, and then hit their heads with his shoe just as the swineherd received the sixty-eighth kiss.

"Go out of my sight," said the emperor, for he was very angry; and both the princess and the swineherd were banished from the empire. There she stood and cried, the swineherd scolded her, and the rain came down in torrents.

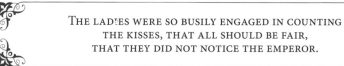

THE LADIES WERE SO BUSILY ENGAGED IN COUNTING THE KISSES, THAT ALL SHOULD BE FAIR, THAT THEY DID NOT NOTICE THE EMPEROR.

"Alas, unfortunate creature that I am!" said the princess.

"Alas, unfortunate creature that I am!" said the princess, "I wish I had accepted the prince. Oh, how wretched I am!"

The swineherd went behind a tree, wiped his face, threw off his poor attire and stepped forth in his princely garments; he looked so beautiful that the princess could not help bowing to him.

"I have now learned to despise you," he said. "You refused an honest prince; you did not appreciate the rose and the nightingale; but you did not mind kissing a swineherd for his toys; you have no one but yourself to blame!"

And then he returned into his kingdom and left her behind. She could now sing at her leisure:

"A jolly old sow once lived in a sty.
Three little piggies had she . . ."

Holger Danske

In Denmark, close by the Oeresund, stands the old castle of Kronborg; hundreds of ships, English, Russian, and Prussian, pass through the sound every day and fire salutes to the old castle—"Boom, boom!"—and the old castle returns their salutes with cannons, for in the language of cannons "Boom" means "Good-day" and "Thank you." In the winter-time no ships can sail by there, for then the water is frozen right across to the Swedish coast, and has quite the appearance of a high-road. There the Danish and Swedish flags are streaming in the wind, and Danes and Swedes bid each other "Good-day" and "Thank you," not with cannons, but with cordial shaking of hands; each comes to buy the bread and cake of the other, for you know other people's bread and butter tastes better than one's own. But the old castle of Kronborg is by far the most beautiful sight of all; there Holger Danske is sitting in a deep, dark cellar, into which nobody can go. He is clad in an armor of iron and steel, and rests his head on his strong arms; his long beard hangs down over the marble table, and has grown through it. He sleeps and dreams, but in his dream he sees all that is going on in Denmark. Every Christmas-eve an angel of God comes to him and tells him that all he has dreamed is true, and that he might go on sleeping, as Denmark is in no real danger; but should it ever get into trouble, the old Holger Danske will rise and burst the table in withdrawing his beard. Then he will strike with his sword, so that the dint of his strokes will be heard through all the countries of the world.

An old grandfather was telling all this about Holger Danske to his little grandson, and the little boy knew that all his grandfather said was true. While the old man spoke he busily carved a large wooden figure, intended to represent Holger Danske and to be fixed to the prow of a ship, for he was a carver in wood—that is to say, a man who carves the figures of persons in wood, which are to be fixed to the fronts of ships according to the names they receive. Now he had carved Holger Danske, who was standing there so proudly with his long beard, holding his broad sword in one hand while the other rested on the Danish arms.

The old man said so much about distinguished Danish men and women that it seemed to his little grandson in the end as if he knew quite as much as Holger Danske, who after all was only dreaming. And when the child was put to bed he thought so much about all he had heard, that he pressed his chin against the counterpane, believing he had a long beard which had grown through it.

The grandfather went on working: he was carving the last part of the figure, the arms of Denmark. When he had finished and looked at the whole and thought of all he had read and heard of, and what he had told his little grandson, he nodded, wiped his spectacles and put them on again, saying: "Well, well, Holger Danske will not come in my lifetime, but the little boy there in bed may have a chance of seeing him one day, when there is really need." The old man nodded again; the more he looked at his figure of Holger Danske, the more he was satisfied with his work; it seemed to him to become colored, and the armor to gleam like iron and steel; the hearts in the Danish arms turned more and more red, and the lions with the golden crowns on their heads were leaping.*

"Indeed, there is no more beautiful coat of arms in the world," said the old man. "The lions represent strength, the hearts kindness and love!" He looked at the uppermost of the lions and thought of King Canute, who subjected the great England to the Danish throne; the second lion reminded him of Waldemar, who united Denmark and conquered the Wendish territories; when he looked at the third lion he thought of Margaret, who united Denmark with Sweden and Norway. When he looked at the red hearts they seemed to glow more than before; they became flames which moved, and in his mind he followed each of them.

The first flame led him into a narrow dark prison; there sat a prisoner, a beautiful woman, Eleanor Ulfeld,† the daughter of Christian the Fourth, and the flame took the shape of a rose on her bosom, and became one with the heart of this noblest and best of all Danish women.

"That is a heart indeed in Denmark's arms," said the old grandfather. And his mind followed the second flame far out into the sea, where the cannons roared and smoke enveloped the ships; it fixed itself in the shape of the ribbon of an order to the breast of Hvitfeld‡ when he blew himself up with his ship in order to save the fleet.

---

*The Danish arms consist of three lions between nine hearts.

†Eleanor was the wife of Corfitz Ulfeld, who was accused of high treason. The only crime of this high-minded woman was her faithful love to her unhappy husband. She passed twenty-two years in a dreadful prison, and was only delivered after the death of her prosecutor, Queen Sophia Amelia.

‡When Hvitfeld's ship, the *Danebrog,* in the battle on the Kjöge Bay, 1710, caught fire, this gallant man blew himself up in order to save the town and the Danish fleet, against which the ship was drifting.

The third flame led him to the miserable huts in Greenland, where the missionary Hans Egede* ruled in word and deed with love; the flame became a star on his breast—that was another heart of the Danish coat of arms.

The old man's mind hastened on in front of the fourth flame; he knew where it would go. In the wretched room of a peasant woman stood Frederick the Sixth, and wrote his name with chalk on a beam; the flame was burning on his breast and in his heart, and there in the peasant's room his heart became a heart of the Danish arms.

The old man wiped his eyes, for he had known King Frederick with his silvery locks and honest blue eyes, and loved him; he folded his hands and was silent for a moment. Just then the old man's daughter-in-law entered the room, and said: "It is late; you must go to rest; supper is ready."

"The figure you have carved is very beautiful, Holger Danske, and our whole old coat of arms," she continued. "I feel as if I have seen this face before."

"No, that is impossible," said the grandfather; "but I have seen it, and I have endeavored to carve it in wood as I have kept it in my memory. It was when the English were in the port, on the memorable second of April when we gave proof that we were all old Danes. On board the *Denmark*, where I fought in the squadron of Steen Bille, there was a man by my side whom the balls seemed to fear. He merrily sang old songs and fought as if he were more than a man. I remember him still very well, but whence he came and whither he went nobody knows. I have often thought that he was perhaps Holger Danske himself, who had swam down from Kronborg in order to help us in the hour of danger; that was my idea, and that is his likeness."

And the figure cast a great shadow all over the wall and part of the ceiling; it seemed as if the real Holger Danske was casting it, for it moved; but this might also have been caused by the flame, which did not burn steadily. And the daughter-in-law kissed the old man and led him to the big easy chair near the table; and there she and the old man's son, who was the father of the little boy in bed, had their supper. The grandfather spoke of the Danish lions and the Danish hearts, of their strength and kindness; he declared that there existed yet another strength besides that of the sword; he pointed to the shelves filled with old books, where Holberg's comedies stood which were so much read and so amusing, it seemed almost as if all the persons of bygone days could be recognized in them.

---

* Hans Egede went in 1721 to Greenland, and worked there as a missionary for fifteen years under very hard conditions.

"He, too, knew how to strike a blow," said the grandfather, "for he ridiculed as much as he could the follies and prejudices of the people." Then the grandfather nodded towards the looking-glass where the almanac with the picture of the Round Tower* was hanging, and said: "Tycho Brahe was also a man who made use of the sword, not to cut flesh and bone, but to make the path on the sky through the stars more distinct. And *he,* whose father belonged to my trade, the old wood-carver's son, *he* whom we have often seen with his white curls and broad shoulders, he who is known all over the world—he could shape the stone; but I can only carve wood. Well, well, Holger Danske can appear in many shapes, so that all the world hears of Denmark's strength. Let us drink Bertel's† health!"

The little boy in bed saw distinctly the old castle of Kronborg and the Oeresund, the real Holger Danske who was sitting deep below with his beard grown to the marble table and dreaming of all that happens here above, Holger Danske was also dreaming of the humble little room where the wood-carver sat; he heard all that was said, and nodded in his dream, saying: "Yes, remember me, ye Danish people—keep me in your memory. I shall return to you in the hour of danger!"

And outside before the Kronborg the bright day shined; the wind carried the sounds of the bugle over from the neighboring country; the ships sailed by and saluted "Boom, boom!" and from the Kronborg it echoed "Boom, boom!" But Holger Danske did not awake, however strong the cannons roared, for it was only "Good-day" and "Thank you." They must fire more strongly if they wish to wake him up; but one day he will wake up, for there is still life in Holger Danske.

* Observatory at Copenhagen.

† Bertel Thorwaldsen, the famous sculptor.

The Flying Trunk

There was once a merchant who was so rich that he could pave the whole street, and almost a little lane too, with silver. But he did not do so; he knew how to employ his money differently. If he spent a shilling, he got back four; such a clever merchant was he—till he died.

His son now got all this money. He lived merrily, went masquerading every night, made kites out of dollar-notes, and played at ducks and drakes on the sea-shore with gold pieces instead of stones. In this manner the money could easily come to an end, and it did so. At last he possessed no more than four shillings, and had no other clothes than a pair of slippers and an old dressing-gown. His friends now no longer troubled themselves about him, as they could not of course walk along the streets with him; but one of them, who was good-natured, sent him an old trunk, with the remark, "Pack up!" That was indeed very nice of him, but he had nothing to pack up, so he sat down in the trunk himself.

It was a wonderful trunk. As soon as you pressed the lock, the trunk could fly. He pressed, and away it flew with him through the chimney, high up above the clouds, farther and farther away. But as often as the bottom creaked a little he was in great terror lest the trunk might go to pieces; in that case he would have turned a mighty somersault.

Heaven preserve us! In this manner he arrived in the country of the Turks. He hid the trunk in the wood under the dry leaves, and then went into the town. He could do so very well, for among the Turks everybody went about like that—in a dressing-gown and slippers. Meeting a nurse with a little child, he said, "I say, you Turkish nurse, what grand castle is that close by the

One of them, who was good-natured, sent him an old trunk, with the remark, "Pack up!"

It was a wonderful trunk. As soon as you pressed the lock, the trunk could fly.

town, in which the windows are so wide open?"

"The Sultan's daughter lives there," she replied. "It was prophesied that she would be very unhappy about a lover, and therefore no one may go to her, unless the Sultan and Sultana are there too."

"Thank you," said the merchant's son; and going out into the wood, sat down in his trunk, flew up on the roof and crept through the window into the Princess's apartments. She was lying on the sofa asleep, and was so beautiful that the merchant's son could not help kissing her. At this she awoke, and was greatly terrified; but he said he was a Turkish god, who had come down to her from the sky, and that pleased her.

They sat down next to one another, and he told her little stories about her eyes: that they were the most glorious dark lakes, in which thoughts were swimming about like mermaids. And he told her of her forehead, that it was a mountain of snow with the most splendid halls and images.

THEY SAT DOWN NEXT TO ONE ANOTHER, AND HE TOLD
HER LITTLE STORIES ABOUT HER EYES:
THAT THEY WERE THE MOST GLORIOUS DARK LAKES,
IN WHICH THOUGHTS WERE SWIMMING ABOUT LIKE MERMAIDS.

They were indeed fine stories! Then he asked the Princess for her hand, and she said "Yes" at once.

"But you must come here on Saturday," she said. "The Sultan and the Sultana will be here to tea then. They will be very proud at my marrying a Turkish god. But mind you bring a very pretty little tale with you, for my parents like them immensely. Mother likes them moral and high-flown, but father likes merry ones, at which he can laugh."

"Yes, I shall bring no other marriage gift than a story," said he, and so they parted. But the Princess gave him a sword ornamented with gold pieces, and the latter were very useful to him.

So he flew away, bought himself a new dressing-gown, and sitting down in the wood made up a story: it was to be ready by Saturday, and that was no easy task. By the time he had got it ready Saturday had come. The Sultan, the Sultana and the whole Court were at the Princess's to tea. He was received very graciously.

"Will you tell us a tale?" said the Sultana. "One that is deep and instructive."

"But something to laugh at, too," said the Sultan.

"Certainly," he replied, and commenced. And now pay attention:

"Once upon a time there was a box of matches which were very proud of their high descent. Their genealogical tree—that is to say, the great fir-tree, of which each of them was a little splinter—had been a high old tree in the forest. The matches were now lying between a tinder-box and an old iron pot, and they were telling about their youth. 'Yes,' said they, 'when we were upon the green branches, then we were really upon the green branches. Every morning and evening there was diamond tea, that was the dew: we had sunshine the whole day long, and when the sun shined the little birds had to tell stories. We could very well see that we were rich too, for the other trees were only dressed in summer, while our family had means for green dresses both in summer and winter.

" 'But one day the woodman came; that was the great revolution; and our family was split up. The head of the family received a post as mainmast on a splendid vessel which could sail round the world, if it wished; the other branches settled in different places, and we now hold the office of kindling a light for the common herd. That is how such grand people as we have come down to the kitchen.' "

"My fate shaped itself in another way," said the iron pot next to which the matches were lying. "From the time I first came into the world, much scrubbing and cooking has gone on inside me. I look after the material wants of life, and occupy the first place in the house. My only pleasure is to be on the shelf after dinner, very nice and clean, and to carry on a sensible conversation with my comrades. But with the exception of the pail, which now and then gets taken down into the yard, we always live within our four walls. The only one who brings us any news is the market basket, but it speaks very unassuringly about the government and the people; indeed, only the other day an old pot fell down from fright and broke into pieces. It is a Liberal, I tell you!"

"Now you're talking too much," interrupted the tinder-box, and the steel struck against the flint, so that it gave out sparks. "Had we not better have a pleasant evening?"

"Yes, let us talk about who is the grandest," said the matches.

"No, I don't like to talk about myself," objected the pot. "Let us get up an evening's entertainment. I will begin by telling a story of every-day life—something that any one can take an interest in and derive pleasure from, too.

"On the Baltic by the Danish coast—"

"That's a pretty beginning!" said all the plates. "That will be a story which we shall like."

"Yes, I passed my youth there, in a quiet family. The furniture was polished, the floor was scrubbed, and every fortnight clean curtains were hung up."

"How interesting you make your story," said the broom. "One can hear at once that the teller is a man who has moved much among women. Something so pure runs through it all."

"Yes, that is so," said the pail, and jumped for joy, so that the water splashed all over the floor.

And the pot continued telling its story, the end of which was just as good as the beginning.

All the plates rattled for joy, and the broom got some green parsley out of the dust-hole and made a wreath for the pot, for it knew that this would make the others angry. "If I present him with a wreath to-day," it thought, "he will have to give me one to-morrow."

"Now I will dance," said the tongs, and did so. Heavens! how high she could lift up one leg. The old chair-cushion in the corner burst when he saw it. "Shall I get a wreath too?" asked the tongs; and she got one.

"Still, they're only common people," thought the matches.

Now the tea-urn was asked to sing; but she said she had caught cold and could not sing unless she were boiling. That was mere affectation, however; she would not sing unless she were standing on the table with the family.

By the window was stuck an old goose-quill, with which the maid wrote. There was nothing remarkable about it, except that it had been dipped far too deep into the ink. But it was proud of that. "If the tea-urn won't sing," it said, “let her alone. Outside there is a nightingale in a cage which can sing. It is true that it has learned nothing, but we’ll leave that out of the question this evening.”

“I don’t think it at all right,” said the tea-kettle—he was kitchen singer and half-brother to the tea-urn—” that such a foreign bird should be heard. Is that patriotic? Let the market-basket decide.”

“I should only be angry,” said the market-basket; “there is such a conflict going on within me as no one would believe. Is this a proper way in which to pass an evening? Would it not be more sensible to put the house in order? Every one ought to go to his own place, and I would lead the game. That would be quite another thing.”

“Yes, let us make a noise,” they all said. Then the door opened, and the servant came in, at which they all stood still; not one stirred. But there was not a single pot who did not know what he could do and how grand he was. “Yes, if I had liked,” each one thought, “we might have had a right merry evening.”

The maid took the matches and lit the fire with them. Heavens! what sparks they threw out, and how they burst into flame!

“Now, everybody can see that we are first,” they thought. “How we shine, and with what light!” And they were burned up.

“That was a fine story,” said the Sultana. “I feel quite transplanted to the kitchen among the matches. Yes, now you shall have our daughter.”

“Indeed you shall,” said the Sultan; “you shall marry our daughter on Monday.” And they made him feel quite one of the family.

The wedding was settled, and on the evening before it the whole city was illuminated. Biscuits and cakes were thrown among the people; the street boys stood upon their toes, shouting “Hurrah” and whistling on their fingers. It was uncommonly grand.

“Well, I suppose I shall have to treat them to something too,” thought the merchant’s son. So he bought some rockets and crackers, and every kind of fireworks that you can think of, put them in his trunk and flew up to the sky with them.

Bang, bang! How they went off and cracked!

All the Turks jumped so high that their slippers flew over their ears; such a display they had never yet seen. Now they could understand that it was the god of the Turks himself who was to marry the Princess.

As soon as the merchant’s son had come down again into the wood with his trunk, he thought, “I’ll just go into the town to hear what impression it made.” And it was natural that he should wish to know that.

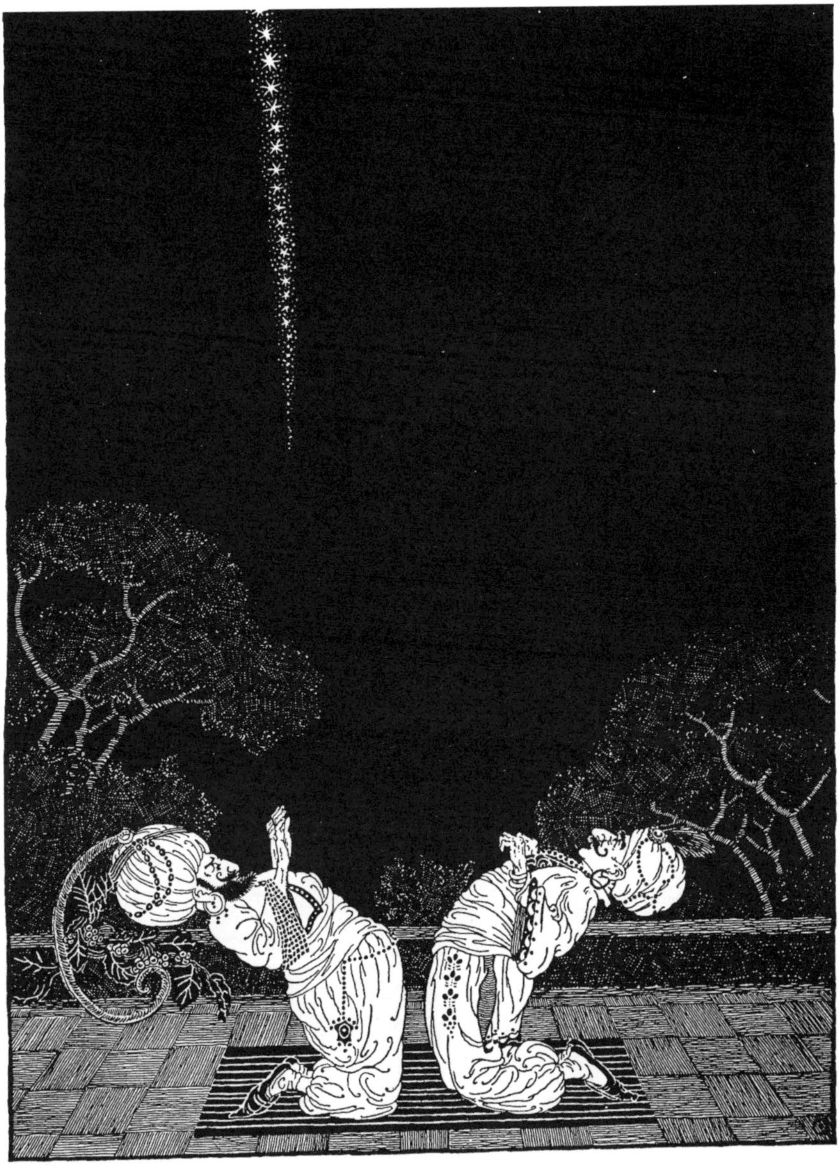

All the Turks jumped so high that their slippers flew over their ears; such a display they had never seen.

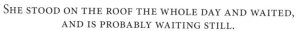

She stood on the roof the whole day and waited, and is probably waiting still.

What stories the people did tell! Every one whom he asked about it had seen it in his own way; but all thought it beautiful.

"I saw the god of the Turks himself," said one. "His eyes were like shining stars, and his beard like foaming water."

"He flew in a mantle of fire," said another. "The sweetest little cherubs peeped out of its folds."

Indeed they were fine things that he heard, and on the following day he was to be married.

So he went back to the wood to get into his trunk; but what had become of it? The trunk was burnt. A spark from the fireworks had fallen into it and had set it alight, and now the trunk lay in ashes. He could not fly any more, nor get to his bride.

She stood on the roof the whole day and waited, and is probably waiting still. But he wanders through the world telling tales, which are, however, no longer such merry ones as the one he told about the matches.

The Fir-Tree

Far out in the forest grew a pretty little fir-tree. It had a favorable place; the sun shined brightly on it, and there was plenty of fresh air, while many taller comrades, both pines and firs, were thriving around it. The little fir-tree longingly desired to grow taller! It was indifferent to the warm sun and the fresh air, it took no notice of the peasant children, who ran about and chattered, when they had come out to gather strawberries and raspberries. Often they came with a basket full, and had threaded strawberries on a straw like beads; then they used to sit down near the little fir-tree and say: "What a pretty little tree this one is!" But this the tree did not like to hear at all.

In the following year it grew taller by a considerable shoot, and the year after by another one, for by the number of shoots which fir-trees have, we may discover how many years they have grown.

"Oh, that I were as tall a tree as the others!" sighed the little tree; "then I might spread out my branches far around, and look with my crown out into the wide world! The birds would build their nests in my boughs, and when the wind blew I could proudly nod, just like the others yonder!"

It took no delight in the sunshine, in the birds, nor in the red clouds which in the morning and evening passed over it. When the winter had come and the snow was lying white and sparkling on the ground, often a hare came running and jumped right over the little tree—oh, that annoyed it so much! But two winters passed, and in the third the little tree was already so high that the hare had to run round it. "To grow, to grow, to become tall and old, this is the most desirable thing in the world," thought the tree.

Every year in autumn woodcutters came and felled several of the biggest trees; the young tree, now well grown, shuddered, for the tall magnificent trees fell to the ground with a crash; and when their branches were hewn off, the trees looked so naked, long and slender, they were hardly to be recognized. Then they were placed upon carts, and horses drew them out of the wood. Whither were they going? What was to become of them? In spring, when the swallows and storks returned, the tree asked them: "Can you not tell me whither they have taken them? Have you not met them?"

The swallows knew nothing about them; but the stork looked pensive, nodded his head and said: "Yes. I think I know. When I left Egypt I passed by many new ships, and on the ships were splendid masts; I suppose these were the trees, for they smelled like fir-trees, and they looked very stately indeed!"

"I wish I were tall enough to go over the sea! I should like to know what the sea is. What does it look like?"

"To explain that," replied the stork, "would take me too long," and thus saying he flew away.

"Enjoy thy youth!" said the sunbeams; "take pleasure in thy vigorous growth, in the fresh life that is within thee."

The wind kissed the tree, and the dew shed tears over it; but the fir-tree did not understand them.

About Christmas-time people cut down many trees which were quite young and smaller than the fir-tree, which had no rest and always wished to be off. These young trees, the very best that could be found, kept all their branches; they were placed upon carts and drawn out of the wood by horses.

"What are they doing with them?" asked the fir-tree. "They are not taller than I am—nay, there was one much smaller! Why did they retain all their branches? Where are they conveying them to?"

"We can tell you; we know!" chirped the sparrows. "Down below in the town we have looked through the windows! We know where they are taken to! They come to the greatest splendor you can imagine! We have looked in at the windows and have seen them standing in the middle of a warm room covered with the most beautiful things: gilded apples, gingerbread, toys, and many, many wax candles."

"And then," asked the fir-tree, trembling all over, "what happens after that?"

"Why, that is all we have seen! But that was very beautiful."

"I wonder whether I am destined to receive such great splendor," exclaimed the fir-tree merrily. "That is far better than crossing the sea! How much I am longing for the time! I wish Christmas had arrived! Now I am tall and have grown to a good length like the others which they took away last year! I wish I were already placed on the cart or in the warm room adorned with all the bright and beautiful things! And then there is something much better and brighter to come, or why would they decorate the trees so beautifully? Yes, indeed, there is something more splendid and grand to follow! But what can it be? Oh, how I suffer with longing; I hardly know how I feel."

"Enjoy our presence," said the air and the sunshine; "delight in thy young life here in the forest."

But the tree did not enjoy anything, it grew and grew; winter and summer it was green, and people who saw it said that it was a beautiful tree.

Christmas came at last, and the tree was the first to be cut down. The ax entered deeply into its stem; the tree fell groaning to the ground; a pain and a faintness overcame it; it was unable to think of the happiness to come, it was sad that it had to leave its home, the spot where it had grown up; it knew well enough that it would never see again the dear old comrades, the little bushes and the flowers, and perhaps not even the birds. Parting was not at all pleasant. The tree did not recover until it was taken from the cart in a court-yard with other trees and heard a man say: "This one is very fine, we only want this one."

Two servants in livery soon came and carried the tree into a large, beautiful room. The walls were all covered with pictures, and by the side of the tile-stove stood big Chinese vases with lions on the lids; there were rocking-chairs, couches covered with silk, on a large table were displayed picture-books and toys of very great value—at least, so the children said. The fir-tree was put into a large vessel filled with sand; but nobody could see that it was a vessel, for it was covered all over with green cloth and placed on a handsome carpet of many colors. How the fir-tree trembled! What was to happen now? The young ladies of the house, aided by the servants, adorned the tree. They hung on its branches little nets cut out of colored paper and filled with sweets; gilded apples and walnuts were fastened to the tree, as if they grew on it, and more than a hundred small candles, red, blue, and white, were fixed to the branches. Dolls looking exactly like human beings—the tree had never seen anything of the like before—were hanging in the green foliage, and on the very top of the tree they fixed a glittering star of tinsel. It was very beautiful.

"To-night," they all said—"to-night it will shine!"

"Oh, that the evening had come!" thought the tree. "I wish the candles were lighted! And what will happen then? I wonder if the trees will come from the wood to look at me, or if the sparrows will look in at the windows. Am I to grow fast here and remain winter and summer adorned as I am now?"

Indeed, that was not a bad guess! Its longing made its bark ache; barkache for a tree is just as bad as a headache for us.

At last the candles were lighted. What a blaze of light! What a splendor! The tree trembled so much with joy in all its branches that one of the lights set fire to one of its boughs and scorched it.

"Heaven preserve us!" exclaimed the young ladies, and quickly extinguished the flame.

Now the tree was no longer allowed to tremble! That was dreadful. It was so afraid lest it might lose some of its ornaments; it was quite dazzled by all the splendor. Then the folding-doors were thrown open, and the children rushed into the room as if they wished to upset the tree; the elders followed.

For a moment the children stood silent with surprise, but only for a moment; then they shouted for joy till the room rang; they danced joyfully round the tree, and present after present was taken down from it.

"What are they doing?" thought the tree. "What is to happen?" The candles burned gradually down to the boughs on which they were fastened and were put out, and then the children were allowed to plunder the tree. Oh, how they rushed at it; all its branches cracked, and had it not been fastened with the glittering star to the ceiling, they would have upset it. The children were dancing about with their beautiful toys. Nobody took any notice of the tree, except the old nurse, who came and looked at the branches, but only to see if there was not a fig or an apple left on them.

"A story! a story!" cried the children, while they pulled a small stout man towards the tree. He seated himself just underneath the tree, "for there we are in its green shade" he said, "and it will be an advantage to the tree to listen! But I shall only tell one story. Would you like to hear Ivede-Avede or Humpty Dumpty, who fell downstairs, but came to honors after all and married the princess?"

"Ivede-Avede!" cried some, "Humpty Dumpty!" cried others; there was a good deal of crying and shouting. Only the fir-tree was quite silent and thought to itself: "Am I not to take part in this?" but it had already done what it was expected to do.

And the man told the story of Humpty Dumpty who fell downstairs, and after all came to honors and married the princess. And the children clapped their hands and cried: "Go on, tell us another!" They wished also to hear the story of Ivede-Avede, but he only told that of Humpty Dumpty. The fir-tree was standing quite silent and thoughtful; the birds of the wood had never told such stories. "Humpty Dumpty fell downstairs, and yet married the princess. Thus it happens in the world," thought the fir-tree, and believed that it was all true, because such a nice man had told the story. "Well, well! Who knows? Perhaps I shall also fall downstairs and marry a princess!" And it looked forward with joy to being adorned again on the following day with toys, glitter, and fruit.

"To-morrow I shall not tremble!" it thought; "I shall enjoy all my splendor thoroughly. To-morrow I shall hear the story of Humpty Dumpty again, and perhaps also that of Ivede-Avede."

All night the tree was standing silent and thoughtful. In the morning the man-servants and housemaids entered the room. "Now," thought the tree, "they will adorn me again!" But they dragged it out of the room, upstairs into the garret, and placed it there in a dark corner, where no daylight reached it. "What does this mean?" thought the tree. "What am I to do here? What can I hear in such a place?" and it leaned against the wall, and thought and thought. And, indeed, it had time enough to think; for days and nights passed, but nobody came upstairs, and when at last somebody did come, it was only to store away some big chests. Thus the tree was quite hidden; one might have thought that they had entirely forgotten it.

"Now it is winter," thought the tree. "The ground is so hard and covered with snow that people cannot plant me again! Therefore, I think, they shelter me here until spring comes. How thoughtful! How kind people are to me! I only wish it was not quite so dark and so dreadfully lonely here! Not even a small hare is to be seen! How nice it was in the wood, when the snow covered the ground and the hare was running by; I should not even mind his jumping right over me, although then I could not bear the thought of it. It is awfully lonely here, indeed!"

"Squeak, squeak," a little mouse said just then, creeping timidly forward; another one soon followed. They sniffed at the fir-tree and slipped into its branches.

"Oh, that it were not so bitter cold," said the mice, "then we should feel quite comfortable here. Don't you think so, old fir-tree?"

"I am not old at all!" replied the fir-tree; "there are many much older than myself."

"Where do you come from?" asked the mice; "what do you know?" for they were very inquisitive. "Tell us about the most beautiful place on earth! Have you been there? Have you been in the pantry where cheeses lie on the shelves, and hams hang from the ceiling, where one can dance on tallow candles, and go in thin and come out fat?"

"I have not been there," said the tree; "but I know the wood where the sun shines and the birds sing." And then the tree told the mice all about its youth. The little mice, who had never heard anything like it before, listened attentively and exclaimed:

"You have seen a great deal, indeed; how happy you must have felt!"

"Do you think so?" said the tree, and reflected on its own story. "After all, those days were not unhappy." Then it told them all about Christmas-eve, when it was so beautifully adorned with cake and lights.

"You must have been very happy, you old fir-tree," replied the mice.

"I am not old at all," repeated the tree, "I only left the wood this winter; I am somewhat forward in my growth."

"How well you can tell stories," said the little mice. Next night they returned with four more little mice, whom they wished to hear what the tree had to relate; the more the tree told them, the more it remembered distinctly all that had happened, and it thought, "Those days were happy indeed, but they may come again. Humpty Dumpty fell downstairs, and married the princess after all; perhaps I may also marry a princess!" And then the fir-tree thought of a pretty little birch in the wood, which appeared to it a beautiful princess.

"Who is Humpty Dumpty?" asked the little mice. And then the tree had to relate the whole tale. It remembered every word of it, and the little mice were so delighted that they nearly jumped to the top of the tree for joy. The next night many more mice came to listen to the tree; and on Sunday two rats came; they, however, said the story was not pretty. The little mice were very sorry, for they began to think less of it.

"Do you know only that one story?" asked the rats.

"Only that one," said the tree, "and that I heard on the happiest night of my life; but then I did not know how happy I was."

"That is a very poor tale," said the rats. "Do you not know one about bacon and tallow candles—a sort of store-room story?"

"No," said the tree.

"We do not care for this one"; thus saying, the rats went off.

In the end also the little mice stayed away, and the tree sighed and said: "How pleasant it was to see all the lively little mice sitting round me when I talked! Now all this is passed. I should be very pleased if they came to fetch me away from here."

But whenever would that happen? One morning people came to tidy the garret; the chests were put aside, the tree was dragged out of its corner and thrown roughly to the ground; a man-servant carried it at once towards the staircase, where the sun was shining.

"Now life is beginning again," thought the tree; it felt the fresh air and the first sunbeams, and soon it was carried into the courtyard. All happened so quickly that the tree forgot to look at itself; there was so much about it to look at. The courtyard bordered on a garden, where all plants were in flower; the roses hung fresh and fragrant over the small fence; the lime-trees were blooming, and the swallows flew about, saying, "Twit, twit, twit, my husband has come!" but they did not mean the fir-tree.

"Now I shall live," exclaimed the fir tree joyfully, spreading out its branches; but alas! they were all withered and yellow; and it lay between weeds and nettles. The star of gilt paper was still fixed to its top and glittered in the sunshine. Some of the bright children who had been dancing round the tree so merrily on Christmas-eve were playing in the courtyard. One of the smallest came and tore the gilt star off.

"Look, what is still sticking to the ugly fir-tree!" said the child, treading on the branches, which cracked under its boots. And the tree looked at all the fresh and beautiful flowers in the garden; it looked at itself and wished that it had remained in the dark corner of the garret; it remembered its bright youth in the forest, the delightful Christmas-eve, the little mice, which had so quietly listened to the story of Humpty Dumpty.

"All is over," said the old tree. "Oh, that I had enjoyed myself while I could do so! All is passed away."

A man-servant came and chopped the tree into small pieces, until a large bundle was lying on the ground; then he placed them in the fire, under a large copper, where they blazed up brightly; the tree sighed deeply, and each sigh was as loud as a little pistol-shot; the children, who were playing near, came and sat down before the fire, and looking into it cried, "Pop, pop." But at each little shot, which was a deep sigh, the tree thought of a summer day in the wood, or a winter night there, when the stars sparkled; it remembered the Christmas-eve and Humpty Dumpty, the only fairy tale which it had heard and knew to tell, and then it was all burned up.

The boys played in the garden, and the smallest had fixed the gilt star which had adorned the tree on its happiest night on his breast. Now all had come to an end, the tree had come to an end, and also the story, for all stories come to an end!

The Darning Needle

There was once upon a time a darning needle, which thought itself so fine that it imagined that it ought to be a sewing needle. "Take care that you hold me tightly," said the darning needle to the fingers which took it up. "Do not drop me, for if I fall on the ground one will certainly not find me again, I am so fine!"

"That's what you say," said the fingers, and seized her round the body.

"Look out! I am coming with a suite!" said the darning needle, and dragged a long thread after it; but there was no knot in the thread. The fingers directed the needle straight towards the cook's slipper. The upper leather was torn and had to be mended.

"That's degrading work," said the darning needle; "I shall never get through it; I shall break, I shall break!" And really it broke. "Did I not tell you so?" said the darning needle, "I am too fine."

"Now it's good for nothing," said the fingers; but yet they had to hold it. The cook fixed a knob of sealing-wax to the needle, and fastened her neckerchief with it. "So! now I am a scarf-pin," said the needle. "I knew very well that I should come to honor; when one is worthy one gets on in the world!" And then it laughed to itself; but one never sees when a darning needle laughs. It sat there as proudly as if it was in a state carriage, and looked in all directions.

"May I ask if you are made of gold?" it inquired of a pin, its neighbor. "You have a bright exterior, and a head of your own, although it is but small! You must endeavor to grow, for it is not every one who receives a knob of sealing-wax!" Thus saying, the darning needle raised itself so proudly that it fell out of the neckerchief, straight into the sink which the cook was rinsing down. "Now I am going on my travels," said the darning needle, "I hope I shall not be lost!" But it was lost indeed. "I am too fine for this world," it said, when it was lying in the gutter, "but I know who I am, and that is always a little pleasure." And the darning needle kept its proud bearing, and did not lose its cheerful temper. All sorts of things passed over it; chips, straws, and bits of old newspaper. "Look how they sail," said the darning needle, "they do not know what is underneath them! I am sticking fast here. See, there goes a chip, thinking of nothing in the world but itself—a chip! There is a straw drifting by; how it turns round and round! Don't think only of yourself; you might easily run against a stone. There floats a piece of newspaper; and although what is printed upon it was forgotten long ago, it gives itself airs. I am sitting here patiently and quietly; I know who I am, and that I shall continue to be!"

One day something lay by the side of it which glittered so splendidly that the darning needle thought it was a diamond; but it was only a piece of a broken glass bottle, and because it was so bright the darning needle spoke to it, and introduced itself as a scarf-pin. "I suppose you are a diamond?"—"Yes, something of that kind." And then they both thought each other something very precious; they spoke of the pride of the world.

"I have been in a girl's box," said the darning needle, "and this girl was a cook; she had five fingers on each hand, but I have never seen anything so conceited as these fingers! And yet they were only there to take me out of the box, and put me back again."

"Were they very distinguished?" asked the piece of glass. "Distinguished!" said the darning needle; " no, but haughty. They were five brothers, all born fingers. They held proudly together, although they were of different lengths. The first, the thumb, was short and thick; it stood out of the rank, and had only one joint in its back and could only make one bow; but it said, if it was cut off a man's hand he could not be a soldier. Sweet-tooth, the second finger, was put into sweet and sour dishes, pointed to the sun and the moon, and made the downstrokes when the fingers wrote. Longman, the third, looked over the heads of all the others. Gold rim, the fourth, wore a golden girdle round the waist; and little Playman did nothing at all, and was proud of it. They did nothing but brag, and therefore I left them."

"And now we sit here and glitter," said the piece of glass. At the same moment more water rushed into the gutter; it overflowed, and carried the piece of glass away. "So, now it is promoted," said the darning needle, "but I remain here; I am too fine; but that is my pride, and I have good reason for it!" And it sat there proudly and had many great thoughts. "I am almost inclined to think I am the child of a sunbeam, I am so fine! It seems to me as if sunbeams were always looking for me here under the water also! I am so fine that my mother cannot find me. If I had my old eye, the one that broke off, I believe I should cry, but I shall not do it—it is not considered good breeding to cry."

One day, a few urchins lay grubbing in the gutter, where they found old nails, farthings, and suchlike treasures. It was dirty work, but it caused them great pleasure. "Oh!" cried one, who had pricked himself with the darning needle, "look, what a fellow."

"I am not a fellow, I am a miss," said the darning needle, but nobody listened to it. The sealing wax had come off and the needle had turned black; but black makes one look thinner, and therefore it thought itself finer than ever.

"Here comes an egg-shell drifting along," said the boys, and they stuck the darning needle firmly into it. "White walls, and I am black myself," said the darning needle; "that is very becoming; now one can see me at least. I wish I may not become seasick and break." But it did not become seasick, nor did it break.

"It is a good thing against seasickness if one has a steel stomach, and does not forget that one is something better than a man. Now my seasickness is past; the finer one is, the more one can bear!"

"Crack," cried the eggshell, as a heavy cart went over it.

"Good heavens!" said the darning needle, "how it presses! Now I shall become seasick after all. I am breaking!"

But it did not break, although the heavy cart passed over it; it lay there full length, and there it may stay.

Big Claus and Little Claus

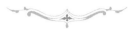

In a village there once lived two men, who had both the same name. Both were called Claus, but the one had four horses and the other had only a single one. So, to distinguish them from each other, he who had four horses was called "Big Claus," and he who had only one "Little Claus." Now let us hear what happened to both, for it is a true story.

In a village there once lived two men, who had both the same name.

Throughout the whole week Little Claus had to plow for Big Claus and lend him his only horse; then in return Big Claus lent him his four, but only once a week, and that was on Sunday. Hurrah! how Little Claus cracked his whip over all the five horses; they were indeed as good as his, on that one day. The sun shined beautifully, all the bells in the church steeple were ringing, and the people, dressed in their best, were going to church, with their hymn-books under their arm, to hear the vicar preach. They saw Little Claus, who was plowing with five horses, and he was so happy that he kept on cracking his whip and shouting, "Gee-up, all my horses!"

"You must not talk like that," said Big Claus, "only one of them is yours!"

But as soon as some one went by Little Claus forgot that he ought not to say so, and cried: "Gee-up, all my horses!"

"Well, now I must ask you to leave off saying that," said Big Claus; "for if you say it once more, I shall strike your horse on the head, so that it will die on the spot; it will be all over with him then."

"I will really not say so any more," said Little Claus. But as soon as people came near again, and nodded him "Good-day," he felt happy, and thought how very fine it looked to have five horses to plow his field; so he cracked his whip once more and cried, "Gee-up, all my horses!"

"I'll gee-up your horses!" said Big Claus, and taking a heavy bar struck Little Claus's only horse on the head, so that it fell down dead on the spot.

"Oh, now I have no longer any horse," said Little Claus, and began to cry. He then took the hide from off his horse and let it dry well in the wind, put it into a sack which he slung across his shoulder, and went to the town to sell it.

He had a very long way to go, through a great, dark wood, and a violent storm came on; he lost his way entirely, and before he came to the right road again it was evening, and much too far to reach the town or to return home before nightfall.

Close to the road lay a large farm; the shutters were up before the windows, but the light could still shine through at the top. "I daresay I shall be able to get permission to stay there for the night," thought Little Claus, and went up and knocked.

The farmer's wife opened the door, but when she heard what he wanted, she told him to be off, saying that her husband was not at home, and that she did not take in strangers.

"Well, then I must lie down outside," said Little Claus, and the farmer's wife shut the door in his face.

Close by stood a large haystack, and between this and the house was a small shed covered with a flat thatched roof.

"Oh, now I no longer have any horse," said Little Claus, and he began to cry.

"I can lie down there," thought little Claus, when he spied the roof; "that will make a splendid bed. I don't suppose the stork will fly down and bite my legs." For a live stork was standing high up on the roof, where it had its nest.

Little Claus now crept up on the shed, where he lay and turned himself over to settle down comfortably. The wooden shutters before the windows did not reach to the top, and so he could see right into the room.

There was a big table laden with wine and roast meat and a splendid fish; at this table were seated the farmer's wife and the sexton, but no one else. She was filling his glass, and he was pegging away with his fork at the fish, for it was his favorite dish.

"How ever could I get some of it, too?" thought Little Claus, and stretched his head out towards the window. Heavens! what a fine cake he saw in there! That was indeed a feast!

Now he heard some one riding from the high road towards the house; that was the woman's husband, who was coming home. He was a very good man, but he had the strange peculiarity that he could never bear to see a sexton; if he caught sight of a sexton he would get quite mad. It was also for this reason that the sexton had gone to see the wife to bid her Good-day, because he knew that her husband was not at home, and the good woman therefore placed before him the best fare that she had. But when they heard the husband coming they were startled, and the woman begged the sexton to creep into a great empty chest. He did so, because he knew that the poor man could not bear to see a sexton. The woman hastily hid all the fine things and the wine in her oven, for if her husband had seen them, he would certainly have asked what it meant.

"Ah me!" sighed Little Claus up on his shed when he saw the good things vanishing.

"Is any one up there?" asked the farmer, and cast his eyes up to Little Claus. "What are you lying there for? You had better come with me into the room."

Then Little Claus told how he had lost his way, and begged to be allowed to stay there for the night.

"Most certainly!" said the farmer; "but we must first have something to live on."

The woman received them both in a very friendly manner, laid the cloth on a long table, and gave them a large dish of porridge. The farmer was hungry and ate with a good appetite, but Little Claus could not help thinking of the fine roast meat, fish, and cake which he knew were in the oven. Under the table, at his feet, he had placed the sack containing the horse-hide, which, as we know, he was going to sell in the town. He did not care for the porridge, and therefore trod upon his sack so that the dry hide creaked.

"Hush!" said Little Claus to his sack, treading, at the same time, on it again, when it creaked louder than before.

"What is it that you have in your sack?" asked the farmer.

"Oh, that's a magician!" said Little Claus. "He says we should not eat any porridge, as he has conjured the whole oven full of roast meat, fish and cake."

"Gracious me!" said the farmer, and quickly opened the oven, where he saw all the nice dainty fare which his wife had hidden there, but which he believed the magician in the sack had conjured up for them. The woman dared not say anything, but put the things on the table at once, and so they both ate of the fish, the roast meat and the cake. Little Claus then trod on his sack again, so that the hide creaked.

"What does he say now?" asked the farmer.

"He says that he has also conjured three bottles of wine for us, and that they are standing in the corner near the oven." The woman was now obliged to bring out the wine which she had hidden, and the farmer drank and became very merry. A magician, such as Little Claus had in his sack, he would have very much liked to possess.

"Can he conjure up the devil too?" asked the farmer; "I should like to see him, for I am merry now."

"Yes," said Little Claus, "my magician can do anything that I ask of him. Can't you?" he asked, and trod on the sack to make it creak. "Do you hear? He says, 'Yes,' but the devil is very ugly; we had better not see him."

"Oh, I'm not at all afraid. I wonder what he is like."

"He will take the form of a sexton."

"Ugh!" said the farmer, "that's awful! I must tell you that I cannot bear to see a sexton. But that's nothing; I know that it's the devil, so I can easily put up with it. Now I have courage. But he must not come too near to me."

"Then I will ask my magician," said Little Claus, and treading on the sack held his ear to it.

"What does he say?"

"He says that if you open the chest which is standing in the corner there, you will see the devil crouching inside; but you must hold the lid so that he does not escape."

"Will you help me to hold it?" he said, and went up to the chest in which the woman had hidden the real sexton, who was sitting inside in a great fright.

The farmer opened the lid a little, and looked in under it. "Ugh!" he cried, and sprang back. "Yes, now I've seen him; he looked exactly like our sexton. Nay, that was terrible."

After that they were obliged to drink, and so they drank till far into the night

"You must sell me the magician," said the farmer. "Ask what you like for him. I'll give you a whole bushel full of money at once."

"No, I can't do that," said Little Claus. "Just think, how much profit I can get out of this magician."

"I should so much like to have him," said the farmer, and went on begging.

"Well," said Little Claus at last, "as you have been so good as to give me shelter to-night, I'll do it. You shall have the magician for a bushel full of money, but I must have the bushel heaped up."

"That you shall have," said the farmer. "But you must take the chest there with you. I won't keep it in my house an hour; one can never know, perhaps he is still in there."

Little Claus gave the farmer his sack containing the dry hide, and received for it a bushel full of money, heaped up too. The farmer even gave him a trunk as well, to carry away the money and the chest.

"Good-bye!" said Little Claus, and went away with his money and the large chest in which the sexton was still concealed.

On the other side of the wood was a large, deep river; the water flowed so rapidly that it was scarcely possible to swim against the stream. A large new bridge had been built across it; Little Claus stopped on the middle of this, and said quite loud so that the sexton in the chest could hear it:

"Whatever am I to do with this stupid chest? It's as heavy as if there were stones in it. I shall only get tired by dragging it farther; I'll throw it into the river. If it swims home to me, well and good, and if it doesn't, it won't matter much."

He then took hold of the chest with one hand and lifted it up a little, as if he wanted to throw it into the water.

"No, don't do that!" cried the sexton in the chest. "Let me out first."

"Ugh!" said Little Claus, and pretended to be frightened. "He's still inside! Then I must throw him into the river quickly, so that he drowns."

"Oh no, no!" shouted the sexton. "I'll give you a whole bushel full of money, if you let me go."

"Oh, well! that's different," said Little Claus, and opened the chest. The sexton crept out quickly, threw the empty chest into the water, and went to his home, where Little Claus received a bushel full of money; he had already received one from the farmer, so he now had his trunk full of money.

"See, I was well paid for the horse!" he said to himself, when he shook out all the money into a heap in his room at home. "That will make Big Claus angry, when he hears how rich I have become through my single horse; but I won't tell him all about it."

He then sent a boy to Big Claus to borrow a bushel measure.

"What can he want with that?" thought Big Claus, and smeared some tar on the bottom, so that something of whatever was measured would remain sticking to it. And so it happened, too; for when he got the bushel measure back, three new silver shilling pieces were sticking to it.

"What's that?" said Big Claus, and immediately ran to Little Claus.

"Where did you get so much money from?"

"Oh! that's for my horse-hide; I sold it yesterday evening."

"That's really well paid!" said Big Claus, and running quickly home, took an ax, and struck all his four horses on the head; he then flayed them, and drove to the town with the hides.

"Hides! Hides! Who'll buy hides!" he cried through the streets. All the shoemakers and tanners came running up and asked what he wanted for them.

"A bushel of money for each," said Big Claus.

"Are you mad?" they all cried. "Do you think we have money by the bushel?"

"Hides! Hides! Who'll buy hides!" and to all who asked him what the hides cost, he answered: "A bushel of money."

"He wants to fool us," they all said; so the shoemakers took their straps, and the tanners their leather aprons, and gave Big Claus a sound thrashing.

"Hides! Hides!" they jeeringly called after him; "yes, we'll tan your hide, till the red liquor runs down from you. Out of the town with him!" they cried, and Big Claus had to run as fast as he could, for he had never had such a sound thrashing before.

"Well," he said, when he got home, "Little Claus shall pay me for that; I'll strike him dead for it."

Little Claus's grandmother, who lived with him, had died. She had really been very cross and bad to him, but still he was sorry, and took the dead woman and laid her in his warm bed to see whether she did not come to life again. He would let her lie there the whole night; he himself would go to sleep upon a chair in the corner, as he had often done before.

As he was sitting there in the night, the door opened, and Big Claus came in with his ax. He well knew where Little Claus's bed stood, went straight up to it, and struck the grandmother on the head, thinking that it was Little Claus.

"There," he said, "now you shall not make a fool of me again," and went home.

"That is a very wicked man," thought Little Claus. "He wanted to kill me. It is lucky for grandmother that she was dead already, else he would have taken her life."

He then dressed his grandmother in her Sunday clothes, borrowed a horse of his neighbor and harnessed it to the cart; then he put his grandmother on the back seat, in order that she could not fall out as he drove, and so they rode away through the wood. By sunrise they had arrived at a large inn; here Little Claus stopped and went in to get something to drink. The landlord had a great deal of money: he was a very good man, too, but as passionate as if he were filled with pepper and tobacco.

"Good morning!" he said to Little Claus. "You got into your clothes early to-day."

"Yes," said Little Claus, "I am going to the town with my grandmother; she is sitting outside on the cart, I can't bring her into the room. Will you give her a glass of mead? But you must speak very loud, for she can't hear well."

"Yes, certainly I will," said the landlord, and poured out a large glass of mead, which he took out to the dead grandmother, who was placed upright in the cart.

"Here is a glass of mead from your son," said the landlord. The dead woman, however, did not answer a word, and sat still.

"Don't you hear?" shouted the landlord, as loud as he could; "here is a glass of mead from your grandson."

He shouted it out once more and then still once more, but as she did not move at all from her place he became angry and threw the glass in her face, so that the mead ran down her nose and she fell backwards in the cart; for she had only been placed upright and not tied fast.

"Hallo!" cried Little Claus, rushing out and seizing the landlord by the throat; "you have killed my grandmother. Look here, there is a large hole in her forehead."

"Oh, what a misfortune!" cried the landlord, wringing his hands. "All this comes of my hot temper. My dear Little Claus, I will give you a bushel of money and have your grandmother buried as if she were my own; but keep silent, or they will cut off my head and that would be so unpleasant." So Little Claus got a bushel of money, and the landlord buried his grandmother as if she had been his own.

When Little Claus came home again with all the money, he at once sent his boy over to ask Big Claus to lend him a bushel measure.

"What's that?" said Big Claus. "Have I not killed him? I must go and see for myself." So he himself took the bushel measure over to Little Claus.

"Tell me where you got all that money," he said, and opened his eyes wide when he saw what had been added.

"You didn't kill me, but my grandmother," said Little Claus; "I have sold her and got a bushel of money for her."

"That's really well paid," said Big Claus; and hurrying home, took an ax and killed his grandmother on the spot. Placing her in the cart, he drove with her to the town where the apothecary lived, and asked him whether he could buy a dead body.

"Who is it, and where did you get it?" asked the apothecary.

"It's my grandmother," said Big Claus. "I killed her to get a bushel of money for her."

"Heaven preserve us!" said the apothecary. "You are mad. Don't talk like that, or you will lose your head." And then he explained to him what a wicked deed he had done, and what a bad man he was, and that he ought to be punished; this frightened Big Claus so, that he rushed out of the shop into the cart, lashed his horses and drove home. But the apothecary and all the people thought he was mad, and so let him drive where he liked.

"You shall pay me for that!" said Big Claus, when he got on the high road outside the town. "Yes, you shall pay me for it, Little Claus." As soon as he reached home he took the largest sack that he could find, went over to Little

Claus, and said, "You have made a fool of me again. First I killed my horses, then my grandmother. That's all your fault, but you shall not fool me again." With that he took hold of Little Claus round the body and put him in his sack, then took him on his back, and called out to him: "Now I am going to take you away to drown you."

It was a long way that he had to go before he came to the river, and Little Claus was not very light to carry. The road led close by the church, and the organ was pealing and the people were singing beautifully. So Big Claus put down his sack with Little Claus in it close to the church door, and thought it might be a very good thing to go in and hear a psalm before going any farther. Little Claus could not possibly get out of the sack, and all the people were in the church; so he went in.

"Oh dear! oh dear!" sighed Little Claus in the sack, turning and twisting about; but it was impossible for him to untie the string. By-and-bye an old cattle-driver with snow-white hair passed by, with a long staff in his hand. He was driving a herd of cows and oxen before him, and these, stumbling against the sack in which Little Claus lay, it was thrown over. "Ah me!" sighed Little Claus, "I am still so young, and am going already to Heaven."

"And I, poor man," said the driver, "who am already so old, cannot get there yet."

"Open the sack," called out Little Claus; "get in instead of me, and you will go to Heaven immediately."

"With all my heart," said the driver, and untied the sack, out of which Little Claus crept at once.

"But will you look after my cattle?" asked the old man, as he got into the sack; upon which Little Claus tied it up and went away with all the cows and oxen.

Soon afterwards Big Claus came out of the church and took his sack on his back again, although it seemed to him to have become lighter, for the old cattle-driver was only half as heavy as Little Claus. "How light he is to carry now! That is because I have heard a psalm." So he went to the river, which was deep and wide, threw the sack, with the old driver in it, into the water, and called out after him, for he believed that it was Little Claus: "Lie there! You will not fool me again." He then went home; but when he came to the place where two roads crossed, he met Little Claus, who was driving his cattle along.

"What's that?" said Big Claus. "Haven't I drowned you?"

"Yes!" said Little Claus. "You threw me into the river scarcely half an hour ago."

"But where did you get these beautiful cattle?" asked Big Claus.

"These are sea-cattle," said Little Claus. "I will tell you the whole story, and thank you for having drowned me, for now I am up in the world and am really rich. How frightened I was while I was in the sack! the wind whistled in my ears as you threw me down from the bridge into the cold water. I immediately sank to the bottom, but did not hurt myself, for down there grows the finest soft grass. I fell on that and the sack was opened at once; a most lovely maiden, with snow-white clothes and a green wreath around her wet hair, took me by the hand and said, "Are you there, Little Claus? Here you have some cattle to begin with. A mile farther on the road there is another large herd, which I will give you." Then I saw that the river formed a great highway for the people of the sea. Down at the bottom they were walking and driving straight from the sea right up into the land, as far as the place where the river ends. It was full of lovely flowers and the freshest grass; the fish, which swam in the water, shot past my ears, just as the birds do here in the air. What lovely people there were there, and what fine cattle grazing in the valleys and on the hills!"

"But why did you come up again to us so quickly?" asked Big Claus. "I shouldn't have done so, if it is so fine down there."

"Well," said Little Claus, "that was good policy on my part. You heard me say that the sea-maiden told me there was a herd of cattle for me a mile farther on the road. Now by the road she meant the river, for she cannot go anywhere else. But I know what windings the river makes, first here and then there, so that it is a long way round; it is much shorter by landing here and cutting across the field back to the river. I save almost half a mile in that way, and get to my cattle more quickly."

"Oh, you are a lucky man," said Big Claus. "Do you think that I should get some cattle too if I went to the bottom of the river?"

"Yes, I think so," said Little Claus. "But I can't carry you in the sack to the river; you are too heavy for me. If you will walk there yourself and creep into the sack, I will throw you in with the greatest pleasure."

"Thank you," said Big Claus; "but if I don't get any sea-cattle when I reach the bottom, I promise you I'll give you a sound thrashing."

"Oh, don't be as bad as that!" So they both went to the river. When the cattle, who were thirsty, saw the water, they ran as fast as they could, to get down to the stream.

"See how they hurry!" said Little Claus. "They are longing to get back to the bottom."

" Yes, but help me first," said Big Claus, "else I'll thrash you"; and he crept into a large sack which had been lying across the back of one of the oxen. "Put a stone into it, or I am afraid I shall not sink to the bottom," he added.

"That's all right!" said Little Claus; but he put a large stone into the sack all the same, tied the string tightly, and then pushed. Plump! there lay Big Claus in the river, and immediately sank to the bottom.

"I don't think he'll find the cattle," said Little Claus, and went home with those that he had.

He put a large stone into the sack...
tied the string tightly, and then pushed.

The Last Dream of the Old Oak

(A Christmas Story)

In a wood, high up on the steep shore, near the open sea, stood a very old oak tree. It was three hundred and sixty-five years old, but all this long time had not appeared any longer to the tree than the same number of days to us human beings. We are awake in the daytime, we sleep at night, and then we have our dreams. It is different with a tree; it is awake during three seasons, and only begins to sleep towards the winter. Winter is its resting-time, its night after a long day, consisting of spring, summer, and autumn.

On many a warm summer day the ephemera—the fly that lives but one day—danced round its crown, lived and felt happy in the sunshine, and then the little creature rested a moment in quiet contentment on one of the large fresh oak leaves, and the oak tree would say: "Poor little one! your whole life is but one day! How very short! It is sad indeed!"

"Sad? What do you mean by that?" the ephemera used to ask. "All around me it is so wonderfully light, warm, and beautiful, and that makes me glad."

"But only one day, and then it is all over!" "Over," repeated the ephemera; "What does *over* mean? Is it not over with you too?"

"No; I live perhaps thousands of your days, and my days consist of entire seasons! That is so long that you are unable to reckon it up!"

"No. I don't understand you! You have thousands of my days, but I have thousands of moments in which I can be merry and happy. Does all the splendor of this world cease to exist when you die?"

"No," said the tree; "that will probably last much longer—indefinitely longer than I am able to imagine."

"But then we have both the same time to live, only we reckon differently." And the ephemera danced and flew about in the air, rejoicing in the possession of its wonderful wings of gauze and velvet; it enjoyed the warm air, which was saturated with the spicy fragrance of the clover fields, the dog roses, the lilac and honeysuckle, the garden hedges, thyme, the primrose, and the mint.

The fragrance was so strong that the ephemera was almost intoxicated with it. The day was long and beautiful, full of joy and sweet pleasures, and when the sun set the little fly always felt agreeably tired of all the delight. Its wings would no longer support it, and gently and slowly it glided down on the waving blades of grass, nodded as an ephemera can nod, and fell asleep, peacefully and joyfully. It was dead. "Poor little ephemera," said the oak, "that was really too short a life."

The same dance, the same questions and answers, the same falling asleep, occurred again on every summer day; all repeated itself through whole generations of ephemeras, which all felt equally merry and happy.

The oak stood awake in the spring, its morning; the summer, its midday; and the autumn, its evening; soon its resting-time, night, was approaching. The winter was at hand. Already the storms sang "Good night! good night!" Here dropped a leaf, there dropped a leaf. "We will stir you and shake you! Go to sleep, go to sleep! We shall sing you to sleep, we shall shake you to sleep, and surely it will do your old twigs good; they will crackle with delight and joy. Sleep sweetly! sleep sweetly! It is your three hundred and sixty-fifth night; properly speaking you are only a stripling! Sleep sweetly! The clouds will throw snow down and make you a covering to keep your feet warm! Sleep sweetly—and pleasant dreams!"

The oak stood there, deprived of its foliage, to go to rest for the whole long winter and to dream many a dream; all was of something that had happened to it, as in the dreams of human beings. The large tree was once small—nay, an acorn had been its cradle. According to human calculation, it was now living its fourth century; it was the largest and best tree in the wood, and over-towered by far all the other trees with its crown. It was seen from a great distance out at sea, and served as a landmark to the sailors. Of course, it had no idea that so many eyes looked for it. High up in its green crown the wood-pigeon built her nest, and the cuckoo made its voice heard; and in autumn, when its leaves looked like hammered copper, the birds of passage rested themselves there before they flew across the sea. Now, however, it was winter; the tree stood there without leaves, and one could see how crooked and knotty the branches were that grew out of the stem. Crows and jackdaws came and sat alternately on it while they talked about the hard times which were now beginning, and how difficult it was to find food in the winter.

Towards the holy Christmas time the tree dreamed a most beautiful dream. It had a distinct notion of the festive time, and it seemed to the tree as if all the church bells round about were merrily pealing, and as if all this took place on a bright, mild, and warm summer day. Fresh and green its mighty crown spread forth, the sunbeams were playing between the leaves and branches, the air was filled with the fragrance of herbs and blossoms; colored butterflies chased each other, the ephemeras danced about as if all was only there for them to enjoy. All the tree had seen happening round it during many years passed before it in a festive procession. It saw the knights and noble ladies of bygone days on horseback, with waving plumes on their heads, the falcons on their wrists, riding through the wood; the bugle sounded, the hounds barked; it saw hostile warriors in colored garments, with glittering arms, spears, and halberds, pitching tents and striking them again; the watch-fires were burning while they sang and slept under the branches of the oak tree; it saw lovers in quiet happiness meet at its trunk in the moonlight and cut their names, their initials, into the dark-green bark. Guitars and Æolian harps were once—many, many years ago—hung in the branches of the oak by merry travelers; now they were hanging there again, and their wonderful sounds rang forth. The wood-pigeons cooed as if they wished to tell what the tree was feeling, and the cuckoo called out to it how many days it had yet to live. Then the tree felt new life streaming into it, down to the smallest root and high up into the topmost branches and leaves. It felt how it spread and extended—nay, it felt, by means of its roots, that there was also warmth and life deep below in the earth; its force was increasing, it grew higher and higher, the trunk shot up, there was no resting; more and more it grew, the crown became fuller, spread out, and raised itself, and in measure as the tree grew, its happiness and its longing to reach higher and higher increased, right up to the bright warm sun. It had already grown up into the clouds, which sailed under it like flights of birds of passage, or large white swans. Every leaf of the tree had the gift of sight, as if they had eyes to see. The stars became visible to it in broad daylight; they were large and sparkling, each of them glittered as mildly and clearly as a pair of eyes; they recalled to its memory well known kind eyes—children's eyes, lovers' eyes—who had met under the tree. It was a marvelous moment, so full of joy and delight! And yet amidst all this joy the tree felt a desire, a longing wish, that all the other trees down in the wood—all the bushes, all the herbs and flowers—might be able to rise with it, see all this splendor, and feel this joy. The great majestic oak, with all its grandeur, was not quite happy without having them all, great and small, around it, and these feelings of longing passed through all the leaves and branches as vigorously as they would pass through a human breast. The crown of the tree was rocking to and fro as if it were seeking something in its deep longing; it was looking back. Then it smelled the fragrance of the thyme, and soon the still stronger scent of the honeysuckle and violet; it seemed as if the cuckoo was answering it.

Yes, through the clouds the green tops of the wood became visible, and below the oak recognized the other trees—how they grew and rose. Bushes and herbs shot high up, several tearing themselves up by the roots and flying up the quicker. The birch tree was the quickest of all; like a white flash of lightning its slender stem shot up in a zigzag line, the branches surrounding it like green gauze and flags. The whole wood, even the brown feathery reed, grew up; the birds followed and sang, and on a long blade of grass which fluttered in the air like a green silk ribbon sat a grasshopper, cleaning his wings with his legs; the cockchafers and the bees were humming; every bird was singing as well as it could; sounds and songs of joy and gladness rose up to Heaven.

"But where is the little blue flower that grows near the water," cried the oak, "and the harebell and the little daisy?" Indeed, the old oak wished to have them all around it.

"Here we are! Here we are!" echoed from all sides.

"But where is the beautiful thyme of last summer?—and wasn't there a bed of snowdrops here last year?—and the crab-apple that bloomed so beautifully, and the splendor of the woods during the whole year! Oh! that it were only born now, that it were only here now; then it could be with us!"

"We are here! We are here!" sounded voices still higher, as if they had flown up in advance.

"No! that is too beautiful to be believed!" exclaimed the old oak. "I have them all, both great and small; not one is forgotten! How is all this happiness imaginable? How is it possible?"

"In God's eternal kingdom it is possible and imaginable," sounded through the air.

The old tree, which was incessantly growing, felt its roots tearing themselves away from the earth. "That is right so, that is the best of all," said the old tree. "No fetters are holding me any longer; I can rise to the highest light and splendor, and all my beloved ones are with me, both great and small. All! All!"

That was the dream of the old oak, and while it thus dreamed a terrible storm was raging over land and sea—on holy Christmas Eve. The sea was rolling heavy waves against the shore; the tree, which crackled and groaned, was torn out of the ground by the roots at the very moment when it was dreaming that its roots tore themselves out of the earth. It fell to the ground. Its three hundred and sixty-five years had now passed away like the one day of the ephemera.

On Christmas morn, when the sun rose, the storm had abated. All the church bells were merrily pealing; out of every chimney top, even from the smallest and humblest cottage, the smoke rose up in blue clouds, like the smoke which rose from the altars of the Druids when they offered thank-offerings. The sea became gradually calm; and on board a large ship which had been struggling all night with the storm, and happily got through it, all the flags were hoisted as a sign of Christmas joy.

"The tree is gone! The old oak, our landmark on the coast," said the sailors, "it has fallen during last night's storm. Who can replace it? No one!"

Such a funeral oration, short and sincere, was pronounced on the tree, which lay stretched out on the snow near the shore; and over it passed the sound of the psalms from the ship—songs of Christmas joy, and of the redemption of the human soul through Christ, and of eternal life:

"Christians, awake! salute the happy morn.
Whereon the Savior of the world was born;
Rise to adore the mystery of love
Which hosts of angels chanted from above.
Hallelujah. Hallelujah."

Thus sounded the old hymn, and every one on board the ship felt himself edified by song and prayer, as the old tree had done in its last most beautiful dream, on Christmas morn.

The Little Mermaid

Far out in the ocean the water is as blue as the petals of the finest cornflower, and as transparent as the purest glass. But it is very deep, much deeper indeed than any anchor-chain can fathom; many steeples would have to be piled one on the top of the other in order to reach from the bottom to the surface of the water. Down there live the sea-folks.

Down there live the sea-folks.

You must not think that there is nothing but the bare white sand at the bottom of the ocean; no, on the contrary, there grow the most peculiar trees and plants, having such pliable trunks, stalks, and leaves that they stir at the slightest movement of the water, as if they were alive. All the big and small fishes glide through their branches as birds fly through the trees. Where the ocean is deepest stands the sea-king's castle; its walls are built of coral, and the high arched windows are cut out of the clearest amber; the roof is covered all over with shells, which open and close according as the current of the water sets. It looks most beautiful, for each of them is filled with pearls of priceless value; a single one of them would be a fit ornament for a queen's diadem.

The sea-king had been a widower for many years, and his aged mother was keeping house for him. She was a clever woman, but she was very proud of her noble birth; therefore she wore twelve oysters on her tail, while other distinguished sea-folks were only allowed to wear six. In every other respect she deserved unmingled praise, especially for her tender care of the sea-princesses, her grand-daughters. They were six in number, and the youngest was the most beautiful of all. Her skin was as clear and delicate as the petals of a rose, her eyes as blue as the sea in its greatest depth; but she also, like the others, had no legs—her body ended in a fish-tail. All day long the princesses used to play about in the spacious halls of the castle, where flowers blossom from the walls. When the large amber windows were thrown open the fishes came swimming to the princesses, as the swallows sometimes fly in when we open the windows; the fishes were so tame that they ate out of their hands, and suffered the princesses to stroke them.

In front of the castle was a large garden in which bright red and dark blue flowers were growing; the fruit glittered like gold, and the flowers looked like flames of fire; their stalks and leaves were continually moving. The ground was covered with the finest sand, as blue as the flame of sulphur. A peculiar blue light was shed over everything; one would rather have imagined one's self to be high up in the air, having above and below the blue sky, than at the bottom of the sea. When the sea was calm one could see the sun; it looked like an immense purple flower, from which the light streamed forth in all directions.

Each of the little princesses had her own place in the garden, where she was allowed to dig and to plant at her pleasure. One gave her flower-bed the shape of a whale, another preferred to form it like a little mermaid; but the youngest made hers as round as the sun, and her flowers were also of the purple hue of the sun. She was a peculiar child, always quiet and sensitive; while her sisters thought a great deal of all sorts of curious objects which they received from wrecked ships, she only loved her purple flowers, and a beautiful figure, representing a boy, carved out of clear white marble, which had come from some wreck to the bottom of the sea. She had planted a red weeping willow close by the marble figure, which throve well and was hanging over it with its fresh branches reaching down to the blue sand and casting a violet-colored shadow. Like the branches, this shadow was continually moving, and it gave one the impression as if the top and the roots of the tree were playing together and trying to kiss each other.

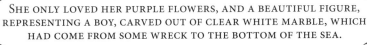

She only loved her purple flowers, and a beautiful figure, representing a boy, carved out of clear white marble, which had come from some wreck to the bottom of the sea.

The little mermaid liked most of all to hear stories about mankind above, and the grandmother had to tell her all she knew about ships, towns, and animals; she was very much surprised to hear that on earth the flowers were fragrant (the sea-flowers had no smell) and that the woods were green, that the fishes which one saw there on the trees could sing beautifully and delight everybody. The grandmother called the little birds fishes; otherwise her grand-daughters would not have understood her, as they had never seen a bird.

"When you are fifteen years old," said the grandmother, "you will be allowed to rise up to the surface of the sea and sit on the cliffs in the moonlight, where the big ships will be sailing by. Then you will also see the woods and towns."

In the following year the eldest princess would complete her fifteenth year; the other sisters were each one year younger than the other; the youngest therefore had to wait fully five years before she could go up from the bottom of the sea and look at the earth above. But each promised to tell her sisters what she liked best on her first visit; for their grandmother, they thought, did not tell them enough—there were so many things on which they wished to be informed. None of them, however, longed so much to go up as the youngest, who had to wait the longest time, and was always so quiet and pensive. Many a night she stood at the open window and looked up through the dark blue water, watching the fishes as they splashed in the water with their fins and tails. She could see the moon and the stars—they looked quite pale, but appeared through the water much larger than we see them. When something like a dark cloud passed over her and concealed them for a while, she knew it was either a whale, or a ship with many human beings, who had no idea that a lovely little mermaid was standing below stretching out her white hands towards the keel of their ship.

The eldest princess now completed her fifteenth year, and was allowed to rise up. When she came back she had to tell about hundreds of things: the greatest pleasure, she said, was to lie in the moonlight on a sandbank, when the sea was calm, and to look at the near coast and the large town where the lights sparkled like many hundreds of stars; to hear the music and noise caused by the clamor of carriages and human voices, to see the many church-steeples and to listen to the ringing of the bells. The youngest sister listened attentively to all this, and when she again, at night, stood at the open window and looked up through the dark-blue water, she thought of the great town, with all its bustle and noise, and imagined she heard the ringing of the bells in the depth of the sea.

In the following year the second sister's turn came to rise up to the surface of the sea and to swim whither she pleased. She came up just as the sun was setting, and this aspect she considered the most beautiful of all she saw. The whole sky looked like gold, and she could not find words to describe the beautiful clouds. Purple and violet, they were sailing by over her head; but even quicker than the clouds she saw a flight of wild swans flying towards the sun; she followed them, but the sun sank down and the rosy hue on the surface of the water and in the clouds vanished.

The year after, the third sister rose up. She was the boldest of all, and swam up the mouth of a broad river. She saw beautiful green hills covered with vines. Strongholds and castles peeped out of the splendid woods; she heard the birds sing, and the sun was shining so warmly that she had often to dive down and cool her burning face. In a little creek she found a troop of human children playing; they were quite naked, and splashed in the water; she wished to play with them, but they ran away, terrified. Then a little black animal, a dog, came—she had never seen one before—and barked so dreadfully at her that she was frightened, and hurried back as fast as she could to the open sea. But she could never forget the stately woods, the green hills, and the nice children who could swim, although they had no fish-tails.

The fourth sister was not so daring; she remained out in the open sea, and declared that there it was most pleasant to stay. There, she said, one could look around many miles, and the sky appeared to one like an immense glass globe. She had also seen ships, but only from a great distance; they looked to her like seagulls. The playful dolphins, she said, threw somersaults, while the big whales spouted up the sea-water through their nostrils, as if many hundred fountains were playing all around her.

Now the fifth sister's turn came, and as her birthday was in winter she saw something different from her sisters on her first visit. The sea looked quite green; enormous icebergs were floating around her—every one of them was like pearl, she said, although they were much higher than the church steeples built by men. They had the most peculiar shapes and glittered like diamonds. She had seated herself on one of the highest, and while the wind was playing with her hair she noticed how the ships were tossed about; towards the evening the sky became covered with black clouds, it lightened and thundered, and the big ice-blocks reflected the flashes of lightning while they were tossed up by the roaring sea. The sailors reefed all their sails, for they were terrified and anxious; but she was sitting quietly on the floating iceberg, and watching how the flashes of lightning descended zigzag into the foaming sea.

The first time one of the sisters came to the surface, all the new and beautiful things charmed her; but now, being as grown-up girls allowed to rise whenever they pleased, all this became indifferent to them, and after a month they declared that it was best down below in their own home. On many a night the five sisters would rise to the surface of the water arm in arm, in a row, and sing, for they had beautiful voices, much finer than any human being ever has; and when a storm was approaching, and they thought that some ships might be wrecked, they swam in front of them, singing of the beautiful things at the bottom of the sea, and bidding the people not to be afraid, but come down. The people, however, did not understand them, and mistook their singing for the noise of the wind; they never saw the treasures below, for when the ship went down they were drowned, and only arrived dead at the sea-king's castle. When her sisters thus went up arm-in-arm, the youngest princess used to stand alone and follow them with her eyes; then she often felt as if she must cry; but mermaids have no tears, therefore they suffer much more than we do.

"Oh! that I were already fifteen years old," she said; "I know I shall love the world above, and the people that dwell in it, very much."

At last she was fifteen. "You are now grown up," said her grandmother, the old dowager-queen, to her; "now let me adorn you like your sisters." She placed a wreath of white lilies on her head, the petals of the flowers being half-pearls; and in order to show her high rank the old lady caused eight oysters to be fixed to her grand-daughter's tail.

"They hurt me, Granny," said the little mermaid. "Never mind, my child, pride must suffer pain," replied the old lady. The little princess would have gladly taken off all her ornaments and the heavy wreath; her purple flowers would have suited her much better, but she could not offend her grandmother. "Farewell!" she said, and rose up as lightly as a bubble. The sun had just set when she lifted her head out of the water, but the clouds were still colored like purple and gold; the evening-star sparkled beautifully through the rose-tinted atmosphere; the air was mild and fresh, and the sea perfectly calm. There was a big ship with three masts lying before her; only one sail was set, as not a breath of air was stirring; the sailors were sitting about on deck and in the rigging. There were music and dancing on board, and when it became dark many hundreds of colored lamps were lighted, and it looked as if the flags of all nations were floating in the air. The little mermaid swam up close to the cabin windows, and when the waves lifted her up she could see many well dressed people through the clear panes. The most beautiful of them was a young prince with large black eyes—he certainly seemed not older than sixteen; it was his birthday, and that was the cause of all this rejoicing. The sailors were dancing on deck, and when the young prince stepped out of the cabin-door hundreds of rockets were thrown up into the air, and became for some moments as bright as day. The little mermaid was frightened, and dived under the water; but soon she lifted up her head again, and then it seemed to her as if all the stars were falling down from the sky. She had never seen such a display of fireworks. Large Catherine-wheels turned rapidly round, splendid fiery fishes flew through the air, and all was reflected by the bright calm sea. On the ship it was so light that one could distinctly see everything, even the smallest rope. And the young prince was so beautiful! He shook hands with the people and smiled graciously, while the music sounded dreamily through the starry night.

It became very late, but the little mermaid could not turn her eyes away from the ship and the beautiful prince. The colored lamps were extinguished; no more rockets were sent up nor cannons fired off. But in the sea, deep below, was a strange murmuring and humming, while the little mermaid was rocking on the waves and looking into the cabin. Soon the wind began to blow; one sail after another was furled; the waves rose up high; flashes of lightning were seen in the distance; a terrible storm was approaching. Then all the sails were reefed. The large ship in its rapid course was tossed about like a nutshell by the waves, which rose up as high as mountains, as if they would roll over the top of the masts. The ship dived like a swan down between the waves, and was then carried up again by them to a great height. The little mermaid thought it was a pleasant journey; not so the sailors. The ship creaked and groaned; her strong planks, were bending under the weight of the heavy waves which entered into her; the mainmast was broken like a reed; the ship lay over on her side, and the water rushed over her. The little mermaid then perceived that the crew was in danger; she herself had to be careful, lest the posts and planks floating about on the water might hurt her. For moments it was so dark that one could distinguish nothing, but when it lightened everything was visible. The little mermaid was looking out for the prince; she saw him sink down into the depths when the ship broke up. She was very pleased, for now she thought he would come down to her. But soon she remembered that men cannot live in the water, and that he would arrive dead at her father's castle. No, he must not die! Heedless of the beams and planks floating on the waters, she dived down to the bottom, and came up again in search of the prince. At last she found him; his strength was failing him; he was no longer able to swim in the storm-tossed sea; his arms and legs became powerless; his beautiful eyes closed; he would surely have died had not the little mermaid come to his assistance. She held up his head, and let the waves drift them where they would.

She held up his head,
and let the waves drift them where they would.

Next morning the storm had abated, but not a plank was visible of the ship anywhere; the sun rose purple and radiant out of the water, and seemed to impart new life to the prince's cheeks; his eyes, however, remained closed. The mermaid kissed his beautiful forehead, stroked back his wet hair; he looked to her very much like the white marble figure in her little garden at home. She kissed him again and again, and wished that he were alive.

Now she had before her eyes the dry land, where high mountains towered into the clouds, while the snow was glittering on their summits, and looking like swans resting there. Down on the coast were magnificent green woods, and quite in the foreground stood a church or a convent—she did not know which; but at any rate it was a building. Lemon and orange trees were growing in the garden, and high palms stood before the gate. The sea formed a little bay here and was quite calm, although very deep; she swam straight to the cliff, where the fine white sand had been washed ashore, and put, him down, taking special care that his head was raised up to the warm sunshine. Then all the bells began to ring in the large white building, and many young girls passed through the garden. The little mermaid swam farther out, hid herself behind some rocks, covered her hair and breast with sea-foam, lest anybody might see her little face, and watched to see who would come to the poor prince. After a while a young girl came to the spot where the prince was lying; at first she seemed very much frightened, but she soon recovered herself, and called some people. The little mermaid saw that the prince came back to life, and smiled at all who stood around him, but at her he did not smile; he little knew that she had saved him. She was very sad; and when they had taken him into the large building, she dived down and so returned to her father's castle.

She had always been silent and pensive; now she was still more so. Her sisters asked her what she had seen when she went up for the first time, but she told them nothing. Many a morning and many an evening she returned to the spot where she had left the prince; she saw how the fruit in the garden became ripe and was gathered, how the snow melted on the high mountains; but she never caught sight of the prince, and each time she returned home she was more mournful than before.

Her only consolation was to sit in her little garden, and to put her arms round the marble figure which resembled the prince, but she no longer looked after her flowers. Her garden became a wilderness; the plants straggled over the paths, and twined their long stalks and leaves round the trunks and branches of the trees, so that it became quite dark and gloomy.

At last she could bear it no longer, and confided her troubles to one of her sisters, who of course told the others. These, and a few other mermaids who mentioned it confidentially to their intimate friends, were the only people who were in the secret. One of them knew the prince, and could tell them where his kingdom was. She also had witnessed the festival on board the ship.

"Come, dear sister," said the other princesses; and arm-in-arm, in a long row, they rose up to the spot where the prince's castle stood. It was built of bright yellow stone, and had broad marble staircases, one of which reached right down to the sea. Magnificent gilt cupolas surmounted the roof, and in the colonnades, running all round the building, stood lifelike marble statues. Through the clear panes in the high window could be seen splendid halls, where costly silk curtains and beautiful tapestry hung, and the wall was covered with paintings so exquisite that it was a pleasure to look at them. In the center of the largest hall a fountain played; its jets rose as high as the glass cupola in the ceiling, through which the sun shined upon the water and the beautiful plants growing in the great basin.

Now she knew where he dwelt, and near there she passed many an evening and many a night on the water. She swam much closer to the shore than any of the others would have ventured; nay, she even went up the narrow canal under the magnificent marble balcony which threw a large shadow on the water. Here she sat and gazed at the young prince, who thought that he was quite alone in the moonlight. Often she saw him sailing in a stately boat, decorated with flags, and with music on board. She listened from behind the green rushes; and when the wind caught her long silver-white veil, and people noticed it, they imagined it was a swan opening its wings. Many a time at night, when the fishermen were upon the sea with torches, she heard them say many good things about the prince, and she was glad that she had saved his life when he was drifting half-dead upon the waves; she remembered how his head had rested on her bosom, and how fervently she had kissed him, but he knew nothing about it, and did not even dream of her. Her love for mankind grew from day to day, and she longed more and more to be able to live among them, for their world seemed to her so much larger than hers. They could cross the sea in large ships, and ascend mountains towering into the clouds. The lands which they possessed, both woods and fields, stretched farther than her eyes could reach. There were still so many things on which she wished to have information, and her sisters could not answer all her questions; therefore she asked her grandmother, who knew the upper world very well, and appropriately styled it "the countries above the sea."

"If human beings are not drowned," asked the little mermaid, "can they live for ever? Do they not die as we do down here in the sea?"

"Yes" replied the old lady. "They also die, and their life is even shorter than ours. We sometimes live to be three hundred years old; but when we cease to exist here we are turned into foam on the surface of the water, and have not even a grave in the depth of the sea among those we love. We never live again; our souls are not immortal; we are like the green seaweed, which, when once severed from its root, can never grow again. Men, on the other hand, have a soul which lives for ever after the body has become dust; it rises through the sky, up to the shining stars. As we rise out of the sea, and behold all the countries of the earth, so they rise to unknown glorious regions which we shall never see."

"Why have we not also an immortal soul?" asked the little mermaid, sorrowfully. "I would gladly give all the years I have yet to live, if I could be a human being only for one day, and to have the hope of seeing that marvelous country beyond the sky."

"You must not dream of that," replied the old lady. "We are much happier and better off than mankind above."

"Then I shall die, and drift on the sea as foam, never hearing the music of the waves, or seeing the beautiful flowers and the red sun. Is there not anything I can do in order to obtain an immortal soul?"

"No!" said the grandmother. "Only if a man would love you so much that you would be dearer to him than father or mother, if he would cling with all his heart and all his love to you, and let the priest place his right hand into yours, with the promise to be faithful to you here and to eternity, then his soul would flow over into your body, and you would receive a share of the happiness of mankind. He would give you a soul and yet keep his own. But that can never happen! What is beautiful here below, your fish tail, they consider ugly on earth—they do not know any better; up there one must have two clumsy limbs, which they call legs, in order to be beautiful."

The little mermaid sighed, and looked at her fish-tail mournfully. "Let us be merry," said the old lady. "Let us dance and make the best of the three hundred years of our life. That is truly quite enough; afterwards repose will be more pleasant. Tonight we will have a court ball."

Such a splendid sight is never seen on earth. The walls and the ceiling of the large ballroom were of thick transparent glass. Several hundred enormous shells, purple and bright green, stood at each side in long rows, filled with blue fire, which lit up the whole room and shined through the walls so that the sea outside was quite illuminated; one could see countless fishes, of all sizes, swimming against the glass walls; the scales of some gleamed with purple, others glittered like silver and gold. A broad stream ran through the middle of the ballroom, upon which the sea-folks, both men and women, danced to the music of their own sweet songs. Human beings have not such beautiful voices. The little mermaid sang best of all, and the whole court applauded with fins and tails. For a moment she felt a joy in her heart at the thought that she possessed the most beautiful voice of all living on earth or in the sea. But soon her mind returned to the world above; she could not forget the beautiful prince, nor cease grieving that she did not possess an immortal soul like his. Therefore she stole out of her father's castle; and while within the others enjoyed songs and merriment, she sat sorrowfully in her little garden.

Then she heard a bugle sound through the water, and thought, "Surely now he is sailing above, he who fills my mind, and into whose hands I should like to entrust my fate. I will dare all in order to obtain him and an immortal soul! While my sisters are dancing in my father's castle I will go to the sea-witch, whom I have always feared so much; perhaps she can advise and help me."

Then the little mermaid left her garden and went out to the roaring whirlpools where the witch dwelt. She had never gone that way before; no flowers, no seaweed even, was growing there—only bare gray sandy soil surrounded the whirlpools, where the water rushed round like mill-wheels and drew everything it got hold of down into the depths. She had to pass right through these dreadful whirlpools in order to reach the witch's territory. For a good part of the way the road led over warm bubbling mud; this the witch called her peat-moor. Behind this her house stood, in a strange wood, for all the trees and bushes were polypes—half-animals and half-plants. They looked like snakes, with many hundred heads, growing out of the ground. All the branches were slimy arms with fingers like supple worms, every limb was moving from the root to the highest branch, all they could seize out of the sea they clutched and held fast, never letting it go again. The little mermaid stopped timidly in front of them; her heart was beating with fear, she nearly turned back again; but then she thought of the prince and the immortal soul, and regained her courage. She twisted her long flowing hair round her head, lest the polypes might seize it; she crossed her hands upon her breast, and shot through the water like a fish, right past the dreadful polypes, which stretched out their supple arms and fingers after her. She saw that each of them had seized something and held it tightly with hundreds of little arms. The polypes held in their arms white skeletons of people who had perished at sea and had sunk into the depth, the oars of ships, and chests, skeletons of land animals, and a little mermaid whom they had caught and strangled: this latter was the most dreadful sight to the little princess.

Then she came to a big marshy place in the wood, where large fat water-snakes were rolling about, and showing their ugly light yellow bodies.

In the middle of this place stood a house, built with the white bones of shipwrecked people; there the sea-witch sat, letting a toad eat out of her mouth, as we should feed a little canary with sugar. The ugly fat water-snakes she called her little chickens, and allowed them to crawl all over her.

"I know very well what you want," said the sea-witch. "It is silly of you, but you shall have your way; you will become wretchedly unhappy, my beautiful princess. You wish to get rid of your fish-tail and have two limbs instead, which men use for walking, that the young prince may fall in love with you and that you may gain him, and an immortal soul." Thus saying the old witch laughed loud and hideously, so that the toads and the snakes fell to the ground, where they wriggled about. "You are just in good time," said the witch; "if you had come to-morrow after sunrise, I should not have been able to help you for a whole year. I will prepare you a drink, and you must swim ashore before the sun rises, and sit down and drink it; then your tail will disappear and shrink together into what mankind call legs; but it will hurt you, as if a sharp sword pierced you. Every man who sees you will say that you are the most beautiful girl he has ever seen. You will keep your gracefulness, and no dancer will be able to move as lightly as you; but at each step that you take you will feel as though you trod on a sharp knife, and as if your blood must flow. If you are ready to suffer all this, I will help you."

"Yes!" said the little mermaid, with a trembling voice; and she thought of the prince and the immortal soul.

"But remember," said the witch, "if you have once received a human form you can never become a mermaid again; you will never be able to return again to your sisters and to your father's castle; and if you fail to gain the prince's love, so that he forgets, for your sake, father and mother, clings to you with body and soul, and makes the priest join your hands, that you become man and wife, you will not obtain an immortal soul. On the first morning after he has wedded another, your heart will break, and you will become foam on the water."

"I will have it," said the little mermaid, and turned as pale as death.

"But you must pay me," said the witch, "and it is not a little that I ask. You have the most beautiful voice of all who live at the bottom of the sea; you may think you can bewitch him with it; but this voice you must give me. I will have the best thing you possess in exchange for my costly drink, for I must give you my own blood, that the drink may be strong enough, and as cutting as a two-edged sword."

"If you take my voice," said the little mermaid, "what is left to me?"

"Your fine figure," said the witch, "your gracefulness and your speaking eyes—with these you may easily capture a human heart. Now, have you lost your courage? Put out your little tongue, that I may cut it off in payment, and I will give you the wonderful drink."

"Do it," said the little mermaid; and the witch placed her pot on the fire to prepare the draft.

"Cleanliness is a good thing " she said, and scoured the kettle with snakes which she had tied into a bundle; then she pricked herself in the breast and let her black blood drop into it. The steam rose up in the strangest shapes; any one who could have seen it, would have been frightened to death. Every moment the witch threw new things into the pot, and when it boiled the sound was like the weeping of a crocodile. At last the drink was ready, and looked like the clearest water.

"There it is," said the witch, and cut the little mermaid's tongue off; so now she was dumb, and could neither sing nor speak. "If the polypes should seize you when you go back through my wood," said the witch, "you have only to throw one drop of this fluid over them, and their arms and fingers will break into a thousand pieces." But the little mermaid had no need of it; the polypes shrunk back in fear at the sight of the sparkling drink, which shined in her hand like a glittering star.

Thus she passed quickly through the wood and the marsh and the roaring whirlpools. She could see her father's castle; the torches in the ballroom were all extinguished; they were all asleep; she dared not go to them; now she was dumb and on the point of leaving them for ever, she felt as though her little heart would break. She stole into the garden, took a blossom from each of her sisters' flower-beds, kissed her hands a thousand times towards the castle, and rose up through the dark blue sea. The sun had not yet risen when she reached the prince's castle and went up the magnificent marble steps. The moon was shining more brightly than usual. The little mermaid took the burning draft, and felt as though a two-edged sword pierced her tender body; she fainted, and lay there as if dead. When the sun rose out of the sea she awoke and felt a sharp pain, but just before her stood the beautiful young prince. He fixed his black eyes upon her, so that she cast hers down, and noticed that her fish tail had disappeared, and that she had, instead, two of the prettiest feet any girl could wish for. As she had no clothes she wrapped herself in her long hair. The prince asked her who she was, and where she came from; she looked at him sweetly and yet mournfully with her dark blue eyes, for she was unable to speak. Then he took her by the hand and led her into the castle. At every step she took she felt, as the witch had told her in advance, as if she trod upon needles and knives; but she suffered it willingly, and stepped as lightly as a soap-bubble at the prince's side, who, with all the others, admired her graceful movements.

They gave her splendid dresses of silk and muslin to put on, and she was the most beautiful of all women in the castle; but she was mute, and could neither sing nor speak. Lovely slaves, dressed in silk and gold, came to sing before the prince and his royal parents. One sang better than all the rest, and the prince clapped his hands and smiled at her. Then the little mermaid became sorrowful; she knew that she had been able to sing much more sweetly, and thought, "Oh! if he only knew that in order to be with him I have sacrificed my voice for ever!"

Then the slaves danced graceful dances to the loveliest music; and the little mermaid lifted her beautiful white arms, balanced herself on tiptoe, and glided, dancing, over the floor; none of them could equal her. At every movement her beauty became still more apparent, and her eyes spoke more deeply to the heart than the songs of the slaves. All were charmed, especially the prince, who called her his little foundling. She danced again, and again, although she felt, whenever her feet touched the ground as though she trod upon sharp knives. The prince wished her always to remain with him, and gave her permission to sleep on a velvet cushion before his door.

He had her dressed like a page, that she might accompany him on horseback. They rode through the fragrant woods, where the green boughs touched their shoulders and the birds sang in the fresh foliage. She climbed with the prince to the summits of the high mountains, and although her tender feet bled so much that even others could see it, she smiled and followed him until they saw the clouds sailing beneath their feet, like a flight of birds traveling to foreign countries. At home, in the prince's castle, when the others slept at night, she went out on the broad marble staircase; it was cooling for her burning feet to stand in the cold sea-water, and then she thought of those below in the deep. One night her sisters came up arm in arm; they sang mournfully as they floated on the water; she beckoned to them, and they recognized her and told her how much she had grieved them. After this she saw them every night, and once she also saw her old grandmother, who had not come up to the surface for many, many years, and the sea-king with his crown on his head. They stretched out their hands towards her, but they did not venture so close to the land as her sisters.

The prince cared more for her from day to day; he loved her as one would love a dear good child, but he never had the least thought of marrying her; and yet she had to become his wife before she could obtain an immortal soul, otherwise she would turn to foam on the sea the morning after his wedding.

"Don't you love me most of all?" the mermaid's eyes seemed to say when the prince took her in his arms and kissed her beautiful forehead.

"Yes, I care most for you," he said, "for you have the best heart of them all. You are most devoted to me, and resemble a young girl whom I once saw, but whom I shall certainly not find again. I was on board a ship which was wrecked; the waves washed me ashore near a sacred temple, where several young girls officiated. The youngest of them found me on the beach, and saved my life. I only saw her twice; she would be the only girl in the world I could love; but you are like her, and you almost efface her likeness from my heart. She belongs to the sacred temple, and therefore my good fortune has sent you to me. Let us never separate."

"Alas! he does not know that I have saved his life," thought the little mermaid. "I carried him across the sea towards the wood where the temple stands; I was sitting behind the foam, looking to see if any one would come to him. I saw the beautiful girl whom he loves better than me." She sighed deeply, for she could not weep. "The girl belongs to the sacred temple, he has said. She will never come out into the world; they will never meet again; but I am near him, and see him every day. I will care for him, love him, and sacrifice my life for him."

But soon the rumor spread that the prince was to marry the beautiful daughter of a neighboring king, and that was why they were equipping a magnificent ship. They say the prince is traveling to see the neighboring king's country, but in reality he goes to see his daughter. A large suite is to accompany him. The little mermaid shook her head and smiled; she knew the prince's thoughts much better than the others. "I must travel," he had said to her; "I must go and see the beautiful princess, for my parents wish it; but they will not compel me to marry her. I cannot love her; she is not like the beautiful girl in the temple, whom you resemble. Should I one day select a bride, I should prefer you, my dumb foundling with the eloquent eyes." And he kissed her ruby lips, and played with her long tresses, and placed his head on her bosom, so that she began to dream of human happiness and an immortal soul.

"You are not afraid of the sea, my dumb child?" he said to her when they were standing on the stately ship that was to take him to the neighboring king's country. He told her of the storm and of the calm, of the strange fishes in the deep, and of the marvelous things divers had seen there. She smiled at his words, for who knew more about the things at the bottom of the sea than she did? In the moonlight night, when all were asleep except the man at the wheel, she sat on board, gazing down into the clear water.

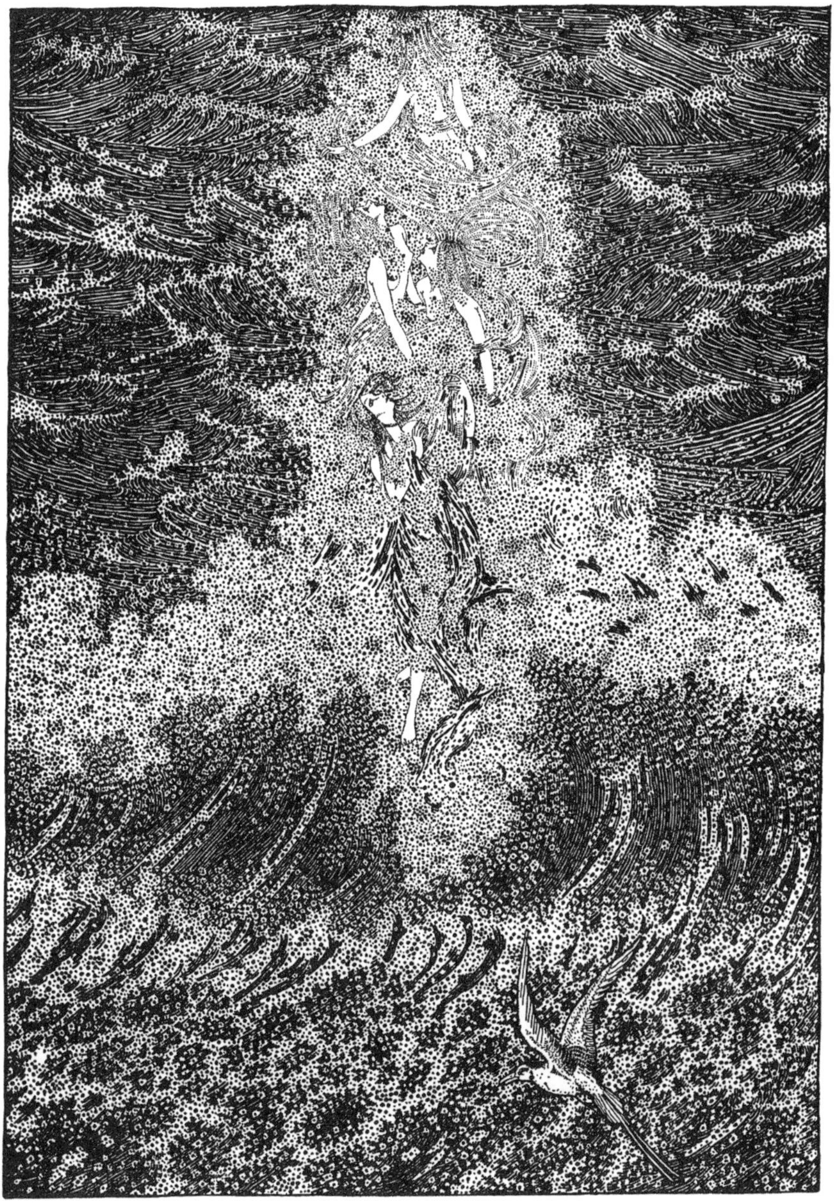

Her sisters came up to the surface, looked mournfully at her, and wrung their white hands.

Then she imagined she saw her father's castle; and her grandmother with her silver crown on her head, looking up through the violent currents at the ship's keel. Her sisters came up to the surface, looked mournfully at her, and wrung their white hands. She beckoned them, smiled, and wished to tell them she was comfortable and happy, but a sailor boy approached her, and her sisters dived under, so that he thought the white objects he had seen were foam on the surface of the water.

The next morning the ship arrived in the harbor of the neighboring king's splendid city. All the church bells were merrily pealing, trumpets were sounding from the high towers, while the soldiers paraded, with colors flying and bayonets glittering. Every day another festivity took place; balls and entertainments followed one another; but the princess had not yet come. They said she was being educated in a sacred temple far away, where she was learning every royal virtue. At last she arrived. The little mermaid was anxious to see her beauty, and did not fail to acknowledge it when she saw her. She had never seen a lovelier being; her complexion was clear and delicate, and behind dark lashes smiled a pair of dark blue, faithful-looking eyes.

"You are she who saved me when I was lying like a dead body on the beach," said the prince, and he pressed his blushing bride to his heart. "I am too happy," he said to the little mermaid. "My greatest hopes have been realized. You will be glad to hear of my happiness, for you have always been so kind to me." The little mermaid kissed his hand, and felt as if her heart was going to break. She knew that she was to die on his wedding morning, and turn to foam on the sea.

The church bells pealed, heralds rode through the streets and announced the engagement. On all the altars sweet-smelling oil burnt in costly silver lamps. The priests swung their censers; bride and bridegroom joined hands, and received the bishop's blessing. The little mermaid was dressed in silk and gold, and carried the bride's train; but her ears did not hear the festive music, her eyes did not see the sacred ceremony; she thought of the night of her death, and all that she had lost in this world.

The very same evening bride and bridegroom went on board the ship; the cannons roared; the flags streamed in the wind; in the middle of the ship a beautiful tent of purple and gold was erected for the royal couple.

The sails swelled in the wind, and the ship glided gently and lightly through the smooth sea. When it became dark, colored lamps were lit, and the sailors danced merrily on deck. The little mermaid could not help thinking of the first time she rose to the surface, when she had witnessed the same splendor and joy; she danced madly, hovering like a swallow when it is pursued. All applauded her, for she had never danced so well. It was like sharp knives cutting her tender feet, but she did not feel it; her heart suffered much greater pain. She knew that it was the last evening that she was to be with him—him for whom she had deserted her relatives and her home, sacrificed her sweet voice, and daily suffered endless pain, while he had not the slightest idea of it. It was the last night that she could breathe the same air with him, and see the deep sea and the starry sky; eternal night, without thought or dream, was waiting for her who had not been able to gain a soul. On board the ship joy and merriment lasted till long past midnight; she laughed and danced while her heart was full of thoughts of death. The prince kissed his beautiful bride, and she fondly touched his dark curls, and arm in arm they retired to rest in the magnificent tent.

Then all became still on board; only the man at the wheel remained at his post. The little mermaid rested her white arms on the railing of the ship, and looked towards the east for the morning dawn; the first sunbeam she knew would kill her. She saw her sisters rising out of the waves; they were as pale as herself; their beautiful long hair was no longer fluttering in the wind—it was cut off. "We have given it to the witch, that we might help you, and save you from death to-night. She has given us a knife; here it is! Look how sharp it is! Before the sun rises you must thrust it into the prince's heart, and when the warm blood spurts upon your feet, they will grow together again into a fish-tail, and you will be a mermaid once more; then you can come back to us, and live your three hundred years before you become dead salt sea-foam. Hasten! You or he must die before the sun rises. Our grandmother is so grieved, her white hair has also been cut off by the witch's scissors. Kill the prince and return to us! Hasten! Do you see that red streak in the sky? In a few minutes the sun will rise, and then you must die!"

Then they heaved a mournful sigh, and disappeared in the waves.

The little mermaid drew back the purple curtain at the door of the tent, and saw the beautiful bride lying with her head on the prince's breast. She bent down and kissed his forehead, and looked up to the sky, where daybreak was approaching; then she looked at the sharp knife, and again at the prince, who murmured his bride's name in his dreams. Only she was in his thoughts, and the knife trembled in the little mermaid's hand. Suddenly she threw it far out into the sea, and where it fell the waves looked red, and it seemed as if drops of blood were spurting up out of the water. As she was passing away she looked once more at the prince, then threw herself down from the ship into the sea, and felt her body dissolving into foam.

The sun rose out of the sea, and his rays fell with gentleness and warmth upon the cold sea-foam; the little mermaid felt no pain of death. She saw the bright sun, and above her were hovering hundreds of transparent beings; their language was melodious, but so ethereal that no human ear could hear them, and no earthly eye could see them; they were lighter than air, and floated about in it without wings. The little mermaid noticed that she had a body like theirs, which rose higher and higher out of the foam.

"Where am I coming to?" she asked, and her voice sounded like that of the other beings—so ethereal that no earthly music could equal it. "To the daughters of the air," replied the others. "The mermaids have no immortal souls, and can never obtain one unless they gain the love of human beings; their eternal existence depends on another's power. The daughters of the air have no immortal soul either, but they can obtain one for themselves by good actions. We fly to the hot countries where the poisonous vapors kill mankind, and bring them cool breezes. We spread the fragrance of the flowers through the air, and refresh and heal them. When we have striven for three hundred years to achieve all the good that is in our power, we obtain an immortal soul, and share the eternal happiness of mankind. You poor little mermaid, you have striven with all your heart for the same object; you have endured and suffered; now you have risen to the aerial world; and now, after three hundred years of good works, you will gain an immortal soul for yourself."

And the little mermaid raised her eyes up to the sun and felt tears in them for the first time.

On the ship there was life and noise once more; she saw how the prince and his beautiful bride were looking for her; mournfully they gazed at the glittering foam, as if they knew that she had thrown herself into the waves. Invisibly she kissed the bride's forehead and caressed the prince; then she rose with the other children of the air up to the rosy cloud which sailed through the ether.

"After three hundred years we float thus into the eternal Kingdom of God!"

"But we may get there sooner," whispered one of the daughters of the air. "Invisibly we penetrate into the houses of human beings, where they have children, and for every day on which we find a good child that causes its parents joy and deserves their love, God shortens our period of probation. The child does not know when we fly through the room, and if we smile for joy, one of the three hundred years is taken off; but if we see a naughty or wicked child, we must shed tears of sorrow, and every tear augments our period of probation by one day.

The Old Street Lamp

Have you ever heard the story of the old street lamp? It is not particularly amusing, it is true, but still it is worth hearing for once.

It was a very honest old lamp, that had done its duty for many, many years, but was now to retire from active service. It felt like an old ballet-dancer who dances for the last time, and who on the morrow will sit in her garret forgotten. The lamp was very anxious indeed about the next day, for it knew that it was to appear for the first time in the Town Hall and be examined by the burgomaster and the council to see whether it was fit for further service or not.

It was to be decided whether it was in future to show its light for the inhabitants of one of the suburbs, or in some factory in the country; its way might even lead straight to an iron foundry to be melted down. In the latter case anything might indeed be made of it, but the thought whether it would then retain the recollection of having formerly been a street lamp troubled it terribly. Whatever might happen to it, this much was certain: that it would be separated from the watchman and his wife, who looked upon it as belonging to their family. When the lamp was hung up for the first time, the watchman was a sturdy young man; it happened at the very same hour when he first entered on his duties. Yes, it was certainly a long time ago, that it became a lamp and he a watchman. The wife was at that time rather proud. Only when she went by in the evening would she deign to notice the lamp; in the daytime, never. But now, of late years, when they all three, the watchman, his wife, and the lamp, had grown old, the wife had also tended it, cleaned it, and provided it with oil. The old couple were thoroughly honest; never had they cheated the lamp of one drop of its proper measure of oil.

It was its last evening in the street, and on the morrow it was to go to the Town Hall; these were two gloomy thoughts. No wonder that it did not burn brightly. But many other thoughts passed through it too. To how much had it lent its light! How much it had seen! Perhaps quite as much as the burgomaster and the council. But it did not give utterance to these thoughts, for it was a good, honest old lamp, which would never have hurt any one, least of all the authorities. It thought of many things, and from time to time its flame flickered up. At such moments it had a feeling that it, too, would be remembered.

"There was that handsome young man—it is certainly a long time ago—who had a letter on pink paper with gilt edges. It was so daintily written, as if by a lady's hand. Twice he read it and kissed it and looked up at me with eyes which plainly said, 'I am the happiest of men!' Only he and I knew what was written in this first letter from his love. Yes, there is still another pair of eyes that I remember. It is something wonderful how thoughts jump about. There was a funeral procession in the street; the young beautiful lady lay on a grand hearse in a coffin covered with flowers and wreaths, and the number of torches darkened my light. The people stood in crowds along the houses, and all followed the funeral as it passed. But when the torches were out of my sight and I looked round, a single person still stood leaning against my post, weeping. Never shall I forget those mournful eyes that looked up to me!" These and similar thoughts occupied the old street lamp, which was burning to-day for the last time.

The sentry who is relieved from his post at least knows his successor and may whisper a few words to him. The lamp did not know who was to succeed it, and yet it might have given a few useful hints regarding rain and fog, and some information as to how far the rays of the moon fell upon the pavement, and from what side the wind generally blew, and many other things.

On the bridge of the gutter stood three persons who wished to introduce themselves to the lamp, believing that the latter itself had the bestowal of the office it filled. The first person was a herring's head, which could shine in the dark too. He thought it would be a great saving of oil if he were stuck up on the post. Number two was a piece of rotten wood, which also shines in the dark. It believed itself to be descended from an old stock, once the pride of the forest. The third person was a glow-worm; whence it had come the lamp could not understand, but there it was, and it could give light too. But the rotten wood and the herring's head swore by all that they held sacred that it only gave light at certain times, and could therefore not be taken into account.

The old lamp declared that none of them gave sufficient light to fill the post of a street lamp; but none of them believed that. They were therefore very glad to hear that the office could not be given away by the lamp itself, declaring that it was much too decrepit to choose aright.

At the same moment the wind from the street corner came rushing along and passed through the air-holes of the old lamp. "What do I hear?" he said; "you are going away to-morrow? Do I meet you to-day for the last time? Then I must give you something at parting; I am now going to blow into your brain-box in such a way that in future you will not only be able to remember all that you have seen and heard, but it will be so bright within you that you will be able to see all that is read about, or spoken of, in your presence."

"Oh, that is really much, very much," said the old lamp. "I thank you heartily. I only hope I shall not be melted down."

"That won't happen just yet," said the wind. "Now I am blowing memory into you; if you get many presents like that, you will be able to pass your old days very pleasantly."

"I only hope I shall not be melted down," said the lamp. "Or should I, in that case, also retain my memory?"

"Old lamp, be sensible," said the wind, and blew.

At that moment the moon came out from behind some clouds.

"What do you give the lamp?" asked the wind.

"I give nothing," answered the moon. "I am on the wane, and the lamps have never given me light; on the contrary, I have often given the lamps light." With these words it again hid itself behind the clouds to escape from further demands.

A drop now fell down upon the lamp as if from the roof; the drop declared that it came from the gray clouds, and that it was also a present, and perhaps the best of all. "I will penetrate you so thoroughly that you will have the power to turn into rust and to crumble away in a single night, if you wish it."

This seemed to be a very bad present to the lamp, and the wind thought the same. "Does no one give any more? Does no one give any more?" he blew as loud as he could.

There fell a bright shooting star, forming one long band of light.

"What was that?" cried the herring's head. "Didn't a star fall down? I verily believe it went into the lamp. Really, if such high-placed personages compete for this post, we may say good night and betake ourselves home."

And they all three did so. The old lamp shed a wonderfully strong light. "That was a splendid present!" it said. "The bright stars, which have always been my greatest joy, and which shine as I have never been able to shine, although I have tried with all my might, have yet noticed me, the poor old lamp, and have sent me a present, consisting in the power of letting those I love see all that I remember, and which I myself see as plainly as if it stood before me. And herein lies true pleasure; for joy that cannot be shared with others is only half joy."

"Such sentiments do you honor," said the wind. "But for that, wax lights will be necessary. If these are not lit up in you, your rare powers will be of no use to others. Do you see?—the stars have not thought of that; they take you and every other light to be wax candles. But I must go down." And the wind went down.

"Good heavens! Wax lights!" said the lamp. "I never had such things till now, and don't suppose I shall get them in the future. I only hope I shall not be melted down."

The next day—well, the next day we shall do better to pass over. The next evening the lamp was reclining in an armchair. Guess where. At the old watchman's. He had begged of the burgomaster and council, in consideration of his long and faithful services, the favor of being allowed to keep the old lamp, which he himself had set up and lit for the first time on his first day of office, four-and-twenty years ago.

He looked upon it as his child, for he had no other; and the lamp was given to him.

Now it lay in the armchair, near the warm stove. It seemed as if it had got bigger, for it occupied the chair all alone.

The old people sat at supper and cast kindly glances at the old lamp, which they would gladly have given a place at the table.

They certainly only occupied a cellar, six feet below the ground, and one had to go along a stone passage to get to the room. But inside it was very comfortable and warm, strips of cloth having been nailed along the door. Everything was clean and neat; there were curtains round the little bedsteads and before the little windows. On the window-sill stood two curious flower-pots which Christian the sailor had brought from the East and West Indies. They were only of clay, and represented two elephants whose backs were wanting; in their place there sprang up from the earth with which one figure was filled the most beautiful chives: that was the kitchen garden. Out of the other grew a large geranium: that was the flower garden. On the wall hung a large colored picture: the Congress of Vienna. There they had all the kings and emperors at once. A kitchen clock with heavy weights went "tick, tick," and always went fast too; but the old people thought that this was much better than going slow. They ate their supper, and the street lamp lay, as we have said, in the armchair close to the stove. It seemed to the lamp as if the whole world had been turned round and round. But when the old watchman looked at it and spoke of what they two had gone through together—in rain and fog, in the short bright summer nights, as well as in the long nights of winter, when the snow came down and one longed to be back in the cellar—then the old lamp felt all right again. It saw everything as plainly as if it were now taking place; yes, the wind had provided it with a capital light.

The old people were very active and industrious; not an hour was spent in idleness. On Sunday afternoons some book or other was brought out—preferably a book of travels. And the old man read aloud of Africa, of the great forests, of the elephants which run about wild; and the old woman listened intently, with stolen glances at the clay elephants which served as flower-pots.

"I can almost picture it to myself," said she. And the lamp heartily wished that a wax candle had been there, and could have been lit up within it; then the old woman could have seen everything to the smallest detail, just as the lamp saw it: the high trees, the branches all closely interwoven, the naked black people on horseback, and bands of elephants trampling down the reeds and bushes with their broad clumsy feet.

"What is now the use of all my powers if I get no wax light?" sighed the lamp. "They have only oil and tallow candles, and that won't do."

One day a great heap of wax candle-ends came down into the cellar; the largest pieces served as lights, the small ones the old woman used for waxing her thread. So there were wax candles enough, but it occurred to no one to put a little piece into the lamp.

"Here stand I with my rare powers," thought the lamp. "I carry everything within me, and cannot let them take part in it; they do not know that I am able to transform bare walls into the most gorgeous tapestries, into the most beautiful woods, into everything they can wish for." The lamp was, however, kept clean, and stood shining in a corner where it caught everybody's eye. Strangers considered it a great piece of rubbish; but the old people did not mind that: they loved the lamp.

One day—it was the old watchman's birthday—the old woman approached the lamp, smiling to herself, and said: "I'll have some illuminations to-day in honor of my old man." And the lamp rattled its metal frame and thought: "Well, at last they have a bright idea." But the idea only went as far as oil, and no wax candle came forth. The lamp burned the whole evening, but now saw only too well that the gift of the star would remain a lost treasure for all its life. Then it had a dream—with such faculties there was, of course, nothing wonderful in that. It seemed to it that the old people were dead, and that it had itself come to the iron foundry to be melted down. It felt quite as terrified as the time when it had to go to the Town Hall to be inspected by the burgomaster and the council. But although the power had been given it to fall into rust and dust at will, still it did not do so. It was put into the furnace and turned into an iron candlestick to hold wax candles—as beautiful a candlestick as any one could wish for. It had received the shape of an angel holding a large bouquet, and in the middle of the bouquet the wax candle was to be placed. The candlestick had a place given to it on a green writing-table. The room was very comfortable: many books stood round it, and the walls were hung with beautiful pictures; it belonged to a poet. Everything that he thought or wrote showed itself round about him. Nature changed itself into thick dark forests, into smiling meadows where the storks strutted about, into a ship on the billowy sea, into the clear sky with all its stars.

"What powers lie in me!" said the old lamp, awakening. "I could almost wish to be melted down. But no! that must not be as long as the old people are alive. They love me for my own sake; they have cleaned me and provided me with oil. I am indeed quite as well off as the whole Congress, in the contemplation of which they also take pleasure."

And since that time it enjoyed more inner peace, and that the honest old street lamp had well deserved.

The Little Elder-Tree Mother

There was once a little boy who had caught cold; he had gone out and got wet feet. Nobody had the least idea how it had happened; the weather was quite dry. His mother undressed him, put him to bed, and ordered the teapot to be brought in, that she might make him a good cup of tea from the elder-tree blossoms, which is so warming. At the same time, the kind-hearted old man who lived by himself in the upper story of the house came in; he led a lonely life, for he had no wife and children; but he loved the children of others very much, and he could tell so many fairy tales and stories, that it was a pleasure to hear him.

"Now, drink your tea," said the mother; "perhaps you will hear a story."

"Yes, if I only knew a fresh one," said the old man, and nodded smilingly. "But how did the little fellow get his wet feet?" he then asked.

"That," replied the mother, "nobody can understand." "Will you tell me a story?" asked the boy. "Yes, if you can tell me as nearly as possible how deep is the gutter in the little street where you go to school."

"Just half as high as my top-boots," replied the boy; "but then I must stand in the deepest holes."

"There, now we know where you got your wet feet," said the old man. "I ought to tell you a story, but the worst of it is, I do not know any more."

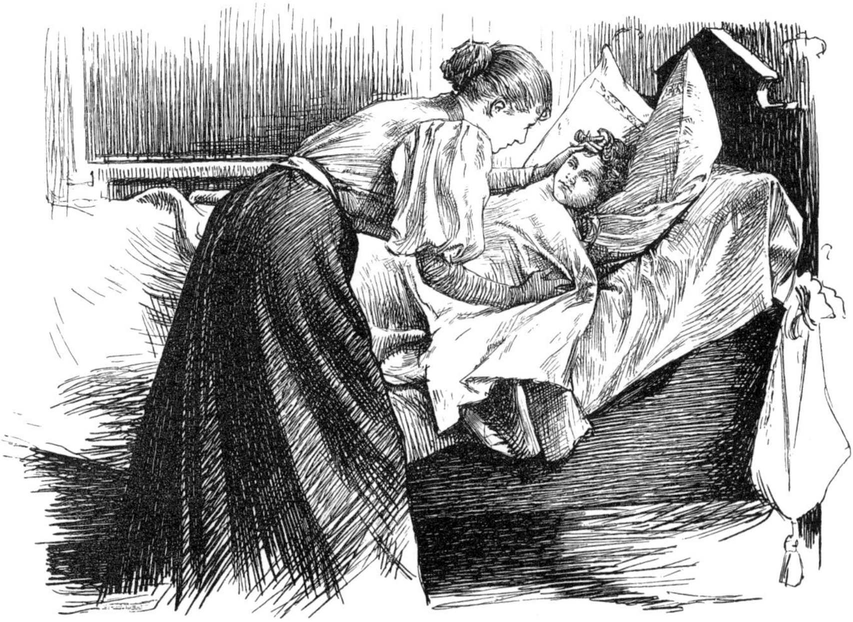

His mother undressed him, put him to bed, and ordered the teapot to be brought in.

"You can make one up," said the little boy. "Mother says you can tell a fairy tale about anything you look at or touch."

"That is all very well, but such tales or stories are worth nothing! No, the right ones come by themselves and knock at my forehead saying: 'Here I am.'"

"Will not one knock soon?" asked the boy; and the mother smiled while she put elder-tree blossoms into the teapot and poured boiling water over them. "Pray, tell me a story."

"Yes, if stories came by themselves; they are so proud, they only come when they please.—But wait," he said suddenly, "there is one. Look at the teapot; there is a story in it now."

And the little boy looked at the teapot; the lid rose up gradually, the elder-tree blossoms sprang forth one by one, fresh and white; long boughs came forth; even out of the spout they grew up in all directions, and formed a bush—nay, a large elder-tree, which stretched its branches up to the bed and pushed the curtains aside; and there were so many blossoms and such a sweet fragrance! In the midst of the tree sat a kindly-looking old woman with a strange dress; it was as green as the leaves, and trimmed with large white blossoms, so that it was difficult to say whether it was real cloth, or the leaves and blossoms of the elder-tree.

There were so many blossoms and such a sweet fragrance!

"What is this woman's name?" asked the little boy.

"Well, the Romans and Greeks used to call her a Dryad," said the old man; "but we do not understand that. Out in the sailors' quarter they give her a better name; there she is called elder-tree mother. Now, you must attentively listen to her and look at the beautiful elder tree."

"Just such a large tree, covered with flowers, stands out there; it grew in the corner of a humble little yard; under this tree sat two old people one afternoon in the beautiful sunshine. He was an old, old sailor, and she his old wife; they had already great-grandchildren, and were soon to celebrate their golden wedding, but they could not remember the date, and the elder-tree mother was sitting in the tree and looked as pleased as this one here. 'I know very well when the golden wedding is to take place,' she said; but they did not hear it—they were talking of bygone days.

"'Well, do you remember?' said the old sailor, 'when we were quite small and used to run about and play—it was in the very same yard where we now are—we used to put little branches into the ground and make a garden.'

"'Yes,' said the old woman, 'I remember it very well; we used to water the branches, and one of them, an elder-tree branch, took root, and grew and became the large tree under which we are now sitting as old people.'

"'Certainly, you are right,' he said; 'and in yonder corner stood a large water-tub; there I used to sail my boat, which I had cut out myself—it sailed so well; but soon I had to sail somewhere else.'

"'But first we went to school to learn something,' she said, 'and then we were confirmed; we wept both on that day, but in the afternoon we went out hand in hand, and ascended the high round tower and looked out into the wide world right over Copenhagen and the sea; then we walked to Fredericksburg, where the king and the queen were sailing about in their magnificent boat on the canals.'

"'But soon I had to sail about somewhere else, and for many years I was traveling about far away from home.'

"'And I often cried about you, for I was afraid lest you were drowned and lying at the bottom of the sea. Many a time I got up in the night and looked if the weathercock had turned; it turned often, but you did not return. I remember one day distinctly: the rain was pouring down in torrents; the dustman had come to the house where I was in service; I went down with the dust-bin and stood for a moment in the doorway, and looked at the dreadful weather. Then the postman gave me a letter; it was from you. Heavens! how that letter had traveled about. I tore it open and read it; I cried and laughed at the same time, and was so happy! Therein was written that you were staying in the hot countries, where the coffee grows. These must be marvelous countries. You said a great deal about them, and I read all while the rain was pouring down and I was standing there with the dust-bin. Then suddenly some one put his arm round my waist.'

"Then suddenly some one put his arm round my waist."

"'Yes, and you gave him a hearty smack on the cheek,' said the old man.

"'I did not know that it was you—you had come as quickly as your letter; and you looked so handsome, and so you do still. You had a large yellow silk handkerchief in your pocket and a shining hat on. You looked so well, and the weather in the street was horrible!'

"'Then we married,' he said. 'Do you remember how we got our first boy, and then Mary, Niels, Peter, John, and Christian?'

"'Oh yes; and now they have all grown up, and have become useful members of society, whom everybody cares for.'

"'And their children have had children again,' said the old sailor. 'Yes, these are children's children, and they are strong and healthy. If I am not mistaken, our wedding took place at this season of the year.'

"'Yes, to-day is your golden wedding-day,' said the little elder-tree mother, stretching her head down between the two old people, who thought that she was their neighbor who was nodding to them; they looked at each other and clasped hands. Soon afterwards the children and grandchildren came, for they knew very well that it was the golden wedding-day; they had already wished them joy and happiness in the morning, but the old people had forgotten it, although they remembered things so well that had passed many, many years ago. The elder tree smelled strongly, and the setting sun illuminated the faces of the two old people, so that they looked quite rosy; the youngest of the grandchildren danced round them, and cried merrily that there would be a feast in the evening, for they were to have hot potatoes; and the elder mother nodded in the tree and cried 'Hooray' with the others."

"But that was no fairy tale," said the little boy who had listened to it.

"You will presently understand it," said the old man who told the story. "Let us ask little elder-tree mother about it."

"That was no fairy tale," said the little elder-tree mother; "but now it comes! Real life furnishes us with subjects for the most wonderful fairy tales; for otherwise my beautiful elder-bush could not have grown forth out of the teapot."

And then she took the little boy out of bed and placed him on her bosom; the elder branches, full of blossoms, closed over them; it was as if they sat in a thick leafy bower which flew with them through the air; it was beautiful beyond all description. The little elder-tree mother had suddenly become a charming young girl, but her dress was still of the same green material, covered with white blossoms, as the elder-tree mother had worn; she had a real elder blossom on her bosom, and a wreath of the same flowers was wound round her curly golden hair; her eyes were so large and so blue that it was wonderful to look at them. She and the boy kissed each other, and then they were of the same age and felt the same joys. They walked hand in hand out of the bower, and now stood at home in a beautiful flower garden. Near the green lawn the father's walking-stick was tied to a post. There was life in this stick for the little ones, for as soon as they seated themselves upon it the polished knob turned into a neighing horse's head, a long black mane was fluttering in the wind, and four strong slender legs grew out. The animal was fiery and spirited; they galloped round the lawn. "Hooray! now we shall ride far away, many miles!" said the boy; "we shall ride to the nobleman's estate where we were last year." And they rode round the lawn again, and the little girl, who, as we know, was no other than the little elder-tree mother, continually cried, "Now we are in the country! Do you see the farmhouse there, with the large baking stove, which projects like a gigantic egg out of the wall into the road? The elder tree spreads its branches over it, and the cock struts about and scratches for the hens. Look how proud he is! Now we are near the church; it stands on a high hill, under the spreading oak trees; one of them is half dead! Now we are at the smithy, where the fire roars and the half-naked men beat with their hammers so that the sparks fly far and wide. Let's be off to the beautiful farm!"

And they passed by everything the little girl, who was sitting behind on the stick, described, and the boy saw it, and yet they only went round the lawn. Then they played in a side-walk, and marked out a little garden on the ground; she took elder-blossoms out of her hair and planted them, and they grew exactly like those the old people planted when they were children, as we have heard before. They walked about hand in hand, just as the old couple had done when they were little, but they did not go to the round tower nor to the Fredericksburg garden. No; the little girl seized the boy round the waist, and then they flew far into the country. It was spring and it became summer, it was autumn and it became winter, and thousands of pictures reflected themselves in the boy's eyes and heart, and the little girl always sang again, "You will never forget that!" And during their whole flight the elder-tree smelled so sweetly; he noticed the roses and the fresh beeches, but the elder-tree smelled much stronger, for the flowers were fixed on the little girl's bosom, against which the boy often rested his head during the flight.

"It is beautiful here in spring," said the little girl, and they were again in the green beechwood, where the thyme breathed forth sweet fragrance at their feet, and the pink anemones looked lovely in the green moss. "Oh! that it were always spring in the fragrant beechwood!"

"Here it is splendid in summer!" she said, and they passed by old castles of the age of chivalry. The high walls and indented battlements were reflected in the water of the ditches, on which swans were swimming and peering into the old shady avenues. The corn waved in the fields like a yellow sea. Red and yellow flowers grew in the ditches, wild hops and convolvuli in full bloom in the hedges. In the evening the moon rose, large and round, and the hayricks in the meadows smelled sweetly. "One can never forget it!"

"Here it is beautiful in autumn!" said the little girl, and the atmosphere seemed twice as high and blue, while the wood shined with crimson, green, and gold. The hounds were running off, flocks of wild fowl flew screaming over the barrows, while the bramble bushes twined round the old stones. The dark-blue sea was covered with white-sailed ships, and in the barns sat old women, girls, and children picking hops into a large tub; the young ones sang songs, and the old people told fairy tales about goblins and sorcerers. It could not be more pleasant anywhere.

"Here it's agreeable in winter!" said the little girl, and all the trees were covered with hoar-frost, so that they looked like white coral. The snow creaked under one's feet, as if one had new boots on. One shooting star after another traversed the sky. In the room the Christmas tree was lit, and there were song and merriment. In the peasant's cottage the violin sounded, and games were played for apple quarters; even the poorest child said, "It is beautiful in winter!"

And indeed it was beautiful! And the little girl showed everything to the boy, and the elder-tree continued to breathe forth sweet perfume, while the red flag with the white cross was streaming in the wind; it was the flag under which the old sailor had served. The boy became a youth; he was to go out into the wide world, far away to the countries where the coffee grows. But at parting the little girl took an elder-blossom from her breast and gave it to him as a keepsake. He placed it in his prayer-book, and when he opened it in distant lands it was always at the place where the flower of remembrance was lying; and the more he looked at it the fresher it became, so that he could almost smell the fragrance of the woods at home. He distinctly saw the little girl, with her bright blue eyes, peeping out from behind the petals, and heard her whispering, "Here it is beautiful in spring, in summer, in autumn, and in winter," and hundreds of pictures passed through his mind.

Thus many years rolled by. He had now become an old man, and was sitting, with his old wife, under an elder-tree in full bloom. They held each other by the hand exactly as the great-grandfather and the great-grandmother had done outside, and, like them, they talked about bygone days and of their golden wedding. The little girl with the blue eyes and elder-blossoms in her hair was sitting high up in the tree, and nodded to them, saying, "To-day is the golden wedding!" And then she took two flowers out of her wreath and kissed them. They glittered at first like silver, then like gold, and when she placed them on the heads of the old people each flower became a golden crown. There they both sat like a king and queen under the sweet-smelling tree, which looked exactly like an elder-tree, and he told his wife the story of the elder-tree mother as it had been told him when he was a little boy. They were both of opinion that the story contained many points like their own, and these similarities they liked best.

"Yes, so it is," said the little girl in the tree. "Some call me Little Elder-Tree Mother; others a Dryad; but my real name is 'Remembrance.' It is I who sit in the tree which grows and grows. I can remember things and tell stories! But let's see if you have still got your flower."

And the old man opened his prayer-book; the elder-blossom was still in it, and as fresh as if it had only just been put in. Remembrance nodded, and the two old people, with the golden crowns on their heads, sat in the glowing evening sun. They closed their eyes and—and—

Well, now the story is ended! The little boy in bed did not know whether he had dreamed it or heard it told; the teapot stood on the table, but no elder-tree was growing out of it, and the old man who had told the story was on the point of leaving the room, and he did go out.

"How beautiful it was!" said the little boy. "Mother, I have been to warm countries!"

"I believe you," said the mother; "if one takes two cups of hot elder-tea it is quite natural that one gets into warm countries!"

And she covered him up well, so that he might not take cold. "You have slept soundly while I was arguing with the old man whether it was a story or a fairy tale!"

"And what has become of the little elder-tree mother?" asked the boy.

"She is in the teapot," said the mother; "and there she may remain."

The Neighboring Families

One would have thought that something important was going on in the duck-pond, but it was nothing after all. All the ducks lying quietly on the water or standing on their heads in it—for they could do that—at once swam to the sides; the traces of their feet were seen in the wet earth, and their cackling was heard far and wide. The water, which a few moments before had been as clear and smooth as a mirror, became very troubled. Before, every tree, every neighboring bush, the old farmhouse with the holes in the roof and the swallows' nest, and especially the great rose-bush full of flowers, had been reflected in it. The rose-bush covered the wall and hung out over the water, in which everything was seen as if in a picture, except that it all stood on its head; but when the water was troubled everything got mixed up, and the picture was gone. Two feathers which the fluttering ducks had lost floated up and down; suddenly they took a rush as if the wind were coming, but as it did not come they had to lie still, and the water once more became quiet and smooth. The roses were again reflected; they were very beautiful, but they did not know it, for no one had told them. The sun shined among the delicate leaves; everything breathed forth the loveliest fragrance, and all felt as we do when we are filled with joy at the thought of our happiness.

"How beautiful existence is!" said each rose. "The only thing that I wish for is to be able to kiss the sun, because it is so warm and bright. I should also like to kiss those roses down in the water, which are so much like us, and the pretty little birds down in the nest. There are some up above too; they put out their heads and pipe softly; they have no feathers like their father and mother. We have good neighbors, both below and above. How beautiful existence is!"

The young ones above and below—those below were really only shadows in the water—were sparrows; their parents were sparrows too, and had taken possession of the empty swallows' nest of last year, and now lived in it as if it were their own property.

"Are those the ducks' children swimming there?" asked the young sparrows, when they saw the feathers on the water.

"If you must ask questions, ask sensible ones," said their mother. "Don't you see that they are feathers, such as I wear and you will wear too? But ours are finer. Still, I should like to have them up in the nest, for they keep one warm. I am very curious to know what the ducks were so startled about; not about us, certainly, although I did say 'peep' to you pretty loudly. The thick-headed roses ought to know why, but they know nothing at all; they only look at themselves and smell. I am heartily tired of such neighbors."

"Listen to the dear little birds up there," said the roses; "they begin to want to sing too, but are not able to manage it yet. But it will soon come. What a pleasure that must be! It is fine to have such cheerful neighbors."

Suddenly two horses came galloping up to be watered. A peasant boy rode on one, and he had taken off all his clothes except his large broad black hat. The boy whistled like a bird, and rode into the pond where it was deepest, and as he passed the rose-bush he plucked a rose and stuck it in his hat. Now he looked dressed, and rode on. The other roses looked after their sister, and asked each other, "Where can she be going to?" But none of them knew.

"I should like to go out into the world for once," said one; "but here at home among our green leaves it is beautiful too.

The whole day long the sun shines bright and warm, and in the night the sky shines more beautifully still; we can see that through all the little holes in it."

They meant the stars, but they knew no better.

"We make it lively about the house," said the sparrow-mother; "and people say that a swallows' nest brings luck; so they are glad of us. But such neighbors as ours! A rose-bush on the wall like that causes damp. I daresay it will be taken away; then we shall, perhaps, have some corn growing here. The roses are good for nothing but to be looked at and to be smelled, or at most to be stuck in a hat. Every year, as I have been told by my mother, they fall off. The farmer's wife preserves them and strews salt among them; then they get a French name which I neither can pronounce nor care to, and are put into the fire to make a nice smell. You see, that's their life; they exist only for the eye and the nose. Now you know."

In the evening, when the gnats were playing about in the warm air and in the red clouds, the nightingale came and sang to the roses that the beautiful was like sunshine to the world, and that the beautiful lived for ever. The roses thought that the nightingale was singing about itself, and that one might easily have believed; they had no idea that the song was about them. But they were very pleased with it, and wondered whether all the little sparrows could become nightingales.

"I understand the song of that bird very well," said the young sparrows. "There was only one word that was not clear to me. What does 'the beautiful' mean?"

"Nothing at all," answered their mother; "that's only something external. Up at the Hall, where the pigeons have their own house, and corn and peas are strewn before them every day—I have dined with them myself, and that you shall do in time, too; for tell me what company you keep and I'll tell you who you are—up at the Hall they have two birds with green necks and a crest upon their heads; they can spread out their tails like a great wheel, and these are so bright with various colors that it makes one's eyes ache. These birds are called peacocks, and that is 'the beautiful.' If they were only plucked a little they would look no better than the rest of us. I would have plucked them already if they had not been so big."

"I'll pluck them," piped the young sparrow, who had no feathers yet.

In the farmhouse lived a young married couple; they loved each other dearly, were industrious and active, and everything in their home looked very nice. On Sundays the young wife came down early, plucked a handful of the most beautiful roses, and put them into a glass of water, which she placed upon the cupboard.

"Now I see that it is Sunday," said the husband, kissing his little wife. They sat down, read their hymn-book, and held each other by the hand, while the sun shined down upon the fresh roses and upon them.

"This sight is really too tedious," said the sparrow-mother, who could see into the room from her nest; and she flew away.

The same thing happened on the following Sunday, for every Sunday fresh roses were put into the glass; but the rose-bush bloomed as beautifully as ever. The young sparrows now had feathers, and wanted very much to fly with their mother; but she would not allow it, and so they had to stay at home. In one of her flights, however it may have happened, she was caught, before she was aware of it, in a horse-hair net which some boys had attached to a tree The horse-hair was drawn tightly round her leg—as tightly as if the latter were to be cut off; she was in great pain and terror. The boys came running up and seized her, and in no gentle way either.

"Its only a sparrow," they said; they did not, however, let her go, but took her home with them, and every time she cried they hit her on the beak.

In the farmhouse was an old man who understood making soap into cakes and balls, both for shaving and washing. He was a merry old man, always wandering about. On seeing the sparrow which the boys had brought, and which they said they did not want, he asked, "Shall we make it look very pretty?"

At these words an icy shudder ran through the sparrow-mother.

Out of his box, in which were the most beautiful colors, the old man took a quantity of shining leaf-gold, while the boys had to go and fetch some white of egg, with which the sparrow was to be smeared all over; the gold was stuck on to this, and the sparrow-mother was now gilded all over. But she, trembling in every limb, did not think of the adornment. Then the soap-man tore off a small piece from the red lining of his old jacket, and cutting it so as to make it look like a cock's comb, he stuck it to the bird's head.

"Now you will see the gold-jacket fly," said the old man, letting the sparrow go, which flew away in deadly fear, with the sun shining upon her. How she glittered! All the sparrows, and even a crow—and an old boy he was too—were startled at the sight; but still they flew after her to learn what kind of a strange bird she was.

Driven by fear and horror, she flew homeward; she was almost sinking fainting to the earth, while the flock of pursuing birds increased, some even attempting to peck at her.

"Look at her! Look at her!" they all cried.

"Look at her! Look at her!" cried her little ones, as she approached the nest. "That is certainly a young peacock, for it glitters in all colors; it makes one's eyes ache, as mother told us. Peep! that's 'the beautiful.'" And then they pecked at the bird with their little beaks so that it was impossible for her to get into the nest; she was so exhausted that she could not even say "Peep!" much less "I am your own mother!" The other birds, too, now fell upon the sparrow and plucked off feather after feather until she fell bleeding into the rose-bush.

"Poor creature!" said all the roses; "only be still, and we will hide you. Lean your little head against us."

The sparrow spread out her wings once more, then drew them closely to her, and lay dead near the neighboring family, the beautiful fresh roses.

"Peep!" sounded from the nest. "Where can mother be so long? It's more than I can understand. It cannot be a trick of hers, and mean that we are now to take care of ourselves. She has left us the house as an inheritance; but to which of us is it to belong when we have families of our own?"

"Yes, it won't do for you to stay with me when I increase my household with a wife and children," said the smallest.

"I daresay I shall have more wives and children than you," said the second.

"But I am the eldest!" exclaimed the third. Then they all got excited; they hit out with their wings, pecked with their beaks, and flop! one after another was thrown out of the nest. There they lay with their anger, holding their heads on one side and blinking the eye that was turned upwards. That was their way of looking foolish.

They could fly a little; by practice they learned to improve, and at last they agreed upon a sign by which to recognize each other if they should meet in the world later on. It was to be one "Peep!" and three scratches on the ground with the left foot.

The young one who had remained behind in the nest made himself as broad as he could, for he was the proprietor. But this greatness did not last long. In the night the red flames burst through the window and seized the roof; the dry straw blazed up high, and the whole house, together with the young sparrow, was burned. The two others, who wanted to marry, thus saved their lives by a stroke of luck.

When the sun rose again and everything looked as refreshed as if it had had a quiet sleep, there only remained of the farmhouse a few black charred beams leaning against the chimney, which was now its own master. Thick smoke still rose from the ruins, but the rose-bush stood yonder, fresh, blooming, and untouched, every flower and every twig being reflected in the clear water.

"How beautifully the roses bloom before the ruined house," exclaimed a passer-by. "A pleasanter picture cannot be imagined. I must have that." And the man took out of his portfolio a little book with white leaves: he was a painter, and with his pencil he drew the smoking house, the charred beams and the overhanging chimney, which bent more and more; in the foreground he put the large, blooming rose-bush, which presented a charming view. For its sake alone the whole picture had been drawn.

Later in the day the two sparrows who had been born there came by. "Where is the house?" they asked. "Where is the nest? Peep! All is burned and our strong brother too. That's what he has now for keeping the nest. The roses got off very well; there they still stand with their red cheeks. They certainly do not mourn at their neighbors' misfortunes. I don't want to talk to them, and it looks miserable here—that's my opinion." And away they went.

On a beautiful sunny autumn day—one could almost have believed it was still the middle of summer—there hopped about in the dry clean-swept courtyard before the principal entrance of the Hall a number of black, white, and gaily-colored pigeons, all shining in the sunlight. The pigeon-mothers said to their young ones: "Stand in groups, stand in groups! for that looks much better."

"What kind of creatures are those little gray ones that run about behind us?" asked an old pigeon, with red and green in her eyes. "Little gray ones! Little gray ones!" she cried.

"They are sparrows, and good creatures. We have always had the reputation of being pious, so we will allow them to pick up the corn with us; they don't interrupt our talk, and they scrape so prettily when they bow."

Indeed they were continually making three foot-scrapings with the left foot and also said "Peep!" By this means they recognized each other, for they were the sparrows from the nest on the burned house.

"Here is excellent fare!" said the sparrow. The pigeons strutted round one another, puffed out their chests mightily, and had their own private views and opinions.

"Do you see that pouter pigeon?" said one to the other. "Do you see how she swallows the peas? She eats too many, and the best ones too. Curoo! Curoo! How she lifts her crest, the ugly, spiteful creature! Curoo! Curoo!" And the eyes of all sparkled with malice. "Stand in groups! Stand in groups! Little gray ones, little gray ones! Curoo, curoo, curoo!"

So their chatter ran on, and so it will run on for thousands of years. The sparrows ate lustily; they listened attentively, and even stood in the ranks with the others, but it did not suit them at all. They were full, and so they left the pigeons, exchanging opinions about them, slipped in under the garden pickets, and when they found the door leading into the house open, one of them, who was more than full, and therefore felt brave, hopped on to the threshold. "Peep!" said he; "I may venture that."

"Peep!" said the other; "so may I, and something more too!" And he hopped into the room. No one was there; the third sparrow, seeing this, flew still farther into the room, exclaiming, "All or nothing! It is a curious man's nest all the same; and what have they put up here? What is it?"

Close to the sparrows the roses were blooming; they were reflected in the water, and the charred beams leaned against the overhanging chimney. "Do tell me what this is. How comes this in a room at the Hall?" And all three sparrows wanted to fly over the roses and the chimney, but flew against a flat wall. It was all a picture, a great splendid picture, which the artist had painted from a sketch.

"Peep!" said the sparrows, "it's nothing. It only looks like something. Peep! that is 'the beautiful.' Do you understand it? I don't."

And they flew away, for some people came into the room.

Days and years went by. The pigeons had often cooed, not to say growled—the spiteful creatures; the sparrows had been frozen in winter and had lived merrily in summer: they were all betrothed, or married, or whatever you like to call it. They had little ones, and of course each one thought his own the handsomest and cleverest; one flew this way, another that, and when they met they recognized each other by their "Peep!" and the three scrapes with the left foot. The eldest had remained an old maid and had no nest nor young ones. It was her pet idea to see a great city, so she flew to Copenhagen.

There was a large house painted in many gay colors standing close to the castle and the canal, upon which latter were to be seen many ships laden with apples and pottery. The windows of the house were broader at the bottom than at the top, and when the sparrows looked through them, every room appeared to them like a tulip with the brightest colors and shades. But in the middle of the tulip stood white men, made of marble; a few were of plaster: still, looked at with sparrows' eyes, that comes to the same thing. Up on the roof stood a metal chariot drawn by metal horses and the goddess of Victory, also of metal, was driving. It was Thorwaldsen's Museum.

"How it shines! how it shines!" said the maiden sparrow. "I suppose that is 'the beautiful.' Peep! But here it is larger than a peacock." She still remembered what in her childhood's days her mother had looked upon as the greatest among the beautiful. She flew down into the courtyard: there everything was extremely fine. Palms and branches were painted on the walls, and in the middle of the court stood a great blooming rose-tree spreading out its fresh boughs, covered with roses, over a grave. Thither flew the maiden sparrow, for she saw several of her own kind there. A "peep" and three foot-scrapings—in this way she had often greeted throughout the year, and no one here had responded, for those who are once parted do not meet every day; and so this greeting had become a habit with her. But to-day two old sparrows and a young one answered with a "peep " and the thrice-repeated scrape with the left foot.

"Ah! Good-day! Good-day!" They were two old ones from the nest and a little one of the family. "Do we meet here? It's a grand place, but there's not much to eat. This is 'the beautiful.' Peep!"

Many people came out of the side rooms where the beautiful marble statues stood and approached the grave where lay the great master who had created these works of art. All stood with enraptured faces round Thorwaldsen's grave, and a few picked up the fallen rose-leaves and preserved them. They had come from afar: one from mighty England, others from Germany and France. The fairest of the ladies plucked one of the roses and hid it in her bosom. Then the sparrows thought that the roses reigned here, and that the house had been built for their sake. That appeared to them to be really too much, but since all the people showed their love for the roses, they did not wish to be behindhand. "Peep!" they said, sweeping the ground with their tails, and blinking with one eye at the roses, they had not looked at them long before they were convinced that they were their old neighbors. And so they really were. The painter who had drawn the rose-bush near the ruined house, had afterwards obtained permission to dig it up, and had given it to the architect, for finer roses had never been seen. The architect had planted it upon Thorwaldsen's grave, where it bloomed as an emblem of 'the beautiful' and yielded fragrant red rose-leaves to be carried as mementoes to distant lands.

"Have you obtained an appointment here in the city?" asked the sparrows. The roses nodded; they recognized their gray neighbors and were pleased to see them again. "How glorious it is to live and to bloom, to see old friends again, and happy faces every day. It is as if every day were a festival." "Peep!" said the sparrows. "Yes, they are really our old neighbors; we remember their origin near the pond. Peep! how they have got on. Yes, some succeed while they are asleep. Ah! there's a faded leaf; I can see that quite plainly." And they pecked at it till it fell off. But the tree stood there fresher and greener than ever; the roses bloomed in the sunshine on Thorwaldsen's grave and became associated with his immortal name.

The Shepherdess and the Sweep

Have you ever seen a very old wooden cupboard, blackened by age, and decorated with many carved arabesques and foliage? Such a one stood in a sitting-room; it was a legacy from the great-grandmother, and was covered all over with carved roses and tulips. Upon it one could see the most peculiar figures, and little stagheads with antlers were projecting from them. In the center of the cupboard stood a carved man; he looked, indeed, very ridiculous, and he grinned, for one could not possibly call it laughing; he had legs like a goat, little horns on his forehead, and a long beard. The children in the room used to call him Under-General-Commander-War-Sergeant-in-Chief Billy Goatlegs. That was a name difficult to pronounce, and there are very few who obtain such a title; but to have such a man cut out was certainly something. There he was! He looked continually towards the table underneath the looking-glass, where a sweet little shepherdess of porcelain was standing. Her shoes were gilded, her dress was adorned with a red rose; she wore a golden hat and crook; in short, she was very beautiful. Close by her stood a little chimney-sweep, as black as coal, and he, too, was of porcelain.

He was as clean and nice as any other person; that he was a sweep was only because he was to represent one; the porcelain modeler might just as well have made him a prince, if he had liked.

There he was standing with his ladder, and his face was as white and rosy as a girl's; properly speaking, that was wrong, for it ought to have been a little blackened. He was close by the shepherdess, and both were standing on the spots where they had been placed. As they were thus brought together, they had become engaged. They were very suitable for each other; both were young, of the same porcelain and equally fragile.

Close by stood another figure, which was three times as large as this couple; it was an old China-man who could nod. He, too, was made of porcelain, and pretended to be the grandfather of the little shepherdess, but he had no proof of it. He claimed to have power over her, and therefore he had nodded to the Under-General-Commander-War-Sergeant-in-Chief Billy Goatlegs, who paid his addresses to the little shepherdess.

"You will have a husband," said the old China-man, "who, I incline to think, is of mahogany. He can make you Mrs. Under-General-Commander-War-Sergeant-in-Chief Billy Goatlegs; he has a whole cupboard full of silver-plate, which he keeps in secret compartments."

Close by stood another figure, which was three times as large as this couple; it was an old China-man who could nod.

"I do not wish to go into the dark cupboard," said the little shepherdess. "I have heard it said that he has eleven China-women inside the cupboard."

"Then you may well become the twelfth," said the China-man. "To-night, as soon as it rattles in the cupboard, you shall be married, as truly as I am a China-man." Then he nodded again and fell asleep.

But the little shepherdess cried and looked at her beloved one, the porcelain chimney-sweep.

"I entreat you," she said to him, "to take me far, far away, for we cannot stay here."

"I will do anything you please," said the little sweep. "Let us be off at once. I think I shall be able to keep you by my trade!"

"I wish we had already safely got down from the table," she said. "I shall not be happy, until we are far away."

And he comforted her, and showed her how she must put her little feet on the carved corners and the gilded ornaments of the leg of the table; he aided her with his little ladder, and soon they arrived on the floor. When they looked towards the old cupboard, they noticed that there was a great deal of noise in it; all the carved stags put their heads further out, lifted up their antlers, and twisted their necks. The Under-General-Commander-War-Sergeant-in-Chief Billy Goatlegs jumped up with excitement, and called out to the old China-man: "Look, there they are running away." Then they were terribly frightened, and leapt quickly into the drawer of the window-seat.

He aided her with his little ladder.

In this drawer were three packs of cards, but none of them was complete, and a little doll's theater, which was built up as well as circumstances permitted. There a comedy was being performed, and all the ladies, diamonds, clubs, hearts, and spades, were sitting in the front row and fanning themselves with their tulips; all the knaves were standing behind them, showing that they had a head below as well as above, as all playing-cards have. The comedy was about two people who were not to marry each other. The shepherdess shed tears over it, for it was exactly her own story.

"I cannot stand this any longer," she said, "I must get out of the drawer." But when they got out and looked up towards the table, the old China-man was awake and shook his whole body, which was all one piece.

"Now the old China-man is coming," cried the little shepherdess, and fell down on her porcelain knees, she was so much afraid.

"I have an idea," said the sweep. "Shall we creep into the big pot-pourri vase yonder in the corner? There we can repose on roses and lavender, and throw salt into his eyes when he comes."

"That will not save us," she said, "for I know that the old China-man and the pot-pourri vase were one day engaged, and there always remains a certain friendly feeling between people who have once been on such terms. No, we have no alternative; we must go out into the wide world."

"Have you really the courage to go with me out into the wide world?" asked the sweep. "Have you ever thought how large the world is, and that we shall never return here?"

"Yes, certainly," was her reply.

Then the sweep looked her straight into the face and said: "My way leads through the chimney. Have you really the courage to go with me through the stove, through the iron case as well as through the pipes? Through them we get out into the chimney, and then I know my way very well. We shall get so high up, that they can no longer reach us; on the very top is a hole which leads out into the wide world."

He then led her to the stove-door.

"How black it looks!" she said; but she went with him, not only through the iron case, but also through the pipes, where it was pitch dark.

"Now we are in the chimney," he said. "Look up above you, there is a beautiful star shining."

It was a real star in the sky which was shining straight down upon them, as if it wished to show them the way. They climbed and crept on; it was a dreadful way and very high up. He held her tightly and pointed the best places out to her, where she could put her little porcelain feet safely down; at last they reached the rim of the chimney-pot and sat down, for they were very tired, and that was not wonderful.

The sky, with all its stars, was high above them, the roofs of the town spread out at their feet. They could see very far, far out into the world. The poor shepherdess had not thought that it would be like this; she leaned her head on her sweep and began to cry so bitterly that all the gilt came off her girdle.

"That is too much," she said. "I cannot stand it. The world is too large! I wish I were again on the table underneath the looking-glass. I shall not be happy until I have got back there. I have gone out with you into the wide world, now you can take me back again, if you really care so much for me as you say."

The sweep reasoned with her, talked about the old China-man and the Under-General-Commander-War-Sergeant-in-Chief Billy Goatlegs; but she sobbed bitterly, and kissed her little sweep so much, that he could not do otherwise than give in, although it was foolish.

So they returned, with great difficulties, through the chimney, and crept through the pipes and the iron case: that was very unpleasant. When they had arrived in the dark stove they stood and listened behind the door to hear what was going on in the room. But there all was quiet; they peeped in, and there the old China-man was lying on the floor. He had fallen down from the table when he wished to run after them, and was broken into three pieces; the whole back had come off in one piece, and the head had rolled into a corner. The Under-General-Commander-War-Sergeant-in-Chief Billy Goatlegs stood still in the place where he had always been, and meditated.

"That is terrible," said the little shepherdess. "The old grandfather is broken to pieces, and that is all our fault. I shall never get over this." And then she wrung her hands.

He had fallen down from the table . . . and was broken into three pieces.

"He can be riveted," said the sweep. "He can be riveted again. Do not be too frightened. If they cement his back and put a good strong rivet into his neck, he will be as good as new, and may still say many disagreeable things to us."

"Do you think so?" she asked. Then they crept up to the table and returned to their former places.

"Here we are again on the same spot," said the sweep. "We might have saved all the trouble."

"Oh, that grandfather were riveted again!" said the shepherdess. "Is that very expensive?"

And he was riveted. The people had his back cemented, and a good strong rivet was put into his neck; he was as good as new again, but he could no longer nod.

"You seem to have become haughty since you broke to pieces," said the Under-General-Commander-War-Sergeant-in-Chief. "I think you have no cause to be so conceited. Am I to have her, or am I not?"

The sweep and the little shepherdess looked quite piteously at the old China-man; they feared lest he might nod again. But he could not do so. It was very unpleasant for him to tell the people that he had a rivet in his neck. Thus the two lovers remained together, blessed the grandfather's rivet, and loved each other till they broke to pieces.

The Wicked Prince

There lived once upon a time a wicked prince whose heart and mind were set upon conquering all the countries of the world, and on frightening the people: he devastated their countries with fire and sword, and his soldiers trod down the crops in the fields and destroyed the peasants' huts by fire, so that the flames licked the green leaves off the branches, and the fruit hung dried up on the singed black trees. Many a poor mother fled, her naked baby in her arms, behind the still smoking walls of her cottage; but also there the soldiers followed her, and when they found her, she served as new nourishment to their diabolical enjoyments; demons could not possibly have done worse things than these soldiers! The prince was of opinion that all this was right, and that it was only the natural course which things ought to take. His power increased day by day, his name was feared by all, and fortune favored his deeds.

He brought enormous wealth home from the conquered towns, and gradually accumulated in his residence riches which could nowhere be equalled. He erected magnificent palaces, churches, and halls, and all who saw these splendid buildings and great treasures exclaimed admiringly: "What a mighty prince!" But they did not know what endless misery he had brought upon other countries, nor did they hear the sighs and lamentations which rose up from the debris of the destroyed cities.

The prince often looked with delight upon his gold and his magnificent edifices, and thought, like the crowd: "What a mighty prince! But I must have more—much more. No power on earth must equal mine, far less exceed it."

He made war with all his neighbors, and defeated them. The conquered kings were chained up with golden fetters to his chariot when he drove through the streets of his city. These kings had to kneel at his and his courtiers' feet when they sat at table, and live on the morsels which they left. At last the prince had his own statue erected on the public places and fixed on the royal palaces; nay, he even wished it to be placed in the churches, on the altars, but in this the priests opposed him, saying: "Prince, you are mighty indeed, but God's power is much greater than yours; we dare not obey your orders."

"Well," said the prince, "then I will conquer God too." And in his haughtiness and foolish presumption he ordered a magnificent ship to be constructed, with which he could sail through the air; it was gorgeously fitted out and of many colors; like the tail of a peacock, it was covered with thousands of eyes, but each eye was the barrel of a gun. The prince sat in the center of the ship, and had only to touch a spring in order to make thousands of bullets fly out in all directions, while the guns were at once loaded again. Hundreds of eagles were attached to this ship, and it rose with the swiftness of an arrow up towards the sun. The earth was soon left far below, and looked, with its mountains and woods, like a cornfield where the plow had made furrows which separated green meadows; soon it looked only like a map with indistinct lines upon it; and at last it entirely disappeared in mist and clouds. Higher and higher rose the eagles up into the air; then God sent one of his numberless angels against the ship. The wicked prince showered thousands of bullets upon him, but they rebounded from his shining wings and fell down like ordinary hailstones. One drop of blood, one single drop, came out of the white feathers of the angel's wings and fell upon the ship in which the prince sat, burned into it, and weighed upon it like thousands of hundredweights, dragging it rapidly down to the earth again; the strong wings of the eagles gave way, the wind roared round the prince's head, and the clouds around—were they formed by the smoke rising up from the burnt cities?—took strange shapes, like crabs many, many miles long, which stretched their claws out after him, and rose up like enormous rocks, from which rolling masses dashed down, and became fire-spitting dragons.

The prince was lying half-dead in his ship, when it sank at last with a terrible shock into the branches of a large tree in the wood.

"I will conquer God!" said the prince. "I have sworn it: my will must be done!"

And he spent seven years in the construction of wonderful ships to sail through the air, and had darts cast from the hardest steel to break the walls of Heaven with. He gathered warriors from all countries, so many that when they were placed side by side they covered the space of several miles. They entered the ships and the prince was approaching his own, when God sent a swarm of gnats—one swarm of little gnats. They buzzed round the prince and stung his face and hands; angrily he drew his sword and brandished it, but he only touched the air and did not hit the gnats. Then he ordered his servants to bring costly coverings and wrap him in them, that the gnats might no longer be able to reach him. The servants carried out his orders, but one single gnat had placed itself inside one of the coverings, crept into the prince's ear and stung him. The place burnt like fire, and the poison entered into his blood. Mad with pain, he tore off the coverings and his clothes too, flinging them far away, and danced about before the eyes of his ferocious soldiers, who now mocked at him, the mad prince, who wished to make war with God, and was overcome by a single little gnat.

The Galoshes of Fortune

A Beginning

In a house in East Street, Copenhagen, not far from the King's New Market, a very large party had assembled; evidently the host aimed at receiving invitations in return, as he had invited so many people. Half of the guests had already sat down at the card-tables, while the others seemed to be waiting for the answer to their hostess's question, "What shall we do now?" The entertainment had advanced far enough for the people to be getting more and more animated. Among various other subjects, the conversation turned upon the Middle Ages. Some held the opinion that the Middle Ages were more interesting than our own time; and Counselor Knapp stood up for this opinion so warmly, that the lady of the house sided with him at once, and both eagerly declaimed against Oerstedt's treatise in the Almanac "On Ancient and Modern Times," in which the main preference is given to our own age. The Counselor held that the times of the Danish King Hans were the best and most prosperous.

While this was the subject of the conversation, which was only interrupted for a moment by the arrival of a newspaper containing nothing worth reading, let us look into the anteroom, where the cloaks, sticks, and galoshes belonging to the guests were lying. Here two women were sitting, the one young, the other more advanced in years. One might have thought they were servants who had come to accompany their mistresses home; but upon looking more closely at them, one was soon convinced that they were not common servants; their appearance was too dignified, their skins too delicate, and their dresses too elegant. They were two fairies.

The youngest was not Fortune herself, it is true, but the handmaid of one of her ladies in waiting, who carried the smaller gifts about. The elder one looked somewhat gloomy; she was Care, who always transacts all her business personally, for only then does she know that it is well done.

They were telling each other where they had been during the day. Fortune's messenger had only carried out some unimportant commissions; for instance, she had saved a new hat from a shower of rain, obtained a bow from a titled nonentity for an honest man, etc.; but she had now something of greater consequence to do. "I must also tell you," she said, "that to-day is my birthday, and in honor of it a pair of galoshes have been entrusted to me, which I am to bring to mankind. These galoshes have the property, that whoever puts them on is instantly transported to the place and age where he or she most desires to be; every wish regarding time or place of existence is at once realized, and thus man can for once be happy here below."

"Believe me," said Care, "he will be most unhappy, and bless the moment when he is once more rid of the galoshes."

"Is that your opinion?" replied the other. "Now I shall put them down at the door; some one will take them, and become the happy man."

Such was their conversation.

What Happened to the Counselor

It was late; Counselor Knapp, deeply lost in thought over the time of King Hans, wished to go home; but fate so arranged matters that, instead of his own galoshes, he put on those of Fortune, and walked out into East Street.

The magic power of the galoshes instantly carried him back to the times of King Hans, and his feet sank deeply into the mud and mire of the street, which was not paved in those days.

"It is awfully dirty here," said the Counselor; "why, the good flagstones are gone and the lamps are all out."

The moon had not yet risen high enough; the atmosphere was somewhat thick, so that all the surrounding objects were not to be recognized in the darkness. When he came to the next corner, he found a lamp before a picture of the Holy Virgin, but the light it gave was so small that he only noticed it when he was passing underneath it, and his eyes fell upon the painted figures of the Mother and Child.

"That is evidently a curiosity shop," he thought, "and they have forgotten to take in their sign."

Several people in the costume of that age then passed by him.

"How funnily they are dressed up! No doubt they are returning from a masquerade."

Suddenly the sound of drums and fifes struck his ears. He saw the flaring light of torches, and stopped. A very extraordinary procession passed before him. First marched a band of drummers, beating their instruments with great skill; they were followed by attendants with cross-bows and lances. The principal person in the procession was a clergyman. The astonished Counselor asked what all this meant, and who the clergyman was.

"The Bishop of Zealand," was the answer.

"Good heavens!" sighed the Counselor, "what does the Bishop intend to do?" Then he shook his head; he could not believe it possible that the man was the bishop.

Still torturing his brains on this point, he passed through East Street and over High Bridge Place. The bridge, which he used to cross in order to reach Castle Square, was nowhere to be found; he at last reached the bank of a shallow river, where he saw two men with a boat.

"Would the gentleman like to cross over to the Holm?" they asked him.

"To the Holm?" said the Counselor, who was quite unconscious that he lived in a different age. "I wish to go to Christian's Port, in Little Turf Street."

The two men stared at him.

"Only tell me where the bridge is," he said. "It is unpardonable that they have not lighted the lamps here, and it is as muddy as if it were a marsh."

The more he talked to the boatmen, the less intelligible their language became to him.

"I do not understand your Bornholmish," he said at last in an angry tone, and left them. He could not find the bridge, nor was there any rail-fence. "It is a downright shame that things are in such disorder here," he said. He had never thought his age more miserable than he did this evening. "I think it will be best for me to take a droske,"* he thought. But where were the cabs? None were visible. "I shall have to return to King's Newmarket to find a vehicle, otherwise I shall never reach Christian's Port." Then he went back to East Street, and had nearly come to the end of it, when the moon broke through the clouds.

"Good heavens! What strange building have they erected here!" he exclaimed when he saw the East Gate, which in those days stood at the end of East Street. He found, however, one of the wickets still open, and passed through it, in the hope of reaching the King's Newmarket; but there were wide meadows before him, with a few bushes growing upon them, and a broad canal or river streaming through them. A few wretched wooden huts, belonging to Dutch sailors, stood on the opposite bank. "Either what I see is a *fata morgana,* or I am intoxicated," lamented the Counselor. "If I only knew what all this means!" He returned again, firmly believing that he was ill. Walking back through the same streets, he looked more closely at the houses, and noticed that most of them were only built of lath and plaster, and had thatched roofs.

* A cab is called "droske" in Copenhagen.

"I do not feel at all well"; he sighed, "and yet I have only taken one glass of punch. But punch does not agree with me, and it is altogether wrong to serve punch with hot salmon. I shall tell the agent's wife so. Would it be wise to go back now, and let them know how I feel? No, no, it would look too ridiculous; and then, after all, the question is, if they are still up." He looked for the house, but was unable to find it.

"This is dreadful; I cannot even recognize East Street again. I do not see a single shop; there are only wretched old houses, as if I were in Roeskilde or Ringstedt. There is no longer any doubt; I am ill, and it is useless to stand on ceremonies. But where in all the world is the agent's house? It is no longer the same; but in yonder house I see some people still up. Alas! I am very ill." He soon arrived at a half-opened door, and saw the light inside. It was an inn of that period, a sort of public-house. The room looked very much like a Dutch bar: a number of people, sailors, citizens of Copenhagen, and a few scholars, sat there in lively conversation, with their mugs before them, and paid little attention to the Counselor coming in.

"I beg your pardon," said the Counselor to the landlady, "I have been suddenly taken ill; would you kindly send for a cab to drive me to Christian's Port?"

The woman looked at him and shook her head. Then she addressed him in German. The Counselor, supposing that she could not speak Danish, repeated his request in German; this, in addition to his dress, made the woman feel sure that he was a foreigner; but she understood that he was unwell, and brought him a jug of water: it tasted very much of sea-water, although it had been fetched from the well outside.

The Counselor rested his head upon his hand, drew a deep breath and thought over all the strange things around him.

"Is that this evening's number of the *Day?*"* he asked mechanically when he saw the woman putting a large piece of paper aside.

She did not know what he meant, but she gave him the paper. It was a woodcut representing a phenomenon which had been seen in the city of Cologne.

"That is very old," said the Counselor, and became quite cheerful at the sight of this old curiosity. "How did you get this rare cut? It is highly interesting, although the whole is but a fable. These phenomena are now explained as polar lights; they probably are caused by electricity."

Those who sat next to him, and heard his speech, looked at him with great surprise, and one of them rose, politely raised his hat, and said in a serious tone, "You are certainly a very learned man, monsieur."

---

* Evening paper at Copenhagen.

"Not at all," replied the Counselor; "I can only talk about things that everybody is supposed to understand."

"*Modestia* is a fine virtue," said the man. "Moreover, I have to add to your explanation *mihi secus videtur;* yet in the present case I willingly suspend my *judidum.*"

"May I ask with whom I have the honor to speak?" replied the Counselor.

"I am a Bachelor of Divinity," said the man.

This answer was enough for the Counselor; title and dress were in accordance with each other. "Surely," he thought, "this man is an old village schoolmaster, such a specimen as one still meets with sometimes in the upper parts of Jutland."

"Although here we are not in a *locus docendi*" began the man again, "I request you to take the trouble to give us a speech. You are surely well read in the ancients."

"Oh, yes," replied the Counselor, "I am very fond of reading old and useful books, but I am also interested in new ones—with the exception of every-day stories, of which we have so many in reality."

"Every-day stories?" asked the Bachelor of Divinity.

"Why, yes; I mean the modern novels."

"Oh!" said the man, smiling, "they certainly contain a great deal of wit, and are read at Court. The King especially likes the romance by Iffven and Gaudian which treats of King Arthur and his valiant Knights of the Round Table. He has made jokes about it to his courtiers."

"This one certainly I have not read yet," said the Counselor. "It must be quite a new one, published by Heidberg."

"No," replied the man, "Heidberg is not the publisher, but Gotfred of Gehmen."*

"Is he the author?" asked the Counselor; "that is a very old name. Was it not the name of the first Danish printer?"

"Yes, he is our first printer," said the scholar.

So far everything went fairly well; now one of the citizens spoke of the dreadful plague which had raged a few years ago, meaning that of the year 1484. The Counselor thought he spoke of the cholera, and so they could discuss it, unaware of the fact that each spoke of something else. The war against the freebooters had happened so lately that it was unavoidably mentioned; the English pirates, they said, had seized some ships that were in the harbor. The Counselor, in the belief that they meant the events of 1801, was

* First printer and publisher in Denmark, under the reign of King Hans.

strongly against the English. The latter part of the conversation, however, did not go off so smoothly; they could not help contradicting each other every moment; the good Bachelor of Divinity was dreadfully ignorant, so that the simplest remark of the Counselor seemed to him too daring or too fantastic. They often looked at each other in astonishment, and when matters became too difficult, the scholar began to talk Latin, hoping to be better understood, but all was of no avail.

"How do you feel now?" asked the landlady, pulling the Counselor's sleeve. Only then his memory returned; in the course of the conversation he had forgotten all that had happened.

"Good heavens! where am I?" he said, and he felt quite dizzy when he thought of it.

"Let us have claret, mead, or Bremen beer," cried one of the guests. "And you shall drink with us."

Two girls came in; one had on a cap of two colors. They poured the wine out, and made curtsies. The Counselor felt a cold shiver run down his back. "What does all this mean?" he said. But he had to drink with them, they asked him so politely. He was quite in despair, and when one of them said that he was intoxicated, he did not doubt it for a moment, and only requested them to get him a droske. Now they thought he spoke the Muscovite language. Never in his life had he been in such rude and vulgar company. "One would think that the country had gone back to Paganism," he thought; "this is the most terrible moment in all my life."

Just then the idea struck him that he would stoop under the table and creep towards the door. He carried this out, but when he was near the door, the others discovered his intention; they took hold of his feet, and to his great good fortune, pulled off the galoshes, and at once the whole enchantment was broken.

The Counselor distinctly saw a street lamp burning, and behind it a large building; it all seemed familiar and grand to him. He was in East Street, as we know it now, and was resting on the pavement with his legs towards the door, and opposite sat the watchman, asleep.

"Goodness gracious! have I really lain herein the street dreaming?" he said. "Yes, this is East Street. How beautifully light and pleasant it looks! That glass of punch must have had a dreadful effect upon me."

Two minutes later, he sat in a cab, and drove to Christian's Port. He thought of all the anguish he had suffered, and praised the present, his own age, with all his heart, as being, in spite of its shortcomings, much better than the age in which he had existed a short while ago.

The Watchman's Adventures

"Well, I never!" said the watchman; "there are a pair of galoshes. They evidently belong to the lieutenant who lives up there, for they are close by his door." The honest man would gladly have rung the bell and returned them to their owner, for there was still a light upstairs, but he did not wish to wake up the other people in the house, so he left them there. "I am sure a pair of such things must keep one's feet very warm," he said. "How nice and soft the leather is!" They fitted his feet exactly. "How strange things are in this world! This man, now, might go into his warm bed, and yet he does not do so, but walks up and down in his room. He is a fortunate man. He has neither wife nor child; he is out every evening. I wish I were in his place, I should certainly be happy."

No sooner had he uttered this wish than the galoshes carried it out; the watchman became the lieutenant in body and mind.

There he was, standing upstairs in the room, holding a sheet of pink notepaper between his fingers, on which was written a poem—a poem from the lieutenant's own pen. Who has not had, once in his life, a poetical moment? Then, if one writes down one's thoughts, they are poetry.

Such poems people only write down when they are in love, but a prudent man never has them printed. To be a lieutenant, poor and in love—this forms a triangle; or one might better describe it as half the broken die of fortune. That is just what the lieutenant thought at this moment, and therefore leaned his head against the window frame and sighed. "The poor watchman down in the street is much happier than I. He does not know what I call want. He has a home, a wife and children, who share his joys and sorrows. I should be much happier if I could change places with him, and live with only his hopes and expectations. I am sure he is much happier than I."

Instantly the watchman became a watchman again, for, through the galoshes of Fortune, he had become, body and soul, the lieutenant; but as such he felt less contented than before, and preferred what he had despised a short time ago. He was a watchman again.

"That was a hideous dream," he said, "but very curious; I felt as if I were the lieutenant up there, and that was by no means a pleasure. I missed my wife and children, who are always ready to smother me with their kisses."

He sat down again and nodded; he could not quite get over the dream; the galoshes were still on his feet. A shooting star passed over the sky.

"There it goes" he said, "and yet there are plenty left. I should like to look a little more closely at these things, especially at the moon, for she would not slip so easily out of one's hands. The student my wife does washing for, says that when we are dead we shall fly from one planet to another. That is wrong, although it would not be at all bad. I wish I could take a little leap up there. I should not mind leaving my body here on the steps."

There are some things in this world that must be spoken of with caution, and one ought to be still more careful when one has the galoshes of Fortune upon one's feet. Now, let us see what happened to the watchman.

Everybody knows how quickly one can move from one place to another by steam, having experienced it either on a railway or a steamboat. But this speed is not more than the crawl of the sloth or creeping of a snail in comparison to the swiftness with which light travels. It flies nineteen million times faster than the quickest railway engine. Death is an electric shock to our hearts: the delivered soul vanishes away on the wings of electricity. Sunlight requires about eight minutes and a few seconds to perform a journey of more than ninety-five millions of miles; the soul travels as quickly on the wings of electricity. The distance between the various celestial bodies is not greater to it than we should find the distance between the houses of friends living in the same town quite close together. The electric shock to our hearts costs us our bodies, unless we have by chance the galoshes of Fortune on our feet, like the watchman.

In a few seconds the watchman had traversed the distance of two hundred and sixty thousand miles to the moon, which consists, as everybody knows, of much lighter material than our earth; something like new-fallen snow, as we should say. He had arrived on one of the numerous circular mountains which one sees on Dr. Maedler's large map of the moon. The inside was a basin of about half a mile in depth. Down below was a town; to get an idea of its appearance, the best thing would be to pour the white of an egg into a glass of water; the substance here was just as soft, and formed similar transparent towers, domes, and terraces, floating in the thin air like sails. Our globe hung above his head, like a dark red ball.

He soon noticed a great many beings, surely intended to be what we call "men," but they were very different from us. If they had been arranged in rank and file, and painted, one would certainly say, "What a beautiful arabesque!" They also had a language, but how could the soul of a watchman be expected to understand it? Nevertheless, it did understand the moon-language, for a soul has much greater faculties than we commonly suppose. Have we not frequent proof of its dramatic power in dreams? Then all our friends appear to us in their own character and voice, so exactly like the reality that we should have great difficulty in imitating them in our waking hours. Does not our soul often recall persons of whom we have not thought for years?

Suddenly they appear before our mental eyes in such living reality that we are able to recognize their minutest peculiarities. Truly, our soul's memory is a dreadful thing, for it will be able one day to recall every sin, every evil thought, we ever had; and then we shall have to give an account of every light word which was in our hearts or on our lips.

Thus the watchman's soul understood the language of the inhabitants of the moon very well. They were discussing our earth, and had doubts as to its being inhabited; they asserted the air there must be too thick for any moon-being to live in. They were of opinion that the moon only was inhabited; that it was *the* celestial body where the ancient inhabitants of the world lived.

They also talked politics; but let us leave them, and return to East Street, and see what happens to the watchman's body. He was still sitting motionless on the steps, his staff having fallen out of his hand, while his eyes looked fixedly towards the moon, where his honest soul was rambling about.

"What's o'clock, watchman?" asked one of the passers-by. But the watchman gave no answer. Then the man gently filliped his nose, which caused him to lose his equilibrium, and fall, full length, on the ground, like a dead man. His comrades were frightened; he seemed quite lifeless, and remained in the same condition. The incident was reported and discussed, and later on in the morning the body was taken to the hospital.

It might have turned out a capital joke if the soul had come back and looked for its body in East Street, without being able to find it. Probably it would first go to the Police Station, from thence to the Lost Property Office, that inquiries might be made, and in the end repair to the hospital. But we need not trouble our minds on that point, for souls are most clever when they act on their own responsibility; only the bodies make them stupid.

As I have stated, the watchman's body was carried to the hospital; there it was taken to the room where the bodies were washed, and naturally, the first thing they did was to take off the galoshes, whereupon the soul was obliged to return to the body. It at once started straight for the body, and in a few moments the man was alive again. He declared that he had never in all his life passed such a dreadful night, and not for any amount of money would he care to have such sensations again; but he got over it all right.

He was able to leave the hospital the same day, but the galoshes remained there.

A Critical Moment—A Most Extraordinary Journey

Every inhabitant of Copenhagen knows the entrance to Frederick's Hospital, but as probably also some people who have not seen Copenhagen will read this story, it will be well to give a short description of it.

Towards the street the hospital is surrounded by an iron railing of considerable height, the thick bars of which stand so far apart that sometimes, as the story goes, some of the most slender young medical assistants have squeezed themselves through and paid little visits to town. Their heads were the most difficult to be brought through, and therefore here, as in other things in this world, those who had the smallest heads were the best off. This information will be sufficient for our narrative.

The hospital is surrounded by an iron railing of considerable height, the thick bars of which stand so far apart that sometimes, as the story goes, some of the most slender young medical assistants have squeezed themselves through and paid little visits to town.

One of the volunteers, of whom one could only say that he had a great head in the physical sense, was on watch one evening; the rain was pouring down; but in spite of these two obstacles he wished to go out.

Just for a quarter of an hour, he thought; he need not trouble the porter, especially if he could slip through the bars. He noticed the galoshes which the watchman had forgotten; it did not strike him in the least that they were those of Fortune; they would render him good service in the bad weather, he thought, and so put them on. The point was now, if he could squeeze himself through the bars—he had never tried before. They were now in front of him.

"I wish I had my head outside," he said, and instantly,

although it was very thick and large, it glided smoothly through the bars; the galoshes seemed to know how to do that very well; now he tried to pass his body through too, but this was impossible.

"I am too stout," he said; "I thought my head was the worst; but it is my body that I can't get through."

Now he tried to withdraw his head again, but he was unable to do so; he could move his neck about comfortably, and this was all. At first he felt very angry, but soon became discouraged. The galoshes of Fortune had placed him in this awkward position, and, unluckily, it never came into his mind to wish himself free again. Instead of wishing, he struggled to get his head out of the bars, but all his attempts were in vain. The rain was pouring down; not a soul was to be seen in the street; he could not reach the bell at the porter's lodge. How could he get out? He felt certain he would have to stop there until the next morning, then they would be obliged to send for a blacksmith to file through the iron bars. But all this would take time; all the charity children would be going to their school opposite, all the inhabitants of the adjoining sailor's quarter would flock together to see him in the stocks; there would be a large crowd, no doubt! "Ugh!" he cried, "the blood is rushing to my head; I must go mad! Yes, I am going mad; oh, I wish I were free, then perhaps I might feel better." He ought to have said this sooner, for the thought was scarcely expressed when his head was free, and he rushed up to his room, quite upset by the fright which the galoshes had caused him.

Now we must not think it was all over for him. No; the worst was still to come.

The night and the following day passed; nobody claimed the galoshes. In the evening a recital was to take place on the platform of a private theater in a far-off street. The house was filled in every part; the volunteer from the hospital was among the audience, and seemed to have entirely forgotten what had happened to him the night before. He had put on the galoshes, as no one had claimed them, and they rendered him good service, for the streets were very dirty. A new poem, entitled "Aunty's Spectacles," was being recited, in which the spectacles were described as enabling the person who wore them in a large assembly to read the people like cards, and to predict from them all that would happen in the coming year.

The spectacles pleased him; he would have very much liked to have such a pair. He thought, one might perhaps be able to look straight into people's hearts, if one made good use of them, and that surely would be much more interesting than to see what would happen in the coming year; the latter, one would be sure to see, but not the former.

"I think if I could look into the hearts of the ladies and gentlemen in the first row, they would seem to me to form a sort of large warehouse; oh, how my eyes would wander about in it! In the heart of that lady, sitting there, I am sure I should find a milliner's shop, in the next one the shop is empty, but a cleaning out would do it no harm. Would there also be some shops with solid articles to be found in them?" "Yes, yes," he sighed, "I know one in which everything is genuine, but there is already a clerk in it, and that, in fact, is the only thing I have to find fault with. One might be invited to come into various others and inspect them. I wish I could pass like a little thought through these hearts!"

That was the catch-word for the galoshes; the volunteer shrunk together, and at once began a most extraordinary journey through the hearts of the occupiers of the first row. The first heart through which he passed belonged to a lady; it seemed to him that he was in one of the rooms of an orthopedic museum, where the plaster casts of deformed limbs are arranged on the walls, the only difference being, that while in the museum the casts are formed when the people enter, they were formed and kept in this heart after they had left. There were casts of the bodily and mental deformities of the lady's female friends carefully preserved.

Quickly he glided into another lady's heart. It appeared to him to be like a large holy church; the white dove of innocence fluttered over the high altar. He would have gladly knelt down, but he had no time—he had to go into the next heart; the sound of the organ was still ringing in his ears, and he felt he had become a new and better man, so that he did not feel unworthy to enter the next sanctuary, where he saw a sick mother in a miserable garret-room. But God's bright sun was shining through the window, splendid roses were growing in the little flower-box on the roof, and two sky-blue birds were singing of the joys of childhood, while the sick mother implored God to bless her daughter.

Then he crept on all-fours through an overcrowded butcher's shop; wherever he turned there was nothing but meat. It was the heart of a rich and respectable man, whose name you will certainly find in the directory.

Thence he came into the heart of this gentleman's wife; it was nothing but an old dilapidated pigeon-house. The husband's portrait served as a weathercock, and was connected with the doors, so that they opened and shut whenever he turned his head.

In the next heart he found a cabinet of mirrors, like those one sees in the castle of Rosenburg. But the mirrors magnified in an incredible degree. The insignificant *I* of the proprietor sat in the center of the floor, like the Dalai-Lama, admiringly contemplating his own greatness.

Next he thought he had entered a narrow case, full of pointed needles, and said, "No doubt, this is the heart of an old maid." But such was not the case; it belonged to a young officer with several orders, whom people considered a man of intellect and heart. The poor volunteer was quite dizzy when he came out of the last heart in the row; he could not collect his thoughts, and fancied his too strong imaginative powers had run away with him.

"Good heavens!" he sighed, "I have a strong tendency to go mad, without doubt, and in here it is intolerably hot; the blood is rushing to my head." Just then he remembered his critical situation the evening before, when he had stuck fast between the bars of the hospital railing.

"Surely that was when I caught it," he thought; "I must do something for it in time. Perhaps a Russian bath would do me good. I wish I were already on the top-shelves."

There he lay on the top-shelf of the vapor-bath, fully dressed, with boots and galoshes still on, and the water dropped down from the ceiling on his face.

"Ugh!" he cried, and jumped down to take a plunge-bath.

The attendant cried out loudly in his surprise at seeing a man with all his clothes on.

The volunteer fortunately had enough presence of mind to whisper in his ear, "It is for a bet."

Upon arriving home, he at once placed a large mustard plaster on his neck and another on his back, to draw out the madness.

The next morning he had a very sore back, and that was all he gained through the galoshes of Fortune.

The Clerk's Transformation

The watchman, whom surely we have not yet forgotten in the meantime, remembered the galoshes which he had found, and carried with him to the hospital.

He went to fetch them, and when neither the lieutenant nor anybody else in the same street recognized them as their property, he took them to the police-office.

"They look exactly like my own galoshes," said one of the clerks, looking at the galoshes, and placing them by the side of his own. "It requires more than a shoemaker's eye to distinguish the difference"

"Mr. Clerk," said an attendant, who entered the room with some papers. The clerk turned round and spoke to the man; afterwards, when he looked at the galoshes again, he was uncertain whether the pair on the left or on the right were his. "The wet ones must be mine," he thought; but in this he was wrong—they were the galoshes of Fortune; and after all it is not so wonderful, for a police-clerk can make mistakes like anybody else.

He put the galoshes on, thrust some papers into his pocket, took some others under his arm (the latter he was to read at home, and make abstracts of their contents), and went out. By chance. it was Sunday morning, and splendid weather. "A trip to Fredericksburg would do me good," he thought, and thither he bent his steps.

No one could be more quiet and steady than this young clerk. We will not grudge him the little walk; after so much sitting, it will no doubt be beneficial to him. At first he walked on mechanically without thinking of anything at all, and therefore gave the galoshes no opportunity of proving their magic powers. In the Avenue he met an acquaintance, a young Danish poet, who told him that he intended to start the next day for a summer tour.

"Are you really off again?" asked the clerk. "You are indeed a luckier and freer man than one of us. You can go wherever you like, but we always have a chain to our feet."

"But it is fastened to the bread-tree," replied the poet. "You need not have a care for the morrow, and when you grow old you will receive a pension."

"But you are better off, after all," said the clerk. "It must be a pleasure to sit down and write poetry. Everybody has something pleasant to say to you, and you are your own master. Come and try what it is like to be obliged to sit in court and listen to all sorts of frivolous cases."

The poet shook his head; the clerk did the same, and so they parted, each retaining his own opinion.

"They are peculiar people, these poets," thought the clerk. "I should very much like to try and enter into such a nature, and become a poet myself, for I am certain I should not write such lamentations as the others. To-day is a splendid spring day for a poet! The air is exceptionally clear, the clouds look beautiful, and the green grass has such a fragrance. For many years I have not felt as I do now."

From these remarks we see that he had already turned a poet. To express such feelings would in most cases be considered ridiculous. It is foolish to think a poet is a different being from other men; there may be some among the latter who have far more poetical minds than professional poets. But a poet has a better memory, he can retain ideas and thoughts until they are clearly fixed and expressed in words; and that others cannot do. But the transition of an ordinary nature to a poetical one must needs be noticeable, and so it was with the clerk.

"What a delicious fragrance!" he said. "How much it reminds me of the violets at Aunt Laura's. That was when I was a small boy. Dear me! I have not thought of that for a long time. Good old lady! She used to live near the canal. She always kept a green branch or a few green shoots in water, however hard the winter was. The violets smelled sweet when I was putting hot pennies against the frozen window-panes to make peep-holes. And I had a fine view through them. There lay the ships out in the canal, frozen in and deserted by their crews; a lonely crow was the only living thing on board. But when spring came, all became alive; with cries and shouting the ice was burst, the ships were tarred and rigged, and then they started for distant lands. I have always remained here, and shall always be obliged to do so, and sit in a police office, while other people take passports for abroad. That's my fate." And he sighed deeply. Suddenly he stopped. "Good heavens! what can be the matter with me? I have never thought and felt like this. The spring air must be the cause of it. It alarms me, and yet it is not disagreeable!" He felt in his pockets for his papers "They will soon make me think of something else," he said, and his eyes glided over the first page:

"'Mrs. Sigbirth: Original Tragedy, in Five Acts,'" he read. "What's this? It's my own handwriting. Have I written this tragedy? 'The Intrigue on the Promenade; or, Fast Day: a Vaudeville.' But wherever have I got these things? Somebody must have put them into my pocket. And here is a letter."

It was from a theatrical manager; the plays were refused, and the letter was written in not over-polite language.

"H'm—H'm," said the clerk, and seated himself on a bench. His thoughts were very elevated, and his nerves highly strung. Involuntarily he plucked a flower growing near him; it was a common daisy. What botanists tell us in many a lecture, this flower tells us in a minute. It told the story of its birth, of the power of the sunlight, which, spreading out the fine petals, compels them to breathe forth sweet fragrance. Then he thought of the struggle of life, which in the same way awakens feelings in our breast. Air and light are the flower's lovers, but light is the favored one. It turns towards the light, and when light vanishes, it folds its petals and sleeps in the arms of the air.

"Light adorns me," said the flower.

"But the air enables thee to breathe," whispered the poet.

A little way off, a boy was splashing with a stick in the water of a marshy ditch, so that the drops of water flew up to the green branches; the clerk thought of the millions of animalcule which were thrown up in each drop of water, which, considering their size, must produce in them the same feeling as if we were thrown up high into the clouds. When the clerk thought of the great change that had taken place in him, he smiled.

"I am asleep and dreaming! It is strange how naturally one can dream and all the time one knows that he is only dreaming. I hope I may be able to remember this dream to-morrow when I am awake. I feel unusually excited. What a clear perception I have of everything, and how free I feel! But I am sure, should I remember anything of it to-morrow, it will seem stuff and nonsense; something of the like has happened to me before. All the clever and beautiful things one hears of and speaks about in dreams, are like the underground treasure; when one digs it up, it looks rich and beautiful, and in the daylight it is but stones and faded leaves. "Ah!" he sighed sadly, and looked at the singing birds hopping merrily from branch to branch, "they are much better off than I! Flying is a fine art. Happy is he who has been born with wings. If I could transform myself into a bird, I should choose to be a lark."

Immediately his coat-tails and sleeves became wings, his clothes feathers, and the galoshes, claws; he noticed it and smiled to himself. "Well, now! I see that I am dreaming, but I never had such a foolish dream!"

He flew up into the green branches and sang, but there was no poetry in his song; the poetical mind was gone. The galoshes, like anybody else who wishes to do a thing well, could only do one thing at a time. He wished to be a poet: he became one. Then he desired to be a little bird, and by becoming one, his former character disappeared.

"This is charming indeed," he said. "In the daytime I sit at the police office among the most uninteresting official papers; at night I can dream, and fly about as a lark in the park of Fredericksburg. One might really write a popular comedy about all this."

Then he flew down into the grass, turned his head from side to side, and pecked the flexible blades of grass with his beak, which, in proportion to his present size, appeared to him as large as palm-leaves in North Africa. The next moment all became as dark as night around him. Something, as it seemed to him, of enormous size was thrown over him; it was a sailor boy's cap. A hand then came underneath the cap, and seized the clerk by the back and wings so tightly that he cried out. In his fright he instinctively shouted out, "You rascal, I am a clerk in the police office." But this only sounded to the sailor boy like "Tweet, tweet." He tapped the bird on its beak and walked off.

In the avenue he met two schoolboys of the upper class—that is, from the social point of view; for as far as their abilities were concerned they belonged to the lowest class in the school; they bought the bird for a small sum, and thus the clerk was brought back to Copenhagen.

"It is a good thing that I am dreaming," said the clerk, "otherwise I should certainly feel very angry! First I was a poet, now I am a lark. Surely the poetical nature has transformed me into this little bird! It is a very poor story, especially if one falls into boys' hands. I should very much like to know how it will end."

The boys took the bird into a very elegantly furnished room; a stout, amiable-looking lady received them. She was not at all pleased to see that they had brought home such a common field bird, as she called the lark. She would only allow them to keep it for the day, and they had to put the bird into an empty cage near the window.

"Perhaps it will please Polly," she added, and nodded to a large green parrot which was proudly rocking itself in its ring in a beautiful brass cage. "To-day is Polly's birthday," she said foolishly, "the little field-bird wants to congratulate it."

Polly did not reply a single word, and continued to rock itself, but a pretty canary, which had been brought away from its warm native country only last summer, began to warble sweetly.

"Squaller!" cried the lady, and threw a white cloth over the cage.

"Tweet, tweet," it sighed; "this is a terrible snowstorm." And then became silent.

The clerk, or, as the lady called him, the field-bird, was put into a small cage close by the canary and not far from the parrot. All that Polly could say (and it sounded sometimes most comical) was, "No, let us be men." What it said besides was no more intelligible than the warbling of the canary; but the clerk, being now a bird himself, understood his comrades very well.

"I flew about beneath green palms and flowering almond-trees," sang the canary. "I used to fly with my brothers and sisters over the beautiful flowers and smooth clear lakes, at the bottom of which one could see the plants waving their leaves. I also saw many fine-looking parrots, which could tell the most amusing tales."

"They were wild birds," replied the parrot, "they were not educated. No, let us be men. Why don't you laugh? When the lady and all the other people laugh you ought to do so also. It is a great shortcoming not to be able to appreciate fun. No, let us be men."

"Do you remember the handsome girls who used to dance in the tents near the flowering trees?" asked the canary. "Have you forgotten the sweet fruit, and the cooling juice of the wild herbs?"

"Oh, yes, I remember it all," replied the parrot; "but I am much more comfortable here. I have good food, and am well treated; I know I am clever, and I do not ask for more. Let us be men. You are a poet, as men call it; I possess sound knowledge and wit; you are a genius, but you lack discretion. You rise up to those high notes of yours, and then they cover you over. They dare not treat me like that. I was more expensive. My beak gains me consideration, and I can be witty. No, let us be men."

"Oh, my warm native country," sang the canary. "I will sing of your dark green trees, your calm bays, where the branches kiss the smooth, clear water. I will sing of all my shining comrades' joy, where the plants grow by the desert springs."

"Leave off those mournful strains," said the parrot. "Sing something that makes one laugh. By laughing you show that you possess the highest mental accomplishments. Have you ever seen a horse or a dog laugh? No, they can cry out; but laugh—only man has the gift of laughing." Then it laughed "Ha, ha, ha!" and added, "Let us be men."

"You poor little gray bird of the North," said the canary, "you are a prisoner here, like us. Although it is cold in your woods, you have freedom there. Fly away; they have forgotten to close the door of your cage, and the top window is open. Fly away!"

The clerk instinctively obeyed, and hopped out of the cage. At the same moment the half-open door leading into the next room creaked, and stealthily, with green shining eyes, the cat came in and chased him. The canary fluttered in the cage, the parrot opened its wings, and cried, "Let us be men." The clerk felt a mortal fright and flew out through the window, over houses and streets, until he was obliged to rest himself a little.

The house opposite his resting-place seemed familiar to him; the windows stood open; he flew in—it was his own room.

He perched himself on the table, and said, "Let us be men," involuntarily imitating the parrot. Instantly he became the clerk again, but he was sitting on the table.

"Oh dear," he said, "I wonder how I came up here, and fell asleep. That was a disagreeable dream. After all, it was nothing but stuff and nonsense."

The Best Thing the Galoshes Did

The next day, early in the morning, when the clerk was still in bed, somebody knocked at his door; his neighbor, a young student of theology, who lived in the same story, walked in.

"Lend me your galoshes," he said; "it is damp in the garden, but the sun shines so brightly that I should like to smoke a pipe out there." He put on the galoshes and was soon in the garden below, in which a plum-tree and a pear-tree were growing. Even such a small garden is considered a wonderful treasure in the center of big cities.

The student walked about in the garden; it was only six o'clock, and from the street he heard the sound of a post-horn.

"Traveling, traveling," he exclaimed. "That is the most desirable thing in the world, that is the aim of all my wishes. The restlessness which I often feel would be cured by traveling. But I ought to be able to go far away. I should like to see beautiful Switzerland, to travel through Italy, and—"

It was well that the galoshes acted instantly, otherwise he might have gone too far, not only for himself, but for us too.

He was traveling in the heart of Switzerland, closely packed with eight others in a diligence. He had a headache, his neck was stiff with fatigue, the blood had ceased to circulate in his feet, they were swollen, and the boots pinched. He was half-asleep and half-awake. In his right-hand pocket he carried his letters of credit; in his left, the passport; and some gold coins sewn in a little bag he wore on his chest. Whenever he dozed off he woke up imagining he had lost one or other of his valuables, and started up suddenly; then his hand would move in a triangle from the right over the breast to the left, to feel if they were still in their places. Umbrellas, sticks and hats were swinging in a net in front of him, and almost entirely deprived him of the view, which was very imposing; he looked at it, but his heart sang what, at least, one poet we know of has sung in Switzerland, although he had not yet printed it—

"I dreamed of beauty, and I now behold it
Mont Blanc doth rise before me, steep and gray!
Were my purse full, I should esteem it
The greatest joy in Switzerland to stay."

Grand, serious, and dark was all nature around him. The pine-woods looked as small as heather on the high rocks, the summits of which towered into the misty clouds; it began to snow; an icy wind was blowing.

"Ugh!" he shivered, "I wish we were on the other side of the Alps; there it would be summer, and I should have raised money on my credit notes. I am so anxious about my money that I do not enjoy Switzerland. Oh! I wish I had already come to the other side."

And there he was on the other side, in Central Italy, between Florence and Rome. The lake Thrasymene lay before his eyes, and looked in the evening light like fiery gold between the dark blue mountains. Here, where Hannibal defeated Flaminius, vines were peacefully growing; by the wayside, lovely half-naked children watched over a herd of swine under the flowering laurel-trees. If we could describe this picture correctly, all would exclaim, "Beautiful Italy!"

But neither the student, nor any of his traveling companions in the carriage of the vetturino, said anything of the sort. Venomous flies and gnats flew into the carriage by thousands; they tried to drive them away with myrtle branches, but in vain; the flies stung them nevertheless. There was not one among them whose face was not swollen from their painful stings. The poor horses looked dreadful; the flies covered them in swarms, and it was only a momentary relief when the coachman dismounted and swept the flies off.

Now the sun set, and a sudden icy cold pervaded all nature—much like the cold air in a tomb when we enter it on a hot summer day; the mountains round about appeared wrapped in that peculiar green which we see in some old oil paintings, and which, if we have not witnessed it in the south, we believe to be unnatural. It was a superb spectacle, but the travelers' stomachs were empty and their bodies exhausted with fatigue; all they were longing for was good night quarters, but what could they find? They looked more longingly for this than they did at the magnificent scenery before them.

The road led through an olive grove, much like a road between pollard willow trees at home. Here was at last a lonely inn. A dozen crippled beggars were lying down before it; the liveliest of them looked, to use one of Marryat's phrases, "like the eldest son of Hunger having just come of age"; the others were either blind or had paralyzed feet, and crept about on their hands, or they had crippled arms and fingerless hands. That was misery in rags, indeed!

"*Excellenza miserabili*" they sighed, and stretched forth their crippled limbs. The landlady herself, barefooted and with disorderly hair and a soiled blouse, received the guests.

The doors were fastened with strings; the floors of the rooms consisted of bricks, and were broken in many places; bats flew about under the ceilings, and there was a vile odor within.

"Lay the table down in the stable," said one of the travelers. "There, at least, we know what we breathe."

The windows were opened to allow the fresh air to enter; but the crippled arms and continual lamenting, "*Miserabili excellenza*" came in quicker than the air. Many inscriptions covered the walls; half of them were not in favor of the *Bella Italia!*

Supper, when served, consisted of watery soup, with pepper and rancid oil. The latter was the chief ingredient in the salad. Musty eggs and fried cockscombs were the best dishes; even the wine had a peculiar taste; it was a nauseous mixture.

At night the travelers' boxes were placed against the door, and one of them had to watch while the others slept. It was the student's turn to watch.

Oh, how unbearably close the room was! The heat was oppressive; the gnats buzzed and stung, the *miserabili* outside groaned in their dreams.

"Traveling," said the student, "would be a pleasure if one had no body. If the body could rest and the mind fly about. Where-ever I go I feel a want that oppresses me; I wish for something better than the moment can give me; something better—nay, the best; but where and what is it?"

No sooner had he uttered this wish than he was at home again. The long white curtains were hanging before the window, and in the middle of the room stood a black coffin; in it he slept the sleep of death. His wish was fulfilled; his body rested, his spirit was free to travel.

"Consider no man happy until he rests in the grave," were the words of Solon. In this case their truth was confirmed. Every dead body is a sphinx of immortality. The sphinx in the black coffin answered the questions which the student two days before had written down:

"O Death, than stern dark angel, we do find
Nought but the tombs that thou dost leave behind!
Will not the soul on Jacob's ladder upward pass,
Or only rise as sickly churchyard grass?

"The world doth seldom see the greatest woes—
Ye lonely suffering ones! ye now repose!
Your hearts were often more opprest by care,
Than by the earth your coffin-lid doth bear."

Two beings were moving about in the room; we know them already. One was the fairy Care, the other was the messenger of Fortune. They bent over the dead.

"Now you see," said Care, "what happiness your galoshes have brought to mankind!"

"They, at least, brought a lasting gift to him who slumbers here," answered Fortune's messenger.

"Oh, no," said Care. "He passed away at his own wish; he was not summoned. His mental power was not strong enough to discern the treasures Fate had destined him to discover. I will render him a good service now."

And she pulled the galoshes from his feet; the sleep of death was at once ended; the awakened man raised himself. Care disappeared, and with her the galoshes; probably she considered them her property.

The Bell

In the narrow streets of a large town people often heard in the evening, when the sun was setting, and his last rays gave a golden tint to the chimney-pots, a strange noise which resembled the sound of a church bell; it only lasted an instant, for it was lost in the continual roar of traffic and hum of voices which rose from the town. "The evening bell is ringing," people used to say; "the sun is setting!" Those who walked outside the town, where the houses were less crowded and interspersed by gardens and little fields, saw the evening sky much better, and heard the sound of the bell much more clearly. It seemed as though the sound came from a church, deep in the calm, fragrant wood, and thither people looked with devout feelings.

A considerable time elapsed: one said to the other, "I really wonder if there is a church out in the wood. The bell has indeed a strange sweet sound! Shall we go there and see what the cause of it is?" The rich drove, the poor walked, but the way seemed to them extraordinarily long, and when they arrived at a number of willow trees on the border of the wood they sat down, looked up into the great branches and thought they were now really in the wood. A confectioner from the town also came out and put up a stall there; then came another confectioner who hung a bell over his stall, which was covered with pitch to protect it from the rain, but the clapper was wanting.

When people came home they used to say that it had been very romantic, and that really means something else than merely taking tea. Three persons declared that they had gone as far as the end of the wood; they had always heard the strange sound, but there it seemed to them as if it came from the town. One of them wrote verses about the bell, and said that it was like the voice of a mother speaking to an intelligent and beloved child; no tune, he said, was sweeter than the sound of the bell.

The emperor of the country heard of it, and declared that he who would really find out where the sound came from should receive the title of Bellringer to the World, even if there was no bell at all.

Now many went out into the wood for the sake of this splendid berth; but only one of them came back with some sort of explanation. None of them had gone far enough, nor had he, and yet he said that the sound of the bell came from a large owl in a hollow tree. It was a wisdom owl, which continually knocked its head against the tree, but he was unable to say with certainty whether its head or the hollow trunk of the tree was the cause of the noise.

He was appointed Bellringer to the World, and wrote every year a short dissertation on the owl, but by this means people did not become any wiser than they had been before.

It was just confirmation-day. The clergyman had delivered a beautiful and touching sermon, the candidates were deeply moved by it; it was indeed a very important day for them: they were all at once transformed from mere children to grown-up people; the childish soul was to fly over, as it were, into a more reasonable being.

The sun shined most brightly; and the sound of the great unknown bell was heard more distinctly than ever. They had a mind to go thither, all except three. One of them wished to go home and try on her ball dress, for this very dress and the ball were the cause of her being confirmed this time, otherwise she would not have been allowed to go. The second, a poor boy, had borrowed a coat and a pair of boots from the son of his landlord to be confirmed in, and he had to return them at a certain time. The third said that he never went into strange places if his parents were not with him; he had always been a good child, and wished to remain so, even after being confirmed, and they ought not to tease him for this; they, however, did it all the same. These three, therefore, did not go; the others went on. The sun was shining, the birds were singing, and the confirmed children sang too, holding each other by the hand, for they had no position yet, and they were all equal in the eyes of God. Two of the smallest soon became tired and returned to the town; two little girls sat down and made garlands of flowers, they, therefore, did not go on. When the others arrived at the willow trees, where the confectioner had put up his stall, they said: "Now we are out here; the bell does not in reality exist—it is only something that people imagine!"

Then suddenly the sound of the bell was heard so beautifully and solemnly from the wood that four or five made up their minds to go still further on. The wood was very thickly grown. It was difficult to advance: wood lilies and anemones grew almost too high; flowering convolvuli and brambles were hanging like garlands from tree to tree; while the nightingales were singing and the sunbeams played. That was very beautiful! But the way was unfit for the girls; they would have torn their dresses. Large rocks, covered with moss of various hues, were lying about; the fresh spring water rippled forth with a peculiar sound. "I don't think that can be the bell," said one of the confirmed children, and then he lay down and listened. "We must try to find out if it is!" And there he remained, and let the others walk on.

They came to a hut built of the bark of trees and branches; a large crab-apple tree spread its branches over it, as if it intended to pour all its fruit on the roof, upon which roses were blooming; the long boughs covered the gable, where a little bell was hanging. Was this the one they had heard? All agreed that it must be so, except one who said that the bell was too small and too thin to be heard at such a distance, and that it had quite a different sound to that which had so touched men's hearts.

He who spoke was a king's son, and therefore the others said that such a one always wishes to be cleverer than other people.

Therefore they let him go alone; and as he walked on, the solitude of the wood produced a feeling of reverence in his breast; but still he heard the little bell about which the others rejoiced, and sometimes, when the wind blew in that direction, he could hear the sounds from the confectioner's stall, where the others were singing at tea. But the deep sounds of the bell were much stronger; soon it seemed to him as if an organ played an accompaniment—the sound came from the left, from the side where the heart is. Now something rustled among the bushes, and a little boy stood before the king's son, in wooden shoes and such a short jacket that the sleeves did not reach to his wrists. They knew each other: the boy was the one who had not been able to go with them because he had to take the coat and boots back to his landlord's son. That he had done, and had started again in his wooden shoes and old clothes, for the sound of the bell was too enticing—he felt he must go on.

"We might go together," said the king's son. But the poor boy with the wooden shoes was quite ashamed; he pulled at the short sleeves of his jacket, and said that he was afraid he could not walk so fast; besides, he was of opinion that the bell ought to be sought at the right, for there was all that was grand and magnificent.

"Then we shall not meet," said the king's son, nodding to the poor boy, who went into the deepest part of the wood, where the thorns tore his shabby clothes and scratched his hands, face, and feet until they bled. The king's son also received several good scratches, but the sun was shining on his way, and it is he whom we will now follow, for he was a quick fellow. "I will and must find the bell," he said, "if I have to go to the end of the world."

Ugly monkeys sat high in the branches and clenched their teeth. "Shall we beat him?" they said. "Shall we thrash him? He is a king's son!"

But he walked on undaunted, deeper and deeper into the wood, where the most wonderful flowers were growing; there were standing white star lilies with blood-red stamens, sky-blue tulips shining when the wind moved them; apple trees covered with apples like large glittering soap bubbles: only think how resplendent these trees were in the sunshine! All around were beautiful green meadows, where hart and hind played in the grass. There grew magnificent oaks and beech-trees; and if the bark was split of any of them, long blades of grass grew out of the clefts; there were also large smooth lakes in the wood, on which the swans were swimming about and flapping their wings. The king's son often stood still and listened; sometimes he thought that the sound of the bell rose up to him out of one of these deep lakes, but soon he found that this was a mistake, and that the bell was ringing still farther in the wood. Then the sun set, the clouds were as red as fire; it became quiet in the wood; he sank down on his knees, sang an evening hymn and said: "I shall never find what I am looking for! Now the sun is setting, and the night, the dark night, is approaching. Yet I may perhaps see the round sun once more before he disappears beneath the horizon. I will climb up these rocks, they are as high as the highest trees!" And then, taking hold of the creepers and roots, he climbed up on the wet stones, where water-snakes were wriggling and the toads, as it were, barked at him: he reached the top before the sun, seen from such a height, had quite set. "Oh, what a splendor!" The sea, the great majestic sea, which was rolling its long waves against the shore, stretched out before him, and the sun was standing like a large bright altar out there where sea and Heaven met—all melted together in the most glowing colors; the wood was singing, and his heart too. The whole of nature was one large holy church, in which the trees and hovering clouds formed the pillars, the flowers and grass the woven velvet carpet, and Heaven itself was the great cupola; up there the flame color vanished as soon as the sun disappeared, but millions of stars were lighted; diamond lamps were shining, and the king's son stretched his arms out towards Heaven, towards the sea, and towards the wood. Then suddenly the poor boy with the short-sleeved jacket and the wooden shoes appeared; he had arrived just as quickly on the road he had chosen. And they ran towards each other and took one another's hand, in the great cathedral of nature and poesy, and above them sounded the invisible holy bell; happy spirits surrounded them, singing hallelujahs and rejoicing.

Thumbelina

Once upon a time there was a woman who wished very much to have a very small child, but she did not know where to get one. So she went to an old witch and said to her: "I would so very much like to have a small child; can you tell me where I can get one?"

"Oh, we shall soon be able to manage that," said the witch. "Here is a barleycorn; it is not of the same kind that grows in the farmer's field, or that the chickens get to eat. Put it into a flower-pot, and you will see something." "Thank you," said the woman, and gave the witch twelve shillings, for that was the price of it. Then she went home and planted the barleycorn; immediately there grew up a large handsome flower, looking like a tulip; the leaves, however, were tightly closed, as though it were still a bud. "It is a beautiful flower," said the woman, kissing its red and yellow leaves; but as she kissed it the flower opened with a bang. It was a real tulip, as could now be seen; but in the middle of the flower, on the green velvety pistils, sat a tiny maiden, delicately and gracefully formed. She was scarcely half a thumb's length high, and therefore she was called Thumbelina.

A neat polished walnut-shell served Thumbelina for a cradle, blue violet leaves were her mattresses, and a rose-leaf her blanket. There she slept at night, but in the daytime she played about on the table, where the woman had put a plate with a wreath of flowers round it, the stalks of which stood in water. On this water floated a large tulip-leaf, and on this she could sit and row from one side of the plate to the other, having two white horse-hairs for oars. It looked wonderfully pretty. She could sing, too, and indeed, so tenderly and prettily as had never been heard before.

One night, as she was lying in her pretty bed, an old toad came creeping in through the window, in which there was a broken pane. The toad was a very ugly one, large and wet; it hopped down upon the table, where Thumbelina lay sleeping under the red rose-leaf.

"She would be a pretty wife for my son," said the toad, taking the walnut-shell in which Thumbelina was sleeping, and hopping with it through the window, down into the garden.

There flowed a great wide brook, the margin of which was swampy and marshy, and here lived the toad with her son. Ugh! he was so ugly and nasty, and looked just like his mother. "Croak, croak! Crek-kek-kex!" was all that he could say when he spied the graceful little girl in the walnut-shell.

"She would be a pretty wife for my son," said the toad, taking the walnut-shell in which Thumbelina was sleeping.

"Don't speak so loud, else you'll wake her," said the old toad. "She might run away from us, for she is as light as swan's-down, so we will put her on one of the broad leaves of the water-lily in the brook; that will be just like an island for her, she is so light and small. She will not be able to run away from there while we are getting ready the state-room under the marsh, where you are to live and keep house."

Out in the brook there grew a great many water-lilies with broad green leaves, which looked as though they were floating on the water; the leaf which lay farthest off was the largest, to this the old toad swam out, and laid the walnut-shell with Thumbelina upon it.

Tiny Thumbelina woke early in the morning, and when she saw where she was she began to cry very bitterly; for there was water on every side of the great green leaf, and she could not get to land.

The old toad was sitting in the marsh decking out her room with reeds and yellow flowers—it was to be made very pretty for the new daughter-in-law; then she swam out with her ugly son to the leaf where Thumbelina was. They wanted to fetch her pretty bed, which was to be placed in the bridal chamber before she herself entered it. The old toad bowed low in the water before her and said: "Here you have my son; he will be your husband, and you will live in great splendor down in the marsh." "Croak, croak! Crek-kek-kex!" was all that the son could say. Then they took the pretty little bed and swam away with it, leaving Thumbelina sitting alone on the green leaf, crying, for she did not want to live with the nasty old toad, or have her ugly son for a husband. The little fishes swimming down in the water had both seen the toad and also heard what she had said; so they put out their heads, for they wanted to see the little girl too. As soon as they saw her they thought her so pretty that they felt very sorry that she was to go down to the ugly toad. No, that should never be! They assembled together down in the water, round the green stalk that held the leaf on which the tiny maiden stood, and with their teeth they gnawed away the stalk; the leaf floated away down the stream with Thumbelina—far away, where the toad could not reach her.

Thumbelina sailed by many towns, and the little birds sitting in the bushes saw her and sang, "What a lovely little girl!" The leaf went floating away with her farther and farther, and so Thumbelina traveled right out of the country.

The old toad bowed low in the water before her and said: "Here you have my son."

A pretty little white butterfly kept fluttering around her, and at last sat down upon the leaf. Thumbelina pleased him, and she was very glad of it, for now the toad could not reach her, and it was so beautiful where she was; the sun was shining on the water, making it sparkle like the brightest silver. She took her girdle, and tied one end of it round the butterfly, fastening the other end of the ribbon to the leaf; it glided along much quicker now, and she too, for of course she was standing on it.

A great cockchafer came flying along, who spied her, and immediately clasped his claws round her slender waist and flew up with her into a tree. The green leaf floated down the stream, and the butterfly with it; for he was bound fast to the leaf and could not get away.

A pretty little white butterfly kept fluttering around her . . . Thumbelina pleased him, and she was very glad of it, for now the toad could not reach her.

Heavens! how frightened poor Thumbelina was when the cockchafer flew up into the tree with her. But she was mostly grieved for the sake of the beautiful white butterfly which she had bound fast; in case he could not free himself, he would be obliged to starve. But the cockchafer did not care about that. He sat down with her on the largest green leaf of the tree, gave her the honey from the flowers to eat, and told her that she was very pretty, although she was not at all like a cockchafer.

Later on all the other cockchafers who lived in the tree came to pay a visit; they looked at Thumbelina and said, "She has not even more than two legs; that looks miserable!" "She hasn't any feelers," said another. "She has such a narrow waist, and looks quite human. Ugh, how ugly she is!" said all the lady cockchafers; and yet Thumbelina was very pretty—even the cockchafer who had carried her off admitted that. But when all the others said she was ugly, he at last believed it too, and would no longer have her; she might go where she liked. So they flew from off the tree with her and put her upon a daisy; she wept because she was so ugly that the cockchafers would not have her, and yet she was the loveliest little girl that one could imagine—as delicate and as tender as the most beautiful rose-leaf.

The whole summer through poor Thumbelina lived alone in the great forest. She wove herself a bed out of blades of grass, and hung it under a shamrock, in order to be protected from the rain; she gathered the honey out of the flowers for food, and drank of the dew that was on the leaves every morning. In this way summer and autumn passed, but now came winter—the long, cold winter. All the birds who had sung so beautifully about her flew away; the trees became bare and the flowers faded. The large shamrock under which she had lived dried up, and there remained nothing of it but a withered stalk; she was dreadfully cold, for her clothes were in tatters, and she herself was so small and delicate. Poor little Thumbelina, she would be frozen to death. It began to snow, and every snow-flake that

A great cockchafer came flying along, who spied her, and immediately clasped his claws round her slender waist and flew up with her into a tree.

fell upon her was like a whole shovelful thrown upon us; for we are so tall, and she was only an inch long. So she wrapped herself in a dry leaf, but that tore in half and would not warm her; she was shivering with cold.

Close to the wood to which she had now come lay a large cornfield; but the corn was gone long since, and only the dry naked stubbles stood up out of the frozen ground. These were like a forest for her to wander through, and oh! how she was trembling with cold. In this state she reached the door of a field-mouse who occupied a hole under the corn stubbles. There the mouse lived comfortably, had a whole room full of corn, a splendid kitchen and larder. Poor Thumbelina stood before the door like a little beggar girl, and asked for a piece of a barleycorn, for she had not had a bit to eat for two days.

"You poor little creature!" said the field-mouse—for she was really a good old mouse—"come into my warm room and dine with me."

Now, being pleased with Thumbelina, she said: "If you like, you can stay with me the whole winter, but you must keep my room clean and neat, and tell me tales, for I am very fond of them." And Thumbelina did what the good old field-mouse wished, and in return was treated uncommonly well.

"Now we shall soon have a visit," said the field-mouse; "my neighbor is in the habit of visiting me once a week. He is even better off than I am; has large rooms, and wears a beautiful black velvety fur. If you could only get him for a husband you would be well provided for. But he cannot see. You must tell him the prettiest stories that you know."

But Thumbelina did not trouble herself about it; she did not think much of the neighbor, for he was only a mole.

He came and paid a visit in his black velvety fur. He was so rich and so learned, said the field-mouse, and his dwelling was twenty times larger than hers; he possessed great learning, but he could not bear the sun and the beautiful flowers. Of the latter he seldom spoke, for he had never seen them.

Thumbelina had to sing, and she sang: "Cockchafer, cockchafer, fly away," and "When the parson goes afield." So the mole fell in love with her because of her beautiful voice: but he said nothing, for he was a prudent man.

A short time before, he had dug a passage through the earth from his house to theirs, and the field-mouse and Thumbelina received permission to take a walk in this passage as often as they liked. But he begged them not to be afraid of the dead bird which lay there. It was an entire bird, with feathers and beak, who had probably died only a short time before, and was buried just where the mole had made his passage.

The mole took a piece of decayed wood in his mouth, for that glimmers like a light in the dark, and then went on in front, and lighted them through

A short time before, he had dug a passage through the earth from his house to theirs, and the field-mouse and Thumbelina received permission to take a walk in this passage.

the long dark passage. When they came to the spot where the dead bird lay, the mole thrust his broad nose against the ceiling and pushed the earth up, so that a large hole was made, through which the light could shine down. In the middle of the floor lay a dead swallow, with its beautiful wings pressed close to its sides and its feet and head drawn under its feathers; the poor bird had certainly died of cold. This grieved Thumbelina very much; she was very fond of all the little birds who had sung and twittered so beautifully to her all the summer. But the mole kicked him with his crooked legs, and said, "He doesn't pipe any more now. How miserable it must be to be born a little bird! Thank Heaven, that can happen to none of my children; such a bird has nothing but his tweet, and is obliged to starve in winter."

"Yes, you may well say that as a sensible man," said the field-mouse. "What does the bird get for all his twittering when winter comes? He must starve and freeze. But I suppose that is considered very grand."

Thumbelina said nothing; but when the two others had turned their backs upon the bird, she bent down, and putting the feathers aside which covered its head, she kissed him upon his closed eyes.

"Perhaps it was he who sang so beautifully to me in the summer," she thought. How much pleasure he has given me, the dear, beautiful bird!"

The mole now stopped up the hole through which the daylight shined in, and then accompanied the ladies home. But at night Thumbelina could get no sleep; so she got up from her bed and wove a fine large carpet of hay, which she carried along, and spread out over the dead bird. She also laid the tender stamina of flowers, which were as soft as cotton, and which she had found in the field-mouse's room, around the bird, so that he might lie warm.

"Good-bye, you beautiful little bird," she said. "Good-bye and many thanks for your beautiful singing in summer, when all the trees were green and the sun shined down warm upon us." Then she laid her head upon the bird's heart. But the bird was not dead; he was only lying there benumbed, and having now been warmed again was coming back to life.

In autumn all the swallows fly away to warm countries; but if there is one who is belated, it gets so frozen that it drops down as if dead, and remains lying where it falls, and soon the cold snow covers it.

Thumbelina trembled, so frightened was she, for the bird was big, very big, compared with her, who was only an inch long. But she took courage, and laying the cotton more closely round the poor swallow, she fetched a leaf of mint which she herself had used as a blanket, and laid it over the bird's head.

The next night she again stole up to him; he was alive, but very weak, and could open his eyes only for a short moment to look at Thumbelina, who stood before him with a piece of decaying wood in her hand, for she had no other lantern.

"Thank you, my pretty little child," said the sick swallow to her. "I have been so beautifully warm. Soon I shall get my strength back and will then be able to fly about in the warm sunshine outside."

"Oh!" said she, "it is cold outside; it is snowing and freezing. Stay in your warm bed; I will take care of you."

Then she brought the swallow some water in a leaf of a flower. This the swallow drank, and told her how he had torn one of his wings on a thorn-bush, and had therefore been unable to fly so quickly as the other swallows who had flown far away to warm countries. So he had at last fallen to the ground, but could not remember anything more, and did not at all know how he had come there.

So he remained down there the whole winter, and Thumbelina nursed and tended him with all her heart; neither the mole nor the field-mouse knew anything about it, for they did not like the poor swallow at all.

As soon as spring came, and the sun warmed the earth, the swallow said good-bye to Thumbelina, who opened the hole which the mole had made up above. The sun shined in beautifully upon them, and the swallow asked her whether she would go with him; she could sit upon his back, he said, and they would fly far into the green forest. But Thumbelina knew that it would grieve the old field-mouse if she left her like that. "No, I cannot," she said.

"Good-bye, good-bye, you good pretty little girl!" said the swallow, and flew out into the sunshine. Thumbelina looked after him, and the tears came into her eyes, for she was very fond of the poor swallow.

"Tweet, tweet," sang the bird and flew into the green forest. Thumbelina was very sad. She got no permission to go out into the warm sunshine. The corn which had been sown on the field over the house of the field mouse grew up high into the air; it was a thick wood for the poor little girl who was only an inch high.

"Now you are a bride, Thumbelina," said the field-mouse. "Our neighbor has asked for your hand. What a great piece of luck for a poor child! Now you will have to make your outfit, both woollen and linen clothes; for you must lack nothing when you are the mole's wife."

Thumbelina had to turn the spindle, and the field-mouse hired four spiders to weave for her day and night. Every evening the mole used to visit them, and was always saying that at the end of the summer the sun would not shine so warm by a long way, that it was burning the earth as hard as a stone. Yes, when the summer was over he would celebrate his marriage with Thumbelina. But the latter was not at all pleased, for she could not bear the tiresome mole. Every morning when the sun rose, and every evening when it set she stole out to the door, and when the wind parted the ears of corn, so that she could see the blue sky, she would think how bright and beautiful it was out there, and would have a great longing to see the dear swallow again. But he never came back; he had probably flown far away into the beautiful green wood.

When autumn came, Thumbelina had her whole outfit ready.

"You are to be married in four weeks," said the field-mouse to her. But Thumbelina wept, and said she would not have the tiresome mole.

"Fiddlesticks!" said the field-mouse; "don't be obstinate, or I will bite you with my white teeth. He is a fine man whom you are going to marry. The Queen herself has not such black velvety fur. He has a full kitchen and cellar. Be thankful for it!"

Now the wedding was to take place. The mole had already come to fetch Thumbelina; she was to live with him deep down under the earth, and never come out to the warm sunshine, for that he did not like. The poor little girl was very sad; she was now to say good-bye to the beautiful sun, which, while she lived with the field-mouse, she had always had permission to look at from the door. "Good-bye, bright sun!" she said, and stretched her arms out high,

The field-mouse hired four spiders to weave for her day and night. Every evening the mole used to visit them.

and walked a little way off from the house of the field-mouse, for now the corn was cut and there remained only the dry stubbles. "Good-bye, good-bye!" she said, and wound her arms round a little red flower which was still blooming there. "Greet the little swallow for me, if you see him." "Tweet, tweet," suddenly sounded above her head; she looked up, and saw the little swallow, who was just flying by. When he spied Thumbelina, he was very pleased; she told him how unwilling she was to marry the ugly mole, and that she would have to live deep down under the earth, where the sun never shined. She could not held crying in telling it.

"The cold winter is coming now," said the little swallow; "I am flying away to warm countries; will you come with me? You can sit on my back; then we shall fly away from the ugly mole and his dark room, far away over the mountains, to warm countries, where the sun shines more beautifully than here, where it is always summer and there are glorious flowers. Do fly with me, dear little Thumbelina—you who saved my life when I lay frozen in the dark underground cellar."

"Yes, I will go with you," said Thumbelina; and she seated herself on the bird's back, with her feet on his outspread wing, binding her girdle fast to one of his strongest feathers. Then the swallow flew up into the air, over forest and sea, high up over the great mountains, where snow always lies. And Thumbelina began to freeze in the cold air, but then she crept under the bird's warm feathers, and only put out her little head to admire all the beauty beneath her.

She seated herself on the bird's back.

At last they came to the warm countries. There the sun shined far brighter than here, the sky seemed twice as high, and in the ditches and on the hedges grew the finest green and blue grapes. In the woods hung citron and oranges; the air was heavy with the scent of myrtle and mint, and on the high roads the prettiest little children ran and played with large colored butterflies. But the swallow flew still farther, and it became more and more beautiful. Under the most majestic green trees by the blue lake stood a marble castle of dazzling whiteness, all of the olden time. Vines wound themselves round the tall pillars, and up above there were a number of swallows' nests, and in one of these lived the swallow who was carrying Thumbelina.

"This is my house," said the swallow. "But it would not be proper for you to live with me here, and my arrangements are not such as you would be satisfied with. Pick out for yourself one of the most beautiful flowers that are growing down there; then I will put you into it, and you shall have everything as nice as you can wish.'

"That is glorious!" she said, clapping her little hands.

There lay a large white marble pillar which had fallen to the ground and broken into three pieces; between these grew the finest large white flowers. The swallow flew down with Thumbelina, and set her upon one of the broad petals. But what was her surprise! There in the middle of the flower sat a little man, as white and transparent as if he were made of glass; he wore the prettiest golden crown on his head, and had splendid little wings on his shoulders;

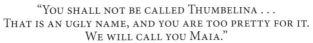

"You shall not be called Thumbelina . . .
That is an ugly name, and you are too pretty for it.
We will call you Maia."

he himself was no bigger than Thumbelina. He was the angel of the flower. In every flower lived such a little man or woman; but this one was the king of all.

"Heavens! how beautiful he is!" whispered Thumbelina to the swallow. The little prince was very frightened at the sight of the swallow, for it was a giant bird compared to him, who was so small and delicate. But when he spied Thumbelina he was greatly pleased; she was the prettiest little girl he had ever seen. He therefore took his golden crown from off his head, and put it upon hers, asking her what her name was, and whether she would be his wife; then she should be queen of all the flowers. He was indeed quite a different man to the son of the toad, and the mole with the black velvety fur. She said "Yes" to the grand prince. And out of every flower came a lady and a gentleman, so dainty that they were a pleasure to behold. Each one brought Thumbelina a present; but the best of all was a pair of beautiful wings from a large white fly; these were fastened on to Thumbelina's back, and now she too could fly from flower to flower. There was much rejoicing, and the little swallow sat up in his nest, and was to sing the bridal song; this he did as well as he could, although in his heart he was sad, for he was so fond of Thumbelina, and would have liked never to separate himself from her.

"You shall not be called Thumbelina," said the Flower Angel to her. "That is an ugly name, and you are too pretty for it. We will call you Maia."

"Good-bye, good-bye!" said the little swallow with a heavy heart, and flew away from the warm countries back to Denmark. There he had a little nest over the window where the man lives who can tell tales. To him he sang "Tweet, tweet." That is how we know the whole story.

Little Tuk

Well, yes, that was little Tuk. That was not his name, but when he could not yet speak he called himself Tuk, which he meant for Charlie; and that does very well, but one must know it. He had to look after his little sister Gustava, who was much younger than himself, and at the same time he had to learn his lessons; these two things, however, would not go very well together. The poor boy sat there with his little sister on his knee, singing to her all the songs he knew, and glancing now and then into his geography book which lay open before him. The next morning he had to know all the towns of Zealand by heart, and all that any one can be expected to know about them.

Then his mother came home, who had been out, and took little Gustava herself. Tuk went as quickly as possible to the window, and read so zealously that he had almost read his eyes out; it became darker and darker, but the mother had no money to buy candles.

"There goes the old washerwoman from over the way," said the mother, looking out of the window. "The poor woman can hardly drag herself along, and has to carry a pail full of water from the well; be a good boy, Tuk, my child, run over and help the old woman. Will you?"

And Tuk ran quickly over and helped her; but when he came back to the room it had become quite dark, and as there could be no question about light, he was to go to bed; his bed was an old settle. He was lying upon it thinking of his geography lesson of Zealand, and of all the master had said. Of course he ought still to be learning, but that was impossible. He therefore put the geography book under his pillow, because he had heard that this helps one a great deal when one wants to learn a lesson; the only thing is, one can't depend upon it. There he was lying and thinking and thinking, and then it seemed to him suddenly as if some one kissed him on the eyes and mouth. He slept, and yet he did not sleep; he felt as if the old washerwoman looked at him with her kind eyes and said: "It would be a great pity if you did not know your lesson to-morrow! You have helped me; therefore I will now help you, as God always helps every one." And suddenly the book under Tuk's pillow began to move. "Cluck, cluck!" It was a hen which came crawling out, and she was from Kjöge.* "I am a Kjöge-hen," she said, and then she told him how many inhabitants the town had, and of the battle that had taken place there, although this latter was not worth mentioning.

Then he heard a rattling noise and a plump—something fell down. It was a wooden bird, the parrot that was used at the shooting competition in Prästöe.† It said that there were as many inhabitants in that town as it had nails in its body; it was very proud too. "Thorwaldsen has been living quite close to me. Plump! here I am, quite comfortable!"

But now little Tuk was no longer lying in bed, but sat on horseback, and went off at a gallop. A magnificently dressed knight, with a shining plume on his helmet, held Tuk before him on the saddle, and so they rode through the wood to the old town of Wordingborg,‡ and that was a large lively town; on the king's castle were high towers, and light streamed from all the windows. Inside there was singing and dancing, for King Waldemar danced with the gaily-dressed Court ladies. Now it became morning, and as the sun rose, the whole city and the king's castle, tower after tower, sank down; and at last one single tower stood on the hill where the castle had been standing. The town was very small and poor, and the boys came out of school with their books under their arms, and said: "Two thousand inhabitants"; but that was not true, for there were not so many in the town.

And little Tuk was again in bed, and did not know if he was dreaming or not, but somebody stood close by his side. "Little Tuk, little Tuk," a voice said. It was a sailor who spoke, but he was as small as if he were a midshipman, although he was not one. "I have to greet you from Corsör; that's a rising town, and is very lively; it has steamboats and mail-coaches—formerly they said that it was ugly, but that is no longer true."

"I am situated upon the sea," said Corsör;§ "I have high-roads and pleasure-grounds, and I am the birthplace of a poet who was witty and entertaining, qualities that not all poets possess. Once I wished to equip a ship that was to go all round the world; but it did not do it, although it might have done it. In addition, I smell sweetly, for close by my gates grow the most splendid rose trees."

---

* Kjöge is a small town in the bay of the same name.

† Prastöe is a little town, only known because the Castle of Nysoe, where Thorwaldsen lived, is in its immediate neighborhood.

‡ Wordingborg is known for the ruins of the old castle. Under King Waldemar it was a flourishing town.

§ Corsör; a small town on the Great Belt.

Little Tuk looked, but all was red and green before his eyes; when the confusion of colors had passed by, he all at once saw a wooded slope near a bay, and high above it stood a beautiful old church with two high pointed spires. Springs of water flowed out of the slope in numerous jets, so that there was continual splashing. Close by sat an old king with a golden crown on his long hair. He was King Hroar, near the springs, close by the city of Roeskilde,* as one now calls it. And over the slope went all the kings and queens of Denmark, hand in hand, with their golden crowns on their heads, up to the old church, and the organ was playing, and the springs rippled. Little Tuk saw and heard everything. "Don't forget the towns," said King Hroar.

All at once everything was gone again, but whither? It seemed to Tuk as if some one turned over the leaves of a book. And there stood an old peasant woman before him, who came from Soröe,"† where the grass grows in the market-place. A gray linen apron was hanging over her head and back, and was very wet; it must have been raining. "Yes, it has," she said, and she could tell many amusing passages from Holberg's comedies and of Waldemar and Absolom. But all at once she shrank together and nodded her head as if she wanted to jump. "Croak," she said; "it is wet, it is wet; Soröe is as quiet as a grave!" Suddenly she became a frog. "Croak!" And then she turned an old woman again. "One must dress oneself according to the weather," she said. "It is wet! It is wet! My town is like a bottle—one has to go in at the neck, and come out at the neck again! Formerly, I had most splendid fishes, and now I have fresh rosy-cheeked boys at the bottom of the bottle, who learn wisdom, Hebrew, Greek. Croak!" That sounded as if the frogs croaked, or as if some one walked over the marshes with large boots—always the same sound, so monotonous and tiresome, that little Tuk fell asleep, and that could not do him any harm. But even in this sleep came a dream, or something of that kind. His little sister Gustava, with her blue eyes and golden curly hair, had suddenly become a tall slender girl, and could fly without having any wings; and then they flew right across Zealand, with its green woods and blue lakes.

"Do you hear the cock crow, little Tuk? Cock-a-doodle-doo.' The cocks fly up from Kjöge! You shall have a large farmyard one day! You will never suffer want or hunger! And you will take the cake, as people say: you will become a rich and happy man. Your house will rise like the tower of King Waldemar, and will be richly adorned with marble statues like those at

---

* Roeskilde was once the capital of Denmark.

† Soröe, a small beautifully-situated town; the Danish poet Holberg founded an academy here.

Prastöe. Understand me well: your name shall travel with glory all over the world, like the ship that was to sail off from Corsör, and at Roeskilde—"don't forget the towns!" said King Hroar—"there you will speak well and cleverly, little Tuk; and when they place you at last in your grave you will sleep peacefully."

"As if I lay in Soröe," said little Tuk, and then he woke up.

It was broad daylight, and he could no longer remember his dream, but that was not necessary, for one must not know what is to come in future. He quickly jumped out of bed and read his book, and there, all at once, he knew his whole lesson.

The old washerwoman just then peeped in at the door, nodded kindly to him, and said: "Many thanks, you good child, for your assistance! May God realize your beautiful dream!"

Little Tuk did not remember what he had dreamed, but God knew it.

A Cheerful Temper

My father left me the best inheritance any man can leave to his son—a cheerful temper. But who was my father? Why, that really has nothing to do with the cheerful temper. He was lively and quick, although somewhat stout and fat; in fact, he was in body and mind the very opposite to what one would expect from a man of his calling. But what was his position, what services did he render to the community? Why, if that were to be written down and printed at the very beginning of a book, some people in reading it would be likely to lay it aside and say there is something unpleasant about it; I don't like anything of that sort. And yet my father was neither a knacker nor a hangman; on the contrary, his office was such that it placed him at the head of the most distinguished citizens of the town, and he was fully entitled to be there, for it was his proper place. He must needs be the foremost of all—before the bishop, nay, even before princes of royal blood, because he was a hearse-driver.

There, now I have betrayed the secret! and I must confess that, when one saw my father sitting high up on the box of Death's bus, clad in his long wide black cloak, having a black-trimmed three-cornered hat on, and then looked into his face, which was as round and smiling as a picture of the sun, one could not think of mourning and the grave; for his face said: "It doesn't matter, never mind—it will go much better than one thinks." So, you see, from him I have my cheerful temper and also the habit of often going to the churchyard: and that is quite amusing, if one goes thither in good spirits. I forgot to say that I also take in the *Advertiser*, as he used to do.

I am no longer young—I have neither wife nor child, nor a library, but I read, as I have mentioned, the *Advertiser;* that suffices me. It is my favorite newspaper, as it was my father's.

The *Advertiser* is a most useful paper, and contains really everything a man requires to know; therein you find who preaches in the churches and in new books; it tells you about charitable institutions, and contains many harmless poetical attempts. Marriages are desired, and meetings brought about. All is so simple and natural! One can indeed live very happily and be buried, if one reads the *Advertiser*—nay, at the end of one's life one has such a heap of paper that one can comfortably lie on it, if one does not care to rest on wood shavings.

The *Advertiser* and the churchyard were always the two things that most elevated my mind, and best nourished my good temper.

Everybody can peruse the *Advertiser* by himself, but let him go with me to the churchyard. Let us go there when the sun is shining and the trees are green; let us walk about between the graves. Every one of them is a closed book with its back turned up; one can read its title, which says all the book contains, and yet says nothing at all. But I know my way; I learned much from my father, and something I know from my own experience. I have it all written down in a book, which I have made for use and pleasure; there is something written about them all, and about a few more.

Now we are at the churchyard.

Here, behind the railings, painted out in white, where one day a rose-tree stood—it is gone now, and only a little bush of evergreen from the neighbor's grave stretches a few straggling branches in, lest it be quite bare—rests a very unfortunate man, and yet he was, as people call it, well-off when he was alive; he had sufficient to live comfortably, and something to spare, but the world—that is to say "art"—used him too badly. When he went in the evening to the theater to enjoy a play thoroughly, he nearly went out of his mind when the machinist put too strong a light into one of the cheeks of the moon, or when the canvases representing the sky were hanging in front of the scene instead of behind, or if they made a palm appear in a garden at Copenhagen, or a cactus plant in Switzerland, or beech-trees in the northern regions of Norway. What does it matter to any one? Who would trouble his mind about anything of that sort? All is only a play which is intended to amuse people. Sometimes the people applauded too much in his opinion, sometimes not enough. "That is wet wood to-night," he used to say, "it will not catch fire"; and when he looked round to see what sort of people were there, then he found that they laughed in the wrong places, when they were not expected to laugh at all. All this angered him, pained him, and made him miserable; and now he rests in the grave.

Here rests a man who was very lucky in life; I mean to say that he was a nobleman of high birth, and that was his luck, for otherwise he would not have turned out anything at all. Nature orders all things so wisely that it is a pleasure to think of it! He used to wear a coat richly embroidered with silk; and one might very well have compared him with a precious bell-pull in a drawing-room. As such, a bell-pull generally has a good strong string behind it; so he had a substitute to do his work for him, and he does it, in fact, still for some other man of that type. Yes, yes; all is so well arranged in this world, one has good reason to have a cheerful temper.

Now here rests—it is very sad indeed—a man who exercised his brains for sixty-seven years in perpetual search for a good idea; at last, according to his own opinion, he had one, and was so pleased with himself that he died for joy. So his good idea was of no use to any one, for nobody heard anything at all about it. I am inclined to think that this good idea will prevent him from resting quietly in the grave; for suppose it was such that it could only be well explained at breakfast-time, and that, being a dead man, he can only rise about midnight—according to the common notion about ghosts—it is not suitable for the time; nobody laughs at it, and the man must take his good idea again down with him into his grave.

Here rests a miser: in her lifetime this woman was so dreadfully stingy that she used to get up at night and mew in order to make people believe she kept a cat.

Here rests a young lady of good family, who liked immensely to sing in society: when she sang *"Mi manca la voce,"* it was the only true thing she said in her life.

Here rests a maiden of another kind. Yes, indeed, love does not listen to reason! She was to be married; but that's an everyday story. Let the dead rest.

Here lies a widow who had a sweet voice, but bitterness in her heart. She used to visit the families in the neighborhood and try to find out their short-comings, and she was very zealous in this pursuit.

What you see here is a family grave. All the members of this family were so much of one opinion that when the whole world and all the newspapers said a certain thing was *so,* and the little boy came home from school and said it was *not so,* he was right, because he belonged to the family. And you can be sure, if it happened that the cock of this family crowed at midnight, they said it was morning, even if the watchman and all the clocks of the town were announcing the midnight hour.

The great poet Goethe concludes his "Faust" with the words: "May be continued"; we may say the same about our walk through the churchyard. I often come here; and when any of my friends or non-friends go too far, I go out to the churchyard, select a plot of ground, and consecrate it to him or to her, whomsoever I wish to bury; then I do bury them immediately, and they remain there dead and powerless until they return as new and better people. I write down their lives and deeds into my book in my own fashion; everybody ought to do so. Nobody should be vexed; if his friends do something foolish, let him bury them at once and keep his good temper. He can also read the *Advertiser,* which is a paper written by the people, although their hands are sometimes guided.

When the time comes that I myself and the story of my life are to be bound in the grave, I wish they may write upon it the epitaph:

A Cheerful Temper.

The Little Match Girl

It was terribly cold; it snowed and was almost dark on this, the last evening of the year. In the cold and darkness, a poor little girl, with bare head and naked feet, went along the streets. When she left home, it is true, she had had slippers on, but what was the use of that? They were very large slippers; her mother had worn them till then, so big were they. So the little girl lost them as she sped across the street, to get out of the way of two carts driving furiously along. One slipper was not to be found again, and a boy had caught up the other and run away with it. So the little girl had to walk with naked feet, which were red and blue with cold. She carried a lot of matches in a red apron, and a box of them in her hand. No one had bought anything of her the live-long day; no one had given her a penny.

Shivering with cold and hunger, she crept along, poor little thing, a picture of misery.

The snow-flakes covered her beautiful fair hair, which fell in long tresses about her neck: but she did not think of that now. Lights were shining in all the windows, and there was a tempting smell of roast goose, for it was New Year's Eve. Yes, she was thinking of that.

In a corner formed by two houses, one of which projected beyond the other, she crouched down in a little heap. Although she had drawn her feet up under her, she became colder and colder; she dared not go home, for she had not sold any matches nor earned a single penny.

She would certainly be beaten by her father, and it was cold at home, too; they had only the roof above them, through which the wind whistled, although the largest cracks had been stopped up with straw and rags.

Her hands were almost numb with cold. One little match might do her good, if she dared take only one out of the box, strike it on the wall and warm her fingers. She took one out and lit it. How it sputtered and burned!

It was a warm, bright flame, like a little candle, when she held her hands over it; it was a wonderful little light, and it really seemed to the child as though she was sitting in front of a great iron stove with polished brass feet and brass ornaments. How the fire burned up, and how nicely it warmed one! The little girl was already stretching ou t her feet to warm these too, when—out went the little flame, the stove vanished, and she had only the remains of the burned match in her hand.

She struck a second one on the wall; it threw a light, and where this fell upon the wall, the latter became transparent, like a veil; she could see right into the room. A white table-cloth was spread upon the table, which was decked with shining china dishes, and there was a glorious smell of roast goose stuffed with apples and dried plums. And what pleased the poor little girl more than all was that the goose hopped down from the dish, and with a knife and fork sticking in its breast, came waddling across the floor straight up to her. Just at that moment out went the match, and only the thick, damp, cold wall remained. So she lighted another match, and at once she sat under the beautiful Christmas tree; it was much larger and better dressed than the one she had seen through the glass doors at the rich merchant's. The green boughs were lit up with thousands of candles, and gaily-painted figures, like those in the shop-windows, looked down upon her. The little girl stretched her hands out towards them and—out went the match. The Christmas candles rose higher and higher till they were only the stars in the sky; one of them fell, leaving a long fiery trail behind it.

What pleased the poor little girl more than all was that the goose hopped down from the dish, and with a knife and fork sticking in its breast

"Now, some one is dying," thought the little girl, for she had been told by her old grandmother, the only person she had ever loved, and who was now dead, that when a star falls a soul goes up to Heaven.

She struck another match on the wall; it was alight once more, and before her stood her old grandmother, all dazzling and bright, and looking very kind and loving.

"Grandmother!" cried the little girl. "Oh! take me with you. I know that you will go away when the match is burnt out; you will vanish like the warm stove, like the beautiful roast goose, and the large and splendid Christmas-tree." And she quickly lighted the whole box of matches, for she did not wish to let her grandmother go. The matches burned with such a blaze that it was lighter than day, and the old grandmother had never appeared so beautiful nor so tall before. Taking the little girl in her arms, she flew up with her, high, endlessly high, above the earth; and there they knew neither cold, nor hunger, nor sorrow—for they were with God.

But in the cold dawn, the poor little girl was still sitting—with red cheeks and a smile upon her lips—in the corner, leaning against the wall: frozen to death on the last evening of the Old Year. The New Year's sun shined on the little body. The child sat up stiffly, holding her matches, of which a box had been burnt. "She must have tried to warm herself," some one said. No one knew what beautiful things she had seen, nor into what glory she had entered with her grandmother on the joyous New Year.

The poor little girl was still sitting . . . in the corner, leaning against the wall.

The Story of the Year

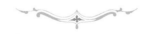

It was in the latter part of the month of January. A violent snowstorm was raging; the snow whirled along the streets and lanes and covered the outside of the window-panes all over, while it fell down in larger masses from the roofs of the houses.

All the people in the street were seized with a sudden haste; they hurried along, often jostling against one another or falling into one another's arms, holding on tightly, so as to be safe for a moment at least. Carriages and horses looked as if they were powdered all over with sugar; the footmen were standing with their backs to the carriages, in order to shelter their faces from the cutting wind; foot-passengers eagerly sought the protection of the vehicles which moved slowly forward through the deep snow. When at last the storm had abated, and narrow paths were cleared along the fronts of the houses, people nevertheless often came to a dead stop when they met, neither wishing to step aside into the deep snow to make room for the other to pass.

Still and silently they were standing face to face, till at last they mutually arrived at the tacit compromise of exposing each one foot to the snow-heaps.

Towards the evening the wind ceased to blow; the sky looked as if it had been swept, and became higher and more transparent; the stars seemed to be quite new, and some of them were shining marvelously bright and clear; it was freezing so much that the snow creaked, and soon it was covered with a crust strong enough to carry the sparrows at daybreak, when they hopped up and down, where the snow had been shovelled away; but there was very little food to be found, and it was bitterly cold.

"Twit," said one to another, "this is what they call a new year; it is much worse than the last, and we might just as well have kept the old one. I am very dissatisfied, and I think I have good cause to be so."

"Yes; people were running about and firing salutes in honor of the new year," said a little sparrow, shivering with cold. "They were throwing pots and dishes against the doors, and were nearly out of their minds for joy, because the old year was gone. I was glad of it too, for I hoped we should soon have warmer days again; but nothing of the sort has happened yet; on the contrary, it freezes much harder than before. I think they must have made a mistake in their calculation of the time."

"There is no doubt about it," said a third, an old gray-headed bird. "They have a thing they call a calendar, which is entirely their own invention, and that is why they wish to regulate everything according to it; but that can't be so easily done. When Spring comes the new year begins; that is the course of nature—I go by that."

"But when will Spring come?" asked the others.

"It will come when the stork comes back; but he is very uncertain. Nobody here in town knows anything about him; they are better informed in the country. Shall we fly thither and wait? There we are certainly much nearer to Spring."

"That is all very well," said one of the sparrows, who had hopped about and chirped for a long time, without really saying anything. "I have found here in town comforts which I fear I should have to go without in the country. Near here, in a courtyard, live some people who had the happy thought of attaching two or three flower-pots to their house, so that their open ends are close to the wall, while the bottoms of the pots stand out; a hole is cut into each of them large enough for me to fly in and out; there my husband and I have built our nest, and there we have reared all our young ones. These people have of course done all this to have the pleasure of seeing us, otherwise I am sure they would not have done it. For their own pleasure, also, they strew out bread-crumbs, and thus we have food: we are, as it were, provided for. Therefore I think my husband and I will stay, although we are very discontented—yes, I think we shall stay."

"And we shall fly into the country to see if Spring is not yet coming." And off they went.

In the country the winter was harder still, and the glass showed a few degrees more cold than in town. The piercing wind swept over the snow-covered fields. The peasant sat in his sleigh, with his hands wrapped in warm mittens, beating his arms across his chest to get warm, while his whip was lying on his knees; the lean horses ran so fast that they steamed; the snow creaked, and the sparrows hopped about in the ruts and froze. "Twit! When will Spring come? It takes a very long time."

"A very long time," resounded from the nearest snow-covered hill far over the field; it might have been an echo which one heard, or perhaps the language of the wonderful old man who sat in wind and weather on the top of snow-heaps; he was quite white, dressed like a peasant in a coarse white coat of frieze; he had long white hair, was very pale, and had large clear eyes.

"Who is the old man yonder?" asked the sparrows.

"I know," said an old raven sitting on the post of a railing, who was condescending enough to acknowledge that we are all small birds in the sight of the Lord, and who was therefore ready to talk to the sparrows and to give them information. "I know who the old man is. It is Winter, the old man of last year: he is not dead, as the calendar says, but is guardian to the young prince Spring, who is coming. Yes, Winter is still swaying his scepter. Ugh! the cold makes you shiver, you little ones, does it not?"

"Yes; but is it not as I said?" asked the sparrow. "The calendar is only the invention of men, it is not arranged according to nature. They ought to leave such things to us, who are more sensitive."

Week after week passed by; the frozen lake was motionless, and looked like molten lead; damp, icy mists were hanging heavily over the country; the large black crows flew about in long rows without making a noise; it was as if everything in nature was asleep. Then a sunbeam glided over the icy surface of the lake, and made it shine like polished tin. The snow covering the fields and the hill no longer glittered as before; but the white man, Winter himself, was still sitting there and looking unswervingly southward; he did not notice that the snowy carpet sunk, as it were, into the ground, and that here and there little green spots came forth, and on these spots the sparrows flocked together.

"Twit, twit! is Spring coming now?"

"Spring!" It sounded over field and meadow, and through the dark woods, where bright green moss was shining on the trunks of the trees; and the two first storks arrived from the south, carrying on their backs two lovely little children, a boy and a girl; they kissed the earth in greeting, and wherever they set their feet, white flowers sprang forth out of the snow; hand in hand they went to the old ice-man, Winter, and tenderly clung to his breast. In a moment they had all three disappeared, while the whole country round them was enveloped in a thick damp mist, dense and heavy, which covered everything like a veil. Gradually the wind began to blow, and rushed with a roar against the mist and drove it away with violent blows; the sun shined brightly.

Winter had disappeared, but Spring's lovely children had seated themselves on the throne of the year.

"This is the new year!" cried the sparrows. "Now we shall get our due, and damages in addition, for the severe winter."

Wherever the two children directed their steps, green buds burst forth on the bushes and trees; the grass was shooting up; the cornfields became day by day greener and more lovely to look at. The little girl strewed flowers all around—there were no end of them in her frock, which she held up; however jealously she strewed them, they seemed to grow there. In her great zeal she poured forth a snow of blossoms over apple and pear trees, so that they stood there in all their splendor, before the green leaves had time to grow forth.

And she clapped her hands, and the boy followed her example; flocks of birds came flying, nobody knew where they came from, and chirped and sang: "Spring has come!"

That was wonderful to see. Many an old woman came out of her doorway into the sunshine, and basked in it, looking at the yellow flowers, blooming everywhere in the fields, and thinking that it was just like that in her young days; the world grew young again to her. "It is a blessing to be out here to-day," she said.

The wood still wore its dark green garments, made of buds, but the thyme had already come out, filling the air with sweet fragrance, and there were plenty of violets, anemones and primroses: every blade of grass was full of sap and strength. Truly that was a marvelous carpet, on which one could not help wishing to rest. There the two Spring children sat down hand in hand, singing and smiling, and continually growing. A mild rain fell down from Heaven; they did not notice it, the rain-drops mingled with their own tears of joy.

The two lovers kissed each other, and in a moment the green of the wood became alive. When the sun rose again all the woods were green.

Hand in hand the betrothed wandered under the fresh hanging roof of leaves, wherever the sunbeams and shadows produced a change of color in the green.

What delicate tints, what a sweet fragrance the new leaves had! The clear stream and brooks rippled merrily between the velvet-like rushes and over the colored pebbles. "So it was for ever and shall ever remain so," said all Nature. The cuckoo sang, the lark flew up—it was a beautiful Spring; but the willow trees wore woollen mittens over their blossoms; they were exceedingly careful, and that is tiresome.

Days and weeks passed by, and the heat came, as it were, rolling down; hot waves of air passed through the corn and made it yellower from day to day. The white water-lily of the north spread its large green leaves over the surface of the streams and lakes, and the fishes sought shade beneath them. In a spot where the trees of the wood sheltered it stood a farmer's cottage; the sun shined on its walls and warmed the unfolded roses, and the black juicy berries with which the cherry-trees were loaded. There sat the lovely wife of Summer, the same that we have seen as child and bride; her glances were fixed on the rising dark clouds, which, like mountains, in wave-like outlines, dark blue and heavy, were rising higher and higher. From three sides they came, continually growing, and seemed very much like a petrified reversed ocean gradually settling down on the forest, where everything, as if by magic, had become quiet. Not a breath of air was stirring; every bird was silent, there was an earnest expectation in the whole of Nature, but on the paths and roadways people in carriages, on horseback, and on foot, hastened to reach a shelter.

Suddenly there came a flash of light, as if the sun broke through the clouds again, flaming, dazzling, all-devouring; and then again it became dark, and the thunder rolled. Rain came pouring down in torrents; darkness and light, absolute silence and terrible noise, followed each other in quick succession. The wind moved the long, feather-like reeds on the moor like the waves of the sea; the branches of the trees were concealed in watery mist. Grass and corn lay beaten down and swamped, looking as if they could never rise again. Then the rain gradually ceased, the sun burst forth, drops of water glittered on the stalks and leaves like pearls, the birds began to sing, the fishes darted out of the water, the gnats played in the sunshine and out on a stone in the foaming water stood Summer himself, the strong man, with vigorous limbs, and wet, dripping hair, refreshed by the bath, basking in the sunshine.

All Nature seemed born anew, and stood forth in rich, strong, beautiful splendor; it was Summer, warm, sweet Summer.

Sweet and agreeable was the fragrance streaming forth from the rich clover field; the bees were humming yonder round the ruins of the old meeting-place; a bramble-bush wound itself round the stone altar, which, washed by the rain, was glittering in the sunshine, thither flew the queen with the whole swarm to prepare wax and honey. Only Summer saw it, and his vigorous spouse; for them the altar-table was covered with Nature's offerings.

The evening sky looked like gold; no church dome was ever so bright, and the moon was shining between the evening red and the dawn. It was Summer!

And days and weeks passed oy. The shining scythes of the reapers glittered in the cornfields, the branches of the apple-trees were bending under the weight of the red and yellow fruit; the hops smelled sweetly and hung in large clusters, and under the hazel bushes, where the nuts grew in big bunches, sat Summer, with his serious wife.

"What a wealth!" she said; "blessings are spread everywhere. Wherever one turns it is pleasant to abide; and yet—I do not know why—I am longing for peace, rest; I cannot express what I feel. They are already plowing again. Men are insatiable; they always wish to gain more and more. See, the storks come in flocks and follow at a little distance behind the plows; it is the bird of Egypt which carried us through the air. Do you still remember when we two came hither to this northern land? We brought with us flowers, lovely sunshine, and green woods. The wind has dealt very roughly with them; they are becoming brown and dark like the trees of the south, but they do not carry golden fruit like those."

"You would like to see the golden fruit?" asked Summer. "Look up, then." He lifted his arm, and the leaves of the trees became red and golden. A splendor of color was spread over all the woods; the dog-rose hedge glittered with scarlet hips, the elder-trees were full of large bunches of dark-brown berries, the horse-chestnuts fell down out of their dark-green husks, and on the ground below violets were blooming for the second time.

But the queen of the year grew quieter and paler. "It is blowing very cold," she said; "the night brings damp mists. I am longing for the country where I passed my childhood."

And she saw the storks fly away. Not a single one remained; and she stretched out her hands after them, as if she wished to retain them. She looked up at the empty nests—in one a long-stalked cornflower, in another the yellow rape-seed were thriving, as if the nest was only intended to protect them and serve as a fence for them; and the sparrows flew up into the storks' nest.

"Twit! What has become of the master and his wife? They cannot bear it if the wind blows a little, and therefore they have left the country. I wish them a happy journey."

The leaves in the wood became more yellow day by day, and fell down one after another. The violent autumn winds were blowing; the year was far advanced, and on a couch of dry leaves rested the queen of the year, and looked with mild eyes at the sparkling stars, while her husband stood by her side. A gust of wind made the leaves rustle; a great many of them fell down, and suddenly she was gone; but a butterfly—the last of the year—flew through the cold air.

Damp fogs came, icy winds were blowing, and the dark long nights set in. The ruler of the year stood there, with white locks, but he was not aware of it; he thought snowflakes were falling from the clouds.

A thin layer of snow was spread over the green fields, and the church bells were pealing forth the Christmas chimes.

"The bells are telling of Christ's birth," said the ruler of the year. "Soon the new rulers will be born, and I shall go to rest, like my wife: to rest in the shining star."

And out in the green pinewood the Christmas angel consecrated the young trees which he selected to serve at his festival.

"May there be joy in the homes under the green branches," said the old ruler of the year: in a few weeks his hair had become as white as snow. "The time for my rest draws near, and the young couple of the year will receive my crown and scepter."

"You are still in power," said the Christmas angel; "you must not yet go to rest. Let the snow still cover and warm the young seed. Learn to bear the thought that honor is done to another while you are still the ruler. Learn to be forgotten and yet to live. The hour of your deliverance approaches with Spring." "When is Spring coming?" said Winter. "He will come when the stork returns."

And Winter, ice-cold and broken down, with white locks and still whiter beard, was sitting on the top of the hill, where his predecessor had sat, and looked towards the south. The ice cracked, the snow creaked, the skaters enjoyed themselves on the smooth surface of the lake and the black of the ravens and crows stood in strong contrast to the white ground. Not a breath of air was stirring. Old Winter clenched his fists in the cold air, and the ice on the rivers and lakes was several feet thick.

Then the sparrows came out of town again and asked: "Who is the old man yonder?" And the raven was there again, or perhaps his son, which comes to the same thing, and replied to them: "It is Winter, the old man from last year. He is not dead, as the calendar says, but is the guardian of Spring, who is approaching."

"When will Spring come?" asked the sparrows; "then we shall have a better time and milder *regime;* the old one was good for nothing."

And Winter nodded pensively towards the dark leafless woods, where every tree showed the graceful outline of its branches, and during the long winter night icy fogs descended—the ruler dreamed of his young days, of his manhood, and at daybreak the whole forest was glittering with hoar-frost; that was Winter's summer dream, but the sunshine soon made the frost melt and drop down from the branches.

"When will Spring come?" asked the sparrows.

"Spring!" echoed the snow-covered hills: the sun shined more warmly, the snow melted, the birds chirped, "Spring is coming."

And the first stork came flying through the air, a second soon followed: each had a lovely child on his back. They descended in an open field, kissed the ground and kissed the silent old man; and as Moses disappeared on the mount, so he disappeared, carried away by the clouds.

The story of the year was ended.

"This is all very fine," said the sparrows; "it is beautiful too; but it is not according to the calendar, and therefore it must be wrong."

"There Is No Doubt About It"

What was a terrible affair!" said a hen, and in a quarter of the town, too, where it had not taken place. "That was a terrible affair in a hen-roost. I cannot sleep alone to-night. It is a good thing that many of us sit on the roost together." And then she told a story that made the feathers on the other hens bristle up, and the cock's comb fall. There was no doubt about it.

But we will begin at the beginning, and that is to be found in a hen-roost in another part of the town. The sun was setting, and the fowls were flying on to their roost; one hen, with white feathers and short legs, used to lay her eggs according to the regulations, and was, as a hen, respectable in every way. As she was flying upon the roost, she plucked herself with her beak, and a little feather came out.

"There it goes," she said; "the more I pluck, the more beautiful do I get." She said this merrily, for she was the best of the hens, and, moreover, as has been said, very respectable. With that she went to sleep.

It was dark all around, and hen sat close to hen, but the one who sat nearest to her merry neighbor did not sleep. She had heard and yet not heard, as we are often obliged to do in this world, in order to live at peace; but she could not keep it from her neighbor on the other side any longer. "Did you hear what was said? I mention no names, but there is a hen here who intends to pluck herself in order to look well. If I were a cock, I should despise her."

Just over the fowls sat the owl, with father owl and the little owls. The family has sharp ears, and they all heard every word that their neighbor hen had said. They rolled their eyes, and mother owl, beating her wings, said: "Don't listen to her! But I suppose you heard what was said? I heard it with my own ears, and one has to hear a great deal before they fall off. There is one among the fowls who has so far forgotten what is becoming to a hen that she plucks out all her feathers and lets the cock see it."

"*Prenez garde aux enfants!*" said father owl; "children should not hear such things."

"But I must tell our neighbor owl about it; she is such an estimable owl to talk to." And with that she flew away.

"Too-whoo! Too-whoo!" they both hooted into the neighbor's dove-cot to the doves inside. "Have you heard? Have you heard? Too-whoo! There is a hen who has plucked out all her feathers for the sake of the cock; she will freeze to death, if she is not frozen already. Too-whoo!"

"Where? where?" cooed the doves.

"In the neighbor's yard. I have as good as seen it myself. It is almost unbecoming to tell the story, but there is no doubt about it."

"Believe every word of what we tell you," said the doves, and cooed down into their poultry-yard. "There is a hen—nay, some say that there are two—who have plucked out all their feathers, in order not to look like the others, and to attract the attention of the cock. It is a dangerous game, for one can easily catch cold and die from fever, and both of these are dead already."

"Wake up! wake up!" crowed the cock, and flew upon his board. Sleep was still in his eyes, but yet he crowed out: "Three hens have died of their unfortunate love for a cock. They had plucked out all their feathers. It is a horrible story; I will not keep it to myself, but let it go farther."

"Let it go farther," shrieked the bats, and the hens clucked and the cocks crowed, "Let it go farther! Let it go farther!" In this way the story traveled from poultry-yard to poultry-yard, and at last came back to the place from which it had really started.

"Five hens," it now ran, "have plucked out all their feathers to show which of them had grown leanest for love of the cock, and then they all pecked at each other till the blood ran down and they fell down dead, to the derision and shame of their family, and to the great loss of their owner."

The hen who had lost the loose little feather naturally did not recognize her own story, and being a respectable hen, said: "I despise those fowls; but there are more of that kind. Such things ought not to be concealed, and I will do my best to get the story into the papers, so that it becomes known throughout the land; the hens have richly deserved it, and their family too."

It got into the papers, it was printed; and there is no doubt about it, one little feather may easily grow into five hens.

Ole Luk-Oie

There is no one in the world who knows so many stories as Ole Luk-Oie. He can tell them beautifully!

Towards evening time when children are still sitting nicely at table or on their stools, Ole Luk-Oie comes. He creeps up the stairs very quietly, for he always walks in his socks; he opens the doors gently, and whish! he squirts sweet milk into the children's eyes in tiny drops, but still quite enough to prevent them from keeping their eyes open and therefore from seeing him. He steals behind them, and blows softly on their necks, and this makes their heads heavy. Of course it does not hurt them, for Ole Luk-Oie is the children's friend; he only wants them to be quiet, and that they are not until they have been put to bed. He wants them to be quiet only to tell them stories. When the children are at last asleep, Ole Luk-Oie sits down upon their bed. He has fine clothes on; his coat is of silk, but it is impossible to say of what color, for it shines green, red and blue, according as he turns. Under each arm he carries an umbrella; the one with pictures on it he opens over good children, and then they dream the most beautiful stories all night; but the other, on which there is nothing at all, he opens over naughty children, and then they sleep as though they were deaf, so that when they awake in the morning they have not dreamed of the least thing.

Now we shall hear how during one week Ole Luk-Oie came to a little boy named Hjalmar every evening, and what he told him. There are seven stories: for there are seven days in the week.

Monday

"Look here," said Ole Luk-Oie in the evening, when he had put Hjalmar to bed; "I'll just make things look nice."

And all the flowers in the flower-pots grew into large trees, stretching out their long branches across the ceiling and along the walls, so that the room looked like a beautiful arbor; and all the branches were full of flowers, every flower being finer than a rose, and smelling sweetly. If one wanted to eat them, they were sweeter than jam. The fruits shined like gold, and there were cakes simply bursting with currants. Nothing like it had ever been seen before. But at the same time terrible cries were heard coming from the table-drawer in which Hjalmar's schoolbooks lay.

"Whatever is the matter?" said Ole Luk-Oie, going to the table and opening the drawer. It was the slate, upon which a terrible riot was going on amongst the figures, because a wrong one had got into the sum, so that it was nearly falling to pieces; the pencil hopped and skipped at the end of its string, as if it were a little dog who would have liked to help the sum, but it could not. And from Hjalmar's copy-book there also came the sounds of woe, terrible to hear. On every page there stood at the beginning of each line a capital letter, with a small one next to it; that was for a copy. Now next to these stood some other letters which Hjalmar had written, and these thought they looked just like the two first. But they lay there as if they had fallen over the pencil-lines upon which they ought to have stood.

"Look, this is the way you ought to hold yourselves up," said the copy. "Look, slanting like this, with a powerful up-stroke."

"Oh, we should like to," said Hjalmar's letters; "but we can't, we are too weak."

"Then you must take some medicine," said Ole Luk-Oie.

"Oh, no," they cried, and stood up so gracefully that it was a pleasure to see them.

"Well, we cannot tell any stories now!" said Ole Luk-Oie; I must drill them. One, two! one, two!" And in this way he drilled the letters. They stood up quite gracefully, and looked as nice as only a copy can do. But when Ole Luk-Oie had gone and Hjalmar looked at them in the morning, they were just as weak and miserable as before.

Tuesday

As soon as Hjalmar had gone to bed, Ole Luk-Oie touched all the furniture in the room with his little magic squirt, whereupon it immediately began to talk.

Every piece spoke about itself, with the exception of the spittoon, which stood quietly there and got very angry at their being so vain as to talk only about themselves, to think only about themselves, and to take no notice whatever of it, which stood modestly in the corner and allowed itself to be spat upon.

Over the wardrobe hung a large picture in a gilt frame; it was a landscape. There might be seen large old trees, flowers in the grass, and a wide river flowing round the wood, past many castles, and far out into the stormy sea.

Ole Luk-Oie touched the picture with his magic squirt, and the birds immediately began to sing, the branches of the trees to move, and the clouds to sail past; their shadows could be seen gliding along over the landscape.

Then Ole Luk-Oie lifted Hjalmar up to the frame and put his little feet into the picture, right among the high grass; there he stood. The sun shined down upon him through the branches of the trees. He ran to the water and got into a small boat which was lying there; it was painted red and white, the sails glittering like silver; and six swans, wearing golden crowns round their necks and brilliant blue stars on their heads, drew the boat along, past the green wood where the trees tell of robbers and witches, and where the flowers speak of the dainty little elves and of what the butterflies have told them.

Most lovely fishes, with scales like silver and gold, swam after the boat; now and then they took a jump, making the water splash. Birds, blue and red, small and large, also followed, flying in two long rows.

The gnats danced and the cockchafers said: "Boom, boom!" They all wanted to follow Hjalmar, and each had a story to tell.

What a pleasant voyage it was! At times the woods were thick and dark, at times full of sunlight and flowers like the most beautiful garden. There were great castles built of glass and of marble, and on the balconies stood princesses, who were all little girls whom Hjalmar knew very well, and with whom he had formerly played. Every one of them stretched out her hands, offering him the prettiest sugar-heart that you could find in a sweetstuff shop. Hjalmar caught hold of one side of the sugar-heart as he sailed by, and the princess also holding on tightly, each got a piece of it; she the smallest, Hjalmar the biggest. At every castle little princes were keeping guard, shouldering their golden swords and showering down raisins and tin-soldiers; it was easy to see that they were real princes.

Sometimes Hjalmar sailed through forests, sometimes through great halls or through the middle of a town; he also came to the town in which lived the nurse who had carried him when he was still a little boy and who had always been so good to him. She nodded and beckoned to him, and sang the pretty little verse which she had herself composed and sent to Hjalmar:

"I think of thee full many a time.
My own dear darling boy;
To kiss thy mouth, thine eyes, thy brow,
Was once my only joy.

"I heard thee lisp thy first sweet words,
Yet from thee I was torn;

May Heaven be e'er that angel's shield
Whom in my arms I've borne."

And all the birds sang too, the flowers danced on their stalks, and the old trees nodded as if Ole Luk-Oie were also telling them stories.

Wednesday

How the rain was pouring down outside! Hjalmar could hear it in his sleep, and when Ole Luk-Oie opened one of the windows the water came up to the window-sill. It formed quite a lake, and a most splendid ship lay close to the house.

"If you would like to sail with us, little Hjalmar," said Ole Luk-Oie, "you can reach foreign countries to-night, and get back here by the morning."

Then Hjalmar suddenly found himself dressed in his Sunday clothes in the middle of the beautiful ship; the weather at once became fine, and they sailed through the streets, cruised round the church, and were soon sailing on a great stormy sea. They sailed until they lost sight of land, and could see only a flight of storks which were coming from Hjalmar's home and going to warm climates. They were flying in a line one after another, and had already come very far. One of them was so tired that his wings could scarcely carry him any longer; he was the last in the line, and was soon left a long way behind, finally sinking lower and lower with outspread wings. He flapped them once or twice more, but it was of no use; first he touched the rigging of the vessel with his feet, then he slid down from the sail, and at last he stood on the deck.

The cabin-boy took him and put him into the fowl-coop with the hens, ducks, and turkeys; there stood the poor stork, a prisoner among them.

"Look at the fellow," said all the fowls, and the turkey-cock puffed himself out as much as he could, and asked him who he was; the ducks waddled backwards and jostled each other, quacking: "What a fool! What a fool!" And the stork told them about the heat of Africa, about the pyramids, and about the ostrich who runs across the desert like a wild horse; but the ducks did not understand him, and nudged each other, saying: "I suppose we all agree that he is very stupid."

"Of course he is very stupid," said the turkey; and then he gobbled. So the stork was silent and thought of his Africa.

"What beautifully thin legs you have," said the turkey-cock. "What do they cost a yard?"

"Quack, quack, quack!" grinned all the ducks; but the stork pretended not to have heard it.

"You might laugh anyhow," said the turkey-cock to him; "for it was very wittily said. But perhaps it was too deep for you. Ha, ha! he is not very clever. We will keep to our interesting selves." And then he gobbled, and the ducks quacked. It was irritating to hear how they amused themselves.

But Hjalmar went to the fowl-coop, opened the door and called the stork, who hopped out to him on the deck. He had now had a good rest, and he seemed to nod at Hjalmar, as if to thank him. He then spread his wings and flew to the warm countries; but the hens cackled, the ducks quacked, and the turkey-cock turned red as fire in his face.

"To-morrow we shall make soup of you," said Hjalmar; and with that he awoke and found himself between his linen sheets. But it was a strange journey upon which Ole Luk-Oie had taken him that night.

Thursday

"Do you know what?" said Ole Luk-Oie; "only don't be frightened, and you will see a little mouse here." And he held out his hand with the pretty little animal in it. "She is come to invite you to a wedding. There are two little mice, who are going to enter the state of matrimony to-night. They live under the floor of your mother's pantry, which must be a fine place to dwell in."

"But how can I get through the little mouse-hole in the floor?" asked Hjalmar.

"Let me look after that," said Ole Luk-Oie. "I will soon make you small." And then he touched Hjalmar with his little magic squirt, making him immediately smaller and smaller, until at last he was only as big as a finger. "Now you can borrow the clothes of the tin soldier; I think they will fit you, and it looks well to wear a uniform when you are in company."

"So it does," said Hjalmar, and in a moment he was dressed like the prettiest little tin soldier.

"Will you be good enough to sit in your mother's thimble?" said the little mouse; "then I shall have the honor of drawing you along."

"Dear me! will you take so much trouble yourself?" said Hjalmar; and in that fashion they drove to the mouse's wedding.

At first they came to a long passage under the floor, just high enough to enable them to drive along with the thimble, and the whole passage was illuminated with lighted tinder.

" Doesn't it smell delightful here?" asked the mouse, who was drawing him along. "The passage is smeared with bacon-rind. There can be nothing nicer!"

They now came into the hall where the wedding was to take place. On the right-hand side stood all the little lady-mice whispering and squeaking as though they were having rare fun; on the left stood all the gentlemen-mice stroking their whiskers with their paws. In the middle of the hall could be seen the bride and bridegroom standing in the hollowed-out rind of a cheese; they were kissing each other in a shameless manner before the eyes of all, for they were already betrothed and on the point of being married.

More strangers were continually arriving; the mice were almost treading each other to death, and the bridal pair had placed themselves right in the doorway, so that it was impossible to go in and out. The whole room, like the passage, had been besmeared with bacon-rind, and that was all the refreshments; for dessert, however, a pea was shown, in which a mouse of the family had bitten the name of the bridal pair—that is to say, of course only the initials. But what a novel idea it was!

All the mice agreed that it had been a splendid wedding, and that the conversation had been most agreeable.

Then Hjalmar drove home again. He had certainly been in distinguished society, but he had also had to huddle himself up a good deal, to make himself small, and to wear the uniform of a tin soldier.

Friday

"You would hardly believe how many grown-up people there are who would only be too pleased to have me," said Ole Luk-Oie. "Particularly those who have done something bad. 'Dear little Ole,' they say to me, 'we cannot close our eyes, and so we lie awake the whole night and see all our wicked deeds sitting like ugly little goblins on the bedstead, and squirting hot water over us; we wish you would come and drive them away, so that we could get a good sleep.' Then they sigh deeply. 'Indeed we would willingly pay for it; good-night, Ole, the money is on the window-sill.'"

"But I don't do it for money," said Ole Luk-Oie.

"What are we going to do to-night?" asked Hjalmar.

"Well, I don't know whether you would like to go to another wedding to-night; it is of quite a different kind to last night's. Your sister's big doll—the one that looks like a man and is called Hermann—is going to marry the doll Bertha. Besides this it is the bride's birthday, and therefore they will receive a great many presents."

"Yes, I know that," said Hjalmar. "Whenever the dolls want new clothes, my sister says it is a birthday or a wedding; that has happened quite a hundred times already."

"Yes, but to-night is the hundred and first wedding, and when that number is reached, everything is over. That is why this one will be quite unlike any other. Only just look!"

And Hjalmar looked upon the table. There stood the little doll's house with lights in the windows, and all the tin soldiers presenting arms in front of it. The bride and bridegroom were sitting on the floor and leaning against the leg of the table; they seemed very thoughtful, and for this they had perhaps good cause.

Ole Luk-Oie, dressed in grandmother's black gown, married them. When the ceremony was over, all the furniture in the room began to sing the following beautiful song, written by the lead-pencil to the air of the soldiers' tattoo:

"We'll troll the song out like the wind.
Long live the bridal pair!
They're both so dumb, so stiff and blind.
Of leather made, they'll wear.
Hurrah, hurrah, though deaf and blind
We'll sing it out in rain and wind."

And now came the presents; they had, however, declined to accept any eatables, love being enough for them to live on.

"Shall we take a country-house, or would you rather travel?" asked the bridegroom. To settle this, the swallow, who had traveled a great deal, and the old hen, who had hatched five broods of chicks, were asked for their advice.

The swallow spoke of the beautiful warm countries, where the grapes grow large and full, where the air is so mild and the mountains have such colors as are never seen on them in our country.

"But still they have not our broccoli," said the hen. "I was once in the country for a whole summer with all my chicks; there was a sand-pit, into which we might go, and scrape up, and then we were admitted to a garden full of broccoli. Oh, it was grand! I cannot imagine anything nicer."

"But one head of cabbage is just like another," said the swallow; "and then we very often have bad weather here."

"Well, one gets used to that," said the hen.

"But it is cold here, and it freezes."

"That is good for cabbages," said the hen. "Besides, it can be warm here too. Didn't we have a summer, four years ago, that, lasted five weeks? It was almost too warm to breathe. And then we have not poisonous animals, as they have there; and we are free from robbers. He must be a wicked man who does not think that our country is most beautiful. He really does not deserve to be here."

And then the hen wept and added: "I have traveled too. I rode for more than twelve miles in a coop. Traveling is by no means a pleasure."

"The hen is a sensible woman," said the doll Bertha. "I don't in the least care for mountain traveling myself, for you only go up and down again. No, we will go into the gravel-pit outside the gate and take a walk in the cabbage-garden."

And so they did.

Saturday

"Shall I hear any stories to-night?" asked little Hjalmar, as soon as Ole Luk-Oie had sent him to sleep.

"We have no time for any this evening," said Ole Luk-Oie, opening his beautiful umbrella over him. "Just look at these China-men!"

The umbrella looked like a large Chinese bowl with blue trees and pointed bridges, and with little China-men nodding their heads.

"We must have the whole world cleaned up by to-morrow morning," said Ole Luk-Oie, "for it is a holiday, it is Sunday. I will go to the church-steeple and see whether the little church goblins are polishing the bells, so that they may sound sweetly; I will go out into the fields and see whether the wind is blowing the dust off the grass and the leaves; and what is the most necessary work of all, I must fetch down the stars to polish them. I take them in my apron; but first each one must be numbered, and the holes in which they are fixed must also be numbered, so that they may be put back in their right places. They would otherwise not hold fast and we should have too many falling stars, one tumbling down after another.

"Look here; do you know, Mr. Ole Luk-Oie," said an old portrait which hung on the wall in Hjalmar's bedroom, "I am Hjalmar's great-grandfather? I thank you for telling the boy tales; but you must not put wrong ideas into his head. The stars cannot be taken down. The stars are worlds, just like our earth, and that is the beauty of them."

"Thank you, old great-grandfather," said Ole Luk-Oie; "thank you. You are the head of the family; you are its founder; but I am still older than you. I am an old heathen; the Greeks and Romans called me the God of Dreams. I have visited the grandest houses, and still go there. I know how to deal both with the humble and the great. Now, you may tell your stories." And Ole Luk-Oie went away and took his umbrella with him.

"Well! One must not even give one's opinion any more," grumbled the old portrait.

And Hjalmar awoke.

Sunday

"Good evening," said Ole Luke-Oie. Hjalmar nodded and sprang up to turn his great-grandfather's portrait against the wall, so that it could not interrupt, as it had done yesterday.

"You must tell me some stories about the five green peas who lived in one pod; about the leg of the cock which went courting the leg of the hen; and about the darning-needle who was so grand that she fancied she was a sewing-needle.

"You can have too much of a good thing," said Ole Luk-Oie. "You know very well that I prefer showing you something. I will show you my brother. He is also called Ole Luk-Oie, but he never comes to any one more than once, but when he does come to them, he takes them with him on his horse and tells them stories. He only knows two; one is so extremely beautiful that no one in the world can imagine anything like it; the other is most awful and horrible—it cannot be described."

Then Ole Luk-Oie lifted little Hjalmar up to the window, saying: "Now you will see my brother, the other Ole Luk-Oie. They call him Death. Do you see, he does not look so bad as in the picture books, where they make him out to be a skeleton. That splendid hussar uniform that he is wearing is embroidered with silver; a black velvet mantle floats behind him over the horse. See at what a gallop he rides."

And Hjalmar saw how this Ole Luk-Oie rode away, taking both young and old upon his horse. Some he placed before him and others behind, but he always asked first:

"How is your report for good behavior?"

"Good," they all replied.

"Yes, but let me see it myself," said he; and then each one had to show him his book of reports. All those who had "Very good" and "Excellent" were placed in front upon the horse and heard the delightful story; but those who had "Pretty good" and "Middling" had to get up behind and listen to the horrible tale; they trembled and wept, and wanted to jump down from the horse, but could not do so, because they had immediately grown fast to it.

"But Death is most beautiful Ole Luk-Oie," said Hjalmar. "I am not afraid of him."

"Neither should you be," said Ole Luk-Oie; "only take care that you get good reports."

"Well, that's instructive," muttered the great-grandfather's portrait. "It is of some use to give one's opinion occasionally."

Now he felt satisfied.

And that is the story of Ole Luk-Oie; perhaps he will tell you some more to-night himself.

Soup from a Sausage-Peg

"That was an excellent dinner yesterday," said an old mouse of the female sex to another who had not been present at the festive meal. "I sat number twenty-one from the old mouse-king; that was not such a bad place! Would you like to hear the *menu?* The courses were very well arranged: moldy bread, bacon-rind, tallow candles, and sausage—and then the same things over again. It was just as good as having two banquets. Everything went on as jovially and as good-humoredly as at a family gathering. There was absolutely nothing left but the sausage-pegs; the conversation turned upon these, and at last the expression 'soup from sausage skins,' or, as the proverb runs in the neighboring country, 'soup from a sausage-peg,' was mentioned. Now every one had heard of this, but no one had tasted such soup, much less prepared it. A very pretty toast to the inventor was drunk; it was said that he deserved to be made an overseer of the poor. That was very witty, wasn't it? And the old mouse-king rose and promised that the young female mouse who could prepare the said soup in the most tasty way should be his queen; he gave her a year and a day for the trial."

"That wasn't bad!" said the other mouse; "but how is the soup prepared?"

"Ah! how is it prepared?" That was just what all the other female mice, both young and old, were asking. They would all have liked to be queen, but they did not want to take the trouble to go out into the wide world to learn how to prepare the soup, and yet that was what would have to be done. But every one is not ready to leave home and family; and out in the world cheese-rinds are not to be had for the asking, nor is bacon to be smelled every day. No, one must suffer hunger, perhaps even be eaten up alive by a cat.

Such were probably the considerations by which the majority allowed themselves to be deterred from going out into the world in search of information. Only four mice gave in their names as being ready to start. They were young and active, but poor; each of them intended to proceed to one of the four quarters of the globe, and it would then be seen to which of them fortune was favorable. Each of the four took a sausage-peg with her, so that she might be mindful of her object in traveling; the sausage-peg was to be her pilgrim's staff.

They set out at the beginning of May, and not till the May of the following year did they return, and then only three of them; the fourth did not report herself, nor did she send any word or sign, notwithstanding that the day of trial had arrived.

"Yes, every pleasure has its drawback," said the mouse-king; then he gave orders that all the mice for many miles round should be invited. They were to assemble in the kitchen, and the three traveled mice should stand in a row alone; a sausage-peg, hung with black crepe, was erected in memory of the fourth, who was missing. No one was to give his opinion before the mouse-king had said what was to be said.

Now, we shall hear!

What the First Little Mouse Had Seen and Learned on Her Travels

"When I went out into the wide world," said the little mouse, "I thought, as a great many do at my age, that I already knew all there was to be known. But that was not so; years must pass before one gets as far as that. I went straight to the sea. I went in a ship that sailed to the north. I had been told that a ship's cook must know how to make the best of things at sea, but it is easy to make the best of things if one has plenty of sides of bacon and great tubs of salt pork and moldy flour; one has delicate living there, but one does not learn how to make soup from a sausage-peg. We sailed on for many days and nights; the ship rocked fearfully, and we did not get off without a wetting either. When we at last reached our destination I left the vessel; it was up in the far north.

"It is a strange thing to leave one's own corner at home, to sail in a ship which is only a kind of corner too, and then to suddenly find oneself more than a hundred miles away in a strange land. I saw great trackless forests of pines and birches, that smelled so strong that I sneezed and thought of sausages. There were great lakes there too. The waters when looked at quite close were clear, but from a distance they appeared black as ink. White swans lay upon them; they lay so still I thought they were foam, but when I saw them fly and walk I recognized them. They belong to the same race as the geese; one can easily see that by their walk—no one can deny his descent. I kept to my own kind. I associated with the forest and field mice, who by the way know very little, especially as regards cooking, and yet that was just what I had gone abroad for. The idea that soup might be made from a sausage-peg seemed to them so extraordinary that it at once spread from mouth to mouth through the whole wood. That the problem could ever be solved they thought an impossibility, and least of all did I think that there, and the very first night too, should I be initiated into the manner of preparing it. It was the height of summer, and that, said the mice, was why the forest smelled so strongly, why the herbs were so fragrant, the lakes so clear and yet so dark, with the swans floating upon them.

"On the edge of the wood, surrounded by three or four houses, a pole as high as the mainmast of a ship had been set up, and from the top of it hung wreaths and fluttering ribbons—it was a maypole. Lads and lasses danced around the tree, and sang as loudly as they could to the music of the fiddler. All went merrily in the sunset and by moonlight, but I took no part in it—what has a little mouse to do with a May-dance? I sat in the soft moss and held my sausage-peg fast. The moon threw its rays just upon a spot where stood a tree covered with such exceedingly fine moss that I may almost say it was as fine and soft as the mouse-king's fur; but it was green, and that is good for the eyes.

"All at once the most charming little people came marching out. They did not reach higher than my knee, and though they looked like human beings they were better proportioned. They called themselves elves, and wore fine clothes of flower-leaves trimmed with the wings of flies and gnats, which did not look at all bad. Directly they appeared they seemed to be looking for something—I did not know what; but at last some of them came up to me, the chief among them pointing to my sausage-peg, and saying: 'That is just the kind of one we want! It is pointed—it is excellent!' And the more he looked at my pilgrim's staff the more delighted he became.

" 'To lend,' I said, 'but not to keep.'

" 'Not to keep!' they all cried; then they seized the sausage-peg, which I let go, and danced off with it to the spot with the fine moss, where they set it up in the midst of the green. They wanted to have a maypole too, and that which they now had seemed cut out for them. Then it was decorated; what a sight that was!

"Little spiders spun golden threads round it, and hung it with fluttering veils and flags, so finely woven and bleached so snowy white in the moonshine that it dazzled my eyes. They took the colors from the butterflies' wings and strewed these over the white linen, and flowers and diamonds gleamed upon it so that I did not know my sausage-peg again; there was certainly not another maypole in the whole world like that which had been made out of it. And now only came the real great party of elves. They wore no clothes at all—it could not have been more genteel. I was invited to witness the festivities, but only at a certain distance, for I was too big for them.

"Then began a wonderful music! It seemed as if thousands of glass bells were ringing, so full, so rich that I thought it was the singing of the swans;

I even thought I heard the voice of the cuckoo and the blackbird, and at last the whole wood seemed to join in. There were children's voices, the sound of bells, and the song of birds; the most glorious melodies and all that was lovely came out of the elves' maypole—it was a whole peal of bells, and yet it was my sausage-peg. That so much could have been got out of it I should never have believed, but it no doubt depends upon what hands it gets into. I was deeply moved; I wept, as a little mouse can weep, for pure joy.

"The night was far too short, but up yonder they are not any longer about that time of year. In the morning dawn the light breezes sprang up, the surface of the woodland lake became ruffled, and all the dainty floating veils and flags floated in the air. The wavy garlands of spiders' web, the hanging bridges and balustrades, or whatever they are called, vanished as if they were nothing; six elves carried my sausage-peg back to me, asking me at the same time whether I had any wish that they could fulfill. So I begged them to tell me how to make soup from a sausage-peg.

" 'How we do it?' asked the chief of the elves, smiling. 'Why, you have just seen it. You hardly knew your own sausage-peg again.'

" 'They only mean that for a joke,' I thought, and I told them straight away the object of my journey and what hopes were entertained at home respecting this brew. 'What advantage,' I asked, 'can accrue to the mouse-king and to the whole of our mighty kingdom by my having witnessed this splendor? I can't shake it out of the sausage-peg and say: "Look, here is the sausage-peg; now comes the soup!" That would be a kind of dish that could only be served up when people had had enough.'

"Then the elf dipped his little finger in the cup of a blue violet and said to me: 'Pay attention! Here I anoint your pilgrim's staff, and when you return home and enter the mouse-king's castle, touch the warm breast of your king with it, and violets will spring forth and cover the whole of the staff, even in the coldest winter time. And with that I think I have given you something to take home with you, and even a little more!' "

But before the little mouse said what this "a little more" was, she touched the king's breast with her staff, and in truth the most beautiful bunch of violets burst forth. They smelled so strongly that the mouse-king immediately ordered the mice who stood nearest the chimney to put their tails into the fire to make a smell of burning, for the scent of the violets was not to be borne, and was not of the kind they liked.

"But what was the 'more' of which you spoke?" asked the mouse-king.

"Well," said the little mouse, "that is, I think, what is called 'effect.' " And thereupon she turned the sausage-peg round, and behold, there was no longer a single flower to be seen upon it: she held only the naked peg, and this she lifted like a conductor's baton.

"'Violets,' the elf told me, 'are to look at, to smell, and to touch. Hearing and taste, therefore, still remain to be considered.' Then the little mouse beat time, and music was heard—not such as rang through the forest at the elves' party, but such as is to be heard in the kitchen. What a sound of cooking and roasting there was! It came suddenly, as if the wind were rushing through all the victuals, and as if the pots and kettles were boiling over. The fire-shovel hammered upon the brass kettle, and then—suddenly all was quiet again. The low subdued singing of the tea-kettle was heard, and it was wonderful to listen to: they could not quite tell whether the kettle was beginning to boil or leaving off. The little pot bubbled up and the big pot bubbled up; the one did not care for the other, and it seemed as if there were no rhyme or reason in the pots. Then the little mouse waved her baton more and more wildly—the pots foamed, threw up large bubbles, boiled over; the wind roared and whistled through the chimney—ugh! it became so terrible that the little mouse even lost her stick."

"That was a heavy soup!" said the mouse-king.

"Isn't the dish coming soon?"

"That is all," answered the little mouse, with a bow.

"All! Well, then let us hear what the next has to say!" said the king.

What the Second Little Mouse Had to Tell

"I was born in the castle library," said the second mouse. "I and several members of our family have never had the good fortune to get into the dining-room, let alone the larder; it was only on my travels and here to-day that I saw a kitchen. Indeed we often had to suffer hunger in the library, but we acquired much knowledge. The rumor of the royal prize offered to those who could make soup from a sausage-peg reached our ears, and then my old grandmother brought out a manuscript that she could not read herself, but which she had heard read out, and in which was written: 'If one is a poet, one can make soup from a sausage-peg.' She asked me whether I was a poet. I felt that I was innocent in that respect, and she said that then I must go out and manage to become one. I again asked what I was to do, for it was quite as difficult for me to find that out as to make the soup. But my grandmother had heard a good deal read out, and she said three things above all were necessary: 'Understanding, imagination, and feeling. If you can manage to attain these three, you are a poet, and then the matter of the sausage-peg will be an easy one for you.'

"I departed and marched towards the west, out into the wide world, to become a poet.

"Understanding is of the most importance in everything—that I knew; the other two qualities are held in much less esteem, and I therefore went in quest of understanding first. Yes, where does it dwell? 'Go to the ant and learn wisdom,' said a great king of the Jews; that I had learned in the library, so I did not stop till I came to the first great ant-hill, and there I lay upon the watch to become wise.

"The ants are a very respectable little people; they are understanding all over. Everything with them is like a well-worked sum in arithmetic that comes right. To work and to lay eggs, they say, means both to live and to provide for posterity, and so that is what they do. They divide themselves into clean and dirty ants; the ant-queen is number one, and her opinion the only correct one. She contains the wisdom of all the world, and it was important for me to know that. She spoke so much, and it was so clever, that it seemed to me like nonsense. She said that her ant-hill was the highest thing in the world, though close beside it stood a tree which was higher, much higher—that was not to be denied, and so nothing was said of it. One evening an ant had lost herself on the tree and had crawled up the trunk—not so far up as the crown, but still higher than any ant had reached till then; and when she turned round and came home again she told of something far higher that she had come across out in the world. But this all the ants thought an insult to the community, and the ant was therefore condemned to be muzzled and to be kept in solitary confinement for life. But shortly afterwards another ant came across the same tree and made the same journey and the same discovery. She spoke about it with deliberation, but unintelligibly, as they called it; and as she was, besides, a much-respected ant and one of the clean ones, she was believed; and when she died an egg shell was erected to her memory, for they had a great respect for the sciences. I saw," continued the little mouse, "that the ants always ran about with their eggs on their backs. One of them once dropped her egg, and though she took great pains to pick it up again, she did not succeed; just then two others came up who helped her with all their might, so that they nearly dropped their own eggs in doing so. But then they immediately stopped in their efforts, for one must think of one's self first—and the ant-queen declared that in this case both heart and understanding had been shown. 'These two qualities,' she said, 'give us ants a place in the first rank among all reasoning beings; we all possess understanding in a high degree, and I have the most of all.' And with that she raised herself on her hind legs, so that she could not fail to be recognized. I could not be mistaken: I swallowed her. 'Go to the ants to learn wisdom'—now I had the queen!

"I now went closer to the large tree I have already mentioned several times. It was an oak, with a tall trunk and a full wide-spreading crown, and was very old. I knew that here dwelt a living being, a woman called a Dryad, who is born with the tree and dies with it. I had heard of this in the library; now I beheld such a tree, and one of these oak maidens. She uttered a terrible cry when she saw me so close to her. Like all women, she was very much afraid of mice; but she had more cause to be so than others, for I could have gnawed the tree through, on which her life depended. I spoke to the maiden in a friendly cordial way, and inspired her with courage; she took me in her dainty hand, and when I had told her why I had gone out into the wide world, she promised me that very evening I should probably have one of the two treasures of which I was still in quest. She told me that Phantasy was her intimate friend, that he was as handsome as the God of Love, and that he rested many an hour under the leafy branches of the tree, which then rustled more strongly than ever over the two. He called her his Dryad, she said, and the tree his tree; the beautiful gnarled oak was just to his taste, the roots spread themselves deeply and firmly in the ground, and the trunk and the crown rose high up into the fresh air; they knew the driving snow, the keen winds, and the warm sunshine, as these should be known. 'Yes,' continued the Dryad, 'the birds up there in the crown sing and tell of foreign countries they have visited, and on the only dead bough the stork has built his nest—that is very ornamental, and one hears a little too about the land of the pyramids. All this pleases Phantasy, but it is not enough for him; so I myself have to tell him about the life in the woods, and have to go back to my childhood's days when I was young and the tree was frail, so frail that a stinging-nettle overshadowed it; and I have to tell everything till now that the tree has grown big and strong. Now sit you down under the green thyme yonder and pay attention; and when Phantasy comes I'll find some opportunity to pinch his wings and to pull out a little feather; take the feather—no better one has been given a poet for a pen—and it will suffice you!'

"And when Phantasy came, the feather was pulled out, and I seized it," said the little mouse. "I put it in water and held it there till it got soft. It was very hard to digest even then, but still I nibbled it up at last. It is very easy to gnaw one's self into being a poet, though there are many things that one has to swallow. Now I had two—understanding and imagination—and through these two I knew that the third was to be found in the library; for a great man has said and written that there are novels which exist purely and solely to relieve people of their superfluous tears, and are therefore a kind of sponge to suck up the feelings. I remembered a few of those books which had always looked particularly appetizing, and were well thumbed and greasy; they must have absorbed an infinite deal of emotion.

"I betook myself back to the library, and devoured, so to speak, a whole novel—that is, the soft or essential part of it; but the crust, the binding, I left. When I had digested it, and another one besides, I noticed what a stirring there was inside me, and I devoured a piece of a third novel. And now I was a poet. I said so to myself and told it to others too. I hnd headache and stomach-ache, and I don't know what aches I didn't have. Then I began to think what stories might be made to refer to a sausage-peg, and a great many pegs and sticks and staves and splinters came into my thoughts—the ant-queen had possessed an extraordinary understanding. I remembered the man who put a white stick into his mouth by which he could make both himself and the stick invisible. I thought of wooden hobby-horses, of stock rhymes, of breaking the staff over any one, and of goodness knows how many expressions of that kind concerning staves, sticks, and pegs. All my thoughts ran upon pegs, sticks, and staves, and if one is a poet—and that I am, for I have tortured myself till I have become one—one must be able to make poetry on these things too. I will therefore be able to serve you up a peg—that is, a story—every day in the week; yes, that is my soup!"

"Let us hear what the third one has to say!" ordered the mouse-king.

"Peep! peep!" was heard at the kitchen door, and a little mouse—it was the fourth of the mice who had competed for the prize, the one whom the others believed to be dead—shot in like an arrow. She threw the sausage-peg with the crepe right over. She had been running day and night, had traveled on the railway by goods train, having watched her opportunity, and yet she had arrived almost too late. She pressed forward, looking very crumpled; she had lost her sausage-peg, but not her voice, for she began to speak at once, as if they had been waiting only for her and wanted to hear her only—as if everything else in the world were of no consequence whatever. She spoke at once and went on till she had said all she had to say. She appeared so unexpectedly that no one had time to object to her speech while she was speaking. Let us hear what she said.

What the Fourth Mouse Had to Tell, Before the Third One Had Spoken

"I immediately betook myself to the largest town," she said; "the name has escaped me—I have a bad memory for names. From the railway station I was taken with some confiscated goods to the town-hall, and when I arrived there, I ran into the gaoler's dwelling. The gaoler was talking of his prisoners, especially of one who had uttered some hasty words. About these words other words had been spoken, and then again others, and these again had been written down and recorded.

" 'The whole thing is soup from a sausage-peg,' " said the gaoler; " 'but the soup may cost him his neck!' "

"Now this gave me some interest in the prisoner," said the little mouse, "so I seized an opportunity and slipped in to him; there is a mouse-hole behind every locked door! The prisoner looked very pale, and had a long beard and large sparkling eyes. The lamp flickered and smoked, and the walls were so used to that, that they grew no blacker for it. The prisoner was scratching pictures and verses in white upon black, but I did not read them. I believe he felt very dull, and I was a welcome guest. He lured me with bread-crumbs, with whistling, and with gentle words. He was very glad to see me: I gradually began to trust him, and we became friends. He shared his bread and water with me, gave me cheese and sausage, and I lived well; but I must say that after all it was principally the good company that kept me there. He let me run about in his hand, on his arm, and right up his sleeve; he let me creep about in his beard, and called me his little friend. I really began to like him—such things are mutual! I forgot what I had gone out into the wide world to seek, and left my sausage-peg in a crack in the floor; it lies there still. I wanted to stay where I was; if I went away, the poor prisoner would have no one at all, and that is too little in this world. I stayed, but he did not. He spoke to me very sadly the last time, gave me twice as much bread and cheese as usual, and threw me kisses; he went and never came back. I don't know his history. 'Soup from a sausage-peg!' the gaoler had said, and to him I now went. He certainly took me in his hand, but he put me into a cage, into a tread-mill. That's awful! One runs and runs and gets no farther, and is only laughed at.

"The gaoler's daughter was a most charming little girl with a head of curls like the finest gold, and such joyous eyes and such a smiling mouth! 'You poor little mouse,' she said; and peeping into my hateful cage she drew out the iron pin, and I sprang down upon the window-sill and so out upon the gutter of the roof. Free! free! I thought only of that, and not of the object of my travels.

"It was dark—night was drawing near. I took up my lodgings in an old tower where a watchman and an owl dwelt. I trusted neither, and least of the two the owl. That animal is like a cat, and possesses the great failing of eating mice; but one may be mistaken, and that I was. She was a respectable, highly-educated old owl; she knew more than the watchman, and quite as much as

I. The owl children made a fuss about everything. 'Don't make soup from a sausage-peg,' the old one would say; those were the harshest words she could bring herself to utter, such tender affection did she cherish for her own family. Her behavior inspired me with such confidence that I sent her a 'peep!' from the crack where I sat; this confidence pleased her very much, and she assured me that I should be under her protection, and that no animal would be allowed to do me harm. She would eat me herself in winter, she declared, when food got scarce.

"She was in every way a clever woman; she explained to me that the watchman could only shriek through the horn that hung loose at his side, saying, 'He is terribly conceited about it, and thinks he is an owl in the tower. He wants to look big, but is very little! Soup from a sausage-peg!'

"I begged the owl to give me the recipe for the soup, and then she explained it to me: 'Soup from a sausage-peg,' she said, 'is only a human expression, and can be used in different ways. Every one thinks his own way is the most correct, but the whole thing really means nothing.'

"Nothing!" I exclaimed. I was struck. The truth is not always agreeable, but truth is above everything, and the old owl said so too. So I thought it over, and soon perceived that if I brought home that which is above everything, I should bring far more than soup from a sausage-peg. And thereupon I hastened away, so that I might get home in time and bring the highest and best, that which is above everything—the truth. The mice are an enlightened little people, and the mouse-king is above them all. He is capable of making me queen—for the sake of truth!"

"Your truth is a lie!" said the mouse who had not yet spoken. "I can prepare the soup, and I will prepare it too."

How It Was Prepared

"I didn't travel," said the third mouse; "I remained in the country, and that's the right thing to do. There is no necessity to travel—one can get everything just as good here. I remained; I did not get my information from supernatural beings, did not gobble it up, nor yet learn it from owls. I have evolved mine from my own thoughts. Now just you get the kettle put upon the fire. That's it. Now some water poured into it! Quite full—up to the brim! So—now more fuel! Let it burn up, so that the water boils—it must boil over and over! That's it! Now throw the peg in. Will the king now be pleased to dip his tail into the boiling water and stir it with that tail? The longer the king stirs, the stronger the soup will become. It costs nothing. It requires no other ingredients—only stirring!"

"Can't any one else do that?" asked the king.

"No," said the mouse, "it is only the king's tail that contains the power."

And the water boiled and spluttered, and the mouse-king placed himself close to the kettle—there was almost danger attached to it—he put out his tail, as the mice do in the dairy when they skim a pan of milk, and then lick their creamy tails; but he only put his tail in as far as the hot steam, then he quickly sprang down from the hearth.

"It's understood, of course, that you are to be my queen!" he cried; "but we'll leave the soup till our golden wedding; in this way the poor of my kingdom, who will have to be fed then, will have something to look forward to with pleasure, and for a long time, too."

Then they held the wedding. But several of the mice said as they were returning home, "that was really not to be called soup from a sausage-peg after all, but rather soup from a mouse's tail." This and that of what had been told they thought very good; but the whole thing might have been different. "Now I would have told it so—and so—and so!"

These were the critics, and they are always so wise—afterwards.

This story went out all over the wide world, and opinions differed about it, but the story itself remained as it was. And that is the best thing in both great things and small, even with regard to soup from a sausage-peg—not to expect any thanks for it.

The Beetle

The emperor's favorite horse was shod with gold; he had a golden horseshoe on each foot. But why was that?

He was a beautiful creature, with slender legs, bright intelligent eyes, and a mane that hung down like a veil over his neck. He had carried his master through the smoke of powder and the rain of bullets, and had heard the balls whistling past; he had bitten, kicked, and taken part in the fight when the enemy pressed forward, and leaping with the emperor across the fallen horse of one of the foe, had saved the bright golden crown and the life of the emperor—and that was worth more than all the bright gold. And that is why the emperor's horse had golden horseshoes.

A beetle came creeping out. "First the great, then the small," said he; "but size is not everything." And with that he stretched out his thin legs.

"Well, what do you want?" asked the smith. "Golden shoes," replied the beetle.

"Why, you must be out of your senses!" cried the smith. "You want golden shoes too?"

"Certainly—golden shoes!" said the beetle. "Am 1 not as good as that creature there, that is waited on, and brushed, and has food and drink put before him? Don't I belong to the imperial stables too?"

"But why has the horse golden shoes?" asked the smith. "Don't you understand that?"

"Understand? I understand that it is a personal slight for me," said the beetle. "It is done to vex me, and I will therefore go out into the wide world."

"Go along!" said the smith.

"You rude fellow!" said the beetle; and then he went out of the stable, flew a short distance, and soon afterwards found himself in a beautiful flower garden, fragrant with roses and lavender.

"Isn't it beautiful here?" asked one of the little lady-bugs that were flying about with their red shield-shaped black-spotted wings. "How sweet it is here, and how lovely!"

"I have been used to better than that," said the beetle. "You call this beautiful? Why, there's not even a dunghill."

Then he went on, under the shadow of a big gilliflower, where a caterpillar was creeping along.

"How beautiful the world is!" said the caterpillar; "the sun is so warm, and everything so happy! And when I one day fall asleep and die, as they call it, I shall awake as a butterfly."

"What things you do fancy!" said the beetle. "To fly about as a butterfly! I come from the emperor's stable, but no one there—not even the emperor's favorite horse, that wears my cast-off golden shoes—fancies anything like that. Get wings! Fly! Well, we'll fly now!" And away flew the beetle. "I don't want to be vexed, but I am all the same," he said, as he flew off.

Soon afterwards he fell upon a great lawn; here he lay awhile, and pretended to be asleep, but at last he really dozed off.

Suddenly a heavy shower of rain fell from the clouds. The noise awoke the beetle, and he wanted to creep into the earth, but could not, for he was being turned over and over. First he was swimming on his stomach, then on his back, and flying was not to be thought of; he despaired of getting away from the place alive. So he lay where he lay, and remained there. When the rain had left off a little, and the beetle had blinked the water out of his eyes, he saw the gleam of something white; it was linen laid out to bleach. He reached it and crept into a fold of the damp linen. It was certainly not so comfortable here as in the warm dunghill in the stable, but nothing better happened to be at hand, and so he stayed where he was—stayed a whole day and a whole night, and the rain stayed too. Towards morning he crept out; he was greatly annoyed at the climate.

On the linen sat two frogs, their bright eyes sparkling with pure joy.

"This is glorious weather," said one. "How refreshing! And the linen keeps the water together so beautifully. My hind legs are itching to swim."

"I should like to know," said the other, "whether the swallow which flies about so far has ever found a better climate than ours in her many travels abroad. So nice and damp! It is really like lying in a wet ditch. Whoever doesn't like this can't be said to love his native country."

"Have you then never been in the emperor's stable?" asked the beetle. "There the dampness is warm and fragrant: that's the climate for me! But you can't take it with you when you travel. Is there no dung-heap in the garden here, where people of rank, like myself, can feel at home and take up their quarters?"

The frogs either could not or would not understand him. "I never ask twice!" exclaimed the beetle, after he had already asked three times and received no answer.

Thereupon he went a little further, and came across a piece of broken pottery which should certainly not have been lying there, but which, as it lay, afforded a good shelter against wind and weather. Here lived several families of earwigs; they did not require much—only company. The females are full of tenderest maternal love, and every mother therefore praised her child as the most beautiful and cleverest.

"Our little son is engaged to be married!" said one mother. "Sweet innocence! It is his sole ambition to get into a parson's ear some day. He is so artless and loveable; his engagement will keep him steady. What joy for a mother!"

"Our son," said another mother, "had hardly crept out of the egg, when he was off on his travels. He's all life and spirits; he'll run his horns off. What joy for a mother! Isn't it so, Mr. Beetle?" They recognized the stranger by the cut of his wings.

"You are both right!" said the beetle, and then they begged him to enter the room; that is to say, to come as far as he could under the piece of pottery.

"Now you see my little earwig too," cried a third and a fourth mother. "They are the sweetest children, and very playful. They are never naughty, except when they occasionally have pains in their inside; unfortunately, one gets those only too easily at their age."

In this manner every mother spoke of her baby, and the babies joined in too, and used the little nippers that they have in their tails to pull the beetle by his beard.

"Yes, they're always up to something, the little rogues!" said the mothers, boiling over with maternal affection. But this bored the beetle, and so he asked whether it was much farther to the dunghill.

"Why, that's out in the wide world, on the other side of the ditch," answered an earwig; "I hope none of my children will go so far—it would be the death of me."

"I'll try to get as far anyhow," said the beetle; and he went off without saying good-bye, for that is considered the most polite way. By the ditch he met several of his kind—all beetles.

"We live here!" they said. "We are very comfortable. May we ask you to step down into the rich mud? The journey has no doubt been very fatiguing for you?"

"Very," said the beetle. "I have been exposed to the rain, and have had to lie on linen, and cleanliness always weakens me very much. I have pain too in one wing through having stood in the draft under a broken piece of pottery. It is really quite a comfort to get once more among one's own kindred."

"Perhaps you come from the dung-heap?" asked the eldest.

"O-ho! from higher places!" cried the beetle. "I come from the emperor's stable, where I was born with golden shoes on my feet. I am traveling on a secret mission, but you must not ask me any questions about it, for I won't betray the secret."

With that the beetle stepped down into the rich mud. There sat three young beetle maidens; they giggled, because they did not know what to say.

"They are all three still disengaged," said the mother; and the young beetle maidens giggled again, this time from bashfulness.

"I have not seen greater beauties in the imperial stables," said the beetle, taking a rest.

"Don't you spoil my girls for me, and don't speak to them unless you have serious intentions. But about that I have no doubt, and so I give you my blessing!"

"Hurrah!" cried all the other beetles, and our beetle was now engaged. The engagement was immediately followed by the wedding, for there was no reason for delay.

The following day passed very pleasantly, and the one after that fairly so; but on the third day the time had come to think of food for the wife, and perhaps even for the children.

"I have allowed myself to be taken in," thought the beetle; "nothing is therefore left for me but to take others in, in return."

So said, so done. Away he went, and stayed out the whole day and the whole night—and his wife sat there, a lonely widow.

"Oh!" said the other beetles, "that fellow whom we received into our family is a thorough vagabond; he went away and left his wife sitting there, to be a burden upon us."

"Well, then she must be passed off as unmarried again, and stay here as my child," said the mother. "Fie on the villain who deserted her!"

In the meantime the beetle had gone on traveling, and had sailed across the watery ditch on a cabbage-leaf. In the morning two people came to the ditch; when they spied him, they picked him up, turned him over and over, and looked very wise, especially one of them—a boy. "Allah sees the black beetle in the black stone and in the black rock. Isn't it written so in the Koran?" Then he translated the beetle's name into Latin, and enlarged upon its species and nature. The second person, an older scholar, was for taking him home with them. But the other said that they had specimens quite as good as that, and this, our beetle thought, was not a polite thing to say—so he suddenly flew out of the speaker's hand. His wings being now dry, he flew a pretty long distance and reached a hotbed, where, one of the windows of the glass-house being ajar, he slipped in comfortably and buried himself in the fresh manure.

"How delightful it is here!" he said.

Soon after, he fell asleep and dreamed that the emperor's favorite horse had fallen and had given him his golden horseshoes, with the promise to have two more made for him.

That was very acceptable. When the beetle awoke, he crept out and looked about him. What splendor there was in the hothouse! In the background were palm trees, growing to a great height; the sun made them look transparent, and under them what a wealth of verdure and bright flowers, red as fire, yellow as amber, and white as driven snow!

"There is an incomparable splendor in these plants," said the beetle; "how fine they will taste when they decay! This is a good larder! There must certainly be relatives of mine living here. I'll have a look round to see if I can find any one to associate with. Proud I am, and that is my pride." And now he strolled about in the hothouse, and thought of his beautiful dream of the dead horse, and the golden horseshoes he had inherited.

Suddenly a hand seized the beetle, pressed him, and turned him over and over.

The gardener's son and a little girl who played with him had come up to the hotbed, had spied the beetle, and wanted to have some fun with him. First he was wrapped up in a vine-leaf, and then put into a warm trousers-pocket. There he cribbled and crabbled about with all his might; but for this he got a squeeze from the boy's hand, and that taught him to be quiet. Then the boy ran off to the great lake at the end of the garden. Here the beetle was put into an old half-broken wooden shoe, in which a little stick was placed for a mast, and to this mast the beetle was bound by a woollen thread. Now he was a sailor and had to sail. The lake was very large, and to the beetle it seemed an ocean; he was so terrified by it that he fell on his back and kicked out with his feet. The little ship sailed away, and the current of the water seized it. But when it went too far from the shore, the little boy would turn up his trousers, go into the water, and fetch it back to the land. But at last, just as it was setting out to sea again in full sail, the children were called away for something important; they hastened to obey, and running away from the lake, left the little ship to its fate. This drifted farther and farther away from the shore, and farther out into the open sea; it was terrible for the beetle, for he could not get away, being bound to the mast. Then a fly paid him a visit. "What lovely weather!" said the fly. "I'll rest here and bask in the sun; it's very pleasant for you here."

"You talk of what you don't understand! Don't you see that I'm tied fast?"

"But I'm not," said the fly, and flew off.

"Well, now I know the world," said the beetle. "It's a base world. I'm the only honest one in it. First, they refuse me golden shoes; then I have to lie on wet linen and stand in a draft; and, to cap all, they fasten a wife on to me. Then, when I have taken a quick step out into the world, and learn how comfortable one can be there, and how I ought to have it, up comes a human boy, binds me fast, and leaves me to the wild waves, while the emperor's favorite horse prances about in golden shoes. That vexes me most of all! But one must not count on sympathy in this world. My career is very interesting; but what's the use of that if nobody knows it? The world doesn't deserve to be made acquainted with my story, for it ought to have given me golden shoes in the emperor's stable when the emperor's favorite horse was being shod, and I stretched out my legs too. If I had received golden shoes I should have been an ornament to the stable; now the stable has lost me, the world has lost me—all is over!"

But all was not over yet. A boat, in which there were some young girls, came rowing up.

"Look, there's an old wooden shoe sailing along," said one of the girls.

"There's a little creature tied up in it!" cried another.

The boat came quite close to our beetle's little ship, and the young girls fished it up out of the water. One of them drew a small pair of scissors out of her pocket, cut the woollen thread without hurting the beetle, and when she got to the shore placed him in the grass.

"Creep, creep. Fly, fly—if you can," she said. "Freedom is a glorious thing."

The beetle flew up and went through the open window of a large building; there he sank down, tired and exhausted, upon the fine, soft, long mane of the emperor's horse that was standing in the stables where both he and the beetle were at home. The beetle clung fast to the mane, sat there quite still for a short time, and recovered.

"Here I sit on the emperor's favorite horse—sit on him just like an emperor. But what was I going to say? Ah, yes! I remember. It's a good idea, and quite correct. Why does the emperor's horse have golden shoes? That's what the smith asked me. Now the answer is clear to me. The horse had golden horseshoes on my account!"

And now the beetle was in a good temper. "Traveling opens one's brains," he said.

The sun's rays came streaming into the stable upon him, and made things bright and pleasant.

"The world is not so bad after all, when you come to examine it," said the beetle, "but you must know how to take it."

Yes, the world was beautiful, because the emperor's favorite horse had only received golden shoes so that the beetle might become his rider. "Now I will go down to the other beetles and tell them how much has been done for me. I will relate to them all the disagreeable things I went through in my travels abroad, and tell them that I shall now remain at home till the horse has worn out his golden shoes."

The Garden of Paradise

Once upon a time there was a king's son. No one had so many fine books as he; he could read in them about everything that had happened in this world, and see pictures of it all in beautiful engravings. He could get information upon every nation and every country; but there was not a word to say where the Garden of Paradise was to be found, and that happened to be just what he thought most about. His grandmother had told him when he was still little, and was about to go to school for the first time, that every flower in this Garden of Paradise was made of the nicest cake, and that the pistils contained the finest wines; that history was written on some of them, and geography or tables on others, so that one had only to eat cake to know one's lesson. The more one ate, the more history, geography, and tables one would learn.

At that time he believed it. But soon, when he was a bigger boy, and had learned more and become wiser, he understood well enough that there must be quite a different kind of delight in the Garden of Paradise.

"Oh, why did Eve pluck from the tree of knowledge? Why did Adam eat of the forbidden fruit? If I had been he, it would not have happened. Sin would never have come into the world." He said this then, and he still said so when he was seventeen years old. The Garden of Paradise occupied all his thoughts.

One day he was walking in the wood alone, for that was his greatest pleasure. The sun went down, and the sky became clouded over. The rain came down as though the whole of Heaven were a single sluice-gate, out of which the water poured; and it was as dark as it is only at night in the deepest well. He often slipped on the wet grass, and often fell over the smooth stones which protruded from the wet rocky ground. Everything was dripping with water; there was not a dry thread on the poor prince. He was obliged to clamber over great boulders, where the water welled up out of the high moss. He was almost fainting, when he heard a strange rushing sound and saw before him a large illuminated cave. There was such a large fire burning in the middle that a stag could have been roasted before it. And indeed this was being done. A splendid stag with long horns had been placed upon a spit and was being slowly turned between two felled pine-trunks. An elderly woman, tall and strong, looking like a man in woman's clothes, was sitting by the fire and throwing on one piece of wood after another.

"Come nearer," she said; "sit down by the fire, so that your clothes may dry."

"There's a terrible draft here," said the prince, sitting down on the floor.

"It will be worse when my sons come home," answered the woman. "You are here in the Cave of the Winds; my sons are the four winds of the world. Can you understand that?"

"Where are your sons?" asked the prince.

"Well, it is difficult to answer when people ask stupid questions," said the woman. "My sons do just as they like: now they are playing at shuttle-cock with the clouds up there in the king's hall." And with these words she pointed upwards.

"Indeed!" said the prince. "But I must say you speak rather gruffly, and are not so gentle as the women I usually have about me."

"Well, I suppose they have nothing else to do. I must be hard, if I wish to keep my boys in order; but that I can do, although they are obstinate fellows. Do you see these four sacks hanging on the wall? They are as frightened of those as you used to be of the rod behind the mirror. I can bend those boys together, I tell you, and then I pop them into the sack; we make no ceremony about it. Then they sit there and dare not stir out before I think fit. But here we have one of them."

It was the North-Wind, who brought in icy coldness; large hailstones skipped upon the floor, and snowflakes fluttered around. He wore bearskin trousers and jacket, and a sealskin cap came down over his ears; long icicles hung down from his beard, and one hailstone after another slid down from the collar of his jacket.

"Don't go near the fire at once," said the prince. "You might get your hands and face frostbitten."

"Frostbitten?" said the North-Wind, and laughed out loud. "Cold is my greatest pleasure. And pray what tailor's son may you be? How did you come into the Cave of the Winds?"

"He is my guest," said the old woman; "and if you are not satisfied with this explanation, you will find your way into the sack. Do you understand me now?"

That settled the matter; and the North-Wind told whence he came, and where he had been almost a whole month.

"I come from the Polar Sea," said he. "I have been on Bear Island with the Russian walrus-hunters. I sat at the helm and slept when they set sail from the North Cape, and when I awoke now and then the stormy petrel was flying about my legs. What a strange bird that is! It makes a quick stroke with its wings, holds them stretched out and unmoved, and is then in full flight."

"Come, don't make your tale too long," said the mother of the winds. "So you came to Bear Island?"

"It is a beautiful place. The ground would do for dancing on, smooth as china. The half-thawed snow mixed with a little moss, sharp stones and the skeletons of walruses and ice-bears lay all around, as well as giant arms and legs covered with moldy green. One would have believed that the sun had never shined upon it at all. I blew the fog off a little in order to see the hut. It was built of wreckage, covered over with walrus hides, the flesh side of which had been turned outwards; a live polar bear was sitting on the roof growling. I went to the shore, and looking into the birds' nests, saw the naked young ones, who were crying with their beaks wide open. I blew down into their thousand throats, and they learned to keep their beaks shut. A little farther off, the walruses were rolling about like live entrails, or giant worms with swine-heads and teeth a yard long."

"You tell your story beautifully, my son," said the mother. "My mouth waters when I listen to you."

"Then the hunting began. The harpoon was thrust into the breast of the walrus, so that the steaming blood rushed over the ice like a fountain. Then I remembered my sport too. I blew and made my ships, the towering icebergs, shut in the boats. Hey! How the men whistled and shouted; but I whistled still louder. They were obliged to throw the bodies of the dead walruses, the boxes and the cordage out upon the ice. I shook snow-flakes over them, and let them float southwards, in their hemmed-in vessels, with what they had caught, to taste the seawaters. They will never come to Bear Island again."

"Then you have been doing mischief," said the mother of the winds.

"The good that I have done others may tell about," said he. "But here we have my brother from the West. I like him best of all: he smells of the sea, and brings a fine coldness with him."

"Is that the little Zephyr?" asked the prince.

"It is indeed Zephyr," said the old woman. "But he is by no means little. Years ago he was a pretty boy, but that time is now past."

He looked like a savage, and wore a padded hat, so that he should not hurt himself in falling. In his hand he held a mahogany club, hewn in the mahogany forests of America. It was no plaything!

"Where do you come from?" asked his mother.

"From the forest-wastes," said he, "where the water-snake lies in the wet grass and people seem to be unnecessary."

"What did you do there?"

"I looked into the deepest river and saw how it hurled itself from the rocks, became dust and flew up to the clouds to carry the rainbow. I saw the wild buffalo swimming in the stream, and how the current carried him away. He floated along with a flock of wild ducks, who flew into the air when they came to the waterfall. But the buffalo had to go down; that pleased me, and I raised a storm that shivered the oldest trees into splinters."

"And is that all you have done?" asked the old woman.

"I have turned somersaults in the savannahs; I have stroked the wild horses, and shaken down the coker-nuts. Dear me! what stories I could tell. But one must not say everything that one knows. You know that very well, old lady." And he kissed his mother so boisterously that she almost fell backwards. He was a terribly wild boy.

The South-Wind now came in, wearing a turban and the flowing mantle of a Bedouin.

"It is very cold out here," said he, throwing some more wood upon the fire. "It is easy to see that the North-Wind came in first."

"It is hot enough here to roast an ice-bear," said the North-Wind.

"You are an ice-bear yourself," answered the South-Wind.

"Do you want to be put into the sack?" asked the old woman. "Sit down on that stone there, and tell me where you have been."

"In Africa, mother," he answered. "I went lion-hunting with the Hottentots in the country of the Kaffirs. Grass grows on the plains there as green as an olive. The ostrich ran a race with me, but I am still quicker than he. I came to the desert and to the yellow sand, where it looks just like the bottom of the sea. I met a caravan: they were killing their last camel to get some drinking water, but they got only a little, after all. The sun burned from overhead and the sand from underfoot. The far-stretching desert was boundless. I danced about in the fine loose sand, and whirled it up into great pillars. What a dance that was! You should have seen how despondently the dromedary stood there, and how the trader drew his caftan over his head. He threw himself down before me as before Allah, his god. Now they are buried; a pyramid of sand is heaped up over them all. When I blow that away, the sun will bleach their white bones; then travelers will see that human beings have been there before. Otherwise that would not be believed in the desert."

"Then you have only done evil," said his mother. "Into the sack with you!" And before he knew where he was she had caught the South-Wind round the body, and popped him into the sack. He rolled himself over and over on the ground, but she sat down on him, and he had to lie still.

"These boys of yours are lively," said the prince. "They are," she answered, "but I know how to keep them in order. Here comes the fourth!"

This was the East-Wind, dressed like a China-man. "Oh, so you come from that quarter?" said his mother. "I thought that you had been in the Garden of Paradise."

"I am not going there until to-morrow," said the East-Wind. "That will be a hundred years since I have been there. I come from China now, where I danced round the porcelain tower and made all the bells jingle. The officials were being beaten in the street; bamboo canes were split across their shoulders, and they were all people from the first to the ninth grade. They shouted: 'Many thanks, my paternal benefactor.' But the cry did not come from their hearts, and I jingled the bells and sang: *'Tsing, tsang, tsu!'* "

"You are mischievous," said the old woman. It is a good thing that you are going to the Garden of Paradise to-morrow; you always leam better manners there. Take a good draft at the fountain of wisdom, and bring a bottleful home for me."

"I will!" said the East-Wind. "But why have you put my brother of the south into the sack? Out with him! He must tell me about the phoenix bird; the princess in the Garden of Paradise always likes to hear about it, when I pay her a visit every hundred years. Open the sack, and then you will be my sweetest mother, and I will give you two bags full of tea, as green and as fresh as I picked it on the spot where it grew."

"Well, for the sake of the tea, and because you are my pet boy, I will open the sack." She did so, and the South-Wind crept out; but he looked quite dejected, because the stranger prince had seen his disgrace.

"Here is a palm-leaf for the princess," said he. "This leaf was given me by the phoenix, the only bird of that kind in the world. It has traced upon it with its beak the whole story of its life during the hundred years that it has lived. Now she can read for herself how the phoenix bird set fire to its nest and sat in it while it was consumed by the flames, like a Hindoo widow. How the dry twigs crackled! What a smoke and a vapor there were! At length all had been destroyed by the flames; the old phoenix bird had become ashes. But its egg lay red and glowing in the fire; suddenly it burst with a great clap, and the young one flew out, and that one now reigns over all birds, and is the only phoenix bird in the world. It has bitten a hole in the palm-leaf I gave you; that is its greeting to the princess."

"Let us eat something," said the mother of the Winds. So they all sat down together and ate of the roast stag. The young prince sat by the side of the East-Wind, and therefore they soon became good friends. "I say," said the prince, "just tell me what princess that is of whom you were talking so much just now, and where is the Garden of Paradise situated?"

"Ho, ho!" said the East-Wind; "would you like to go there? Well, then, fly with me to-morrow. But I must tell you this: no human being has been there since the time of Adam and Eve. I suppose you know them from your Bible history?"

"Of course," said the prince.

"At that time, when they were driven out, the Garden of Paradise sank into the earth; but it retained its warm sunshine, its balmy air, and all its beauty. The fairy queen lives there now; there lies also the Island of Happiness, where Death never comes and where all is beautiful. If you get upon my back to-morrow, I will take you with me; I think we shall be able to manage it. But leave off talking now, because I want to go to sleep."

And then they all went to sleep.

Early in the morning the prince awoke, and was not a little surprised to find himself already high above the clouds. He was sitting on the back of the East-Wind, who held him fast; they were so high up in the air that forests and meadows, rivers and seas looked as though painted on a map.

"Good morning," said the East-Wind. "You might just as well sleep a little longer, because there is not much to be seen on the flat country beneath us, unless you have a mind to count the churches. They stand like little lumps of chalk on the green board." What he called a green board were the fields and meadows.

"It was very rude of me not to say good-bye to your mother and your brothers," said the prince.

"Such things are excusable if one is asleep," said the East-Wind. And thereupon they flew along still faster. It could be heard by the tree-tops, for when they flew over them all the branches and the leaves rustled; it could be heard by the sea and the lakes, for wherever they flew the waves rose higher, and the great ships dipped low into the water, like swans swimming.

Towards evening, when it was getting dark, the large towns were an extremely pretty sight, with all the lights being kindled, first here and then there. It was just like watching all the little sparks as they vanish one after another from a burnt piece of paper. At this the prince clapped his hands; but the East-Wind begged him not to do so, and rather to hold on tight, as otherwise he might easily fall, and remain hanging from the top of a church steeple. The eagle in the dark forests flew very lightly, but the East-Wind flew more lightly still. The Cossack on his little steed sped very swiftly across the plain, but the prince rode more swiftly still. "Now you can see the Himalayas," said the East-Wind. "They are the highest mountains in Asia, and we shall soon reach the Garden of Paradise." Then they turned more towards the south, and soon the air was balmy with spices and flowers. Figs and pomegranates were growing wild; red and white grapes hung from the wild vines. Here they both descended and stretched themselves on the soft grass, where the flowers nodded to the wind, as if they wanted to say, "Welcome!"

"Are we now in the Garden of Paradise?" asked the prince. "Dear me! no," answered the East-Wind. "But we shall soon get there. Do you see yonder cliff and the wide cave in front of which the vines hang like a long green curtain? We must go through there to get in. Wrap yourself up in your cloak; the sun burns here; but one step farther, and it will be as cold as ice.
The bird which flies past the cave has one wing in the warmth of summer, and the other in the cold of winter."

"Indeed! So that is the way to the Garden of Paradise," said the prince. They now entered the cave. Oh, how icy cold it was! But it did not last long; the East-Wind spread out his wings, and they shined like the brightest fire. What a cave it was! The great boulders, from which the water trickled down, hung above them in the strangest forms. In one place it was so narrow that they had to creep along on hands and feet, and in another as high and wide as in the open air. It looked like subterranean chapels with mute organ-pipes and petrified organs.

"I suppose we are going to the Garden of Paradise by the road of Death?" asked the prince. But the East-Wind answered not a syllable, only pointing forwards, where the most beautiful blue light was streaming towards them. The boulders above became more and more hazy, till at last they looked like a white cloud in the moonlight. Now they breathed a beautiful balmy air, as fresh as on the mountains, as fragrant as among the roses of the valley. A

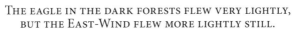

The eagle in the dark forests flew very lightly,
but the East-Wind flew more lightly still.

"So that is the way to the Garden of Paradise."

river flowed there, as clear as the air itself, and the fish were like silver and gold. Purple eels, which gave forth blue sparks with every movement, were playing beneath the surface, and the broad leaves of the water-lily had all the colors of the rainbow. The flower itself was a glowing orange colored flame, which was fed by the water, just as oil keeps a lamp continually burning. A strong marble bridge, so delicately and artistically carved as though it were of lace and seed-pearls, led over the water to the Island of Happiness, where the Garden of Paradise was.

The East-Wind took the prince in his arms, and carried him across. The flowers and leaves sang the most beautiful songs of his childhood, but with such sweet modulations as no human voice can command. Were they palm-trees or gigantic water-plants that grew here? The prince had never before seen trees so large and full of sap, and hanging there in long garlands were the most wonderful creepers, such as are only found, painted in colors and gold, on the margins of old missals or wound about initial letters. They were the strangest compounds of birds, flowers, and stalks. Close by, on the grass, stood a group of peacocks with their bright tails spread out. It was really so!

But when the prince touched them he found that they were not birds, but plants; they were large plantain-leaves, that shined here like the majestic tail of the peacock. Lions and tigers sprang like agile cats in and out of the green hedges, which were as fragrant as the flowers of the olive-tree; but they were tame. The wild wood-pigeon shined like the finest pearl, and beat her wings against the lion's mane; the antelope, so shy elsewhere, stood by and nodded its head, as if it wished to join them in their play.

There now appeared the Fairy of Paradise. Her raiment was resplendent as the sun, and her face wore a smile like that of a glad mother when she is happy on account of her child. She was young and fair, and the loveliest maidens, each wearing a bright star in her hair, followed her. The East-Wind gave her the leaf on which the phoenix bird had written, and it made her eyes sparkle with joy. She took the prince by the hand, and led him into her castle, where the walls had colors like those of the brightest tulip petals when they are held in the sunlight. The ceiling itself was a large shining flower, and the more one looked up at it the deeper seemed to be its cup. The prince went to the window and looked through one of the panes: there was the Tree of Knowledge, and Adam and Eve standing close by. "Were they not driven out?" he asked. And the Fairy smiled and explained to him that Time had stamped its picture on every pane; but not as pictures are generally seen. Here there was life in them. The leaves of the trees moved; the people came and went just as anything is seen in a mirror. And he looked through another pane and saw Jacob's dream, with the ladder reaching up to Heaven, and angels with great wings were floating up and down. Indeed, everything that had happened in this world lived and moved in the glass panes; such artistic pictures could only be engraved by Time.

The fairy smiled and led him to a large lofty hall, the walls of which appeared to be transparent. Here were many portraits, one more beautiful than the other. Millions of happy faces were seen, all smiling and singing in beautiful harmony. The top ones were so small that they looked smaller than the smallest rose-buds when they are drawn, no larger than a pin's head on paper. In the middle of the hall stood a large tree with luxuriant branches hanging down; golden apples peeped out like oranges from between the green leaves. It was the Tree of Knowledge, of whose fruit Adam and Eve had eaten. From each leaf there trickled a bright red dew-drop; it looked as if the tree were weeping tears of blood.

"Let us get into the boat now," said the fairy, "and we will have some refreshments on the billowy water. Our bark will not move from the spot, but all the countries of the earth will glide past before our eyes."

There now appeared the Fairy of Paradise.
Her raiment was resplendent as the sun, and her face
wore a smile like that of a glad mother.

And it was wonderful to behold how the whole coast moved. First came the high, snow-clad Alps, with clouds and dark fir-trees; the horn sent forth its melancholy note, and the shepherd sang lustily in the valley. Then the banana-trees trailed their long hanging branches over the boat; black swans swam upon the water, and the strangest animals and flowers appeared on the river-bank: it was New Holland, the fifth quarter of the globe, which with a view of its blue mountains now swept by. One could hear the chant of the priests and see the savages dancing to the sound of the drums and the bone trumpets. The pyramids of Egypt, their tops reaching the clouds, ruined pillars and sphinxes, half buried in the sand, sailed past in like manner. The Northern Lights shined out over the extinct volcanoes of the Arctic regions: a firework display which no one could imitate. The prince was very happy, for he saw a hundred times as much as we can tell of here.

"And can I always stay here?" he asked.

"That depends upon yourself," answered the fairy. "If you do not wish to do, as Adam did, what is forbidden, you can always stay here."

"I will never touch the apples on the Tree of Knowledge," said the prince.

"There are thousands of kinds of fruit here, just as fine as they are. Try yourself, and if you are not strong enough, go back with the East-Wind, who brought you here. He is now about to fly back, and will not let himself be seen here for a hundred years; that time will pass for you in this place as if it were a hundred hours, but it is a long time to resist temptation. Every evening when I leave you, I must call to you: "Come with me!" I must beckon you to me with my hand. But stay where you are. Do not go with me, or else your desire would grow stronger at every step. You would then reach the hall where the Tree of Knowledge grows; I sleep under its fragrant, hanging branches. You will bend over me, and I must smile, but if you press a kiss upon my mouth, Paradise will sink deep into the earth, and be lost to you. The piercing wind of the desert will whistle round you, and the cold rain will trickle upon your head. Sorrow and trouble will be your lot."

"I will stay here," said the prince. And the East-Wind kissed him on the forehead and said: "Be strong; then we shall meet each other here again after a hundred years. Farewell, farewell!" And the East-Wind spread out his great wings; they shined like lightning in harvest-time, or like the North-Light in winter.

"Farewell, farewell!" re-echoed all the flowers and trees. Rows of storks and pelicans flew like waving ribbons, and accompanied him to the boundaries of the garden.

"Now let us begin our dances," said the fairy. "Towards the end, when I am dancing with you, and the sun is sinking, you will see me beckon you, and hear me call to you to come with me. But do not do so. For a hundred years I must repeat it every evening; on every occasion, as soon as the time is past, you will have gained more strength, and at last you will no longer even think of it. To-night is the first time; now I have warned you."

The fairy then led him into a large hall of white transparent lilies; the yellow stamina in each flower formed a little golden harp, from the strings of which came notes like those of a flute. The most beautiful maidens, graceful and slender, clad in wavy gauze, so that their charming limbs could be seen, glided through the dance, and sang how beautiful it was to live, that they would never die, and that the Garden of Paradise would flourish for ever.

The sun was setting; the whole sky became the color of gold, and gave the lilies the appearance of the most lovely roses. The prince drank the sparkling wine which the maidens handed him, and felt a happiness that he had never experienced before. He saw the background of the hall open itself, and the Tree of Knowledge standing in a splendor which blinded his eyes; the singing there was soft and sweet, like his mother's voice, and it seemed as though she were singing: "My child, my beloved child!"

Then the fairy beckoned to him, and called so sweetly, "Come with me! Come with me!" that he rushed towards her, forgetting his promise, forgetting it already on the first evening, while she beckoned and smiled. The fragrance, the spicy fragrance, all around became stronger; the harps sounded much sweeter, and it seemed as if the millions of smiling heads in the hall, where the tree grew, nodded and sang: "One should know everything. Man is lord of the earth." And they were no longer tears of blood that fell from the leaves of the Tree of Knowledge; they were brilliant red stars, which the prince thought he saw. "Come with me! Come with me!" sang the quivering tones, and with every step the prince's cheeks burned more hotly, his blood rushed more quickly through his veins. "I must," said he. "It is no sin—can be none. Why may I not follow beauty and joy? I will see her sleep; there is no harm done if I refrain from kissing her. And I shall not kiss her. I am strong; I have a firm will."

And the fairy, throwing aside her dazzling raiment, bent back the boughs, and a moment after she was concealed behind them.

"I have not yet sinned," said the prince; "neither will I do so."

And then he drew the boughs aside; she was already asleep, as beautiful as only the fairy in the Garden of Paradise can be. She smiled in her dream, but he bending down over her, saw tears trembling between her eyelids.

"Do you weep on my account?" he whispered. "Do not weep, you lovely creature. Now only do I understand the bliss of Paradise. It is rushing through

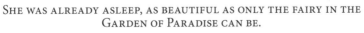

She was already asleep, as beautiful as only the fairy in the Garden of Paradise can be.

my blood, through my thoughts; I feel the strength of the cherub and of eternal life in my earthly body. May eternal night come over me! One minute such as this is riches enough!" And he kissed the tears from her eyes; his mouth touched hers.

There came a crash of thunder more deep and terrible than had ever been heard. Everything rushed together; the beautiful fairy, the blooming Garden of Paradise sank, sank lower and lower. The prince saw it sink into the black night; it shined in the distance like a twinkling little star. Icy coldness ran through his limbs; he closed his eyes and lay for a long time as one dead.

The cold rain beat into his face, the sharp wind flew about his head, and his senses returned. "What have I done!" he sighed. "I have sinned, like Adam—sinned, so that Paradise has sunk far away." He opened his eyes and still beheld the star in the distance, the star that shined like the lost Paradise—it was the morning-star in the heavens. He rose and found himself in the great forest near the Cave of the Winds; the mother of the winds was sitting beside it; she looked angry and raised her hand in the air.

"Already, on the first evening," she said. "I thought as much! Well, if you were my son you would go into the sack."

"He shall go in," said Death. He was a strong old man, with a scythe in his hand and with large black wings. "He shall be laid in the coffin, but not yet. I will only mark him, and let him wander about a little while longer in the world to repent of his sins and to become good and better. But I shall come one day when he least expects it, put him into the black coffin, place it on my head and fly up to the star. There too blooms the Garden of Paradise, and if he is good and pious, he shall enter; but if his thoughts are wicked and his heart is still full of sin, he will sink deeper with his coffin than Paradise sank, and I shall fetch him up only every thousand years, so that he either sinks still deeper or reaches the star—that star which shines yonder."

A Story

In the garden all the apple-trees were in blossom. They had hastened to bring forth flowers before they got green leaves, and in the yard all the ducklings walked up and down, and the cat too; it basked in the sun and licked the sunshine from its own paws. And when one looked at the fields, how beautifully the corn stood and how green it shined, without compassion! and there was a twittering and a fluttering of all the little birds, as if the day were a great festival; and so it was, for it was Sunday. All the bells were ringing, and all the people went to church, looking cheerful, and dressed in their best clothes. There was a look of cheerfulness on everything. The day was so warm and beautiful that one might well have said: "God's kindness to us men is beyond all limits." But inside the church the pastor stood in the pulpit, and spoke very loudly and angrily. He said that all men were wicked, and God would punish them for their sins, and that the wicked, when they died, would be cast into hell, to burn for ever and ever. He spoke very excitedly, saying that their evil propensities would not be destroyed, nor would the fire be extinguished, and they should never find rest. That was terrible to hear, and he said it in such a tone of conviction; he described hell to them as a miserable hole where all the refuse of the world gathers. There was no air beside the hot burning sulphur flame, and there was no ground under their feet; they, the wicked ones, sank deeper and deeper, while eternal silence surrounded them! It was dreadful to hear all that, for the preacher spoke from his heart, and all the people in the church were terrified. Meanwhile, the birds sang merrily outside, and the sun was shining so beautifully warm, it seemed as though every little flower said: "God, Thy kindness towards us all is without limits." Indeed, outside it was not at all like the pastor's sermon.

The same evening, upon going to bed, the pastor noticed his wife sitting there quiet and pensive.

"What is the matter with you?" he asked her.

"Well, the matter with me is," she said, "that I cannot collect my thoughts, and am unable to grasp the meaning of what you said to-day in church—that there are so many wicked people, and that they should burn eternally. Alas! eternally—how long! I am only a woman and a sinner before God, but

I should not have the heart to let even the worst sinner burn for ever, and how could our Lord do so, who is so infinitely good, and who knows how the wickedness comes from without and within? No, I am unable to imagine that, although you say so."

It was autumn; the trees dropped their leaves, the earnest and severe pastor sat at the bedside of a dying person. A pious, faithful soul closed her eyes for ever; she was the pastor's wife.

. . . "If any one shall find rest in the grave and mercy before our Lord you shall certainly do so," said the pastor. He folded her hands and read a psalm over the dead woman.

She was buried; two large tears rolled over the cheeks of the earnest man, and in the parsonage it was empty and still, for its sun had set for ever. She had gone home.

It was night. A cold wind swept over the pastor's head; he opened his eyes, and it seemed to him as if the moon was shining into his room. It was not so, however; there was a being standing before his bed, and looking like the ghost of his deceased wife. She fixed her eyes upon him with such a kind and sad expression, just as if she wished to say something to him. The pastor raised himself in bed and stretched his arms towards her, saying, "Not even you can find eternal rest! You suffer, you best and most pious woman?"

The dead woman nodded her head as if to say "Yes," and put her hand on her breast.

"And can I not obtain rest in the grave for you?"

"Yes," was the answer.

"And how?"

"Give me one hair—only one single hair—from the head of the sinner for whom the fire shall never be extinguished, of the sinner whom God will condemn to eternal punishment in hell."

"Yes, one ought to be able to redeem you so easily, you pure, you pious woman," he said.

"Follow me," said the dead woman. "It is thus granted to us. By my side you will be able to fly wherever your thoughts wish to go. Invisible to men, we shall penetrate into their most secret chambers; but with sure hand you must find out him who is destined to eternal torture, and before the cock crows he must be found!" As quickly as if carried by the winged thoughts they were in the great city, and from the walls the names of the deadly sins shined in flaming letters: pride, avarice, drunkenness, wantonness—in short, the whole seven-colored bow of sin.

"Yes, therein, as I believed, as I knew it," said the pastor, "are living those who are abandoned to the eternal fire." And they were standing before the magnificently illuminated gate; the broad steps were adorned with carpets and flowers, and dance music was sounding through the festive halls. A footman dressed in silk and velvet stood with a large silver-mounted rod near the entrance.

"Our ball can compare favorably with the king's," he said, and turned with contempt towards the gazing crowd in the street. What he thought was sufficiently expressed in his features and movements: "Miserable beggars, who are looking in, you are nothing in comparison to me."

"Pride," said the dead woman; "do you see him?"

"The footman?" asked the pastor. "He is but a poor fool, and not doomed to be tortured eternally by fire!"

"Only a fool!" It sounded through the whole house of pride: they were all fools there.

Then they flew within the four naked walls of the miser. Lean as a skeleton, trembling with cold and hunger, the old man was clinging with all his thoughts to his money. They saw him jump up feverishly from his miserable couch and take a loose stone out of the wall; there lay gold coin in an old stocking. They saw him anxiously feeling over an old ragged coat in which pieces of gold were sewn, and his clammy fingers trembled.

"He is ill! That is madness—a joyless madness—besieged by fear and dreadful dreams!"

They quickly went away and came before the beds of the criminals; these unfortunate people slept side by side, in long rows. Like a ferocious animal, one of them rose out of his sleep and uttered a horrible cry, and gave his comrade a violent dig in the ribs with his pointed elbow, and this one turned round in his sleep:

"Be quiet, monster—sleep! This happens every night!"

"Every night!" repeated the other. "Yes, every night he comes and tortures me! In my violence I have done this and that. I was born with an evil mind, which has brought me hither for the second time; but if I have done wrong I suffer punishment for it. One thing, however, I have not yet confessed. When I came out a little while ago and passed by the yard of my former master, evil thoughts rose within me when I remembered this and that. I struck a match a little bit on the wall; probably it came a little too close to the thatched roof. All burned down—a great heat rose, such as sometimes overcomes me. I myself helped to rescue cattle and things, nothing alive burned, except a flight of pigeons, which flew into the fire, and the yard dog, of which I had not thought; one could hear him howl out of the fire, and this howling I still hear when I wish to sleep; and when I have fallen asleep, the great rough dog comes and places himself upon me, and howls, presses, and tortures me. Now listen to what I tell you! You can snore; you are snoring the whole night, and I hardly a quarter of an hour!" And the blood rose to the head of the excited criminal; he threw himself upon his comrade, and beat him with his clenched fist in the face.

"Wicked Matz has become mad again!" they said amongst themselves. The other criminals seized him, wrestled with him, and bent him double, so that his head rested between his knees, and they tied him, so that the blood almost came out of his eyes and out of all his pores.

"You are killing the unfortunate man," said the pastor, and as he stretched out his hand to protect him who already suffered too much, the scene changed. They flew through rich halls and wretched hovels; wantonness and envy, all the deadly sins, passed before them. An angel of justice read their crimes and their defense; the latter was not a brilliant one, but it was read before God, Who reads the heart, Who knows everything, the wickedness that comes from within and from without, Who is mercy and love personified. The pastor's hand trembled; he dared not stretch it out, he did not venture to pull a hair out of the sinner's head. And tears gushed from his eyes like a stream of mercy and love, the cooling waters of which extinguished the eternal fire of hell.

Just then the cock crowed.

"Father of all mercy, grant Thou to her the peace that I was unable to procure for her!"

"I have it now!" said the dead woman. "It was your hard words, your despair of mankind, your gloomy belief in God and His creation, which drove me to you. Learn to know mankind! Even in the wicked one lives a part of God—and this extinguishes and conquers the flame of hell!"

The pastor felt a kiss on his lips; a gleam of light surrounded him—God's bright sun shined into the room, and his wife, alive, sweet and full of love, awoke him from a dream which God had sent him!

The Dumb Book

In the high-road which led through a wood stood a solitary farm-house; the road, in fact, ran right through its yard. The sun was shining and all the windows were open; within the house people were very busy. In the yard, in an arbor formed by lilac bushes in full bloom, stood an open coffin; thither they had carried a dead man, who was to be buried that very forenoon. Nobody shed a tear over him; his face was covered over with a white cloth, under his head they had placed a large thick book, the leaves of which consisted of folded sheets of blotting-paper, and withered flowers lay between them; it was the herbarium which he had gathered in various places and was to be buried with him, according to his own wish. Every one of the flowers in it was connected with some chapter of his life.

"Who is the dead man?" we asked.

"The old student," was the reply. "They say that he was once an energetic young man, that he studied the dead languages, and sang and even composed many songs; then something had happened to him, and in consequence of this he gave himself up to drink, body and mind. When at last he had ruined his health, they brought him into the country, where someone paid for his board and residence. He was gentle as a child as long as the sullen mood did not come over him; but when it came he was fierce, became as strong as a giant, and ran about in the wood like a chased deer. But when we succeeded in bringing him home, and prevailed upon him to open the book with the dried-up plants in it, he would sometimes sit for whole days looking at this or that plant, while frequently the tears rolled over his cheeks. God knows what was in his mind; but he requested us to put the book into his coffin, and now he lies there. In a little while the lid will be placed upon the coffin, and he will have sweet rest in the grave!"

The cloth which covered his face was lifted up; the dead man's face expressed peace—a sunbeam fell upon it. A swallow flew with the swiftness of an arrow into the arbor, turning in its flight, and twittered over the dead man's head.

What a strange feeling it is—surely we all know it—to look through old letters of our young days; a different life rises up out of the past, as it were, with all its hopes and sorrows. How many of the people with whom in those days we used to be on intimate terms appear to us as if dead, and yet they are still alive—only we have not thought of them for such a long time, whom we imagined we should retain in our memories for ever, and share every joy and sorrow with them.

The withered oak leaf in the book here recalled the friend, the schoolfellow, who was to be his friend for life. He fixed the leaf to the student's cap in the green wood, when they vowed eternal friendship. Where does he dwell now? The leaf is kept, but the friendship does no longer exist. Here is a foreign hothouse plant, too tender for the gardens of the North. It is almost as if its leaves still smelled sweet! She gave it to him out of her own garden—a nobleman's daughter.

Here is a water-lily that he had plucked himself, and watered with salt tears—a lily of sweet water. And here is a nettle: what may its leaves tell us? What might he have thought when he plucked and kept it? Here is a little snowdrop out of the solitary wood; here is an evergreen from the flower-pot at the tavern; and here is a simple blade of grass.

The lilac bends its fresh fragrant flowers over the dead man's head; the swallow passes again—"twit, twit"; now the men come with hammer and nails, the lid is placed over the dead man, while his head rests on the dumb book—so long cherished, now closed for ever!

The Ugly Duckling

The country was looking beautiful. It was summer; the wheat was yellow, the oats were green, the hay stood in stacks on the green meadows, and the stork strutted about on his long red legs chattering Egyptian, for he had learned that language from his mother. All around the fields and meadows were large forests, and in the middle of these forests deep lakes. Yes, it was really glorious out in the country. In the sunshine one could see an old country seat surrounded by deep canals, and from the wall, right down to the water, there grew large burdock leaves, which were so high that little children could stand upright under the tallest. It was as wild there as in the thickest wood. A duck, who was hatching her young, sat on her nest here, but she got very tired of waiting for the young ones to come. She rarely had visitors, for the other ducks preferred swimming about in the canals to waddling up and sitting down under a burdock leaf to gossip with her.

A duck, who was hatching her young, sat on her nest here, but she got very tired of waiting for the young ones to come.

At last one egg cracked after another. "Chick, chick"; all the yolks were alive, and the little heads peeped out.

"Quack, quack!" said the duck; so they all hurried up as fast as they could, and looked about on all sides under the green leaves. Their mother let them look as much as they liked, because green is good for the eyes.

"How large the world is," said all the little ones; for, of course, they had much more room now than in the egg.

"Do you think this is the whole world?" said the mother; "why, that stretches far beyond the other side of the garden, right into the parson's field, but I have never been there yet. I suppose you are all here?" she continued, getting up. "No, you are not; the largest egg is still lying here. How long will this last? I'm getting tired of it!" And so saying she sat down again.

"Well, how are you getting on?" said an old duck, who had come to pay her a visit.

"This egg takes such a long time," answered the sitting duck; "it will not break. But just look at the others; are they not the daintiest ducklings that were ever seen? They all look like their father, the rascal—he doesn't come to pay me a visit."

"Let me see the egg that will not break," said the old duck. "Depend upon it, it is a turkey's egg. I was once deceived in the same way myself, and had a

At last one egg cracked after another. "Chick, chick"; all the yolks were alive, and the little heads peeped out.

lot of trouble and bother with the young ones, for they are afraid of the water. I couldn't get them into it; I quacked at them and I hacked at them, but it was of no use. Let me see the egg. Yes, that is a turkey's egg. Let it alone and rather teach the other little ones to swim."

"I'll just sit on it a little while longer," said the duck; "having sat so long now, I may as well sit a few days more."

"As you like," said the old duck, and went away.

At last the big egg broke. "Tweet, tweet," said the young one, creeping out. It was very big and ugly. The duck looked at it. "That's a mighty big duckling," said she; "none of the others look like that; could he be a young turkey-cock? Well, we shall soon get to know that; he will have to go into the water, if I have to push him in myself."

The next day the weather was gloriously fine; the sun shined down on all the green leaves, and the mother duck went down to the canal with her whole family. She sprang with a splash into the water, and as she went "Quack, quack!" one duckling after another jumped in. The water closed over their heads, but they soon came up again, and swam beautifully; their legs moved by themselves, and all were in the water. Even the ugly little gray one was swimming too.

"No, he is not a turkey," said the duck; "look how beautifully he moves its legs, and how upright he holds itself; he is my own child. And if you only look at him properly, he is really very pretty. Quack, quack! Come with me;

I will take you into society, and introduce you to the duck-yard; but mind you always keep near me, so that no one treads on you; and beware of the cat."

So they came into the duck-yard. There was a terrible noise inside, for there were two families who were fighting about the head of an eel; and after all the cat got it.

"You see, such is the way of the world," said the mother-duck, sharpening her beak, for she, too, wanted the eel's head. "Now, use your legs," said she; "try to hurry along, and bend your necks before the old duck there; she is the most distinguished of all here. She is of Spanish blood, that is why she is so fat; and you see she has a red rag round her leg. That is something extremely grand, and the greatest distinction a duck can attain; it is as much as to say that they don't want her to get lost, and that she may be recognized by man and beast. Hurry up! Don't turn your feet inwards; a well-educated duckling turns his feet outwards as much as possible, just like his father and mother. Look, like that! Now bend your neck and say 'Quack!'"

And they did as she told them; but the other ducks all around looked at them and said, quite loud: "Look there! Now we are to have that lot too; as if we were not enough already. And, fie! how ugly that one duckling is; we will not stand that." And one of the ducks immediately flew at him, and bit him in the neck.

"Leave him alone," said the mother; "he is doing no one any harm."

"Yes, but he is too big and strange-looking," said the duck who had bitten him; "and therefore he must be whacked."

"They are pretty children which the mother has," said the old duck with the rag round her leg; "they are all fine, except one, which has turned out badly. I wish she could hatch him over again."

"That cannot be, your highness," said the duckling's mother; "he is not handsome, but he has a very good heart, and swims as beautifully as any other; indeed, I may say, somewhat better. I think he will grow prettier and get to look a little smaller in time. He has lain too long in the egg, and therefore not received the right shape." And with this she scratched the little one's neck and smoothed his feathers. "Besides," she said, "he is a drake, and therefore it does not matter so much. I think he will become very strong and fight his way through the world."

"The other ducklings are very pretty," said the old duck; "pray make yourselves at home, and if you find an eel's head, you may bring it to me."

So now they felt at home. But the poor duckling who had been the last to leave his shell, and who was so ugly, was bitten, pushed, and made a fool of, and that by the hens as well as by the ducks. "He is too big," they all said, and the turkey-cock, who had come into the world with spurs, and therefore thought himself an emperor, puffed himself up like a ship in full sail, and bore down upon him, gobbling and getting quite red in the face. The poor duckling did not know where to stand or where to go; he was distressed at being so ugly and the jest of the whole duck-yard.

So passed the first day, and afterwards things grew worse and worse. The poor duckling was chased about by all; even his sisters were unkind to him, and kept on saying: "If only the cat would catch you, you hideous creature!" And his mother said, "Would that you were far away!" The ducks bit him, the hens beat him, and the girl who had to feed the poultry kicked him away with her foot.

Things grew worse and worse. The poor duckling was chased about by all.

So he ran and flew over the hedge, frightening away the little birds in the bushes. "That is because I am so ugly," thought the duckling, closing his eyes, but running on just the same. So he came to a great moor, where some wild ducks lived; here he lay the whole night, being tired and sorrowful.

Towards morning the wild ducks flew up and gazed at their new comrade.

"Pray, who are you?" they asked, and the duckling turned in all directions, and greeted them as well as he could.

"You are exceptionally ugly!" said the wild ducks; "but that does not matter to us as long as you do not marry into our family."

Poor thing! he was really not thinking of marrying, but only wanted permission to lie among the reeds and drink a little moor water. So he lay two whole days; then two wild geese, or rather ganders, came by; they had not long crept out of their shell, and that is why they were so bold.

"Listen, comrade," they said; "you are rather ugly but we like you very well; will you come with us and be a bird of passage? On another moor near this place there are some nice sweet wild geese, all females too, every one of whom can say 'Quack!' You would be in a fair way to make your fortune there, ugly as you are."

"Bang! bang!" went a gun, and the two wild ganders fell down dead among the reeds, and the water became red with their blood. "Bang! bang!" came again, and whole flocks of wild geese flew up out of the reeds. Once more came a shot. There was a great hunting party going on, and the huntsmen were lying all round the moor; some were even sitting up in the branches of the trees, which stretched far out over the reeds. The blue smoke dispersed itself into the thick trees and far out over the water, like clouds; the hounds came splashing across the moor, the reeds and the rushes bending in all directions. What a fright the poor duckling was in! He turned his head to put it under his wing, but at the same moment a terribly large dog stood quite close to him, his tongue hanging far out of his mouth, his eyes gleaming angrily, hideously. Craning forward straight at the duckling, he showed his sharp teeth, and—splash! splash! he was gone again, without touching him.

At the same moment a terribly large dog stood quite close to him.

"Oh, how thankful I am!" sighed the duckling; "I am so ugly that even the dog will not bite me."

And so he lay still while the shots whistled through the reeds, one report following another.

It was late in the day before all was quiet, but the poor little one did not dare to stir even then; he waited several hours more before he looked round, and then hurried away from the moor as fast as he could. He ran over fields and meadows, though there was such a storm raging that it was difficult for him to get along at all.

In the evening he reached a wretched little peasant's hut; it was in such bad repair that it did not know itself on which side to fall, and therefore remained standing. The wind whistled so round the duckling that he was obliged to sit down in order to withstand it, and it grew worse and worse. He then noticed that the door had fallen from one of its hinges, and hung so to one side that he could creep into the room through the gap, which he did.

Here lived a woman with her tom-cat and her hen. The tomcat, whom she called her little son, could put his back up and purr; he could even give out sparks, but that was only when he was stroked the wrong way. The hen had very small short legs and was therefore called "Chickling Short-legs"; she laid good eggs, and the woman loved her like her own child. The next morning they immediately noticed the strange duckling, and the tom-cat began to purr and the hen to cluck.

"What's the matter?" said the woman, looking round; but she could not see well, and took the duckling to be a fat duck who had lost her way. "That's indeed a rare catch," said she. "Now I can have duck's eggs. I hope it's not a drake. That we must find out."

And so the duckling was taken on trial for three weeks, but no eggs came.

The tom-cat was master in the house, and the hen was mistress, and they used always to say "We and the world," for they believed themselves to be the half, and by far the better half too. The duckling thought that it was possible to be of another opinion, but that the hen would not allow.

"Can you lay eggs?" she asked.

"No."

"Well, then you will have the goodness to be quiet."

And the tom-cat said, "Can you set your back up, purr and give out sparks?"

"No."

"Then you may have no opinion when reasonable people are speaking."

So the duckling sat in the corner and was in a bad humor; here the fresh air and the sunshine came in to him, and excited in him such a strong desire to swim on the water that he could not help telling the hen of it.

"What are you thinking of?" asked the latter. "You have nothing to do, and that is why you get these fancies. Either lay eggs or purr, and then they will pass away."

"But it is so nice to swim on the water," said the duckling; "so delightful to let it close over your head and to dive to the bottom."

"Well, that seems a fine pleasure," said the hen. "I think you must be mad. Ask the tom-cat—he is the wisest creature I know—whether he likes to swim on the water or to dive under. I won't speak of myself. Ask even our mistress, the old woman; there is no one in the world wiser than she. Do you think she has a longing to swim and to let the water close over her head?"

"You don't understand me," said the duckling.

"We don't understand you? Who then would be able to understand you? I don't suppose you pretend to be wiser than the tom-cat and the old woman—I won't speak of myself at all. Don't get silly things into your head, child, and be thankful for all the kindness that has been shown you. Have you not come into a warm room, and are you not in the society of those from whom you can learn something? But you are a fool, and it is disagreeable to have anything to do with you. Believe me, I wish you well. I tell you unpleasant things, and it is in this way that one's real friends may be known. Only learn to lay eggs or to purr and send out sparks."

"I think I shall go out into the wide world," said the duckling.

"Well, do so," said the hen.

So the duckling went; he swam upon the water, he dived down, but none of the animals took any notice of him, on account of his ugliness.

The autumn now came; the leaves in the wood turned yellow and brown; the wind caught them and made them dance about; and up in the air it was very cold. The clouds were heavy with hail and snow-flakes, and the raven sat on the hedge and croaked with cold; indeed, it made one shiver only to think of it. The poor duckling had by no means a good time. One evening—there was a glorious sunset—a flock of beautiful large birds came out of a thicket. The duckling had never seen such handsome ones; they were of dazzling whiteness, with long slender necks. They were swans; and uttering a peculiar cry they spread their long, splendid wings and flew away out of the cold region to warmer countries and open seas.

They rose so high, that a strange feeling came over the ugly young duckling. He turned round and round in the water like a wheel, stretched his neck high up in the air after them, and uttered such a loud and peculiar cry that he was quite frightened by it himself! Oh! he could not forget the beautiful happy birds, and when he could see them no longer he dived down to the bottom; on coming up again he was almost beside himself. He did not know what the birds were called, nor whither they were flying; yet he loved them as he had never loved any one before. He did not envy them at all. How could it occur to him to wish himself such loveliness as that? He would have been quite happy if only the ducks had suffered him to be among them—the poor, ugly creature.

The winter became cold, very cold. The duckling was obliged to swim about in the water to prevent it from freezing over entirely, but every night the opening in which he swam became smaller and smaller. It froze so hard that the ice cracked; the duckling was obliged to use his legs continually, so that the hole should not close up. At last he got tired, lay quite still, and froze fast in the ice.

The duckling was obliged to use his legs continually, so that the hole should not close up.

Early next morning a peasant came by, and seeing what had happened, went up, broke the ice in pieces with his wooden shoe, and carried the duckling home to his wife. There he revived.

The children wanted to play with him; but the duckling thought they wished to do him some harm, and in his terror jumped right into the milk-pail, so that the milk flew about the room. The farmer's wife clapped her hands at him, upon which he flew into the butter-vat, then down into the meal tub, and out again. What a sight he looked! The woman screamed and struck at him with the tongs, and the children, all laughing and screaming, knocked each other down in trying to catch him. It was a good thing for him that the door was open, and that he could slip out among the bushes into the freshly fallen snow. There he lay, quite worn out.

But it would be too sad to relate all the trouble and misery that the duckling had to endure during the severe winter. He was lying on the moor among the reeds when the sun began to shine warmly again. The larks were singing; it was beautiful spring.

Then once more the duckling was able to use his wings; they were much stronger, and carried him along more swiftly than before, and ere he was aware of it, he found himself in a large garden, where an elder-tree scented the air, and bent its long green branches down to the winding canal. Oh, what beauty, what vernal freshness was here! And out of the thicket came three splendid white swans; they ruffled their feathers and swam lightly on the water. The duckling knew the splendid creatures, and was seized with a strange sadness.

"I will fly to them, to those royal birds! And they will kill me, because I, who am so ugly, dare to come near them. Better to be killed by them than to be bitten by the ducks, beaten by the hens, kicked by the girl who minds the poultry-yard, and to suffer so much in winter." So he flew into the water and swam towards the beautiful swans. They perceived him, and shot down upon him with all their feathers up. "Only kill me," said the poor creature, bowing his head to the level of the water and awaiting his death. But what did he see in the clear water? He saw beneath him his own image, no longer an awkward dark gray bird, ugly and deformed, but a swan himself.

"Only kill me," said the poor creature, bowing his head to the level of the water and awaiting his death.

It matters little whether one has been born in a duck-yard so long as one has been hatched from a swan's egg.

He felt quite happy at having suffered so much trouble and care. Now only could he rightly value the good fortune that greeted him. And the large swans swam round him and stroked him with their beaks.

Some little children came into the garden and threw bread and corn into the water. The youngest one cried, "There is a new one"; and the other children also shouted with glee, "Yes, a new one has come," dancing about and clapping their hands. They ran to their father and mother, and bread and cake was thrown into the water, while every one said, "The new one is the finest; so young and so beautiful!" And the old swans bowed down before him.

Then he felt quite ashamed, and put his head under his wing; he really did not know what to do. He was all too happy, but not at all proud. He remembered how he had been persecuted and despised, and now he heard every one saying that he was the most beautiful of all beautiful birds. Even the elder-tree bowed down before him till its branches touched the water, and the sun shined warm and bright. Then he shook his feathers, stretched his slender neck, and from the bottom of his heart joyfully exclaimed, "I never even dreamed of such happiness when I was still the ugly duckling."

Even the elder-tree bowed down before him till its branches touched the water.

Under the Willow-Tree

The country round the little town of Kjöge, in Zealand, is very bare. It is true that the town lies by the sea-shore, which is always beautiful, but still it might be more beautiful there than it really is: all around are flat fields, and it is a very long way to the forest. Still, when one is quite at home in a place, one can always find some attraction in it, for which one afterwards longs, even when in the most charming spot in the world. And we must freely confess that it looked very pretty in summer at the extreme edge of the little town, where a few humble gardens skirt the rivulet which flows into the sea there; this was also the opinion of two children who lived next to each other and played here, making their way through the gooseberry bushes to get to each other.

In one garden stood an elder-tree, in the other an old willow, and it was especially under the latter that the children were very fond of playing; this they were allowed to do, although the willow stood near the rivulet and they might easily have fallen into the water. But the eye of God watches over the little ones—otherwise it would be a bad look-out for them. They were, however, very careful with regard to the water; in fact, the boy was so afraid of it that it was impossible in summer-time to get him to go into the sea, in which the other children were very fond of splashing about. Accordingly, he was constantly being teased and laughed at, and had to bear it patiently. Once Johanna, the little girl who lived next door, dreamed that she was sailing in a boat and that Kanut waded out to her, so that the water first came up to his neck, then closed over his head, and that at last he disappeared altogether. From the moment when little Kanut heard of this dream, he would no longer bear the jeers of the other boys; for he was not afraid of going into the water now. Had not Johanna dreamed it? It is true that he never did it, but from that time the dream was his pride.

Their parents, who were poor people, often came together, and Kanut and Johanna played in the gardens and on the high road, where, beside the ditch stood a row of willow-trees, looking, it is true, far from beautiful with their polled tops, but then they were not there for ornament, but for use. The old willow in the garden was much finer, and under that the two children usually sat. In the little town itself there is a large market-place, and at the time of the annual fair this was covered with whole streets of tents and booths full of silk ribbons, boots, and all that one could wish for. There was a terrible crowd; and as it generally rained too, one could easily distinguish the odor of the peasants' frieze jackets, mingled, however, with the more agreeable fragrance of honey-cakes and gingerbread, of which there was a booth full. The best of it all was that the man who sold the cakes always lived during fair-time with little Kanut's parents, and there was generally a present of a piece of gingerbread now and then, of which Johanna, of course, got her share. But it was still more charming that the gingerbread dealer could tell tales about every possible thing, even about his gingerbread; indeed, one evening he told a story about it which made such a deep impression upon the children that they never forgot it, and therefore it is perhaps best that we should hear it too, especially as it is only a short one.

"On the counter," he said, "lay two cakes of gingerbread, one in the shape of a man with a hat, the other in the shape of a young woman without a hat; both their faces were on the side that was turned uppermost, and they were to be looked at only on that side, and not on the other, for people should never be looked at from the wrong side. The man carried on his left side a bitter almond—that was his heart; the maiden, on the other hand, was all honey-cake. They both lay as samples on the counter, and lay there so long, that at last they fell in love with each other; but neither told the other, as they ought to have done, if they had wanted anything to come of it.

" 'He is a man—he ought to speak first,' she thought, but would have been quite satisfied, if she had only known that her love was returned. His ideas were far more extravagant, as is always the case with men. He dreamed that he was a real street boy, that he possessed four pennies, and that he bought the young woman and ate her up.

"And so they lay for days and weeks upon the counter and got dry, the thoughts of the young woman growing more and more tender and womanly.

" 'It is enough for me that I have lain on the same counter with him,' she thought, and—crack!—she broke right in two.

" 'If she had only known of my love, she would have held together a little longer,' thought he.

"That is the story, and here they are both," said the cake-seller. "They are remarkable for their history and for their silent love, which never led to anything. You may have them!" Saying which he gave Johanna the man, who was whole, and Kanut received the broken maiden; but the children were so affected by the story that they did not have the heart to eat the pair of lovers.

On the following day they took them into the churchyard, and sat down by the church wall, which is covered, summer and winter, with the most luxuriant ivy, as with a rich carpet. Here they stood the two gingerbread cakes between the green creepers in the sunshine, while they told a group of other children the story of the silent love which was so silly; that is to say, the love was silly, for of course the story was beautiful—on that they were all agreed. But when they looked at the gingerbread pair again, a big boy, purely out of mischief, had eaten up the broken maiden. The children wept about it, and afterwards—probably in order that the poor lover should not remain in the world alone—they ate him up too; but they never forgot the story.

The two children were always together by the elder-tree and under the willow, and the little girl sang the most beautiful songs with a voice as clear as a bell; Kanut, on the contrary, had not a note in him, but he knew the words, and that is at least something. The people of Kjöge, even to the wife of the fancy goods dealer, stood still and listened when Johanna sang. "What a very sweet voice the little girl has!" they would say.

Those were glorious days, but they did not last for ever. The neighbors became separated. The little girl's mother was dead, and her father intended to marry again—in the capital, too, where he had been promised a living somewhere as messenger, which post was said to be a very lucrative one. The neighbors parted in tears; that is to say, the children wept, but their parents promised to write to one another at least once a year.

Kanut was apprenticed to a shoemaker, for such a big boy could not be allowed to walk about idle any longer; and he was also confirmed.

Oh! how he would have liked to have been in Copenhagen with little Johanna on that joyous day, but he remained in Kjöge, and had never been to Copenhagen, although the capital is only five miles distant from the little town; but when the sky was clear Kanut had seen the towers of the city far away across the sea, and on his confirmation day he distinctly saw the golden cross on the church of the Virgin glittering in the sun.

How often his thoughts were with Johanna! Did she ever think of him? he wondered. Yes. Towards Christmas a letter came from her father to Kanut's parents, saying that they were getting on very well in Copenhagen, and that Johanna might look forward to great fortune on account of her fine voice; she had been engaged to sing at the theater, and was already earning a little money by that, out of which she sent her dear neighbors in Kjöge a whole dollar for a merry Christmas Eve; she had herself added in a postscript that they were to drink to her health, and in the same postscript was also written: "Kind regards to Kanut."

The whole family wept, and yet all this was so pleasant; but they wept for joy. Johanna had occupied Kanut's thoughts every day, and now he was convinced that she also thought of him, and the nearer the time came when he should have finished his apprenticeship, the more clearly did it appear to him that he loved Johanna dearly and that she must be his wife. At these thoughts a smile would come over his face and he would draw the thread twice as fast and press his foot against the knee-strap; he ran the awl deep into his finger, but that was nothing. He certainly did not intend to play the dumb lover, as the two gingerbread cakes had done; that story should be a good lesson for him.

Now he was a journeyman and his knapsack was packed; at length, for the first time in his life, he was to go to Copenhagen, where he already had a master. How surprised and pleased Johanna would be! She was now seventeen years old—he nineteen.

He wanted to buy a gold ring for her before leaving Kjöge, but it occurred to him that much finer things of that kind could be bought in Copenhagen. So he took leave of his parents, and on a rainy day late in autumn he set out on foot from his native town; the leaves were falling from the trees, and he arrived in the great city at his new master's, soaked through. He intended to pay his visit to Johanna's father on the following Sunday. The new journeyman's clothes were brought out and the new hat from Kjöge was put on; Kanut looked very well in it, having till that time always worn a cap. He found the house that he was looking for, and went up so many steps that it made him quite giddy to see how the people were piled on top of each other in the great city.

Everything in the room had a prosperous look, and Johanna's father received him in a very friendly manner; to the wife he was of course a stranger, but she shook hands with him, and gave him some coffee.

"Johanna will be pleased to see you," said the father; "you have indeed grown a very nice young man. Now you shall see her; she is a girl who causes me much pleasure, and with God's help will do so still more. She has her own room, and pays us for it." The father himself knocked politely at the door, as if he were a stranger, and then they went in.

And how pretty everything was in there! Such a little room was certainly not to be found in all Kjöge; the queen herself could not have a more charming one. There were carpets, there were window-curtains right down to the ground, and even a velvet chair, and all around flowers and pictures, and a mirror into which there was almost danger of stepping, for it was as large as a door. Kanut saw all this at a glance, and yet he saw only Johanna; she was a grown-up girl, and quite different from what Kanut had imagined her, but much more beautiful. In all Kjöge there was not a single maiden like her. How elegant she was, and how very strangely she looked at Kanut, but only for a moment, for the next she rushed towards him, as though she were about to kiss him! She certainly did not do so, but she was very near it. Yes, she certainly rejoiced at the sight of her old playmate. There were actually tears in her eyes, and then she had much to ask and much to talk about, from Kanut's parents down to the elder-tree and the willow, which she called elder-mother and willow-father, as if they had been people too; there was indeed no reason why they should not pass off as such, as well as the gingerbread cakes. Of these she also spoke, and of their silent love, as they lay upon the counter and broke in two, and at that she laughed quite heartily; but the blood mounted up into Kanut's cheeks and his heart beat quicker than ever. No, she was not proud at all. It was through her too—he saw that very well—that her parents invited him to spend the whole evening there; she poured out the tea and gave him a cup herself. Presently she took a book and read aloud, and it seemed to Kanut that the piece that she read was all about his love, so well did it fit in with his thoughts; then she sang a simple song, but it came from her lips like a story, and her own heart seemed to be overflowing with it. Yes, she was certainly fond of Kanut. The tears rolled down his cheeks—he could not help it, and he was unable to utter a single word; he appeared to himself as if he were struck dumb, and yet she pressed his hand and said: "You have a good heart, Kanut—always remain as you are."

That was an evening without its like; to sleep after it was impossible—neither did Kanut do so.

At parting, Johanna's father had said: "Now, I hope you will not forget us altogether. You will not allow the whole winter to pass before coming to see us?" So he could very well go again on the following Sunday, and he intended to do so. But every evening, after working hours—and they worked by candle-light too—Kanut went into the town; he walked through the street in which Johanna lived, and looked up at her windows, which were almost always lit up. Once he plainly saw the shadow of her face on the curtain—that was an eventful night. His master's wife did not like his roaming about every evening, as she called it, and she shook her head; but the master smiled, saying, "He is a young man."

"We shall see each other on Sunday, and I will tell her how she fills my heart and thoughts, and that she must be my little wife; it is true I am only a poor journeyman shoemaker, but I may become a master. I will work and strive—yes, I will tell her so. Nothing comes of silent love; that I learned from the gingerbread cakes." So thought Kanut.

Sunday came, and Kanut came, but how unfortunate it was! they were obliged to tell him that they were all invited out for that evening. Johanna pressed his hand and asked, "Have you been to the theater? You must go there. I sing on Wednesday, and if you can get out on that day, I will send you a ticket. My father knows where your master lives."

How kind it was of her! And on Wednesday afternoon he received a sealed envelope, without a word inside it, except the ticket; and in the evening Kanut went to the theater for the first time in his life. And what did he see? Johanna, so beautiful and charming, married, it is true, to a strange man, but that was all play-acting—something that they pretended; that Kanut knew, otherwise she would not have had the heart to send him a ticket so that he might see it; and all the people clapped their hands and shouted, and Kanut also shouted "Hurrah!"

Even the King smiled at Johanna, as if he were pleased with her. Heavens! how small Kanut felt; but he loved her very tenderly, and she was also fond of him—that he knew; but the man must say the first word—even the gingerbread maiden had been of that opinion. Indeed there was a great deal in that story.

As soon as Sunday came he went again, feeling as though he were going to take the sacrament; Johanna was alone, and received him. So it could not have chanced more luckily.

"I am glad that you have come," she said. "I was already thinking of sending my father to you, but I had an idea that you would come to-night; for I must tell you that I am going to France on Friday. I must, if I wish to do anything in the future."

But it seemed to Kanut as if the room were turning round and round; he felt as though his heart was going to burst. It is true no tears came into his eyes, but one could plainly see how grieved he was. "Dear honest, faithful soul!" she said; and with that Kanut's tongue was loosed, and he told her how dear she was to him, and that she must be his wife. While he uttered these words, he saw Johanna change color and turn pale; she let go his hand and replied earnestly and sadly: "Do not make yourself and me unhappy, Kanut. I will always be a kind sister to you, upon whom you can rely; but no more than that." And she passed her soft hand over his hot brow. "God gives us strength to bear much, if we but will it."

At that moment her step-mother entered the room.

"Kanut is quite beside himself at my going away," said Johanna. "Be a man"; and with that she laid her hand upon his shoulder. One would have thought that they had spoken only of the journey and of nothing else. "You are a child," she continued; "but now you must be good and reasonable, as under the willow-tree, when we were both children."

But it seemed to Kanut as though the world were out of joint; his thoughts were like a loose thread, fluttering to and fro in the wind. He stayed, not knowing whether they had asked him to stay; but they were kind and good, and Johanna poured him out some tea, and sang. The songs did not have the old ring, but were still so infinitely beautiful, almost heartbreaking. At last Kanut went; he did not offer her his hand, but she took it, saying, "I suppose you will give your sister your hand at parting, my old playmate." She smiled through the tears which were running down her cheeks, and repeated the word "Brother." Yes, that was indeed a beautiful consolation. Such was their parting.

She sailed to France; Kanut walked about in the dirty streets of Copenhagen. His shopmates asked him why he went about looking so miserable, and told him that he, a young fellow, ought to go out and enjoy himself with them.

They went together to a dancing saloon; there were many pretty girls, but none at all like Johanna, and here, where he had thought to forget her, she was most of all in his thoughts. "God gives us strength to bear much, if we but will it," she had said, and a kind of devotion came over him. He folded his hands; the violins struck up, and the girls danced around in a circle. Suddenly he started; it seemed to him as if he were in a place where he ought not to have taken Johanna, for after all she was with him there in his heart. So he went out, walked about the streets, and went past the house where she had lived; all was dark there—it was dark, empty, and lonesome everywhere. The world went its way, and Kanut went his.

Winter came and the waters froze over; it seemed as if everything were preparing itself for burial.

But when spring returned, and the first steamer went out, a longing seized Kanut to go far out into the world, but not to France.

He buckled on his knapsack and wandered far into Germany, from town to town, knowing no rest neither peace; only when he reached the beautiful old town of Nüremberg did he seem to become master again of his feet. He controlled himself sufficiently to stay there.

Nüremberg is a wonderful old town, looking as though it were cut out of an old picture-book. The streets run just as they themselves please, and the houses do not care about standing evenly in rows. Bow-windows and small turrets, scroll-work and statues project over the pavement, and high up from the roofs, gutters, in the form of dragons and long-legged dogs, run out into the middle of the street. Here on the market-place stood Kanut with his knapsack on his back; he was standing near one of the old fountains with the beautiful biblical and historical figures which are to be seen between the sparkling jets of water. A pretty servant-maid was just getting some water, and gave Kanut a draft; having a handful of roses, she also gave him one, and this seemed to him to be a good omen.

From the neighboring church the sound of the organ came out towards him; it sounded so homelike, that it seemed to come from the church at Kjöge, and he went into the great cathedral. The sun shined in between the tall slender pillars through the stained-glass windows; Kanut's thoughts were filled with devotion, and a peaceful calm came over his soul.

He sought out a good master in Nüremberg, and stayed with him and learned the German language.

The old ditches round the town have been turned into small kitchen-gardens, but the high walls with their heavy towers are still standing. The ropemaker twists his rope on the wooden galleries along the inner side of the city wall, and here all around the elder grows up out of holes and crevices. It stretches its branches over the small lowly houses lying beneath, and in one of these lived the master with whom Kanut worked; the elder-tree hung its branches over the little attic window at which the young man sat.

Here he passed a summer and a winter; but when spring came it was no longer to be borne. The elder blossomed, and its fragrance reminded him so of home that it seemed as if he were again in the gardens of Kjöge: so Kanut left his master for another who lived farther in the town, where no elder-tree grew.

His workshop was near an old walled bridge, opposite an ever-splashing low water-mill; the rushing stream flowed past, hemmed in by houses which were all provided with old crumbling balconies. It looked as if the houses wanted to shake them all down into the water. Here no elder grew; here there was not even a flower-pot with a little green. But just opposite the workshop there stood a large old willow, clinging, as it were, to the house, so as not to be torn away by the stream, and stretching its boughs out over the water, like the willow-tree in the garden at Kjöge.

Yes, he had indeed removed from elder-tree mother to willow father; the tree here, especially on moonlight evenings, had something about it that went to his heart; it was, however, by no means the moonlight, but the old tree itself.

Anyhow, he could not bear it. Why not? Ask the willow-tree, ask the blossoming elder. And so he bade his Nüremberg master good-bye and went farther.

He never spoke to any one of Johanna, hiding his grief within him, and laying a deep significance upon the story of the two gingerbread cakes. Now he understood why the little man had had a bitter almond on his left side, for he himself had also a bitter taste there; and Johanna, who had always been so kind and friendly, she was honey-cake all over. It seemed as though the strap of his knapsack was so tight that he could hardly breathe; he loosened it, but it was no better than before. He saw only half the world around him; the other half he carried within him. That was how the matter stood.

It was only when he caught sight of the high mountains that his heart became lighter. Tears came into his eyes, and his thoughts turned towards the things about him.

The Alps seemed to him to be the folded wings of the earth; what if they should unfold themselves, these great pinions with their variegated pictures of dark forests, rushing torrents, clouds and masses of snow? On the last day the earth will lift up its great wings, soar up to Heaven, and burst like a soap-bubble in the light that streams from the Throne. "Oh! would that it were the last day!" sighed Kanut.

Silently he wandered through the land that seemed to him like a grass-grown orchard. Pretty young lacemakers nodded to him from the wooden balconies of the houses, the mountain-tops glowed in the red sunset, and when he saw the green lakes, overshadowed by the dark trees, he thought of the coast in the bay of Kjöge, and his heart was filled with sadness, but not with pain.

And farther on he saw the Rhine rolling along like a great wave, dashing itself into foam, and, with the rainbow fluttering overhead like a loose ribbon, transforming itself into snow-white masses of clouds; it seemed to him as though this was the place where the clouds were made, and he thought of the water-mill at Kjöge, where the waters rush and foam.

He would gladly have remained here in the quiet town on the Rhine, but there were far too many elder and willow trees. He therefore proceeded farther, across the great lofty mountains, through the clefts in the precipices, and along paths which hung upon the sides of the rocks like swallows' nests. The waters rushed along far beneath him, and the clouds lay at his feet; he marched along in the warm summer sun, over thistles, alpine roses and snow, saying farewell to the lands of the North, and entering the region of blossoming chestnut-trees, vineyards, and fields of maize. The mountains formed a wall between him and all his recollections; and this was as it should be.

Before him lay a great magnificent city which they called Milan, and here he found a German master, who gave him employment; they were an old, pious couple in whose shop he worked, and they grew very fond of the quiet young journeyman, who spoke little, but worked the more, and who lived in such a pious and Christian way. It also seemed to him as though Heaven had taken the heavy burden from his heart.

His greatest pleasure was to occasionally ascend the mighty marble cathedral which seemed to him to be built of snow from his home, and shaped into images, tapering spires, and open halls adorned in many colors; from every corner, every spire and every niche the white statues smiled down upon him. Above him was the blue sky, beneath him lay the city and the far-stretching green plains of Lombardy, and towards the north were the high mountains with their eternal snows. At such moments he would think of the church at Kjöge, with its red ivy-clad walls, but he did not wish himself away; here, behind the mountains, he longed to be buried.

He had lived in Milan a year, and three years had passed since he had left home, when one day his master took him into the town, not to the circus to see the riding, but to the grand opera, and it was a building, too, worth seeing. The finest silken curtains hung down from seven balconies, and from the floor to the dizzy heights of the roof sat the grandest ladies with bouquets in their hands, as if they were going to a ball; the gentlemen were all in full dress, and many of them adorned with gold and silver. It was as light as in the brightest sunshine; the music was beautiful, and everything was much grander than in the theater at Copenhagen, although Johanna was there. But surely it was magic! The curtain went up, and here she was too! Here was Johanna, all dressed in gold and silk, with a golden crown on her head. She sang as only an angel can sing, coming down to the footlights as far as she could.

She smiled as only Johanna could smile, and looked straight at Kanut.

The poor fellow seized his master's hand and shouted "Johanna"; but no one else heard him, the music drowning everything. His master nodded, saying, "Yes, her name is Johanna"; and with that he took out a printed paper and showed Kanut her name, written out at length.

No, it was not a dream. Every one applauded and threw flowers and wreaths to her, and every time that she went off, she was called back; she was continually going off and coming on.

In the street the people crowded round her carriage and drew it along; Kanut was among the foremost and shouted the most lustily. When they had reached her house, which was all beautifully illuminated, he stood at the carriage-door, which sprang open, and Johanna got out. The light fell upon her sweet face, and she, though deeply moved, smilingly returned her thanks in a kind, friendly way. Kanut looked her straight in the face, and she looked full into his, but she did not know him. A man, on whose breast sparkled a star, gave her his arm—they were betrothed, people said.

Then Kanut went home and packed his knapsack; he felt that he must get back to his native place, to the elder and the willow-tree. Under that dear old willow-tree!—One can run over a whole lifetime in an hour.

The old couple begged him to stay, but no words could keep him back. It was all in vain that they reminded him of the coming winter, and told him that snow had already fallen on the mountains; he would be able, he said, to get along, with his knapsack on his back and supported by his staff, in the track of the slow rolling wagons, for which a way would have to be made.

He marched along towards the mountains, and crossing them descended into the valley; though wearied, he saw neither village nor house, and continued his march northwards. The stars gleamed overhead, his knees gave way, and his head became dizzy; down in the valley stars shined forth too, and it seemed as if the sky were also beneath him. He felt ill; the stars below became more numerous, and grew brighter and brighter, moving to and fro. It was a little town in which lights were flickering, and when he comprehended this he exerted his remaining strength and reached a miserable inn.

He remained there for the night and for the whole of the following day, for his body required rest and nourishment; it was thawing, and rain was falling in the valley. But early on the next morning a minstrel came into the village playing an air from Kanut's home, and then it was impossible for him to tarry any longer. He continued his journey towards the north, marching for days and days with such haste as if he were anxious to get home before all were dead there; but to no one did he speak of his longing; no one would have believed in the sorrow of his heart, the deepest sorrow that can exist. Such grief is not for the world, it is not entertaining—not even for friends; and he was a stranger in the strange lands through which he was passing to his home in the north.

It was evening; he was walking along the public high-road. The frost was beginning to make itself felt, and the country was becoming more and more flat, with more fields and meadows. By the road stood a large willow-tree; everything looked so very home-like that he sat down under it. He felt very tired, his head began to nod, and his eyes closed in slumber, but still he knew that the willow-tree stretched its hanging branches out over him; the tree seemed to him to be an old mighty man. It seemed to be old willow-father himself, who took him up in his arms, and carried him, his tired son, back to the old homeland, to the open bleak shore of Kjöge, to the garden of his childhood's days. It was indeed the willow-tree itself, from Kjöge, which had wandered out in the world to seek him; now it had found him, and had led him back to the little garden by the brook, and here stood Johanna in her splendor, as he had last seen her, and crying out "Welcome" to him.

Before him stood two peculiar forms, although they seemed much more human than when he had seen them in his childhood, for they too had altered; they were the two gingerbread cakes, the man and the woman, turning their right side towards him and looking very well.

"Many thanks," said they to Kanut. "You have loosened our tongues to freely express our thoughts, otherwise nothing would come of them, and now something has come of them: we are engaged."

Then they went hand in hand through the streets of Kjöge and looked very respectable even on their wrong side—there was no fault to be found with them. They walked straight towards the church, Kanut and Johanna following; the latter also went hand in hand, and the church stood there just as ever, with its red walls, clad with green ivy. Both the great doors of the church flew open, the organ pealed forth, and they walked up the broad aisle.

"Our master first," said the gingerbread bridal pair, making way for Kanut and Johanna, who knelt down at the altar; she bent her head over his face and icy-cold tears fell from her eyes. It was the ice round her heart melting by his strong love; the tears fell upon his burning cheeks and—awoke him, and he found himself sitting under the old willow-tree, in a strange land, on a cold wintry evening. From the clouds fell icy hail and beat upon his face.

"That was the most beautiful hour of my life," said he, "and it was—a dream. Oh God! let me dream again!" He closed his eyes once more; he slept and dreamed.

Towards morning snow fell. The wind blew it in drifts over him, but he slept on. The villagers going to church found a working lad sitting by the roadside; he was dead, frozen to death—under the willow-tree.

Ib and Christine

Near the clear stream called the Gudenau, in North Jutland, in the forest which extends from its banks far into the country, there rises a high ridge of land stretching like a wall through the wood. To the west of this stands a farm-house, surrounded by some poor arable land; the sandy soil may be seen through the spare rye and ears of barley that grow there. Some years ago some people lived here who cultivated the fields, and kept, moreover, three sheep, a pig, and two oxen; in fact, they supported themselves very well, and had enough to live on, if one takes life as it comes. Indeed, they might even have managed to keep two horses, but, like the other peasants of the neighborhood, they said: "A horse eats its head off"—that is to say, it eats as much as it earns. Jeppe Jänsens cultivated his fields in summer; in winter he made wooden shoes, and then he had an assistant, a journeyman who, like him, knew how to make the shoes strong, though light and "fashionable." They cut out shoes and spoons, and that brought in money, so it would have been unfair to the Jeppe Jänsens to call them poor people.

Little Ib, a boy seven years old, the only child in the house, would sit by and look at the men at work, whittling away at a stick, and occasionally cutting his fingers. But one day Ib had succeeded so well with two bits of wood that they looked like little wooden shoes, and these he intended to give to little Christine. And who was little Christine?

She was the boatman's little daughter, as dainty and delicate as a nobleman's child; if she had been dressed as such, no one would have believed that she lived in the hut on the neighboring heath. There dwelt her father, who was a widower, and earned his living by carrying firewood in his large boat from the forest to the neighboring estate of Silkeborg, with its fine eel-fisheries and eel-weir, and sometimes even as far as the distant hamlet of Randers. He had no one who could have taken care of Christine; therefore the little girl was almost always in the boat with him, or in the wood amongst the ferns and blackberry bushes. Occasionally, when he went to the little town, he would take Christine, who was a year younger than Ib, across the heath to Jeppe Jänsens'.

Ib and Christine agreed very well in everything; they shared each other's bread and blackberries when they were hungry, and they dug up the earth together, running, creeping and playing about everywhere. One day they even ventured quite alone up the high ridge and a long way into the wood; once they found a few snipe's eggs there, and that was a great event.

Ib had never yet been on the heath where Christine's father lived, nor had he been on the river. But at last he was to go; Christine's father had invited him, and on the evening before the excursion he followed the boatman across the heath to his house.

Early the next morning both the children were sitting high up on the pile of firewood in the boat, eating bread and blackberries, while Christine's father and his assistant sent the boat along by means of poles. They had the current with them, and they glided swiftly along the stream and across the lakes which it forms. The latter often seemed entirely shut in by woods, reeds and water-plants, but still always afforded a thoroughfare, even though the old trees bent-down over the water, and the oaks stretched forward their peeled boughs, looking as if they had turned up their sleeves to show their knotty, naked arms. Old alders, which had been washed away from the banks by the current, clung fast by their roots to the bed of the river, and looked like little wooded islands; while the water-lilies rocked themselves on the stream. It was a glorious journey, and at last they reached the great eel-weir, with the water rushing through the sluices. It was too beautiful, thought Ib and Christine.

In those days there was no factory there, nor any town: only the great old farmyard was to be seen, with its scanty fields and its few servants and a small number of cattle; and the rush of the water through the weir and the cries of the wild ducks were the only life stirring at Silkeborg. After the firewood had been unloaded, Christine's father bought a bundle of eels and a slaughtered sucking-pig, all were put into a basket and placed in the back of the boat. Then they went back again up the stream, but the wind was in their favor, and when they had hoisted the sails, it was as good as if they were being towed by two horses.

When they reached a point on the river near which the boatman's assistant lived, not far from the bank, the boat was made fast, and both men landed, after impressing upon the children to remain quiet. But the children did not obey—at least only for a very short time. They wanted to peep into the basket in which the eels and the sucking-pig lay. They must needs take the pig out, hold it in their hands, and feel and touch it; and as they both wanted to do this at the same time, they happened to let it fall into the water, and away floated the pig with the stream. Here was a terrible calamity!

Ib sprang ashore and ran a little distance away from the boat, and Christine sprang after him, crying, "Take me with you!" In a few moments they were deep in the bushes, and could no longer see either the boat or the bank; they ran on a little farther, and then Christine fell down and began to cry. But Ib picked her up again.

"Follow me," he said. "There's the house over there."

But the house was not over there. They wandered farther and farther, over the dry rustling last year's leaves, over fallen branches that cracked under their little feet. Soon they heard a loud piercing cry. They stood still and listened, and then the cry of an eagle echoed through the wood. It was a horrible scream, and it frightened them; but before them, there in the wood, grew the finest blackberries in immense numbers. This was too inviting for them to do otherwise than stop, so they stayed and ate blackberries till they had black mouths and black cheeks. Again they heard the cry that had startled them before.

"We shall get into trouble about the pig," said Christine. "Come, let us go home," said Ib; "it is here in the wood." And they went on. They came to a road, but it did not lead them home, and as it was growing dark they got frightened. The wonderful stillness that reigned all around was broken by the ugly cries of the horned owl and other birds. At last they both lost themselves in some bushes. Christine cried, and Ib cried, and when they had both cried some time they lay down on the dry leaves and fell asleep.

The sun was high in the heavens when the two children awoke. They felt frozen, but near their bed, on the hill, the sun shined through the trees, and there they would go to warm themselves; thence too, thought Ib, they would be able to see his parents' house. But they were far from the house, in quite another part of the wood. They climbed up the hill, and found themselves on a slope by a clear transparent lake; the fish were near the surface in great numbers illumined by the sun's rays. The sight of all this was as unexpected as it was sudden. Close beside them grew a nut-bush full of the finest hazel-nuts; these they picked, cracked them, and ate the nice fresh kernels, which had only just been formed. But there was yet another surprise, another fright, in store for them. Out of the bushes came a tall old woman with jet black shining hair, and the whites of her eyes shined like those of a Moor. On her back she carried a bundle and in her hand was a knotted stick: she was a gypsy. The children did not understand at first what she said. She took three large nuts out of her pocket and told them that these contained the finest and most beautiful things: they were wishing-nuts.

Ib looked at her, and as she spoke so friendly, he summoned up courage and asked her whether she would give him the nuts. The woman gave them to him, and picked herself some more, a whole pocketful, from the nut-bush.

Ib and Christine stared at the three wishing-nuts with wondering eyes.

"Can there be a cart with two horses in this nut? " asked Ib.

"Yes, there is a golden carriage and golden horses," answered the woman.

"Then give me the nut," said Christine; and Ib gave it to her, while the strange woman tied it in her neckerchief for her.

"Can there be a pretty little neckerchief in this nut, like the one Christine has round her neck?" asked Ib.

"There are neckerchiefs in it," said the woman. "There are fine dresses, stockings, a hat, and a veil."

"Then I want that one too," said Christine; and Ib gave her the second nut too. The third was a little black thing.

"You must keep that," said Christine, "and it is a pretty one too."

"What is in it?" asked Ib.

"The best of all things for you," replied the gypsy woman. And Ib held the nut very tight. The woman promised to lead the children to the right path, so that they could find their way home; and now they went on, certainly in quite another direction to that which they should have taken, but that is no reason why the old woman should be suspected of having wished to steal the children.

In the wild paths through the woods they met the forest ranger, who knew Ib, and with his help Ib and Christine got home, where there had been great anxiety about them. They were pardoned and forgiven, although they had indeed both deserved to "get into trouble"—first, for having let the pig fall into the water; and secondly, for having run away.

Christine was taken back to her father on the heath, and Ib remained in the farmhouse on the edge of the wood near the great ridge.

The first thing he did in the evening was to take out of his pocket the little black nut that contained the "best of all things." Placing it carefully between the door and the door-post, he closed the former upon it; the nut cracked right enough, but there was not much kernel to be seen. It looked as if it were filled with snuff or rich black earth; it was a bad one, or worm-eaten, as people call it.

"Yes, I thought as much," said Ib. "How could there be room in the little nut for the best of all? Christine will get just as little out of her two nuts—neither fine clothes nor a golden carriage."

Winter came on, and the new year began; indeed, several years went by. At last Ib was to be confirmed, and therefore he used to go over to the clergyman's in the village to be taught during a whole winter. About this time the boatman one day visited Ib's parents, and told them that Christine was going into service, and that it was really a piece of luck for her to fall into such hands and to get such a good place with such nice people; for, only fancy, she was going to the rich innkeeper's at Herning, far in the west, many miles from Ib. There she was to assist the hostess in the housekeeping, and afterwards, if she took to it, and was confirmed there, the worthy couple would adopt her as their daughter.

So Ib and Christine took leave of one another—"the engaged couple," people called them; and at parting she showed him that she still had the two nuts which he had given her during their adventure in the wood, and she also told him that she kept in a drawer the little wooden shoes which he had carved and given to her when a boy. With this they parted.

Ib was confirmed. But he remained in his mother's house, for he had become a clever maker of wooden shoes; in summer he looked after the field, for which his mother no longer kept a man. He did it all alone too, for his father had died long ago.

Only very rarely, and mostly through a postillion or an eel-fisher, did any news come from Christine. But she was getting on very well at the rich innkeeper's, and after she had been confirmed she wrote her father a letter in which she sent her compliments to Ib and his mother. In the letter she also spoke of some new linen and a fine dress that had been given her by her employers. All this was certainly good news.

One day in the following spring there was a knock at the door of Ib's mother, and there stood the boatman and Christine. She had come over to spend the day; a carriage had to go from the inn at Herning to the next village, and she had taken the opportunity to go and see her friends once more. She was as handsome as a grand lady, and had fine clothes on, which had been well made and expressly for her. She stood there in all her finery, and Ib was in his everyday clothes. He could not bring a word out; he certainly caught her hand and held it in his own, and was heartily glad; but he could not get his tongue to move. Christine, however, could, and went on talking and talking, and kissed Ib right on the lips without more ado.

"Did you know me again at once, Ib?" she said; but even when they were afterwards quite alone, and he still stood there holding her hand, he could only say: "You have become quite a grand lady, and I look so rough. How often I have thought of you, Christine, and of the old times!"

Arm-in-arm they sauntered up the great ridge and looked out across the stream towards the heath and the great hills covered with flowers. Although Ib said nothing, yet by the time they parted it had become clear to him that Christine must be his wife. Had they not been called the "engaged couple" from their childhood? It seemed to him that they were really betrothed, even though neither of them had ever said a word on the matter.

They could only stay together a few hours longer, for Christine had to go back to the next village, whence the carriage was to start early next morning for Herning. Her father and Ib accompanied her as far as the village. It was a fine moonlight night, and when they reached their journey's end, and Ib was holding Christine's hand in his own, he could not let it go. His eyes sparkled, but the words fell slowly from his lips; still, they came from the depths of his heart, and he said, "If you have not become too fine, Christine, and can make up your mind to live in my mother's house as my wife, then we shall get married some day; but we can wait a little while yet."

"Yes, let us leave it like that for a time, Ib," she said, as she pressed his hand, and he kissed her on the lips.

"I trust you, Ib," said Christine, "and I believe that I love you. But I will sleep upon it."

With that they parted. On the way back Ib told the boatman that he and Christine were as good as engaged, and the boatman said that it was what he had always foreseen; he went home with Ib that night and stayed till the morning. Nothing more was said of the engagement.

A year passed, in the course of which two letters were exchanged between Ib and Christine. "True till death" was written at the bottom.

One day the boatman came in to Ib to bring him a greeting from Christine. What else he had to say came out rather slowly, but it was to the effect that all was well—indeed, more than well—with Christine; that she was now a pretty girl, courted and beloved.

The innkeeper's son had been home on a visit; he was employed in the office of some great institution in Copenhagen. He was very fond of Christine, and she thought him very nice; his parents too were not unwilling to give their consent; but it weighed upon Christine's heart that she was so much in Ib's thoughts, and she had therefore "decided to refuse this good fortune," said the boatman.

At first Ib did not say a word, but he turned as white as the wall, and shook his head a little. Then he said slowly: "Christine must not refuse this good fortune."

"Well, then, write her a few words," said the boatman.

And Ib sat down to write, but he could not put the words as he wished to, and first he altered, and then tore up, what he had written. But the next morning a letter lay ready for Christine, running thus:

> "I have read the letter you have written to your father, and learn from it that all is well with you, and that you may attain even greater good fortune. Look into your heart, Christine, and consider well what awaits you if you take me: what I have is but little. Do not think of me, or of my position, but of your own welfare. You are bound to me by no promise, and if you have given me one in your heart, I release you from it. May joy pour out its treasures upon you, Christine! Heaven will no doubt console my heart.
>
> "Ever your sincere friend,
>
> "Ib."

The letter was sent off, and Christine duly received it.

In the course of November the banns were published in the church on the heath, as well as in Copenhagen, where the bridegroom lived; and to

Copenhagen Christine traveled, accompanied by her mother-in-law, because the bridegroom could not, on account of business, undertake the long journey into the interior of Jutland. Christine met her father in a village on the way, and here the two took leave of each other. A good deal was spoken about the matter on different occasions, but Ib made no remarks upon it, and his mother said he had been very thoughtful of late. Thoughtful he had indeed become, and therefore the three nuts came into his mind which he had received from the gypsywoman, and two of which he had given to Christine. They had been wishing-nuts, and in one of hers had lain a golden carriage and horses, and in the other the most beautiful clothes. It was right—all that splendor would now be hers in the capital. Her part had come true, while to him (Ib) the nut had offered black earth. "The best of all things" for him, the gypsy had said. Yes, it was right—that too had come true. The black earth was the best for him. Now he understood clearly what the woman had meant. The dark grave, in the black earth, was the best place for him.

Again years passed—not very many, but they seemed long ones to Ib. The old innkeeper and his wife died, one after another, and the whole of their property, many thousands of dollars, went to their son. Now Christine could indeed have the golden carriage and plenty of fine clothes.

During two long years that followed no letter came from Christine, and when her father at last received one, it was by no means written in prosperity and joy. Poor Christine! Neither she nor her husband had been able to keep the money together; there was no blessing in it—because they had sought none.

Again the wild flowers bloomed and faded, and again the ferns dried up. The snow had swept for many winters across the heath and over the ridge at the foot of which Ib dwelt, sheltered from the rough winds. The spring sun shined once more; and as Ib guided the plow across his field it cut into what he believed to be a fire-stone. A great black lump like a plane came out of the ground, and when Ib took it up he found it was metal, and the place where the plow had cut into it gleamed brightly. It was a great heavy golden armlet of antiquity. A giant's grave had been disturbed, and now one of his costly ornaments was laid bare. Ib showed it to the clergyman, who explained to him the value of what he had found; he then betook himself to the district judge, who reported the discovery to the director of the museum and advised Ib to deliver up the treasure in person.

"You have found in the earth the best thing you could find," said the judge.

"The best thing!" thought Ib. "The very best thing for me, and in the earth! Well, if that is the best, the gypsy-woman was right in what she foretold me."

So Ib went with the ferry-boat from Aarhuus to Copenhagen. To him, who had only once or twice crossed the river that rolled by his home, this seemed a journey across the ocean.

He arrived in Copenhagen. The value of the gold he had found was paid out to him; it was a large sum—six hundred dollars. And Ib from the heath walked about in the great city.

On the evening before the day he had arranged to return with the captain, Ib lost his way in the streets and took quite a different direction from the one he had intended to go. He had strayed into a poor little street in the suburb of Christianshafen. There was not a soul to be seen. At last a very little girl came out of one of the miserable dwellings. Ib asked the little one the way to the street he wanted; she looked at him shyly, and began to cry bitterly. He asked her what was the matter, but he could not understand her answer. As they walked along the street and passed beneath a lamp, the light fell right upon the child's face, and a strange feeling came over him, for it was Christine that stood before him in the flesh, just as he remembered her in the days of their childhood.

He went with the little girl into the wretched house, and ascended the narrow, rickety staircase that led to a little attic high up under the roof. The air was close and almost suffocating; no light was burning, and from one corner came heavy sighs and groans. Ib struck a light with the help of a match. It was the child's mother, who lay groaning on the miserable bed.

"Can I do anything for you?" asked Ib. "The little girl brought me up here, but I am a stranger in the city. Are there no neighbors or others whom I could fetch?" He lifted up the sick woman's head and smoothed her pillow.

It was Christine from the heath!

For years her name had not been mentioned yonder, for that would have disturbed Ib's peace of mind, and according to all reports there was nothing good to tell. The wealth her husband had inherited from his parents had made him arrogant and turned his brain. He had given up his appointment and had traveled about in foreign countries for six months; on his return he had run into debt and still gone on living in great style. The coach rode more and more heavily, till at last it toppled over altogether. His numerous friends and merry table-companions declared that it served him right, for he had kept house like a madman. One morning his body was found in a canal.

The hand of Death was already on Christine. Her youngest child, only a few weeks old, hoped for in prosperity and born in misery, was already in its grave, and now it had come to this with Christine herself; she lay deserted and sick unto death in a miserable room—in poverty which she might have borne in her younger years, but which she now felt the more keenly, being used to better things. It was her eldest child, also a little Christine, who suffered hunger and want with her, and who had led Ib to her.

"I am tormented by the thought that I am dying and am leaving my poor child behind," she sighed. "Alas! what will become of her?" More she could not utter.

Ib took another match and lighted a piece of candle that he found in the room, and the flame lit up the miserable dwelling.

Then he looked at the little girl and thought of Christine when she was young; for her sake he could love this child who was a stranger to him. The dying woman looked at him and her eyes grew larger and larger: did she recognize him? He never knew, for no other word passed her lips.

It was in the forest by the river Gudenau, in the neighborhood of the heath. The air was thick and dark, and there was no bloom on the heather; the storms of autumn drove the yellow leaves out of the wood into the stream and across the heath towards the boatman's hut, now inhabited by strangers. But at the foot of the ridge, well sheltered by high trees, stood the little farm-house, whitewashed and painted, and within it the turf blazed up in the chimney. There was sunlight there too, the bright light of a child's eyes—and the notes of the spring birds rang out in the woods echoed from its smiling cherry lips. Life and joy reigned within; little Christine was there, sitting on Ib's knee. Ib was her father and mother, for her own parents had gone from her as a dream passes from the mind of both man and child. Ib sat in the pretty neat house, a prosperous man, while the mother of the little girl lay in the churchyard at Copenhagen where she had died in poverty.

Ib was wealthy; he had laid by for a rainy day, and he had his little Christine too.

Twelve by the Mail

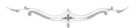

It was intensely cold, the sky was studded with stars, there was no breath of air stirring.

"Boom!" An old earthen pot was flung against the neighbor's door. "Bang, bang!" A gun was fired off. They were greeting the New Year. It was New Year's Eve! The church-clock was striking Midnight.

It was intensely cold, the sky was studded with stars, there was no breath of air stirring.

"Ta-ta-ra, ta-ta-ra!" The heavy mail-coach came lumbering up and stopped before the gate of the town. There were twelve passengers in it, for all seats were occupied.

"Hip, hip, hurrah!" cried the people in the houses of the town, where they were keeping New Year's Night, and rose when the clock struck twelve with their glasses in their hands, drinking the health of the New Year.

"A Happy New Year to you!" was the cry. "A pretty wife! plenty of money! no trouble and sorrow!"

Such were the good wishes expressed amid clinking of glasses. There was singing and ringing! Before the gate of the town stopped the mail-coach with twelve guests, the passengers.

And who were these strangers? Each of them had his passport and luggage with him; they even brought presents for you, for me, and for all the inhabitants of the little town. But who were they, what did they intend to do, and what did they bring with them?

"Good morning!" they called out to the sentry at the town-gate.

"Good morning!" answered the sentry, for the clock had already struck twelve o'clock.

"Your names? your business?" the sentry asked the first who left the coach.

An old earthen pot was flung against the neighbor's door.

"Look for yourself in my passport," replied the man. "I am I!" And he was indeed a man, clad in a large bearskin and wearing fur boots. "I am the man on whom many people set their hopes. Come and see me to-morrow and I shall give you a New Year's gift. I throw coppers and silver among the people, and give balls—to wit, thirty-one; but more nights I cannot sacrifice. My ships are frozen in, but in my office it is warm and pleasant. My name is January; I am a merchant, and carry all my accounts with me."

Then the second alighted from the coach. He was a jovial fellow; he was theatrical manager, arranger of masquerades and all sorts of amusements that one could think of. His luggage consisted of a big cask.

"We shall drive the cat out of this cask at carnival time," he said. "I shall give you and myself pleasure. We shall be merry every day. I have not too long to live—in fact, of all the family my life is the shortest, for I shall only become

They were keeping New Year's Night, and rose when the clock struck twelve with their glasses in their hands, drinking the health of the New Year.

twenty-eight days old. Sometimes they allow me one day more, but I don't trouble myself about that. Hurrah!"

"You must not shout so!" said the sentry.

"Why shouldn't I?" replied the man. "I am Prince Carnival, traveling under the name of Februarius."

Then the third left the coach. He looked the very picture of fasting; he carried his nose very high, for he was related to the "forty knights," and he was a weather-prophet. But this is not a remunerative trade, and therefore he was in favor of fasting. He had a bunch of violets in his button-hole, but it was very small.

"March, March!" cried the fourth after him, slapping his shoulders, "do you not smell something? Come quick into the guardroom; they are drinking punch there, which is your favorite beverage; I can smell it outside. March, Mr. Martius!" But it was not true, he only wished to tease him by making him an April fool; for with such merriment the fourth generally made his entrance into the town. He looked very smart, worked but very little, and kept more holidays than others. "I wish there was a little more steadiness in the world," he said, "but sometimes one is in good, sometimes in bad, humor, always according to circumstances; one has continually to change one's dress, for sometimes it rains and sometimes the sun shines. I am a sort of house-agent and undertaker; I can laugh and weep according to circumstances. I have my summer-clothes here in my portmanteau, but it would be foolish to put them on. Here I am! On Sundays I take a walk in shoes and white silk stockings, and with a muff."

After him a lady alighted from the coach. Her name was Miss May. She wore a summer dress and galoshes, her frock was of a light green, and anemones adorned her hair; she smelled so strongly of thyme that the sentry could not help sneezing. "Health and prosperity to you," she said, greeting him. How pretty she was! She was a singer, but not a theatrical vocalist, nor a ballad-singer; she was a songstress of the grove; she roamed about in the green forests and sang for her own pleasure and amusement.

"Now comes the young married woman," they cried from inside the coach, and a young, beautiful and distinguished-looking woman stepped out. One could see that Mrs. June was not accustomed to do much for herself, but rather to be waited upon. On the longest day in the year she gave a great dinner-party, that her guests might have time to eat the numerous courses which were served. Although she had her own carriage, she traveled like the others by the mail, in order to show people that she was not haughty. But she was not unaccompanied, for her younger brother Julius was with her. He looked very well fed, wore summer clothes and a straw hat. He had but little luggage, as it was burdensome to carry in the great heat; he had only a pair of bathing-drawers with him.

Then the mother alighted, Mrs. August, a wholesale fruiterer, the proprietress of many fish-ponds and a farmer, wearing a large crinoline; she was stout and hot, worked hard, and carried the beer out to her laborers in the field herself. "In the sweat of thy brow thou shalt eat thy bread," she used to say; "that is written in the Bible. When the work is done follow the excursions into the country, dance and play under the green trees, and the harvest festivals." She was an excellent housekeeper.

After her a man came out of the coach who was a painter; he was the famous colorist, September; he would repair to the woods and change the color of the leaves according to his ideas; and soon it gleamed with crimson, russet, and gold. The master could whistle like a starling; he was a quick worker, and decorated his beer-jug with a twining branch of hops, so that it looked beautiful; he had a strong sense of beauty. There he stood with his color-box, which made up his whole luggage.

He was followed by a landowner, who only thought of plowing and preparing the field in the seed-month, and who was fond of field sports. Mr. October had his dog and gun with him, and carried nuts in his game-bag. "Crack, crack!" He had a great deal of luggage, including even an English plow; he talked about agriculture, but on account of the coughing and groaning of his neighbor one could not hear much of it.

It was November who coughed so much when he got out. He suffered a great deal from colds, and blew his nose continually; and yet he declared that he must accompany the servant-girls to their new places and initiate them into their winter service; his cold, he thought, would soon be better when he began wood-cutting, for he was a master woodcutter, and the president of the guild. He passed his evenings cutting wood for skates, for he knew well, he said, that in a few weeks these articles would be in great demand for the people's amusement.

Finally, the last passenger made her appearance—the old mother December, carrying a foot-warmer with her. The old woman was shivering with cold, but her eyes were as bright as two stars. She held a flower-pot in her arm, in which a little fir-tree was growing. "This tree," she said, "I will take care of and cherish, that it may thrive and grow very tall, till Christmas-eve; it must reach from the floor to the ceiling, and will be covered with glittering lights, gilded apples, and cut-out figures. The foot-warmer warms me like a stove; I shall take a story-book out of my pocket and read it aloud, until all the children in the room are quiet, and all the little figures on the tree become alive; and the little wax angel on the top of the tree opens his wings of tinsel, flies down from his green resting-place, and kisses all the children and grown-up people in the room. Nay, he also kisses the poor children who stand outside in the street and sing the Christmas song of the "Star of Bethlehem."

"Well, the coach may drive off," said the sentry, "now we have all the twelve. And the luggage cart may come up."

"First let the twelve come in to me," said the captain of the guard, "one after the other. I shall keep their passports here; they are all available for one month; when it is gone I shall give them a character on the passports. Now, Mr. January, please walk in."

And Mr. January accepted the invitation.

When a year is gone, I shall tell you what the twelve passengers have brought you, myself, and all of us. At present I do not know it, and perhaps they do not know it themselves; for it is a strange time we live in.

The Metal Pig

In the city of Florence, not far from the *Piazza del Granduca,* runs a little cross-street, called, I think, *Porta Rosa.* In this street, in front of a kind of market-hall where vegetables are sold, there lies a pig artistically wrought out of metal. The fresh clean water pours from the mouth of the animal, which has become a blackish green from age; only the snout shines as if it were polished, and that it is too by many hundreds of children and beggars, who lay hold of it with their hands as they put their mouth to the animal's snout to drink. It it quite a picture to see the well-shaped animal clasped by a pretty and half-naked boy who lays his red lips against its snout.

Every one who comes to Florence can easily find the place; he need only ask the first beggar he comes across for the metal pig, and he will find it.

It was an evening late in winter. The mountains were covered with snow; but it was moonlight, and moonlight in Italy is as good as the light of a dark northern winter's day, and indeed better, for the air is bright and exhilarating, while in the north the cold gray leaden skies seem to press us to the earth, to the cold, damp earth, which will one day press upon our coffin.

In the garden of the grand duke's castle, where thousands of roses bloom, even in winter, a little ragged boy had been sitting under the pines all day long—a boy who might serve as a type of Italy, pretty and smiling, but yet suffering. He was hungry and thirsty, but no one gave him anything, and when it got dark and the garden had to be closed, the gatekeeper drove him out. For a long time he stood dreaming on the bridge that crosses the Arno, gazing at the stars that were reflected in the water between him and the splendid marble bridge *Delia Trinità.*

He made his way towards the metal pig, and, half kneeling down, wound his arms round it, then putting his mouth to the shining snout, drank the fresh water in deep drafts. Close by lay some salad leaves and a few chestnuts; these were his supper. There was no one in the street but himself; it belonged to him alone, and somewhat comforted he lay down upon the pig's back, bending forward so that his curly head rested on that of the animal, and before he knew it he was asleep.

It was midnight—the metal pig stirred, and he heard it say distinctly, "You little boy! hold on tight, for I am going to run," and away it ran with him; it was a wonderful ride. First they reached the *Piazza del Granduca,* and the metal horse that carries the duke's statue neighed aloud, while the painted coats-of-arms on the council-house looked like transparent pictures, and Michaelangelo's David swung his sling; there was a strange life stirring. The metal groups representing Perseus and the Rape of the Sabine women stood there as if they were alive; a cry of deadly anguish escaped them and re-echoed across the splendid square.

At the *Palazza degli Uffizi,* in the arcade, where the nobility assemble for the carnival festivities, the metal pig stopped. "Hold tight," said the animal, "hold tight, for we are going upstairs.

The little boy spoke not a word, for he was half trembling and half delighted. They passed through a long gallery in which the boy had been before. The walls were hung with pictures, and here stood statues and busts, all in the most excellent light, as if it were broad day; but the most beautiful of all was when the door of a side-room opened. The little boy remembered the beautiful things he had seen there, but that night everything was in its highest splendor. There stood a lovely woman, as beautiful as only Nature or the greatest master of sculpture could form her. She moved her glorious limbs, dolphins sprang about her feet, and immortality shined out of her eyes. The world calls her the Venus de Medici. At her side are marble statues in which the spirit of life has entered into the stone. There are handsome undraped figures of men—one is sharpening a sword, and is called the Grinder; the Wrestling Gladiators form another group, the sword being sharpened and the struggle being for the Goddess of Beauty.

The boy was dazzled by so much splendor; the walls were radiant with colors, and everything had life and movement. The picture of Venus was there in duplicate, the earthly one as yielding and as amorous as when Titian had pressed her to his heart. It was wonderful to behold. They were two beautiful women; their graceful limbs reclined on soft pillows, their bosom heaved, and their heads moved so that their rich tresses fell upon their well-shaped shoulders, while the dark eyes expressed the feelings that were coursing through their veins; but none of the pictures ventured to leave their frames entirely. The Goddess of Beauty herself, the Gladiators, and the Grinder remained in their places, for the halo of glory that shined out from the Madonna, Jesus, and John restrained them. The sacred pictures were no longer pictures; they were the saints themselves.

What splendor and what beauty they passed in going from hall to hall! The boy saw it all, for the metal pig went step by step through all this glory and magnificence. Every fresh sight effaced the remembrance of the last, but one picture impressed itself deeply upon his soul, and particularly on account of the happy smiling children it represented—he had seen it once by daylight.

Many, no doubt, pass this picture with indifference, and yet it contains a treasure of poetry. It is Christ descending into Hell; but these are not the damned by whom he is surrounded—they are heathens. The picture was painted by Angiolo Bronzino, a native of Florence. The most beautiful thing about it is the expression on the children's faces—the full confidence that they will get to Heaven. Two little ones are already embracing; one stretches out his hand to another, who stands below him, and points to himself as if he were saying: "I am going to Heaven." The elder ones look uncertain, though hopeful, or humbly bow down in adoration before the Lord Jesus. Longer than upon any other did the boy's gaze rest upon this picture, and the metal pig stopped before it. A low sigh was heard; did it come from the picture or from the animal? The boy lifted up his hands towards the smiling children; then the pig ran away with him—away through the open vestibule.

"Thanks and blessings upon you, you beautiful creature," said the little boy, caressing the metal pig as it ran down the steps.

"Thanks and blessings upon yourself," said the pig. "I have helped you and you have helped me, for only when I have an innocent child on my back I have the power to run. You see that I may even go under the rays of the lamp that hangs before the image of the Virgin, though I may not venture into the church. But if you are with me I can look in from without through the open doors. Don't get down from my back, for if you do I shall lie dead as you see me in the daytime at the *Porta Rosa*.

"I will stay with you, my dear creature," said the boy, and so they went on in hot haste through the streets of Florence, out into the square before the church of Santa Croce. The folding-doors flew open, and the light shined forth from the altar through the church into the deserted square.

A wonderful blaze of light streamed out from a monument in the left aisle, around which a thousand moving stars formed as it were a halo of glory. A coat of arms stands proudly on the grave—a red ladder on a blue ground—and seemed to glow like fire; it was the grave of Galileo. The monument is very simple, but the red ladder on the blue ground is full of meaning—an emblem as it were of art, the path of which always leads up a burning ladder, and to Heaven. All the prophets of the mind soar up towards Heaven, like Elijah.

To the right, in the aisle, every figure on the magnificent tombs seemed endowed with life. Here stood Michaelangelo, there Dante with a laurel wreath upon his brow, Alfieri and Macchiavelli; these great men, the pride of Italy, lie side by side.* It is a grand church, far more beautiful than the marble cathedral at Florence, though not so large.

It seemed as if the marble draperies of the statues moved, as if these great figures held up their heads and regarded, amidst song and music, the bright altar blazing with light, where white-robed choristers swung the golden censers; the strong fragrance streamed out of the church into the open square.

The boy stretched out his hand towards the stream of light, and in a twinkling the metal pig hurried away with him; he had to cling tightly, and the wind whistled about his ears; he heard the church doors creaking on their hinges as they closed, and at the same time he seemed to lose consciousness—he felt an icy shudder pass through him, and he opened his eyes.

It was morning, and he was still sitting on the metal pig, which stood in the *Porta Rosa*, but he had slipped half off his back.

Fear and trembling seized the boy at the thought of her whom he called mother, and who had sent him out yesterday to get some money; he had nothing, and he was hungry and thirsty. Once more he put his arms round the

*Opposite the grave of Galileo is that of Michaelangelo. On the monument is his bust and three figures representing Sculpture, Painting, and Architecture. Close by is Dante's monument (the body itself was interred at Ravenna), on which is seen Italy pointing to a colossal statue of the poet, while Poetry weeps over his loss. A few steps farther is Alfieri's monument, adorned with laurels, the lyre and masks, while a figure of Italy weeps over his bier. Macchiavelli closes the series of celebrated men.

pig's neck, kissed it on the snout, and, nodding to it, wandered away into one of the narrowest streets, hardly wide enough for a laden donkey. A great iron-clamped door stood ajar; passing through this, he went up some stone stairs with dirty walls and a rope for a balustrade, till he reached an open gallery hung with rags. From here a flight of steps led down into the yard, where there was a fountain with great iron wires running to all the stories of the house; by this means one pail after another was swung up, while the roller creaked and the pail danced about so that the water splashed down into the yard. Here again a tumble-down stone staircase led upwards; two Prussian sailors were descending quickly, and almost knocked the poor boy down. They were returning from their nocturnal carouse. A woman, plump but no longer young, with rich black hair, followed them.

"What do you bring home?" she asked the boy.

"Don't be angry," he pleaded; "I got nothing—nothing at all." And he seized his mother's dress, as if to kiss it. They went into the little room; I will not describe it, but only say that there stood in it a pot with handles—called a *marito*—filled with burning coals. This she took in her arms, warmed her fingers, and pushed the boy with her elbow.

"You must have got some money," she said.

The boy wept, and she kicked him so that he cried aloud.

"Will you be quiet, or I'll break your screaming head?" and she lifted up the fire-pot that she held in her hands.

The boy bent down to the ground with a cry of terror. At this a neighbor came in, also with a *marito* in her arms. "Felicita," she said, "what are you doing to the child?"

"The child is mine," answered Felicita. "I can murder him if I like, and you too, Giannina." And she again lifted up her fire-pot. The other woman raised hers to defend herself, and both pots crashed together so violently that the fragments, fire and ashes, flew all over the room; at the same moment the boy rushed out at the door, across the yard and out of the house.

The poor child ran till he could scarcely breathe; he stopped at the church, whose great doors had opened before him last night, and went in. All was bright as the boy knelt down by the first grave on the right, that of Michaelangelo, and soon he was sobbing aloud.

People came and went, and Mass was performed, but no one noticed the boy; only one elderly citizen stood still, looked at him—and then went away like the rest.

Hunger and thirst tormented the child, and he was quite faint and ill; so he crept into a corner between the marble monuments and went to sleep.

Towards evening he was awakened by some one pulling his sleeve, and jumping up, he found the old citizen before him.

"Are you ill? Where do you live? Have you been here all day?" were a few of the many questions that the old man put to him. They were answered, and the old man took him into his little house, which was close by in a side-street. They entered a glove-maker's workshop, in which the wife was busily sewing when they arrived. A little white poodle, so closely shaven that his pink skin could be seen, was capering about upon the table and gambolled before the boy.

"Innocent souls recognize each other," said the woman, caressing both the dog and the boy. The latter was given food and drink by the good people, and they said they would permit him to stay with them for the night, promising him that next day Father Giuseppe should go and speak to his mother. He was given a humble little cot; but for him, who had often been obliged to sleep on the hard stone ground, it seemed like a royal couch. How sweetly he slept, dreaming of the beautiful pictures and of the metal pig!

Next morning Father Giuseppe went out; the poor child was by no means glad, for he knew that the object of this errand was to send him back to his mother. He kissed the lively little dog, and the woman nodded at them both.

What news did Father Giuseppe bring? He spoke with his wife for a long time, and the latter nodded and stroked the boy. "He is a beautiful child," said she. "He may become a good glove-maker like you are, and he has such delicate and pliable fingers. The Madonna intended him for a glove-maker."

So the boy stayed in the house, and the woman herself taught him to sew; he ate well, slept well, became very cheerful, and began to tease Bellissima, as the little dog was called. The woman threatened him with her finger, scolded him and got angry. That went to the boy's heart, and he sat thoughtful in his little room. This looked out into the street where skins were being dried; thick iron bars were before the windows. He could not sleep; the metal pig was continually running in his mind, and suddenly he heard a pit-a-pat outside. That must be a pig, he thought. So he ran to the window, but there was nothing to be seen; it had passed already.

"Help the signor to carry his box of colors," said madam the following morning to the boy, when her young neighbor, the artist, passed, carrying the box and a large canvas rolled up. The boy shouldered the box and followed the painter, who took the way leading to the gallery, and went up the same steps which were so well known to the boy since the night he had ridden on the metal pig. He knew the statues and the pictures, the beautiful marble Venus and the one who lived on the canvas; he again saw the Madonna, Jesus and John.

They stopped before the picture by Bronzino, in which Christ is descending into Hell, and the children are all smiling around him in sweet expectation of Heaven. The poor boy smiled too, for here he was in his Heaven!

"You may go home now," said the artist when the boy had stood there till the other had set up his easel.

"May I look at your painting?" asked the boy. "May I see how you get the picture upon this white canvas?"

"I'm not going to paint yet," replied the man, taking up his black chalk. His hand moved quickly, his eye measuring the great picture, and although only a thin line was visible, the figure of Christ was already on the canvas, as in the painted picture.

"But why don't you go home?" said the painter; and silently the boy walked home, sat down at the table and learned to sew gloves.

But the whole day his thoughts were in the picture gallery, and therefore he pricked his fingers and was very awkward, though he did not tease Bellissima. When evening came, and the house-door stood open for a moment, he slipped out; it was still cold, but a very fine bright starlight night. Away he wandered through the already deserted streets, and was soon standing before the metal pig, over which he bent, kissed its polished snout, and seated himself on its back. "You blessed creature," he cried, "how I have longed for you! We must have a ride to-night."

The metal pig lay motionless, and the fresh stream gushed forth from his mouth. The boy was sitting on his back like a rider, when something pulled him by the clothes. He looked down, and there was Bellissima, the little clean-shaven Bellissima, barking as if it wanted to say, "Do you see, I'm here too; why are you sitting there?" No fiery dragon could have startled the boy so much as did the little dog in this place. Bellissima in the street, and undressed too, as the old dame called it! What would be the end of it? The dog only went out in winter enveloped in a little lambskin which had been cut out for him and sewn. The skin, which was adorned with bows and bells, was fastened with a red ribbon round his neck and under his body. In this costume the dog looked like a little kid when in winter he got permission to trip out with his mistress. Now Bellissima was out and undressed too: what would be the end of it? All the boy's fancies had vanished, but still he kissed the metal pig and then took Bellissima in his arms. The little creature was trembling with cold, so the boy ran as fast as he could.

"What are you running away with there?" cried two soldiers whom he met and at whom Bellissima barked. "Where did you steal that pretty dog?" they asked, taking it from him.

"Oh, give it me back," pleaded the boy.

"If you did not steal it, you may go home and say that the dog may be had at the guard-house." They gave him the name of the street and went away with Bellissima.

This was a great calamity. The boy did not know whether he should jump into the Arno, or go home and confess all; they would certainly kill him, he thought. "But I will gladly be killed; then I shall go to Jesus and the Madonna." So he went home, principally for the sake of getting killed. The door was closed, and he could not reach the knocker. There was no one in the street, but a stone lay there, and with this he banged at the door.

"Who's there?" cried somebody inside.

"It's I," he said "Bellissima is gone. Open the door and kill me."

Everybody was terror-stricken concerning poor Bellissima, but especially madam. She immediately looked at the wall, where the dog's coat generally hung, and there was the little lambskin.

"Bellissima at the guard-house," she cried aloud. "You wicked child! How did you entice it out? It will freeze. The delicate little thing among those rough soldiers!"

Her husband had to go after it at once—the woman lamented and the boy wept. All the inmates of the house came together, and among them the painter. He took the boy between his knees, cross-questioned him, and in fragments got to know the whole story of the metal pig and the picture gallery: it was pretty unintelligible. He comforted the little fellow, and tried to pacify the old woman; but she was not satisfied till her husband arrived with Bellissima, who had been among the soldiers. There was great rejoicing, and the painter caressed the boy and gave him a handful of pictures.

Oh! what beautiful bits and comical heads there were, and the metal pig was actually among them too! Oh, nothing could be more delightful! It had been put there on the paper by a few strokes, and even the house behind it was also given.

Whoever could draw and paint, could collect the whole world round him! The first spare moment he had on the following day the boy seized a pencil and tried to copy the drawing of the metal pig on the back of one of the pictures. He succeeded; it was rather crooked, it is true, rather up and down, one leg thick and another thin, but still it was recognizable, and he rejoiced at it himself. The pencil would not go just as it should—he saw that very well; the following day a second metal pig stood by the side of the first, and it looked a hundred times better. The third was already so good that every one could recognize it.

But the glove-sewing went on very badly, and the orders given in the town were but slowly got out; the metal pig had taught the boy that all pictures can be drawn on paper, and the city of Florence is a picture-book for any one who will turn over its pages. On the *Piazza del Trinità* stands a slender pillar, on the top of which is the Goddess of Justice, blindfolded, and holding the scales in her hand. She was soon on paper, and it was the glove-maker's young apprentice who had put her there.

His collection of pictures increased, but still it contained only drawings of things without life, when one day Bellissima came springing up to him. "Stand still," he said, "then you shall be made beautiful and get into my collection."

But Bellissima would not stand still, so it had to be bound fast. Its head and tail were tied, but as it still barked and jumped, the string had to be pulled tighter. Just then his mistress came in.

"You wicked boy! The poor creature!" was all that she could utter. She pushed the boy aside, kicked him, and turned him out of the house, calling him a most ungrateful good-for-nothing, and a very wicked child, and tearfully she kissed her little half-strangled Bellissima.

Just at that moment the painter came down the stairs; and this is the turning-point of the story.

In the year 1834 there was an exhibition in the Academy of Arts at Florence. Two pictures placed side by side attracted a number of spectators. The smaller of the two represented a merry little boy, who sat drawing, with a small white, curiously shorn poodle for his model; but the animal would not stand still, and was therefore tied up with a string, both by its head and tail. There was a life and truth about the picture that appealed to every one. The painter, it was said, was a young Florentine, who had been picked up from the streets when a child, and brought up by an old glove-maker, and had taught himself to draw. A now celebrated painter had discovered this talent, as the boy was being sent away for tying up madam's pet, the little poodle, and taking it for his model.

The glove-maker's apprentice had become a great painter; that was evident from the picture, but especially from the larger one beside it. Here there was only a single figure, a ragged but handsome boy, who was lying asleep in the streets, leaning against the metal pig in the *Porta Rosa*. All the spectators knew the spot. The child's arms rested upon the pig's head; he was fast asleep, and the lamp which hung before the image of the Madonna threw a strong effective light upon his pale, handsome face. It was a wonderfully beautiful picture, and was set in a large gilt frame, on the corner of which was hung a laurel wreath; but a black band was wound among the green leaves and a long streamer of crepe hung down from it.

A few days before, the young artist had—died!

The Bond of Friendship

We have just returned from a short journey, and already we feel the wish to take a longer one. Whither? To Sparta, Mycene, or Delphi? There are hundreds of places the mere name of which makes the heart desire to travel. One has to ascend mountains on horseback, through shrubs and bushes; the single traveler appears to be a whole caravan. He rides in front himself, with a guide, while a pack-horse carries trunk, tent, and provisions; a few armed men follow in the rear for his protection. No inn with soft beds is waiting for him at the end of the fatiguing day's journey; the tent is often his shelter in Nature's grand wilderness, and the guide prepares him a meal of rice, fowls, and curry for his supper. Thousands of gnats swarm round the little tent; it is a miserable night, and on the morrow the way leads across swollen rivers. Stick to your horse, that the water does not carry you away!

What reward do you receive for all these hardships? The greatest and richest. Nature reveals herself in all her grandeur; every spot is historical; the eyes and the mind revel. The poet can sing hymns of praise, the painter can represent it on rich canvases, but the impression of the reality which enters into the soul of the spectator and remains there for ever neither can reproduce.

I have endeavored in many small sketches to delineate a picture of a small portion of Athens and its surroundings, and yet how colorless is the whole! How little does it represent Greece, this mourning genius of beauty, the grandeur and sadness of which the stranger can never forget.

The solitary shepherd, high up on the rocky slope, would perhaps, better than I with my pictures, give an idea to him who wishes to know something about the country of the Hellenes.

"Let him speak," says my Muse.

Well, then! A beautiful peculiar custom shall furnish the shepherd up in the mountains with a subject for his story, namely:

"The Bond of Friendship"

"Our house was built of clay, but the doorposts consisted of squared marble pillars found on the spot where the house was built. The roof almost reached down to the ground. Now it is dark brown and ugly, but when it was made it consisted of flowering oleander and fresh bay branches fetched from the mountain slopes. Round our dwelling it was narrow; walls of rock rose steeply up, bare and black looking; round their summits clouds were often hanging, like white living beings. I never heard a singing bird here, nor did men dance to the sound of the bagpipe; but the place was sacred from time immemorial—its very name reminded us of it, for it was called Delphi. The dark gloomy mountains were all covered with snow. The highest—the one that reflected the red evening sun longest—was Parnassus; the brook near our house rushed down from it, and was also, one day, sacred; now the donkey sullies it with its feet, but the current rolls on and becomes clear again. How well I remember every spot in its sacred deep solitude! In the middle of the cottage a fire was lit, and when the ashes lay high and glowing, bread was baked in it. When the snow was piled up so high round our cottage that it was almost hidden, then my mother was at her brightest, then she would hold my head between her hands, kiss my forehead, and sing songs which she never sang at other times, for the Turks, our masters, would not suffer it. She sang:

"'On the summit of Olympus, in the wood of dwarf firs, lived an old stag; its eyes were heavy with tears. It wept red, green, and pale blue tears, and a roebuck passed. 'What ails thee, that thou weepest such red, green, and pale blue tears?' 'The Turks have taken our city. They have wild hounds for their hunt, a goodly pack.' 'I will chase them over the islands,' said the young roebuck; 'I will chase them over the islands into the deep sea.' But ere the sun set the roebuck was slain, and before nightfall the stag was chased and dead.'

"And when my mother thus sang her eyes became wet, and on her long lashes hung a tear, but she concealed it and then baked our black bread in the ashes. Then I clenched my fist and said, 'Let us kill the Turks.' But she repeated from the song: 'I will chase them over the islands into the deep sea.' But ere the sun set the roebuck was slain, and before nightfall the stag was chased and dead.

"Several days and nights we had been lonely in our cottage when my father came. I knew he would bring me shells from the Gulf of Lepanto, or perhaps a knife, sharp and glittering. This time he brought us a child, a little naked girl, whom he carried beneath his sheepskin coat. She was wrapped in a skin, and all the little one possessed when this was taken off and she lay in my mother's lap were three silver coins attached to her black hair. My father told us about the Turks who had slain the child's parents; he told us so much that I dreamed of it all night. My father was himself wounded. My mother dressed his arm; the wound was deep, and the thick sheepskin was stiff with frozen blood. The little girl was to be my sister. How radiantly beautiful she was! My mother's eyes were not softer than hers. Anastasia, as she was called, was to be my sister, for her father was united to mine, in accordance with an old custom which we still keep. They had in their youth become brothers, and had chosen the most beautiful and most virtuous girl in the whole neighborhood to consecrate their bond of friendship. I often heard of this strange good custom.

"Now the little girl was my sister, she sat on my knee. I brought her flowers and feathers of the field-birds; we drank together from the waters of Parnassus, and slept head to head under the laurel roof of the cottage, while my mother sang yet full many a winter of the red, green, and pale-blue tears. But I did not yet understand that it was my nation whose thousandfold sorrows were reflected in those tears.

"One day three Franks arrived. Their dress was different from ours. They had their beds and tents on horses, and more than twenty Turks, all armed with sabers and guns, accompanied them, for they were friends of the Pasha, and they had letters of safe-conduct from him. They only came to see our mountains, to ascend Parnassus in snow and clouds, and to look at the strange black steepy rocks surrounding our hut. There was not room enough for them inside, nor could they bear the smoke, which passed along the ceiling and escaped through the low door; they pitched their tents on the narrow place near our hut, roasted lambs and birds, and partook of strong sweet wines; but the Turks were not allowed to drink them.

"When they started I accompanied them some distance, and my little sister Anastasia hung in a goatskin upon my back. One of the prankish gentlemen placed me against a rock, and drew us so strikingly well as we stood there that we looked like one being. I had never thought of it, but Anastasia and I were really one; she always lay on my knee or hung on my back, and when I dreamed she appeared in my dreams.

"Two nights after this, other people armed with knives and guns came to our hut. They were Albanese, courageous men, as my mother said. They only stayed a short time; my sister Anastasia sat on the knee of one of them. When they were gone she had two instead of three silver coins in her hair. They wrapped tobacco in strips of paper and smoked it; the eldest spoke of the way they were to take, and was uncertain about it.

"But one way had to be chosen; they went off and my father accompanied them. Soon afterward we heard the report of guns, and after a little while again; then soldiers rushed into our hut, and took my mother, myself, and Anastasia prisoners; the robbers, they said, had stayed with us, and my father was their guide, therefore we were to follow them. I saw the bodies of the robbers, I saw my father's body, and cried until I fell asleep. When I awoke we were in prison, but the room was not worse than our own hut. They gave me onions and resinous wine, which they poured out of a tarred sack; ours at home was not any better.

"I do not know how long we were kept in prison; but many days and many nights passed. When we were released it was holy Eastertide; I carried Anastasia on my back, for my mother was ill, and could only walk very slowly, and it was a long way down to the sea, at the Gulf of Lepanto. We entered a church which shined with pictures on a golden background; they represented angels, which were very beautiful, but it seemed to me that our little Anastasia was just as beautiful. In the center of the floor stood a coffin filled with roses: 'Our Lord Christ lies there represented by beautiful flowers,' said my mother; and the priest announced: 'Christ has risen from the dead!' All the people kissed one another, every one of them held a burning candle, I myself received one, and so did little Anastasia; bagpipes sounded, and the men danced hand in hand out of the church, while the women were roasting the Easter lamb outside. We were invited to share the meal; I sat by the fire, when a boy older than myself kissed and embraced me saying: 'Christ has risen!' Thus Aphtanides and I saw each other for the first time.

"My mother could make fishing nets, and by this she earned a good deal at the Gulf, and we remained a long time by the sea—the beautiful sea, which tasted like tears, and the colors of which reminded me of the tears of the stag, for indeed it was sometimes red, sometimes green, and then blue again.

"Aphtanides knew how to guide a boat, and when I was sitting in it with my little Anastasia it was gliding over the water like a cloud over the sky. When the sun set the mountains assumed a deeper blue; one range of mountains rose above the other, and in the far distance stood Parnassus covered with snow. Its summit glittered in the evening sun like red-hot iron; it looked as if the light came from its inside, for still, long after the sun had set, it shined in the blue shimmering air. The white sea-birds touched the surface of the water with their wings, and it was indeed as quiet here as between the black rocks near Delphi. I was lying on my back in the boat, while Anastasia rested on my breast, and the stars over us sparkled much more brightly than the lamps in our church. They were the same stars and stood in exactly the same places above me, which I saw when sat before our hut at Delphi. At last it seemed to me as if I were still there! Then there was a splash in the water and the boat rocked to and fro; I uttered a loud cry, for Anastasia had fallen in, but just as quickly Aphtanides jumped in after her, and lifted her up to me! We undressed her, wrung the water out of her clothes, and then put them on again; all this Aphtanides did. We remained on the water until her things were dry, and nobody heard anything about our anxiety for our little foster-sister, whose life Aphtanides had saved.

"The summer came. The sun burned so hot that the leaves on the trees were scorched; I thought of our cool mountains and of their fresh water; my mother too was longing for them, and one night we started to return thither. What calm, what quietness! We walked on through the high thyme, which still smelled sweetly, although the sun had burned its leaves. All was quiet and deserted; only a shooting star told us there was life up there in the sky. I do not know whether the clear blue air which gave light, or whether it was the rays of the stars; we could easily distinguish the outlines of the mountains. My mother kindled a fire and fried onions which she had brought with her; my little sister and I slept in the thyme, without fear of the ugly smidraki,* from the throat of which fire spurts forth, and much less of the wolf and the jackal; my mother sat by our side and this I considered sufficient protection.

"We reached our old home, but the hut was a heap of ashes—a new one had to be built. Some women helped my mother, and in a few days walls were erected and a new roof of oleander made. My mother made many bottle cases of bark and skins—I kept the sheep of the priests;‡ Anastasia and the little tortoises were my playmates. One day we had a visit from our beloved Aphtanides; he had longed to see us so much, and he stayed with us two whole days.

"After a month he came again, and told us that he wished to go on board a ship to Patras and Corfu. He had come to say good-bye to us: he brought a large fish for our mother. He knew many things to tell us, not only of the fishermen at the Gulf of Lepanto, but also of the kings and heroes which one day ruled over Greece as the Turks do now.

"I have seen a bud on a rose-bush come out and develop into a flower in the course of days and weeks; it became one before I thought how large, fine, and red it was. The same thing happened to me concerning Anastasia. She was a beautiful tall girl, and I a strong lad. The wolf-skins on the couches of my mother and Anastasia I had myself taken from the animals which I had shot.

"Years passed. Then one night Aphtanides came: he was as slender as a reed, strong and brown; he kissed us all, and told us much about the great sea—of Malta's fortifications, and of Egypt's strange tombs. It sounded wonderful, like a legend of the priests. I looked up to him with a sort of reverence.

---

*According to the Greek superstition this monster originates from the uncut stomach of slaughtered sheep which are thrown on the fields.

‡A peasant who can read often becomes a priest, and then he is addressed as " Most holy sir." The inferior class kiss the ground on which he walks.

" 'How much you know!' I said. 'How well you can tell it!'

" 'You have after all told me the best one day,' he said; 'you have spoken to me of something that has never been out of my thoughts, of the fine old custom—the bond of friendship; I wish very much to follow this custom. Brother, let us go to the church, as your father and Anastasia's father once did. Your sister Anastasia is the most beautiful, most innocent girl: she shall consecrate us! No nation has better customs than we Greeks!'

"Anastasia blushed like a young rose, and my mother kissed Aphtanides. About an hour's walk from our hut, where loose mold lies on the rocks and some trees give shade, stood the little church; a silver lamp was hanging before the altar.

"I had put on my best clothes, the white fustanella fell in rich folds over my hips, the red jacket fitted tight and close, the tassel on my fez cap was silver, and my knife and pistols stuck in my girdle. Aphtanides wore the blue costume of a Greek sailor; a silver plate, with a figure of the Virgin Mary hung on his breast; his sash was as precious as only rich gentlemen can wear. Everyone could see that we went to some celebration. We entered the small solitary church, where the rays of the evening sun fell on the burning lamp and on the colored pictures on golden backgrounds. We knelt on the altar-steps, and Anastasia came before us; her long white dress hung loosely and lightly round her beautiful form; her white neck and bosom were covered with a chain of old and new coins, forming a kind of collar. Her black hair was tied into a single knot, held together by a head-dress consisting of silver and gold coins, found in ancient temples. No Greek girl had a finer ornament: her face beamed, her eyes were like two stars.

"We all three prayed silently; then she asked us: 'Will you be friends in life and death?'

" 'Yes,' we replied.

" 'Will you, whatever may happen, remember: my brother is part of me, my secret, my happiness is his; devotion, perseverance, every virtue in me belongs to him, as well as to me?'

"And we repeated our 'Yes!'

"She placed our hands together, kissed us on the forehead, and we prayed again silently. Then the priest came out of the door close to the altar, and blessed us all three, while a hymn was sung by the other holy men behind the altar screen. The bond of eternal friendship was concluded. When we rose I saw my mother crying bitterly near the church door.

"How bright it was in our little hut, at the springs of Delphi!

"The evening before his departure, Aphtanides and I were pensively sitting on the slope of the rock; his arm was slung round my waist, mine round his neck; we spoke of the distress of Greece, and of the men in whom she could trust. Every thought of our souls lay clearly before us both. Then I seized his hand.

" 'One thing I have yet to tell you—one thing, which was up to the present only known to God and myself! My whole soul is love! A love much stronger than that which I feel for my mother and for you!'

" 'And whom do you love?' asked Aphtanides, his face and neck turning crimson.

" 'I love Anastasia!' I said. His hand trembled in mine; he turned as pale as a dead body. I saw it; I understood him, and I thought that also my hand trembled. I bent down to him, kissed his forehead, and whispered:

" 'I have never told her about it; perhaps she does not love me! Brother think that I saw her daily; she has grown up by my side—one with my soul!'

" 'And yours she shall be!' he said. 'Yours! I must not deceive you, and I will not do so. I love her also—but tomorrow I am off. In a year we shall see each other again, and then you will be married—don't you think so? I have a little gold; it shall be yours—you must, you shall take it.'

"Silently we walked over the rocks; it was late in the evening when we arrived at my mother's hut. Anastasia raised the lamp as we entered; my mother was not there. She looked sorrowfully at Aphtanides. 'To-morrow you will go from us," she said, 'how sad it makes me.'

" 'Makes you sad?' he said—his words seemed to express a pain as great as my own. I was unable to speak, but he seized her hand and said:

" 'Our brother loves you, he is dear to you! His silence is the best proof of his love.'

"Anastasia trembled, and burst into tears. Then I only saw her, only thought of her, flung my arms round her, and said:

" 'Yes, I love you!'

"She pressed her lips to mine, and placed her arms round my neck; but the lamp had fallen on the floor: it was dark around us, as dark as in the heart of poor Aphtanides.

"Before daybreak he got up, kissed us all, and departed. He had given his money to my mother for us. Anastasia was my betrothed, and in a few days became my wife."

The Red Shoes

Once upon a time there was a little girl, pretty and dainty. But in summer-time she was obliged to go barefooted because she was poor, and in winter she had to wear large wooden shoes, so that her little instep grew quite red.

In the middle of the village lived an old shoemaker's wife; she sat down and made, as well as she could, a pair of little shoes out of some old pieces of red cloth. They were clumsy, but she meant well, for they were intended for the little girl, whose name was Karen.

Karen received the shoes and wore them for the first time on the day of her mother's funeral. They were certainly not suitable for mourning; but she had no others, and so she put her bare feet into them and walked behind the humble coffin.

Just then a large old carriage came by, and in it sat an old lady; she looked at the little girl, and taking pity on her, said to the clergyman, "Look here, if you will give me the little girl, I will take care of her."

Karen believed that this was all on account of the red shoes, but the old lady thought them hideous, and so they were burned. Karen herself was dressed very neatly and cleanly; she was taught to read and to sew, and people said that she was pretty. But the mirror told her, "You are more than pretty—you are beautiful."

One day the Queen was traveling through that part of the country, and had her little daughter who was a princess, with her. All the people, among them

Karen too, streamed towards the castle, where the little princess, in fine white clothes, stood before the window and allowed herself to be stared at. She wore neither a train nor a golden crown, but beautiful red morocco shoes; they were indeed much finer than those which the shoemaker's wife had sewn for little Karen. There is really nothing in the world that can be compared to red shoes!

Karen was now old enough to be confirmed; she received some new clothes, and she was also to have some new shoes. The rich shoemaker in the town took the measure of her little foot in his own room, in which there stood great glass cases full of pretty shoes and white slippers. It all looked very lovely, but the old lady could not see very well, and therefore did not get much pleasure out of it. Among the shoes stood a pair of red ones, like those which the princess had worn. How beautiful they were! and the shoemaker said that they had been made for a count's daughter, but that they had not fit her.

"I suppose they are of shiny leather?" asked the old lady. "They shine so."

"Yes, they do shine," said Karen. They fit her, and were bought. But the old lady knew nothing of their being red, for she would never have allowed Karen to be confirmed in red shoes, as she was now to be.

Everybody looked at her feet, and the whole of the way from the church door to the choir it seemed to her as if even the ancient figures on the monuments, in their stiff collars and long black robes, had their eyes fixed on her red shoes. It was only of these that she thought when the clergyman laid his hand upon her head and spoke of the holy baptism, of the covenant with God, and told her that she was now to be a grown-up Christian. The organ pealed forth solemnly, and the sweet children's voices mingled with that of their old leader; but Karen thought only of her red shoes. In the afternoon the old lady heard from everybody that Karen had worn red shoes. She said that it was a shocking thing to do, that it was very improper, and that Karen was always to go to church in future in black shoes, even if they were old.

On the following Sunday there was Communion. Karen looked first at the black shoes, then at the red ones—looked at the red ones again, and put them on.

The sun was shining gloriously, so Karen and the old lady went along the footpath through the corn, where it was rather dusty.

At the church door stood an old crippled soldier leaning on a crutch; he had a wonderfully long beard, more red than white, and he bowed down to the ground and asked the old lady whether he might wipe her shoes. Then Karen put out her little foot too. "Dear me, what pretty dancing shoes!" said the soldier. "Sit fast, when you dance," said he, addressing the shoes, and slapping the soles with his hand.

The old lady gave the soldier some money and then went with Karen into the church.

And all the people inside looked at Karen's red shoes, and all the figures gazed at them; when Karen knelt before the altar and put the golden goblet to her mouth, she thought only of the red shoes. It seemed to her as though they were swimming about in the goblet, and she forgot to sing the psalm, forgot to say the "Lord's Prayer."

Now every one came out of church, and the old lady stepped into her carriage. But just as Karen was lifting up her foot to get in too, the old soldier said: "Dear me, what pretty dancing shoes!" and Karen could not help it, she was obliged to dance a few steps; and when she had once begun, her legs continued to dance. It seemed as if the shoes had got power over them. She danced round the church corner, for she could not stop; the coachman had to run after her and seize her. He lifted her into the carriage, but her feet continued to dance, so that she kicked the good old lady violently. At last they took off her shoes, and her legs were at rest.

At home the shoes were put into the cupboard, but Karen could not help looking at them.

Now the old lady fell ill, and it was said that she would not rise from her bed again. She had to be nursed and waited upon, and this was no one's duty more than Karen's. But there was a grand ball in the town, and Karen was invited. She looked at the red shoes, saying to herself that there was no sin in doing that; she put the red shoes on, thinking there was no harm in that either; and then she went to the ball, and commenced to dance.

But when she wanted to go to the right, the shoes danced to the left, and when she wanted to dance up the room, the shoes danced down the room, down the stairs through the street, and out through the gates of the town. She danced, and was obliged to dance, far out into the dark wood. Suddenly something shined up among the trees, and she believed it was the moon, for it was a face. But it was the old soldier with the red beard; he sat there nodding his head and said: "Dear me, what pretty dancing shoes!"

She was frightened, and wanted to throw the red shoes away; but they stuck fast. She tore off her stockings, but the shoes had grown fast to her feet. She danced and was obliged to go on dancing over field and meadow, in rain and sunshine, by night and by day—but by night it was most horrible.

She danced out into the open churchyard; but the dead there did not dance. They had something better to do than that. She wanted to sit down on the pauper's grave where the bitter fern grows; but for her there was neither peace nor rest. And as she danced past the open church door she saw

She wanted to sit down on the pauper's grave where the bitter fern grows.

an angel there in long white robes, with wings reaching from his shoulders down to the earth; his face was stern and grave, and in his hand he held a broad shining sword.

"Dance you shall," said he, "dance in your red shoes till you are pale and cold, till your skin shrivels up and you are a skeleton! Dance you shall, from door to door, and where proud and wicked children live you shall knock, so that they may hear you and fear you! Dance you shall, dance!"

"Mercy!" cried Karen. But she did not hear what the angel answered, for the shoes carried her through the gate into the fields, along highways and byways, and unceasingly she had to dance.

One morning she danced past a door that she knew well; they were singing a psalm inside, and a coffin was being carried out covered with flowers. Then she knew that she was forsaken by every one and damned by the angel of God.

She danced, and was obliged to go on dancing through the dark night. The shoes bore her away over thorns and stumps till she was all torn and bleeding; she danced away over the heath to a lonely little house. Here, she knew, lived the executioner; and she tapped with her finger at the window and said:

"Come out, come out! I cannot come in, for I must dance."

And the executioner said: "I don't suppose you know who I am. I strike off the heads of the wicked, and I notice that my ax is tingling to do so."

"Don't cut off my head!" said Karen, "for then I could not repent of my sin. But cut off my feet with the red shoes."

And then she confessed all her sin, and the executioner struck off her feet with the red shoes; but the shoes danced away with the little feet across the field into the deep forest.

And he carved her a pair of wooden feet and some crutches, and taught her a psalm which is always sung by sinners; she kissed the hand that had guided the ax, and went away over the heath.

"Now, I have suffered enough for the red shoes," she said; "I will go to church, so that people can see me." And she went quickly up to the church-door; but when she came there, the red shoes were dancing before her, and she was frightened, and turned back.

During the whole week she was sad and wept many bitter tears, but when Sunday came again she said: "Now I have suffered and striven enough. I believe I am quite as good as many of those who sit in church and give themselves airs." And so she went boldly on; but she had not got farther than the churchyard gate when she saw the red shoes dancing along before her. Then she became terrified, and turned back and repented right heartily of her sin.

"I don't suppose you know who I am.
I strike off the heads of the wicked,
and I notice that my ax is tingling to do so."

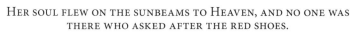

Her soul flew on the sunbeams to Heaven, and no one was there who asked after the red shoes.

She went to the parsonage, and begged that she might be taken into service there. She would be industrious, she said, and do everything that she could; she did not mind about the wages as long as she had a roof over her, and was with good people. The pastor's wife had pity on her, and took her into her service. And she was industrious and thoughtful. She sat quiet and listened when the pastor read aloud from the Bible in the evening. All the children liked her very much, but when they spoke about dress and grandeur and beauty she would shake her head.

On the following Sunday they all went to church, and she was asked whether she wished to go too; but, with tears in her eyes, she looked sadly at her crutches. And then the others went to hear God's Word, but she went alone into her little room; this was only large enough to hold the bed and a chair. Here she sat down with her hymn-book, and as she was reading it with a pious mind, the wind carried the notes of the organ over to her from the church, and in tears she lifted up her face and said: "O God! help me!"

Then the sun shined so brightly, and right before her stood an angel of God in white robes; it was the same one whom she had seen that night at the church-door. He no longer carried the sharp sword, but a beautiful green branch, full of roses; with this he touched the ceiling, which rose up very high, and where he had touched it there shined a golden star. He touched the walls, which opened wide apart, and she saw the organ which was pealing forth; she saw the pictures of the old pastors and their wives, and the congregation sitting in the polished chairs and singing from their hymn-books. The church itself had come to the poor girl in her narrow room, or the room had gone to the church. She sat in the pew with the rest of the pastor's household, and when they had finished the hymn and looked up, they nodded and said, "It was right of you to come, Karen."

"It was mercy," said she.

The organ played and the children's voices in the choir sounded soft and lovely. The bright warm sunshine streamed through the window into the pew where Karen sat, and her heart became so filled with it, so filled with peace and joy, that it broke. Her soul flew on the sunbeams to Heaven, and no one was there who asked after the red shoes.

A Rose from Homer's Grave

In all the songs of the East the love of the nightingale for the rose is spoken of; they describe how the winged songster serenades his fragrant flower in the silent starlight night.

Not far from Smyrna, under high plane-trees, where the merchant drives his heavily-loaded camels, which proudly raise their long necks and stride with heavy step over the sacred ground, I saw a hedge of roses in full bloom; wild pigeons flew about in the high branches of the trees, and when a sunbeam glided over their wings they glittered like mother-of-pearl. There was one rose in the hedge which was more beautiful than all the others, and this rose the nightingale was entreating for love; but the rose was silent—a dewdrop lay, like a tear of compassion on its petals, the branch on which it grew was bending down over several large stones.

"Here sleeps the greatest singer that ever lived on earth!" said the rose. "On this grave I will breathe forth sweet fragrance and strew my petals over it when the wind scatters them! The singer of Troy became the earth from which I grew forth!—I, a rose from Homer's grave, am too sacred to bloom for a poor nightingale!" And the nightingale sang itself to death.

A camel-driver came to the spot with his loaded camels and his black slaves; his little son found the dead bird and buried the songster in the grave of the great Homer; the rose trembled in the wind. The evening came; the rose folded its petals closer together and dreamed!

It had been a beautiful sunny day; a troop of strangers approached, they had made a pilgrimage to Homer's grave. Among them was a singer from the north, from the home of fogs and of the *aurora borealis;* he broke the rose off, pressed it tightly in a book, and carried it with him into another part of the world—into his distant native country. The rose withered for grief, and lay between the leaves of the book which he opened at home and said: "Here is a rose from Homer's grave!"

This the flower dreamed, and when it awoke it trembled in the wind, so that a dewdrop fell from its petals on the singer's grave. The sun rose, and the flower was more beautiful than ever; the day turned out very hot and it was still in its warm Asia. Then steps were heard: strangers from France came, as the rose had seen them in its dream, and among them was also a poet from the north: he plucked the rose, pressed a kiss on its beautiful mouth, and carried it with him to the home of fog and *aurora borealis.* This flower now rests in his Iliad like a mummy, and as in a dream, it heard him say as he opened the book, "Here is a rose from Homer's grave."

The Jewish Girl

In a charity school, among other children, sat also a little Jewish girl. She was a good intelligent child, the quickest in the school; but she had to be excluded from one of the subjects taught in that school—that is to say she was not allowed to take part in religious instruction, for it was a Christian school.

The little girl was allowed in the meantime to open her geography book, or to work out some calculation for the following day, but that was soon done, and when she had got through her geography lesson, the book, it is true, remained open before her, but she no longer read it; she listened attentively to the words of the Christian master, who soon perceived that she was more attentive than any of the other children.

"Read your book, Sarah," said the master, reproving her gently; but her black radiant eyes remained fixed upon him, and when once he addressed a question to her, she knew more about the subject than any of the other children. She had heard, understood, and pondered his words in her heart.

Her father, a poor but honest man, had brought his daughter to the school on the condition that she was not to be instructed in the Christian religion. But as it would perhaps have caused trouble, or made the other children discontented, if they had sent her out of the room during this lesson, she remained there; but henceforth this could no longer be permitted. The master went to her father, and explained to him that either he would have to take his daughter away from the school, or he must not be surprised if Sarah became a Christian. "I can no longer remain an idle spectator of the child's beaming eyes, and of her devoutness and longing of her soul for the Gospel," said the teacher.

The father burst into tears: "I know but little of the law of my fathers," he cried, "but Sarah's mother was firm in the faith, a daughter of Israel, and I have promised her on her deathbed that our child should never be baptized. I must keep my vow; it is to me like a covenant with God!"

And thus the little Jewish girl left the Christian school.

Years had passed. In one of the smallest provincial towns there lived, as servant in a humble household, a poor girl of Mosaic creed; her hair was as black as ebony, her eyes as dark as night, and yet full of that brightness and light so peculiar to the daughters of the East. It was Sarah. The expression in the face of the grown-up girl was still the same as that of the child, when sitting on the school-bench, and listening attentively to the words of the Christian teacher.

Every Sunday the sound of the organ and the singing of the congregation sounded across the street into the house where Sarah was industriously and conscientiously at work. "Thou shalt keep the sabbath holy!" said the voice of the law in her heart; but her sabbath was a working day with the Christians, and this did not seem to suffice her. "Does God reckon by days and hours?" she thought in her soul, and when this idea was once awakened in her mind it was a consolation to her that on the Christian Sunday her hour of devotion was less disturbed; and when the sound of the organ and the singing entered the kitchen where she was at work, even this place became sacred to her. Then she read in the Old Testament, the treasure and comfort of her people; but she read only this, for she faithfully remembered what her father and her teacher had told her when she left school, about the vow which her father had made to her dying mother that she should never be baptized, nor deny the faith of her fathers. The New Testament was to remain a closed book for her, and yet she knew a great deal of it, and the Gospel resounded in her, with the recollections of her childhood.

One evening she sat in a corner of the room; her master was reading aloud, and she could listen to him, because it was not the Gospel, but an old storybook which he read. The book told about a Hungarian knight taken prisoner by a Turkish pasha, who had him yoked with his oxen to the plow, and driven with lashes of the whip, ill-treated him beyond measure, and almost let him die of thirst. The knight's faithful wife at home sold her jewels, and mortgaged her castle and land; his friends collected large sums; the ransom demanded for his release was almost more than they could pay, but at last it was collected, and the knight rescued from servitude and shame. Ill and suffering, he arrived at his home.

But soon there was a fresh appeal to fight against enemies of Christendom; the news also came to the knight, who was still alive, and he could no longer rest and remain at home. They had to lift him on his war-horse; his cheeks colored, his strength seemed to return and he went forth to battle and to victory.

And the very same pasha, who had him yoked before the plow, now became his prisoner, and was taken to his dungeon. But hardly an hour had passed before the knight stood before the captured pasha, and asked him: "What do you think now awaits you?"

"I know well," replied the Turk; "retaliation!"

"Yes; the retaliation of the Christians," replied the knight. "Christ's doctrine teaches us to forgive our enemies, and to love our neighbor, for God is love. Go in peace; return to your home; I give you back to your beloved ones. But be in future mild and humane towards those who suffer!"

Then the prisoner burst into tears: "How could I think such kindness possible! Shame and torture seemed to wait for me, seemed so certain—I took poison which I secretly carried about me, I shall succumb to its effects in a few hours. I must die; it is impossible to save me! But before I die teach me the doctrine which gives room to such immeasurable love; it is grand and divine! Grant me that I may die in this doctrine—as a Christian!" And his request was granted to him.

Such was the legend which the master read from the old storybook. All those present listened with great attention; but she who sat still in the corner—Sarah, the Jewish girl—felt her heart inspired; large tears came into her radiant black eyes, she sat there with the same feeling of piety with which she had sat in the school, she felt the sublimeness of the Gospel, and tears rolled over her cheeks.

But, however, the last words of her dying mother came before her, "Let not my child become a Christian," sounded in her heart with the words of the law, "Honor thy father and thy mother." "I am not received into the community of the Christians," she said to herself; "they tease me as a Jewish girl; the neighbor's boys did so only last Sunday, when I stopped before the church door and looked in, when the altar candles were burning and the congregation singing! Yes, ever since I was at school I have felt the power of Christianity, a power which is like a sunbeam, and which, however much I close my eyes, penetrates into my heart! But I will not grieve you in your grave, mother; I will not break my father's vow, I will not read the Bible of the Christians! Have I not the God of my fathers? To Him I will remain faithful!"

Years passed by once more. Her master died. The widow came into difficult circumstances. The maid was to be dismissed. But Sarah did not leave the house—she became the support in need, and kept the home together; she worked till late at night, and gained the daily bread through the industry of her hands, for there was no relation to assist the family, and the widow became weaker from day to day and was tied to a sick-bed for months. Sarah worked and sat also, nursing and watching by the bedside of the sick woman. She was gentle and good, an angel of blessing to the poverty-stricken household.

"There on the table lies the Bible," said the sick woman to Sarah. "Read me a little from it; the night seems to me so long, so long—and I am thirsting for the word of God!"

And Sarah bowed her head. She took the book, folded her hands round the Bible of the Christians, opened it and read to the sick woman; tears often came into her eyes, but they were radiant and beaming; and it became light in her heart. "Mother," she whispered, "your child must not receive the baptism of Christians, not be received into their community. You have wished it, and I will honor your wish—we are one on this point here below; but beyond this earth there is a higher union in God; He leads and guides us beyond death! He descends to earth, and when He has let it suffer thirst, He showers fertility over it. I understand it! I do not know myself how I learned to understand it! But it is through Him, through Christ!"

She trembled all over when she pronounced the holy name, and a baptism as of fiery flames overcame her and overwhelmed her body; she struggled convulsively; her limbs gave way, and she sank, fainting, weaker than the sick woman whom she nursed.

"Poor Sarah!" said the people, "she is exhausted from work and night watching!"

She was carried into the hospital of the poor. There she died, and from there she was borne to the grave, but not to the churchyard of the Christians, there was no place for a Jewish girl; outside, near the wall, they dug a grave for her.

God's sun, which shines over the graves of the Christians, also throws his rays over the Jewish girl's grave outside the wall, and when the psalms sound over the churchyard, they also pass over her solitary resting-place, and the call to the resurrection also appeals to her who who sleeps there, in the name of Christ, our Lord, who spake to His disciples:

"John baptized you with water, but I will baptize you with the Holy Ghost!"

The Lovers

A top and a little ball lay together among other toys in a drawer. The top said to the little ball one day, "Shall we be sweethearts, as we are lying together here in the same drawer?" But the little ball, which was covered with red morocco, and thought as much of itself as any young lady, would not even reply to such a proposal.

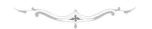

A top and a little ball lay together among other toys in a drawer.

On the next day the little boy to whom the toys belonged took the top, painted it red and yellow, and drove a nail with a brass head into it, so that the top looked very beautiful when it was spinning round.

"Look at me," it said to the little ball. "What do you say to this? Shall we be sweethearts now? We are so well suited to each other; you jump and I dance. No two people could be happier than we two."

"Really, do you think so?" replied the little ball. "You evidently do not know that my father and mother were morocco slippers, and that I have a Spanish cork in my body."

"Very well, but I am made of mahogany," said the top. "The mayor himself has turned me, for he has a lathe of his own which causes him a great deal of pleasure."

"Can I depend upon this being true?" asked the little ball.

"May I never be whipped again, if I do not speak the truth," replied the top.

"You know very well how to plead your cause," said the little ball. "But I cannot comply with your wishes, for I am as good as engaged to a swallow. Whenever I fly up into the air it puts its head out of the nest and asks me: 'Will you?' And in myself I have already said 'Yes,' and that is as much as half an engagement; but I will promise never to forget you."

"What is the good of that to me?" said the top; and they spoke no more to each other.

Soon after this conversation the boy took out the little ball. The top saw it flying high up into the air, like a bird, till it was no longer visible: it always came back, and every time it touched the ground it made a high leap; this was either because it was desirous to fly up again, or because it had a Spanish cork in its body.

When the boy threw it up for the ninth time, the little ball did not come back; he looked everywhere for it, but could not find it—it was gone.

"I know very well where it has gone to," sighed the top, "it is in the swallow's nest, and has married the swallow."

The more the top thought of this, the more it loved the little ball; and its love increased for the very reason that its wish could not be fulfilled, for the little ball had married another; and the top twirled round and hummed, and was continually thinking of the little ball, which, to its imagination, became more and more beautiful. Thus the years passed by, and its love grew quite old.

The boy took out the little ball. The top saw it flying high up into the air, like a bird.

The top itself was no longer young; but one day it was gilded all over, and looked more beautiful than it had ever done before. Now it was a golden top, and leaped and twirled till it hummed. But suddenly it jumped too high and was gone.

They sought it everywhere, even in the cellar, but it was not to be found.

Where was it?

It had jumped into the dust-bin, where all sorts of rubbish were lying: old cabbage stalks, dust and dirt, that had fallen down through the gutter.

"Here, I am well placed indeed! Here my gilding will soon disappear. Oh, what company I have come into!" And then it looked at a long naked cabbage stalk and at a peculiar round thing that was much like an old apple; but it was no apple—it was an old ball which had lain for many years in the gutter and was soaked through with water.

"Heaven be thanked! here is an equal at last; somebody to whom one can talk," said the little ball, and looked at the gilded top. "I was originally covered with morocco, and sewn by the hands of a young lady, and have a Spanish cork in my body; but nobody will think so now. I was on the point of marrying a swallow, but then I dropped into the gutter, and there I remained more than five years, and was thoroughly soaked through. You can believe me, it was a very long time for a little ball."

But the top said nothing; it thought of its old love, and the more the little ball talked, the more it became certain that this was its old sweetheart. Just then the servant came to throw some rubbish into the dust-bin. "Ah, there is the gilt top," she said.

Thus the top came again to respectability and honor, but the little ball was never heard of again. The top did not mention its old love any more, for love vanishes when one's sweetheart has lain five years in the gutter and become soaked through; one does not recognize it again, if one meets it in the dust-bin.

"Oh, what company I have come into!"

A Picture from the Rampart

It is autumn, we are standing on a rampart and look out on the sea; we see the many ships and the Swedish coast on the other side of the sound which, in the light of the sinking sun, rise high above the surface of the sea; behind us the wood limits our view; stately trees surround us, and the yellow leaves flutter down from the branches. Below, at the foot of the rampart, stand gloomy buildings, surrounded by high walls, within it is very narrow and dismal, but it is much more dismal beyond that grating in the wall; there sit the prisoners, the worst criminals.

A ray of the sinking sun enters the bare cell of one of these prisoners. The sun shines upon the good and the evil. The sullen stubborn culprit throws a glance of disgust on the cold ray. A little bird flies towards the grating. The little bird chirps to the unjust as well as to the just; it utters nothing more than a short, "twit, twit," sits down on the wall, beats with its wings, and plucks a feather out of one of them, puffs itself up, and makes the feathers on its neck and breast rise.

And the wicked man on the chain looks at it; his hardened face assumes a milder expression; a thought rises in his breast which he cannot himself explain, but this thought is connected with the sunbeam and the fragrance of the violets which in spring grew plentifully along the wall. Now the bugles of the hunters sound sweet and full. The little bird flies away, frightened; the sunbeam gradually vanishes and it becomes dark again in the cell, dark in the wicked man's heart; but the sun has shined into it, the little bird has chirped into it! Continue to sound, ye bugles of the hunters, continue to sound! The evening is mild, and the sea gently rocks its smooth surface.

A Leaf from Heaven

High up in the thin clear air flew an angel with a flower from the garden of Heaven. While he kissed the flower a tiny little leaf dropped down on the soft mold in the midst of a wood, took root at once, and brought forth new shoots among the other plants.

"What a curious little shoot that is!" they said. And none of them would recognize it, neither thistles nor nettles.

"Oh, that is probably a sort of garden plant," they said, and began to mock at it as a garden plant.

"Whither will you go?" asked the high thistles, the leaves of which were all armed with thorns.

"You are going rather far—that is stuff and nonsense! We are not here to support you!"

Winter came, and snow covered the plant; but the snow that covered it looked as bright as if the sun was shining underneath it. When spring came, a beautiful flowering plant was seen; there was no other like it in the wood. Now the Professor of Botany, who could show in black and white that he was what he was, came out into the wood. He looked at the plant and tasted it, but he could not find it in any of his works on botany; he was unable to find out to which class it belonged.

"It must be a new species," he said. "I don't know it; it is not yet embodied in the system."

"Not accepted in the system!" said the thistles and nettles. The large trees that were standing round both saw and heard it, but they said nothing—neither good nor evil; and that is the wisest thing to do when one does not know.

Then came through the wood a poor innocent girl; her heart was pure, her mind enlarged by faith. Her whole inheritance was an old Bible, and from its leaves the voice of God spoke to her. When people wish to harm us, it is said about Joseph, "They imagined evil in their hearts, but God turned it into good." When we are wrongfully suffering, or misunderstood and mocked, we hear the words of Him—the purest and best—whom they calumniated and nailed to the cross, where He prayed: "Father, forgive them: they know not what they do!"

The girl stopped before the marvelous plant, the green leaves of which smelled sweet and refreshing; its flowers shined in the bright sunlight like a colored firework, and from each it sounded as if there was a source of melody in it that thousands of years would not be able to exhaust. With pious devotion she looked at the wonderful work of God; she bent one branch down to look well at the flower and to breathe in its fragrance. Her mind was enlightened, it gladdened her heart; she would have very much liked to pluck a flower, but she could not make up her mind to do so—she thought how soon it would fade with her. Then she took only one single green leaf and put it into her Bible at home: there it lay, fresh and green, and never withered. It was kept among the pages of the Bible; with the Bible it was placed under the young girl's head when, a few weeks later, she was lying in her coffin with the holy calm of death on her pious face, as if it was impressed upon it that she was now standing before her Creator.

But out in the wood the marvelous plant was thriving; it looked almost like a tree, and all birds of passage bowed before it.

"That's now affecting the foreigner," said the thistles and burrs. "We can't behave like that here in this country."

The black wood-snails spat upon the flower. Then came the swineherd. He was gathering thistles and shrubs to burn for ashes; he took the marvelous plant, with roots and all, into his bundle.

"Now it shall be useful." he said, and then walked off.

For a long time the king of the country had suffered from despondency; he was industrious and hard-working, but it did not help him. They read deep learned books to him, and also the lightest, most amusing literature they could find; but it was all to no purpose. Then one of the wisest men in the world, whom they consulted, sent a messenger to tell them that there was still a means by which they might give him ease and cure him: "In his own kingdom was a plant of heavenly origin growing in the wood; it looked so and so—one could not possibly mistake it."

"Oh, it has come into my bundle and has been turned to ashes long ago," said the swineherd; "but I did not know any better."

"You did not know any better! Oh, ignorance of ignorances!"

The swineherd might apply these words to himself, for to him and no one else they referred. Not a single leaf was to be found—the only one was in the dead girl's coffin, and nobody knew about it.

The king himself, in his melancholy mood, went out to the place in the wood.

"Here the plant stood," he said. "It is a sacred place."

And the place was railed in with a golden fence, and a sentinel was posted by it.

The Professor of Botany wrote a long treatise upon the heavenly plant, and he was very well paid for it, which was good for him and for his family. And that's the best of the whole story, for the plant had disappeared. And the king remained melancholy and dismal, but he had always been so, the sentinel said.

The Princess and the Pea

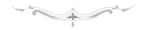

Once upon a time there was a prince who wanted to marry a princess; but she would have to be a real princess. He traveled all over the world to find one, but nowhere could he get what he wanted. There were princesses enough, but it was difficult to find out whether they were real ones. There was always something about them that was not as it should be. So he came home again and was sad, for he would have liked very much to have a real princess.

One evening a terrible storm came on; there was thunder and lightning, and the rain poured down in torrents. Suddenly a knocking was heard at the city gate, and the old king went to open it.

It was a princess standing out there in front of the gate. But, good gracious! what a sight the rain and the wind had made her look. The water ran down from her hair and clothes; it ran down into the toes of her shoes and out again at the heels. And yet she said that she was a real princess.

It was a princess standing out there in front of the gate.

"Well, we'll soon find that out," thought the old queen. But she said nothing, went into the bed-room, took all the bedding off the bedstead, and laid a pea on the bottom; then she took twenty mattresses and laid them on the pea, and then twenty eider-down beds on top of the mattresses.

On this the princess had to lie all night. In the morning she was asked how she had slept.

"Oh, very badly!" said she. "I have scarcely closed my eyes all night. Heaven only knows what was in the bed, but I was lying on something hard, so that I am black and blue all over my body. It's horrible!"

Now they knew that she was a real princess because she had felt the pea right through the twenty mattresses and the twenty eider-down beds.

Nobody but a real princess could be as sensitive as that.

So the prince took her for his wife, for now he knew that he had a real princess; and the pea was put in the museum, where it may still be seen, if no one has stolen it.

There, that is a true story.

The pea was put in the museum, where it may still be seen,

The Old Church Bell

In Würtemburg, a country in Germany, where the acacias bloom by the highroad, and apple and pear trees bend in autumn under their burden of ripe fruit, lies the little town of Marbach; although it belongs to the number of small towns, it is charmingly situated on the Neckar, the river which passes villages, old feudal castles and vineyards in its rapid course, as it hurries on to add its water to the proud Rhine.

It was in the latter part of autumn; the leaves were, it is true, still on the vine, but they were already tinged with red. Heavy rain-clouds were passing over the country, the chilly autumn winds increased in power and coldness. It was indeed no agreeable time for poor people.

The days became shorter and duller, and if it was dark outside in the open air, it was much more so inside the little old-fashioned houses. One of these houses turned its gable towards the street, and stood there with its small, low windows, poor and insignificant; the family who lived in this house were also poor, but they were brave and industrious, and they feared and loved God. The mother lay in pain and anguish, for the hour approached when God would give her another child. From the church-tower opposite the deep festival peal sounded in her ear. It was a sacred hour, the sound of the bell filled the praying woman with devotion and faith; from the depth of her heart her thoughts rose up to God, and in the same hour her little son was born. She was filled with infinite joy, and the church-bell opposite pealed forth, as it were, her joy over town and country. Two bright baby eyes looked at her, and the little one's hair shined like gold. The child was received on earth with the sound of the bell on the gloomy November day. Mother and father kissed him, and wrote in their Bible: "On the 10th of November 1759, God gave us a son"; later on was added that he had received in holy baptism the names of "Johann Christoph Friedrich."

And what became of the little fellow, the poor boy from the insignificant town of Marbach? Well, then nobody knew, not even the old church bell, although it was hanging so high, and had first sung and sounded over him—over him who was to sing one day the most beautiful "Song of the Bell."

The boy grew up, and the world grew older with him; the parents settled later on in another town, but some dear friends of theirs remained in little Marbach, and therefore one day mother and son started for Marbach to pay visits. The boy was then only six years old, but he already knew many passages from the Bible, and from the Psalms, and many a night when he was sitting on his little cane-chair he had listened when his father read aloud Gellert's "Fables" or from Klopstock's "Messiah"; both he and his sister, who was two years older, had shed hot tears over Him who suffered death for us all on the cross.

Upon this first visit to Marbach, the little town had not much altered, and indeed they had only lately left it. The houses stood there as formerly, with their pointed gables and their projecting walls, the one story standing out farther than the other, and with their low windows; only in the churchyard new graves had been added, and down below on the grass, close by the wall, lay the old bell. It had fallen down from its high position, was cracked, and could no longer ring, and a new bell had been put up in its place.

Mother and son had entered the churchyard. They stopped before the old bell, and the mother told the boy how it had been useful for centuries, how it had rung for christenings, weddings and funerals: it had announced festivals and joys, and the terrors of fire—nay, it had sung of the most eventful moments of whole human lives. And the boy never forgot what his mother had told him, and it sounded, sang, and echoed in his breast, until he gave vent to his feelings as a man. The mother also told him how the old bell had been her comfort and her joy in her anguish, how it had sung and sounded when he had been given to her as a babe. The boy looked at the large old bell with a certain reverence; he bent over it and kissed it, old, cracked, and thrown away as it was, standing among grass and nettles. And the boy who grew up in poverty, tall and slender, with reddish hair and a face covered with freckles, kept the old bell in remembrance; yes, so he looked, but his eyes were as clear and blue as the deepest water. And how did he get on? Very well, so well that many people would envy him. We find him again received with the highest favor in the military school, even into the division where the sons of the nobility were sitting: that was honor and good fortune enough! He wore gaiters, a stiff neckcloth, and a powdered wig; and knowledge was instilled into him, although it was by the commands "March! Halt! Front!" All this was likely to result in something.

The old bell had been almost forgotten in the meantime; it was evident that it had to return once more to the foundry, but what would then become of it? Why, that was impossible for any one to predict, and it was equally impossible to say what would be heard of the bell which echoed in the young breast of the boy from Marbach; but it was a sounding metal, and it rung so that its sound was heard far over the world; and the narrower the school-room became, the louder the "March! Halt! Front!" was heard, the louder it sounded in the youth's breast. It burst forth in the circle of his comrades, and was heard far beyond the limits of his own country. But that was not why he had received a scholarship in the military school, and free clothing and food. Had he not already been selected for the place which he was one day to occupy in the big clockwork, where we all have a place for general usefulness? How little we understand ourselves! How, then, should others, even the best men, understand us? But it is just the pressure that forms the precious stone. The pressure was here—but would the world be able one day to recognize the jewel?

In the capital of the dukedom a splendid festival took place. Thousands of lamps and lights shined brightly there, rockets flew up, leaving behind them a train of fiery sparks; the splendor of this day is still kept alive in the memory of mankind, and through him, the pupil of the military school, who then in tears and pain, unnoticed, made the attempt to reach a foreign territory. He had either to leave his own country, his mother and all his dear ones, or to sink down in the stream of generality. The old bell had a good time of it; it was lying under the shelter of the church wall at Marbach, well preserved, almost forgotten. The wind was blowing over it and might then already have told of him on whose birth the bell had rung, told how icily it had blown over him in the wood of a neighboring country, where he had sunk down exhausted with fatigue, having with him all his riches and hopes for the future: some written pages of "Fiesco"; the wind might have told of his only patrons, who were all artists, and they stole away while the contents of those leaves were read, to converse over a game of skittles; the wind might have related about the pale fugitive who passed weeks and months in the miserable country inn, where the landlord raged and drank, and vulgar amusements took place while he sang of the ideal.

Difficult days, dark days! The heart itself must suffer and pass through the trials of which it is to sing. Dark days and cold nights also passed over the old bell; it did not feel them, but the bell in the human breast is affected by these miseries. How was the young man getting on? What happened to the old bell? The bell was carried far away, much farther than its sound might have been heard formerly from its high place in the belfry; and the young man?—Well, the bell in his breast sounds farther than even his foot was destined to wander and his eye to see; it rung and continually rings all over the ocean, all over the globe. But let us first see about the church bell. It was taken away from Marbach; it was sold as old copper destined for a foundry in Bavaria; but how and when did this happen? In the capital of Bavaria, many years after the bell had fallen down from the tower, it was said that it was to be melted and used in casting the memorial statue of one of the most eminent men who had ever lived in Germany. And look, how all this came about; strange and wonderful things happen in this world! In Denmark, on one of those green islands where the beech woods rustle and many barrows are to be seen, a very poor boy was born; he had walked in wooden shoes when he carried his father's dinner, wrapped in an old faded handkerchief, out to him at the wharves where he carved ships' figure-heads; this poor child had become the pride of his country; he knew how to carve out of marble such wonderful things that they astonished the whole world; and to this very man the honorable task had been entrusted of shaping in clay a beautiful and majestic figure, to be afterwards cast in bronze, to produce the statue of him whose name the father had once written in his Bible as Johann Christoph Friedrich.

The glowing metal flowed into the mold; the old bell—nobody thought of its home and vanished sounds—flowed also into the mold, and formed the head and breast of the statue as it now stands before the royal castle in Stuttgart, in the place where he whom it represents had walked about, struggling and suffering, harassed by the world, he, the boy from Marbach, the pupil of the Karlschule, the fugitive, Germany's great immortal poet, who sang of the liberator of Switzerland and of the inspired maiden of France.

It was a beautiful sunny day; colors were streaming down from the towers and roofs in the royal city of Stuttgart; in honor of the festival the church bells pealed merrily; one bell alone was silent, it shined in the bright sunshine from the face and the breast of the statue of glory. Just a hundred years had passed since the day when the church bell had rung consolation and joy to the mother, when she gave birth to her son in the poor cottage, who was, later on, the rich man, whose treasures the world blesses—the poet who sang the praise of noble women, the singer of the sublime and magnificent—Johann Christoph Friedrich Schiller.

The Silver Shilling

Once upon a time there was a shilling which came out of the Mint quite bright, springing and ringing, "Hurrah! Now I'm off into the wide world." And into the wide world it certainly went.

The child held it in its warm hands, and the miser in his cold trembling clutches; the old man turned and turned it, goodness knows how many times, while youth immediately let it roll again. The shilling was of silver, and had very little copper about it, and had now been a whole year in the world—that is, in the country in which it had been coined. But one day it went traveling abroad; it was the last coin of its country in the purse which its traveling master carried. The gentleman himself did not know that he still had the shilling, till he came across it.

"Why, here's still a shilling from home," he said; "well, it can make the journey with me."

The shilling sprang and rang for joy, as it was put back into the purse. Here it lay among strange companions which were always coming and going, one making way for the other, but the shilling from home always left in the purse—that was a distinction.

Several weeks had already passed, and the shilling had gone far out into the world without exactly knowing where it was, though it learned from the other coins that they were French and Italian. One said that they were now in this town, another in that, but the shilling could form no idea of all this; he who lives in a sack sees nothing of the world, and that was just its lot. But one day, as it was lying there, it noticed that the purse was not closed, and so it crept up to the opening to have a look round. Now it ought certainly not to have done that, but it was inquisitive, and it had to pay for it. It slipped out into the pocket; and when the purse was taken out at night, the shilling still lay where it had fallen, and went out into the passage with the clothes. There it fell upon the floor; no one heard it and no one saw it.

The next morning the clothes were taken back into the room; the gentleman put them on and continued his journey, while the shilling remained behind. It was found and was to go into service again, so it went out with three other coins. "It is pleasant, after all, to have a look round in the world," thought the shilling, "and become acquainted with other people and other ways."

"What kind of a shilling is this?" were the words it heard at that moment. "That isn't a coin of the realm. It's bad! It's no use!"

Now begins the story of the shilling, as afterwards told by itself.

"'Bad! No use!' These words went through and through me. I knew that I had a good ring and had been properly struck. The people must either have been mistaken or they could not have meant me. But they did mean me though! I was the one they called bad and of no use. 'I must pass it in the dark,' said the man who had received me, and so I was passed in the dark and abused in the daytime. 'Bad, no good! We must try and get rid of it.'

"I trembled between people's fingers every time I was to be passed off on the sly as a coin of the realm. 'Miserable shilling that I am!' I thought. 'Of what use is my silver, my value and my impression, if all that is regarded as worthless?'

"In the eyes of the world one is only what the world takes one to be. It must be horrible to have a bad conscience and creep along in wicked ways, if I, who was quite innocent, felt so miserable because I merely appeared bad. Each time I was brought out I shuddered to think of the eyes that would look at me, for I knew that I should be thrust back and thrown upon the counter as if I were a deception and a cheat. Once I came to a poor old woman who had received me as her pay for a hard day's work, but she could not get rid of me at all. No one would take me—I was a great trouble to the woman. 'I shall really be obliged to deceive some one with the shilling,' she said; 'with the best will in the world I can't lay by such a sum. The rich baker must have it; he can best afford it, but what I'm doing is wrong, after all.'

"To cap all, I have to lie heavy on that woman's conscience," I sighed. "Had I then really changed so in my old age?"

"The woman betook herself to the rich baker's, but he knew far too well what a good shilling was, to take me; so he threw me back right into the woman's face, and she got no bread for me. I felt heartily grieved that I had been coined in such a way as to cause others distress—I, who in my younger days had been so happy in the certainty of my value, and in the consciousness of my true impression. I became as sad as a poor shilling can be, whom no one will take. The woman took me home again, and, looking at me in a kind, friendly way, said, 'No, I will not deceive any one with you. I will bore a hole through you, so that every one may see you are bad. And yet it just occurs to me that you may perhaps be a lucky shilling. The idea seems to have got into my head of itself, and I am almost forced to believe it. I will bore a hole through the shilling and put a string through it, and hang it round the neck of the neighbor's little boy for a lucky shilling.' And she bored a hole through me; it is by no means pleasant to have a hole bored through one, but much may be borne if it is done with a good intention. A string was passed through me, and I became a kind of medal; I was hung round the child's neck and the child smiled at me, and kissed me, and I lay all night on its warm, innocent bosom.

"When morning came, the child's mother took me up in her fingers, and as she looked at me, I could feel very well that she had her own thoughts about me. She brought out a pair of scissors and cut the string.

"'A lucky shilling!' she said. 'Well, we shall soon find that out!' And she laid me in vinegar till I turned quite green; then she stopped up the hole, rubbed me a little, and went to the lottery-collector, when it was getting dark, to buy a ticket that should bring her luck.

"How wretched I was! There was a feeling within me as if I were going to break, for I knew that I should be called bad and thrown down—right before a whole crowd of shillings and coins, too, who lay there bearing inscriptions and figures of which they might be proud. But that degradation was spared me. There were a number of people at the collector's, and he had a great deal to do; so I was thrown chinking into the drawer with the other money. I don't know whether the ticket won, but this I do know, that the very next morning I was recognized as a bad shilling, laid aside, and sent out to deceive and go on deceiving. Such treatment is hardly to be endured when one really has a good character, and that I certainly had.

"For years I passed in this way from hand to hand, and from house to house, always abused and always unwelcome; no one trusted me and I lost confidence in myself and in the world. It was a terrible time! One day a traveler, a stranger, arrived, and I was passed to him. He was simple-hearted enough to take me for a current coin, but when he wanted to pass me on, I again heard the cry, 'No use! Bad!'

"'I received it as a good one,' said the man, looking at me closely; suddenly his whole face smiled, and that no other face had done when it looked at me. 'Why, how's that?' he said. 'That's one of the coins of my own country—a good honest shilling from home—and they have bored a hole through it, and call it bad. That's very funny! I'll keep you and take you home with me.'

"I felt a thrill of delight, for I had been called a good honest shilling, and was to be taken home again, where every one would recognize me, and know that I was made of good silver and bore a true stamp. I could have thrown out sparks for joy, but you see it is not in my nature to do so; steel can do that, but not silver.

"I was wrapped up in fine white paper so that I should not get mixed up with the other coins and go astray; and on festive occasions, when countrymen met together, I was handed round and good things were said about me. They said I was very interesting: it is certainly wonderful that one may be interesting without saying a single word.

"At last I reached home. All my troubles were at an end, and joy returned to me, for I was of good silver and had the right stamp. I had no more trials to undergo, although a hole had been bored through me, as though I were bad; but that does not matter as long as one is really not so. Everything comes right in the end, if we only wait long enough—that's my belief!" said the shilling.

The Girl Who Trod on a Loaf

The story of the girl who trod on a loaf of bread in order to avoid soiling her shoes, and how she was punished for it, is well known; it is written down—nay, even printed. Ingé was the girl's name; she was a poor child, but proud and haughty; there was a bad foundation in her, as the saying is. Already, when quite a small child, it amused her greatly to catch flies, pull their wings off, and to transform them into creeping things. Later on she took cockchafers and beetles, stuck them on a needle, and held a green leaf or a little piece of paper close to their feet. Then the poor animal seized it, and turned it over and over in its struggles to get free from the needle. "Now the cockchafer is reading," said Ingé, "look how it turns the leaf over." As years passed by she became rather worse than better, but she was beautiful, and that was her misfortune; otherwise something else might have happened to her than what really happened.

"Your bad disposition ought to be thoroughly rooted out," her own mother said to her. "As a child you have often trampled upon my apron, but I am afraid you will one day trample on my heart."

And that she really did.

She went into the country, and entered the service of some rich people who treated her like their own child, and dressed her accordingly; she looked very well, but her haughtiness increased.

When she had been there about a year, her mistress said to her: "Ingé, you ought to go for once to see your parents."

And Ingé went off, but only in order to show herself in her native place; she wished people to see how grand she had become. But when she came to the entrance of the village and saw the young men and girls chatting there, and her own mother near them, resting on a stone, and having a bundle of sticks in front of her which she had picked up in the wood, Ingé turned back; she was ashamed to think that she, who was so well clad, had a poor ragged woman for a mother, who picked up sticks in the wood. And she was not sorry that she returned; she was only angry.

Again six months passed by, and her mistress said: "You ought to go home again and visit your parents, Ingé. I will give you a large loaf of bread for them. I am sure they will be pleased to see you."

Ingé put her best dress and her new shoes on, raised her skirt, and walked very carefully that she might be clean and neat about the feet and for that no one could find fault with her. But when she came to the point where the path runs over the moor, where it was muddy, and where many puddles had formed, she threw the loaf down and trod on it, in order to keep her shoes clean; but while she was thus standing with one foot on the loaf and the other raised up in order to go on, the loaf sank down with her deeper and deeper, and she entirely disappeared. A large puddle with bubbles on it was all that was left to show where she had sunk. That is the story.

But what became of Ingé? She sank down into the ground, and came to the Marsh Woman below, where she was brewing. The Marsh Woman is a sister of the Elfin Girls, who are known well enough, for there are songs and pictures of them; but of the Marsh Woman people only know that when in the summer mists rise in the meadows, she is brewing below. Ingé sank down to the Marsh Woman's brewery, but there nobody can bear to stay long. The dung hole is a splendid drawing-room compared to the Marsh Woman's brewery. Every vessel smells so disagreeably that one almost faints, and in addition the barrels are so closely packed that if there were a small opening between them through which one might creep, it would be impossible because of the wet toads and fat serpents which abide there. In this place Ingé arrived; all the horrible creeping things were so icy cold, that she shuddered all over, and then she became more and more rigid. She stuck fast to the loaf, which dragged her down as an amber button attracts a straw.

The Marsh Woman was at home. There were visitors at the brewery, for Old Bogey and his grandmother inspected it. And Old Bogey's grandmother is a wicked old woman, who is never idle; she never rode out on visits without having her needlework with her, and also here she had not forgotten it. She sewed little bits of leather to be attached to men's shoes, so that they continually wander about without being able to settle anywhere; she embroidered cobwebs of lies, and made crochet-work of foolish words which had fallen to the ground: all this was for men's disadvantage and destruction. Yes, indeed! She knew how to sew, to embroider, and to crochet—this old grandmother.

She saw Ingé, put her spectacles on, and looked at her again.

"That's a girl who possesses talents," she said; "and I request you to let me have the little one as a memento of my visit here. She will make a suitable statue in my grandson's ante-room."

And she was given to her, and thus Ingé came into still lower regions. People do not go there directly, but they can get there by a circuitous road, when they have the necessary talents. That was an endless ante-room; one felt quite dizzy if one looked forward or backward. A crowd of people, exhausted to death, were standing here and waiting for the gate of mercy to be opened to them. They had to wait a long time. Large, fat, waddling spiders spun cobwebs, which lasted thousands of years, over their feet, and cut like iron foot-traps and copper chains; besides this, every soul was filled with everlasting restlessness—a restlessness of misery. The miser was standing there, and had forgotten the key of his money-box; the key was in the keyhole, he knew that. It would lead us too far to enumerate all the tortures and misery which were seen there. Ingé felt inexpressible pain when she had to stand there as a statue; it was as if she had been tied to the loaf.

"That is the consequence of trying to keep one's feet clean and tidy," she said to herself. "Look how they stare at me!"

And indeed the eyes of all were fixed upon her; their wicked desires were looking out of their eyes and speaking out of their mouths, without a sound being heard. They were dreadful to look at.

"It must be a pleasure to look at me!" thought Ingé. "I have a pretty face and fine clothes." And then she turned her eyes, for she could not move her neck—it was too stiff. She had forgotten that she had been much soiled in the Marsh Woman's brewery. Her dress was covered with slime; a snake had fixed itself in her hair, and hung down her back; out of every fold of her dress a toad looked forth, croaking like a short-winded pug-dog. That was very disagreeable. "But the others down here look just as dreadful," she thought, and thus consoled herself.

The worst of all, however, was the terrible hunger she felt. Could she not stoop down and break off a piece from the loaf on which she was standing? No, her back was stiff, her arms and hands were rigid, her whole body was like a pillar of stone; she could only turn her eyes in her head, but right round, so she could also see behind her. It was an awful aspect. And then flies came and ran to and fro over her eyes. She blinked, but they did not fly away, for they could not, as their wings were torn off, and they were transformed into creeping things. It was a horrible pain, which was increased by hunger, and at last it seemed to her as if there was nothing left in her body. "If this is to last much longer," she said, "I shall not be able to bear it." But she had to bear it. Then a hot tear fell upon her head, and rolled over her face and her breast, down to the loaf upon which she stood; and another tear fell, and many others more. Who do you think was weeping for Ingé? Her mother was still alive! The tears of grief which a mother sheds over her child always reach it, but they do not redeem; they burn and augment the torture—this unbearable hunger, and not to be able to reach the loaf upon which she was standing with her feet! She had a feeling as if her whole interior had consumed itself. She was like a thin hollow reed which takes in every sound; she heard everything distinctly that was spoken about her on earth, but what she heard was hard and evil. Although her mother shed a great many tears over her, and was sad, she could not help saying, "Pride goes before a fall. That was your misfortune, Ingé. You have much grieved your mother."

Her mother and all on earth knew of the sin which she had committed; they knew that she had trod on the loaf, and that she had sunk and disappeared, for the cowherd had seen it from the slope near the marsh land.

"How you have grieved your mother, Ingé!" said the mother. "I had a sort of presentiment."

"I wish I had never been born!" thought Ingé; "it would have been much better. Of what use are my mother's tears now?" She heard how her master and mistress, the good people who had taken care of her like parents, said that she was a sinful child who had despised God's gifts, and trod upon them with her feet. The gates of mercy would be very slowly opened to her!

"They ought to have chastised me, and driven out the whims, if I had any," thought Ingé.

She heard that a song was composed about her—the haughty girl who had trod on a loaf to keep her shoes clean—and that it was sung all over the country.

"That one must bear so much evil, and have to suffer so much!" thought Ingé. "Others ought to be punished too for their sins! But, of course, then there would be much to be punished. Alas! how I am tortured!"

Her mind now became harder than her exterior. "In such company," she said, "it is impossible to become better, and I don't wish to become better. Look how they stare at me!" Her mind was full of wrath and malice against all men. "At last those up there have something to talk about! Alas! how I am tortured!"

The tears of grief which a mother sheds over her child always reach it, but they do not redeem; they burn and augment the torture.

She also heard how her story was told to children, and how the little ones called her wicked Ingé. They said she was so ugly and wicked she ought to be severely punished. Again and again hard words were uttered about her by children Yet, one day, while grief and hunger were gnawing her hollow body, she heard her name pronounced and her story told to an innocent child—a little girl—and she also heard that the little one burst into tears at the story of the haughty, vain Ingé.

"But will Ingé never come up again?" asked the little girl.

"No, never," was the answer.

"But if she says 'please,' and asks pardon, and promises never to do it again?"

"Then, yes; but she will not ask to be pardoned," they told the child.

"I should like her so much to do it," said the little girl, and was quite inconsolable. "I will give my doll and all my toys if she may only come up. It is too terrible—poor Ingé."

These words touched Ingé to the depth of her heart; they did her good. It was the first time any one had said, "Poor Ingé," and did not add anything about her faults. A young innocent child cried and asked mercy for her. She felt very strange; she would have much liked to cry herself, but she could not do it: she was unable to cry, and that was another torture.

While years passed on above, no change took place below. She more rarely heard words from above; she was less spoken of. Then suddenly one day a sigh reached her ear: "Ingé! Ingé! how sad you have made me. I have said it would be so!" It was the last sigh of her dying mother. Sometimes she heard her name mentioned by her former master and mistress, and these were pleasant words when the lady said: "Shall I ever, see you again, Ingé? One does not know where one comes to!"

But Ingé was convinced that her kind mistress would never come to the place where she was.

Again a long while passed—a long bitter time. Then Ingé heard her name pronounced once more, and saw two stars sparkling above her. These were two kind eyes which had closed on earth. So many years had passed since the little girl had been inconsolable and had wept over "poor Ingé," that the child had become an old woman, whom God was calling back again, and in the hour when thoughts of various periods of her life came back to her mind she remembered how she had once as a little child cried bitterly when she heard the story of Ingé. And the old lady had such a lively recollection, in the hour of death, of the impression the story had made upon her that she exclaimed: "My God and Lord, have I not sometimes, like Ingé, trampled Thy blessings under my feet, without thinking it wrong? Have I not walked about with haughtiness? But in Thy mercy Thou hast not let me sink, but supported me. Oh, do not forsake me in my last hour!" The eyes of the old lady closed, and the eyes of her soul opened to see hidden things. She, whose last thoughts Ingé had so much occupied, saw now how deep she had sunk, and at this sight the pious woman burst into tears; in Heaven she was standing like a child and crying for poor Ingé! And these tears and prayers resounded like an echo in the hollow outside shell that enclosed the fettered tortured soul; the never-dreamed-of love from above overwhelmed her; an angel of God was shedding tears over her. Why was this granted her?

The tortured soul collected as it were in thought every action she had done on earth, and Ingé trembled in tears such as she had never wept. Grief at herself filled her, she felt as if the gates of mercy could never be thrown open to her; and while in contrition she recognized this, a beam of light rushed down to her in the precipice with a force much stronger than that of the sunbeam which melts the snowman that boys have put up, and much quicker than the snowflake melts that falls on the warm lips of a child, and becomes a drop of water; the petrified shape of Ingé dissolved into mist—a little bird flew up with the quickness of lightning into the upper world.

But the bird was timid and shy towards all that surrounded it; it was ashamed of itself, ashamed to face the living creatures, and quickly concealed itself in a dark hole in an old weather-beaten wall. There it sat and cowered, trembling all over and unable to utter a single sound: it had no voice. It sat there a long time before it could see all the splendor around it; indeed it was very beautiful! The air was fresh and mild, the moon threw her silvery light over the earth; trees and bushes breathed forth fragrance, and the place where it sat was pleasant; its feathers were pure and fine. How love and brightness pervaded all creation! The bird wanted to burst into song, and to sing forth all that filled its breast, but was unable to do it; it would gladly have sung like the cuckoo and nightingale in spring. But God, who hears the soundless hymn of praise of the worm, also heard the notes of praise which filled its breast, as the psalms of David were heard before they were expressed in word and tune.

For weeks these soundless songs stirred in the bird's breast; a good deed had to be performed to make them burst forth!

Holy Christmastime approached. A peasant set up a pole near the wall and tied a bunch of oats to it, that the birds of the air might also have a pleasant Christmas and a good feed in this blissful time. When the sun rose on Christmas morn and shined upon the oats, the twittering birds flew in flocks round the pole. Then also a "tweet, tweet" sounded from a hole in the wall—the swelling thought became a sound, the weak "tweet, tweet," a whole song of joy, the thought of a good deed was called to life, the bird left its hiding-place; in Heaven it was known what sort of bird this was!

The winter was hard, the water frozen over, and the birds and the animals in the wood had little food. Our little bird flew over the highroad, and found a grain of corn here and there in the ruts the sleighs made, and a few crumbs at the halting-places; it ate but few, but called all the other starving sparrows that they might have some food. It flew into the towns, looked all round, and where a loving hand had strewn bread-crumbs on a window-sill for the birds, it only ate a single crumb, leaving all to the other birds.

In the course of the winter the bird had gathered so many crumbs and given them to other birds, that altogether they equalled the weight of the whole loaf on which Ingé had trodden to keep her shoes clean. And when the last bread-crumb was found and given away, the gray wings of the bird turned white and expanded.

"There flies a sea-swallow over the water," said the children who saw the white bird; it dived down into the sea and then rose up again into the bright sunshine; it glittered, and it was impossible to see what became of it—they said it flew into the sun.

Two Brothers

In one of the Danish islands, where old Thingstones, the seats of justice of our forefathers, still stand in the cornfields; and huge trees rise in the forests of beech, there lies a little town whose low houses are covered with red tiles. In one of these houses strange things were brewing over the glowing coals on the open hearth; there was a boiling going on in glasses, and a mixing and distilling, while herbs were being cut up and pounded in mortars. An elderly man looked after it all.

"One must only do the right thing," he said; "yes, the right—the correct thing. One must find out the truth concerning every created particle, and keep to that."

In the room with the good housewife sat her two sons; they were still small, but had great thoughts. Their mother, too, had always spoken to them of right and justice, and exhorted them to keep to the truth, which she said was the countenance of the Lord in this world.

The elder of the boys looked roguish and enterprising. He took a delight in reading of the forces of nature, of the sun and the moon; no fairy tale pleased him so much. Oh, how beautiful it must be, he thought, to go on voyages of discovery, or to find out how to imitate the wings of birds and then to be able to fly! Yes, to find that out was the right thing. Father was right, and mother was right—truth holds the world together.

The younger brother was quieter, and buried himself entirely in his books. When he read about Jacob dressing himself in sheepskins to personify Esau, and so to usurp his brother's birthright, he would clench his little fist in anger against the deceiver; when he read of tyrants and of the injustice and wickedness of the world, tears would come into his eyes, and he was quite filled with the thought of the justice and truth which must and would triumph.

One evening he was lying in bed, but the curtains were not yet drawn close, and the light streamed in upon him; he had taken his book into bed with him, for he wanted to finish reading the story of Solon. His thoughts lifted and carried him away a wonderful distance; it seemed to him as if the bed had become a ship flying along under full sail. Was he dreaming, or what was happening? It glided over the rolling waves and across the ocean of time, and to him came the voice of Solon; spoken in a strange tongue, yet intelligible to him, he heard the Danish motto: "By law the land is ruled."

The genius of the human race stood in the humble room, bent down over the bed and imprinted a kiss on the boy's forehead: "Be thou strong in fame and strong in the battle of life! With truth in thy heart fly towards the land of truth!"

The elder brother was not yet in bed; he was standing at the window looking out at the mist which rose from the meadows. They were not elves dancing out there, as their old nurse had told him; he knew better—they were vapors which were warmer than the air, and that is why they rose. A shooting star lit up the sky, and the boy's thoughts passed in a second from the vapors of the earth up to the shining meteor. The stars gleamed in the heavens, and it seemed as if long golden threads hung down from them to the earth.

"Fly with me," sang a voice, which the boy heard in his heart. And the mighty genius of mankind, swifter than a bird and than an arrow—swifter than anything of earthly origin—carried him out into space, where the heavenly bodies are bound together by the rays that pass from star to star. Our earth revolved in the thin air, and the cities upon it seemed to lie quite close to each other. Through the spheres echoed the words:

"What is near, what is far, when thou art lifted by the mighty genius of mind?"

And again the boy stood by the window, gazing out, while his younger brother lay in bed. Their mother called them by their names: "Anders Sandoe" and "Hans Christian"

Denmark and the whole world knows them—the two brothers Oersted.

The Old Tombstone

In a small provincial town, about the time of year when people are wont to say "the evenings are drawing in," the whole family circle was one night assembled in the house of a man of some property.

The weather was still mild and warm; a lamp burned on the table, and the long curtains hung down before the open windows, by which stood many flower-pots; outside in the open air it was a most glorious moonlight night. But they were not talking about this. They were talking about an old large stone which lay below in the yard close by the kitchen-door, and upon which the maids used to stand the copper-kitchen utensils after scouring them, so that they might dry in the sun, and around which the children were fond of playing. It was, in fact, an old tombstone.

"Yes," said the master of the house, "I believe the stone comes from the old convent churchyard, for these, as well as the pulpit, the memorial tablets and the tombstones in the church, were all sold. My father bought the slabs, which were hewn in two and used as paving-stones; but this stone was kept back and has been lying in the yard ever since."

"You can easily see that it's a tombstone," said the eldest of the children. "We can still make out an hour-glass and part of an angel, but the inscription that stood below it is almost entirely effaced; the only thing that is still readable is the name of *Preben* and a capital *S* just after it, and the name of *Martha* a little farther on. The rest is all indistinct, and even those names are only plain when it has been raining or when we have washed the stone."

"Dear me! that must be the tombstone of Preben Schwane and his wife," said the old man; he was so old that he might very well have been the grandfather of all those in the room. "They were among the last people who were buried in the churchyard of the convent. They were a venerable old couple; I remember them from my boyhood's days. Everybody knew them and every one loved them, for they were the oldest people here in the town. People said they had a mint of money, and yet they dresssed very simply and in the coarsest stuffs, but their linen was always dazzlingly white. They were a fine old couple, were Preben and Martha! It did you good to see them both sitting on the bench at the top of the high stone steps in front of the house, nodding at the passers-by. They were very good to the poor; they clothed them and fed them, and in their benevolence there was judgment and true Christianity.

The old lady died first; I remember the day well. I was a little boy, and had gone with my father to old Preben's house, and just as we got there she died. The old man felt it very much and cried like a child. The body lay in the room next to the one in which we were, and the poor husband spoke to my father and to a few neighbors who were there, saying how lonely the house would now be, and how good and faithful his poor wife had been; he told them how they had gone through life together for many years, and how they had first come to know each other and to fall in. love. As I have said, I was only a boy, and stood by listening to what the others said; but I was filled with a strange emotion when I heard the old man speak, and saw how he gradually brightened up, and how his cheeks flushed as he told of the days of their courtship, of her beauty, and of the many little innocent subterfuges he had invented to meet her. Then he spoke of the wedding-day; his eyes sparkled and he seemed to live that happy time over again, while she lay in the little room close by—dead—an old woman; and he was an old man speaking of the days of hope. Yes, yes, such is life! At that time I was only a child, and now I am old—as old as Preben Schwane. Time passes, and all things change. I well remember the day of her funeral; old Preben walked close behind the coffin.

A few years before, the old couple had had their tombstone prepared, and their names and an inscription put upon it—all but the date. The stone was taken to the churchyard in the evening and laid upon the grave; a year later it was lifted, and old Preben was laid beside his wife. They did not leave behind them anything like the wealth people had expected; what there was went to distant relations, to such as had never been heard of till then. The old wooden house with the bench at the top of the high stone steps, under the lime-tree, was pulled down by the Corporation: it was too old and tumble-down to be left standing. When the same fate afterwards befell the convent church, and the churchyard too fell into ruin, Preben and Martha's tombstone, like everything else, was sold to whoever would buy it; and that is how it comes that the stone has not been cut in two and used like many others, but still lies in the yard below—a scouring bench for the maids and a place for the children to play upon. The paved street now passes over the resting-place of old Preben and his wife. No one thinks of them any more!"

And the old man, who related all this, shook his head mournfully. "Forgotten! Everything will be forgotten!" he said.

Then they spoke in the room of other things; but the youngest child, a boy with large grave eyes, got upon a chair behind the curtains, and looked out into the yard, where the moon was shedding its bright light upon the old stone—the old stone which had always seemed to him so tame and flat, but which now lay there like a great leaf out of a book of chronicles.

All that the boy had heard about old Preben and his wife was now concentrated in the stone: he gazed at it, and looking up at the bright moon and out into the clear air, it seemed to him as if the countenance of Heaven shined out over the earth.

"Forgotten! Everything will be forgotten!" was again repeated in the room, and at the same moment an invisible angel kissed the boy's breast and forehead, and whispered to him:

"Preserve the seed that has been entrusted to thee, that it may bloom and ripen! Preserve it well! By thee, my child, shall the effaced inscription of the weather-beaten tombstone be handed down to future generations in bright letters of gold. The old couple shall again wander arm-in-arm and smiling through the old streets, and sit with rosy cheeks upon the high bench under the lime-tree, nodding to rich and poor. The seed of this hour shall ripen in the course of years into a lovely poem. The good and the beautiful is not forgotten; it lives in legend and in song."

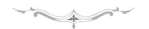

The Snowman

"It is so bitterly cold that my whole body creaks," said the snowman. "The wind is wonderfully invigorating. How that glowing thing up there is staring at me!" He meant the sun, who was just setting. "He shall not make me wink; I will hold the pieces tightly." For you must know that he had two large triangular pieces of red tile in the place of eyes in his head; an old rake represented his mouth, and therefore he had also teeth.

"It is so bitterly cold that my whole body creaks," said the snowman.

He was born amidst the cheering of the boys, and greeted by the tinkling of sleigh-bells and the cracking of whips.

The sun set, the full moon rose large, round and clear on the blue sky. "There he is again on the other side!" said the snowman. Of course he fancied the sun was showing himself again. "I thought I had cured him of staring. Now let him hang there, and give me a light, that I may see myself. I wish I knew how to move, I should so much like to walk about. If I could, I should like to go down and slide on yonder ice, as I have seen the boys do; but I don't know how—I can't even walk."

"Away, away!" barked the old dog in the yard; he was somewhat hoarse, and could no longer well pronounce the proper "Wow, wow." He had become hoarse when he used to live indoors and lie all day long under the warm stove. "The sun will soon teach you how to run; I have seen him teach your predecessor last year, and his predecessors before him. Away, away, they are all gone."

"I do not understand you, friend," said the snowman. "Do you mean to say that she up there is to teach me walking?" He meant the moon. "I have certainly seen her walk a little while ago when I looked her straight in the face, but now she comes creeping from the other side."

"You are dreadfully ignorant," replied the dog, "but that is no wonder, for you have only just been put up. She whom you see up there is the moon; he whom you have seen going off a little while ago was the sun; he is returning to-morrow, and is sure to teach you how to run down into the ditch. We shall soon have a change in the weather, I feel it by the pain I have in my left hind leg; the weather is going to change."

"I do not understand him," said the snowman, "but it strikes me that he speaks of something disagreeable. He who was so staring at me and afterwards went off—the sun, as he calls him—is not my friend; so much I know for certain."

"Away, away," barked the dog; turned three times round himself, and crept back into his kennel to sleep.

The weather really changed. On the next morning the whole country was enveloped in a dense fog; later on an icy wind began to blow, it was bitter cold; but when the sun rose, what a splendor! Trees and bushes were covered with a hoar-frost, they looked like a wood of white coral; all the branches seemed to be strewn over with shiny white blossoms. The many delicate boughs and twigs, which are in the summer completely hidden by the rich foliage, were all visible now. It looked very much like a snowy white cobweb; every twig seemed to send forth rays of white light. The birch-tree moved its branches in the wind, as the trees do in the summer; it was marvelously beautiful to look at.

And when the sun rose the whole glittered and sparkled as if small diamonds had been strewn over them, while on the snowy carpet below large diamonds or innumerable lights seemed to shine even more white than the snow.

"How charming!" said a young girl who stepped out into the garden with a young man. Both stopped near the snowman, and then looked admiringly at the glittering trees. "There is no more beautiful scene in the summer," she said, and her eyes were beaming. "And we can't possibly have such a fellow there in the summer," replied the young man, pointing at the snowman.

The girl laughed, nodded at the snowman, and then both walked over the snow, so that it creaked under their feet like starch.

"Who were these two?" asked the snowman of the dog. "You are longer in the yard than I; do you know them?"

"Certainly I do," replied the dog. "She has stroked me, and he has given me a meat-bone. I shall never bite those two."

"But what are they?" asked the snowman again.

"Lovers," was the dog's answer. "They are going to live together in one kennel, and gnaw on the same bone. Away, away!"

"Are they beings like ourselves?" asked the snowman.

"They are members of the master's family," replied the dog. "Of course one knows very little if one has only been born yesterday. I can see that from you! I have the age and the knowledge too. I know all in the house. I also knew a time when I was not obliged to be chained up here in the cold. Away, away!"

"The cold is splendid," said the snowman. "Go on, tell me more; but you must not rattle so with the chain, for you make me shudder if you do."

"Away, away!" barked the dog. "They say I was once a dear little boy. Then I used to lie on a chair covered with velvet, up in the mansion, or sit on the mistress's lap; they kissed me upon the mouth and wiped my paws with an embroidered handkerchief. They called me Ami, dear sweet Ami. But later on I became too big for them, and they gave me to the housekeeper; thus I came down into the basement. You can look in at the window from the place where you are standing. You can look down into the room where I was one day master, for master I was at the housekeeper's. The rooms were not so grand as above in the mansion, but they were more homely; I was not continually touched and pulled about by the children, and the food was just as good, if not better, than at the mansion. I had my own cushion, and there was a stove in the room, which is at this time of the year the best thing in the world. I used to creep under the stove; there was enough room for me. I am still dreaming of this stove. Away, away!"

"Does a stove look nice?" asked the snowman. "Does it resemble me?"

"The very contrary of you! It is as black as a raven and has a long neck with a broad brass band round it. It eats so much fuel that the fire comes out of its mouth. One must keep at its side, close by or underneath it; there one is very comfortable. Perhaps you can see it from your place."

The snowman looked and noticed something, brightly polished with a broad brass band round it; in its lower parts the fire was visible. A strange feeling overcame the snowman; he had no idea what it was, nor could he explain the cause of it; but all beings, even those who are not snowmen, know it.

"Why did you leave her?" asked the snowman, for he had a notion that the stove was a woman. "How could you leave such a place?"

"I was compelled to," replied the dog; "they threw me out of the house and fastened me up here with the chain. I had bitten the youngest son of the squire in the leg, because he pushed away the bone which I was gnawing with his foot. Bone for bone, I think. But this they took very ill of me, and from this time forward I was chained up. And I have lost my voice, too—do you not hear how hoarse I am? Away, away! I can no longer bark like other dogs. Away, away! That was how it ended."

The snowman was no longer listening to him; he looked unswervingly at the basement into the housekeeper's room, where the stove was standing on its four iron legs, as high as the snowman.

"What a strange noise I hear within me," he said. "Shall I never get in there? It is such an innocent wish of mine, and they say innocent wishes are sure to be fulfilled. I must go in there, and lean against her, even if I must break the window."

"You will never get in there," said the dog, "and if you come close to the stove you are gone. Away, away!"

"I am already now as good as gone," replied the snowman, "I believe I am fainting."

The snowman was all day long looking in at the window. In the dawn the room appeared still more inviting; a gentle light shined out of the stove, not like that of the moon or the sun, but such light as only a stove can produce after being filled with fuel. When the door of the room was opened, the flame burst out at the mouth of the stove—that was its custom. And the flame was reflected on the white face and breast of the snowman, and made him appear quite ruddy.

"I can no longer stand it," he said; "how well it suits her to put out her tongue!"

The night was long, but it did not appear so to the snowman, for he was standing there deeply lost in his pleasant thoughts, which were so freezing that it creaked.

In the morning the window-panes of the basement were covered with ice; the most beautiful ice-flowers that one could wish for were upon them; but they concealed the stove.

The ice on the window-panes would not thaw; the snowman could not see the stove which he imagined to be such a lovely woman. It groaned and creaked within him; it was the very weather to please a snowman; but he did not rejoice—how could he have been happy with this great longing for the stove?

"That is a dreadful disease for a snowman," said the dog; "I suffered myself from it one day, but I have got over it." "Away, away!" he barked. "We shall soon have a change in the weather," he added.

The weather changed; it was beginning to thaw. The warmer it became, the more the snowman vanished away. He said nothing, he did not complain; that is the surest sign.

One morning he broke down; and lo! in the place where he had stood, something like a broomstick was sticking in the ground, round which the boys had built him up.

"Well, now I understand why he had such a great longing," said the dog; "I see there is an iron hook attached to the stick, which people use to clean stoves with; the snowman had a stove-scraper in his body, that has moved him so. Now all is over. Away, away!"

And soon the winter was gone. "Away, away," barked the hoarse dog, but the girls in the house were singing:

"Thyme, green thyme, come out, we sing.
Soon will come the gentle spring;
Ye willow trees, your catkins don:
The sun shines bright and days roll on.
Cuckoo and lark sing merrily too,
We also will sing Cuckoo! cuckoo!"

And nobody thought of the snowman.

The Wild Swans

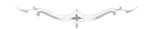

Far from here, where the swallows fly when it is winter with us, there lived a king who had eleven sons, and one daughter, called Elise. The eleven brothers were princes, and went to school with stars on their breasts and swords at their sides. They wrote with diamond pencils on gold slates, and learning by heart came as easy to them as reading; one could see at once that they were princes. Their sister Elise sat upon a little plate-glass stool, and had a picture-book that had been bought for half a kingdom.

Oh, the children were extremely well cared for, but it was not to be always so. Their father, who was king of the whole country, married a wicked queen, who did not love the poor children at all. That they found out the very first day. There were grand doings at the castle, and the children were playing at "visiting"; but instead of having as many cakes and roasted apples as they used to have, the queen gave them only some sand in a teacup and told them they could pretend it was something.

The following week she took little Elise to live with some peasants in the country, and it was not long before she told the king so much that was untrue about the poor princes that he would have nothing more to do with them.

They became eleven beautiful wild swans.

"Go out into the world and gain your own living," said the wicked queen. "Fly, like the great dumb birds!" But she could not make matters as bad as she wished, for they became eleven beautiful wild swans.

With a strange cry they flew out of the castle windows, far away over the park and into the wood.

It was still early in the morning when they passed the place where their sister Elise lay sleeping in the peasant's hut. Here they hovered about the roof, stretched their long necks and flapped their wings; but no one heard or saw them. They were obliged to go farther, high up in the clouds, out into the wide world; so they flew on to a great dark forest which extended as far as the seashore.

Poor little Elise stood in the peasant's hut playing with a green leaf, for she had no other plaything. She pricked a hole in the leaf, and looking up at the sun through it, she seemed to see her brothers' bright eyes, and whenever the warm sunbeams fell upon her cheeks she thought of all their kisses.

One day passed just like the other. When the wind blew through the great edge of rose bushes before the house it would whisper to the roses: "Who can be more beautiful than you?" But the roses would shake their heads and say "Elise!" And when the old woman sat before the door on Sundays reading her hymn-book, the wind would turn over the leaves and say to the book: "Who can be more pious than you?" And the hymn-book would answer, "Elise." It was the pure truth too, what the roses and the hymn-book said.

When she was fifteen years old she was to go home; and when the queen saw how beautiful she was she disliked her more than ever. She would gladly have changed her into a wild swan like her brothers; but she did not dare to do so at once, because the king wished to see his daughter.

Early in the morning the queen went into the bath, which was built of marble and furnished with soft cushions and the most splendid coverings. She took three toads, and, kissing them, said to one: "Get on Elise's head when she enters the bath, so that she may become dumb like you." "Get on her forehead," she said to the other, "and let her become ugly like you, so that her father may not know her!" "Rest on her heart!" she whispered to the third; "let her become wicked, so that she may be tormented." Putting the toads into the clear water, which immediately turned green, she called Elise, undressed her, and made her get in too. As Elise dived under, one of the toads got into her hair, another upon her forehead, and the third upon her breast. She, however, appeared not to notice them, and as soon as she stood up, three red poppies were floating on the water. Had the creatures not been poisonous and kissed by a witch, they would have been changed into red roses. But having rested on her head, her forehead, and her heart, they were bound to become flowers of some kind. She was too pious and innocent for sorcery to have any power over her.

When the wicked queen saw that, she rubbed Elise all over with walnut juice, so that she became dark brown, smeared an evil-smelling salve over her pretty face and entangled her glorious hair. It was impossible to recognize the beautiful Elise.

When her father saw her he was quite startled, and said she was not his daughter. No one knew her except the watch-dog and the swallows; but they were merely poor animals who had nothing to say.

Then poor Elise wept and thought of her eleven brothers who were all away. She stole out of the castle sorrowfully, and walked the whole day over fields and moors till she reached the great forest. She did not know where to go, but she felt extremely miserable and longed for her brothers: she supposed that they, like her, had been driven out into the world, and she determined to seek and find them.

She had been in the forest only a short time when night came on; then she entirely lost her way. So she lay down on the soft moss, said her evening prayer, and leaned her head against the stump of a tree. A deep silence reigned, the air was mild, and all around in the grass and in the moss there gleamed, like green fire, hundreds of glow-worms; when she touched a branch gently with her, hand, the glimmering insects fell down upon her like falling stars.

All night long she dreamed of her brothers; they were playing again as when they were children, writing with the diamond pencils on the golden slates and looking at the beautiful picture-book that had cost half a kingdom. But on the slate they did not make, as formerly, noughts and strokes; they wrote, instead, of the daring deeds they had done and of all they had seen and gone through. And in the picture-book everything was alive; the birds sang, and the people came out of the book and spoke to Elise and her brothers. But when she turned over a leaf, they immediately jumped back, so that there should be no confusion.

When she awoke, the sun was already high in the heavens. It is true she could not see it, for the branches of the tall trees were so closely entwined overhead. But the sunbeams played among them like a wavy golden veil, while the foliage gave forth a sweet fragrance and the birds almost sat upon her shoulders. She heard the splashing of water, for there were a number of large springs which all flowed into a lake having the softest sand for its bed. Although thick bushes grew all around it, the deer had made an opening in one place, and through this Elise went down to the water.

It was so clear that if the wind had not moved the branches and bushes one would have believed that they were painted on the surface; so distinctly was every leaf reflected in it, both those upon which the sun shined and those which were in the shade.

As soon as Elise perceived her own face, she was quite startled, so brown and ugly did it look; but when she wetted her little hand and rubbed her eyes and forehead, her skin appeared as white as before. Then she undressed and got into the fresh water. A more beautiful king's daughter than she could not be found in the wide world.

When she had dressed herself again and plaited her long hair, she went to the bubbling spring, drank out of the hollow of her hand, and wandered far into the forest, without knowing whither. She thought of her brothers, and of the good God who would certainly not forsake her. He had made the wild crabapples grow to feed the hungry, and now led her to a tree the branches of which bent under the weight of their fruit. Here she made her mid-day meal, put some props under the branches, and then penetrated into the darkest part of the forest. It was so still that she could hear her own footsteps, as well as the rustling of every dry leaf that bent under her feet. Not one bird was to be seen, not a single ray of the sun could penetrate the thick dark foliage. The tall stems stood so close together, that when she looked straight before her, it seemed as if she was enclosed by palisades on all sides. Here was a solitude such as she had never known before.

The night became very dark; not a single little glow-worm glimmered in the moss. Sorrowfully she laid herself down to sleep. Then it seemed to her as though the boughs above her were parted, and the good God looked down upon her with kindness, and little angels peeped out from above and behind Him.

When she awoke in the morning she did not know whether she had dreamed it or whether it had really happened.

After walking a few steps she met an old woman with some berries in her basket; the old woman gave her some of them, and Elise asked whether she had not seen eleven princes riding through the forest.

"No," replied the old woman; "but yesterday I saw eleven swans with golden crowns on their heads swimming in the river close by."

And she led Elise a short distance farther to a slope, at the foot of which a streamlet wound its way. The trees on its banks stretched their long leafy branches out towards each other, and where by their natural growth they could not reach across, the roots had been torn out of the earth, and hung, entwined with the branches, over the water.

Elise bade the old woman farewell, and went along the stream to the place where it flowed out to the great open shore.

The whole glorious sea lay before the young girl, but not one sail appeared upon it: not a single boat was to be seen. How was she to get any farther? She gazed on the innumerable little pebbles on the shore; the water had worn them all smooth and round. Glass, iron stones, everything that was lying washed together there, had received its shape from the water, which was, however, softer than her dainty hand.

"It rolls on unweariedly, and thus it makes hard things smooth. I will be just as indefatigable. Thanks for your lesson, you clear rolling waves; my heart tells me that some day you will carry me to my brothers."

Upon the seaweed that had been washed ashore lay eleven white swans' feathers, which Elise collected into a little bunch. Some drops of water lay upon them: whether they were dewdrops or tears no one could tell. It was very lonely on the sea-shore, but she did not feel it, for the sea afforded constant variety; indeed, more in a few hours than the lovely inland lakes presented in a whole year. When a great black cloud came it seemed as if the sea wished to say: "I can look black too"; and then the wind would blow and the waves turn their white linings outside. But when the clouds shined red, and the winds slept, then the sea was as smooth as a rose-leaf; sometimes green, sometimes white. But however peaceful it might be, there was always a slight movement on the shore; the water would heave gently, like the bosom of a sleeping child.

Just as the sun was about to set, Elise saw eleven wild swans, with golden crowns on their heads, flying towards the land; they flew one behind the other, and looked like a long white ribbon. Then Elise ascended the slope and hid behind a bush; the swans descended close to her and flapped their great white wings.

As the sun sank beneath the water, the swans' feathers suddenly disappeared, and there stood eleven beautiful princes—Elise's brothers.

She uttered a loud cry, for although they had altered very much, she knew that they were, and felt that they must be, her brothers. She sprang into their arms and called them by their names; and the princes felt very happy when they saw their little sister, and recognized her too, who was now so tall and beautiful. They laughed and wept, and soon they had told each other how wickedly their stepmother had behaved towards them all.

"We brothers," said the eldest, "fly about as wild swans when the sun is in the heavens; as soon as it has set, we again return to our human shape. We therefore have to be very careful to find a safe resting-place by sunset, for if at that time we should be flying up towards the clouds, we should be hurled down into the depths in our human form. We do not live here; there is a country just as beautiful as this across the sea, but it is a long way off. We have to cross the great ocean, and there is no island on our way where we can rest for the night; only one little rock rises up from the waters midway, and that is only just large enough to accommodate us if we stand very close together. When the sea is very rough, the water dashes up right over us, but still we thank Heaven for this resting-place. There we pass the night in our human form; if it were not for this rock we could never visit our dear native land, for we require two of the longest days in the year for our flight. Only once a year are we permitted to visit our home; we may stay here for eleven days and fly over the great forest from whence we can see the castle in which we were born, and where our father lives, and catch a glimpse of the high church-tower where our mother lies buried. Here it seems as if even the trees and bushes were related to us; here the wild horses career across the steppes as we saw them do in our childhood; here the charcoal-burner sings the old songs to which we danced when children; here is our native land, hither we feel drawn, and here we have found you, dear little sister. We can stay here two days longer; then we must away across the sea to a glorious country, which, however, is not our native land. How can we get you away? We have neither ship nor boat."

"In what manner can I release you?" asked their sister. And they sat talking nearly the whole night, taking only a few hours' slumber. Elise was awakened by the beating of the swans' wings as they rustled above her. Her brothers were again transformed, and flew in great circles, and at last went far away; but one of them, the youngest, remained behind, and the swan laid his head in her lap and she stroked his wings; the whole day they were together. Towards evening the others came back, and when the sun had set they stood there in their natural forms.

"To-morrow we fly away from here, and cannot come back before a whole year has gone by. But we cannot leave you like that. Have you courage to go with us? My arms are strong enough to carry you through the wood; ought not, then, all our wings be strong enough to fly with you across the sea?" "Yes, take me with you," said Elise.

They were occupied the whole night in making a great strong net out of the pliable willow bark and tough reeds. On this Elise laid herself, and when the sun rose, and her brothers were changed into wild swans, they seized the net with their bills and flew with their dear sister, who was still asleep, high up towards the clouds. The sunbeams fell right upon her face, so one of the swans flew over her head so that his broad wings might overshadow her.

They were far away from land when Elise awoke; she thought she was still dreaming, so strange did it seem to her to be carried across the sea, high up in the air. At her side lay a branch with beautiful ripe berries and a bunch of sweet carrots; the youngest of her brothers had picked them and laid them there for her. She smiled at him gratefully, for she recognized him; he it was who flew over her and shaded her with his wings.

They were so high that the largest ship they saw beneath them looked like a white sea-gull lying on the water. A large cloud stood behind them looking just like a mountain, and upon it Elise saw her own shadow and that of the eleven swans in gigantic proportions. It was a picture more splendid than she had ever seen before. But as the sun rose higher and the cloud remained farther behind, the floating shadow picture vanished.

The whole day they flew on like an arrow rushing through the air; but they went slower than usual, for now they had their sister to carry. Bad weather came on and evening drew near; Elise looked anxiously at the setting sun, and still the lonely rock in the ocean was not to be seen. It seemed to her as if the swans were making stronger efforts with their wings. Alas! it was through her that they did not get along fast enough. When the sun had set they must become human and fall into the sea and drown. Then she sent up a prayer to Heaven from the bottom of her heart, but still she perceived no rock. The black clouds came nearer, forming themselves into one great threatening wave, which shot forward as if it were of lead, while continuous flashes of lightning lit up the sky.

The sun was now just at the water's edge. Elise's heart beat fast; suddenly the swans shot down, and so quickly that she thought she should fall, but still they sailed on for a little. The sun was already half below the water when she perceived the little rock beneath her. It looked no larger than if it were a seal putting its head above the water. The sun sank very fast; it looked only like a star as her foot touched the firm ground, and then it vanished like the last spark in a piece of burnt paper. She saw her brothers standing arm in arm around her, but there was only just room enough for them and her, not more.

The sea dashed against the rock and covered them with its spray; the heavens were ablaze with continuous flashes of lightning, and the thunder rolled in peal upon peal; but sister and brothers held each other by the hand and sang psalms, from which they gathered comfort and courage.

In the early dawn the sky was serene and calm; as soon as the sun rose, the swans flew away with Elise from the island. The sea still ran high; it seemed to them, high up in the air, as if the white foam on the dark green sea were millions of swans swimming upon the water.

When the sun rose higher Elise saw before her, half floating in the air, a mountainous land with shining masses of ice on its heights; in the middle of it rose a castle quite a mile long, with row upon row of stately pillars, while beneath waved forests of palms and gorgeous flowers. She asked whether that was the land for which they were making; but the swans shook their heads, for what she beheld was the beautiful but ever-changing castle in the air of the Fata Morgana; into this they might bring no human being. As Elise gazed upon it, mountains, woods, and castle fell into an indistinct heap, and twenty proud churches, all alike, with tall spires and pointed windows, stood in their place. She thought she heard the organ pealing, but it was only the sea that she heard. When she came quite close to the churches they changed to a whole fleet sailing away beneath her, but when she looked down it was only a sea-mist floating on the water. Thus she had a constant change before her, till, at last, she saw the real land for which they were making; there arose the most beautiful blue mountains with cedar forests, cities, and castles. Long before the sun went down she was sitting on a rock in front of a great cave which was overgrown with delicate green creepers looking like embroidered carpets.

"Now we shall see what you dream of here to-night," said the youngest brother showing her her bedroom.

"Heaven grant that I may dream how I can release you," said she. This thought filled her mind completely, and she fervently prayed to Heaven for help; indeed, even in her sleep she continued to pray. Then it seemed to her as if she were flying high up into the air, to the castle among the clouds of the Fata Morgana; and the fairy came towards her, beautiful and radiant, but still bearing a close resemblance to the old woman who had given her berries in the forest and had told her of the swans with the golden crowns.

"Your brothers can be released," she said, "but have you courage and perseverance? Water is indeed softer than your dainty hands, and yet it changes the shape of stones; but it does not feel the pain which your fingers will feel; it has no heart, and therefore does not suffer the anxiety and torment which you must endure. Do you see the stinging-nettle that I hold in my hand? Many of the same kind grow around the cave in which you sleep; now remember that only that kind, and those which grow upon the graves in the churchyard, are of any use. Those you must pluck, although they will make your hands full of blisters. If you tread these nettles underfoot, you will get flax: of this you must plait and weave eleven shirts of mail with long sleeves; throw these over the eleven swans, and the charm will be broken. But remember that from the moment when you begin this task until it is finished, even if it should take years to do, you may not speak; the first word that you utter will go like a deadly dagger straight to your brothers' hearts. Upon your tongue depends their life. Remember all that I tell you!"

And at the same time she touched her hand with the nettle; it was like a burning fire, and awoke Elise. It was broad daylight, and close to where she had slept lay a nettle like the one she had seen in her dream. Then she fell upon her knees to offer up her thanks to Heaven, and went out of the cave to begin her task.

With her delicate hands she caught hold of the hateful nettles; they stung like fire and raised great blisters on her hands and arms; but she would bear it gladly if she could but release her dear brothers. She trod on every nettle with her bare feet and plaited the green flax.

When the sun had gone down her brothers returned and were frightened at finding her so dumb; they believed it was a new charm of their wicked stepmother. But when they saw her hands they understood what she was doing for their sake. The youngest brother wept, and wherever his tears fell she felt no pain and the burning blisters vanished.

She passed the night at her work, for she could not rest until she had released her dear brothers. The following day, while the swans were away, she sat in her solitude; but never before had the time flown so quickly as now. One shirt of mail was already finished, and now she was beginning the second.

Suddenly a hunting-horn was heard among the hills, and she was seized with fear. The sound came nearer and nearer, and she heard the baying of hounds; she fled in terror into the cave, and binding the nettles which she had collected and prepared into a bundle, sat down upon it.

Immediately a great dog came leaping up out of the ravine, and soon afterwards another and yet another; they kept running to and fro, baying loudly. In a few minutes all the huntsmen were before the cave, and the most handsome among them was the king of that country. He went up to Elise, for he had never seen a more beautiful maiden.

"How did you come hither, you lovely child?" he asked.

Elise shook her head; she dared not speak, for her brothers' deliverance and life were at stake. She also hid her hands under her apron, so that the king should not see what she had to suffer.

"Come with me!" he said; "you shall not stop here. If you are as good as you are beautiful I will clothe you in silk and velvet, place a golden crown upon your head, and you shall live in my grandest castle and reign!" Then he lifted her upon his horse. She wept and wrung her hands, but the king said: "I only wish for your happiness. Some day you will thank me for it." With these words he galloped away across the mountains, holding her before him on his horse, and the hunters galloped behind.

When the sun went down, the beautiful royal city with its churches and cupolas lay before them. The king led her into the castle, where great fountains were splashing in the marble halls, and where walls and ceilings were adorned with paintings. But she had no eyes for all this, she only wept and mourned. She passively allowed the women to dress her in royal robes, to plait pearls in her hair, and to draw on dainty gloves over her blistered fingers.

When she stood there in her splendor she was dazzlingly beautiful, so that the courtiers bowed low before her. The king chose her for his bride, although the archbishop shook his head, and whispered that the beautiful forest maiden was certainly a witch who dazzled the eyes and fooled the heart of the king.

The king, however, did not listen to this, but ordered the music to play, the costliest dishes to be served, and the loveliest maidens to dance before them. And she was led through fragrant gardens into splendid halls, but never a smile came upon her lips or from her eyes: she stood there a picture of grief. Then the king opened a little chamber close by, where she was to sleep; it was hung with costly green tapestry and resembled the cave in which she had been. On the floor lay the bundle of flax which she had made from the nettles, and under the tapestry hung the shirt of mail which she had already completed. All these things one of the huntsmen had taken with him as curiosities.

"Here you can dream yourself back in your former home!" said the king. "Here is the work that occupied you there; now, in the midst of all your splendor it will be pleasant for you to recall that time."

When Elise saw the work she was so anxious about, a smile played round her mouth and the blood came back to her cheeks. She thought of her brothers' deliverance, and kissed the king's hand, while he pressed her to his heart and had the marriage feast proclaimed by all the church bells. The beautiful dumb maiden out of the wood became queen of the land.

Then the archbishop whispered evil words into the king's ear, but they did not reach his heart. The marriage was to take place; the archbishop himself had to place the crown upon her head, and he maliciously pressed the narrow circlet down tightly upon her brow so that it pained her. But a heavier band encompassed her heart—sorrow for her brothers. She did not feel bodily pain. Her lips were dumb, for a single word would have caused her brothers to die, but her eyes spoke of tender love for the good handsome king who did everything to please her. He became dearer to her from day to day, and oh! how she wished that she could confide in him and tell him of her sorrows. But she was forced to be dumb, and to remain so until she had finished her task.

Therefore at night she crept away from his side, went into the little chamber which had been decorated like the cave, and wove one shirt of mail after the other. But when she began the seventh, she had no more flax.

She knew that in the churchyard there grew nettles that she could use; but she must pluck them herself, and how was she to get there?

"Oh, what is the pain in my fingers compared to the torture that my heart endures?" thought she. "I must venture it. Heaven will not withdraw its protection from me."

In fear and trembling, as though what she intended doing were a wicked deed, she crept down into the garden in the moonlight night and went through the lanes and the lonely streets to the churchyard. There she saw a circle of vampires sitting on one of the broadest tombstones. These hideous witches took off their rags, as if they were going to bathe, and then digging up the newly-made graves with their long skinny fingers, they snatched out the corpses with fiendish greed and ate the flesh. Elise had to pass close by them, and they fastened their evil glances upon her; but she prayed quietly, collected the stinging nettles, and carried them home to the castle.

Only one person had seen her; it was the archbishop, for he was awake when other people slept. Now he knew that he was right in his opinion, that all was not with the queen as it should be: she was a witch, and therefore she had cast a spell over the king and the people.

He secretly told the king what he had seen and what he feared. And when the hard words fell from his lips the images of the saints in the church shook their heads as though they wished to say, "It is not so; Elise is innocent!" But the archbishop interpreted it in a different way; in his opinion they bore witness against her and shook their heads at her sins. Then two big tears rolled down the king's cheeks; he went home with doubt in his heart and pretended to be asleep in the night. But no peaceful slumber came to his eyelids, and he noticed that Elise got up. Every night she did the same, and every time he followed her softly and saw her vanish into her room.

From day to day his looks grew darker; Elise saw it, but did not understand the reason; but it made her anxious, and what did she not suffer in her heart for her brothers! Her hot tears fell upon the royal velvet and purple; they lay there like glittering diamonds. And all who saw the rich splendor wished to be queen. In the meantime she had almost finished her work; only one shirt of mail was still wanting, but she had no more flax and not a single nettle. Therefore she was obliged to go once more, for the last time, to the churchyard to pluck a few handfuls. She thought with terror of this lonely walk and of the horrible vampires; but her will was firm as well as her faith in Providence.

From day to day his looks grew darker.

Elise went; but the king and the archbishop were following her. They saw her disappear by the gate leading into the churchyard, and when they approached it, they saw the vampires sitting on the tombstone as Elise had seen them; and the king turned aside, for among them he believed her to be whose head had rested on his breast only that evening.

"The people must condemn her," he said: and the people condemned her to be burned.

Out of the splendid regal halls she was led into a dark damp hole, where the wind whistled in through the grated window; instead of velvet and silk, they gave her the bundle of nettles that she had collected. She could lay her head upon them and the hard stinging coats of mail which she had woven were to be her coverlet. But they could have given her nothing more dear to her; she took up her work again and prayed to Heaven. Outside the street-boys sang mocking songs about her; not a soul comforted her with a kind word.

Towards evening there was a rustling of swans' wings close to the grating; it was the youngest of her brothers. He had found his sister, and she sobbed aloud for joy, though she knew that the next night would probably be the last she had to live. But now the work was almost ended, and her brothers were here.

The archbishop now came, to be with her in her last hours: that he had promised to the king. But she shook her head and begged him with looks and gestures to go. That night she had to finish her work, otherwise all would have been in vain; the pain, the tears, and the sleepless nights. The archbishop went away with nothing but evil words for her; but poor Elise knew that she was innocent and went on with her work.

The little mice ran about upon the floor and dragged the nettles up to her feet in order to help in some way too, and the thrush sat upon the window grating and sang all night as merrily as it could, so that Elise should not lose courage.

In the morning twilight, about an hour before sunrise, the eleven brothers stood at the castle gate and requested to be taken before the king. They were told that that could not be; that it was not daylight yet: that the king was asleep and could not be disturbed. They begged and threatened so, that the sentinels came up, and even the king himself came out and asked what the matter was. Just then the sun rose and no brothers were now to be seen, but eleven wild swans flew away over the castle.

The whole people streamed out of the city gates; they were going to see the witch burned. A broken-down old horse drew the cart along on which she sat; they had dressed her in a gown of coarse sackcloth, and her glorious hair hung loose about her beautiful head. Her cheeks were deadly pale; her lips moved slightly, while her fingers were busied with the green flax. Even on the way to her death she did not interrupt the work she had begun; ten shirts of mail lay at her feet, and she was now working at the eleventh. The mob jeered at her.

"Look at the red witch, how she mutters! She has no hymn-book in her hand; no, there she sits with her hideous sorcery—tear it from her into a thousand pieces."

And they all crowded upon her and wanted to tear up the shirts of mail; then eleven wild swans came flying up and sat round her on the cart, beating their great wings. Now the mob fell back terrified. "It is a sign from Heaven! She cannot be guilty," many whispered. But they did not dare to say so aloud.

As the executioner seized her by the hand she quickly threw the eleven shirts of mail over the swans. Immediately eleven beautiful princes stood there. But the youngest had a swan's wing instead of an arm, for one sleeve was wanting in his shirt of mail—that one she had not quite finished.

"Now I may speak," said she. "I am innocent."

And the people who saw what had happened bowed down before her as before a saint; she, however, sank lifeless into her brothers'arms, the suspense, anguish, and pain having told upon her.

"Yes, she is innocent," said the eldest brother, and then he related all that had taken place. While he spoke a fragrance as of millions of roses spread itself in the air, for every piece of wood piled around the stake had taken root and was sending out shoots. There stood a fragrant hedge, tall and thick, full of red roses; on the top was a flower of dazzling whiteness, gleaming like a star. This the king plucked and placed upon Elise's bosom, whereupon she awoke with peace and happiness in her heart.

All the church bells rang of their own accord and the birds came in great flocks. There was a wedding procession back to the castle such as no king had ever seen.

The Snail and the Rose-Tree

Round about the garden ran a hedge of hazel-bushes; beyond the hedge were fields and meadows with cows and sheep; but in the middle of the garden stood a rose-tree in bloom, under which sat a snail, whose shell contained a great deal—that is, himself. "Only wait till my time comes," he said; "I shall do more than grow roses, bear nuts, or give milk, like the hazel-bush, the cows and the sheep."

"I expect a great deal from you," said the rose-tree. "May I ask when it will appear?"

"I take my time," said the snail. "You're always in such a hurry. That does not excite expectation."

The following year the snail lay in almost the same spot, in the sunshine under the rose-tree, which was again budding and bearing roses as fresh and beautiful as ever. The snail crept half out of his shell, stretched out his horns, and drew them in again.

"Everything is just as it was last year! No progress at all; the rose-tree sticks to its roses and gets no farther."

The summer and the autumn passed; the rose-tree bore roses and buds till the snow fell and the weather became raw and wet; then it bent down its head, and the snail crept into the ground.

A new year began; the roses made their appearance, and the snail made his too.

"You are an old rose-tree now," said the snail. "You must make haste and die. You have given the world all that you had in you; whether it was of much importance is a question that I have not had time to think about. But this much is clear and plain, that you have not done the least for your inner development, or you would have produced something else. Have you anything to say in defense? You will now soon be nothing but a stick. Do you understand what I say?"

"You frighten me," said the rose-tree. "I have never thought of that."

"No, you have never taken the trouble to think at all. Have you ever given yourself an account why you bloomed, and how your blooming comes about—why just in that way and in no other?"

"No," said the rose-tree. "I bloom in gladness, because I cannot do otherwise. The sun shined and warmed me, and the air refreshed me; I drank the clear dew and the invigorating rain. I breathed and I lived! Out of the earth there arose a power within me, while from above I also received strength; I felt an ever-renewed and ever-increasing happiness, and therefore I was obliged to go on blooming. That was my life; I could not do otherwise."

"You have led a very easy life," remarked the snail.

"Certainly. Everything was given me," said the rose-tree. "But still more was given to you. Yours is one of those deep-thinking natures, one of those highly gifted minds that astonishes the world."

"I have not the slightest intention of doing so," said the snail. "The world is nothing to me. What have I to do with the world? I have enough to do with myself, and enough in myself."

"But must we not all here on earth give up our best parts to others, and offer as much as lies in our power? It is true, I have only given roses. But you—you who are so richly endowed—what have you given to the world? What will you give it?"

"What have I given? What am I going to give? I spit at it; it's good for nothing, and does not concern me. For my part, you may go on bearing roses; you cannot do anything else. Let the hazel-bush bear nuts, and the cows and sheep give milk; they have each their public. I have mine in myself. I retire within myself and there I stop. The world is nothing to me."

With this the snail withdrew into his house and blocked up the entrance.

"That's very sad," said the rose-tree. "I cannot creep into myself, however much I might wish to do so; I have to go on bearing roses. Then they drop their leaves, which are blown away by the wind. But I once saw how a rose was laid in the mistress's hymn-book, and how one of my roses found a place in the bosom of a young beautiful girl, and how another was kissed by the lips of a child in the glad joy of life. That did me good; it was a real blessing. Those are my recollections, my life."

And the rose-tree went on blooming in innocence, while the snail lay idling in his house—the world was nothing to him.

Years passed by.

The snail had turned to earth in the earth, and the rose-tree too. Even the souvenir rose in the hymn-book was faded; but in the garden there were other rose-trees and other snails. The latter crept into their houses and spat at the world, for it did not concern them.

Shall we read the story all over again? It will be just the same.

She Was Good for Nothing

The mayor stood at the open window. He wore a very fine shirt and cuffs, with a breast-pin stuck in his frill, and was uncommonly well shaved—a piece of his own work. Still, he had given himself a slight cut, and had stuck a piece of newspaper upon it.

"Here! You boy," he cried. The boy was no other than the poor washer-woman's son, who was just passing the house and was respectfully taking off his cap; the peak was broken in the middle, and the cap was evidently used to being rolled up and put in its owner's pocket. In his poor but clean and well-patched clothes, with heavy wooden shoes on his feet, the boy stood there as respectfully as if he were standing opposite the king himself.

"You're a good boy," said the mayor; "you're a civil boy. I suppose your mother is at her washing down by the river, and that's, no doubt, where you are taking what you've got in your pocket. That's a sad habit of your mother's. How much have you there?"

"Half a quartern," said the boy, trembling, and in a low voice. "And this morning she had the same," continued the mayor. "No, it was yesterday," answered the boy. "Two halves make a whole. She is good for nothing. It's very sad that there are such people. Tell your mother that she ought to be ashamed of herself, and mind you don't grow up a drunkard—but I suppose you will. Poor child! Run on!"

And the boy ran on; he kept his cap in his hand, and the wind played among his yellow hair so that great locks of it stood up on end. When he got to the corner he turned down the lane that led to the river, where his mother was standing in the water by her washing bench and beating the heavy linen with a beater. There was a strong current, for the mill-sluices had been opened, and the sheets were floating along with the stream and on the point of overturning the bench. The washerwoman had to place herself against it to keep it up.

"I was very nearly sailing away," she said; "it's a good thing that you came, for I require something to keep my strength up a bit. It's cold here in the water, and I've been standing here six hours already. Have you got anything for me?"

The boy brought out the bottle, and his mother put it to her mouth and took a draft.

"Oh! that does me good! How it warms me! It's just as good as a hot meal, and not so dear. Drink, my boy. You look quite pale, and you're freezing in your thin clothes. One can feel it's autumn. Ugh! how cold the water is! I hope I shall not be ill. No, that will not happen to me. Give me another mouthful and drink some yourself, but only a little drop; you mustn't get used to it, my poor dear child!"

And she went round the plank on which the boy stood, and came ashore. The water dripped down from the straw mat that she had bound round her waist, and from her petticoat.

"I work and toil till the blood runs out at my finger's ends, but I am only too glad to do it if I can bring you up honestly and well, my dear boy."

At that moment a somewhat older woman came along, a miserable-looking object, lame in one leg and with a big false curl hanging down over one eye; this eye was a blind one, and the curl was intended to cover it, but it only made the defect more striking. She was a friend of the washerwoman's, and was called by the neighbors "lame Martha with the curl."

"Poor thing, how you work and stand in the cold water! You really want something to warm you a little, and yet the gossips will cry out about the few drops you drink." And in a few minutes' time all that the mayor had said was laid before the washerwoman, for Martha had heard all, and it had made her angry to hear him talk in that way to the child of its own mother, and of the few drops that she took; and just on that day, too, when he himself was giving a large dinner-party at which there would be wine by the bottle. "Good strong wine! A good many will drink more than they want; but that's not called drinking. They are good, but they call you good for nothing," said Martha.

"Ah, so he spoke to you, my child?" said the washerwoman, and her lips trembled as she spoke. "He says you have a mother who is good for nothing. Perhaps he's right; still he ought not to have told my child so. But a great deal of my misfortune comes from that house."

"Yes, you were in service there when the mayor's parents were alive and lived in that house. That's many years ago. Many bushels of salt have been eaten since then, and one may well be thirsty," said Martha, smiling. "The mayor gives a big dinner to-day; the guests were to have been put off, but it was too late, and the dinner was already cooked. I heard so from the footman. A letter came a little while ago, saying that the younger brother had died in Copenhagen."

"Died!" cried the washerwoman, turning deathly pale.

"Yes, died!" said Martha. "Do you take that so much to heart? It is true, you knew him many years ago when you were in service there."

"Is he dead? He was such a good, kind man! There are not many like him." And the tears rolled down her cheeks. "Oh, great heavens, everything is going round—that's because I emptied the bottle—I couldn't stand so much—I feel quite ill." And she leaned against the plank.

"Good heavens! You are indeed ill," cried the other woman. "Come, try to get over it. No, you are really seriously ill. It will be best for me to take you home."

"But the washing there!"

"I'll look after the washing. Come, give me your arm. The boy can stop and take care of the linen, and I'll come back and finish the few pieces that are left."

The washerwoman's legs gave way beneath her. "I stood too long in the cold water, and I have eaten and drunk nothing since this morning. The fever has hold of me. Oh! heavens, help me to get home! My poor child!" She wept. The boy wept too and soon he was sitting alone by the river beside the damp washing. The two women walked along very slowly, the washerwoman dragging her tottering limbs through the lane, and then turning the corner of the street passed the house of the mayor, just opposite to which she sank down on the stones. A crowd collected, and lame Martha ran into the house for help, while the mayor and his guests came to the window."

"It's the washerwoman!" he said; "she has had a drop too much. She's good for nothing. It's a pity for the pretty boy she has. I really like the boy, but his mother's good for nothing."

The washerwoman came to herself again, and they took her into her humble dwelling where she was put to bed. The kind-hearted Martha made her a jug of spiced ale with some butter and sugar; this medicine she thought was the best. Then she went to the river, and though she meant well she finished the washing very badly—in fact she only pulled the wet things out of the water and put them into a basket.

Towards evening she was sitting in the poor little room with the washerwoman. The mayor's cook had given her some baked potatoes and a fine fat piece of ham for the sick woman; with those Martha and the boy had a good feast while the patient enjoyed the smell which she thought was very nourishing.

The boy was put to bed, in the same one, too, in which his mother lay; but his place was crosswise at her feet, and his blanket consisted of an old carpet made of blue and white patchwork.

The washerwoman now began to feel a little better; the spiced ale had strengthened her, and the smell of the good fare had done her good.

"Thank you, you good soul," she said to Martha. "I want to tell you something when the boy is asleep. I think he sleeps already. How good and sweet he looks as he lies there with his eyes closed! He doesn't know what his mother has gone through, and God grant that he may never hear it. I was in service at the councillor's, the mayor's father, and it happened that the youngest of the sons, who was a student, came home. I was young then, and a wild girl, but honest—that I can say before Heaven. The student was very merry and kind, and a brave-hearted fellow. Every drop of blood in his veins was honest and true, and there was not a better man on earth. He was a son of the house and I was only a servant, but we loved each other truly and honorably; a kiss is no sin after all if people really love each other. And he told his mother all about it, for he worshipped her like a goddess. She was so wise and gentle! He started off on a journey, but before he went he put his gold ring on my finger, and scarcely had he left the house when my mistress sent for me. Her words were earnest but kind, and it seemed as if an angel were speaking to me; she showed me clearly the difference there was between him and me, both mentally and materially.

" 'Now he is attracted by your good looks,' said she, 'but they will fade in time. You have not been educated as he has; you are not each other's equals in mind, and that is the misfortune. I respect the poor; in the sight of God they may occupy a higher place than many of the rich. But here on earth we must take care not to get into a false track as we go onwards, lest our wagon be upset and we get thrown out. I hear that an honest man, a workman, has asked you to marry him—I mean Erick, the glove-maker. He is a widower, has no children, and is well-to-do; think it over.'

"Every word that she said went to my heart like a knife, but the lady was right, and that weighed heavily upon me. I kissed her hand and wept bitter tears, and wept still more when I got to my room and threw myself on the bed. The night that followed was a weary one for me, and God knows what I endured. On the following Sunday I took the communion, so that light might come to me. It seemed just like the act of Providence: as I went out of church, Erick came towards me. There was now no longer any doubt in my soul; we were suited to each other both in rank and in means, indeed he was even a well-to-do man. So I went up to him, took his hand and said: 'Do you still think of me?'

"'Yes, ever and always,' he said.

"'Will you marry a girl who respects and honors, but who does not love you, though that may come later?'

"'That will come,' said he, and upon that I gave him my hand. I went home to my mistress; the gold ring which her son had given me I used to wear next my heart, for I could not put it on my finger during the day but only at night when I went to bed. 1 kissed it till my lips bled, and then I gave it to my mistress, telling her that the banns for the glove-maker and myself would be put up the following week. Then my mistress put her arms round me and kissed me. *She* did not say that I was good for nothing, but at that time I was perhaps better than I am now, although I had not yet been visited by the misfortunes of this world. We were married at Candlemas; for the first year all went well. We had one workman and one apprentice, and you, Martha, were our servant."

"Oh, you were a dear, good mistress," said Martha, "I shall never forget how kind you and your husband were."

"Yes, those were my happy years when you were with us. We had no children then. The student I never saw. Yes, I did though—once! but he did not see me. He was here for his mother's funeral. I saw him standing by the grave, looking as pale as death and very sad, but that was on account of his mother. Later, when his father died, he went to foreign countries and never came here again. He never married, I know that; I believe he became a lawyer. He had forgotten me, and even if he had seen me, he would certainly not have known me again, so miserable do I look now. So it's all for the best."

Then she spoke of her days of trial, and related how misfortune had, as it were, rushed upon them.

"We possessed," she said, "five hundred dollars, and there being a house in the street to be sold for two hundred, we thought it would pay to pull it down and build a new one, and so it was bought. The builder and carpenter estimated the new house to cost a thousand and twenty dollars. Erick had credit, and borrowed the money in the chief town, but the captain who was to have brought it was shipwrecked, and the money went down with him.

"About that time my dear sweet boy, who is sleeping there, came into the world, and my husband was seized with a long and severe illness; for nine months was I obliged to dress and undress him. We were continually going backwards, and got into debt. Everything that we had went, and then my husband died. 1 have worked and toiled and striven for the sake of my child; I have scrubbed steps and washed linen, both coarse and fine, but I was not to be better off—it was God's will. But He will soon take me to Himself, and will not forsake my boy." Then she fell asleep.

Towards morning she felt refreshed and strong enough, she believed, to go back to her work. She had just got into the cold water again when she was seized with a fit of trembling and fainted. And clutching the air convulsively with her hand, she took one step forward and fell down. Her head lay upon the bank, but her feet were in the water; the wooden shoes that she had worn—with a handful of straw in each—floated along with the stream, and so Martha found her when she brought her some coffee.

In the meantime a messenger had been sent to her house by the mayor to say she was to come to him at once, as he had something to tell her. It was too late. A surgeon had been sent for to open a vein, but the washerwoman was dead.

"She has drunk herself to death," said the mayor.

In the letter which brought the tidings of his brother's death, the contents of the will had been given, and according to this, six hundred dollars had been left to the glove-maker's widow, who had once been in service with his parents. The money was to be paid at discretion in large or small sums to her or her child.

"There was some nonsense between my brother and her," said the mayor. "It's a good thing she's gone. Now the boy will get all, and I'll place him with some honest people; he may become a good workman."

And Heaven laid its blessing upon these words.

The mayor sent for the boy, promised to look after him, and added how fortunate it was that his mother had died, for she was good for nothing. They carried her to the churchyard, the churchyard in which the poor are buried Martha strewed some sand on the grave and planted a little rose-tree upon it, and the boy stood beside her.

"My dear mother," he said, his tears rolling down. "Is it true—was she good for nothing?"

"She was good for a great deal," said the old servant, looking up to Heaven. "I have known it for many years, but most of all since the evening before her death. I tell you she was good for a great deal, and God in Heaven will say so too, though the world may say: 'She was good for nothing.'"

The Traveling Companion

Poor John was in great trouble, for his father was very ill and could not be cured. Besides these two there was no one at all in the little room: the lamp on the table was almost out, and it was late at night.

"You have been a good son, John," said the sick father; "the Lord will help you on in the world." He looked at him with his grave loving eyes, took a deep breath, and died: it seemed as if he were asleep. John wept; now he had no one in the world, neither father nor mother, neither sister nor brother. Poor John! He lay on his knees at the bedside, kissed his dead father's hand, and wept many bitter tears; but at last his eyes closed, and he fell asleep with his head resting against the hard bedpost.

Then he dreamed a strange dream. He saw the sun and moon bow down before him; he saw his father alive and well again, and heard him laugh as he always laughed when he was right merry.

A beautiful girl, with a golden crown on her long shining hair, gave him her hand, and his father said: "Do you see what a bride you have obtained? She is the most beautiful maiden in the world." Then he awoke, and all the joy was gone; his father lay dead and cold upon the bed, and there was no one else in the room. Poor John!

The next week the funeral took place. John walked close behind the coffin; he could no longer see the kind father who had loved him so dearly. He heard them throwing the earth down upon the coffin, and gazed upon it till only the last corner was to be seen; but with the next shovelful of earth that too was hidden. Then he felt as if his heart must burst with sorrow. Those

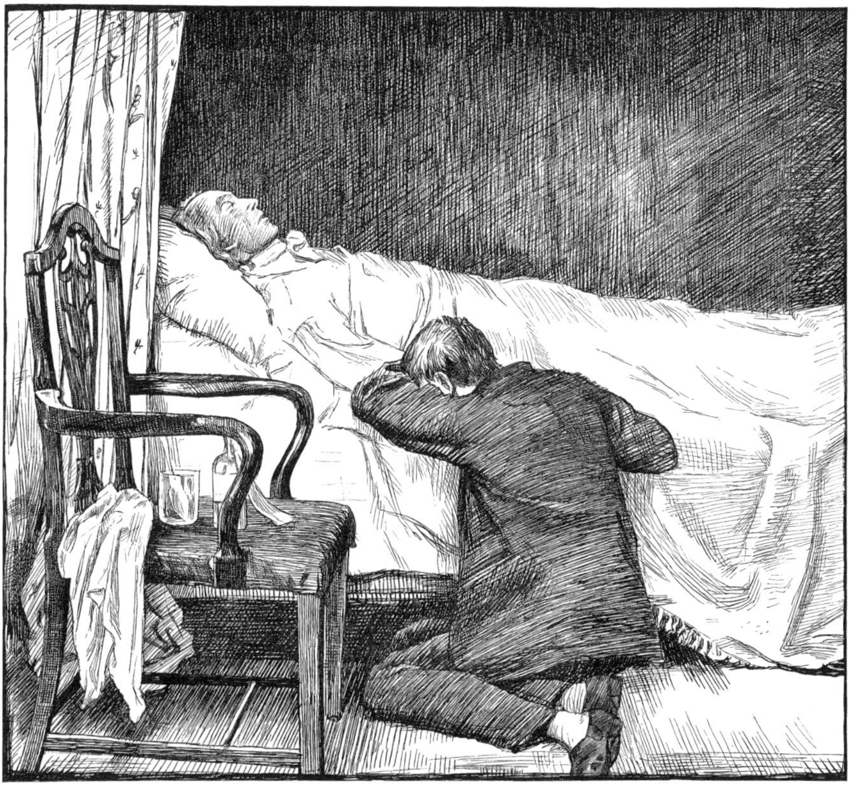

He lay on his knees at the bedside, kissed his dead father's hand, and wept many bitter tears.

around him were singing a psalm in beautiful sacred tones that brought tears into his eyes; he wept, and that did him good in his grief.

The sun shone beautifully upon the green trees, as if it would say: "You must not give way to sorrow any longer, John! Do you see how beautiful the sky is? Up yonder is your father, and he is praying to the good Lord that it may always go well with you."

"I will always be good," said John; "then I shall join my father in Heaven; and what joy it will be when we see each other again! How much shall I then be able to tell him! And he will show me so many things, and explain to me the glory of Heaven, just as he used to instruct me here upon earth. Oh! what joy that will be!"

He saw it all so plainly that it made him smile, while the tears were still running down his cheeks. The little birds sat up in the chestnut-trees and twittered. They were joyous and cheerful, although they too had been present at the funeral; but they knew very well that the dead man was now in Heaven, and that he had wings, larger and more beautiful than theirs. They knew that he was happy now, because he had been good down here on earth, and therefore they were pleased. John saw how they flew far out into the world from the green trees, and he felt a desire to fly with them. But first he cut a large wooden cross to place upon his father's grave, and when he brought it there in the evening he found the grave already strewn with sand and flowers. Strangers had done this, for all loved the good father who was now dead.

Early next morning John packed his little bundle, and carefully placed in his belt his whole inheritance, amounting to fifty dollars and a few silver pennies; with this he intended to start out into the world. But he first went to the church-yard to his father's grave, recited the Lord's Prayer, and said "Farewell!"

In the fields through which he passed all the flowers looked fresh and blooming in the warm sunshine; they nodded in the wind as if they wished to say, "Welcome to the green pastures! Is it not beautiful here?"

But John turned round once more to take a last look at the old church in which he had been baptized when a little child, and where he had gone to service with his father every Sunday, and where he had sung many a psalm. On looking back he saw the goblin of the church, with his little red pointed cap, standing high up in one of the openings of the steeple, shading his face with his bent arm to keep the sun out of his eyes. John nodded him farewell, and the goblin waved his red cap, laid his hand upon his heart, and threw him a great many kisses to show that he wished him well and hoped that he might have a right pleasant journey.

John thought of the many beautiful things he would now see in the great splendid world, and he went farther and farther—farther than he had ever been before. He did not know the places through which he passed nor the people whom he met; he was now in quite a strange land.

The first night he had to lie down to rest upon a haystack in the open fields; he had no other bed. But it was a very nice one, he thought; the king could have no better: the whole field, with the brook, the haystack, and then the blue sky above—what a fine bedroom it made! The green grass, with its little red and white flowers, was the carpet; the elder-bushes and the wild roses were bouquets; and the whole brook, with its clear fresh water, in which the reeds bowed down and wished him good evening and good morning, served him as a wash-hand basin. The moon was really a splendid night-lamp high up under the blue canopy, and it would not set light to the bed-curtains—John could sleep in peace. And he did so too, not waking up till the sun rose and all the little birds round about were singing "Good morning! Good morning! Are you not up yet?"

The bells were ringing for church; it was Sunday. The people were going to hear the sermon, and John went in with them, sang a hymn and listened to the Word of God. He felt as if he were in his own church, in which he had been baptized and where he had sung hymns with his father.

Outside in the church-yard were many graves, and on some there grew long grass. Then he thought of his father's grave, which would one day look like these, for he would not be able to weed it and keep it trim. So he sat down, tearing up the weeds, setting upright the wooden crosses that had fallen down, and restoring to their places the wreaths which the wind had carried from the graves.

"Perhaps some one will do the same to my father's grave, since I cannot do so!" thought he.

At the church-yard gate stood an old beggar leaning on a crutch. John gave him the silver pennies he had, and then went farther on his way into the wide world, happy and contented.

Towards evening a dreadful storm came on. He hastened to get under shelter, but the dark night soon fell, and at last he reached a small church which stood alone upon a little hill.

"I will sit down in a corner here," he said, and went in. "I am tired, and must rest for a little while."

So he sat down, folded his hands, and said his evening prayer; and before he knew it he was asleep and dreaming, while outside it thundered and lightened.

When he awoke it was midnight; the storm was over and the moon was shining in through the windows. In the middle of the church stood an open coffin in which lay a dead man waiting to be buried. John was by no means afraid, for he had a clear conscience, and he knew that the dead hurt no one.

Only the living who do evil are wicked. Two of these living wicked people stood close by the corpse, which had been placed in the church before burial; they had come with the wicked intention of taking the poor man out of his coffin and of throwing him out before the church door.

"Why do you want to do that?" asked John. "That is wicked and bad; let him rest, in God's name."

"Fiddlesticks!" said the two evil-looking men. "He has deceived us. He owes us money which he could not pay; and now that he is dead into the bargain, we shall not get a penny of it: that's why we want revenge. He shall lie like a dog before the church-door."

"I have only fifty dollars," said John. "That is my whole inheritance; but I will gladly give it you, if you promise me, upon your honor, to leave the poor dead man in peace. I daresay I shall manage to get on without the money; I have strong healthy limbs, and the Lord will provide."

"Very well," said the men; "if you will pay his debts, we shall neither of us do him any harm, you may depend upon that." So they took the money that he gave them and went their way, laughing loudly at his simplicity. He then laid the body straight again in the coffin, folded its hands, and bidding it farewell went further into the wood with a light heart.

All around him, wherever the moon shone through the trees, he saw the pretty little elves playing merrily. They were not at all disturbed by him; they knew very well that he was good and innocent, and it is only bad people who never see the elves. Some of them were no taller than a finger's breadth, and had their long yellow hair fastened up with golden combs. Two by two they played at see-saw on the large dew-drops that lay upon the leaves and the tall grass; every now and then a drop rolled down, and then they fell among the long blades of grass, causing much laughter and noise among the rest of the little people. It was delightful! They sang, and John distinctly recognized the pretty songs which he had learned when a little boy. Great gaily-colored spiders, with silver crowns on their heads, were made to spin long suspension bridges from one hedge to another, and palaces that looked like glittering glass in the moonshine when the fine dew fell upon them. And so it went till sunrise. Then the little elves crept into the flower-beds, and the wind seized their bridges and castles, which flew through the air like spiders' webs.

John had just left the wood, when a strong manly voice called out after him: "Hallo, comrade, where are you going to?"

"Out into the wide world!" he replied. "I have neither father nor mother, I am only a poor fellow but the Lord will help me."

"I am going out into the wide world, too," said the stranger. "Shall we keep each other company?"

"Certainly," replied John; and so they went together.

They soon grew very fond of each other, for they were both good men. But John perceived that the stranger was much wiser than himself. He had traveled almost all over the world and could speak of every possible thing that existed.

The sun was already high in the heavens when they sat down under a large tree to eat their breakfast. Just then an old woman came up. She was very old and lame, supporting herself on a crutch; on her back she carried a bundle of firewood that she had collected in the woods. Her apron was

GREAT GAILY-COLORED SPIDERS, WITH SILVER CROWNS ON THEIR HEADS, WERE MADE TO SPIN LONG SUSPENSION BRIDGES FROM ONE HEDGE TO ANOTHER, AND PALACES THAT LOOKED LIKE GLITTERING GLASS IN THE MOONSHINE WHEN THE FINE DEW FELL UPON THEM.

tied up, and John saw that she had three large bundles of ferns and willow-boughs in it. As she came near them, her foot slipped, and she fell with a loud cry, for she had broken her leg, poor old woman.

The sun was already high in the heavens when they sat down under a large tree to eat their breakfast.

John at once suggested that they should carry the old woman to her home; but the stranger, opening his knapsack, took out a box, and said that he had a salve that would heal her leg, and make it strong immediately, so that she would be able to walk home herself, as if she had never broken her leg at all.

But he demanded that in return she should give him the three bundles she had in her apron.

"That would be well paid," said the old woman, shaking her head in a strange manner. She was very unwilling to give up the herbs, but it was certainly unpleasant to lie there with a broken leg. So she gave him the three bundles, and as soon as he had rubbed the salve into her leg she got up and walked much better than before. All this the salve could do. But it was not to be bought at the chemist's.

"What do you want the bundles for?" John asked his companion.

"They are three fine bundles of herbs," he replied. "I am very fond of them, for I am an odd kind of fellow."

They walked on some distance.

"Look how the clouds are gathering," said John, pointing straight before him. "How terribly black they are!"

"No," said his companion, "those are not clouds, they are mountains—the glorious high mountains by which one gets up among the clouds and into the fresh air. Believe me, it is delightful to be there. To-morrow we shall certainly be a good stretch on our way."

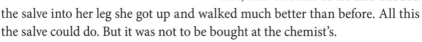

But they were not so near as they looked; they had to walk a whole day long before they reached the mountains, where the dark forests grew up towards the sky, and where there were stones almost as large as a whole town. It would certainly be a great exertion to cross them, so John and his companion turned into an inn to take a good rest, and recruit their strength for the morrow's march.

A great many people were assembled in the roomy bar of the inn, for there was a man giving a puppet-show. He had just put up his little theater, and the people were sitting round in a circle to see the play. A fat butcher had taken the best seat in the first row, and by his side sat his big mastiff—a ferocious-looking animal—staring, like all the others, with all his might.

The show now began; it was a pretty little play, with a king and a queen in it. They sat upon a splendid throne, with golden crowns upon their heads, and long trains to their robes, for their means permitted it. The sweetest little wooden dolls, with glass eyes and great moustaches, stood at all the doors, opening and closing them, so that fresh air might come into the room. It was really a very pretty play. But when the queen got up and walked across the floor, the great mastiff—Heaven knows why!—not being held by the fat butcher, jumped right into the theater, and seized the queen by the waist, making her crack. It was terrible!

The poor showman was very upset and grieved about his queen. She was the most beautiful doll he possessed, and now the ugly mastiff had bitten her head off. But when all the people had gone, the stranger who had come with John said that he would soon make it right again; taking out his box, he rubbed some of the salve that he had used to heal the old woman's broken leg, into the doll. As soon as it had been applied, the doll was whole again; indeed, it could even use all its limbs by itself; there was no longer any need to pull the string. The doll was just like a human being, except that it could not speak. The owner of the little show was delighted; he no longer needed to hold this doll, for it could dance by itself. None of the others could do that.

Later in the night, when all the people in the inn were in bed, some one was heard groaning so terribly and so continuously that every one got up to see who it was. The showman went to his little theater, for it was from that quarter that the groans came. All the wooden puppets, including the king and all the soldiers, lay scattered about; they were groaning terribly, and looking most piteously out of their glass eyes, for they were all most anxious to be besmeared with the salve like the queen, so that they also might be able to move by themselves. The queen immediately fell upon her knees, and holding out her splendid crown, said in imploring tones: "Take this, but anoint my consort and my courtiers!" At this the poor showman could not refrain from weeping; he really felt for her. He promised to give the stranger all the money he should receive for his play on the following evening, if he would only besmear four or five of his best dolls. But the stranger said he desired nothing more than the sword that the showman carried at his side; on that being given him, he besmeared six puppets, which immediately began to dance, and so prettily, that all the young girls who were looking on soon began to dance too. The coachman and the cook, the waiter and the chambermaid, all the guests, and even the shovel and the tongs, joined in; the latter, however, fell over as soon as they had taken the first step. What a merry night it was!

The queen immediately fell upon her knees, and holding out her splendid crown, said in imploring tones: "Take this, but anoint my consort and my courtiers!"

Next morning John left the inn with his companion, ascending the lofty mountains, and going through the vast pine-forests. They got up so high that the church towers far beneath them looked like little blue berries among all the verdure; they could see very far, for many, many miles, places where they had never been. John had never before seen so much of the beauty of this fair world at once. The sun shone warm in the clear blue sky, and when he heard the sweet notes of the horn as it was blown by the huntsmen in the mountains, tears of joy came into his eyes, and he could not refrain from crying: "How good is God to have created so much beauty in the world, and to have given it us to enjoy!"

His comrade too stood there with his arms folded, gazing out over woods and towns, into the warm sunshine.

At that moment they heard a strange sweet sound over their heads, and looking up they saw a large white swan hovering in the air above them and singing as they had never heard a bird sing before. The song, however, grew fainter and fainter; with drooping head the bird slowly sank down at their feet, where the beautiful creature died.

"Two beautiful wings," said John's companion, "so white and large as those which this bird has, are worth money; I will take them with me. Do you see what a good thing it was that I had a sword?"

So he struck off both wings of the dead bird with one blow; he was going to keep them.

They now traveled many, many miles, far across the mountains, till at last they saw a great city before them, with hundreds of steeples that shone like silver in the sun. In the city was a splendid marble castle with a roof of pure gold. There lived the king. John and his companion did not wish to go into the town at once, but stopped at an inn just outside, in order to wash and dress themselves a bit, for they wanted to look neat when they went into the streets.

The landlord told them that the king was a very good man, who never did any one any harm; but as for his daughter—heavens preserve us!—she was a bad princess. She was beautiful enough; nobody was so pretty nor so dainty as she; but what was the use of that? She was a wicked sorceress, who was the cause of many handsome princes losing their lives. She had given everybody permission to woo her. Any one might come, were he prince or beggar; that was all one to her. He was only to guess three things that she happened to be thinking of when she asked him. If he could do so, she would marry him, and he would be king over the whole country when her father died; but if he could not guess the three things, she had him hanged or beheaded. Her father, the old king, was very grieved about it; but he could not prevent her from being so wicked, for he had once declared that he would never have anything to do with her lovers, and that she could do as she liked. Every time a prince came and tried to guess in order to have the princess, he failed, and then he was either hanged or beheaded. Had he been warned in time, he might have gone away without guessing. The old king was so grieved at all the sorrow and misery she caused, that he and all his soldiers spend a whole day on their knees every year, praying that the princess might reform; but that she never would. The old women who drank brandy used to color it black before they drank it—so deeply did they mourn. And more than that they really could not do.

"What a hateful princess!" said John. "She ought really to be flogged—that would do her good. If only I were the old king, she should soon be thrashed."

As they spoke they heard the people shouting "Hurrah" outside. The princess was passing; she was really so beautiful that all the people forgot how wicked she was, and so they shouted "Hurrah." Twelve fair maidens, all in white silk dresses, and each carrying a golden tulip in her hand, rode at her side on black horses. The princess herself was on a white horse adorned with diamonds and rubies. Her riding habit was of pure cloth of gold, and the whip which she held in her hand glittered like a sunbeam. The golden chain around her neck seemed as though composed of small heavenly stars, and her mantle had been made up from more than a thousand butterflies' wings. Nevertheless, she was still more beautiful than her attire.

When John beheld her, he got as red in the face as a drop of blood, and could not say a single word. The princess looked just like the beautiful maiden with the golden crown of whom he had dreamed the night his father died. He thought her so beautiful that he could not help loving her with all his heart. "It could not be true," he said to himself, "that she was a wicked sorceress, who had people hanged or beheaded if they could not guess what she asked them. Every one is free to woo her, even the poorest beggar. Then I will really go to the castle, for I feel that I must."

Every one told him not to go, and warned him that he would certainly share the fate of all the others. His companion, too, tried to dissuade him, but John was of opinion that it would be all right. He brushed his shoes and coat, washed his hands and face, combed his beautiful fair hair, and went into the town alone, and up to the castle.

"Come in," said the old king when John knocked at the door. John went in, and the old king, in his dressing-gown and slippers, came to meet him. He had his crown on his head and held the scepter in one hand and the orb in the other.

"Wait a moment," he said, putting the orb under his arm in order to shake hands with John. But as soon as he heard that he was a suitor, he began to cry so bitterly that both the scepter and the orb fell upon the floor, and he was obliged to dry his eyes on his dressing-gown. Poor old king!

"Pray, don't," he said. "You will share the fate of all the others. Well, you will see." Then he led him out into the princess's pleasure garden. What a terrible sight was there! In each tree there hung three or four princes who had wooed the princess, but had not been able to guess what she had asked them. Every time a gust of wind came, all the skeletons rattled, so that the little birds were startled and never ventured to come into the garden. All the flowers were tied up to human bones, and in the flower-pots were grinning skulls. It was really a strange garden for a princess.

"Now you see it," said the old king. "You will share the same fate. Therefore give up the idea. You will really make me very unhappy, for I take these things much to heart."

John kissed the good old king's hand and said it would be all right, for he was charmed with the fair princess.

Then the princess herself came riding into the courtyard with all her ladies, so they went out to her and bade her "Good-day." She was marvelously fair to look at, and gave John her hand. He loved her still more passionately than before. She could certainly be no wicked sorceress, as all the people wanted to make out. Then they went into the hall and the little pages offered them preserves and ginger-nuts. But the old king was sad and could eat nothing. Besides, the ginger-nuts were too hard for him.

It was arranged that John was to come to the castle again on the following morning; then the judges and the whole council would be assembled to hear the guessing. If it turned out all right he would have to come twice more; but hitherto no one had yet guessed aright the first time, and had all lost their lives.

John was not much concerned about his fate. On the contrary, he was in good spirits, and thought only of the fair princess, feeling sure Heaven would help him—how, he did not know, and preferred not to think about it. He danced along the highroad as he went back to the inn, where his traveling companion was waiting for him.

John did not tire of telling how gracious the princess had been to him, and how beautiful she was. He already longed for the next day, when he was to go to the castle to try his luck at guessing.

But his companion shook his head and was very sad. "I am so fond of you," he said; "we might have stayed together a long while yet, and I am to lose you so soon. Poor dear John! I could weep, but I will not spoil your happiness on the last evening that we shall perhaps spend together. We will be merry, right merry; to-morrow, when you are gone, I will weep undisturbed."

All the people in the town had soon heard that a new suitor for the princess had arrived; and consequently there was great mourning. The theater was closed; all the cake-women tied crepe round their sugar-figures, and the king and the priests lay upon their knees in the churches. There was general mourning, for no other fate awaited John than that which had befallen all the other suitors.

Towards the evening John's companion made a large bowl of punch, and said to him: "Now let us be right merry, and drink to the health of the princess." But when John had drunk two glasses he became so sleepy that it was impossible for him to keep his eyes open; he sank into a deep slumber. His companion lifted him gently from the chair and laid him in the bed. When it had got quite dark he took the two large wings that he had cut off from the swan, and fastened them upon his own shoulders. He then put into his pocket the largest of the bundles which he had received from the old woman who had fallen and broken her leg, and, opening the window, flew over the town to the castle, where he sat down in a corner under the window that belonged to the princess's bedroom.

Stillness reigned throughout the city. As the clock struck a quarter to twelve the window opened, and the princess, with black wings and a long white mantle, flew away over the town to a high mountain. John's companion, making himself invisible, flew after her, and whipped her so with his rod that the blood came at every stroke. What a journey that was through the air! The wind caught her mantle, which spread itself out on all sides like a sail of a ship, and the moon shone through it.

"How it hails! how it hails!" said the princess at each blow she received from the rod; and it served her right. At last she arrived at the mountain and knocked. There was a noise like thunder as the mountain opened and she went in. John's companion followed her, for no one could see him: he was invisible. They went through a long wide passage where the walls shone strangely, for more than a thousand gleaming spiders were running up and down them, making them look as though illuminated with fire. Then they entered a great hall built of silver and gold. Red and blue flowers as large as sunflowers shone on the walls; but no one could pick them, for the stalks were hideous poisonous snakes, and the flowers were flames darting out of their jaws. The whole ceiling was covered with shining glow-worms and sky-blue bats flapping their flimsy wings.

The place looked quite horrible. In the middle of the floor was a throne, borne by four skeleton horses, whose harness had been made by the red fiery spiders. The throne itself was made of milk-white glass, and the cushions were little black mice, who were biting each other's tails. Over it was a canopy of rose-colored spiders' webs studded with pretty little green flies that shone like precious stones. On the throne sat an old sorcerer, with a crown on his ugly head and a scepter in his hand. He kissed the princess on the forehead, gave her a seat by his side on the splendid throne, and then the music began. Great

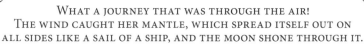

What a journey that was through the air!
The wind caught her mantle, which spread itself out on
all sides like a sail of a ship, and the moon shone through it.

black grasshoppers played on mouth-organs, and an owl beat the drum. It was a ridiculous concert. Little black goblins, each with a will-o'-the-wisp on its cap, danced around in the hall. But no one could see the traveling companion; he had placed himself behind the throne and could hear and see everything. The courtiers, who now entered, looked very noble and grand, but any one with common sense could see what they really were. They were nothing more than broomsticks with cabbages stuck upon them; the sorcerer had blown life into them and given them embroidered robes. But that made no difference; they were only used for show.

After there had been some dancing, the princess told the sorcerer that she had a new suitor, and therefore asked him what she was to think of for him to guess when he came to the castle next morning.

"Listen," said the sorcerer; "I will tell you. You must choose something very easy, for then he will not guess it at all. Think of your shoes. He won't guess that. Have his head chopped off, but don't forget to bring me his eyes when you come to-morrow night, for I want to eat them."

The princess bowed low and said she would not forget the eyes. The sorcerer then opened the mountain and she flew back again; but the traveling companion followed her and whipped her so with the rod that she groaned aloud at the severity of the hailstorm, and made as much haste as she could to get back to her bedroom through the window. The companion then flew back to the inn where John was still asleep, took off his wings and lay down on the bed, for he was naturally very tired.

It was early in the morning when John awoke. His companion got up too, and told that he had had a wonderful dream that night of the princess and her shoe, and therefore begged him to ask her whether she had not thought of her shoe. For that was what he had heard from the sorcerer in the mountain.

"I can just as well ask that as anything else," said John. "Perhaps what you have dreamed is correct, for I trust in Heaven, which I am sure will help me. But still I will bid you farewell, for if I guess wrong I shall never see you again."

Then they embraced each other, and John went into the town and to the castle. The hall was full of people; the judges sat in their armchairs and had eider-down cushions upon which to rest their heads, for they had a great deal to think of. The old king got up and dried his eyes with a white pocket-handkerchief.

Now the princess entered. She was still more beautiful than she had been on the previous day, and greeted every one in the most gracious manner; but to John she gave her hand and said, "Good morning to you."

The courtiers, who now entered,
looked very noble and grand, but any one with common
sense could see what they really were.

Now, John was to guess of what she had thought. Heavens! how kindly she looked at him. But as soon as she heard him utter the word "shoe" she turned deathly pale and trembled all over. But that could not help her, for he had guessed aright.

Gracious! how pleased the old king was—he turned a somersault which it was a pleasure to see. And all the people clapped their hands in his honor and John's, who had guessed rightly the first time.

The traveling companion too was glad when he heard how successful John, had been. But the latter folded his hands and thanked God, who he felt sure would also help him on the two other occasions. On the next day the guessing was again to take place.

The evening was passed like the preceding one. When John was asleep his companion flew after the princess to the mountain and flogged her more severely than the night before, for now he had taken two rods. No one could see him, and he heard everything. The princess was to think of her glove, and this he told John as if he had again heard it in a dream. He was therefore able to guess correctly, and it caused great joy at the castle. The whole Court turned somersaults, just as they had seen the king do on the first occasion. But the princess lay upon the sofa and would not say a single word. Now it depended whether John would be able to guess aright the third time. If he did, he would receive the fair princess's hand, and inherit the whole kingdom after the death of the old king. But if he guessed wrong, he would lose his life, and the sorcerer would eat his beautiful blue eyes.

The evening before the day John went to bed early, said his evening prayer, and slept peacefully. But his companion tied on his wings, hung his sword by his side, took all the three rods, and flew to the castle.

The night was dark and it was so stormy that the tiles flew from off the houses, and the trees in the garden, with the skeletons on them, bent like reeds before the wind. The lightning flashed every moment, and the thunder rolled as though it were one continuous peal all night. The window opened, and the princess flew out. She was as pale as death, but she laughed at the storm and thought it was not bad enough. Her white mantle fluttered in the air like the great sail of a ship, and John's traveling companion whipped her with his three rods till the blood ran down upon the ground and she could scarcely fly any farther. At last, however, she reached the mountain.

"What a terrible hail-storm!" she said; "I have never been out in such weather."

"One can have too much of a good thing," said the sorcerer. Then she told him that John had guessed aright the second time too, and if he did the same the next morning he would have won, and she would never be able to come to the mountain again, or practice such magic arts as she had formerly done; therefore she was very grieved.

"He will not be able to guess it this time," said the sorcerer. "I will think of something for you that he has never thought of, unless he be a greater magician than I. But now let us be merry."

And then he took the princess by both hands, and they danced around with all the little goblins and will-o'-the-wisps in the room. The red spiders ran up and down the walls quite as merrily; and it seemed as if the fiery flowers were throwing out sparks. The owl beat the drum, the crickets whistled, and the black grasshoppers played on mouth-organs. It was a merry ball.

When they had danced enough the princess had to go home, lest she might be missed at the castle. The sorcerer said he would accompany her; they would thus still be together on the way.

Then they flew away through the storm, and the traveling companion broke his three rods across their backs. Never had the sorcerer been out in such a hail-storm. Just outside the castle he bade the princess good-bye, and whispered to her: "Think of my head!" But the companion had heard it, and just as the princess slipped through the window into her bedroom, and the magician was about to turn back, he seized him by his long beard and with his sword struck off his hideous head just at the shoulders, so that the sorcerer did not even see him. He threw the body into the sea to the fishes, but the head he only dipped in the water, and then tying it up in his silk handkerchief he took it with him to the inn and lay down to sleep.

The next morning he gave John the handkerchief and told him not to untie it before the princess asked him what she had thought of.

There were so many people in the great hall of the castle that they stood as close as radishes tied together in a bundle. The councillors sat upon their chairs with the soft cushions, and the old king had new clothes on; his golden crown and the scepter had been polished up, and he looked quite stately. But the princess was pale and wore a black gown, as though she were going to a funeral.

"What have I thought of? " she asked John.

He immediately untied the handkerchief, and was himself startled when he beheld the hideous head of the sorcerer. All the people shuddered, for it was horrible to look at; but the princess sat there like a marble statue, and could not utter a single word. At last she rose and gave John her hand, for he had guessed aright. She looked at no one, but sighed deeply and said: "You are my master now; the wedding shall take place this evening."

"Well, I am pleased," said the old king. "That's just what I wished."

All the people shouted "Hurrah," the band played in the streets, the bells rang, and the cake-women took the black crepe off their sugar figures, for now there reigned great joy. Three roast oxen stuffed with ducks and chickens were put in the middle of the market-place, and every one could help himself to a slice. The fountains ran with the finest wines, and if you asked for a penny roll at the baker's, you got six large buns as a present—and with raisins, too.

In the evening the whole town was illuminated; the soldiers let off cannons, and the boys crackers; there were eating and drinking, toasting and dancing, up at the castle. All the grand lords and ladies danced together; at a great distance they could be heard singing:

"Here are many maidens fair
Dancing all so gladly.
Turning like a spinning-wheel
In the maze so madly;
Dance and jump the whole night through.
Till the sole falls from your shoe."

But the princess was still a witch, and did not care for John at all. His traveling companion had thought of that, and he therefore gave John three feathers from the swan's wings, and a little bottle containing a few drops. He then told him to have a large tub full of water placed before the princess's bed, and when she was about to retire, he must give her a little push, so that she might fall into the water in which he was to dip her under three times, after having first thrown the feathers and the drops into it. This would dispel the charm under which she was, and she would love him dearly.

John did everything that his companion told him. The princess shrieked when he dipped her under the water, and struggled in his hands in the form of a great black swan with sparkling eyes. When she came out of the water for the second time, the swan was white, with the exception of a black ring round its neck. John prayed devoutly to Heaven, and let the water close a third time over the bird's head, and at the same moment it was changed into the most beautiful princess. She was more beautiful than before, and thanked him with tears in her glorious eyes for having dispelled the charm.

The next morning the old king came with his whole Court, and there were congratulations till late in the day. Last of all came John's traveling companion; John embraced him many times, and told him he must not go away, but must remain with him, for he was the cause of his good fortune. But the other shook his head and said quietly and kindly: "No, my time is up. I have only paid my debt. Do you remember the dead man whom the wicked men wanted to ill-treat? You gave everything you possessed, so that he might rest in his grave. I am that dead man!"

Saying this, he vanished.

The wedding lasted a whole month. John and the princess loved each other dearly, and the old king lived to see many happy days, and used to let his little grandchildren ride on his knee and play with his scepter.

And in time John became king over the whole land.

The Last Pearl

We are in a house where all is riches and happiness. The master and mistress, the servants, and even the friends of the family—all feel happy and full of joy, for on this day a son and heir had been born, and mother and child were both doing excellently.

The burning lamp in the bedroom had been shaded, and before the windows heavy silken curtains of costly materials had been drawn. The carpet was as thick and soft as moss, and everything invited to slumber, and was charmingly devised for repose. And so thought the nurse, for she slept; and here she might sleep, for everything was good and blessed. The guardian spirit of the house leaned against the head of the bed; over the child at the mother's breast there spread itself, as it were, a net of shining stars in endless number, and every star was a pearl of happiness. All the lucky stars of life had brought the new-born child their gifts; here sparkled health, wealth, happiness and love—in fact everything that man can wish for on earth. "Everything has been presented here," said the guardian spirit.

"No, not everything," said a voice near him, the voice of the child's good angel. "There is one fairy who has not yet brought her gift; but she will do so some day. Even if years shall have passed, she will bring it; the last pearl is still wanting."

"Still wanting! There must be nothing wanting here, and if it should really be the case, let us go at once to seek the powerful fairy. Come, let us go!"

"She will come, she will come, some day, uninvited. Her pearl may not be wanting; it must be there to complete the wreath."

"Where is she to be found? Where does she dwell? Tell me, I will get the pearl."

"If you really wish it," said the child's good angel, "I will lead you to her at once, wherever she may be. She has no fixed place of abode; at one time she rules in the emperor's castle, at another you will find her in the peasant's humble cot. She passes no one without leaving her trace; to all she brings her gift, be it a world or a toy. To this child also must she come. You think the time is equally long, but not equally profitable. Well, then we will fetch this pearl, the best pearl in all this wealth."

Hand in hand they floated to the palace, where the fairy was now lingering.

It was a large house with gloomy corridors and empty rooms, and a strange stillness reigned therein; a whole row of windows stood open, so that the raw air might enter to its heart's content, the long white curtains moving to and fro in the draft.

In the middle of the room stood an open coffin, and in this lay the body of a beautiful woman, still in the bloom of youth. Fresh roses were strewn upon her, leaving visible only the delicate folded hands and the noble face—glorified in death by the solemn look of inspiration and the return to its Maker.

Around the coffin stood the husband and the children, a whole troop. The youngest child was in its father's arms, and all were taking a last farewell of their mother. The husband kissed her hand, which was now like a withered leaf, but which, till only a short time ago, had worked and striven in diligent love for them all. Tears of sorrow rolled down their cheeks and fell in heavy drops upon the floor; but not a word was spoken. The silence that reigned here covered a world of grief. With silent steps they left the room sobbing.

A candle is burning in the room, and the long red wick stands out far above the flame which flickers in the draft. Strange men come in and place the lid upon the coffin over the body; they drive the nails firmly in, and the blows of the hammer resound through the whole house, re-echoing in hearts that bleed.

"Whither are you leading me?" asked the guardian spirit. "Here dwells no fairy, whose pearls might be counted among the best gifts of life."

"She is here, at this sacred hour," said the angel, pointing to a corner of the room. There, where in her lifetime the mother had had her seat amid flowers and pictures; there, whence she, like a beneficent fairy of the house, had greeted husband, children and friends, whence, like a sunbeam, she had spread joy and cheerfulness, and been the center and heart of all—there now sat a strange woman, clad in long garments. It was affliction, now mistress and mother in the place of her who was gone. A hot tear rolled down into her lap and formed itself into a pearl, glittering with all the colors of the rainbow. The angel seized it, and the pearl shone like a star of sevenfold radiance.

The pearl of affliction—the last, which must not be wanting—for it enhances the splendor and the value of all the others.

Do you see the shimmer of the rainbow, that rainbow that unites Heaven and earth? It is indeed a bridge from here to the world beyond. We gaze upward through the earthly night to the stars, looking forward to perfection. Gaze upon it, the pearl of affliction, for it conceals within it the wings that shall carry us hence.

In the Duck-Yard

A duck once arrived from Portugal. Some said she came from Spain, but that's neither here nor there; it's enough to know that she was called the Portuguese duck, laid eggs, and was killed and cooked—that was her life. All those that crept out of her eggs were afterwards called Portuguese too, and that meant a great deal. Of the whole family there was now only one left in the duck-yard, a yard to which the chickens had access also, and where the cock was really cock of the walk.

"He annoys me with his loud crowing," said the Portuguese duck. "But he is very handsome, there's no denying that, even though he isn't a duckling. He ought to moderate his voice, but that's an art which indicates a higher education, such as only the little singing birds in the lime-trees in the next garden have received. How sweetly they sing! There is something so touching in their song—I call it Portugal. If I only had a little singing bird like that, I should be a good kind mother to it, for it's in my blood, in my Portuguese blood."

While she was still speaking, a little singing bird came head over heels from the roof into the yard. The cat was after it; but nevertheless the bird escaped with a broken wing—that's why it fell into the duck-yard.

"That's just like the cat, she's a wretch!" said the Portuguese duck; "I know her from the time when I had children of my own. That such a creature should be allowed to live and wander about on the roofs! I don't think such things happen in Portugal!"

She pitied the little singing bird, and the other ducks, who were not of Portuguese descent, also pitied him. "Poor little creature!" they said, as they came up one by one. "We certainly cannot sing," they said, "but we have the rudiments of it or something of the sort inside us—we can feel that, even if we don't talk about it."

"But I will talk about it," said the Portuguese duck, "and I'll do something for the little one; it's only duty!" So she got into the water-trough and beat the water so vigorously with her wings that the little singing bird was almost drowned by the bath he got; but the duck meant well.

"That's a good action," she said; "let the others take example by it."

"Peep!" said the little bird, one of whose wings was broken, and who had some difficulty in shaking himself; but he understood very well that the bath had been well-meant. "You are very kind-hearted, madam," he said, though he had no desire for a second bath.

"I have never thought about my heart," continued the Portuguese duck, "but this much I know, that I love all my fellow creatures except the cat, and no one can expect me to love her, for she has eaten two of my little ones. But pray make yourself at home—it's not difficult to do that. I am myself from foreign parts, as you may already have observed by my bearing and my feathers; my drake, however, is a native of this country, and not of my race: but I'm not proud. If any one here in the yard can understand you, I may indeed say that I am that one."

"She has Portulak on the brain!" said a common little duck, who was witty, and the other common ducks thought the word Portulak excellent: it sounded like Portugal, and they nudged each other and said "Quack." It was really too witty! And all the other ducks now made friends with the little singing bird.

"The Portuguese certainly has a greater command of language," they said. "As for us, we don't have such big words continually in our beaks, but our sympathy is just as great. Even if we do nothing for you, we will go about quietly with you, and that we think is the best."

"You have a sweet voice," said one of the oldest. "It must be a beautiful feeling to be able to give pleasure to so many creatures as you can do. It is true I do not understand your singing, and therefore I keep my beak shut; that is surely better than talking nonsense to you, as a great many others do."

"Don't bother him so," said the Portuguese duck, "he wants rest and nursing. Would you like me to give you another bath, my little singing bird?"

"Oh, no! pray let me remain dry," he begged.

"The water cure is the only one that does me any good when I am not well," answered the Portuguese. "Distraction is a good thing too. The fowls next door will soon come and pay a visit, and among them are two Cochin Chinas. They wear breeches, are well educated, and have been imported; therefore they stand higher in my esteem than the others."

The fowls came and with them the cock; to-day he was polite enough not to be rude. "You are a real singing bird!" he said, "and you get what there is to be got out of such a small voice as yours. But you should have more steam power, so that every one may hear you are of the male sex."

The two Cochin Chinas were quite charmed with the singing bird's appearance; he looked very rough after the bath he had had, so that he seemed to them almost like a Cochin China chick. "He's charming!" they exclaimed, and entered into conversation with him, speaking only in whispers, and in the Pa dialect, which is aristocratic Chinese.

"We are of your race," they said; "the ducks, even the Portuguese one, are swimming birds, as you will no doubt have observed. You don't know us yet; very few know us or take the trouble to do so—not even any of the fowls, although we are born to sit a step higher than most of the rest. But that does not trouble us. We quietly go our way among the others, whose principles are certainly not ours, for we always look at things from their favorable side, and only speak of what is good, though it is difficult to find something where there is nothing. Besides us two and the cock, there is no one in the whole poultry-yard who is both talented and polite. That cannot even be said of the inhabitants of the duck-yard. We warn you, little singing bird! Don't trust that one there with the short feathers in her tail; she's cunning. The one pied there crookedly marked on her wings is quarrelsome, and will always have the last word, although she's generally in the wrong. The fat duck over there speaks ill of every one; that is contrary to our nature—if we cannot speak well of a person, we hold our beaks. The Portuguese duck is the only one who has a little education and with whom one can associate, but she's passionate, and talks too much about Portugal."

"What can those two Cochin Chinas always be whispering about?" whispered one duck to its mate, "they annoy me; we have never spoken to them."

Just then the drake came up. He thought the singing bird was a sparrow. "Well, I don't know the difference," he said, "and it's all the same. He's no more than a plaything, and if you have them—why, you have them."

"Don't attach any importance to what he says," whispered the Portuguese duck. "He's very respectable in business matters, and with him business goes before everything else. But now I shall lie down for a rest. That is a duty we owe ourselves so that we may become nice and fat, if we are to be stuffed with apples and plums."

So she lay down in the sun and blinked one eye; she lay very comfortably, felt very comfortable, and, moreover, slept very comfortably too.

The little singing bird occupied himself with his broken wing, and at last he lay down too, pressing himself close to his protectress; the sun shone warm and bright, and he had found a very good place.

But the fowls from next door were wide awake and went about scratching up the earth; to tell the truth, they had paid the visit simply and solely for the sake of getting something to eat. The Cochin Chinas were the first to leave the duck-yard; the other fowls soon followed. The witty duckling said of the Portuguese that the old lady was fast becoming a "dotard of a duck." The other ducks laughed at this till they cackled. "A dotard of a duck!" they whispered; "that's too funny!" Then they also repeated the former joke about Portulak—it was too amusing, they declared, and then they lay down. When they had lain there awhile, something was suddenly thrown into the duck-yard for them to pick. It came down with such a whack! that the whole company started up from their sleep and flapped their wings; the Portuguese awoke too, and rolling over on the other side, pressed the little singing bird very hard.

"Peep!" he said; "you trod very hard upon me, madam!"

"Well, why do you get in my way?" she cried. "You shouldn't be so touchy. I have nerves too, but I have never yet said 'Peep.'"

"Don't be angry!" said the little bird. "The 'peep' dropped from my beak quite unawares."

The Portuguese did not stop to listen to him, but pounced down upon the food and made a good meal. When this was finished, and she lay down again, the little singing-bird came up to her and wanted to be amiable. So it sang:

"I'll fly so far,
Tra-la-la-la!
Singing so fine
Of that heart of thine!"

"Now I want to rest after my dinner," said the Portuguese. "You must conform to the rules of the house. I want to sleep now."

The little singing bird was quite abashed, for he had meant well. When madam awoke later on, he again stood before her with a grain of corn that he had found. He laid it at her feet, but as she had not slept well, she was, of course, in a very bad temper. "Give that to a chick!" she said, "and don't be always standing in my way!"

"Why are you angry with me?" answered the little bird. "What have I done?"

"Done?" repeated the Portuguese duck; "I should like to point out to you that that's not a very genteel expression."

"It was all sunshine here yesterday," said the little bird; "today there is thunder in the air."

"You have very poor notions of time," retorted the duck. "The day is not ended yet. Don't stand there like a fool!"

"But you are looking at me just like the wicked eyes did when I fell down into the yard."

"You impudent fellow!" said the Portuguese duck, "do you compare me with the cat, that beast of prey? There is not a drop of bad blood in me; I have promised to take care of you, and 1 will teach you good manners!"

With that she bit off the singing bird's head, and he lay there dead.

"What does that mean?" she said. "Couldn't he bear that? Well, then he was certainly not made for this world. I have been a mother to him, I know that, for I have a good heart."

Then the cock from next door put his head into the yard and crowed with the strength of a steam-engine.

"You'll kill me with your crowing!" she cried. "It's all your fault; he lost his head, and I am very near losing mine, too."

"There's not much lying where he fell," said the cock.

"Speak respectfully of him!" answered the Portuguese duck. "He had good manners, a voice, and an excellent education. He was affectionate and tender, and that is as becoming to animals as to so-called human beings."

All the ducks crowded round the little dead singing bird. Ducks have strong passions whether they feel envy or pity, and as there was nothing here to envy, pity made its appearance, even in the two Cochin Chinas. "We shall never get such a singing bird again; he was almost a Cochin China," they whispered; and then they wept till they clucked, and all the fowls clucked too, but the ducks went about with the reddest eyes of all.

"We have hearts!" they said; "that no one can deny."

"Hearts!" repeated the Portuguese; "yes, that we have, almost as much as in Portugal."

"Now let's think of getting something in our inside!" said the drake; "that's of most importance. Even if one of the playthings does get broken we have plenty more of them!"

The Shadow

In hot countries the sun is very strong; people turn mahogany brown, and in the hottest countries they are even burned black. This time it was, however, only as far as the hot countries that a learned man from the cold regions had come. He believed that he would be able to walk about there in the same way as he did at home, but he soon found out his mistake. He had to stay at home like other sensible people; the window-shutters and the doors were closed the whole day, and it looked just as if everybody in the house were asleep or had gone out. The narrow street of high houses where he lived was so situated that the sun fell upon it from morning till night, making it really unbearable. The learned man from the cold regions was, although a young man, a wise one; he felt as though he were sitting in a burning oven, and this injured his health, and he became thin. Even his shadow shriveled up and became smaller than it used to be at home; the sun went so far as to take it away altogether, and it only re-appeared in the evening after that luminary had set. It was a pleasure to see it return. As soon as the light was brought into the room the shadow stretched itself up the wall, and even made itself so tall that it reached the ceiling; it was obliged to stretch itself in order to get its strength back. The learned man used to go out upon the balcony to stretch himself, and as soon as the stars appeared in the beautiful clear sky he seemed to come back to life. People now appeared on all the balconies in the street, and in warm countries there is a balcony before every window, for one must have fresh air even if one is accustomed to getting mahogany brown. Then there was life above and below. Below, all the cobblers and tailors—among whom is included everybody else—came out into the street; they brought out tables and chairs and lights. Thousands of lights were lit. One talked, another sang, and some walked about; carriages passed and mules trotted by, the bells which they wear on their harness tinkling merrily. On one side was heard the chant of a funeral procession, on the other the tolling of the church bells. Yes, there was indeed life in the street at such an hour. Only in one house—the one opposite to which the learned man from the north lived—it was very quiet. And yet somebody lived there, for on the balcony there were flowers which bloomed beautifully even in the heat of the sun; this they could not have done if they had not been watered, and there must have been somebody to do that. Besides, the doors were half opened towards evening; but then it was dark, at least in the front room, while music was heard proceeding from the inner one. The learned stranger thought this music particularly fine, but that might have been only a fancy of his, for he thought everything in these warm countries excellent, with the exception of the sun. The stranger's landlord told him that he did not know who had taken the house opposite; no one had ever been seen, and as to the music, it seemed to him terribly tedious. "It is just as if some one were sitting there practicing a piece that he can't play: always the same piece 'I shall play it after all,' he thinks, but he won't play it, however long he may practice."

One night the stranger awoke. He always slept with the balcony door open; the wind blew aside the curtain hanging before it, and it seemed to him as though there were a strange light coming from the balcony of the house opposite. All the flowers shone like flames of the most beautiful colors, and in the midst of the flowers stood a lovely graceful maiden. She seemed to be all aglow, and it quite dazzled his eyes, but he had opened them too wide, having just woke up out of his sleep. With one jump he was out of bed. Softly he crept behind the curtain; but the maiden was gone, the splendor was gone, and the flowers no longer shone, although they stood there as beautiful as ever. The door was ajar, and from inside came such sweet and lovely music that one could really go into raptures about it. It was like sorcery; but who lived there? Where was the actual entrance? For towards both the street and the side-street the whole of the ground floor was taken up by shops, and surely people could not go through these to get upstairs.

One evening the stranger was sitting on his balcony: a light was burning in the room close behind him, and it was therefore natural for his shadow to fall upon the wall of the house opposite. Yes, there it sat, among the flowers on the balcony, and when the stranger moved the shadow moved too.

"I believe my shadow is the only living thing to be seen over there," said the learned man. "See how nicely it sits there among the flowers. The door is only half closed: now my shadow ought to have the sense to go in, have a look round, and then come back and tell me what it has seen. "Yes, you would make yourself useful by doing that," he said in a joke. "Be good enough to go in. Well, why don't you go?" He then nodded to the shadow, and the shadow nodded back. "Well, go! but don't stay away altogether." The stranger got up, and the shadow on the balcony opposite got up too; the stranger turned round, and if any one had paid particular attention to it he would have seen how the shadow went straight through the half-opened balcony door of the opposite house at the same moment that the stranger entered his room and let fall the long curtains.

A light was burning in the room close behind him, and it was therefore natural for his shadow to fall upon the wall of the house opposite.

The next morning the learned man went out to get a cup of coffee and to read the papers. "How's this?" he said when he came into the sunshine. "I've lost my shadow. Then it really went away last night and did not come back; this is most annoying!"

He was vexed; not so much because his shadow was gone, but because he knew that there was already a story of a man without a shadow. Everybody in his own country knew that story, and when he returned home and told his own tale they would say that it was only an imitation, and he did not care about having that said of him. He therefore resolved to say nothing about it, which was very sensible of him.

In the evening he again went out upon his balcony; he had placed the light just behind him, for he knew that a shadow always likes to have its master for a screen, but he could not entice it to come out. He made himself first small and then tall, hut there was no shadow, and there came no shadow. He said "Hem, hem!" but that was of no use either.

It was very, very vexing; but in warm countries everything grows very quickly, and after the lapse of a week he perceived, to his great joy, that a new shadow was growing out of his legs when he walked in the sunshine: the roots must therefore have remained. After three weeks' time he had a tolerable shadow, which continued to grow during his journey back to the north till it was at last so tall and so broad that he could well have spared half of it.

When the learned man came home he wrote books about all that was true, and good, and beautiful in the world; and days and years—many years—passed.

One evening as he was sitting in his room there was a gentle tap at the door. "Come in," he said; but as nobody appeared he got up and opened the door. There stood a man before him so excessively thin that it made him feel quite queer, but as the man was also very well dressed he took him to be an important personage.

"With whom have I the honor of speaking?" he asked.

"Ah!" said the fine gentleman, "I hardly expected that you would recognize me. I have grown so much body that I have both flesh and clothes. I suppose you never thought of seeing me in this condition? Don't you know your old shadow? You doubtless never believed that I would ever come back. Things have gone exceedingly well with me since I saw you last, and I have amassed fortune in every way. I could easily buy myself free from servitude if I wished to do so." He rattled a bunch of valuable seals which hung from his watch, and passed his hand over the massive gold chain which he wore round his neck. And how the diamond rings on his fingers glittered! Everything was real too!

"I am utterly bewildered!" said the learned man. "What does all this mean?"

"Well, certainly nothing usual," answered the shadow. "But you are not like ordinary men yourself, and, as you well know, I have trodden in your footsteps since childhood. As soon as you thought that I was old enough to go out into the world alone I went my own way, and I am now in brilliant circumstances. But a kind of longing came over me to see you once more before you die, and I wanted to see these places again, for one always loves one's native country. I know that you have grown another shadow; have I anything to pay to it or to you? If so, kindly say so."

"But is it really you?" said the learned man. "It is indeed astonishing. I should never have believed that one could ever see one's old shadow again turned into a human being."

"Do tell me what I have to pay," said the shadow, "for I would not like to be in any one's debt."

"How can you talk like that?" said the learned man. "What debt can there be? You are as free as any one else. I am exceedingly glad of your good fortune. Sit down, my old friend, and just tell me how all this came about, and what you have seen in the warm countries and in that house opposite to which we used to live."

"Well, I will tell you," said the shadow, sitting down; "but you must promise me never to tell any one in the town here, wherever you may meet me, that I was once your shadow. I intend to become engaged; I can support more than one family."

"Have no fear," said the learned man; "I will tell no one who you really are. Here is my hand; I promise it upon my honor as a man!"

"Upon my honor as a shadow!" said the other. He was, of course, obliged to speak like that.

It was, however, most wonderful how much of a human being he had become. He was dressed in the finest black cloth, and wore patent leather boots and an opera hat—that is, a hat which can be closed up till it looks all brim and crown. We will say nothing more of the seals, the gold chain, and the diamond rings, with which we are already acquainted. Yes, the shadow was exceedingly well dressed, and it was, in fact, this that made him look quite like a man.

"Now I will tell you all about it," said the shadow; and then he put down his feet with the patent leather boots as hard as he could on the arm of the learned man's new shadow, which was lying like a dog at his feet. This he did either out of pride or because he thought the new shadow might stick to him. But the shadow lying down remained very still, in order that he might hear all about it: he was also desirous to know how he might free himself and become his own master.

"Do you know who lived in the house opposite us?" said the shadow. "That was the most charming of all! It was Poetry. I was there for three weeks, and that is exactly the same as living three thousand years and reading everything that is composed and written. For this I tell you and it is true: I have seen everything, and I know everything."

"Poetry!" cried the learned man. "It is true she only lives as a hermitess in large cities. Poetry! Yes, I saw her for one short moment, but sleep was still in my eyes; she was standing on the balcony radiant as the northern lights, in the midst of flowers with living flames. Tell me, tell me! You were on the balcony. You went in at the door and then—"

"Then I found myself in the front room," said the shadow. "You were sitting on the other side and continually looking across into the room. It was not lit up, but there was a kind of twilight; one door after another stood open in a long row of rooms and halls, and at the end it was so bright that the mass of light would have killed me if I had reached the maiden. But I was prudent; I took my time, and that one is obliged to do."

"And what did you see then?" asked the learned man.

"I saw everything! And I will tell you all about it; but—you must really not put it down to pride on my part—as a free man, and considering the knowledge that I possess, to say nothing of my position and circumstances, I wish you would speak to me a little more respectfully."

"I beg your pardon," said the learned man, "but my way of speaking is an old habit, and it is therefore difficult to drop. You are perfectly right, I will think of it in future. But now do tell me all that you saw."

"All," said the shadow, "for I saw all and I know all."

"How did it look in the inner rooms?" asked the learned man.

"Were they like the cool grove? Were they like a holy temple? Were the halls like the starry heavens seen from the mountain-tops?"

"Everything was there," said the shadow. "I certainly did not go right inside, for I remained in the twilight of the outer room, but that was an excellent position. I saw everything and know everything. I have been in the ante-chamber of the Court of Poetry."

"But what did you see? Did the gods of antiquity pass along the lofty halls? Did you see the combats of the ancient heroes? Did sweet children play there and tell their dreams?"

"I tell you that I was there, and from that you must understand that I saw everything that was to be seen. If you had gone there, you would not have remained a human being, but I became one, and at the same time I obtained a knowledge of my inmost nature, of what is born in me, and the relationship in which I stood to Poetry. When I was still with you I never thought of such things; but you know that whenever the sun rose or set I was often wonderfully tall, and in the moonlight I was almost more noticeable than yourself. At that time I did not understand my inner self; it was made plain to me in the ante-chamber when I became a human being. I came out fully mature, but you were no longer in the warm countries. I was ashamed of myself to go about as a human being in the condition in which I then was. I wanted boots and clothes and the whole of that human outfit that distinguishes a man. I made my way—yes, I think I can trust you with this, for you will not put it into a book—I made my way under the cook's cloak; I hid myself under it, and the woman did not know how much she was hiding. It was only in the evening that I went out, and walked about the streets in the moonlight. I stretched myself up along the wall, which tickles one very pleasantly in the back; I ran up and down, looked through the highest windows into grand halls, as well as through the attic windows which nobody could reach, and I saw what no one saw, what no one was supposed to see. It is really a wicked world after all; 1 would not care to be a man if it were not the generally accepted idea that it is an honor to be one. I saw the most incredible things among men and women, among parents, and 'sweet incomparable children.' I saw what no one knows, but which all would so much like to know: their neighbor's evil deeds. Had I published a newspaper, it would have been read, but I wrote straight to the evil doers themselves, and in every town I came I created terror. They were so afraid of me that they loved me to excess. Professors made me a professor; tailors gave me new clothes (I am well provided); coiners made money for me; women said that I was beautiful—and so I became the man I now am. I must now bid you adieu. Here is my card, I live on the sunny side, and am always at home when it rains." And the shadow went.

"That was very remarkable," said the learned man.

Days and years passed away, and the shadow came again.

"How do you do?" he asked.

"Ah!" sighed the learned man; "I am writing about the true, the good, and the beautiful; but no one cares to hear about such things. I am in despair, for I take it to heart."

"That I never do," said the shadow; "I grow strong and fat as every one should try to be. You don't understand the world, and that makes you ill—you must travel. I am going to make a tour this summer; will you go with me? I should like to have a traveling companion; will you come as my shadow? It would be a great pleasure to me, and I will pay your expenses."

"I suppose you are going very far?" asked the learned man.

"Some might call it so," said the shadow. "A journey will do you a deal of good. Will you be my shadow? You shall have everything paid for you."

"The idea is too mad," said the learned man.

"But so is the world," said the shadow, "and it will remain so."

With that he went away.

Everything went wrong with the learned man; sorrow and trouble followed him, and what he wrote about the true, the good, and the beautiful, was like casting pearls before swine. At length he fell ill.

"You really look like a shadow," people said to him, and at these words a shudder ran through the learned man, for he had his own thoughts on the matter.

"You must go and drink the waters," said the shadow, who one day paid him a visit. "There is no other help for you. I will take you with me for old acquaintance's sake. I will pay your expenses, and you shall write a description of the journey to entertain me on the way. I want to go to a watering-place; my beard does not grow quite as it ought, which is as bad as being ill, for one must have a beard. Now be reasonable, and accept my offer; we will travel as comrades."

And they traveled. The shadow was now master, and the master, shadow. They drove, they rode, and they walked together, sometimes next to each other, sometimes before or behind each other, according to the position of the sun. The shadow always took care to secure the place of honor; the learned man hardly noticed it, for he had a very kind heart and exceedingly mild and friendly manners. One day the master said to the shadow, "As we have become traveling comrades in this way and have also grown up together from childhood, shall we not call each other 'thou?' It sounds so much more familiar."

"What you say," said the shadow, who was now really the master, "is very kind and straightforward; I will now be just as kind and straightforward. You, who are a learned man, know very well how strange nature is. There are some people who cannot bear the smell of brown paper—it makes them ill, while it makes others' flesh creep to hear a pane of glass scratched with a nail; I myself have a similar feeling when I hear you address me as 'thou.' I feel as though I were thrust back into my old position with you—pressed to the earth. You see it is only a matter of feeling, not pride. I cannot let you say 'thou' to me, but I will willingly call you 'thou,' and so your wish will be half fulfilled."

And now the shadow called its former master "thou." "That's rather cool," thought the latter, "that I have to say 'you' to him, while he says 'thou' to me"; but he was obliged to put up with it.

They came to a watering-place where there were a great many strangers, and among them a very pretty princess whose malady consisted in being too sharp-sighted, which was very alarming.

She at once perceived that the new arrival was quite a different kind of person from all the others. "It is said that he is here to make his beard grow, but I recognize the real cause—he cannot cast a shadow."

Her curiosity now being aroused, she immediately entered into conversation with the stranger on the promenade. Being a king's daughter, it was not necessary for her to make any ceremonies, so she told him straight out: "Your illness consists in your being unable to cast a shadow."

"Your royal highness must be well on the road to recovery," said the shadow. "I know that your illness consists in seeing too sharply, but that is past, and you are cured. I have a very uncommon shadow. Don't you see the person who always walks next to me? Other people have common shadows, but I don't like what is common. People often give their servants better cloth for their liveries than they wear themselves, and so I have allowed my shadow to dress himself up like a man; as you see, I have even given him a shadow. It costs a great deal, but I like to have something uncommon."

"What!" said the princess, "can I be really cured? These baths are the best that exist; the waters have quite marvelous powers nowadays. But I sha'n't go from here yet, for it is only just beginning to be amusing; the strange prince—for he must be a prince—pleases me immensely. I only hope his beard won't grow, for if it does he will be off again."

In the evening the king's daughter danced with the shadow in the great ballroom. She was light, but he was still lighter; she had never seen such a dancer before. She told him from what country she came, and he knew the country; he had been there, but she was away at the time. He had looked through the windows of the castle, both the upper and the lower ones; there he had learned one thing and another, and could therefore give the princess answers and make allusions that greatly astonished her. She thought he must be the cleverest man in the world, and she conceived a great respect for all that he knew. And when she danced with him again she fell in love with him; and that the shadow perceived very well, for she almost looked him through and through with her eyes. They danced together once more, and she was nearly telling him of her love, but she was judicious, and thought of her country and her kingdom and of the many people over whom she was to reign.

"He is a clever man," she said to herself; "that is good. And he dances excellently; that is good too. But I wonder whether he has good sound knowledge. That is just as important; he must be examined." And she immediately put a difficult question to him which she herself could not have answered; and the shadow pulled a long face.

"You can't answer me that," said the princess.

"I knew that already when I was a child," said the shadow. "I believe even my shadow, standing by the door there, could answer that."

"Your shadow," said the princess; "that would be very strange."

"I don't say for certain that he can," said the shadow, "but I should almost think so. He has followed me now for so many years, and he has heard so much from me, that I should think so. But your royal highness will permit me to draw your attention to the fact that he is so proud of passing for a man that if he is to be put into a good humor—and that he must be to answer correctly—he should be treated just like a human being.

"I like that!" said the princess.

And now she went up to the learned man at the door and spoke with him about the sun and the moon, about the green forests and nations both near and far, and the learned man answered very wisely and well.

"What a man that must be, who has such a clever shadow!" she thought. "It would be a real blessing for my people and my kingdom if I chose him. I will do so!"

And the matter was soon agreed to between the princess and the shadow, but no one was to know anything of it till she had returned to her country.

"No one; not even my shadow," said the shadow, and for that he had special reasons.

They came to the country where the princess ruled when she was at home. "Listen, my friend," said the shadow to the learned man; "now I am as happy and powerful as any one can become, and now I will do something special for you. You shall live with me in the castle, you shall drive with me in the royal carriage, and you shall have a hundred thousand dollars a year; but you must allow yourself to be called a shadow by each and every one, and may never say that you have ever been a man. And then once every year, when I sit in the sun on the balcony to show myself, you must lie at my feet as befits a shadow; for I will tell you that I am going to marry the princess, and the wedding will take place this evening."

"No, that is too mad!" said the learned man. "I won't do it, and I sha'n't do it; why, it means cheating the whole country and the princess too! I'll tell everything: that I am a man, and that you are a shadow merely dressed up in men's clothes."

"No one would believe you," said the shadow. "Be reasonable, or I'll call out the guard."

"I am going straight to the princess!" said the learned man.

"But I shall go first," said the shadow, "and you'll go to prison." And it was so too, for the sentries obeyed the one whom they knew the princess was going to marry.

"You are trembling," said the princess when the shadow came into her room. "Has anything happened? You must not be ill to-day, just as we are going to get married."

"I have experienced the most terrible thing that can happen to one," said the shadow. "Just fancy—such a poor shadow brain cannot stand much—just fancy, my shadow has gone mad; he imagines that he has become a man, and that—only just fancy!—that I am his shadow."

"How terrible!" said the princess. "He is locked up, I suppose?"

"Of course; I fear he will never recover."

"Poor shadow!" cried the princess. "He is very unfortunate; it would be a real kindness to rid him of his life. And if I consider the matter rightly—how in our time the people are only too ready to take the part of the lower against the higher—it appears to me necessary to have him quietly put away."

"That's really hard, for he was a faithful servant," said the shadow, and he pretended to sigh.

"You are a noble character!" said the princess, and bowed before him.

In the evening the whole city was illuminated, and cannon were fired "Boom!"—and the soldiers presented arms. What a wedding it was! The princess and the shadow came out upon the balcony to show themselves and receive another "Hurrah!" The learned man heard nothing of all these festivities, for he was already executed.

The soldiers presented arms.

The Bottle-Neck

In a narrow crooked street among other abodes of poverty there stood a particularly narrow and tall house built of wood, with which time had played such havoc that it had gone quite out of joint in every direction. The house was inhabited by poor people, but poorest of all were those who occupied the attics under the gable where, before the single little window in the sunshine hung an old bent birdcage which had not even a waterglass, but only a bottle-neck with a cork in it turned upside down and filled with water. An old maid stood at the window; she had adorned the cage with green chickweed, and a little chaffinch hopped from one perch to the other, and sang and twittered to its heart's content. "Yes, it's all very well for you to sing," said the bottle-neck—that is to say, it did not utter these words as we do, for a bottle-neck cannot speak; but that's what it thought to itself in its own quiet mind, just as we human beings talk to ourselves.

"Yes, it's all very well for you to sing, you who have all your limbs whole. You should just try what it's like to lose your body and to have only your neck and mouth left, and a cork stuck into that in addition as I have, and you would certainly not sing. But it's a good thing, all the same, that there's somebody who is happy. I have no reason to sing, and moreover I can't sing. Yes, when I was a complete bottle I could, if I was rubbed with a cork; then I was called a perfect lark, a fine lark. That was when I went to a picnic with the tanner's family, and his daughter was engaged—why, I remember it as if it were only yesterday. I have gone through a great deal, when I come to think of it. I have been through fire and water, deep down into the black earth, and higher up than most of the others, and now I hang here in the air and the sunshine outside a birdcage. Oh, it would be worthwhile hearing my story, but I don't speak aloud of it, because I can't."

And now the bottle-neck related its story, which was remarkable enough. It told the story to itself, or thought it over quietly in its mind; and the little bird sang his song merrily, and down in the street there was a riding and a running, and every one was thinking of his own matters or of nothing at all—only the bottle-neck thought. It thought of the flaming furnace in the manufactory in which it had been blown into life; it still remembered how warm it had been, and how it had gazed into the hissing flames, the place of its birth, and felt a great desire to jump back again into it immediately, and how, as it kept growing cooler, it had gradually found itself getting more comfortable where it was. It had stood in rank and file with a whole regiment of brothers and sisters all out of the same furnace, some of which, however, had been blown into champagne bottles, others into beer-bottles, and that makes a difference. Later, out in the world it may sometimes happen that a beer-bottle may contain the most precious wine, while a champagne bottle be filled with blacking, but by one's form it is always easy to see to what one was born—what is noble will always be noble, even if it has blacking inside it.

All the bottles were packed up and our bottle too. At that time it did not think of ending its career as a bottle-neck, to work its way up to a bird's-glass, which is, however, an honorable existence after all—for in that state one is at least something. The bottle did not see daylight again till it was unpacked with its comrades in the wine-merchant's cellar and rinsed out for the first time; that was a curious sensation. There it lay empty and corkless, with a very strange feeling as if it lacked something, but what it did not know itself. At last it was filled with a fine old wine, provided with a cork and sealed up. It was labelled "first quality," and it felt as if it had just taken the first prize at an examination; but then the wine was good and the bottle too. Youth is the time for poetry, so it sang and rang of things of which it had no knowledge: of the green sunny mountains, where the wine grows, where the merry lads and lasses dress the vines, singing and kissing, and caressing.

How beautiful life is! Of all this the bottle sang and rang like many a young poet, who often does not understand the meaning of the song he sings.

One morning the bottle was sold; the tanner's apprentice had been sent for a bottle of "the best." And then it was placed in a hamper with ham, cheese, and sausage; the finest butter and the finest bread was there too, and the tanner's daughter packed the hamper herself. She was young and pretty; in her brown eyes and upon her lips there played a smile. She had soft delicate hands, beautifully white, but her neck and shoulders were still whiter; you saw at once that she was one of the fairest maidens in the town—and still she was not yet engaged.

The basket lay in the young girl's lap when the family drove out into the forest, the bottle-neck peeping out from between the folds of the white napkin. There was a red seal on the cork, and the bottle looked straight into the girl's face; it also looked at the young sailor who sat next to her. The latter was an old playmate, the son of the portrait-painter. He had just passed his examination as mate with honors, and on the morrow he was to sail far away to foreign shores. A good deal had been spoken about this while the basket was being packed, and just then there was by no means an expression of joy in the eyes and around the mouth of the pretty tanner's daughter. The young people sauntered through the wood talking together. Of what did they speak? Well, that the bottle did not hear, for it was standing in the provision basket. It was a long time before it was brought out, but when that was at length done some pleasant matters had come to pass. Everybody laughed, and the tanner's daughter laughed too; but she spoke less than before, and her cheeks glowed like two red roses.

Then father took the full bottle and the corkscrew in his hand. It is indeed a strange feeling to be drawn like that for the first time. The bottle-neck had never afterwards forgotten that solemn moment, for he was distinctly heard to say "Pop!" as the cork came out—and how he clucked as the wine was poured into the glasses!

"Long life to the betrothed!" said the old man, and every glass was emptied to the dregs, and the young sailor kissed his beautiful bride.

"Health and happiness!" said both the old people, the father and mother.

And the young man filled the glasses again.

"A safe return, and the wedding this day next year!" he cried; and when the glasses were emptied, he took the bottle, lifted it up, and said:

"You have been present on the happiest day of my life, you shall never serve another!"

And he hurled it high into the air.

The tanner's daughter little thought that she should ever see the flying bottle again, and yet it was to be so. It fell into the thick reeds on the margin of a little woodland lake—the bottle-neck still remembered quite plainly how it had lain there for a long time.

"I gave them wine, and they gave me marsh water—but they meant well!"

He could no longer see the lovers and the happy parents, but he heard them singing and rejoicing for a long time. At last two peasant boys came by, and looking among the reeds, saw the bottle and picked it up; now it was given to the eldest brother of these boys, who was a sailor, and who was about to start on a long voyage, and had been home yesterday, at the cottage in the wood, to say good-bye. His mother was busy packing up a few things that he was to take with him on his journey, and which his father was to carry to the town that evening to see his son once more, and to bring him a farewell greeting from himself and the boy's mother. A little bottle of medicated brandy had already been wrapped up and added to the parcel, when the boy entered with a larger and stronger bottle that they had found. It would hold more than the little one, and the brandy being mixed with herbs, would be a capital thing in case of indigestion. It was not red wine such as the bottle had held before that was now poured into it; these were bitter drops, but they were good too—for indigestion, of course. So the large new bottle, and not the little one, was to be taken, and thus the bottle set on its wanderings once more. It went on board with Peter Jensen, and on board the same ship, too, in which the young mate sailed. But he did not see the bottle; and if he had, he would never have recognized it, or suspected that it was the same with which they had solemnized the engagement, and drunk to his safe return.

It is true it could no longer give wine, but it contained something which was just as good; and when Peter Jensen brought it out it was always called "the apothecary" by his messmates. It contained the best medicine, something that was good for the inside, and it gave its aid loyally as long as it had a drop left. That was a pleasant time, and the bottle sang when it was rubbed with the cork, and was called the big lark, "Peter Jensen's lark."

Long days and months rolled by, and the bottle already stood in a corner empty when a storm arose—whether it was on the journey out or home that the bottle could not exactly say, for it had not been on shore at all; great waves came rolling heavily and darkly along, lifting and tossing the ship. The mainmast was torn away; a wave stove in one of the planks, and the pumps became useless. It was black night. The ship sank—but at the last moment the young mate wrote on a sheet of paper: "In Christ's name! We are sinking!" He wrote the name of his betrothed, his own name and that of the ship, put the paper into the first empty bottle that he came across, pressed the cork down tightly, and threw the bottle out into the raging sea. He did not know that it was the same out of which the cup of joy and hope had once been filled for him and her—and now it was tossed on the billows, carrying a farewell greeting and a message of death.

The ship sank with all her crew; the bottle flew along like a bird, for it had a heart within it—a letter of love. And the sun rose and the sun set; and the bottle felt the same sensation as it had when it was being made in the glowing furnace. A longing came over it to fly back into the heat.

It went through calms and fresh storms too; it was, however, hurled against no rock, nor was it swallowed by a shark, but floated about year after year, to the north, sometimes to the south, just as the currents carried it. It was besides its own master, but one gets tired of that.

The written page, the last farewell from the lover to his lass, would only bring trouble when it came into the proper hands; but where were those hands, so white and soft which once spread the cloth on the fresh grass in the wood on the betrothal day? Where was the tanner's daughter? Where indeed was the land, and what land lay nearest? None of these questions could the bottle answer, so it drifted and drifted till at last it got tired of floating about, for that was not its mission at all. But any how it went drifting on till it reached land, a foreign land. It did not understand a word of what was spoken here, for it was not the language it had heard spoken before, and one loses a great deal if one does not understand the language.

The bottle was fished out and examined on all sides; the note that it contained was seen, taken out, turned and twisted, but the people did not understand what there was written on it. They certainly understood that the bottle must have been thrown overboard and that the paper contained something about it; but what it was they could not tell, and the paper was put back into the bottle, and the latter placed in a large cupboard in a large room in a large house.

Every time strangers came, the paper was brought out, and turned and twisted so that the characters, which were only written in pencil, became more and more illegible, and at last no one could see that they were letters. For a whole year more the bottle remained in the cupboard, and then it was placed in the loft and became covered with dust and cobwebs.

How often it thought of better days! of the time when it had poured out the red wine in the fresh green wood, when it had been tossed on the wavy billows carrying a secret, a letter, a farewell sigh within it. Full twenty years did it stand in the loft; it might have stood there longer still, but for the house having to be rebuilt. The roof was taken off, and the bottle was noticed and spoken about, but it did not understand the language. One cannot learn a language by standing up in a loft, even in twenty years. "If I had remained down in the room," it thought, "I should have learned it."

It was now washed and rinsed out, and it was high time too. It felt clear and transparent and young again in its old age, but the paper which it had faithfully borne—that perished in the washing. The bottle was filled with seeds, though it had not the slightest idea what these were, and was corked and well wrapped up. It got to see neither light nor lantern, let alone the sun or moon, and yet one ought to see something when one goes traveling, it thought; but it saw nothing, though it did what was of most importance—it traveled, and reached the place of its destination and was there unpacked.

"What trouble they've taken over there with this bottle," it heard people say, "and I daresay it's broken"; but it was not broken. It understood every word that was said; it was the language it had heard at the furnace, at the wine-merchant's, in the wood and on the ship, the only good old language it could understand. It had come back home, and the language was a greeting of welcome to it. It almost jumped out of the people's hands for joy; it hardly noticed that its cork had been drawn and that it had been emptied and carried to the cellar to be stored there and forgotten.

But there's no place like home, even in the cellar!

It never occurred to the bottle to consider how long it had lain there; it lay comfortably and for years. At last people came down and took all the bottles out of the cellar, and ours among them.

There was a great festivity out in the garden; burning lamps hung in garlands and paper lanterns shone transparent like great tulips. It was a glorious evening, the weather was still and clear; the stars twinkled, and there was a new moon. One could really see the whole round of the moon like a bluish gray disc half encircled in gold, which was a pretty sight for those with good eyes.

The illuminations extended even to the remotest parts of the garden, at least sufficient for any one to be able to find his way by their light. Among the branches of the hedges stood bottles, each containing a burning light, and here too was the bottle we know, the one which was to end as a bottle-neck—a bird's glass. Everything here seemed lovely to it, for it was again out among the green, and in the midst of joy and feasting; it heard music and singing and the noise and murmur of many people, especially from that part of the garden where the lamps burned and the paper lanterns displayed their colored splendor. It certainly stood in a remote path, but that made it the more conspicuous; it held a light and was both ornamental and useful, which is as it should be. In one such hour one forgets twenty years passed in a loft—and it is a good thing to forget.

Close to it there passed a single pair, like the betrothed pair in the wood of long ago, the sailor and the tanner's daughter; the bottle seemed to live all that over again. In the garden walked not only the guests, but other people who were permitted to come and view the festive splendor; among the latter was an old maid who had not a single relative left in the world. Her thoughts were like those of the bottle: she was thinking of the green wood and of two young lovers—two who concerned her very nearly, in whom she had some interest—indeed she was one of them, and that had been the happiest hour of her life, an hour one never forgets, even if one becomes ever such an old maid. But she did not recognize the bottle, neither did the latter notice the old maid; so do we pass each other in this world till we meet again—and meet again they did, for they were both again in the same town.

From the garden the bottle went once more to the wine-merchant's, was again filled with wine and sold to the aeronaut, who was to make an ascent in his balloon on the following Sunday. A great crowd of people were assembled to see the sight; a military band had been engaged, and many other preparations had been made. The bottle saw it all from a basket in which it lay next to a live rabbit; the latter was quite bewildered, for it well knew that it was going up to come down again by means of a parachute. The bottle however knew nothing of the "up" or the "down"; it only saw that the balloon blew itself out bigger and bigger, and that when it could swell no more it began to rise and to become more and more restless, The ropes which held it were cut, and it floated up with the aeronaut, the basket, the bottle and the rabbit, while the music played and all the people shouted "Hurrah!"

"That's a wonderful excursion up into the air!" thought the bottle; "that's a new kind of sailing. But up here there's no fear of running into anything!"

Thousands of people gazed up at the balloon, and the old maid looked up at it too; she was standing at the open window in her attic, under which hung the cage with the little chaffinch, which at that time had no water-glass, but had to content itself with a cup.

In the window itself stood a myrtle in a pot; this had been pushed a little to one side so that it should not fall out, for the old maid was leaning out of the window to look. She distinctly saw the aeronaut in the balloon and how he let down the rabbit by the parachute and then drank to the health of all the spectators, finally hurling the bottle high into the air. She little thought that this was the very bottle she had seen flying up in honor of her and of her friend on that joyful day in the green wood years ago.

The bottle had no time for reflection at so unexpectedly and suddenly reaching the highest point in its career. Steeples and roofs lay far, far beneath it, and the people looked extremely small.

But now it sank and in quite a different fashion to the rabbit: it turned somersaults in the air, and felt so young and so loose and careless; it was still half full of wine, but did not remain so long.

What a journey! The sun shone on the bottle, and all the people were looking at it; the balloon was already a long way off, and soon the bottle was off too, for it fell on one of the roofs and broke, but the pieces had still so much go in them that they could not lie still, but went bounding and rolling along till they reached the yard and there they lay in still smaller pieces; only the bottle-neck remained whole, and that was cut off as if with a diamond.

"That would make a fine bird-glass!" said the people in the cellar; but as they had neither bird nor cage it would be going a little too far to expect them to get both, because they had a bottle-neck which might be used as a glass. But the old maid up in the garret—she might perhaps be able to use it—and so the bottle-neck was taken up to her, and had a cork put into it. What was formerly the top was now at the bottom, as often happens when changes take place; some fresh water was put into it, and it was hung up on the cage of the little bird, which sang and twittered right merrily.

"Yes, it's all very well for you to sing!" said the bottle-neck, which was considered a great curiosity for having been up in a balloon—that was all that was known of its history. Now it hung there as a bird-glass, and heard the noise and bustle of the people down in the street and the voice of the old maid in the room within. An old friend had come to see her and they were speaking—not of the bottle-neck, but of the myrtle in the window.

"No, you must really not spend a dollar for a bridal wreath for your daughter!" said the old maid. "You shall have a pretty little bunch from me, full of blossoms. Look how splendidly my tree blooms. Well, it has grown up from a sprig of myrtle that you gave me on the day of my engagement, and from which I was to have made my own bridal wreath after a year had passed; but that day never came, for the eyes closed that were to have made my life all joy and happiness. My dear one sleeps sweetly in the bed of the ocean. The myrtle grew into an old tree, but I grew still older, and when the tree at length died, I took the last green twig, put it into the ground, and out of it has grown a large tree; and now the myrtle will still serve at a wedding after all—as a bridal wreath for your daughter."

Tears stood in the eyes of the old maid; she spoke of the playmate of her youth, of the engagement in the wood. Many thoughts came to her, but she never thought that, quite close to her before the window, was a remembrance of those times—the neck of the bottle that shouted aloud for joy when the cork flew up with a pop at her betrothal. But the bottle-neck did not recognize her either, for he was not listening to what she said and related—because he was thinking only of her.

Children's Prattle

At the rich merchant's there was a children's party for the children of rich and grand people. The merchant was a learned man; he had once passed the college examination, for his father, who from the first had only been a cattle-dealer, though an honest and industrious man, had kept him to that. The business had brought money, and that money the merchant had managed to increase. He was clever, and he had also a heart, but less was said of his heart than of his piles of money. Grand people visited at the merchant's—people of blood, as the saying is, and people of intellect—people too who had both, and people who had neither. This time there was a children's party and children's prattle, and children, as we know, say what they mean. Among the rest was a beautiful little girl, but she was terribly proud; this the servants had taught her to be, not her parents, for they were much too sensible for that; her father was a Groom of the Bedchamber, and that's something very grand, and she knew it.

"I am a child of the Bedchamber!" she said.

Now she might just as well have been a child of the cellar, for no one can help their birth. Then she told the other children that she was "well born," and said that no one who was not well born could get on in the world; it was no use trying to read and be industrious—if you were not well born, you would never be anything.

"And those whose names end in 'sen,'" she said, "they can never be anything at all. You must put your arms akimbo, and keep these 'sen' at a distance!"

And with that she put her pretty little arms on her hips and stuck her elbows out to show the others how to do it; and her little arms were very pretty, too. She was a sweet little girl.

But the merchant's little daughter got quite angry at these; her father's name was Petersen, and she knew that it ended in "sen," so she said as proudly as she could:

"But my father can buy a hundred dollars' worth of bon-bons and let the children scramble for them; can your father do that?"

"Yes; but my father," said the journalist's little girl, "can put your father and everybody's father in the paper. Everybody is afraid of him, my mother says, for it's my father who rules the paper."

And the little girl looked quite proud, as if she had been a real princess who had something to be proud of.

But outside the door, which was ajar, stood a poor boy looking through the crack. He was so humble that he was not even allowed to go into the room with the others. He had turned the roasting-spit for the cook, and she had allowed him to stand behind the door and to look at the well-dressed children who were enjoying themselves inside—and that was a great deal for him.

"To be one of those!" he thought; and then he heard what they said, and that was enough to make him very miserable. His parents at home had not a penny to spare to buy a paper, let alone write one; and worst of all his father's name, and therefore his own too, ended in "sen"; so he could never be anything at all. That was too sad! But still it seemed to him that he had been born, and very well born too—it could not possibly be otherwise.

So much for that evening.

Many years had passed since then, and in that time children grow up.

In the town stood a beautiful house filled with nothing but beautiful things and treasures. Every one wanted to see it; even those who lived in the country came to town to see it. Now which of the children of whom we have spoken could call that house his own? Well, that's very easy to say. No, no, it's not so very easy after all. The house belonged to the poor little boy who had stood behind the door that evening; you see he had become something in the world, although his name ended in "sen"—*Thorwaldsen.*

And the three other children—the children of blood, of money, and of the pride of intellect? Well, they have nothing to reproach each other with—they are all equal as children; they all turned out well, for Nature had so endowed them. What they had thought and spoken that evening was merely "children's prattle."

The Old House

Down yonder in the street stood an old, old house. It was almost three hundred years old according to the inscription on one of the beams, which bore the date of its erection surrounded by tulips and trailing hops. There one could read whole verses in old-fashioned letters, and over each window a face, making all kinds of grimaces, had been carved in the beam. One story projected a long way beyond the other, and close under the roof was a leaden gutter with a dragon's head. The rain-water was to run out of the jaws, but it ran out of the animal's stomach, for there was a hole in the gutter.

Down yonder in the street stood an old, old house.

All the other houses in the street were still new and neat, with large window-panes and smooth walls. It was plainly to be seen that they wished to have nothing to do with the old house. Perhaps they were thinking: "How long is that tumble-down old thing to remain a scandal to the whole street? The parapet projects so far that no one can see from our windows what is going on on the other side. The steps are as broad as those of a castle, and as high as if they led to a church steeple. The iron railings look like the gate of a family vault, and they have brass knobs too. It is really too silly!"

Opposite, there were some more new neat houses, and they thought just as the others; but at the window sat a little boy with fresh rosy cheeks and clear sparkling eyes, and he was particularly fond of the old house, both by sunshine and by moonlight. And when he gazed across at the wall where the plaster had fallen off, he could make out the strangest pictures of how the street had formerly looked, with its open staircases, parapets, and pointed gables; he could see soldiers with halberds, and gutters in the form of dragons and griffins. It was a house worth looking at, and in it lived an old man who went about in leather knee-breeches, and wore a coat with great brass buttons, and a wig which it was easy to see was a real one. Every morning another old man came to clean the place for him and to run on errands. With this exception, the old man in the knee-breeches lived quite alone in the old house. Occasionally he came to the window and looked out, and the little boy would nod to him, and the old man would nod back, and so they became acquainted and became friends, although they had never spoken to each other. But indeed that was not at all necessary.

The little boy once heard his parents say: "The old man opposite is very well off; but he is alone!"

On the following Sunday the little boy wrapped something up in a piece of paper, went into the street with it, and addressing the old man, who ran errands, said: "Here! will you take this to the old man who lives opposite, from me? I have two tin soldiers; this is one of them, and he shall have it, because I know he is quite alone."

And the old attendant looked pleased, nodded, and took the tin soldier into the old house. Afterwards word was sent over whether the little boy would not like to come himself and pay a visit. His parents gave him leave to do so, and he went over to the old house.

The brass knobs on the staircase railings shone brighter than ever; one would have thought that they had been polished on account of the visit. And it looked just as if the carved trumpeters—for on the door trumpeters had been carved all in tulips—were blowing with all their might; their cheeks were more blown out than before. Yes, they blew, "Ta-ta-ra-ta! The little boy is coming! Ta ta-ra-ta!" And then the door opened. The whole hall was hung with old portraits of knights in armor, and ladies in silk dresses; and the armor clattered and the silk dresses rustled. And then came a staircase which went up a long way and then down a little bit, and then one found oneself upon a balcony, which was certainly very rickety, with large holes and long cracks; out of all these grew grass, for the whole balcony, the courtyard, and the wall was so overgrown with green that it looked like a garden; but it was only a balcony. Here stood old flower-pots which had faces and asses' ears; but the flowers grew just as it pleased them. In one pot pinks were growing over on all sides—that is to say, the green part of them—sprout upon sprout. And they said quite plainly: "The air has caressed me, the sun has kissed me and promised me a little flower on Sunday,—a little flower on Sunday."

And then one came to a room where the walls were covered with pigskin, and on the pigskin golden flowers had been stamped.

"Gilding fades fast.
But pigskin will last!"

said the walls.

And there stood chairs with high backs, all carved and with arms on each side. "Sit down," they said. "Oh, how it cracks inside me! I am certainly getting gouty, like the old cupboard. Gout in the back—ugh!"

And then the little boy came to the room where the old man was sitting.

"Thank you for the tin soldier, my little friend," said he, "and thank you for coming over to me."

"Thanks, thanks!" or rather, "Crick, crack!" said all the furniture. There was so much of it that the pieces almost stood in each other's way to see the little boy.

And in the middle of the wall hung a picture of a beautiful lady, of young and cheerful appearance, but dressed in the old-fashioned way, with powdered hair and clothes that stood out stiff. She said neither "Thanks" nor "Crack," but looked down with kind eyes upon the little boy, who immediately asked the old man, "Where did you get her from?"

"From the second-hand dealer over the way," said the old man. "There are always a lot of portraits hanging there; no one knows who they were or troubles about them, for they are all buried. But I knew this lady many years ago, and now she has been dead and gone these fifty years."

And under the portrait hung, in a frame, a bouquet of faded flower, they were certainly half a century old too—at least they looked so.

And the pendulum of the great clock swung to and fro, and the hands moved, and everything in the room grew older still; but no one noticed it.

"They say at home," said the little boy, "that you are always alone."

"Oh!" replied the old man, "the old thoughts, with all that they bring with them, come and visit me; and now you come too. I am very comfortable, I'm sure!"

And then he took from a shelf a book with pictures; there were long processions and the most wonderful coaches, such as are never seen now-a-days; soldiers like the knave of clubs, and citizens with waving banners. The tailors had a banner with a pair of shears on it, held by two lions, and the shoemakers a banner without any shoes, but with an eagle that had two heads, for shoemakers must have everything in such a way that they can say, "That's a pair!" What a picture-book it was!

The old man went into the next room to get some preserves, apples, and nuts. It was really glorious in the old house.

"I can't stand it any longer!" said the tin soldier, who was standing on the chest of drawers. "It is quite too lonely and dull here. No; when once one knows what family life is, there is no getting accustomed to this kind of thing. I cannot stand it! The day seems already long enough; but the evening is longer still. Here it is not at all like it is at your house, where your father and mother always talked pleasantly, and where you and the other sweet children made a capital noise. Dear me! how lonely it is here at the old man's! Do you think he gets any kisses? Do you think he gets friendly looks or a Christmas tree? He'll get nothing but a grave! I can't stand it!"

"You mustn't look at it from the dark side," said the little boy. "All this seems to me extremely beautiful, and all the old thoughts, with all that they bring with them, come and visit here."

"Yes, but I don't see them and I don't know them," said the tin soldier. "I can't stand it!"

"You must!" said the little boy.

The old man came with a most pleased look on his face, and with the finest preserved fruits and apples and nuts; then the little boy thought no more of the tin soldier.

The little boy came home happy and pleased. Days and weeks passed by, during which there was a great deal of nodding both to and from the old house; then the little boy went across again.

The carved trumpeters blew "Ta-ta-ra-ta! There's the little boy! Ta-ta-ra-ta!" The swords and armor on the old knights' portraits clattered, and the silk dresses rustled; the pigskin told tales, and the old chairs had gout in their backs: "Oh!" It was just like the first time, for over there one day or one hour was just like another.

"I can't stand it!" said the tin soldier. "I have wept tin. It is too dull here. Let me rather go to war and lose my arms and legs. That would be at least a change. I can't stand it! Now I know what it means to be visited by one's old thoughts, with all that they bring with them. I have had visits from mine, and you may believe me, that's no pleasure in the long run. I was at last nearly jumping down from the chest of drawers. I saw you all in the house over there as plainly as if you were really here. It was again Sunday morning, and you children were all standing round the table singing the hymn that you sing every morning. You were standing devoutly with folded hands, and father and mother were also feeling very solemn; then the door opened and your little sister Mary, who is not yet two years old, and who always dances when she hears music and singing, of whatever kind it may be, was brought in. She ought not to have done so, but she began to dance, though she could not get into the right time, for the notes were too long drawn; so she stood first on one leg and held her head forward, but she could not keep it up long enough. You all looked very earnest, though it was rather difficult to do so; but I laughed inwardly, and therefore fell down from the table and got a bump, which I have still. It was certainly not right of me to laugh. All this, and everything else that I have gone through, now passes through me again, and these are, no doubt, the old thoughts with all that they bring with them. Tell me, do you still sing on Sundays? And tell me something about little Mary. And how is my comrade, the other tin soldier? He is certainly a very happy fellow. I can't stand it!"

"You have been given away," said the little boy; "you must stay. Can't you see that?"

Then the old man came with a chest in which there were many things to be seen: little rouge-boxes and scent-boxes and old cards, so large and so thickly gilt as one never sees now-a-days. Many little boxes were opened; the piano too, and on the inside of the lid of this were painted landscapes. But it sounded quite hoarse when the old man played upon it; then he nodded to the portrait that he had bought at the second-hand dealer's, and his eyes sparkled quite brightly.

"I'll go to war! I'll go to war!" cried the tin soldier as loud as he could, and threw himself down upon the floor.

Yes, but where had he gone? The old man looked for him and the little boy looked too, but away he was, and away he stopped. "I'll find him some day," said the old man, but he never did; the flooring was too open and full of holes. The tin soldier had fallen through a crack, and there he now lay as in an open grave.

The day passed, and the little boy came home. Several weeks passed by; the windows were quite frozen up, and the little boy had to breathe upon the panes to make a peep-hole to look at the old house. The snow had blown into all the carvings and inscriptions, and covered the whole staircase, as if there were no one in the house. And there was no one in the house, either: the old man had died! In the evening a carriage stopped at the door, and upon that he was placed in his coffin; he was to rest in his family vault in the country. So he was carried away; but no one followed him, for all his friends were dead. The little boy threw kisses after the coffin as it was driven by.

A few days afterwards an auction was held in the old house, and the little boy saw from his window how the old knights and the old ladies, the flower-pots with the long ears, the chairs and the old cupboards, were carried away. One went this way, another that way; her portrait, that had been bought from the second-hand dealer went back to his shop, and there it remained hanging, for no one cared about the old picture.

In the spring the old house itself was pulled down; it was an old piece of lumber, people said. You could see from the street straight into the room with the pigskin wall-covering, which was torn down all in tatters, and the green of the balcony hung in confusion around the beams, which threatened a total downfall. And now the place was cleared up.

"That's a good thing!" said the neighboring houses.

A noble house was built, with large windows and smooth white walls; but in front of the place where the old house had stood a little garden was laid out and wild vines crept up the neighbors' wall. Before the garden were placed great iron railings with an iron gate, looking very stately. People remained standing before it and looked through. And the sparrows sat in dozens upon the vine branches, all chattering at once as loud as they could, but not about the old house, for that they could not remember, many years having passed—so many, that the little boy had grown into a man, a sturdy man who was a great joy to his parents. He was just married, and had moved with his wife into the house which had the garden in front of it; and here he stood beside her while she planted a field flower which she thought very pretty; she planted it with her little hand, pressing the earth close round it with her fingers "Oh! what was that?" She had pricked herself. Out of the soft ground something pointed was sticking up. It was—just fancy!—the tin soldier, the same that had been lost up at the old man's, that had been roaming about for a long time among old wood and rubbish, and that had now lain already many years in the earth.

The young wife first dried the soldier with a green leaf, and then with her dainty handkerchief, which smelled delightfully.

The tin soldier felt just as if he were waking up out of a swoon.

"Let me see him!" said the young man. He smiled and then shook his head. "No, it can hardly be the same one; but it reminds me of the story of a tin soldier which I had when I was a little boy." And then he told his wife about the old house and the old man, and the tin soldier which he had sent across to him because he was so lonely; and the tears came into the young wife's eyes when she heard of the old house and the old man.

"But it is quite possible that this is the very tin soldier!" said she. "I will take care of him and remember what you have told me; but you must show me the old man's grave."

"I don't know where that is," he replied, "and no one knows. All his friends were dead; no one tended it, and I was only a little boy."

"Oh! how lonely he must have been!" said she.

"Yes, very lonely!" said the tin soldier; "but it is glorious not to be forgotten."

"Glorious!" exclaimed a voice close by; but no one except the tin soldier saw that it came from a rag of the pigskin hangings, which had now lost all its gilding. It looked like wet earth; but still it had an opinion which it expressed as follows:

Out of the ground something pointed was sticking up. It was—just fancy!—the tin soldier.

"Gliding fades fast,
But pigskin will last!"

But the tin soldier did not believe it.

The Farm-Yard Cock and the Weather-Cock

There were two cocks—one on the dung-hill, the other on the roof. They were both arrogant, but which of the two rendered most service? Tell us your opinion—we'll keep to ours just the same though.

The poultry-yard was divided by some planks from another yard in which there was a dung-hill, and on the dung-hill lay and grew a large cucumber which was conscious of being a hot-bed plant.

"One is born to that," said the cucumber to itself. "Not all can be born cucumbers: there must be other things, too. The hens, the ducks, and all the animals in the next yard are creatures too. Now I have a great opinion of the yard cock on the plank; he is certainly of much more importance than the weather-cock who is placed so high and can't even creak, much less crow. The latter has neither hens nor chicks, and only thinks of himself and perspires verdigris. No, the yard cock is really a cock! His step is a dance! His crowing is music, and wherever he goes one knows what a trumpeter is like! If he would only come in here! Even if he ate me up stump, stalk, and all, and I had to dissolve in his body, it would be a happy death," said the cucumber.

In the night there was a terrible storm. The hens, chicks, and even the cock sought shelter; the wind tore down the planks between the two yards with a crash; the tiles came tumbling down, but the weather-cock sat firm. He did not even turn round, for he could not; and yet he was young and freshly cast, but prudent and sedate. He had been born old, and did not at all resemble the birds flying in the air—the sparrows, and the swallows; no, he despised them, these mean little piping birds, these common whistlers. He admitted that the pigeons, large and white and shining like mother-o'-pearl, looked like a kind of weather-cock; but they were fat and stupid, and all their thoughts and endeavors were directed to filling themselves with food, and besides, they were tiresome things to converse with. The birds of passage had also paid the weather-cock a visit and told him of foreign countries, of airy caravans and robber stories that made one's hair stand on end. All this was new and interesting; that is, for the first time, but afterwards, as the weather-cock found out, they repeated themselves and always told the same stories, and that's very tedious, and there was no one with whom one could associate, for one and all were stale and small-minded.

"The world is no good!" he said. "Everything in it is so stupid."

The weather-cock was puffed up, and that quality would have made him interesting in the eyes of the cucumber if it had known it, but it had eyes only for the yard cock, who was now in the yard with it.

The wind had blown the planks, but the storm was over.

"What do you think of that crowing?" said the yard cock to the hens and chickens. "It was a little rough—it wanted elegance."

And the hens and chickens came up on the dung-hill, and the cock strutted about like a lord.

"Garden plant!" he said to the cucumber, and in that one word his deep learning showed itself, and it forgot that he was pecking at her and eating it up. "A happy death!"

The hens and the chickens came, for where one runs the others run too; they clucked, and chirped, and looked at the cock, and were proud that he was of their kind.

"Cock-a-doodle-doo!" he crowed, "the chickens will grow up into great hens at once, if I cry it out in the poultry-yard of the world!"

And hens and chicks clucked and chirped, and the cock announced a great piece of news.

"A cock can lay an egg! And do you know what's in that egg? A basilisk. No one can stand the sight of such a thing; people know that, and now you know it too—you know what is in me, and what a champion of all cocks I am!"

With that the yard cock flapped his wings, made his comb swell up, and crowed again; and they all shuddered, the hens and the little chicks—but they were very proud that one of their number was such a champion of all cocks. They clucked and chirped till the weather-cock heard it; he heard it, but he did not stir.

"Everything is very stupid," the weather-cock said to himself. "The yard cock lays no eggs, and I am too lazy to do so; if I liked, I could lay a wind-egg. But the world is not worth even a wind-egg. Everything is so stupid! I don't even want to sit here any longer."

With that the weather-cock broke off; but he did not kill the yard cock, although the hens said that had been his intention. And what is the moral?" Better to crow than to be puffed up and break off!"

Five out of One Pod

There were once five peas in one pod; the peas as well as the pod were green, and therefore, they thought that the whole world was green, and nothing was more natural. The pod grew larger and so did the peas; they made the best of circumstances, they were all sitting in a row. While the sun shone on the outside of the pod, the rain made it clear and transparent; the weather was mild and pleasant; it was light in the daytime and dark at night, as it should be. The peas, as they were sitting there, grew larger and more pensive; for they must needs do something in the world.

"Are we to sit here for ever?" asked one of them; "I fear sitting here so long will make us hard. I have a certain feeling that there is something outside."

Weeks passed; the peas turned yellow, and so did the pod.

"The whole world turns yellow," they said, and also in this they were quite right.

Suddenly they felt a pull, the pod was wrenched from the stem, came into human hands and glided into the pocket of a jacket, in company with other full pods. "Now we shall soon see daylight," they said; for that was what they were waiting for.

"I should like to know which of us will get on best," said the smallest of the five. "That we shall soon find out."

"What is to be, will be," said the largest.

"Crack," the pod burst open, and the five peas rolled out into the bright sunshine. There they lay in a little boy's hand, who held them tightly, declaring that they were fine peas for his peashooter; and he at once put one in and shot it off."

"Now I am flying out into the wide world, catch me if you can," and away it was.

"I," said the second, "shall fly straightway into the sun, that is a pod one can be proud of, and one that would suit me exactly."

And off it was.

"We shall go to sleep wherever we get to," said the two next ones; "to be sure we shall roll forward."

They certainly did roll forward, and fell to the ground before they were put into the pea-shooter, and yet they were put in all the same. "We shall get on best."

"What is to be will be," said the last, while it was flung out of the pea-shooter; it flew against the weather-beaten sill of a garret window and dropped into a crevice full of moss and soft mold: the moss closed up over it; there it lay, in prison, it is true, but not overlooked by Providence.

"What is to be, will be," it said.

In the little garret lived a poor woman, who went out in the daytime to clean stoves, chop wood, and do other menial services of that kind; she was strong and industrious, but yet she always remained poor. At home in her little room lay her only daughter, who was but half grown up and very weakly and delicate; she had been bedridden for a whole year, and it seemed as if she could neither live nor die.

"She will go to join her little sister," said the woman. "I have only had these two children, and truly it was no easy task to provide for them both; but God has lightened my burden and taken one away from me; now I greatly wish to keep the other; but I am afraid they will not long be separated, and my poor girl will join her sister above."

But the invalid remained there; she lay patient and quietly all day long in bed, while the mother went out to earn their daily bread.

Spring came; one morning early, when the mother was just going to her work, the sun shone so brightly through the window, and his beams fell on the floor of the little room; the sick girl, by chance, turned her eyes towards the lower window pane.

"I wonder what the green thing is which is peeping in at the window; look there how the wind moves it."

The mother went to the window and half opened it. "Good gracious," she exclaimed, "here is actually a little pea that has taken root, and is putting out its leaves. I wonder how it came into the crevice. That is a little garden which will be a pleasure to you."

The invalid's bed was moved close to the window, that she might see the growing plant; the mother went out as usual to her work.

"Mother, dear," said the girl in the evening, "I believe I shall soon be well again; the sun was shining so brightly upon me today; the little pea is thriving so well, I think I shall soon thrive again too, and go out into the sunshine."

"May God grant it," said the mother; but in her heart she did not think it possible; she supported the plant with a little stick, that had inspired her child with new hope of life, lest the wind might break it; then she tied a piece of string on the sill and the upper part of the window-frame, that the pea had something to climb upon when it shot up; it soon began to do so, one could see it grow larger from day to day.

"Truly, it will soon have a flower," said the woman one morning; and from this day forward she began to cherish hopes for her daughter's recovery. She remembered that the child had spoken with more cheerfulness in the last weeks, and that she had sat upright in her bed for the last few days, while she looked with beaming eyes at her little garden, which consisted of a single pea-plant.

One week after this morning the patient was, for the first time, able to be up for a whole hour; she sat happily in the warm sunshine; the window was open, and outside was the little plant with its first pink flowers fully out.

The girl bent over it, and kissed gently the tender leaves. The day seemed to her like a festival.

"God himself has planted it and made it grow, my child, that it might fill our hearts with new hope and joy," said the happy mother, while she looked at the plant as if it had been a good angel.

But now, what about the other peas?

Well, the one that flew out into the wide world and said, "Catch me if you can," fell into the gutter, and from thence it passed into a pigeon's crop, where it lay like Jonah in the whale's stomach.

The two lazy ones reached the same destination; they also were swallowed by pigeons, so they were, at least, in some way useful. The fourth, however, which wished to go up into the sun, dropped into the drain, and there it remained in the dirty water for days and weeks, until it was quite swollen up.

"I am getting so nice and fat," said the pea, "I am nearly bursting. I think no pea has done or can do more than that. I am certainly the most remarkable of the five which were in the pod." And the drain was of the same opinion.

But the girl stood at the garret window with sparkling eyes, and the hue of health on her cheeks; she folded her thin hands over the pea-blossom and thanked God for it.

"I," said the drain, "stand up for my pea."

The Snow-Queen

Story the First
Which Describes the Looking-Glass and the Fragments

Well! We will begin. When we get to the end of the story we shall know more than we do now about a certain wicked goblin. He was one of the very worst, for he was Old Nick himself. One day he was in a very good temper, for he had made a mirror that possessed the power of making everything good and beautiful that was reflected in it shrink to almost nothing, while all that was worthless and bad looked still larger and worse. The most beautiful landscapes appeared like boiled spinach, and the best people looked repulsive, or stood on their heads and had no bodies. Their faces were so distorted that no one could recognize them, and if there was one freckle on any one's face, he might be sure that it would spread all over his nose and mouth. Old Nick thought this extremely amusing. When a good pious thought passed through any one's mind, it was reflected in the mirror as a grin, and the devil could not help laughing at his cunning invention. Those who went to the goblin's school—for he kept a school of his own—related everywhere that a miracle had taken place, and declared that now people could see for the first time how the world and mankind really looked. They carried the mirror about everywhere, till at last there was not a country nor any person who had not been distorted in it. Then they even wanted to fly up to Heaven with it to see the angels, but the higher they flew with the mirror the more hideously did it grin. They could hardly hold it, but still flying upwards, they came near the angels; then the grins of the mirror shook it so terribly, that it slipped from their hands and fell to the earth, where it was shattered into millions and billions of pieces. And now it caused far more unhappiness than before, for some pieces were no larger than a grain of sand. These flew about in the world, and when they got into any one's eyes, they would stay there, and then the people saw everything distorted, or could only see the bad side of a thing; for every fragment of the mirror retained the same power that the whole mirror had possessed. Some people even got a fragment into their heart, and that was a horrible thing; the heart at once became like a lump of ice. Some fragments were so large that they were used for window panes; but it was a bad thing to look at one's friends through such windows. Other pieces were made into spectacles, and when people put these on, it was difficult for them to see straight or to be just; the evil one laughed till his sides shook—it tickled him so. But there were still some of these small fragments floating about in the air. Well, we shall hear about them.

Story the Second
A Little Boy and a Little Girl

In a large town, which contained so many people and houses that there was not room enough for everybody to possess a little garden of his own, and where therefore most of them had to content themselves with flowers in pots, there dwelled two poor children who had a somewhat larger garden than a flower-pot. They were not brother and sister, but they loved each other as much as if they had been. Their parents lived in two attics exactly opposite each other. Just where the roof of one house joined the other, and where a gutter ran between the two, there was a little window in each house; one had only to step across the gutter to get from one window to the other.

The parents of both children had a large wooden box standing outside, in which grew herbs they used in cooking, and a small rose-bush; there was one in each box, and they grew splendidly. The parents hit upon the idea of placing the boxes across the gutter, so that they almost reached from one window to the other, and looked just like two walls of flowers. Scarlet-runners hung down over the boxes, and the rose-bushes put forth long shoots which climbed up round the windows, and becoming entwined with those opposite, formed almost a triumphal arch of foliage and flowers. As the boxes were very high, and the children knew that they might not climb upon them, they often got permission to go out on the roof, and to sit on their little stools under the roses, and there they played prettily.

Winter put an end to this pleasure. The windows were often quite frozen over; but then they would warm a penny on the stove and hold it against the

They carried the mirror about everywhere, till at last there was not a country nor any person who had not been distorted in it.

Just where the roof of one house joined the other, and where a gutter ran between the two, there was a little window in each house.

frozen pane; in this way they made a little round peep-hole, behind which there sparkled a kind gentle eye, one at each window. These were the little boy and the little girl; he was called Kay, and her name was Gerda. In summer they could get to each other in one bound, but in winter they had to go up and down ever so many stairs and through the snow.

"Those are swarms of white bees," said the old grandmother.

"Have they a queen bee too?" asked the little boy, for he knew that the real bees had one.

"Certainly they have," said the grandmother. "She flies where they are thickest. She is the largest of all, and she never remains quiet on the ground; she flies up again into the black clouds. Many a time at midnight does she

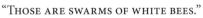

"Those are swarms of white bees."

fly through the streets of the town looking in at the windows, and then they freeze in a wonderful way and look like flowers."

"Oh yes! we have seen that," said both children, and now they knew it was true.

"Can the Snow-Queen come in here?" asked the little girl.

"Only let her come," said the boy; "I'll put her on the warm stove, and then she'll melt."

But grandmother smoothed her hair and told other tales. In the evening, when little Kay was at home and half undressed, he climbed up on a chair to the window, and peeped through the little hole; a few snow-flakes were falling outside, and one of them, the largest, remained lying on the edge of one of the flower-boxes. The snow-flake got larger and larger, and at last grew into a maiden, dressed in the finest white gauze, which was composed of millions of starry flakes. She was very beautiful and dainty, but made of ice—of dazzling, glittering ice. But still she was alive; her eyes sparkled like two stars, but there was no rest nor peace in them. She nodded at the window and beckoned with her hand. The little boy got frightened and jumped down from the chair; then it was just as if a larger bird was flying past the window.

There was a clear frost next day, and then spring came. The sun shone, the trees and bushes budded, the swallows built their nests, the windows were opened, and the little children sat once more in their little garden high up in the gutter on the top of the roof.

How splendidly the roses bloomed that summer! The little girl had learned a psalm in which there was something about roses, and when she came to that part she thought of her own. She sang it to the little boy, and he sang it with her:

"The roses fade and die, but we
Our Infant Lord shall surely see."

The little ones held each other by the hand, kissed the roses and, looking at God's fair sunshine, spoke to it as if the Child Jesus were there. What glorious summer days those were! How beautiful it was out there by those fragrant rose-trees, which seemed to wish that they might never stop blooming!

One day Kay and Gerda were looking at their picture-book full of animals and birds, when just as the clock in the great church-steeple struck five, Kay said:

"Oh! what a shooting pain I felt in my heart, and something has flown into my eye."

The snow-flake got larger and larger, and at last grew into a maiden, dressed in the finest white gauze, which was composed of millions of starry flakes. She was very beautiful and dainty, but made of ice.

The little girl put her arms round his neck; he blinked his eyes—no, there was nothing to be seen.

"I believe it is gone," he said; but gone it was not. It happened to be one of those splinters of glass from the magic mirror which we have not forgotten—that hateful glass that made everything great and good that was reflected in it small and ugly, and in which all that was wicked and bad was made still more so, and every fault magnified.

Poor Kay had got a splinter right into his heart which would now soon become like a lump of ice. He no longer felt any pain, but the splinter was there.

"What are you crying for?" he said. "You look ugly when you cry. There's nothing the matter with me. Good gracious!" he suddenly cried out, "that rose there has a worm in it. And look, this one hangs quite crooked. They are ugly roses, after all. They look like the box in which they grow." And then he kicked the box and tore off the roses.

"Kay, what are you doing?" cried the little girl; and when he saw how frightened she was, he tore another rose off, and then sprang into his window away from dear little Gerda.

When she came to him afterwards with the picture-book, he said that it was only fit for babies in long clothes, and when his grandmother told them tales he always put in a "but." When he could, he would get behind, put on her spectacles, and speak just like her; he could do that wonderfully well, and people laughed at him. Soon he was able to mimic the speech and walk of everybody in the street. Everything that was peculiar or not nice about them, Kay could imitate, and people would say: "What a remarkable head that boy has!" But it was the glass that was in his heart. It was that too that made him tease even little Gerda, who was very fond indeed of him. His games were now different from what they had been before; they became quite sensible ones. One winter's day, when it was snowing, he came in with a large magnifying glass, and holding out one of the tails of his blue coat, let the snow fall upon it.

"Now look through the glass, Gerda," he said; each snowflake was much larger and looked like a splendid flower or a ten-cornered star. It was a beautiful sight. "Do you see how curiously they are made?" said Kay. "They are much more interesting than real flowers. And there is not a single fault in them; their points are absolutely regular. If only they would not melt!"

Soon after this Kay came in wearing thick gloves and with his sleigh on his back; he called out to Gerda, "I have obtained permission to go sleighing in the large square where the other boys play," and away he went.

In the square the most daring boys often tied their sleighs to the carts of the country people, and then they rode a good way with them. That was very fine. While they were in the midst of their play, a large sleigh came along. It was painted white all over, and in it sat some one wrapped in a rough white fur and wearing a rough white cap. The sleigh rode round the square twice, and Kay, quickly binding his little sleigh to it, rode away with it, faster and faster, through the neighboring streets. The person who was driving turned round and nodded to Kay in a friendly manner, just as if they knew each other, and every time that Kay wanted to unfasten his little sleigh, the driver nodded again, and so Kay stayed on and rode out through the city-gates. Then the snow began to fall so thickly that the little boy could not see an inch before him, but still he rode on. At last he tried to undo the rope to get away from the great sleigh, but it was of no use; his little carriage hung fast and flew along like the wind. Then he called out quite loudly, but no one heard him; the snow fell, and the sleigh flew along, now and then giving a jump as if it were driving over hedges and ditches. The boy was quite frightened; he tried to say his prayers, but he could only remember his multiplication table.

The snow-flakes became larger and larger; at last they looked like large white chickens. All at once they fell aside, the large sleigh stopped, and the person who had been driving got up from the seat; the cloak and the cap were made entirely of snow, and they were worn by a lady, tall and slender and dazzlingly white—it was the Snow-Queen. "We have driven fast," she said; "but no one likes to be frozen. Creep under my fur." And placing Kay next to her in the sleigh, she wrapped her cloak around him, and he seemed to be sinking in a snow-drift.

"Are you still cold?" she asked, and kissed him on the forehead. Oh! that kiss was colder than ice, it went right through his heart, which was already fast becoming a lump of ice. He felt as if he were going to die, but it was only for a moment, then he was all right again, and no longer felt the cold all around him.

"My sleigh! Don't forget my sleigh!" That was the first thing he thought of, and it was bound fast to one of the white chickens which flew on behind with the sleigh on its back. The Snow-Queen kissed Kay again, and then he forgot all about little Gerda, his grandmother, and all the folks at home.

"I will not give you anymore kisses now," she said; "else I should kiss you to death."

Kay looked at her, she was so beautiful; he could not imagine a wiser and kinder face. She no longer appeared to him to be of ice as when she sat outside the window beckoning to him; in his eyes she was perfect, and he felt no fear at all. He told her he could do mental arithmetic, and in fractions, too; that he knew how many square miles there were in the country, and the number of its inhabitants. She smiled, and then it occurred to him that it was not enough after all that he knew, and he looked up into the great space above him. She flew on high with him up to the black clouds where the storm was raging and moaning, and it seemed to Kay as if it were singing old songs. They flew across forests and lakes, across sea and land. Under them the cold winds whistled, the wolves howled and the snow crackled, while above them flew the black cawing crows. The moon, large and bright, shone down upon all, and there Kay sat and gazed through the long winter's night; during the day he slept at the feet of the Snow-Queen.

Story the Third
The Flower-Garden of the Sorceress

But how fared it with little Gerda when Kay did not return? Where could he be? No one knew, no one could tell. The boys said that they had seen him tying his sleigh to another larger one which had driven into the streets and out through the gates of the town. No one knew where he was; many tears were shed, especially by little Gerda, who wept much and long. Then they said that he was dead: that he was drowned in the river that flowed not far from the school. Oh! what long dark winter days those were!

Now came spring with its warm sunshine.

"Kay is dead and gone!" said little Gerda.

"I don't believe it!" answered the sunshine.

"He is dead and gone," she said to the swallows.

"We don't believe it," they replied, and at last little Gerda did not believe it either.

"I will put on my new red shoes," she said, one morning, "those that Kay has never seen, and then I will go down to the river and ask after him."

It was still very early; she kissed her old grandmother, who was still asleep, put on her red shoes, and went quite alone through the gates of the town, down to the river.

"Is it true that you have taken away my little playmate from me? I will give you my red shoes, if you give him back to me."

It seemed to her as if the waves nodded in a strange way; so she took off her red shoes, which she liked more than anything she had, and threw them both into the river. But they fell close to the bank, and the little waves carried them back to her; it was just as if the river not having little Kay, would not take from her what she liked best. She, however, thought she had not thrown them in far enough, and so she crept into a boat that lay among the reeds; going to the farthest end of it she threw the shoes in from thence, and the boat, not being fastened, her movement caused it to glide away from the bank. Seeing this, she hastened to get out, but before she reached the other end the boat was more than a yard from the land, and was quickly gliding away.

Little Gerda was quite frightened and began to cry; but no one besides the sparrows heard her, and they could not carry her back to land. However, they flew along the banks, and sang as if to comfort her: "Here we are, here we are!"

The boat drifted along with the stream, and in it sat little Gerda, quite still, with only stockings on her feet; her small red shoes floated behind her, but they could not reach the boat, for it went along too quickly.

The banks on both sides were very pretty; beautiful flowers, old trees, and hills dotted with sheep and cows were there, but not a single human being was to be seen.

"Perhaps the river is carrying me to little Kay," thought Gerda, and then she became more cheerful, stood up and gazed for hours at the beautiful green banks. At last she came to a large cherry-orchard, in which there was a little house with curious red and blue windows; it also had a thatched roof, and outside stood two wooden soldiers who presented arms as she sailed by.

Gerda called out to them, thinking that they were alive, but of course they did not answer. She came quite close to them, for the stream was drifting the boat straight to the land.

Gerda called still louder, and then an old woman came out of the house, supporting herself on a crutch; she wore a large sun-hat, with the most beautiful flowers painted on it.

"Poor little thing!" said the old woman; "how ever did you come upon the great rushing stream, and get carried out so far into the world?" Then the old woman got into the water, and seizing the boat with her crutch, drew it to the shore, and took little Gerda out.

Gerda was pleased to reach dry land again, although she was somewhat afraid of the strange old woman.

"Come and tell me who you are, and where you come from," she said. And Gerda told her all, and the old woman shook her head and said "Hem, hem!" And when Gerda had told her all, and asked her whether she had not seen little Kay, she answered that he had not come by, but that he would probably do so yet. She told Gerda not to be sad, but to eat some cherries, and look at her flowers, which were finer than any in the picture-book, and each of which could tell a story. Then she took Gerda by the hand, led her into the little house, and closed the door.

AN OLD WOMAN CAME OUT OF THE HOUSE, SUPPORTING HERSELF ON A CRUTCH; SHE WORE A LARGE SUN-HAT, WITH THE MOST BEAUTIFUL FLOWERS PAINTED ON IT.

The windows were very high, and the panes were red, blue and yellow, so that the daylight shone through them strangely in all kinds of colors. Upon the table stood the finest cherries, and Gerda was allowed to eat as many of them as she liked. While she ate, the old woman combed her hair with a golden comb, and the bright flaxen locks fell in beautiful ringlets round the small smiling face which looked as round and as blooming as a rose.

"I have long wished for such a dear little girl," said the old woman. "Now you will see how happily we shall live together." And as she combed little Gerda's hair, the child gradually forgot her foster-brother Kay, for the old woman was a sorceress. But she was not a wicked sorceress; she only practiced her charms for amusement, and wished very much to keep little Gerda. She therefore went into the garden, and stretched out her crutch towards all the rose-trees, and although they were blooming beautifully, they all sank into the black ground, and it was impossible to see where they had stood. The old woman was afraid that if Gerda saw the roses, she would think of her own, and then remember little Kay, and run away.

Then she took Gerda out into the flower-garden. How fragrant and lovely it was! Every imaginable flower, and those of every season, too, stood here in perfect bloom; no picture-book could be more richly or finely colored.

Gerda jumped for joy, and played till the sun went down behind the tall cherry-trees; then she was laid in a beautiful bed with red silk pillows embroidered with violets. She slept and dreamed as gloriously as only a queen can do on her wedding-day.

The next day she could again play with the flowers in the warm sunshine, and in this way many days passed. Gerda knew every flower; but although there were so many of them, it seemed as if one were missing, yet which she did not know. One day she was sitting gazing at the old woman's sun-hat with the painted flowers, and it happened that the finest one was a rose. The old woman had forgotten to make it disappear from her hat when she had charmed the others into the earth. But so it is, if one has not perfect command over one's thoughts.

"What! are there no roses here?" cried Gerda, and she ran among the beds searching and searching; but alas! there were none to be found. Then she sat down and wept, and her warm tears falling just on the spot where a rose-tree had sunk down, they moistened the earth, and the tree suddenly shot up as blooming as when it had sunk; Gerda embraced it, kissed the roses, and thought of the beautiful roses at home, and with them of little Kay, too.

"Oh! how I have been detained!" said the little girl. "I wanted to go and find little Kay. Don't you know where he is?" she asked the roses. "Do you think he is dead?"

"No, he is not dead," answered the roses. "We have been in the ground where all the dead are, but Kay was not there."

"Thank you," said little Gerda, and going to the flowers, she looked into their cups and asked: "Do you know where little Kay is?"

But every flower was standing in the sun dreaming its own fairy tale or story, and of these Gerda heard ever so many; none, however, knew anything about Kay.

What says the tiger-lily?

"Do you hear the drum? 'boom, boom!' There are only two notes, always, 'boom, boom!' Listen to the wailing chant of the women, listen to the cry of the priests. The Hindoo widow clad in her long red mantle stands upon the funeral pile; the flames leap up around her and her dead husband. But she thinks of the living one in that circle—of him, her son whose eyes burn more than fire, of him whose looks are greater torture to her heart than the flames which will soon reduce her body to ashes. Can the flame of the heart perish in the flames of the stake?"

"I don't understand that at all," said little Gerda.

"That is my tale," said the tiger-lily.

What says the convolvulus?

"Overhanging the narrow pathway stands an old knight's castle; the thick evergreen climbs up the ruined red walls, leaf upon leaf, right up to the balcony where a beautiful maiden stands. She bends over the balustrade and looks along the path. No rose on the bough is fresher than she; no apple-blossom, when swept from the tree by the breeze, floats lighter than she. How her rich silken garments rustle as she exclaims, " 'Does he not come yet?' "

"Is it Kay you mean?" said little Gerda.

"I am only speaking of my tale, my dream," answered the convolvulus.

What says the little snowdrop?

"Between the trees a board is hanging by some ropes; it is a swing. Two pretty little girls in snow-white dresses and with long green silk ribbons fluttering from their hats are sitting on it swinging. Their brother, who is bigger than they, stands in the swing; he has his arm round the rope to hold himself, for in one hand he has a little dish and in the other a clay pipe. He is blowing soap bubbles; the swing flies on and the bubbles rise in beautiful varying colors. The last is still hanging to the bowl of the pipe and sways in the wind. The swing goes on; a little black dog, as light as the bubbles, stands on his hind legs and wants to get in too. But the swing flies up and the dog falls, barking and angry; they tease him, and the bubbles burst. A swinging plank, and a dissolving airy picture is my song."

"What you relate may be pretty, but you tell it so mournfully, and you don't mention little Kay at all."

What do the hyacinths say?

"There were three beautiful sisters, dainty and transparent. One was dressed in red, another in blue, and the third in white; hand in hand they danced by the silent lake in the bright moonlight. They were not elves but human beings. Attracted by the sweet fragrance, they disappeared into the wood; here the fragrance became stronger. Three coffins, in which lay the beautiful maidens, glided from the thicket of the wood out across the lake; the fire-flies flew all around to light their way, like little floating torches. Do the dancing maidens sleep, or are they dead? The fragrance from the flowers says they are dead, and the evening bell tolls their knell."

"You make me feel quite sad," said little Gerda. "Your scent is so strong that it makes me think of the dead. Is little Kay then really dead? The roses have been down in the ground and they say "No."

"Ding, dong!" tolled the hyacinth bells. "We are not tolling for little Kay, we don't know him; we do but sing our song, the only one we know."

Then Gerda went to the buttercups that were shining out from among the bright green leaves.

"You are bright little suns," said Gerda. "Tell me, do you know where I can find my playmate?"

The buttercups shone so brightly and again looked at Gerda. What song could they sing? It was not about Kay.

"On the first spring day the fair sun shone down so warm on a little courtyard, its rays falling on the white walls of the neighboring house. Close by bloomed the first yellow flower, glittering like gold in the warm sun-beams. The old grandmother sat outside in her chair; her grandchild, a poor but pretty servant-girl, was just going home again after a short visit. She kissed her grandmother, and there was gold, pure gold, in that blessed kiss. Gold, gold everywhere, on the maiden's lips and in the early morning air! You see, that is my little story," said the buttercup.

"My poor old grandmother," sighed Gerda. "Yes, I have no doubt she longs and grieves for me just as she did for little Kay. But I shall soon be home again, and then I will bring Kay with me. It is no use asking the flowers; they only know their own song, and cannot give me any information." And then she tucked up her little dress, so that she might run faster; but the narcissus caught hold of her leg as she was jumping over it. So she stopped to look at the long yellow flower and said, "Perhaps you know something." And she bent down quite close to the flower, and what did it say?

"I can see myself! I can see myself!" said the narcissus. "Oh! how I smell! Up in the little corner room stands a little ballet-girl, half undressed; first she stands on one leg, then on the other, sometimes on both. She treads the whole world under her feet, yet she is nothing but a delusion. She pours some water out of a teapot upon a piece of stuff that she holds in her hand; it is her bodice. Cleanliness is a fine thing. Her white dress hangs on a peg; it has also been washed in the teapot and dried on the roof. She puts it on and ties a saffron-colored kerchief round her neck which makes the dress look whiter. Look how she struts on one stem! I can see myself! I can see myself!"

"I don't care for that at all," said Gerda. "You need not have told me that." And then she ran to the end of the garden.

The door was fastened, but she pressed against the rusty latch so that it gave way; the door opened, and little Gerda sprang out with bare feet into the wide world. She looked back three times, but there was no one following her; at last she could walk no more and sat down on a large stone. When she looked round, the summer was gone and it was late in autumn. It was impossible to see that in the beautiful garden, where there was always sunshine, and where the flowers of every season grew.

"Oh, how I have tarried!" said little Gerda. "Autumn has come already. I must not rest any longer." And she rose to go.

Oh! how tired and sore her little feet were! All around it looked cold and raw. The long willow-leaves were quite yellow, and the dew trickled down like water. One leaf fell after another, and only the sloe-thorn still bore fruit, but it was sour and set one's teeth on edge. Oh! how dark and miserable the whole world looked.

Story the Fourth
The Prince and the Princess

Gerda was obliged to rest again; just opposite the spot where she sat a great crow was hopping on the snow. It had sat looking at her and wagging its head for a long time; at last it said, "Caw, caw! Good-day, good-day!" It could not speak plainer than that, but it meant to be kind to the little girl, and asked where she was going all alone like that in the wide world. Gerda understood the word "alone" very well, and felt how much it expressed; so she related to the crow her whole life and adventures, and asked whether it had seen Kay.

The crow nodded very thoughtfully and said, "It may be, it may be."

"What! Do you think so?" cried the little girl, and almost hugged the crow to death as she kissed it.

"Gently, gently!" said the crow. "I believe—I know. I believe—it may be—little Kay—but he has doubtless forgotten you by this time for the princess."

"Does he live with a princess?" asked Gerda.

"Yes, listen!" said the crow. "But it is so difficult for me to speak your language. If you understand the crow's language* I could tell it you better."

"No, I have never learned it," said Gerda, "but my grandmother understood it and could speak it too. I wish I had learned it."

"It doesn't matter," said the crow. "I will speak as well as I can, but it will be very badly." Then he related what he knew.

"In the kingdom where we now are, there lives a princess who is excessively clever; she has read all the newspapers there are in the world, and forgotten them too, so clever is she. A little while ago she was sitting on the throne, and they say that it is not such a comfortable seat after all. Well, she began to sing a song and it was this: 'Why should I not marry?' Now listen, for there's something in this. She wished to marry, but she wanted a husband who could answer when he was spoken to—one who would not merely stand there and look grand, for that would be too tedious. So she assembled all her court ladies by the beat of the drum, and when they heard what she wished they were very pleased. 'I like that,' said each one; 'I was just thinking about it myself.' You may believe every word I say," added the crow. "I have a tame sweetheart, who goes about freely in the castle, and she told me all about it."

Of course his sweetheart was a crow too. For one crow seeks another, and a crow always remains a crow.

"The newspapers immediately appeared with a border of hearts and the initials of the princess. They said that every good-looking young man was free to go to the castle and talk to the princess; and he who spoke so that it could be heard that he felt at home, and who spoke best, would be chosen for the princess's husband. Yes, yes," said the crow, "you may believe me; it is all as true as I sit here. Young men came in streams. There was a deal of crowding and rushing; but no one succeeded either on the first or on the second day. They could all talk well when they were in the street, but when they entered the castle-gates, and saw the guards in silver and the

* This is a kind of gibberish used by children, and is formed by adding syllables or letters to each word.

footmen in gold on the staircases, and the great halls lighted up, they became confused. And when they stood before the throne where the princess sat, they could only repeat the last word she had uttered, and she had no wish to hear that over again. It was just as if the people had swallowed snuff and went to sleep while they were inside till they came back into the street, for it was only then that they found their tongues again. A whole row of them reached from the city-gates to the palace. I went there myself to see them," said the crow.

"They were hungry and thirsty, but at the castle not even a glass of water was given to them. A few of the wisest had taken some bread and butter with them, but they did not share it with their neighbors, for they thought, "let him look hungry, then the princess will not take him."

"But Kay, little Kay," said Gerda. "When did he come? Was he among the crowd?"

"Wait a bit! We're coming to him now. It was on the third day there came, gaily marching along to the palace, a little personage without horses or carriage; his eyes sparkled just like yours. He had beautiful long hair, but was very poorly dressed."

"That was Kay!" exclaimed Gerda, joyfully. "Oh, then I have found him," and she clapped her hands.

"He had a little knapsack on his back," said the crow.

"No, that must have been his sleigh," said Gerda; "for he went away with that."

"It may have been," said the crow; "I did not look at it so closely. But this I know from my tame sweetheart, that when he passed through the castle-gates and saw the body-guards in silver and the footmen in gold on the staircases, he was not in the least embarrassed. He nodded to them and said: "How tedious it must be to stand on the stairs; I prefer to go in." The halls were brilliant with lights; privy councillors and ambassadors went about barefooted carrying golden vessels. It was enough to make any one feel serious. His boots creaked terribly, but he was not at all afraid."

"That was most certainly Kay," said Gerda. "I know he has new boots on; I heard them creaking in grandmother's room."

"Indeed they did creak," said the crow. "Yet he boldly went straight up to the princess, who was sitting on a pearl as large as a spinning-wheel; and standing all round in a great circle were all the court ladies, with their maids and their maids' maids, and all the courtiers, with their servants and their servants' servants, and the latter each had a man too. The nearer they stood to the door the prouder they were. One hardly dared to look at the men of the servants' servants, who always wear slippers, so proudly did they stand in the doorway."

"That must have been dreadful," said little Gerda. "But did Kay get the princess after all?"

"If I had not been a crow, I would have taken her myself, even though I am engaged. They say he spoke as well as I do when I speak crows' language: so my tame sweetheart told me. He was gay and good-looking. He said he had not come to woo, but only to hear the princess's wisdom. This he thought excellent, and she thought him very nice."

"Certainly that was Kay," said Gerda. "He was so clever; he could do fractions in his head. Oh, will you not take me to the palace?"

"Yes, that's easily said," replied the crow. "But how can we manage it? I'll talk it over with my sweetheart; she'll be able to advise us, for I must tell you that a little girl like you never obtains permission to enter the castle."

"Oh, but I shall," said Gerda. "When Kay hears that I am there, he'll come out at once and fetch me."

"Wait for me by those railings," said the crow, and wagging his head flew away.

It was late in the evening before the crow came back. "Caw, caw," he said. "She sends you her compliments, and here is a little roll for you which she took from the kitchen; there's bread enough there, and you must be hungry. It is impossible for you to enter the castle; you are barefooted. The guards in silver and the footmen in gold would not allow it. But don't cry; you shall get in. My sweetheart tells me there is a narrow back staircase that leads to the sleeping apartments, and she knows how to get the key."

They went into the garden and along the great avenue where the leaves were falling one after another; and when the lights in the castle had been extinguished in the same manner, the crow led little Gerda to a back door which stood ajar.

Oh, how Gerda's heart beat with fear and longing! She felt as if she were about to do something wrong, and after all she only wanted to know whether little Kay was there. Yes, it must be he; she had such a vivid recollection of his bright eyes and his long hair; she could see him smiling as he used to do when they sat under the roses at home.

He would no doubt be glad to see her: to hear what a long way she had come for his sake, and to know how grieved they had all been at home when he had not returned. Oh, what fear and joy she felt!

Now they were on the stairs; a little lamp was burning in a recess, and in the middle of the floor stood the tame crow, turning her head from side to side and looking at Gerda, who curtsied as her grandmother had taught her to do.

"My betrothed has spoken so highly of you, my little lady," said the tame crow; "your career, as people say, is very touching. If you will take the lamp, I will go before you. We will go straight along this way, then we shall meet no one."

"It seems to me as if some one were coming behind us," said Gerda, and something rushed past her like shadows on the wall: horses with flying manes and thin legs, huntsmen, and ladies and gentlemen on horseback.

"They are only dreams," said the crow; "they are come to fetch the thoughts of the lords and ladies out hunting. That's a good thing, for then you can look at them in their beds more safely. But I hope that when you rise to honors and dignities, you will show a grateful heart."

"Of course she will," said the crow from the forest. They now came into the first hall, the walls of which were covered with rose-colored satin, embroidered with flowers. Here the dreams again rushed by them, but so quickly that Gerda was unable to catch a glimpse of the great lords and ladies. Each hall was more splendid than the other; indeed, it was quite bewildering. At last they reached the sleeping apartments. The ceiling here was like a great palm-tree with leaves of costly crystal, and over the middle of the floor, two beds, each of which looked like a lily, hung suspended from a thick golden stem. The one in which the princess lay was white; the other was red, and in this Gerda had to seek for little Kay. She pushed one of the red leaves aside and saw a brown neck. Oh, that must be Kay! She called him loudly by his name, and held the lamp towards him; the dreams on horseback again rushed into the room—he awoke, turned his head, and—it was not little Kay.

The prince resembled him only in the neck; but he was young and handsome. And the princess peeped out of the white lily-leaf and asked who was there. Then little Gerda wept and told her whole story, and all that the crows had done for her.

"Poor child!" said the prince and princess; and then praised the crows, and said that they were not angry with them, but they were not to do so again. They would, moreover, be rewarded.

"Would you like to be free?" said the princess. "Or would you like a permanent appointment as court crows, with permission to have all the leavings in the kitchen?"

Both the crows bowed, and begged for a permanent appointment, for they thought of their old age, and said:

"It would be nice to have some provision for one's old age," as they called it.

And the prince got up from his bed and let Gerda sleep in it; he could not do more than that. She folded her little hands and thought, "How good both men and animals are!" Then she closed her eyes and slept sweetly. All the dreams came flying in again, looking like angels, and drawing a little sleigh, on which sat Kay nodding to her; but it was all only a dream, and was therefore gone again as soon as she awoke.

The following day she was dressed from head to foot in silks and velvets, and was asked to remain in the castle and enjoy herself. But she only begged for a little carriage and one horse, and for a pair of boots, so that she might again go out into the wide world to look for Kay.

She obtained not only the boots but a muff also, and she was neatly dressed. When she was about to go, a new carriage made of pure gold drove up to the door, with the arms of the prince and princess shining upon it like a star, and the coachman, footmen, and outriders—for there were outriders too—all wearing golden crowns on their heads. The prince and princess themselves helped her into the carriage, and wished her every happiness. The crow from the wood, who was now married, accompanied her for the first three miles; he sat at her side, for he could not bear riding backwards. The other crow stood in the doorway flapping her wings: she did not go with them, for she suffered from headache since she had received her permanent appointment and got too much to eat. The carriage was lined inside with sugar-cakes, and under the seat were fruit and ginger-nuts.

"Farewell, farewell!" cried the prince and the princess; and little Gerda wept, and the crow wept. At the end of the first three miles the crow also bade her farewell, and this was the saddest parting of all; he flew into a tree, and flapped his black wings as long as he could see the carriage, which shone like bright sunshine.

Story the Fifth
The Little Robber-Girl

They drove through a dark wood, but the coach was as brilliant as a lighted torch; it dazzled the eyes of some robbers, who could not bear to see it.

"It's gold! It's gold!" they cried, and rushing forward, they seized the horses, killed the little jockeys, the coachmen and the footmen, and pulled little Gerda out of the carriage.

"She is plump and pretty, and has been fed on nuts," said the old robber-woman, who had a long stubbly beard and eyebrows that hung down over her eyes.

"She is as good as a fat little lamb; how nice she will taste!" And then she drew forth her shining knife that glittered horribly.

"Oh!" cried the woman at the same moment; she had been bitten by her own daughter—who was hanging on her back—in such a ferocious way that it would have pleased us to see it. "You ugly brat!" cried her mother, and had no time to kill Gerda.

"She shall play with me!" said the little robber-girl. "She shall give me her muff and her pretty dress, and sleep with me in my bed." And then she bit her mother again, making the robber-woman jump in the air and dance about. All the robbers laughed and said: "Look how she dances with her calf."

"I want to get into the carriage," said the little robber-girl. She would have her own way, too, for she was quite spoiled and very obstinate; so she and Gerda sat in it and drove over stumps and stones farther into the forest. The little robber-girl was as tall as Gerda, but stronger, and had broader shoulders and darker skin; her eyes were black and looked almost sad. She caught little Gerda round the waist and said: "They shall not kill you as long as I am not vexed with you. I suppose you are a princess?"

"No," said Gerda, and told her all that she had gone through, and how she loved little Kay.

The robber-girl looked at her very earnestly, shook her head a little and said, "They shall not kill you, even if I do get vexed with you; I'll do it myself then." And then she dried Gerda's eyes and put both her hands into the beautiful muff, which was soft and warm.

At last the coach stopped in the courtyard of a robber's castle. The walls were cracked from top to bottom; ravens and crows flew out of the open holes, and great mastiffs, each of which looked as if he could swallow a man, jumped up; but they did not bark, for that was forbidden.

In the large old smoky hall a bright fire was burning in the middle of the stone floor; the smoke curled up to the ceiling and had to find a way out for itself. A large cauldron of soup was boiling, and hares and rabbits were roasting on the spit.

"You shall sleep with me and all my little animals to-night," said the robber-girl. They had something to eat and drink, and then went to a corner where there lay some straw and carpets. Above them on laths and sticks were perched more than a hundred pigeons, who all appeared to be asleep, though they moved a little when the two little girls came up.

"All these belong to me," said the little robber-girl, and quickly seizing one of the nearest held it by its feet and shook it till it flapped its wings.

"Kiss it," she cried, beating it into Gerda's face. "Those are the wretches from the wood, those two; they would fly away at once, if they were not kept well locked up. And here is my old sweetheart, 'Ba,'" she said, as she dragged out a reindeer by the horns; it had a bright copper ring round its neck, and was tied up. "We have to hold him tight too, else he would spring away. Every evening I tickle his neck with my sharp knife; that makes him very frightened." And the little girl took a long knife out of a crack in the wall and passed it over the reindeer's neck; the poor animal kicked out, while the little robber-girl laughed and then pulled Gerda into bed with her.

"Are you going to keep the knife with you while you sleep?" asked Gerda, looking at it somewhat timidly.

"I always sleep with my knife," said the little robber-girl. "One never knows what may happen. But tell me again what you told me before about little Kay, and why you went out into the wide world."

And Gerda related it all over again while the wood-pigeons cooed up in their cage, and the other pigeons slept. The little robber-girl put her arm round Gerda's neck, held the knife in the other hand and was soon asleep and snoring. But Gerda could not close her eyes at all; she did not know whether she was to live or die. The robbers sat round the fire, singing and drinking, and the robber-woman turned somersaults. Oh, it was quite a horrible thing for the little girl to see all this!

Then the wood-pigeons said "Coo, coo! We have seen little Kay. A white hen was carrying his sleigh, and he sat in the Snow-Queen's carriage as it drove through the wood quite close to our nest. She blew upon us, and all the other young ones died except us two. Coo, coo!"

"What do you say up there?" cried Gerda, "Whither was the Snow-Queen going? Can you tell me that?"

"She was probably going to Lapland, for there is always snow and ice there. Ask the reindeer, that is fastened up with a rope."

"There is ice and snow, there it is glorious and fine," said the reindeer. "There one can spring about freely in the great shining valleys. There the Snow-Queen has her summer tent; but her finest castle is farther north, nearer the Pole, on the island they call Spitzbergen."

"Oh Kay, little Kay!" sighed Gerda.

"You must lie still," said the robber-girl, "or I shall stick my knife into you."

In the morning Gerda told her all that the wood-pigeons had said, and the little robber-girl looked grave, shook her head and said: "It doesn't matter! It doesn't matter! Do you know where Lapland is?" she asked the reindeer.

"Who should know better than I?" said the animal, and his eyes sparkled. "I was born and bred in Lapland; I have jumped about upon the snow-fields there."

"Listen," said the robber-girl to Gerda; "you see that all our men are away. Only mother is still here, and she will stay. But about mid-day she drinks out of a big bottle and then she sleeps for a little while—then I will do something for you."

Then she jumped out of bed, clasped her mother round the neck, and pulled her beard, saying: "Good morning, my own dear nanny-goat!" Then her mother pulled her nose till it was black and blue; and that was all done out of pure love.

So when the mother had drunk out of her bottle and fallen asleep, the robber-girl went up to the reindeer and said: "It would give me great pleasure to tickle your neck a few times more with my sharp knife, for then you are really too funny; but it doesn't matter. I will loosen your rope and help you out so that you may run to Lapland; but you must put your best leg forward, and take this little girl to the Snow-Queen's castle where her playmate is. You must have heard what she told me, for she spoke loud enough, and you were listening."

The reindeer jumped for joy. The robber-maiden lifted little Gerda on his back and took the precaution to tie her on, and even to give her a little cushion for a seat. "Here are your fur boots, too," she said, "for it will be cold; but the muff I will keep, it is so very pretty. But you shall not freeze on that account. Here you have my mother's large mittens; they will reach right up to your elbows. Get into them! Now you look just like my ugly mother about the hands."

But Gerda wept for joy.

"I can't bear to see you make such grimaces," said the little robber-girl. "You ought to look quite happy now. Here are two loaves and a ham, so you will not starve." These were tied on behind on the reindeer's back; the little robber-girl then opened the door, coaxd in all the big dogs, and cutting the rope with her sharp knife, said to the reindeer: "Now run! But mind you take good care of the little girl!"

And Gerda stretched out her hands with the great mittens to the robber-girl and said "Farewell!"

Then the reindeer galloped away across stumps and stones, through the great wood and across marshes and plains, as quickly as he could. The wolves howled and the ravens croaked, while the sky seemed to be spitting fire.

"Those are my old northern lights," said the reindeer; "see how they flash." And now he galloped along faster still, day and night. The loaves were eaten, and the ham too, and then they came to Lapland.

Story the Sixth
The Lapland Woman and the Finland Woman

They stopped at a little hut; it was a very humble one. The roof sloped down almost to the ground, and the door was so low that the family had to go on hands and knees when they went in and out. There was no one at home but an old woman who was cooking fish over an oil lamp. The reindeer told her Gerda's whole story, but his own first, for that seemed to him of much more importance; and Gerda was so numbed with the cold that she could not speak.

"Poor creatures!" said the woman; "you have still a long way to go. You must travel more than a hundred miles farther, to Finland, for that is where the Snow-Queen lives and where she burns Bengal lights every evening. I will write a few words on a dried stock-fish, for I have no paper. This you can take for me to a Finland woman there; she can give you more information than I."

And when Gerda was warmed and had had something to eat and drink, the woman wrote a few words on a dried stock-fish, and telling Gerda to take care of it, tied her again on the reindeer which galloped away. "Fut! Fut!" was heard up in the sky, and all night long the most beautiful blue northern lights were burning. At last they reached Finland and knocked at the chimney of the woman for whom they had a message; for she had not even a door.

It was so hot inside that the woman, who was small and dirty, wore scarcely anything. She immediately loosened little Gerda's dress and took off her mittens and boots—for else the heat would have been too great for her; she also laid a piece of ice on the reindeer's head, and then read what was written on the stock-fish. She read it three times, and then knew it by heart; so she put the fish into the soup-kettle, for it could be eaten, and she never wasted anything.

Then the reindeer told first his story and then that of little Gerda. The woman blinked her cunning eyes, but said nothing.

"You are very clever," said the reindeer; "I know you can tie all the winds of the world together with a piece of twine. If the sailor unties one knot, he has a fair wind; if he unties another, it blows hard; and if he unties the third and fourth, the storm will tear up a forest. Will you not give the little girl a potion that will make her as strong as twelve men and enable her to conquer the Snow-Queen?"

"As strong as twelve men!" said the woman. "That would not be of much use." Then she went to a bed, took out a large skin and unrolled it; there were strange letters written on it, and the woman read till the sweat ran down from her forehead.

But the reindeer begged again so hard for little Gerda, and Gerda looked at the woman with such pleading and tearful eyes, that her own again began to twinkle, and drawing the reindeer into a corner, she whispered to him, while she placed some fresh ice on his head:

"Little Kay is, it is true, with the Snow-Queen, but finds everything there to his taste and liking, and thinks it the best place in the world. That is, however, because he has a splinter of glass in his heart and a small grain of it in his eye; these will have to come out first, or he will never be a human being again, and the Snow-Queen will retain her power over him."

"But can't you give little Gerda something to enable her to do all this?"

"I can give her no greater power than she already possesses; don't you see how great that is? Don't you see how both men and animals are obliged to serve her, and how well she has got on in the world barefooted? She cannot receive any power from us; she possesses it in her heart; it consists in her being a sweet innocent child. If she cannot herself get to the Snow-Queen and remove the glass from little Kay, we cannot help her. Two miles from here the Snow-Queen's garden begins; thither you can carry the little girl. Put her down by the great bush with the red berries that stands in the snow; don't stand chattering, but hasten to get back here." Then the woman lifted little Gerda upon the reindeer, who ran off as quickly as he could.

"Oh, I have left my boots and my mittens behind!" cried little Gerda.

The piercing cold reminded her of this; but the reindeer did not venture to stop. He ran on till he reached the bush with the red berries; there he put Gerda down and kissed her on her mouth. Large bright tears ran down the animal's cheeks, and then he galloped back as fast as he could. There stood poor Gerda, without shoes or gloves, in the middle of terrible icy Finland.

She ran on as quickly as she could till she met a whole regiment of snow-flakes coming along. They did not fall from the sky, for that was bright and shining with the northern lights; the snow-flakes ran along the ground, and the nearer they came, the larger they grew. Gerda remembered how large and curious the snow-flakes had looked when she saw them through the magnifying glass. But here they were larger still, and more terrible; they were alive; they were the Snow-Queen's outposts, and had the strangest shapes.

Some looked like great ugly porcupines; others like knots of serpents with outstretched heads; others, again, like small fat bears with bristling hair. All were dazzlingly white, and all were live snow-flakes. Then little Gerda said the Lord's Prayer; the cold was so intense that she could see her own breath; it came out of her mouth like smoke. Her breath became thicker and thicker, and took the form of little angels who grew larger and larger as soon as they touched the ground. All had helmets on their heads, and lances and shields in their hands; their numbers increased, and when Gerda had finished her prayer a whole legion stood around her. They thrust their lances against the horrible snow-flakes, so that the latter flew into a hundred pieces; and little Gerda went forward safely and cheerfully. The angels stroked her hands and feet, so that she felt the cold less, and she hastened on to the Snow-Queen's castle.

But now we must first see what Kay is doing. He was by no means thinking of little Gerda, and least of all that she was standing outside the castle.

Story the Seventh
Of the Snow-Queen's Castle, and What Happened There in the End

The walls of the castle were formed of driven snow, and the doors and windows of the cutting winds. There were more than a hundred halls in it, all just as the snowstorm had blown them together. The largest of them extended for several miles; they were all lit up by the strong northern light, and how large and empty, how icy cold and glittering they were! There were never any festivities here, not even a little bear's ball, for which the storm might have been the music, and at which the polar bears could have walked on their hind legs and shown off their grand manners. There were never any little games of snapdragon or touch, nor any tea-parties at which the young lady foxes might gossip. Empty, spacious, and cold were the halls of the Snow-Queen. The northern lights burned so steadily that they could be counted when they stood highest and lowest. In the middle of this empty, endless hall of snow, there was a frozen lake broken into a thousand pieces; but each piece was so like the other that it was a perfect work of art. In the middle of the lake sat the Snow-Queen when she was at home; then she used to say that she sat in the mirror of Understanding, and that it was the only and the best one in the world.

Little Kay was blue with cold, in fact almost black; but he did not notice it, for she had kissed away the icy chills and his heart was like a lump of

She used to say that she sat in the mirror of Understanding, and that it was the only and the best one in the world.

ice. He dragged some sharp, flat pieces of ice to and fro, putting them together in every possible position, for he wanted to make something out of them. It was just as when we have little wooden tablets, and make figures out of them, calling it a Chinese puzzle. Kay was making figures too, and very artistic ones. It was the ice game of reason. In his eyes the figures were very extraordinary and of the greatest importance: the grain of glass in his eye was the cause of that. He made several complete figures which formed a written word; but he could never manage to make the word he wanted—the word "Eternity."

The Snow-Queen had said, "If you can make that figure, you shall be your own master, and I will give you the whole world and a pair of new skates."

But he could not do it.

"Now I must rush off to warm countries," said the Snow-Queen. "I will go and look into the black-pots." She meant the fire-spitting mountains Etna and Vesuvius, as they are called. "I'll whiten them a bit. That will be good for them and for the lemons and grapes too." And away flew the Snow-Queen, leaving Kay alone in the great empty ice-halls so many miles in length. He sat there stiff, and still gazing at the pieces of ice, and thinking till his head was bursting; one would have thought he was frozen.

Just at that moment little Gerda entered the castle by the great gate. Cutting winds kept guard here, but they all seemed asleep; so she entered the great empty cold halls—and there she saw Kay.

She recognized him, flew to him, and clasped him round the neck, and held him tightly while she exclaimed, "Kay, dear little Kay! At last I have found you."

But he sat still, stiff and cold; then little Gerda wept hot tears, which fell upon his breast. They penetrated into his heart, thawed the lump of ice and consumed the little splinter of glass in it. He looked at her, and she sang:

"The roses fade and die, but we
Our Infant Lord shall surely see."

Then Kay burst into tears; he cried so that the grain of glass was washed out of his eye. Now he recognized her and cried joyfully: "Gerda! dear little Gerda! Where have you been all this time? And where have I been?" And he looked all around him. "How cold it is here, and how vast and empty!" he said, as he clung to Gerda, who was laughing and crying for joy. There was such joy that even the ice-blocks danced about; and when they were tired and lay down, they formed themselves into the letters of which the Snow-Queen had said that if he found them out he should be his own master, and she would give him the whole world and a pair of new skates.

And Gerda kissed his cheeks and they became blooming. She kissed his eyes and they shone like hers; she kissed his hands and feet, and he was happy. The Snow-Queen might come home now; there stood his discharge written in glittering ice-blocks.

And they took each other by the hand and went forth from the great castle. They spoke of the grandmother and of the roses upon the roof, and wherever they walked the winds sank to rest and the sun came out. When they reached the bush with the red berries, the reindeer stood waiting there; he had brought anothor young one with him whose udder was full, and this one gave the children its warm milk and kissed them on the mouth. Then they carried Kay and Gerda first to the Finland woman, where they warmed themselves in the hot room and obtained information about the journey home; and then to the Lapland woman who had made new clothes for them and repaired their sleigh.

The reindeer and the young one ran by their side and followed them as far as the boundaries of the country, where the first green leaves were budding; there they parted from the reindeer and the Lapland woman. "Farewell," they all said. And now they once more heard the little birds twittering and saw the green buds of the forest. Out of the latter came riding on a splendid horse which Gerda knew—for it had drawn the golden coach—a young girl, with a bright red cap on her head and pistols in her belt. It was the little robber-girl who had got tired of staying at home, and was now going north, and if that did not suit her, to another part of the world. She recognized Gerda at once, and Gerda recognized her too; it was a joyful meeting.

"You are a fine fellow to go gadding about like that," she said to little Kay. "I should like to know whether you deserve that people should run to the end of the world for your sake."

But Gerda patted her cheeks and asked after the prince and princess.

"They have gone to foreign countries," said the robber-girl.

"And the crow?" asked Gerda.

"Oh, the crow is dead," she replied. "The tame sweetheart is a widow now and wears a piece of black wool round her leg; she mourns very much, but it's all talk! But tell me now how you got on and how you managed to catch him."

And Gerda and Kay told their story.

"Snip, snap, snorum, porum, basilorum!" said the robber-girl, and taking both their hands she promised that if ever she should pass through their city, she would come and visit them. And with that she rode out into the wide world. Gerda and Kay went hand in hand, and wherever they went it was glorious spring with flowers and verdure. The church bells were ringing, and they recognized the high steeples and the great city in which they lived. They entered it, and went to their grandmother's door up the stairs and into the room, where everything stood in exactly the same spot as before. The clock went "tick, tick!" and the hands went round, but as they passed through the door they noticed that they had become grown-up people. The roses on the roof bloomed in at the open window, and there stood the little children's chairs; Kay and Gerda sat down each on their own, and held each other by the hand. They had forgotten the cold empty grandeur of the Snow-Queen's castle like a bad dream. The grandmother sat in God's bright sunshine and read aloud from the Bible: "Except ye become as little children, ye shall in no wise enter into the kingdom of God."

And Kay and Gerda looked into each other's eyes, and all at once understood the old song:

"The roses fade and die, but we
Our Infant Lord shall surely see."

There they both sat, grown up and yet children—children in heart; and it was summer—warm, pleasant summer.

The Pen and the Inkstand

In the room of a poet, where his inkstand stood upon the table, the following words were spoken: "It is wonderful how much can be got out of an inkstand! I wonder what the next thing will be! It is indeed wonderful!"

"It is indeed! It's inconceivable—that's what I always say!" said the inkstand, addressing the pen and the other things on the table that were close enough to hear. "It's wonderful how much can be got out of me! Indeed it's quite incredible. I really don't know myself what the next thing will be when the man once begins to dip into me. A drop from me is sufficient to cover half a page of paper, and what a deal can be got into that space! I am something perfectly marvelous! From me issue all the poet's works—all those characters so lifelike that people fancy they have met them—those inner feelings, that humor, and those delightful descriptions of nature. I myself don't understand it, for I am unacquainted with nature, but it just happens to be in me. From me have issued and still issue those troops of graceful charming damsels, of bold knights on prancing steeds, of blind and lame, and goodness knows what else—I assure you I don't think of any of it."

"You're right there," said the pen, "you don't think at all, for if you did, you would understand that you only furnish the fluid. You give the fluid so that I may write with it and put upon paper the thoughts that dwell in me. It is the pen that writes; no one has any doubt about that, and I should think that most people know as much about poetry as an old inkstand."

"You have but little experience," answered the inkstand; "you have been scarcely a week in use, and are already half-worn out. Do you imagine you are the poet? You are only a servant, and before you came I had a good many of the same kind, both of the goose family and of English make—I know a quill as well as a steel pen. I have had a great many in my service, and shall have many more, when the man comes who makes the movements for me, and writes down what he gets out of me. I should like to know what he will take out of me first!"

"Inkpot!" said the pen.

Late in the evening the poet came home. He had been to a concert where he had heard an eminent violinist with whose glorious playing he was quite filled and enchanted. The artist drew a marvelous wealth of tone from his instrument; first it sounded like the trickling of drops of water, and like a shower of pearls, then like a chorus of twittering birds, and then again it roared like the wind through the pine forests. The poet almost fancied he could hear the moaning of his own heart, but in melodious tones, like the sound of a woman's voice. It seemed as if not only the strings of the violin gave forth sound, but even the bridge and the screws and the sounding-board too. It was a marvelous performance! And though it was a difficult one, it really seemed play—just as if the bow were merely passing to and fro over the strings, and as though any one could have done it. It seemed as if both did all between them; the master who led them and breathed life and soul into them was forgotten, but the poet remembered him, named him, and wrote down his thoughts about it all.

"How foolish it would be of the violin and the bow to boast of their performance! And yet mankind so often does—the poet, the artist, the scientist, the general—they all do so. We are all only instruments upon which the Lord our Master plays; to Him be all the glory. We have nothing of which we may be proud."

Yes, that is what the poet wrote. He wrote it in the form of a parable and called it: "The Master and the Instruments."

"That's one for you, madam," said the pen to the inkstand, when they were both alone again. "I suppose you heard him read what I wrote down?"

"Yes, what I gave you to write," retorted the inkstand. "That was a knock for you, for your arrogance. That you don't even see when you're being made fun of! I gave you a knock from my very inside—I ought to know my own sarcasm!"

"Miserable ink-pot!"

"Wretched writing-stick!"

And each of them felt convinced that he had made a clever retort, and that is a very agreeable feeling—one on which you sleep well, and sleep they did. But the poet did not sleep. Thoughts welled up from within him like the tones from the violin, rolling along like pearls and roaring like the wind through the forests. He recognized his own heart in these thoughts and caught a ray of light from the Eternal Master. To Him be all the honor!

The Puppet Showman

On board the steamer was an elderly man with such a pleasant face, that if it did not belie him, he must have been the happiest man on earth. And he declared he was, I heard it myself out of his own mouth. He was a Dane, the manager of a traveling theater. He had all his company with him in a great big box, for he was a puppet showman. His innate cheerfulness, he said, had been enlightened by a Polytechnic student, and the operation had made him completely happy. I did not understand all this at first, but he afterwards explained the whole story to me, and here it is in his own words:

"It was in the little town of Slagelse; I was giving a performance in the hall of the principal inn, and had a brilliant audience—an entirely juvenile one, with the exception of a couple of old matrons.

"All at once a person dressed in black, looking like a student, enters the hall, takes a seat, laughs out loud at the right places and applauds just at the proper time. He was quite an uncommon spectator. I was very anxious to know what he was, and I learned that he was a student from the Polytechnic Institute at Copenhagen, who had been sent out to teach the people in the provinces. Punctually at eight o'clock my performance was over, for children have to go to bed early, and the convenience of one's audience has to be consulted. At nine o'clock the student began his lecture and experiments, and now I formed part of his audience. It was wonderful to hear and to see. The greater part of it was beyond my scope, but still it made me think that, if men can find out as much as that, they ought to be able to hold out longer on earth than they do now. They were little miracles that he performed, and yet all was done so easily and so naturally. In the days of Moses and the Prophets a Polytechnic student like that would have been one of the sages of the land; in the Middle Ages he would have been burnt at the stake. I did not sleep the whole night, and when I gave another performance on the following evening and the student was there again, I was overflowing with good spirits. I have heard of an actor who when playing a lover's part always thought of only one lady in the audience; he played to her and forgot the rest of the house. Well, the Polytechnic student was my 'she,' my only spectator, to whom alone I played. At the end of the performance all the puppets were called before the curtain, and I was invited by the Polytechnic student to go and take a glass of wine in his room; he spoke of my comedies and I of his science, and I think we were both equally delighted. Perhaps I ought not to say equally, for there was a good deal that he did that he could not always explain—for instance, the fact of a piece of iron becoming magnetic by falling through a spiral. How's that, eh? The spirit enters into it; but where does the spirit come from? I think it's just as it is with people: Providence makes them turn a somersault through the spiral of time, the spirit enters into them, and hey presto! you have a Napoleon, a Luther, or some similar individual. 'The whole world is a series of miracles,' said the student, 'but we are so used to them that we call them every-day matters.' He went on explaining until it seemed as if the top of my head were coming off, and I honestly confessed that if I had not already been an old fellow, I would have entered the Polytechnic Institute at once and learned to examine the world a bit more closely—in spite of my being one of the happiest of men. 'One of the happiest!' exclaimed the student, and he seemed to relish my words. 'Are you happy?' 'Yes,' I said, 'I am happy, and I am welcomed in every town that I enter with my company. It is true I have certainly one wish, and not infrequently it lies like a mountain of lead upon my good spirits: I should like to be the manager of a live troop, of a real company of actors.' 'You wish to have life blown into your puppets, so that they may become real actors and you their manager,' he said. 'Do you think you would be perfectly happy then?' He did not think so, and we discussed all the *pros* and *cons,* and at the end differed as much as ever. And we drank to each other's health in excellent wine, but there was some magic in it, or I would certainly have been tipsy. But I was not; I remained clear-sighted, and the room was filled with sunshine, while sunshine also streamed from the eyes of the Polytechnic student. It made me think of the gods of the ancients, and of their eternal youth, when they still went about on earth and visited us mortals; I told him that too and he smiled—and then I could have sworn that he was a god in disguise, or at least belonging to the family. And he was too! My greatest wish was to be realized; the puppets were to come to life, and I was to be the manager of a living company. After he had promised this we drank to each other's health, and emptied our glasses. Then he packed all my puppets in the box, strapped it on my back, and let me fall through a spiral. I can still hear myself turning somersaults, and there I lay on the ground—I know that quite well—and the whole company jumped out of the box. The spirit had entered into us all; all the puppets had become distinguished artists, for they said so themselves; and I was their manager. Everything was ready for the first performance; the whole company, and the public, too, wanted to speak to me. The dancing lady said the house would fall in if she did not stand on one leg, and being the mistress of the whole company she begged to be treated accordingly. The lady who acted the queen wanted to be treated like a queen off the stage too lest she should get out of practice. The man who had nothing to do but to hand over a letter considered himself as important as the first lover, declaring that the small parts were of as much consequence as the great ones in an artistic whole. The hero wanted parts consisting only of points, for these were always applauded; the prima donna would only act with a red light thrown on her, for she said that suited her, and blue did not. It was like being with flies in a bottle, and I was in the middle of the bottle—I was the manager! My breath left me and so did my senses; I was as miserable as a man can be. It was quite a new race of men among whom I had come, and I only wished I had them all in the box again, and that I had never become a manager. I told them straight out that they were only puppets after all; at this they killed me. I found myself lying on my bed in my room; but how I got there, and more especially how I got away from the Polytechnic student he may know, but I don't. The moon shone in upon the floor, where lay the box upset and all the puppets in a fine confusion—great and small, the whole lot. But I was not idle; out of bed 1 jumped, and they were all popped into the box, some on their head and some on their feet; and shutting down the lid, I seated myself on the top. 'Now you will stay there,' I said, 'and I will take care not to wish you flesh and blood again.' I felt quite light again—I was the happiest of men. The Polytechnic student had thoroughly enlightened me. I sat there on the box as happy as could be, and fell asleep. The next morning—it was really mid-day, for I slept wonderfully long that morning—I was still sitting there happy, and feeling conscious that my former and only wish had been a foolish one. I asked after my Polytechnic student, but he was gone, like the gods of the Greeks and Romans. From that time I have been the happiest of men. I am a lucky manager: my company does not argue, neither does my audience, for it is always satisfied. I can patch my pieces together as I like; I take what pleases me best from each comedy, and nobody troubles himself about it. Pieces that are no longer looked at upon the real stage, but to see which the people flocked like mad thirty years ago, and at which they wept till the tears ran down their cheeks, these I now take up. I place them before the little ones, and they weep just as papa and mamma used to do; only I shorten them a little, for children don't care much about the love-nonsense—they want something sad, but soon over."

The Story of a Mother

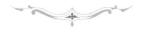

A mother was sitting by her little child; she was very sad, for she was afraid that it was going to die. Its little face was pale, and the little eyes were closed. The child breathed with difficulty, and at times as deeply as if it were sighing, and the mother looked more and more sadly at the little being. There was a knock at the door, and a poor old man came in wrapped up in a large horse-cloth to keep him warm; he had need of it, too, for it was in the depth of winter. Outside every thing was covered with ice and snow, and the wind blew so keenly that it cut one's face.

As the old man was shivering with cold and the child was asleep for a moment, the woman got up and warmed some beer in the oven in a little pot. The old man sat down and rocked the cradle, while the mother also sat down on an old chair next to him, looking at her sick child, who was breathing so heavily, and holding his little hand.

"You don't think I am going to lose it, do you?" she asked. "Heaven will not take it from me."

The old man—it was Death—nodded his head in such a strange way that it might just as well have meant "Yes" as "No." The mother looked down and tears rolled over her cheeks. Her head began to feel heavy; for three days and three nights she had not closed her eyes, and

The wheels of the old clock in the corner went whirring round.

now she slept, but only for a minute; then she jumped up shivering with cold. "What is it?" she asked, looking all around her; but the old man was gone and her little child too. He had taken it with him. The wheels of the old clock in the corner went whirring round; the heavy leaden weight ran right down to the ground, and then the clock stood still.

The poor mother rushed out of the house, calling for her child.

Outside, in the midst of the snow, sat a woman in long black clothes, who said: "Death has been in your room; I saw him hurry away with your little child. He strides along more quickly than the wind, and never brings back what he has taken."

"Only tell me which way he went," said the mother. "Tell me the way, and I will find him."

"I know the way," said the woman in black; "but before I tell it you, you must sing me all the songs you sung to your child. I like those songs; I have heard them before, for I am Night, and saw your tears when you were singing them."

"I will sing them all—all!" said the mother. "But do not detain me now; let me overtake him, so that I may get my child back."

But Night sat dumb and motionless. The mother wrung her hands, singing and weeping. There were many songs, but still more tears. Then Night said: "Go to the right into the dark pine forest; thither I saw Death wend his way with the little child."

In the depths of the forest the road divided, and she did not know in which direction to go. There stood a blackthorn bush, without any leaves, or flowers; for it was winter time, and icicles hung from its boughs.

"Have you seen Death pass by with my little child?"

"Yes," replied the blackthorn bush; "but I shall not tell you which road he took unless you first warm me at your bosom. I am freezing to death here—I am turning into pure ice!"

So she pressed the blackthorn bush close to her bosom in order to thaw it completely. The thorns pierced her flesh and her blood flowed in large drops. But the blackthorn bush put forth fresh green leaves and blossomed in the cold winter's night; so warm is the heart of a sorrowing mother. Then the bush told her which road she was to take.

She came to a great lake upon which there was neither ship nor boat. The lake was not frozen hard enough to bear her, nor was it shallow and even enough for her to wade through it, and yet she must cross it if she wished to find her child. Then she lay down to drink the lake dry, but that was impossible for one person to do. The sorrowing mother, however, thought that perhaps a miracle might be wrought.

"No, that will never do," said the lake. "Let us rather see whether we can come to some agreement. I love to collect pearls, and your eyes are two of the brightest I have ever seen; if you will weep them out into me, I will carry you over to the great hothouse where Death lives and where he grows flowers and trees, each one of which is a human life."

"Oh, what would I not give to get back my child!" said the sobbing mother. She wept still more, and her eyes fell down to the bottom of the lake and became two costly pearls. Then the lake took her up as though she were sitting in a swing, and in one sweep wafted her to the opposite shore, where stood a wonderful house, miles in length. It was difficult to say whether it was a mountain with forests and caves, or whether it had been built. But the poor mother could not see it; she had cried out her eyes.

"Where shall I find Death, who took my little child away?" she asked.

"He has not arrived here yet," said an old gray-haired woman, who was walking to and fro and guarding Death's hothouse. "But how did you find your way here, and who helped you?"

"Heaven has helped me," she answered. "It is merciful, and that you will be too. Where shall I find my little child?"

"I don't know it," said the old woman, "and you can't see. Many flowers and trees have faded during the night, and Death will soon come to transplant them. You know very well that every human being has his tree of life or his flower of life, according to how it has been arranged for each. They look just like other plants, but their hearts beat. Children's hearts can beat too. If you try, perhaps you may be able to recognize the heartbeat of your child. But what will you give me if I tell you what else you must do?"

"I have nothing to give," said the unhappy mother. "But I will go to the end of the world for you."

"I have nothing there for you to do," said the old woman; "but you can give me your long black hair: I daresay you know yourself that it is beautiful; it pleases me. You can have my white locks for it; they are better than nothing."

"Is that all you want?" she said. "I will give you that with pleasure." And she gave her her beautiful hair, receiving for it the snow-white locks of the old woman.

Then they went into Death's great hothouse, where flowers and trees grew strangely intermingled. Here stood some delicate hyacinths under glass bells, and great strong peonies. There grew water-plants, some quite fresh, others somewhat sickly; water-snakes lay upon them, and black crabs clung fast to the stalks. In another place were splendid palm-trees, oaks, and plantains, parsley and blooming thyme. All the trees and flowers bore names; each one was a human life, and the people they represented were still living, some in China, others in Greenland, and all over the world. There were great trees planted in small pots, so that they were cramped and almost bursting the pots; and there was also many a weakly little flower set in rich mold, with moss all round it, and well taken care of and tended. The anxious mother bent down over all the little plants to hear the human heart beating in each, and from among millions she recognized that of her child.

"There it is!" she cried, and stretched out her hand towards a little crocus, which was feebly hanging over on one side.

"Don't touch the flower!" said the old woman, "but stand here, and when Death comes—I expect him every moment—don't let him tear up the plant, but threaten him that you will do the same with the other flowers: that will frighten him! He is responsible for them to Heaven; not one may be pulled up before permission has been given."

Suddenly an icy blast swept through the hall, and the blind mother felt that it was Death who was approaching.

"How could you find the way here?" he asked. "How were you able to come here more quickly than I?"

"I am a mother!" she replied.

Death stretched out his long hand towards the small delicate flower; but she held her hands firmly round it, held them clasped—oh! so closely, and yet full of anxious care lest she should touch one of the petals. Then Death breathed upon her hands, and she felt that this was colder than the cold wind; and her hands sank down powerless.

"You have no power to resist me!" said Death.

"But Heaven has!" said she.

"I only do its will," said Death. "I am its gardener. I take up all its flowers and trees and transplant them into the great Garden of Paradise, into the Unknown Land. How they thrive there and what that life is like I may not tell you."

"Give me back my child!" said the mother, weeping and imploring.

Suddenly she grasped two pretty flowers firmly in her hands and called out to Death: "I will tear up all your flowers, for I am in despair."

"Do not touch them!" said Death. "You say that you are so unhappy, and would you now make another mother as unhappy as yourself?"

"Another mother!" exclaimed the poor mother, and immediately let both flowers go.

"Here are your eyes," said Death. "I fished them up out of the lake; they were sparkling brightly at the bottom; I did not know that they were yours.

Take them back—they are now even brighter than before—and then look down into this deep well. I will utter the names of the two flowers you were about to tear up, and you will see what you were on the point of destroying."

She looked down into the well; it was a glorious thing to see how one of the lives became a blessing to the world, to see how much happiness and joy diffused itself around it. She also saw the life of the other, which consisted in sorrow and want, trouble and misery.

"Both are the will of God!" said Death.

"Which of them is the flower of unhappiness, and which the blessed one?" she asked.

"That I will not tell you," answered Death; "but this you shall learn from me, that one of the flowers is that of your own child. It was the fate of your child that you saw—the future of your own child."

Then the mother shrieked with terror. "Which of them is that of my child? Tell me that! Liberate the innocent child! Release my child from all this misery! Rather take it away! Take it to the Kingdom of God! Forget my tears, forget my entreaties and all that I have done!"

"I don't understand you," said Death. "Will you have your child back, or shall I take it to that place that you do not know?"

Then the mother wrung her hands, and falling on her knees, prayed to the good God: "Hear me not when I pray contrary to Thy will, for Thy will is ever best! Hear me not! Hear me not!"

Her head sank down upon her breast, and Death went with her child to the Unknown Land.

The Child in the Grave

Sorrow was in the house, sorrow in every heart. The youngest child, a boy four years old, the joy and hope of his parents, had died. There still remained to them two daughters—good, charming girls—the elder of whom was just about to be confirmed; but the child one has lost is always the dearest, and in that case it was the youngest, and a son. It was a heavy trial. The sisters mourned as young hearts do, and were especially moved by their parents' grief. The father was bowed down, but the mother was quite overwhelmed by her great sorrow. Day and night she had sat by the sick child, had nursed him, lifted and carried him; she had felt how great a part he was of herself. She could not grasp that the child was dead, that he was to be laid in the coffin and rest in the grave; she had thought God could not take the child from her, and when it really came to pass, and there was no longer any doubt, she said in her feverish pain:

"God did not know it; He has heartless servants here on earth, who act as they please, and who do not hear a mother's prayers."

In her grief she turned from Heaven, and there arose dark thoughts, thoughts of death, of everlasting death, that man became dust in the earth, and that all ended with that. But such thoughts afforded her no hold, nothing to which she could cling, and she sank into the bottomless abyss of despair.

In her saddest moments she could not even weep; she gave no thoughts to the young daughters whom she still had. Her husband's tears fell upon her brow, but she did not look at him; her thoughts were with her dead child—her whole mind and being were alone intent in recalling every remembrance of the little one, every one of his innocent childish words.

The day of the funeral came. For nights before, the mother had not slept; but in the morning twilight of that day she slumbered a little, overpowered by weariness, and in the meantime the coffin was carried to a distant room, and there nailed down, so that she should not hear the sound of the hammer.

When she awoke and wanted to see her child, her husband said to her in tears:

"We have nailed down the coffin; it had to be done."

"If God is hard to me, what can I expect from others?" she exclaimed, amidst tears and sobs.

The coffin was carried to the grave. The disconsolate mother sat with her daughters; she gazed at them and yet did not see them, for her thoughts were no longer busied with her domestic hearth. She gave herself up entirely to grief, and her mind was tossed restlessly to and fro, as a ship without a rudder or steers-man is tossed about by the sea.

So passed the day of the funeral, and similar days of dull heavy pain followed. With tearful eyes and mournful glances the sorrowing daughters and the afflicted husband gazed upon her who was deaf to their words of consolation; and indeed what comfort could they offer her, when they themselves were so heavily bowed down?

It seemed as if she knew sleep no more; and yet that alone would now have been her best friend, have strengthened her body and brought peace to her soul. She was prevailed upon to seek her couch, and she lay there still like one sleeping. One night her husband listened, as he often did, to her breathing, and firmly believed that she had at last found peace and relief. He folded his hands in prayer, and soon fell into a deep sound sleep himself; he did not notice that his wife got up, threw her clothes around her, and crept silently out of the house to reach the place where her thoughts lingered day and night—the grave which held her child. She strode through the garden of the house, and across the fields where a path led to the church-yard. Nobody saw her on her walk, and she had seen no one—her eyes were fixed on one goal.

It was a glorious starlight night. The air was still mild, for it was the beginning of September.

She entered the church-yard and stood by the little grave, which looked like a great nosegay of fragrant flowers. She sat down and bowed her head low over the grave, as if she could have seen through the heavy clay the little child whose smile rose so vividly before her, the sweet expression of whose eyes, even on his bed of sickness, was never to be forgotten. How eloquent had been his look, when she bent down over him and took his little hand, which he himself was no longer able to lift! As she had sat by his bedside, so she now sat by his grave, except that here her tears had free course and fell upon the little mound.

"Do you wish to go down to your child?" said a voice quite close to her—a voice that sounded so clear and deep, it went straight to her heart. She looked up, and beside her stood a man wrapped in a black cloak with the hood drawn deep down over his head, but still she could see his face under it; it was stern but yet inspired confidence, and his eyes beamed with the brightness of youth.

"Yes, down to my child!" she repeated, and a despairing entreaty spoke out of her words.

"Have you the courage to follow me?" asked the form; "I am Death."

She bowed her head in acquiescence. Then in a second it seemed as if the stars above shone with the radiance of the full moon, showing her the bright colors of the flowers on the grave, while the surface of the earth yielded gently and gradually like a waving cloth. She sank, and the form covered her with his black cloak; it was night, the night of death, and she sank deeper than the sexton's spade ever penetrates, while the church-yard stood like a roof over her head.

The end of the cloak was drawn aside, and she stood in a great hall far extending and pleasing to the eye. Twilight reigned around. Suddenly her child appeared before her, and in a second was pressed to her heart, smiling at her and looking more beautiful than she had ever seen him do before. She uttered a cry which, however, remained inaudible.

The sweet strains of heavenly music came swelling alternately quite close at hand and then from afar; never had such angelic tones fallen on her ear. They came from beyond the thick curtain, dark as night, that separated the hall from the great land of eternity.

"My sweet darling mother," she heard her child say. It was the clear, well-known voice, and kiss followed kiss in endless happiness, and the child pointed to the dark curtain.

"It is not so beautiful as that on earth; do you see, mother, do you see them all? Oh, that is happiness!"

But the mother saw nothing where the child pointed—nothing but the dark night. She looked with earthly eyes, and did not see like the child whom God had called to Him. She could hear, too, only the sound—the notes of the music—but the Word, the Word in which she was to believe, she heard not.

"I can fly now, mother, fly with all the other happy children into the presence of the Lord. I would so much like to go; but if you weep as you are weeping now I might be lost to you, and yet I would so much like to go. Will you not let me fly? And you will come to me there very soon, dear mother!"

"Oh, stay! stay!" cried the mother; "only a moment longer, only once more would I look at you, kiss you, and fold you in my arms."

She kissed the child and pressed it to her heart. Then her name was called from above—called in plaintive tones. "Oh, what can this mean?"

"Do you hear?" said the child; "it is father who is calling you."

And again, in a few moments, were heard deep sobs as of weeping children.

"They are my sisters," said the child. "Mother, you surely have not forgotten them?"

And she remembered those she had left behind. Terror seized her; she looked out into space, and forms were continually flitting past. She thought she recognized some of them as they flitted through the Hall of Death towards the dark curtain, where they vanished. Perhaps her husband and daughters would also come flitting by. No, their sighs and lamentations were still heard from above—she had almost forgotten them for the sake of the dead.

"Mother, now the bells of Heaven are ringing," said the child. "Mother, now the sun is rising."

An overpowering light streamed in upon her. The child had vanished, and she was borne upwards. It became cold all around her; and, lifting her head, she saw that she was lying in the church-yard, on the grave of her child. But in this dream God had become a stay for her feet, a light to her spirit; she fell on her knees and prayed.

"O Lord, my God, forgive me for having wished to keep back an eternal soul from its flight, and for having forgotten my duties towards the living whom Thou hast given to me."

At these words it seemed as if her heart found relief. The sun burst forth, a little bird sang overhead, and the church bells rang for early service. All seemed holy around her—chastened like her heart. She acknowledged her God, she acknowledged her duties, and eagerly she hastened home. She bent over her husband, who was still sleeping; her warm tender kiss awoke him, and heartfelt words of affection flowed from the lips of both. She was strong and gentle as a wife can be, and from her came those words of comfort, "God's will is always best."

"Whence did this strength and feeling of consolation come to you so suddenly?" asked her husband.

And as she kissed him and kissed her children she said: "They came to me from God, through the child in the grave."

The Shirt-Collar

There lived once a rich gentleman whose whole goods and chattels consisted of a boot-jack and a hair-brush, but he wore the finest shirt-collar in the world, and it is about this very shirt-collar that we shall hear a story. The shirt-collar had now become so old that it thought of getting married; and it happened that it was sent to the laundress together with a garter.

"Truly," said the shirt-collar, "I have never seen anybody so slender and refined, so tender and nice before! May I ask for your name?"

"I shall not answer you," replied the garter.

"Where do you live?" continued the shirt-collar.

But the garter was somewhat shy, and thought it strange to be expected to answer such questions.

The shirt-collar . . . was sent to the laundress together with a garter.

"I suppose you are a girdle," said the shirt-collar, "a sort of inside girdle. I see you are useful as well as ornamental, my little lady!"

"Do not speak to me," said the garter, "I think I have given you no encouragement to do so!"

"If one is as beautiful as you are," said the shirt-collar, "is this not encouragement enough?"

"Go away, and do not come too close to me!" said the garter, "you look exactly like a man."

"I am a gentleman, indeed," said the shirt-collar, "I possess a boot-jack and a hair-brush!"

But that was not true, for it was his master who possessed these articles.

"Do not come too near me!" said the garter, "I am not accustomed to that."

"Conceited thing!" said the shirt-collar.

Then they were taken out of the washing-tub, stretched and put on a chair in the sunshine to dry, and put on the ironing-board. And now came the hot iron.

"Mistress widow!" cried the shirt-collar, "little mistress widow, I am getting very warm! I am turning quite another being, all my creases are coming

"I possess a boot-jack and a hair-brush!"

And now came the hot iron.

out; you are burning a hole in me! Ugh! I propose to you!"

"Wretch!" said the iron, proudly passing over the shirt-collar, for it imagined itself a steam-engine which was to run on metals and draw carriages. "Wretch!" it repeated.

As the edges of the shirt-collar were a little frayed, the scissors were brought to trim it. "I believe," said the shirt-collar, addressing the scissors, "you must be a first-class dancer. How you can throw your legs up! I have never seen anything more charming; no human being can do what you do."

"I know," replied the scissors.

"You deserve to be made a countess," continued the shirt-collar. "All I possess is a gentleman, a boot-jack, and a hair-brush. I wish, for your sake, that I had an earl's estate."

"What! He will propose to me!" said the scissors, and became so angry, that they cut too deeply into the shirt-collar, and it had to be turned out as useless.

"I shall have to propose to the hair-brush," thought the shirt-collar. One day it said, speaking to the hair-brush: "What remarkably beautiful hair you have, my little lady! Have you never thought of becoming engaged?"

"Of course! How could you have any doubt about this?" replied the hair-brush. "I am engaged to the boot-jack."

"Engaged?" said the shirt-collar. As there was now nobody left to propose to, the shirt-collar began to despise all love-makings.

A long time passed after this; the shirt-collar came at last into the bag of the paper-maker! There was a large company of rags, the fine ones lay apart from the coarse ones, as it ought to be. They had all a great deal to tell, but most of all the shirt-collar, for it was a wonderful bragger.

"I have had no end of love-affairs," said the shirt-collar; "they

"How you can throw your legs up!"

never left me alone; but, of course, I was a distinguished gentleman, and well starched. I possessed a boot-jack and a hair-brush, which I never used. You ought to have seen me—seen me when I was put aside! I shall never forget my first love! It was a girdle, and how fine, soft and nice it was! My first love threw itself for my sake into a large washing-tub. There was also a widow, which loved me very ardently, but I left it and it turned quite black! Then there was a first-class dancer, the very person which inflicted the wound upon me which you still see; it was a very excitable being. My own hair-brush was in love with me—and lost all its hairs because I disappointed it. I have seen a great deal of this sort of thing, but most of all I am sorry for the garter—girdle, I intended to say—which threw itself into a washing-tub. I have a great deal to answer for; it is time that I should be turned into white paper."

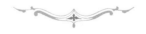

"Have you never thought of becoming engaged?"

And to this the collar was transformed at last, the very same paper on which this story here is printed, because it had bragged so much and told things which were not true. And we ought to remember this, and never imitate the shirt-collar, for who knows if we may not one day also come into the rag-bag and be turned to white paper, upon which our whole story, even its most secret parts, might be printed, so that we should be obliged, like the shirt-collar, to run about and tell it ourselves.

The Butterfly

The butterfly wanted a bride, and he, of course, wished to select a very pretty one from among the flowers. He therefore cast a critical glance over all the flower-beds and found that every flower sat quietly and modestly on her stalk, as became a maiden who is not engaged; but there were a great many there, and the choice threatened to become tedious. The butterfly did not care to take so much trouble, so he flew off on a visit to the daisies.

The French call this little flower "Marguerite"; they know too that Marguerite can prophesy, and that she does this when lovers, as they often do, pluck off one leaf after another, putting to each leaf a question concerning their lovers. "Loves me? Loves me not? Loves me? Loves me not?" and so on. Every one asks in his own language. So the butterfly came to Marguerite too to question her; he did not, however, pull its leaves off, but imprinted a kiss on each, thinking that one gains most by kindness.

"Dear little daisy Marguerite," he said, "you are the cleverest woman among the flowers, for you can prophesy. Pray do tell me which one I shall get. Which will be my bride? When I know that, I will fly straight to her and propose." But Marguerite did not answer. She was angry at his having called her a woman when she was still a maiden; there's a big difference. He asked for the second and the third time; but when she remained dumb and answered not a single word, he would not ask any longer, but flew away to begin his wooing at once.

It was one of the first days of spring, and the snowdrop and crocus were everywhere in bloom.

"They are very pretty," thought the butterfly; "sweet young ladies, but a little too much of the school-girl about them." He, like all boys, looked out for elder girls.

Then he flew off to the anemones. They were a little too bitter for him, and the violets a little too sentimental; the lime blossoms were too small and had too many relations; while the apple blossoms—well, it is true, they looked like roses; but they bloomed to-day, to fade to-morrow, at the first wind that blew. Such a union would be of too short duration, he thought. The pea-blossom was the one that pleased him most; it was red and white and very delicate and dainty, and belonged to the domesticated maidens who look well and are also useful in the kitchen. He was just about to propose when close by the blossom he spied a pod at whose end hung a withered flower. "Who is that?" he asked. "That's my sister," answered the pea-blossom. "Oh, indeed! And you'll look like that later on?" he said, and flew away quite shocked.

The honeysuckle hung in bloom over the hedge—an abundance of young ladies all of one kind with long faces and yellow complexions. No! that kind did not suit him.

But which kind did he like best then?

Spring passed and summer was nearly over, autumn came, and he was still undecided. The flowers now appeared in the most gorgeous apparel, but in vain—they lacked the fresh fragrance of youth. A heart that is no longer young itself requires fragrance, and very little of that is to be found among the dahlias and poppies. So the butterfly turned to the mint near the ground. But this plant has fragrance in every leaf, not only in its blossoms, and smells from top to bottom. "I will take her," said the butterfly. And so he proposed.

But the mint stood stiff and still, and heard what he had to say. At last she said: " Friendship, if you like, but nothing more. I am old and you are old. We might, it is true, live for each other, but as for marrying—no! Don't let us make fools of ourselves in our old age."

So the butterfly got no wife at all. He had been too long choosing, and that's a bad thing to do. He remained an old bachelor.

It was late in autumn, and the weather was rainy and dull. The wind blew cold over the old willow-trees, and made them creak. It was no weather to be flying about in summer costume; nor, indeed, was the butterfly out in the open air. He had chanced to get under cover where there was a fire in the stove, and where it was as warm as it is in summer. He could go on living, but "living is not enough," he said. "One must have sunshine, liberty, and a little flower."

And flying against the window-pane, he was seen, admired, stuck upon a pin, and exhibited in a box of curiosities; they could not do more for him.

"Now I sit on a stalk like the flowers," said the butterfly. "It's not so very pleasant after all. It must be something like this to be married—one sticks fast." With this he consoled himself somewhat.

"That's a poor consolation," said the potted plants in the room.

"But," thought the butterfly, "these potted plants are not to be trusted; they have had too much intercourse with mankind."

The Goblin and the Huckster

Once upon a time there was a real student; he lived in an attic and possessed nothing at all. But once upon a time there was also a real huckster; he lived on the ground-floor, and the whole house belonged to him. The goblin remained friends with him, for at the huckster's they always had a big plum-pudding every Christmas Eve, with a fine large piece of butter in it. That the huckster could afford, and therefore the goblin stayed in the huckster's shop, and that was very interesting. One evening the student came in through the back door to buy some candles and cheese. He had no one to send, so he came himself. He got what he wanted, and the huckster and his wife both nodded him a good evening. Madam was a woman who could do more than merely nod; she had an extraordinary power of speech. The student nodded too, but suddenly stood still reading the sheet of paper in which the cheese was wrapped up. It was a leaf that had been torn out of an old book—a leaf out of a book that ought not to have been torn up, a book that was full of poetry.

"Here's some more of the same kind," said the huckster; "I gave an old woman a little coffee for the book. If you give me twopence you shall have the rest."

"Very well," said the student, "give me the book instead of the cheese; I can eat my bread and butter without cheese. It would be a sin to tear the book up entirely. You are a fine fellow and a practical man, but you know as much about poetry as that cask there."

Now this was very rude, especially towards the cask, but the huckster laughed and the student laughed, for it was only said in fun. But the goblin was angry that people should dare to say such things to a huckster who was a landlord—and who sold the best butter.

When night came and the shop was closed, and all were in bed with the exception of the student, the goblin came out, went into the bedroom, and took madam's tongue away. She did not want it while she was asleep; and on whatever object in the room he placed it that object acquired speech and voice, and told its thoughts and feelings just like madam. But only one object at a time could use it, which was a blessing, otherwise they would all have spoken at once.

The goblin placed the mouthpiece on the cask in which lay the old newspapers. "Is it really true," he asked, "that you don't know anything about poetry?"

"Certainly I do," replied the cask. "Poetry is something they always put at the bottom of newspapers, and which is sometimes cut out. I daresay I have a great deal more of it in me than the student, and yet I am only a poor cask compared to the huckster."

Then the goblin placed the tongue on the coffee-mill. Mercy on us! how it rattled away! And he put it on the butter-cask, and on the till—all were of the same opinion as the waste-paper cask, and the opinion of the majority must be respected.

"Now I'll tell the student." And with these words the goblin stole quietly up the backstairs to the attic where the student lived. The student had still a candle burning, and the goblin peeped through the keyhole and saw him reading in the torn book that he had got from the shop downstairs.

But how light it was up there! Out of the book shone a bright beam, which grew up into a thick stem and into a mighty tree, that rose and spread its branches far over the student. Every leaf was fresh, and every blossom was a beautiful maiden's head, some with dark sparkling eyes, others with wonderfully clear blue ones; every fruit was a shining star, and there was a sound of glorious singing in the student's room.

No, such splendor the little goblin had never dreamed of, let alone seen or heard. He remained standing there on tiptoe, peeping and peeping till the light in the garret went out. Probably the student had blown it out and gone to bed, but the goblin remained standing there all the same, for he could still hear the sweet glorious singing—a beautiful lullaby for the student, who had lain down to rest.

"What an incomparable place this is!" said the goblin; "I never expected such a thing. I should like to live with the student." Then the little man thought it over—he was a sensible little man too—but he sighed: "The student has no plum-pudding," and then he went down again to the huckster's. And it was a good thing too that he did come back, for the cask had almost worn out madam's tongue: it had already spoken out at one side all that was contained in it, and was just about to turn round to give it out from the other side too, when the goblin entered and put madam's tongue back into its right place. But from that time forth the whole shop, from the till down to the firewood, took its views from the cask; and all paid it so much respect, and reposed so much confidence in it, that when the huckster afterwards read the art and dramatic criticism in the newspaper she was foolish enough to believe it came from the cask.

But the goblin no longer sat quietly listening to the wisdom and understanding to be heard down in the shop; no, as soon as the light glimmered down from the garret in the evening, he felt as if the rays were strong cables, drawing him up, and he was obliged to go and peep through the keyhole. There a feeling of greatness came rushing over him, such as we feel beside the ever-rolling sea when the storm sweeps over it, and he burst into tears; he did not know himself why he wept, but a peculiar and very pleasant feeling was mingled with his tears. How wonderfully glorious it must be to sit with the student under that tree! but that could not be—he must content himself with the keyhole, and be glad of that. There he stood in the cold passage with the autumn wind blowing down from the trap-door in the loft; it was cold, very cold, but that the little fellow only felt when the light in the attic was put out and the sounds in the wonderful tree died away. Ugh! then he felt frozen, and he crept down to his warm corner again—it was cozy and comfortable there! When Christmas came, and with it the plum-pudding and the great lump of butter, why, then the huckster was Number One.

But in the middle of the night the goblin was awakened by a terrible noise and a banging at the shutters, against which the people outside were knocking as hard as they could. The night watchman blew his horn, for a great fire had broken out. Was it in the house itself, or at the neighbor's? Where was it? A panic ensued. The huckster's wife was so bewildered that she took her gold earrings from her ears and put them into her pocket so that she might save at least something; the huckster made a dash for his bank-notes, and the maid for her black silk mantle—for her means allowed her that luxury. Every one wanted to save the best thing they had; the goblin wanted to do that too, and in a few leaps he was up the stairs and in the room of the student who was calmly standing at the open window gazing at the fire that raged in the house of the neighbor opposite. The goblin seized the book lying on the table, put it into his red cap, and clasped it with both hands; the greatest treasure in the house was saved, and now he ran up and away, out upon the roof of the house, on to the chimney. There he sat in the light of the flames from the burning house opposite, both hands pressed over his red cap in which the treasure lay, and now he knew the real inclinations of his heart and knew to whom it really belonged. But when the fire was extinguished, and the goblin again began to reflect calmly, well—

"I will divide myself between the two," he said, "I cannot give the huckster up altogether on account of the pudding!"

And that was only human after all. Most of us stick to the huckster for the sake of the pudding.

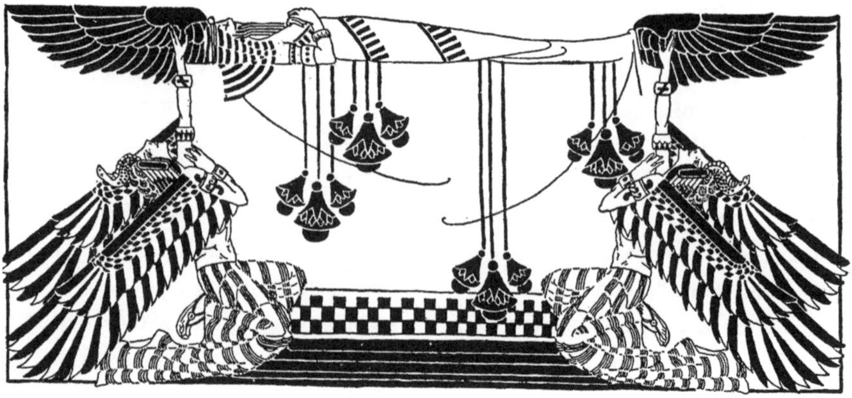

The Marsh King's Daughter

The storks tell their little ones a good many tales about the moor and marsh. As a rule these are suited to the age and understanding of the hearers; the very youngest are satisfied if they have "cribble, crabble, plooramoora" said to them, and think it an excellent story, but the elder ones want something with a deeper meaning, or at least something to do with the family. Of the two oldest and longest tales which have been preserved among the storks, one is known to all of us—that of Moses, whom his mother placed in the Nile, and who was found by the king's daughter, received a good education and became a great man, and of whom it was afterwards not known where he was buried. That is a well-known story.

The second tale is still unknown, perhaps because it is almost an inland one. It has been handed down for thousands of years, from mouth to mouth, from stork-mamma to stork-mamma, and each of them has told it better and better, till at last we tell it best of all. The first stork pair who told it, and who really took part in it, had their summer residence on the wooden house of the Viking, which stands on the wild heath in Wendsyssel; that is to say, if we wish to speak out of the abundance of our knowledge, hard by the great moor in the district of Hjörring, up by the Skagen, the northern point of Jutland. It is said that, once upon a time, this all formed part of the sea, but that there had been an upheaval; the moorland now extends for miles on all sides, surrounded by damp meadows and treacherous swamps, by turf-bogs covered with blackberries and stunted trees. There is always a mist floating over this region, and seventy years ago it was still inhabited by wolves. It is fitly called the "Wild Moor," and one can easily think how dreary and impassable it must have been, and how much marsh and lake there was a thousand years ago. In detail there was exactly the same to be seen here as there is still: the reeds were of the same height, and bore the same kind of long leaves and bluish-brown feathery plumes that they do now; the birch stood there with its white bark and its fine loosely hanging leaves just as it does now; and as regards the living creatures that dwelled here—well, the fly wore its gauzy dress of the same cut as now, and the favorite colors of the stork were white and black, with red stockings. The people, on the other hand, wore coats cut differently from those of to-day, but every one who strode across the treacherous moorland, were he huntsman or follower, master or servant, shared the same fate a thousand years ago as befalls those who venture on it to-day. He sank and went down to the marsh king, as they called him, who ruled down in the great moor kingdom. "Gungel-king" he was also called, but we like marsh king better, and that is what the storks call him too. Very little is known of the marsh king's rule, but perhaps that is a good thing.

Near the moorland, hard by the great arm of the sea that stretches from the German Ocean and the Cattegat, and which is called the Lym Fjord, stood the wooden house of the Viking, with its stone water-tight cellars, its tower, and its three projecting stories. The stork had built his nest on the roof, and there stork-mamma hatched her eggs, and was certain that her sitting would come to something.

One evening stork-papa stayed out rather late, and when he came home he looked very excited and flurried.

"I have something horrible to tell you!" he said to stork-mamma.

"Well, don't!" she said; "remember that I am hatching eggs, and it might be injurious to me; and it has an effect on the eggs."

"You must hear it," he continued. "She has arrived—the daughter of our Egyptian host. She has ventured to make the journey here—and she's gone!"

"She who sprang from the race of the fairies! Do tell me all about it! You know that I cannot bear to be kept waiting long in my hatching time."

"You see, mother, she after all believed what the doctor said and what you told me; she believed that the moor flowers here would heal her sick father, so she flew hither in swan's feathers in company with the other swan-princesses who come to the north every year to make themselves younger. She has come here, and she is gone!"

"You are much too long-winded!" said stork-mamma; "the eggs might catch cold. I can't bear to be kept in such suspense."

"SHE WHO SPRANG FROM THE RACE OF THE FAIRIES!"

"I have been watching," continued stork-papa; "and this evening, as I went into the reeds, there where the marsh ground will bear me, three swans approached. Something in their flight seemed to say to me, 'Look out! that's not altogether a swan, that's only a swan's feathers!' Yes, mother, I am just like you—you know whether it's the right one or not."

"Certainly," she said; "but tell me about the princess; I have heard enough of the swan's feathers."

"Here, in the middle of the moor, there's something like a lake, you know," said stork-papa. "You can see a bit of it if you stretch yourself a little. There, by the reeds and the green slime, lay a great alder stump; upon this the three swans sat down, flapped their wings, and looked about themselves. One of them cast her swan's feathers off, and I immediately recognized her as the princess from our house in Egypt. There she sat with no other covering than her long black hair; I heard her beg the two others to look after the swan's feathers while she dived down into the water to pluck the flower that she thought she saw there. The others nodded, picked up the empty feather dress and took it on their backs. 'Hallo! I wonder what they are going to do with it!' I thought, and she probably thought the same. She got an answer, too, a practical answer—both rose and flew away with her swan's plumage. 'Dive down,' they cried. 'You will never see Egypt again; stay here in the moor.' And with that they tore the swan's plumage into a thousand pieces, so that the feathers whirled about like a snow-storm—and then away they flew, the two faithless princesses!"

"That is indeed terrible!" said stork-mamma; "I can't bear to hear any more of it—but do tell me what happened next."

"The princess wept and wailed aloud; and her tears falling on the alder stump; the latter rose, for it was not a real alder stump, but the marsh king, he who lives and rules in the depths of the moor. I saw it myself—how the tree-stump turned itself round, and then it was no longer a tree-stump: it stretched out its long slimy branches like arms. At this the poor child was terribly frightened, and jumped up and ran away. She hurried across the green slimy marsh, but that will not bear even me, much less her; she sank immediately, and the alder stump dived down too—it was he that dragged her down. Great black bubbles rose up out of the slimy swamp, and then every trace of them vanished. Now the princess is buried in the wild moor, and will never take a flower to Egypt. Your heart would have broken to see it, mother!"

"You ought not to tell me anything of this sort at such a time; it might have a bad effect on the eggs. The princess will soon find some means of escape. Some one is sure to help her. Now if it had been you or I, or even any of our family, it would have been all over with us!"

"You ought not to tell me anything of this sort at such a time; it might have a bad effect on the eggs."

"But still I shall go and see every day whether anything happens," said stork-papa; and so he did.

A long time passed, when one day he saw a green stalk shooting up out of the deep marsh. As soon as it reached the surface of the water, a leaf sprang forth and grew broader and broader. Close by it a bud appeared, and as stork-papa flew over the stalk one morning the bud opened by the power of the strong sunbeams, and in the cup of the flower lay a beautiful child, a little girl, looking as if she had just come out of a bath.

The little girl resembled the Egyptian princess so much that for the first moment or two the stork really thought it was she, but on second thoughts it seemed to him more probable that it must be the daughter of the princess and the marsh king, and that was why she lay in the cup of the water-lily.

"But she cannot possibly remain lying there," thought stork-papa, "and in my nest there are too many persons already. But I have an idea! The Viking's wife has no children, and how often she has wished to have a little child! They always say that the stork brings the little children, and now I will do so for once in real earnest. I'll fly with the child to the Viking's wife—what rejoicing there will be!"

So the stork lifted the little girl out of the flower, flew to the wooden house, and picking a hole in the bladder window with his beak, laid the charming child in the arms of the Viking's wife; then he flew to stork-mamma and told her what he had seen and done, and the little storks listened too, for they were big enough to do so.

"So you see, the princess is not dead, she has sent the little one up here, and now it is provided for."

"I said so from the first!" cried stork-mamma; "but now just think a little of your own family. The time for our departure is drawing near. I already begin to feel an itching in my wings. The cuckoo and the nightingale have already gone, and I heard the quails say that they would be off too, as soon as the wind was favorable. Our little ones will get through the autumn maneuvers well enough unless I am mistaken in them."

The Viking's wife was overjoyed when she woke next morning and found the dear little child in her arms. She kissed it and caressed it, but it cried terribly and struggled with its hands and feet, appearing not to be at all pleased. At last it cried itself to sleep, and as it lay there so still, it looked wonderfully beautiful. The Viking's wife was extremely pleased, and felt light in body and soul; her heart bounded within her, and she felt that her husband and his men who were absent would return as unexpectedly and as suddenly as the child had come.

She and the whole household had therefore enough to do in preparing everything for the reception of her lord. The long colored tapestries which she and her maids had themselves worked, and into which they had woven images of their deities—Odin, Thor, and Freia—were hung up; the slaves polished the old shields that served as ornaments, and cushions were placed on the benches, and dry wood laid on the fireplace in the middle of the hall, so that the flame might be kindled in a moment. The Viking's wife herself set to work too, so that she was very tired when evening came, and soon fell asleep.

When she awoke early in the morning, she was terribly startled to find the child vanished. She jumped up from her couch, lit a pine torch, and looked all round the room; and behold! on that part of the couch where her feet had rested, lay, not the child, but a great ugly frog. At this sight a horrible feeling came over her; she seized a heavy stick to kill the frog; but it looked at her with such strangely mournful eyes that she could not strike the blow. Once more she looked all round the room while the frog croaked in a low feeble manner. The sound made her shudder; and springing from her couch, she ran to the little shutter that served as a window and quickly flung it open. At that moment the sun shone forth, and cast its beams through the opening on to the couch and upon the big frog, and suddenly—behold! it seemed as if the wide mouth contracted and became small and red, the limbs moved and stretched, and assumed the most beautiful shape, and it was her own sweet little child that lay there and no hideous frog.

"What is this?" she said; "have I had a bad dream? Surely it is the little image of myself that is lying there!" and she kissed it and pressed it to her heart, but the child kicked and struggled, and bit like a little wild cat.

Not on that day nor on the following one did the Viking return, although he was certainly on his way home; but the wind was against him, blowing towards the south for the storks. A favorable wind for one is a contrary wind for another.

After a few days and nights had passed, it became clear to the Viking's wife that her child was under a terrible spell. During the day it was as beautiful as a little fairy, though it had a bad savage temper; at night, however, it was a hideous frog, quiet and mournful, with sorrowful eyes. Here were two natures which changed inwardly as well as outwardly with the sunlight; this was because by day the little girl had the outer form of her real mother, but the disposition of her father—at night, on the contrary, her paternal descent made itself visible in the shape of her body, while the mind and heart of her mother became dominant within her. Who would be able to break this spell that some wicked witchcraft had wrought?

The Viking's wife was in great sorrow and trouble about it, and still her heart clung to the little creature of whose condition she felt she would not dare to tell her husband on his return; for he would probably, according to the custom of those times, have the child put out upon the highway, so that any one who liked might take it. The good Viking's wife could not find it in her heart to let this happen, so she resolved that the Viking should only see the child in bright daylight.

One morning there was a great rustling of stork's wings on top of the roof; more than a hundred pairs of storks had rested there from the grand maneuvers, and were now soaring up to travel towards the south.

"All the males fall in!" was the order; "wives and children too!"

"How light we feel!" cried the little storks in chorus; "we are itching down to our very toes, as if we were filled with nothing but live frogs. Oh, how beautiful it is to go traveling abroad."

"Mind you keep close to us as you fly," cried papa and mamma. "Don't open your mouth so much, it's bad for the chest."

And away flew the storks.

At the same moment the blast of the war trumpets sounded across the heath—the Viking had landed with his warriors. They were returning home richly laden with booty, from the Gallic court, where the people, as in the land of the Britons, sang in terror:

"Deliver us from the wild Northmen!"

Life and boisterous merriment now entered the Viking's castle on the moorland. The great cask of mead was carried into the hall, the pile of wood was set alight, and horses were killed; there was to be a great feast. The priest who offered up the sacrifices sprinkled the slaves with the warm blood to consecrate them, the fire crackled, the smoke curled up to the roof and the soot fell in flakes from the rafters; but they were used to all that. The guests were invited and received handsome presents; quarrels and treachery were forgotten. The company drank deep and threw the bones into each other's faces—that was a sign of good humor. The bard, a kind of minstrel—who, however, was also a warrior and who, having taken part in the Viking's expedition knew of what he was singing—sang a song in which all heard their warlike deeds recounted, and in which special praise was given to each. Every verse ended with the refrain:

"Goods and gold, friends untold, all must one day die;
Though man himself must also go, great fame will never die!"

Hereupon they beat their shields, and hammered the table with knives and bones, till the walls rang again.

The Viking's wife sat upon the daïs in the great hall where they feasted; she wore a silken dress, gold armlets and great amber beads. She was in grand array, and the singer mentioned her too in his song, and spoke of the treasure of gold that she had brought her rich husband. The latter was heartily delighted with the lovely child; he had only seen it in its beauty in the daytime, and its wild nature pleased him. He said that the girl might grow up into a powerful woman of doughty deeds who would stand by her husband. She would not even blink if a practiced hand were to strike off her eyebrows with a sharp sword in fun.

The cask of mead was emptied and a fresh one brought in, for these were people who liked to enjoy everything in plenty. They certainly knew the old proverb—"The cattle know when they must leave the pastures, but a foolish man knoweth not the measure of his own stomach"—oh yes! they knew all about that; but one knows one thing and does another. They also knew that "even the welcome guest may outstay his welcome," but still they sat there, for bacon and mead are good things; all went merrily, and at night the serfs slept in the warm ashes, and dipped their fingers in the fat soot and licked them. These were the good old times!

Once more that year the Viking went forth, even though the autumn storms were already beginning to blow. He went with his men to the shores of Britain, calling that a mere pleasure trip across the water, and his wife remained behind with the little girl. This much is certain, that the foster-mother soon got to love the poor frog with the gentle eyes and deep sighs almost more than the beauty who struck out and bit.

The raw damp autumn mist which kills the leaves in the wood already lay upon heath and forest. The "Bird Featherless," as the snow is called, fell in heavy masses, and winter was fast coming on. The sparrows took possession of the stork's nests and talked about the absent owners in their own fashion; but the stork pair and their little ones—what, indeed, had become of them?

The storks were now in the land of Egypt, where the sun sent out its warm rays as it does with us on a fine midsummer day. Tamarinds and acacias bloomed all over the country, and Mahomet's crescent shone brightly down from the cupolas of the temples, where, upon the slender minarets, sat many a stork pair resting after their long journey. Great flocks divided among themselves the nests which lay close to each other on venerable pillars, and on the ruined temple arches of forgotten cities. The date-palm lifted its screen on high as if it wanted to be a sun-shade; the grayish pyramids stood out like shadows in the clear air of the distant desert where the ostrich sped swiftly along, and the lion gazed with his great grave eyes at the marble sphinx that lay half buried in the sand. The waters of the Nile had receded, and the whole river bed was swarming with frogs, a sight that was exactly suited to the taste of the stork families. The young ones thought it was an optical illusion, so delightful did they think everything.

"That's how it is here, and that's how we always live in our warm country," said stork-mamma, and the young ones felt their mouths water.

"Is there anything more to be seen?" they asked; "can we go any farther in the land?"

"There's nothing more to be seen there!" answered stork-mamma. "Beyond this district there are only immense forests whose branches grow entwined, while prickly, trailing plants bar one's steps on all sides; there only the elephant with his clumsy feet can make a path for himself, and the snakes there are too large, and the lizards too quick for us. If you want to go to the desert, you'll get your eyes full of sand at the best of times, but if it blows great guns you will be enveloped in a pillar of sand. Here it is best. Here there are frogs and locusts. Here I shall stay, and you too!"

And they stayed there. The parents sat in the nest which rested on the slender minaret, and at the same time busily occupying themselves in smoothing and cleaning their feathers, and in whetting their beaks on their red stockings. Now and then they stretched out their necks and bowed gravely, lifting their heads with their high foreheads and fine smooth feathers, out of which their brown eyes peeped wisely forth. The young females strutted about among the juicy reeds, glanced slily at the other young storks, made acquaintances, and gulped down a frog at every third step, or dangled a little snake at the end of their beaks; this they thought looked pretty, besides tasting nice. The young males picked quarrels, beat each other with their wings, hacked away with their beaks, and even stabbed each other till the blood gushed forth. In this way soon this and then that couple from among the young ladies and gentlemen was engaged, and that was just what they wanted, and their only object in life; then they occupied a new nest, and soon got into fresh quarrels, for in warm countries everybody is hot-tempered and hasty; but still it was very pleasant, and the old people especially were delighted, for whatever the young ones do is so prettily done. There was sunshine every day, and plenty to eat; there was nothing but pleasure to think of. But in the rich castle, at the Egyptian host's, as they called him, there was no pleasure to be found.

The rich and mighty lord reclined upon his couch in the middle of the great hall with the gaily painted walls—it seemed as if he were lying in a tulip; but he was stiff and crippled in all his limbs, and lay stretched out like a mummy. His family and servants stood around him; he was not dead, but he could hardly be said to be alive. The healing marsh flower from the north, which was to have been sought and brought home by those who loved him most dearly, never came. His beautiful young daughter who had flown in swan's feathers across sea and land, far up into the north, was never to return.

"She is dead for ever," the two snow-maidens had said on their return, and they had made up a story which ran as follows:

"We three together," they said, "flew high up into the air. A hunter saw us, and shot an arrow at us; it hit our young friend and sister; and singing her farewell song, she slowly sank down, a dying swan, into the woodland lake. On the shore of the lake, under a weeping birch-tree, we laid her in the cold earth. But we had our revenge. We bound some fire under the wings of the swallow who had its nest beneath the thatched roof of the hunter; the house burst into flames, and the hunter was burnt with the house. The blaze could be seen right across the lake, as far as the weeping birch, where she now lies in the earth. She will never return to the land of Egypt."

Thereupon the two wept; and when stork-papa heard the story, he rattled his beak, so that it could be heard a long way off.

"All lies and deception!" he cried; "I should like to run my beak deep into their breasts."

"And break it!" added stork-mamma; "then you would look well. Think of yourself first, and then of your family—the rest doesn't concern us."

"Still, I'll sit on the edge of the open cupola to-morrow when the wise and learned men assemble to deliberate upon the sick man's condition; perhaps they'll get a little nearer the truth."

The wise and learned men came together and talked a great deal upon all kinds of things out of which the stork could make absolutely nothing, and nothing came of it either for the sick man or for the daughter in the marshy moor. But still we will just hear what they had to say, for we have to listen to so much in this world.

It would, however, be as well to hear what had happened years before, for then we shall be better versed in the matter, and will know at least as much as stork-papa.

"Love begets life! The highest love begets the highest life! Only by love can this life be saved!" This is what had been said; and it was very wisely and beautifully said, thought the learned men.

"That is a beautiful idea!" stork-papa immediately said.

"I don't quite understand it," replied stork-mamma, "and that is not my fault, but that of the idea; but let that be as it may, I have something else to think of."

Then the learned men had spoken of the love for this and the other, and the distinction between such love and that which lovers feel—and of that existing between parents and children, and of the love of light for the plants when the sunbeam kisses the earth and germs shoot forth—it was all so elaborately and learnedly expounded that it was an impossibility for stork-papa to follow it, let alone repeat it. He became quite full of thought about it, half closed his eyes, and stood on one leg the whole of the following day thinking; the burden of all that learning quite weighed him down.

But one thing stork-papa understood. All, high and low, had spoken out of their inmost heart and said that it was a great misfortune for thousands of people, indeed for the whole country, that this man was lying there ill and could not be cured, and that it would spread joy and blessings if he were to recover. But where did the flower grow which could bring him health? They had all searched for it in learned books, in twinkling stars, in storm and wind; they had searched for it in every byway they could think of, and at last the sages and the learned men, as we have already said, had concluded that "Love begets life, even the life of a father"; in this they had surpassed themselves, and said more than they understood. Then they repeated it, and wrote down as a prescription "Love begets life." But how the mixture which had been prescribed was to be prepared—that, they could not get over. At last they agreed that help must come through the princess, through her who clung to her father with her whole soul, and they even devised how the difficulty was to be overcome. Yes, days and years had now passed since that night when the princess had betaken herself by the waning light of the new moon's brief rays to the marble sphinx, had scraped away the sand from the pedestal, and had gone through the long passage that leads into the depths of one of the great pyramids where one of the mighty kings of old, surrounded by splendor and glory, lies in the wrappings of a mummy. There she was to place her head on the dead king's breast, and then it would be made clear to her where life and deliverance for her father were to be found.

All this she had accomplished, and had learned in a dream that she must bring home from the deep lake on the moorland heath, far north in the land of Denmark—the very spot had been accurately described to her—the lotus flower that takes root in the depths of the water, and that by this her father would be healed. She had therefore flown in swan's plumage from the land of Egypt to the heath, to the wild moor.

Do you see? all this stork-papa and stork-mamma knew, and now we also know more about it than we did before. We know that the marsh king drew her down to himself, and know too that she is dead for ever to her loved ones at home. One of the wisest men among them, too, said just what stork-mamma did, "She will be able to get herself out of the difficulty," and with that they resolved to be satisfied and wait for what might turn up, for they knew of nothing better to do.

"I should like to get away the swan's feathers from the two faithless princesses," said stork-papa; "then at least they would not be able to fly up to the wild moor again and do mischief. I could hide the two suits of swan's feathers up there, till some one has a use for them."

"But where will you hide them?" asked stork- mamma.

"Up in our nest on the wild moor," he replied. "I and our young ones will take it in turns to carry them along with us on our flight, and if they are too heavy for us, there are plenty of places on the way where we can hide them till our next journey. One suit of swan's plumage would certainly be sufficient for the princess, but two are always better. In those northern countries one cannot have too many clothes when traveling."

"No one will thank you for it," said stork-mamma, "but you are master. Except at hatching-time I have nothing to say."

In the Viking's castle on the wild moor, whither the storks directed their flight when spring approached, they had given the little girl the name of Helga; but this name was far too soft for a temper such as was in this case wrapped up in the most beauteous form. Every month this temper showed itself in sharper outlines, and in the course of years, during which the storks were continually making the same journey—in autumn to the Nile, and in spring to the moorland lake—the child grew up into a big girl; and before one was aware of it, she was a lovely maiden of sixteen. The shell was beautiful, but the kernel was hard and harsh; she was as wild as most were in those stern, dark days.

She took a pleasure in sprinkling with her white hands the foaming blood of the horses killed for the sacrifices; in her wild moments she would bite off the head of the black cock that the high priest was about to kill, and to her foster-father she said in full earnest:

"If your enemies were to tear down the roof of your house, while you lay heedlessly buried in sleep, and I were to see or hear it, I would not wake you, even if I could. I could never bring myself to do so, for my ears are still burning with the blow that you—yes, you—gave me years ago. I have not forgotten it."

But the Viking thought she spoke in jest; for, like all others, he was bewitched by her beauty, and did not know that Helga's temper and form changed, or how, without a saddle, she sat like a statue upon her horse as it rushed along on its wild career, and she did not dismount even when it fought with other horses. She would often plunge from the steep banks, dressed as she was, into the rushing stream, and swim down the bay to meet the Viking when his boat steered for home. She would cut off the longest lock of her beautiful hair and plait it into a string for her bow.

"What one does one's self is well done!" she would say.

The Viking's wife possessed a strong will and character, even for those days, but compared to her daughter she was like a weak, timid woman; she knew, however, that it was an evil charm that lay upon the poor child.

Apparently from pure malice Helga would frequently sit on the railings round the well, and when she saw her mother standing on the balcony or come into the courtyard, she would beat the air with arms and legs, and then suddenly slip down into the deep narrow pit; there with her frog-like nature, she would dive beneath the water, and rising, climb up like a cat, and come into the hall dripping with water, so that the green leaves strewn upon the ground floated in the stream that flowed from her.

One thing only imposed a check upon Helga, and that was the evening twilight. Then she would become quiet and thoughtful, and allow herself to be advised and guided, and at that time her inward feelings would draw her towards her mother. When the sun sank, and both the inner and the outer transformation took place, she sat there quiet and sad, shriveled up into the form of a frog. Her body was indeed much larger than that of one of those animals, and it was therefore the more hideous to behold. She looked like a wretched dwarf with the head of a frog and with web-fingers. Her eyes wore a very mournful expression; voice she had none, only a hollow croak, almost like the sobs of a dreaming child. Then the Viking's wife would take her on her lap, and forgetting the hideous form, gaze only into the mournful eyes, and say:

"I could almost wish that you were always my dumb frog-child; you are more terrible when beauty lends you its form."

And the Viking's wife wrote Runic charms against witchcraft and disease, and threw them over the wretched girl; but no cure showed itself.

"It is hardly credible that she was so small, and that she lay in the cup of a water-lily," said stork-papa; "now she is quite grown up and the very cut out of her Egyptian mother—ah! we shall never see her again. After all she was not able to get out of the difficulty, as you and the wise men said she would. Year in, year out, have I flown across the great moorland in all directions, but she never gave a sign that she lived. Yes, I'll tell you now how every year, when I came here a few days before you to mend the nest, and to put this and that in order, I used to fly to and fro across the lake for a whole night, as if I were a bat or an owl, but all in vain. The two coats of swan's feathers which I and the young ones dragged up here out of the Nile country have therefore not been used; we had trouble enough to carry them up here in three journeys, and now they lie here at the bottom of the nest, and should a fire break out some day, and the wooden house be burned, they would be lost."

"And our good nest would be lost too," exclaimed stork-mamma; "you think less of that than of your wretched feathers and your moor-princess. You had better go down into the marsh and stay with her. You are a bad father to your own children; I said that as soon as I hatched our first brood. I only hope that neither we nor our young ones may get an arrow into our wings from that wild girl. Helga does not in the least know what she does. She might take into consideration that we have lived here longer than she has; we never forgot our obligations, and paid our tribute every year—a feather, an egg, and a young one, as we should. Do you think I still go down into the courtyard and wander about everywhere as I once used to do, and as I still do in Egypt, where I am almost a friend of the people, and that I can go so far as to peep into the pots and kettles as I do there? No, I sit up here till I get quite angry with her—the chit!—and I get angry with you too! You ought just to have left her lying in the water-lily; then she would have perished long ago."

"You make yourself out worse than you are," said stork-papa. "I know you better than you know yourself."

With that he gave a hop, and taking two vigorous strokes with his wings, stretched out his legs behind him, and flew, or rather sailed away, without moving his wings. He had already gone some distance when he took a powerful stroke. The sun shone brightly on his fine plumage, and his neck and head were stretched proudly forth—there was a swing and a go in his movements.

"After all, he's handsomer than any of the others," said stork-mamma, "but I will not tell him so."

* * *

The Viking came home early that autumn, laden with booty and bringing prisoners with him. Among the latter was a young Christian priest, one of those who despised the gods of the northern countries.

There had been much talk of late, both in the hall and in the cottage, of the new religion which was spreading far and wide in the south, and which had indeed been brought as far as Hedeby on the Schlei by Saint Ansgarius. Even Helga had heard of the belief in the White Savior, who had out of love for mankind laid down His life for their redemption; but with her it had all gone in at one ear and out of the other, as the saying is. It seemed as if she only understood the meaning of the word love when she lay crouching down in the locked chamber in the miserable form of a frog; but the Viking's wife had heard the story, and the tidings of the Son of the one true God, and had been wondrously moved by it.

The men, on their return from their sea-voyages, had told of the splendid temples hewn out of beautiful stone, which had been erected to glorify Him whose service meant love. Some heavy vessels, artistically wrought out of massive gold, had been taken and brought home. The fragrance of spices still clung to them, for they were incense vessels, which the Christian priests swung before the altar, on which no blood flowed, but where the wine and the consecrated bread was changed into the blood of Him who had laid down his life for the sake of generations still unborn. They had taken the young Christian priest down into the deep dungeons of the castle, and had bound his hands and feet with strips of bark.

The Viking's wife said that he was as beautiful to behold as Baldur, and his distress touched her, but Helga declared that he ought to have cords drawn right through his feet and be tied to the tails of wild oxen.

"Then I would let loose the dogs and halloo! over moor and marsh and across the heath! That would be a sight for the gods! And finer still to follow him in his career!"

But the Viking would not suffer him to die such a death; he intended to have him sacrificed on the morrow, on the bloodstained altar in the grove as a denier and despiser of the great gods. For the first time a human being was to be sacrificed here.

Helga begged for the privilege of sprinkling the images of the gods and the assembled people with the blood of the priest. She sharpened her glittering knife, and when one of the great fierce dogs that ran about the Viking's castle sprang past her, she thrust the knife into his side. "Only to see if it's sharp enough," she said, and the Viking's wife gazed mournfully at the wild wicked girl; and when night fell, and the beauty of form and soul exchanged places in her daughter, she spoke to Helga of her sorrow, in eloquent words that came from the depths of her grieved heart. The hideous frog, in the form of a monster, stood before her; and fixing upon her its sad brown eyes, listened to her words, and seemed to understand them with the sense of a human being.

"Never, not even to my lord and husband, has a word passed my lips of what I suffer through you," said the Viking's wife; "my heart is full of sorrow for you. Stronger and greater than I ever imagined is a mother's love. But love never entered into your feelings—your heart is like the cold wet plants of the marsh."

Then the miserable form trembled, and it seemed as if these words touched an invisible bond between the body and the soul, for great tears came into its eyes.

"Your time of trial will one day come," said the Viking's wife, "and it will be a terrible time for me too. It had been better if you had been put out on the high road, and the night wind had lulled you to sleep."

The Viking's wife wept bitter tears, and went away in anger and sorrow, passing behind the skin which hung loose over the rafter and divided the hall.

The frog sat huddled up in a corner all alone. An unbroken stillness reigned; but at short intervals a half-stifled sigh escaped from Helga's breast; it seemed as if a pain and a new life had been born in her heart. She took a step forward, listened, and then taking another step, grasped with her clumsy hands the heavy bar that was laid across the door. Softly and laboriously she pushed back the door, and just as softly did she draw the bolt that secured the latch, then seizing the flickering lamp that stood in the ante-chamber of the hall. It seemed as if a stronger will lent her power; she drew back the iron bolt from the trap-door leading to the cellar, and crept down to the prisoner. He was asleep; she touched him with her cold clammy hand, and when he awoke and saw the hideous form, a shudder passed over him as if he had seen a ghost. Drawing her knife, she cut the cords that bound his hands and feet, and beckoned him to follow her.

He uttered some holy names, made the sign of the cross, and as the form remained motionless, he spoke as follows:

"Blessed are they who help the needy, for the Lord will deliver them in their hour of need! Who art thou? Whence this animal shape which yet is so full of kind mercy?'

The frog beckoned him to follow, and led him through a lonely corridor, concealed by curtains, to the stable, where it pointed to a horse. He swung himself upon its back, but the frog jumped up too, placing itself before him and holding on by the horse's mane. The prisoner understood her, and at a swift trot they rode out on to the open heath along a path which he would never have found alone.

He forgot the hideous form, and felt only how the Lord's mercy and kindness showed itself through the medium of the monster; he prayed devoutly, and sang sacred lays. At this the unhappy maiden trembled. Was it the effect of prayer and song, or was this shudder called forth by the chilly dawn that was approaching? What were her feelings? She rose, and attempted to stop the horse and jump down; but the Christian priest held her back with all his might, and sang a sacred song, thinking this might break the spell that held her bound in the hideous form of a frog. The horse galloped along more wildly; the heavens became streaked with red, the first sunbeams pierced the clouds, and with the bright stream of light the change in form took place. Helga was again the beauteous maiden with the fiendish, wicked mind. The priest was holding a most lovely young woman in his arms, and this terrified him; he jumped down from the horse and compelled it to stop. This seemed to him a new and dangerous piece of sorcery; but Helga had also dismounted with a single leap, and stood on the ground. Her short gown reached only to her knees; she snatched the sharp knife from her girdle, and rushed quick as lightning upon the astonished priest.

"Only let me get at you!" she cried. "Let me get at you, and my knife shall enter your body. You are pale as straw, beardless slave!"

She pressed in upon him, and they struggled together in fierce combat, but an invisible power seemed to sustain the Christian. He held her fast, and the old oak by which they stood came to his aid, its roots half loosened from the earth acting as bonds for the maiden's feet, which had become entwined in them. Hard by, a spring gushed forth, and the priest sprinkled Helga's face and breast with the fresh water, bidding the unclean spirit go forth, and blessing her in Christian fashion; but the water of faith has no power where its spring does not also flow from within. And yet the power of the Christian became evident even here, for he contended against the struggles of the evil power with more than the simple might of man. His holy actions overpowered her; her arms fell to her side, and she gazed with astonished eyes and pallid cheeks upon him who appeared to be a mighty magician and practiced in secret arts. He seemed to her to be uttering mysterious Runic charms and to be making secret signs in the air. She would not have flinched if he had raised a glittering ax or a sharp knife against her, but now that he made the sign of the cross over her she sat there like a tamed bird, her head sunk upon her breast.

Then he spoke to her in gentle words of the deed of love that she had performed for him in the night, when she had come to him in the form of a hideous frog to loosen his bonds and lead him out to light and life. She too was bound, he said, in closer bonds than those which had held him, but she too should be led to light and life, and that by him. He would take her to Hedeby,* to the holy Ansgarius, and there in the Christian town the spell would be removed. But she should not ride before him on the horse, even if she offered to sit there of her own accord.

"You must sit behind me, not before me! Your magic beauty has a power that is born of evil—I fear it, although I am certain to conquer in the name of the Lord."

He knelt down, and prayed devoutly and fervently. It seemed as if his prayer consecrated the quiet wood into a holy church; the birds sang, as if they belonged to the new congregation, and the wild mint smelled sweetly as if to fill the place of the incense. In a loud voice the priest recited the words:

"May He appear to us who dwell in darkness and the shadow of death, and direct our steps in the paths of peace."

He told her of the deep love that pervaded the whole of nature; and while he spoke, the horse that had carried them both in wild career stood still before the tall bramble bushes, and plucked at them, so that the ripe juicy berries fell down upon Helga's head, offering themselves for refreshment.

She patiently allowed herself to be lifted on the horse, and sat there like a somnambulist who is not awake and yet not asleep. The Christian bound two branches together with bark, in the form of a cross, and held it on high as they rode through the wood, which got thicker as they went on, and at last became a totally trackless wilderness.

Blackthorn-bushes barred the way, so that they had to ride round them. The spring did not grow into a stream, but into a stagnant swamp, around which the horse had also to be led. There was strength and refreshment in the cool forest air, and no mean power lay in the gentle words that were uttered in faith and Christian love from an inward yearning to lead the poor maiden to light and life.

The rain-drops, they say, hollow out the hard stone, and the waves of the sea round the rugged corners of the rocks. The dew of mercy, administered to Helga, softened what was hard and smoothed what was rugged within her. It could not be seen in her, it is true—she did not know it herself; but does the germ in the bosom of the earth, when the refreshing dew and the warm sunbeams fall upon it, know that it carries within it growth and blossom?

---

* The ancient Danish name of the town of Schleswig.

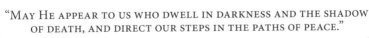

"MAY HE APPEAR TO US WHO DWELL IN DARKNESS AND THE SHADOW OF DEATH, AND DIRECT OUR STEPS IN THE PATHS OF PEACE."

Just as a mother's song enters into a child's mind, and it babbles the words after her without understanding them, until they afterwards collect themselves into thoughts and become clearer and clearer with time, so here too did the Word work which has the power to create. They rode out of the dense forest across the heath and again through pathless woods, and towards evening they came across a robber-band.

"Where did you steal that charming maiden?" cried the robbers, seizing the horse by the bridle and dragging down both the riders. The priest had no other weapon than the knife he had taken from Helga, and with this he struck out to right and left; one of the robbers aimed a blow at him with his ax, but the young priest sprang aside and eluded the glittering blade, which sank deep into the horse's neck, so that the blood gushed forth and the animal fell to the ground. Then Helga, as if she were suddenly waking out of her long deep reverie, threw herself hastily upon the groaning animal.

The priest placed himself before her to defend and protect her; but one of the robbers brought down his heavy iron hammer with such a crash upon the Christian's head, that blood and brains were scattered all around, and he fell lifeless to the ground.

The robbers seized beautiful Helga by her white arms and her slender waist; at that moment the sun went down and its last ray disappeared, and she was changed into the form of a frog. The greenish mouth spread itself over half the face, the arms became thin and clammy, and a broad hand with webbed fingers spread out in the shape of a fan. Then the terrified robbers let her go, and she stood among them a hideous monster, and as it is the nature of the frog to do, she sprang on high, higher than her own height, and disappeared in the thicket. The robbers began to see that this must be either an evil trick of the spirit Loke, or hidden witchcraft, and they hurried away from the spot in terror.

The full moon was already rising. Soon it shone upon and illumined the earth, and out of the thicket crept poor Helga in the wretched form of the frog. She stopped before the body of the Christian priest and before her dead horse, and gazed at them with eyes that seemed to weep, while from the frog's mouth came a croaking that sounded like a child bursting into tears. She threw herself first upon one and then upon the other, fetched water in the hollow of her hand which could hold a good deal on account of the webbed skin, and poured it over them; but dead they were and dead they remained, that she saw. Soon wild beasts would come and tear their bodies, but no! that must not be.

She therefore dug up the earth as much as she could, for she wanted to make them a grave. To do this she had only the branch of a tree and her two hands, while the webbed skin that grew between her fingers got torn and the blood flowed over them. At last she saw that her efforts would not be successful, so she fetched some more water and washed the dead man's face, covered it with fresh green leaves, and gathering together some large branches she spread them over him, scattering dead leaves between the boughs. Then she brought the heaviest stones she could lift, laid them over the dead body and filled up the openings with moss. In this manner, she thought, the mound would be strong and well secured. The night had passed in this hard work—the sun burst forth, and there stood beautiful Helga in all her loveliness, with bleeding hands, and for the first time with tears on her maidenly cheeks. Then in the change that came over her it seemed as if two natures were striving within her. She trembled from head to foot, and looked about her as if she were awakening from a terrible dream. Then she rushed to a slender tree, clung to it for support, and in another moment climbed up like a cat into the topmost branches. There she sat like a startled squirrel, remaining the whole day long in the solitary stillness of the wood, where all is quiet and dead, as they say—dead. Butterflies fluttered around in play, and close to her were numerous ant-hills, each crowded with many hundreds of busy little creatures hurrying to and fro. In the air danced myriads of gnats, swarm upon swarm, and hosts of buzzing flies, lady-bugs, gold beetles and other little winged insects; the eanh-worm crept up out of the damp ground and the moles popped out—for the rest, a deathlike silence reigned all around. No one noticed Helga but the magpies, who flew with cries round the tree-top in which she sat; the birds hopped close up to her on the boughs in bold curiosity, but a glance from her eye was sufficient to put them to flight. They could, however, make nothing of her, neither could she understand herself.

When evening drew near and the sun was sinking, her transformation called her to fresh activity. She slid down from the tree, and as the last sunbeam vanished she stood there in the shriveled form of the frog with the torn webbed skin on her hands But now her eyes were radiant with a splendor that they had scarcely possessed even in the maiden's lovely form—they were the gentle modest eyes of a girl that looked out from the frog's face. They gave proofs of deep feeling and of a human heart; and the lovely orbs overflowed in tears, beautiful tears that brought relief.

Yonder, on the mound she had raised, there still lay the cross made of twigs, the last work of him who now lay dead and cold beneath it. The idea to take up the cross seemed to come to Helga of itself; she planted it between the stones over him and the dead horse.

Sorrowful remembrances caused the tears to burst forth, and in this sad state she traced the same sign in the sand all round the grave, thus making a kind of ornamental border. As she made the sign of the cross with both hands, the webbed skin fell off like a torn glove, and when she washed her hands in the spring and gazed in wonder at their fair whiteness, she again made the same sign in the air between her and the grave. Her lips trembled, her tongue moved; and the name of our Savior, which she had heard spoken and sung so frequently during her ride through the wood, now fell audibly from her. Then the frog-skin dropped off, and she was once more the young beauty; but her head sank wearily and her limbs required rest—she fell into a slumber.

Her sleep, however, was but short. Towards midnight she awoke; before her stood the dead horse, so radiant and full of life that the fire gleamed forth from his eyes and the wound in his neck; close beside the animal stood the murdered Christian priest—"more beautiful than Baldur," the Viking's wife would have said—and yet he seemed to come in flames of fire.

A look so earnest, so piercing and so full of justice, shone out of the great gentle eyes that it seemed to penetrate into every corner of the heart.

Beautiful Helga trembled before this glance, and her memory awoke with a power as if the Day of Judgment had come. All the kindness that had been shown her, every tender word that had been said, sprang up before her; she understood now that it had been love that had sustained her in those days of trial during which every creature formed of the spirit and of dust—soul and clay—fights and struggles. She recognized that she had only obeyed the impulse of her inclinations, and had done nothing for herself; everything had been given her, everything had happened as it were providentially. She bowed deeply, confessing her own deep imperfection before Him who can read every fold of the heart, and at that moment there shot through her a ray from the flame of truth—the flame of the Holy Spirit.

"Thou daughter of the earth!" said the Christian priest, "out of the earth, out of the marsh didst thou come forth—from the earth shalt thou again arise. The sunbeam within thee, conscious of its origin, will return thereunto, for it is not a ray of light proceeding from the sun's body, but a ray that comes from God. I come from the land of the dead. Thou too shalt travel through the deep valleys into the radiant mountain-land where mercy and perfection dwell. I will not lead thee to Hedeby to receive Christian baptism, for thou must break the surface of the water that covers the deep moorland, and draw up to the light the living root of thy being and of thy birth: thou must exercise thine energies, before the consecration may be given thee."

He lifted her upon the horse, and handed her a golden censer like the one she had formerly seen in the Viking's castle, and a strong, sweet fragrance rose from it. The open wound in the forehead of the murdered priest shone like a brilliant diadem; he took the cross from the grave and held it on high as they sped on through the air, over the rustling wood, over the hills where the warriors of old lay buried with their dead chargers. The iron figures rose, sprang forward, and planted themselves on the summits of the hills; the bright circlet of gold with its golden knot shone upon the brow of each in the moonlight, and their mantles fluttered in the wind. The dragon that sat guarding hidden treasures raised his head and gazed after the riders. The goblins and mountain-sprites peeped forth from beneath the hills and the ridges of the fields, flitting to and fro with red, blue, and green flames, like the sparks dying out in a piece of burned paper. Over wood and heath, over river and marsh they flew along, up to the wild moor; over this they swept in great circles. The Christian priest raised on high the cross, which glittered like gold, and from his lips fell pious prayers. Beautiful Helga joined in the hymns, like a child lisping its mother's song. She swung the censer, and a fragrance so strong and so miraculous streamed from it that the reeds and rushes of the moor burst forth into blossom. Every seed shot up out of the deep ground; everything that had life rose up. A veil of water-lilies spread itself out like a worked carpet of flowers, and upon this lay a sleeping woman, young and wondrous fair. Helga thought it was her own image that she saw reflected in the still waters; but it was her mother she beheld, the marsh king's wife, the princess from the banks of the Nile.

The dead Christian priest commanded the slumbering woman to be lifted up on the horse, but the latter sank under the burden, as if its body were a pall fluttering in the wind. The sign of the cross, however, strengthened the airy phantom, and now the three rode away from the lake to the firm land.

Then the cock crowed in the Viking's castle, and the phantom forms dissolved and floated away on the breeze, but mother and daughter stood opposite each other.

"Is it my own reflection that I see in the deep water?" asked the mother.

"Is it my own reflection that is cast upon the gleaming mirror?" cried the daughter; and they approached each other, and were locked in a close embrace. The mother's heart beat quickest, and she understood what the quickened pulses meant.

"My child! The flower of my own heart! My lotus-flower of the deepest waters!"

The dragon that sat guarding hidden treasures
raised his head and gazed after the riders.

And she embraced her child anew and wept; her tears were a fresh baptism of life and love for Helga.

"I came hither in the feathers of a swan, and here I cast the plumage off," said the mother; "I sank through the treacherous moor deep down into the ground, which closed like a wall around me. But soon I felt a fresh stream; a power drew me down deeper, ever deeper, and I felt sleep pressing upon my eyelids. I slept, and dreams surrounded me—it seemed as if I lay again in the pyramids of Egypt, but before me there still stood the swaying alder-stump which had inspired me with such terror on the surface of the marsh above. I gazed at the cracks and wrinkles in the stump, and they shone in colors and assumed the forms of hieroglyphics; it was the case of a mummy that I had before me. At last this burst, and out stepped the thousand-year-old king, the mummy form, black as pitch—a shining black, like that of the wood-snail, or of the rich black slime of the marsh; it was the marsh king, or the mummy of the pyramids—I knew not which. He wound his arms around me, and it seemed as if I must die. I only returned to life when my bosom became warm, and I found upon it a little bird which beat its wings, twittered and sang. The bird flew from my breast up towards the dark heavy roof, but a long green band still bound us together. I heard and understood the tones of its longing: "Freedom! Sunlight! To father!"

Then I thought of my father and the sunny light of home, my life and my love, and I loosened the band and let the bird fly away—home to father. Since that hour I have dreamed no more; I slept a long and deep sleep indeed, till within this hour sweet tones and fragrance raised me and delivered me." Where did the green band from the mother's heart to the wings of the bird flutter now, whither had it been wafted? Only the stork had seen it. The band was the green stalk, the bow was the radiant flower, the cradle of the child that had grown up so lovely, and that was once more pressed to its mother's heart.

And while the two were locked in each other's arms, stork-papa flew around them in smaller and smaller circles, finally darting away in rapid flight to his nest. Bringing thence the coats of swan's feathers that he had saved so many years he threw one to each, the feathers closed around them, and they soared up from the earth, two white swans.

"Now we will talk together," said stork-papa—"now we understand each other, even though the beak of one bird is differently formed from that of the other. It is exceedingly fortunate that you came to-night; to-morrow we should already have been up and away, mother, myself and the little ones—we are flying towards the south. Yes, you may look at me! I am your old friend out of the Nile country, and so is mother too, though she shows it more in her heart than with her beak. She always declared the princess would manage to help herself out, and I and the youngsters carried the swan's feathers up here. But how glad I am, and how lucky it is that I am still here! At break of day we shall be off, a large company of storks. We shall fly first, do you fly close behind us, then you will not lose your way; I and the little ones will keep an eye on you, too."

"And the lotus-flower that I was to bring," said the Egyptian princess, "will fly besides me in the swan's plumage. I shall bring with me the flower of my heart; and thus the riddle has been solved. Homeward! Homeward!"

But Helga declared that she could not leave the Danish land without having once more seen her foster-mother, the kind Viking's wife. Every tender recollection, every kind word, every tear that her foster-mother had wept, rose up in her memory, and at that moment it almost seemed as if she loved that mother best.

"Yes, we must go to the Viking's castle," said stork-papa; "mother and the young ones are waiting for us there. What eyes they will make, and how they will rattle their beaks! Yes, mother doesn't say much; she's very brusque, but she means well. I'll just give a rattle, so that they'll know we're coming."

And stork-papa rattled in first-class style, and he and the swans flew off to the Viking's castle.

In the castle every one was still fast asleep. The Viking's wife had not retired to rest till very late on the preceding evening. She was very anxious about Helga, who had vanished with the Christian priest now fully three days ago. Helga must have assisted him in his flight, for it was her horse that was missing from the stables; but by what power was all this brought about?

The Viking's wife thought of the miracles that were said to be performed by the White Savior, and by those who believed in Him and followed Him. Her fleeting thoughts shaped themselves into a vision, and it seemed to her that she was still sitting awake on her couch and that darkness reigned without. The storm drew near; she heard the sea roaring and rolling in the east and west, like the waves of the North Sea and the Cattegat. The immense snake that encircled the earth in the depths of the ocean quaked convulsively. It was the night of the downfall of the gods—Ragnarok, as the heathens called the Day of Judgment, when all was to pass away, even the great gods. The war-horn sounded, and over the rainbow rode the gods, clad in steel, to fight the last combat. Before them flew the winged Valkyries, and the phantoms of the dead champions brought up the rear. The whole sky around them was ablaze with northern lights, though darkness conquered in the end. It was a terrible hour.

And close to her the terrified Viking's wife seemed to see Helga sitting on the floor in the hideous form of the frog, trembling and clinging to her foster-mother, who took her on her lap and pressed her lovingly in her arms, hideous as she was. The air re-echoed with the blows of swords and clubs, and with the whistling of arrows, as if a hailstorm were passing over them. The hour was come when Heaven and earth were to burst, the stars fall, and all sink into Surtar's sea of fire; but she knew that a new earth and a new Heaven would come, that wavy fields of corn would stand where now the sea rolls over the dreary depths, that the ineffable God would reign! And up to him ascended Baldur, the gentle, the kind, redeemed from the kingdom of the dead; he came—the Viking's wife saw him, she recognized his countenance—it was the imprisoned Christian priest. "White Christian!" she cried aloud, and with this cry she pressed a kiss upon the forehead of the hideous frog-child. Then the frog-skin fell off, and Helga stood before her in all her beauty, lovely and gentle as she had never been before, and with beaming eyes. She kissed her foster-mother's hand, blessing her for all the care and love bestowed on her during the days of trial and sorrow, for the thoughts she had instilled and awakened in her, and for uttering the name which she repeated: "White Christian." Then beautiful Helga arose, a mighty swan, and her wings spread themselves out with a rustling noise like that of a troop of birds of passage in their flight.

Then the Viking's wife awoke and she still heard the same strong beating of wings out in the air. She knew it was about the time when the storks migrate, and that it must be those whose flight she heard. She wished to see them once more and to bid them farewell on their departure. She rose from her couch and stepped out upon the balcony, and now she saw the gable of the side-wing of the house crowded with storks, and all around the castle, over the tall trees, bands of them were wheeling in great circles; but opposite to her and the balcony, by the well where Helga had so often sat and alarmed her by her wildness, sat two swans gazing at her with intelligent eyes. She remembered her dream—it still filled her thoughts as if it were a reality, and she thought of Helga in the form of a swan, thought of the Christian priest, and suddenly felt her heart rejoice.

The swans flapped their wings and bent their necks as though they also wished to send her a greeting, and the Viking's wife spread her arms out towards them as if she understood all this, and smiling through her tears stood sunk in deep thought.

Then all the storks rose with a rustling of wings and a rattling of beaks to start on their journey to the south.

"We shall not wait for the swans," said stork-mamma; "if they want to go with us, let them come. We cannot sit here till the plovers start. There is something fine after all in traveling in families in this way—not like the finches and partridges, where the cock-birds and the hens fly in separate parties, which, to tell the truth, is not at all proper. And what kind of stroke do the swans call that?"

"Well, every one flies in his own fashion," said stork-papa; "the swans fly on the slant, the cranes in a triangle, and the plovers in a snake's line."

"Don't talk of snakes when we are flying up here," said stork-mamma; "that creates desires in the young ones that can't be gratified."

"Are those the high mountains that I have heard about?" asked Helga, in the swan's plumage.

"Those are thunder-clouds that float beneath us," answered her mother

"What white clouds are those that rise so high?" asked Helga once more.

"Those are the mountains perpetually covered with snow, which you see yonder," said her mother; and they flew across the Alps towards the blue Mediterranean.

"Africa's land! Egypt's strand!" joyfully cried the daughter of the Nile in her swan's form, as from the lofty sky she caught sight of her native land looking like a yellowish wavy streak.

And all the birds spied it too and hastened their flight.

"I scent Nile mud and wet frogs," said stork-mamma; "it makes my mouth water. Ah! now you'll taste something, and you'll see the marabu, the ibis, and the crane. They all belong to our family, but they are by far not so beautiful as we. They think themselves very grand, especially the ibis; but he has been spoiled by the Egyptians, who make a mummy of him and stuff him with spices. I would rather be stuffed with live frogs, and so would you, and that you shall be too. Better to have something in one's inside while one is alive than to be the subject of pomp when one is dead. That's my opinion, and mine is generally the right one."

"The storks have come," they said in the rich house on the banks of the Nile, where the royal lord lay on soft cushions under a leopard skin in the open hall, not alive and yet not dead, hoping and waiting for the lotus-flower from the deep moorland in the far north. Relatives and servants stood around his couch.

Into the hall flew two beautiful swans; they had come with the storks. They cast off the dazzling white feathers, and there stood two charming female forms, as like each other as two drops of dew. They leaned over the pale, old invalid, and threw back their long hair, and as fair Helga bent over her grandfather, his cheeks reddened, his eyes sparkled, and life came back to his benumbed limbs. The old man arose well and young again; his daughter and grandchild embraced him as if in a joyful morning greeting after a long, painful dream.

Joy reigned throughout the whole house and in the stork's nest too—in the latter, it is true, principally on account of the good food, consisting of numbers of frogs that seemed to spring in shoals out of the earth. And while the learned men hastily wrote down the story of the two princesses and of the flower of health, as an important event and a blessing for the royal house and the country, the stork-pair told the story to their family in their own way, but only after they had all eaten their fill, for till then they had something else to do than to listen to stories.

"Now you will at last be made something," whispered stork-mamma, "there's no doubt about it."

"What should I be made?" said stork-papa. "What have I done? Nothing at all!"

"You have done more than the others. Without you and the little ones the two princesses would never have seen Egypt again or have effected the old man's cure. You will be made something. They will certainly give you a doctor's degree, and in future our little ones will be born with it, and their children after them, and so on. You already look like an Egyptian doctor—in my eyes!"

The wise and learned men developed the fundamental idea, as they called it, that ran through the whole event: "Love begets life!" This phrase they expressed in different ways. The warm sunbeam was the Egyptian princess who had descended to the marsh king, and from this embrace sprang the flower.

"I can't repeat the words so very exactly," said stork-papa, who had been listening on the roof, and was now telling what he had heard to his own family. "What they said was so complicated, so wise and so deep, that rank and presents were immediately bestowed upon them; even the head cook received a special mark of distinction—probably for the soup."

"And what did you get?" asked stork-mamma. "Surely they will not forget the most important one, and that you certainly are! The learned men have done nothing throughout the whole matter but use their mouths; but you will certainly get your due."

Late in the night, when the gentle peace of sleep lay upon the now happy house there was still some one awake—not stork-papa; although he stood on one leg, and slept as he kept guard—it was Helga. She stood leaning out over the balcony and gazing up into the clear sky, where the great gleaming stars seemed to her larger and purer in luster than those she had seen in the north, though they were the same. She was thinking of the Viking's wife in the wild moorland region, of her foster-mother's gentle eyes, and the tears she had wept over the poor frog-child that now dwelled in splendor under the brilliant stars in the glorious spring air by the waters of the Nile. She was thinking of the love that dwelled in the breast of the heathen woman, of the love begotten for a wretched creature—a savage beast when in human form, and loathsome in its animal shape. She gazed at the gleaming stars, and thought of the radiance that had shone out from the forehead of the dead man when she flew with him through the wood and across the moor. Tones rang in her ears, words she had heard pronounced as they rode along, and she was borne wondering and trembling through the air,—words from the great fountain of love, the highest love, that embraces all mankind.

Much had indeed been bestowed, attained, and won! Fair Helga was absorbed day and night in thoughts of her great happiness, and stood lost in contemplation of it, like a child that hurriedly turns from the giver to the beautiful gifts it has received; she seemed to lose herself in the ever-increasing bliss that might and, she felt sure, would come. Had she not been borne by miracles to greater and greater joy? And one day she was so led away by this idea that she no longer remembered the Giver. It was the exuberance of youth unfolding its wings in bold flight. Her eyes were sparkling; but suddenly a loud noise in the courtyard below checked her thoughts in their wild career. There she saw two great ostriches running round very quickly in narrow circles; she had never seen this animal before—this great, fat, clumsy bird, whose wings looked as if they had been clipped, and the creature itself as if it had suffered violence. She asked what had happened to the animal, and now for the first time she heard the legend that the Egyptians tell of the ostrich.

Once, they say, the ostriches were a race of fine handsome birds, with large strong wings, when one evening the large birds of the forest said to the ostrich:

"Brother, shall we fly to-morrow, God willing, to the river to drink?"

And the ostrich answered, "I will."

At daybreak they flew off, first winging their way upwards, high up towards the sun, to the eye of God—ever higher and higher, the ostrich far in advance of all the other birds. The ostrich flew proudly up towards the light, confident of its strength, but, forgetful of the Giver, it had neglected to say "God willing!"

Then the avenging angel drew aside the veil from the flaming ocean of the sun; and in a second the bird's wings were scorched, and it sank miserably to the ground. The ostrich and all its race has never been able to fly again since; it speeds along when startled, and rushes round in narrow circles. This legend is a warning to mankind that in their thoughts and efforts, in all their actions, they should say "God willing!"

Helga bowed her head in deep meditation, and gazed at the timid circling ostrich, who took a silly pleasure in seeing its own great shadow on the white sunlit wall. And a deep earnestness took root in her heart and mind. A life very rich in present and future happiness was given and won; what was still to happen, yet to come? The best—"God willing!"

Early in the spring, when the storks again flew northwards, fair Helga slipped off her golden bracelet, scratched her name upon it, and beckoning stork-papa to come to her, placed the golden band round his neck and begged him to deliver it to the Viking's wife; from this the latter would, no doubt, understand that her foster-child was alive and happy, and thought of her.

"That's heavy to carry!" thought stork-papa, when he had it round his neck; "but gold and honors are not to be thrown away. The stork brings good fortune; that they will have to admit up yonder."

"You lay gold and I lay eggs," said stork-mamma; "but you lay only once, I lay every year. But neither of us gets any thanks for it. That's what hurts me!"

"But we have the knowledge of having done good, mother!" said stork-papa.

"You can't hang that round your neck," retorted stork-mamma; "it gives neither a good wind nor a good meal."

The little nightingale that sang in the tamarind tree was soon about to depart for the north too. Fair Helga had often heard it singing up yonder by the wild-moor; now she wanted to give it a message, for since she had flown in swan's plumage she understood the language of the birds; and as she had repeatedly spoken it with the storks and the swallows, she felt sure the nightingale would understand her. So she begged the nightingale to fly to the beech wood on the peninsula of Jutland, where the mound of stones and twigs had been reared—she begged it to ask all the little birds to build their nests round the grave, so that their songs should be heard there for ever and ever. And the nightingale flew away—and Time too.

In autumn the eagle stood upon the pyramid, and saw a stately train of richly laden camels approaching, of richly clad warriors on foaming Arab steeds that shone white as silver, with red quivering nostrils, and great thick manes that hung down almost over their slender legs.

Rich guests—a royal prince from Arabia, handsome as a prince should be, entered the stately house upon the roof of which the stork's nest now stood empty; they who dwelled in the nest were now in the far north, but would soon return. And they returned on the very day that was so full of joy and pleasure. A marriage was being celebrated here, and fair Helga was the bride, radiant in silk and jewels; the bridegroom was the young prince from Arabia, and the happy pair sat at the upper end of the table between mother and grandfather.

But the bride was not looking at the bridegroom, with his manly bronzed cheeks around which a black beard curled; she did not gaze into his dark fiery eyes that were fixed on her, but far away at the twinkling star that gleamed down from the heavens.

Then the rustling of strong wings was heard in the air. The storks were coming home, and the old stork-pair; tired as they were from the journey and in want of repose, at once flew down upon the balustrade of the veranda, for they already knew what festivities were going on. As soon as they reached the frontier they had heard that Helga had had their figures painted on the wall—for did they not belong to her story too?

"That is very nice and thoughtful," said stork-papa.

"It's very little," replied stork-mamma; "they could not have done less."

When Helga caught sight of them she got up, and came out upon the veranda to stroke their backs. The old stork-pair wagged their heads and bent their necks, while even the youngest of the young ones felt much honored by this reception.

Helga gazed up at the gleaming star that shone ever brighter; and between it and herself there floated a form, purer even than the air and visible through it. It floated quite close to her—it was the dead Christian priest; he too came to her wedding feast—came from the kingdom of Heaven.

"The splendor and glory there outshines all that is known on earth," he said.

And fair Helga prayed more beseechingly and more fervently than she had ever prayed before, that she might be allowed to gaze in upon it for only a single moment—to catch only one glimpse of the kingdom of Heaven and all its glory.

The priest carried her up amidst splendor and glory, in a wavy sea of melody and thoughts. Not only around her, but within her, was such brightness and music as words cannot express.

"Now we must go back," said he; "you will be missed."

"Only one look more!" she begged. "Only one short minute!"

"We must go down to the earth. The guests will all depart."

"Only one look more! The last!"

And again Helga stood on the veranda; but the marriage torches outside had vanished, the lights in the festive hall were extinguished, the storks were gone—nowhere a guest to be seen—no bridegroom—all as though swept away in those few short minutes.

Terror came over her. She strode through the great empty hall into the next chamber; there slept strange warriors. She opened a side-door that led into her own chamber, and as she thought to step in there, she suddenly found herself in the garden—but it had never looked like that here before; the sky gleamed red—it was the dawn.

Only three minutes in Heaven, and a whole night on earth had passed!

Then she caught sight of the storks; and calling to them, she spoke their language, and stork-papa turned his head towards her, listened and approached.

"You speak our language," he said; "what do you wish? Why are you—a strange woman—here?"

"It is I, Helga! Don't you know me? Three minutes ago we spoke together yonder on the veranda."

"You're making a mistake," said the stork; "you have dreamed all that."

"No, no," she said, and reminded him of the Viking's castle and the great sea, of the journey hither.

Then stork-papa blinked his eyes.

"Why, that's an old story that I have heard tell of my great-grandfather's time! There certainly was such a princess here from the land of Denmark, but she disappeared on the evening of her wedding-day many hundred years ago, and never came back. You can read it for yourself on the monument in the garden yonder; swans and storks have been inscribed upon it, and at the top you will find yourself in white marble."

It was so. Helga saw it, understood it, and fell upon her knees.

The sun burst forth in splendor; and as once the frog-covering used to vanish at its rays and the lovely form appear, so now there rose in the baptism of light a form of beauty, brighter and purer than the air—a ray of light that rose up to its Father.

The body crumbled into dust: a faded lotus flower lay where Helga had stood.

"Well, that was a new end to the story," said stork-papa; "I had certainly not expected that. But I am very pleased with it."

"I wonder what the youngsters will say to it," observed stork-mamma.

"Yes, that's the most important after all!" said stork-papa.

The Loveliest Rose in the World

There lived once a queen, who possessed a garden in which one could find at all seasons of the year the choicest flowers from all parts of the globe. But roses were the favorite flowers of this queen, and therefore she had all possible varieties of them, from the common briar with its fragrant leaves to the finest Provence rose; they grew along the walls of the castle, wound themselves round the pillars and window-frames, climbed up into the passages, and covered the ceilings of the halls; there one could see roses of every fragrance, shape, and color.

But sorrow and mourning dwelled in the castle; the queen lay on the sick-bed, and the physicians declared that she must die.

"There is after all one thing that would save her," said the wisest of them. "If you brought the loveliest rose in the world, the one that is the expression of the greatest and purest love, and showed it to her, before her eyes lose their power, she will not die."

Then people came from everywhere and brought with them the finest roses that grew in their gardens; but nobody had the right one; *the* rose that could save her, had to be fetched out of the garden of love; but which of the many roses there was the one that expressed the highest and purest love?

The poets sang of the loveliest rose in the world; every one of them described another as possessing this quality. A message was sent to every loving heart of every class, age, and station in life in the whole country to ask for this wonderful rose.

"Nobody has yet named the flower," said the wise physician; "nobody has pointed out the place where it is thriving in its marvelous splendor. It is not a rose from the coffins of Romeo and Juliet, nor from the grave of Walburg, although these roses will live for ever in song; it is not a rose that sprang forth from the breast of Winkelried pierced by lances, from the sacred blood running out of the breast of the hero dying for his own country, although no death can be sweeter, no rose more red than the blood that flows for such a sacred cause. Nor is it the wonderful, magic flower of knowledge, to the growing of which many a man devotes many days and sleepless nights of his young life in zealous studies."

"I know where it grows," said a happy mother, coming with her tender child to the queen's bed. "I know where one can find the loveliest rose in the world. The rose, which is the expression of the highest and purest love, grows on the rosy cheeks of my sweet child, when refreshed by sleep he opens his eyes and lovingly smiles at me."

"This is a lovely rose, but there is still one much lovelier," said the wise man.

"Indeed," said one of the women, "I have seen one much more beautiful, I am sure no rose more sacred can bloom anywhere; but it was pale, as pale as the petals of the tea-rose. I saw it on the queen's cheeks; she had taken off her royal crown, and in the long sorrowful night she carried her sick child about, crying and kissing it, and praying to God for its life, as only a mother can pray in her anguish."

"Sacred and wonderful is this white rose of mourning in its power, but it is not the right one."

"No," said the pious old bishop, "I have seen the loveliest rose before the table of our Lord. I saw it shining like an angel's face. The young maidens came to the Lord's table to renew the vow made at their baptism, and on their fresh cheeks were pale and red roses; one was among them who looked up to God with all the purity and love of her soul; I think her face then had the expression of the purest and highest love."

"May God bless her," said the wise man, "but nobody has yet named the loveliest rose in the world."

Just then a child came into the room—he was the queen's little son; his eyes were full of tears, and tears glittered on his cheeks; he carried a large book bound in velvet with silver clasps, which was open.

"Mother, dear," cried the boy, "O listen to what I have read!" He sat down near the bedside, and began to read in the book of Him who gave his life on the cross to save mankind, not only those alive but also those yet unborn.

"There is no greater love than this."

The queen's cheeks colored and her eyes were beaming, for she saw before her eyes the loveliest rose rising from the leaves of the book, the rose which grew out of the Savior's blood at the foot of the cross.

"I see it," she said; "he who beholds this rose, the loveliest in the world, will never die."

The Racers

One prize, nay, two prizes, a small one and a great one, had been offered for the greatest swiftness, not in a single race, but for the greatest swiftness all the year round.

"I obtained the first prize," said the hare; "justice must at least be there, when relatives and good friends are members of the jury; but that the snail has received the second prize I think is almost an insult to me."

"No," declared the fence-post, who had been a witness at the distribution of the prizes, "one must also take into consideration industry and goodwill, as several respectable people said, and I can quite understand it. The snail, it is true, required more than half a year to cross the threshold of the door, but he hurt himself, and broke his collar-bone in the haste, for it cannot be denied that it was haste for him. He has only lived for the race, and carried his house on his back!—and all this is very laudable!—and therefore he obtained the second prize!"

"They ought to have considered my merits," said the swallow. "I should think no one has shown more swiftness than I in flying about; and how far I have been!"

"Yes, that is your misfortune!" said the fence-post. "You are too fickle! You always go abroad when it begins to freeze here; you have no love for your own country! You cannot be considered."

"But if I were to lie all through the winter on the heath," replied the swallow, "if I were to sleep all the time, should I then be considered?"

"Bring a certificate from the old marsh woman, stating that you have passed half your time sleeping in your own country; then you will be considered."

"I think I have well deserved the first prize, not the second only," said the snail. "This at least I know, that the hare has only run because he is a coward; each time he thought there was danger in the air. I, on the contrary, have made racing the task of my life, and in carrying it out I have become a cripple! If the first prize was to have been given to any one, I ought to have been that person. But I do not understand showing off and boasting; on the contrary, I despise it."

"I am able to affirm that every prize, at least my voting for it, had been given with just consideration," said the old boundary-post in the wood who was a member of the jury. "I always do everything in due order, with reflection and calculation. Seven times I had formerly the honor to be present and vote at the distribution of prizes, but only to-day I have had my will. At each distribution I have started from a certain something. For the first prize I always started from the first letter in the alphabet, for the second from the last. If you will be kind enough to pay attention, I will explain to you how one begins at the beginning. Commencing with A, H is the eighth letter, there we have the hare; that is why I have awarded the first prize to the hare. S is the eighth letter from the other end, therefore the snail received the second prize. The next time it will be the turn of I for the first and of R for the second prize! Proper order must be in all things! One must have a certain fixed point."

"I should certainly have voted for myself if I had not been on the jury," said the mule, who was also a juryman. "One must not alone consider the swiftness with which one advances, but also every other quality which one possesses—for instance, how much one is able to drag. But this time I did not wish to lay stress on this point, nor on the cleverness of the hare in his flight, or on his trick when he suddenly makes a jump aside in order to lead people into a wrong track, so that they do not know where he has hidden himself. No, there is something else which is of great importance, and which ought to be considered. I mean that which one calls the beautiful. I pay special attention to the beautiful; I looked at the fine well-grown ears of the hare; it is a real pleasure to see how long they are; it seemed to me as if I saw myself in the days of my childhood, and thus I voted for the hare!"

"Pst," said the fly. "I will not make a speech, I will only say something. I beg to say that in reality I have overtaken more than one hare. A little while ago I smashed the hind legs of one of the youngest of them. I sat on a railway engine; I often do that, for thus one can best observe one's own swiftness. A young hare ran a long time in front of the engine, he had no idea that I was upon it. At last he had to give it up and to leave the rails, but then the engine smashed his hind legs, for I sat upon it. The hare remained there, but I continued my journey. Surely that was beating him! But I don't care for the prize."

"To me it seems," said the wild rose, but it did not say so, for it is not in its nature to say anything, although it would have been good if it had been said; "it seems to me that the sunbeam ought to have had the first and also the second prize. The sunbeam traverses in the twinkling of an eye the immense distance from the sun down to us, and it comes with such force that all nature awakes; it possesses such beauty that we roses all blush and breathe forth sweet fragrance! The honorable members of the jury do not seem to have noticed this at all. If I were a sunbeam I should give each of them a sunstroke, but this would make them mad, and they may become so in another way. I say nothing," thought the wild rose. "Peace reigns in the wood! It is beautiful to bloom, to smell sweet, and to live—to live in song and tradition. The sunbeam outlives us all!"

"What is the first prize?" said the earthworm, who had slept all the time and only now arrived.

"Free admission to a cabbage-garden," said the mule. "I have proposed this prize. The hare was to have it, and therefore I as a thinking and active member of the jury, gave reasonable attention to the utility of the prize to him who was to have it; now the hare is provided for. The snail can sit on the fence and lick up moss and sunshine, and in addition to this has been appointed one of the first jurymen for racing. It is really very important to have a professional in the thing which mankind call a committee! I must say I expect a great deal from the future; and we have already made a very good beginning!"

The Happy Family

The largest green leaf here in the country is certainly the burdock leaf: if you put it round your little waist it is like an apron; and if you lay it upon your head when it rains, it is almost as good as an umbrella, for it is extremely large. One burdock never grows alone; where one grows there are several more, making quite a splendid sight. And all this splendor is food for snails. Of these large white snails, which lived on burdock leaves, the grand people in olden times used to have fricasseé made, and when they had eaten it they would say, "Dear me! how nice it is"; for they really believed it tasted excellent. And that is why burdocks were sown.

Now there was an old country-seat, where snails were no longer eaten. They had died out, but the burdocks had not died out. They grew and grew in all the paths, on all the beds; there was no stopping them any more—it was quite a forest of burdocks. Here and there stood an apple or plum tree; otherwise one would never have thought that it was a garden. Everything was burdock, and among it all lived the two last ancient snails.

They did not know themselves how old they were, but they could very well remember that there had been a great many more of them, that they

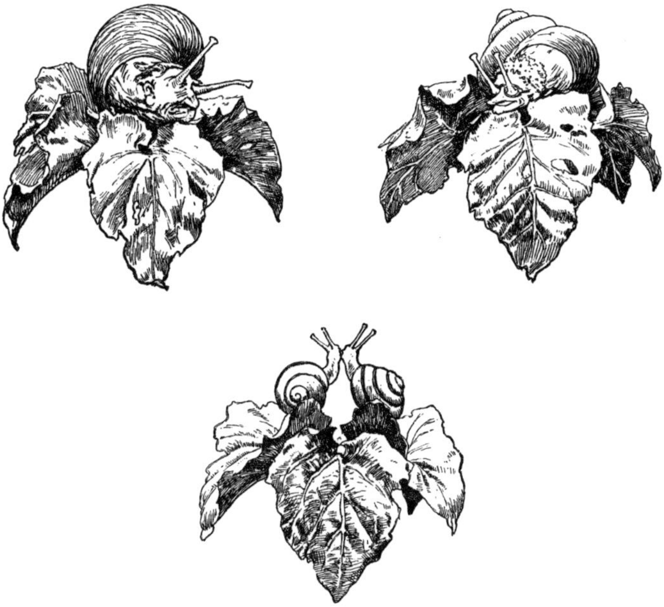

Everything was burdock, and among it all lived the two last ancient snails.

came from a foreign family, and that the forest had been planted for them and theirs. They had never been out of it, but it was known to them that there was something in the world besides, which was called "the Castle"; there one was boiled, became black, and was laid upon a silver dish—but what happened after that they did not know. They could not imagine what it was like to be boiled and laid upon a silver dish, but it was said to be very fine and particularly grand. Neither the cockchafer, nor the toad, nor the earthworm, all of whom they questioned, could give them any information about it; for none of their kind had ever been boiled or laid upon a silver dish.

The old white snails were the grandest in the world: that they knew. The forest was there on their account, and the Castle too, so that they might be boiled and laid upon a silver dish.

They lived very retired and happy, and as they themselves were childless, they had adopted a common little snail, which they brought up as their own child. But the little one would not grow, for it was only a common snail; the old people, however, particularly the mother-snail, declared that it was easy to see how it grew. And she said that if the father could not see that, he was only just to feel the little shell, and on doing so, he found that the mother was right.

One day it rained very hard.

"Listen how it drums upon the burdock-leaves—rum-a-dum-dum, rum-a-dum-dum!" said the father-snail.

"Those are what I call drops!" said the mother-snail. "It is running down the stalk. You see it will get wet here. I'm only glad that we have our good houses, and that the little one has his too. More has really been done for us than for other creatures; it is very plainly to be seen that we are the lords of the world. We have houses from our birth, and the burdock forest was planted for our sakes. I should like to know how far it extends, and what lies outside it."

"There is nothing," said the father-snail, "that could be better than it is with us: I have nothing to wish for."

"Yes!" said the mother. "I should like to be taken up to the Castle, boiled and laid upon a silver dish; that is what happened to all our ancestors, and you may believe that it is something uncommon."

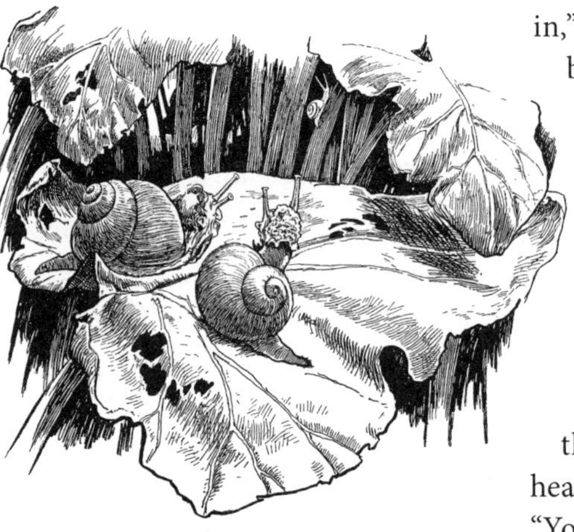

"I'm only glad that we have our good houses, and that the little one has his too."

"The Castle has perhaps fallen in," said the father-snail; "or the burdock forest has grown over it, so that the people cannot come out. But there's not the slightest hurry about it. You're always in too great a hurry, and the little one is beginning to be just the same. Has he not been crawling up that stalk for already three days? It really gives me a headache to look up at him."

"You must not scold him," said the mother-snail. "He crawls along very deliberately: we shall certainly live to have great joy of him, and we old ones have really nothing else to live for. But have you ever thought of where we shall get a wife for him? Don't you think that there are some of our kind still living farther in the burdock forest?

"I daresay there are some black snails there," said the old man; "black snails without houses; but they are too vulgar, and yet they fancy themselves somebody. But we can give the ants the commission; they run to and fro, as though they had some business to do; they will certainly know of a wife for our little one."

"I certainly know the most beautiful one you could have," said one of the ants; but I am afraid the proposal is of no use, for she is a queen."

"That doesn't matter!" said the old people. "Has she a house?"

"She has a castle," answered the ant; "a most beautiful ant-hill with seven hundred passages."

"Many thanks!" said the mother-snail. "Our son shall not go into an ant-hill. If you know of nothing better than that, we will give the white gnats the commission; they fly far around in rain and sunshine; they know the burdock forest in and out."

"We have a wife for him," said the gnats. "A hundred man's paces from here there is a little snail with a house sitting on a gooseberry-bush; she is all alone, and old enough to marry. It is only a hundred man's paces from here."

"Well, let her come to him," said the old people. "He has a burdock forest; she has only a bush."

And so they fetched the little maiden snail. She took eight days in coming; but that was the beauty of it, for by that one could see that she was of the right kind.

Then they had the wedding. Six glow-worms gave as much light as they could; for the rest, things went very quietly, for the old people could not bear much feasting and dissipation. A beautiful speech was, however, made by the mother-snail. The father could not speak; he was too deeply moved. Then they gave the young couple the whole burdock forest as an inheritance, and said what they had always said: that it was the best in the world, and that if they lived honest and upright lives, and multiplied, they and their children would one day be taken to the Castle, boiled black, and laid upon a silver dish. And after this speech had been made, the old people crept back into their houses and never came out again; they slept. The young couple now ruled in the forest and had a numerous progeny. But as they were never boiled and laid upon the silver dish, they concluded that the Castle must have fallen in, and that all the people in the world had died out. And as nobody contradicted them, they knew they were right. The rain fell upon the burdock leaves to play the drum for them, and the sun shone to color the burdock forest for their sake. They were very happy, and the whole family was happy—infinitely happy!

Something

"I want to be something," said the eldest of five brothers; "I want to do something useful in the world. However humble my position may be, if that which I succeed in doing is something good, it will be something. I will make bricks; they are always wanted, and I shall really have done something."

"But that something is not enough," said the second brother; "that which you intend to be is as good as nothing; it is journeyman's work and can be done by a machine. No, then I would rather be a mason—and that is what I have chosen, for it is really something; it is a position. By that one becomes incorporated and a citizen; one has his own banner and his own club-room at the inn. If all goes well I shall employ workmen, I shall become a master, and my wife will be known as the master's wife; that is really something."

"That's nothing at all!" said the third; "that is not any real position, and there are many in a town which are all far above that of a master mechanic. You may be an honest man, but you still belong as a master only to those who are called the common people. No, I know something better than that. I will be an architect, will move in the world of art and speculation, and will rank among the highest in the empire of intellect. I shall certainly have to work my way up from the spade; indeed, I may as well say at once that I shall have to begin as a carpenter's apprentice, and go about as a boy wearing a cap, although I have been used to wearing a silk hat. I shall have to fetch beer and spirits for the common workmen, and they will treat me in an insolent manner. But I shall look upon it all as a mummery and the licence of a masquerade. On the morrow—that is, when I myself am a journeyman—I shall go my own way, and I shall have nothing to do with the others. I shall go to college, learn drawing, and be called an architect. That is something; indeed, it is a great deal. I may attain to some rank, and even have something placed before and after my name, and I shall go on building just as others have built before me. That is a foundation upon which one can rely. And the whole is something."

"But I don't think anything of your something," said the fourth; "I have no wish to sail in another's wake, nor to be a mere copy. I want to be a genius and become greater than all of you together. I will be the creator of a new style, and will bring out the idea of erecting buildings suited to the climate and the materials found in each country, as well as to the nationality of the people and the development of the age, besides building a story more for my own genius."

"But suppose both the climate and the materials of a country are bad?" said the fifth. "That would be a very unfortunate circumstance, for they are of great importance.

"Nationality also may go on extending itself until it becomes affectation, and the development of the age may run wild with you, as youth often does. I clearly foresee that none of you will really become anything, however much you may think so yourselves. But do what you will, I will not be like you. I will keep clear of everything and criticize what you do. There is sure to be something wrong, and not as it should be about everything; that it will be my business to find out and expose. That is something."

This he did, and people said of the fifth brother:

"There is decidedly something about him. He has a good head, but he does nothing."

But it was just that that made him something!

You see, this is only a little story, and yet it will have no end as long as the world exists.

But did nothing further become of these five brothers?

That would have been indeed nothing and not something.

Well, let us hear the tale.

The eldest brother who made bricks soon discovered that to each brick when made there was hanging a little coin, even if only a copper one. But many copper pieces, when laid upon each other, make a silver dollar, and at whatever door you knock with one of these—be it the baker's, the butcher's, or the tailor's—the door flies open and you get what you want. So you see what was hanging to the bricks. Some, it is true, crumbled away or broke in two, but even these could be used.

On the high bank of earth which formed the dyke on the seacoast, a poor woman, named Margaret, wished to build herself a cottage. So all the broken bricks were given her, and a few whole ones too, for the eldest brother had a kind heart, even if he had not risen higher than brick-making. The old woman built her house with her own hands; it is true, it was very small and narrow, and the single window was a little crooked. The door was too low, and the straw roof might have been better thatched; but still it afforded shelter, and from the cottage one could see far out across the sea, which dashed wildly against the dyke. The salt waves sprinkled their foam over the house, which stood there long after he who had made the bricks for it was dead and buried.

The second brother of course knew how to build better than that, for he had been apprenticed to the trade. When he had passed his journeyman's examination, he buckled on his knapsack and started off, singing the journeyman's song of how he should wander abroad and come back as a master.

And that he did too. When he had come back and was a master-builder, he put up one house after the other in the town—a whole street, which when finished looked so well that it was really an ornament to the town. These houses built a house for him in return which was his own property. But how can houses build a house? Ask them, and they would not be able to answer. But people would answer and say, "Certainly, the street has built him his house!" It was small, and the floor was of lime, but when he danced with his bride upon the lime-covered floor, it became bright and polished, and from every stone in the wall there sprang a flower adorning the room as with the most costly tapestry. It was a pretty house, and in it were a happy pair. The banner of his guild waved before it, and the journeyman and apprentices shouted "Hurrah!" Yes, that was something. And then he died, and that was something too.

Now came the architect, the third brother who had first served as an apprentice, had worn a cap and acted as an errand-boy, but had risen from the college to being an architect, and had gained a high-sounding title. Indeed, though the houses in the street had built his brother, the master-builder, a house, the street was named after the architect, and the finest house in the street became his property.

That was something, and he was something—and that with a long title before and behind his name too. His children were called "well-born," and when he died his widow was a lady of rank—that is something! And his name remained up for ever at the corner of the street and lived in everybody's mouth as the name of a street—and that is something too.

Then came the genius, the fourth brother, who wanted to invent something new, something original, and a story on top of that, but he fell down and broke his neck. Still he had a splendid funeral with the banners and band of his guild, while both his obituary in the papers and the street through which the procession passed were strewn with flowers. Three orations were spoken over his grave, the one longer than the other, and that must have pleased him very much, for he was very fond of being talked about. A monument too was erected over his grave, only of one story, it is true, but still that is something.

He, as well as his three other brothers, was now dead; but the youngest, the critic, survived them all, and that was quite correct and as it should be, for in this way he got the last word, and to him it was of great importance to have the last word. What a head he had! people said. At last his hour had come too, and he died and came to the gates of Heaven. Souls always enter in couples, so he was standing there with another soul who also wanted to go in, and it happened to be that of old Dame Margaret who had built the house on the dyke.

"I suppose it is for the sake of contrast that this miserable soul and I must go in together," said the critic. "Well, who are you, my good woman? Do you want to go in too?" he asked.

The old woman curtsied as well as she could; she believed it was Saint Peter himself who was talking to her. "I am a poor old woman without any family; I am old Margaret that lived in the house on the dyke."

"Well, what have you done—what deeds did you perform down there?"

"I have really done nothing at all in the world—nothing that would make these gates open for me. It will be pure mercy if they allow me to slip in."

"In what manner did you leave the world?" he went on to ask, just for the sake of saying something, as he was getting tired of standing there waiting.

"Well, I really don't know how I left it. I was ill and miserable during the last few years, and I suppose I could not stand creeping out of bed and coming suddenly into frost and cold. It was a hard winter, but now I have got through it. There were a few calm days, but very cold, as your honor knows; the ice-mantle lay upon the water as far out as one could see. All the townspeople walked upon it, and I think they said there was skating and dancing; there was certainly music and feasting too, for I heard the sounds in my humble cottage where I lay. And then towards evening the moon rose, but not in its full splendor; I looked from my bed out across the wide sea, and there, just where the sky and the sea met, I saw a strange white cloud rising. I lay gazing at the cloud, and I also saw the small black spot in the middle of it growing larger and larger, and then I knew what it meant, for I am old and experienced. Although that sign is not often seen, I knew it and horror crept over me. I had seen the same thing twice before in my life, and knew that there would be a terrible storm with a spring tide, which would swallow up those poor people who were now drinking, dancing, and making merry. Young and old, the whole town were there; who would warn them if no one noticed the sign, or knew what it meant as I did? I got quite alarmed, and felt such life within me as I had not felt for a long time. Out of the bed I came and got to the window; I could not drag myself any farther from weakness, but I managed to open the windows, and 1 saw the people outside running and dancing on the ice. I also saw the beautiful flags waving in the wind, and I heard the boys shouting "hurrah" and young men and girls singing. It was very merry everywhere, but alas! the white cloud with the black spot. I shouted as loud as I could, but no one heard me; I was too far off from them. Soon the storm must burst, the ice break, and all who were on it be irretrievably lost. They could not hear me, and I could not get out to them; oh! if I could only get them to the shore. Then Heaven sent me the idea of setting light to my bed; it would be better to burn the house down than that so many people should perish miserably. I succeeded in striking a light and the red flames leapt up just as I was fortunate enough to escape by the door. But I remained lying before the threshold and could get no farther. The flames darted out after me, burst out of the window, and leapt up on high through the roof. All the people on the ice saw them, and came running up as fast as they could to help a poor old woman who, as they thought, was being burnt alive. There was not one but ran; I heard them coming, but I also felt a sudden rush of wind and I heard a sound like the roar of heavy cannons. The spring-tide raised the ice covering which split up into a thousand pieces; but the people had reached the dyke where the sparks were flying around me—I had saved them all! But I suppose I could not stand the cold nor the fright, and so now I am come here to the gates of Heaven. They do say that they are sometimes opened even for such a poor old creature as I am, and now I have no longer a house down on the dyke either—but I suppose that fact will not gain me admission here."

Then the gates of Heaven opened, and the angel led the old woman in. Just outside she had dropped one straw—one of the straws of her bed which she had set on fire to save so many lives. It had been changed into the purest gold, and into such gold too as constantly grew up into the finest flowers and leaves.

"Do you see? this is what the old woman brought," said the angel. "What do you bring? Oh yes, I know that you did nothing, that you did not even make a brick. If you could only go back now and manage to produce as much as that! Probably the brick would not be worth much when you had made it, but still, made with a good will, it would be at least something. Anyhow you can't go back, and I can't do anything for you."

Then the poor soul, the old dame who had lived in the house on the dyke, pleaded for him. "His brother gave me the bricks and broken pieces out of which I constructed my humble house, and that was a good deal for poor me. Now, could not all the pieces and the whole bricks be as good as one for him? It is an act of mercy. He has great need of it now, and here is the very fountain of mercy."

"Your brother, he whom you used to call the humblest of you all," said the angel, "he whose honest labor seemed to you the lowliest, sends you this heavenly gift. You shall not be turned away. You shall be permitted to stand outside here and reflect, and to try and better your life on earth; but you shall not enter before you have performed one good deed—something."

"I could have expressed that better," thought the critic, but he did not say it aloud, and that for him was indeed something.

At the Uttermost Parts of the Sea

Large ships were sent high up to the North Pole, in order to find out the uttermost limits, the last sea-shores, and to try how far it was possible for men to advance up there.

They were already sailing for a long, long time, through fogs and ice, and their crews had to bear many hardships; at last the winter had come and the sun had disappeared from those regions; they knew there would now be a night many, many weeks long. As far as the eye could reach it was one single ice block; the ships were anchored to it, the snow was piled up in large heaps, and huts were made of it in the shape of beehives—some as large as the old barrows, some, on the other hand, only big enough to accommodate two or four men. It was, however, not quite dark; the northern lights were shining red and blue, it was a lasting, magnificent firework. The snow glittered and sparkled, so that the night was one single long twilight. When it was brightest the natives came in troops, wonderful to look at in their hairy, rough fur clothing; they came in sleighs, consisting of ice-blocks, and brought hides and skins in large bundles with them; thus the snow huts received warm foot-rugs, for the skins were either used as such or as counterpanes. The sailors made up their beds under the snow roof; while it froze outside till it creaked, very much harder than it freezes with us in the winter. We were still in the latter part of autumn, and they thought of this up there; they remembered the yellow leaves on the trees in their native country. The clock pointed out that it was evening and time for going to bed, and in one of the snow huts two were already stretching themselves out to rest. The youngest of them had with him his best and dearest treasure from home, the Bible which his grandmother had given him on parting. Every night the Holy Scriptures were resting under his head, and he knew from his childhood what was written in it; he read it daily when he was lying on his couch, and often those holy words came into his mind which run: "If I take the wings of the morning, and fly to the uttermost parts of the sea, even there Thou art with me, and Thy right hand shall uphold me!" Under the influence of the eternal Word and of true belief he closed his eyes, and sleep overcame him, and a dream which was a revelation of the Holy Ghost in God.

His soul was alive and active while the body was resting; he felt this life, and it seemed to him as if dear, well-known airs were sounding and gentle summer breezes floating over him, and from his resting-place he saw it shine over him as if it was penetrating from outside through the snow-crust. He raised his head, but the beaming brightness was, however, not the reflection of the snow-crust, but the great wings of an angel, into whose gentle sweet face he gazed up. As if from the cup of a lily the angel rose from the leaves of the Bible, spreading his arms wide, and the walls of the snow-hut sank into the ground as if they were a light, airy veil of fog; the green meadows and hills of home lay around him, with the red-brown woods, in the still sunshine of a beautiful autumn day; the stork's nest was empty, but some apples still hung on the wild crab-tree, although it was already leafless; the red hips glittered, and a starling was whistling in the green cage over the window of a peasant's cottage, his home. The starling was whistling tunes that it had learned, and the grandmother was hanging green leaves on its cage, just as her grandson had always done. The daughter of the village blacksmith, young and beautiful, was standing at the well, drawing water, and nodded to the grandmother, who nodded to her and showed her a letter which had come from far, far away. The letter had come this very morning from the cold region near the North Pole, where the grandson was in the hand of God. They smiled and cried; and he, up there, in the ice and snow, under the wings of the angel, he too smiled and cried in his spirit with them, for he saw and heard them.

The letter was read aloud, and the words from the Holy Scripture: "At the uttermost parts of the sea Thy right hand shall uphold me." Round him sounded a beautiful psalm, and the angel let his wings sink down like a veil over the sleeping man. The vision had disappeared, it was dark in the snow-hut, but the Bible rested under his head, faith and hope dwelled in his heart. God was with him, and he carried his home in his heart—"at the uttermost parts of the sea."

The Tinder-Box

A soldier was marching along the high road—left, right! left, right! He had a knapsack on his back and a sword at his side. He was returning from war, and now on his way home.

When he had gone some distance he met an old witch. She was dreadfully ugly, her underlip was hanging down upon her breast.

"Good evening, soldier," she said; "what a fine sword you have, and what a big knapsack! You are a true soldier, and now you shall have as much money as ever you wish for." "Thank you, old witch," replied the soldier. "Do you see yonder large tree?" asked the witch, pointing out a tree which stood not far from them. "It is hollow inside. You must climb right up to its summit, when you will see a hole; through this hole you can let yourself down and get deep into the tree. I shall tie a rope round your waist, so that I can pull you up when you call out to me."

"What shall I do down in the tree?" asked the soldier.

"Fetch money," said the witch. "You must know that you will find a spacious hall at the bottom of the tree; it is quite light, for there are no less than three hundred lamps burning down there. You will then see three doors; you can open them—the keys are in the locks. If you enter the first room you will find in the middle of the floor a large wooden chest and a dog sitting on it, which has a pair of eyes as large as teacups. Never mind him! I shall give you my blue checked apron; you can spread it on the floor; then go quickly, seize the dog and place him on my apron, open the chest, and take out of it as many coins as you like. They are of copper; if you prefer to have silver, you must go into the second room. There you will see a dog having eyes as large as mill-wheels. But do not be afraid; put him on my apron and take as much money as you like. If, however, you wish to have gold, you can have that too, and as much as you can carry, if you go into the third room. The dog which sits on the chest in this room has eyes as large as a church-steeple. He is a very wicked dog, I can assure you, but you need not fear him. If you put him on my apron he will not hurt you, and you can take as much gold as you like out of the chest."

"That is not at all bad," said the soldier. "But what do you expect me to give you in return, for surely you will not do all this for nothing?"

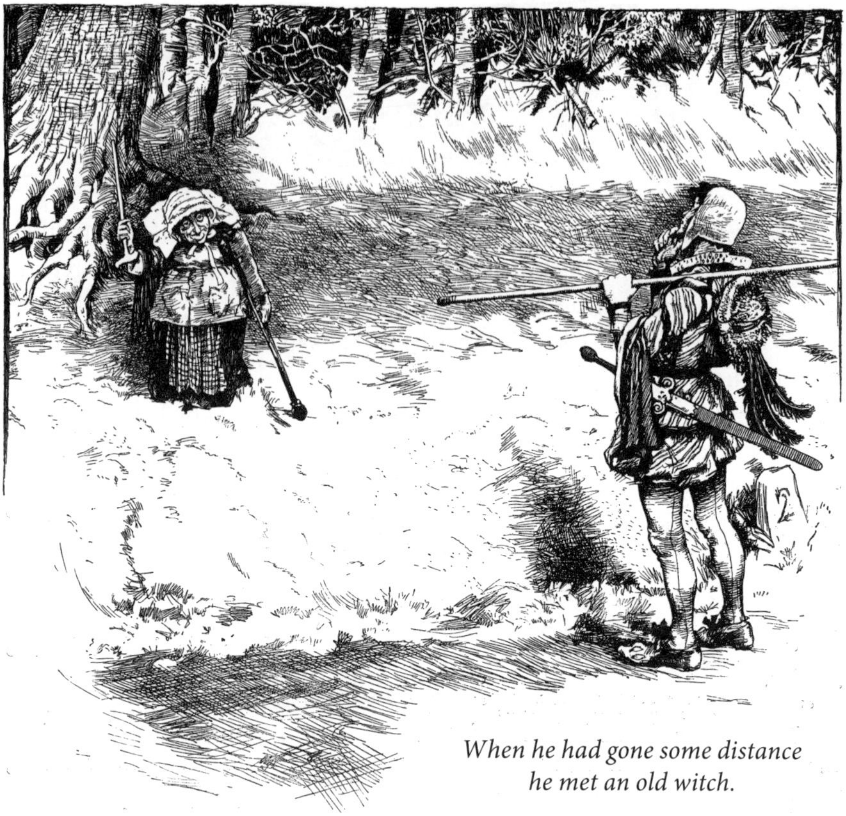

When he had gone some distance he met an old witch.

"Yes," replied the witch. "I shall not ask you for a single shilling. I only want you to bring up for me an old tinder-box which my grandmother forgot when she was down there for the last time."

"Well, then, tie the rope round my waist," said the soldier.

"Here it is," said the witch, "and here is also my blue checked apron."

The soldier then climbed up the tree, descended inside it by the rope, and arrived, as the witch had told him, in the great hall where the three hundred lamps were burning.

He opened the first door. Ugh! there the dog with the eyes as large as teacups was staring at him.

"You are a fine fellow," said the soldier, placed him on the apron of the witch, and took as many coppers as his pockets would hold. Then he locked the chest, put the dog upon it, and went to the second room. Really, there was the dog with the eyes as large as mill-wheels.

"You had better not look at me so hard," said the soldier, "you might strain your eyes," and put the dog on the witch's apron. When he saw the silver in the chest, he threw all the copper he had taken away, and filled his pockets and knapsack with silver. Then he went into the third room. That was dreadful to look at. The dog there had really two eyes as large as church-steeples, which turned in his head like wheels.

"Good evening," said the soldier, and touched his cap, for he had never in his life seen a dog like this. When he had looked at him more closely, he thought "that is enough," lifted him down on the floor, and opened the chest. Good heavens! what a lot of gold there was! There was enough gold to buy the whole town, and all the sweets from all the sweetmeat stalls, in addition to all the tin soldiers, whips, and rocking-horses in the whole world. The soldier quickly threw away all the silver with which he had filled his pockets and knapsack, and replaced it by gold. He filled even his cap and his boots with gold, so that he could scarcely walk. Now he was rich.

He placed the dog again on the chest, shut the door, and called up through the tree.

"Now pull me up, old witch."

"Have you found the tinder-box?" asked the old witch.

"Upon my soul," said the soldier, "that I should really have forgotten." He returned and fetched it. The old witch pulled him up, and soon he was again in the high road, his pockets, boots, knapsack, and cap filled with gold.

"What will you do with the tinder-box?" asked the soldier.

"Do not trouble your mind about that," said the witch. "You have received your reward. Give me the tinder-box."

"Certainly not," replied the soldier. "Tell me quickly what you are going to do with it, or I shall draw my sword and cut your head off."

"No," said the witch.

Then the soldier cut her head off, so that she lay dead on the ground. He tied all his gold up in her apron, took it like a bundle on his shoulders, put the tinder-box into his pocket, and went straight to the nearest town.

It was a very pleasant town. He put up in the best inn, asked for the best rooms and for his favorite dishes; for he was rich, having so much gold.

The servant, who had to clean his boots, thought they were rather shabby old things for such a rich gentleman, for he had not yet bought a new pair. On the next day, however, he purchased decent boots and fine clothes. Thus the poor soldier had become a gentleman, and people talked to him about all the sights of their town, about the king, and about the beautiful princess, his daughter.

The old witch pulled him up, and soon he was again in the high road, his pockets, boots, knapsack, and cap filled with gold.

"Where can one see her?" inquired the soldier.

"Nobody can see her," they all said, "she lives in a strong copper castle with many towers, surrounded by high walls. Nobody but the king himself can pass in and out, for there has been a prophecy that she would marry a private soldier, and the king will prevent that."

"I should very much like to see her," thought the soldier, but he could by no means obtain permission to do so.

He led a merry life, went to the theater, drove in the Royal Gardens, and gave largely to the poor—that was very good of him; he remembered well of former days what it means to have not a single penny. He was now rich, had fine clothes, and soon found many friends, who all told him that he was a splendid fellow and a true gentleman; all this pleased the soldier greatly. As, however, he spent every day a good deal of money, without gaining anything, he had soon nothing left but two shillings; therefore he had to give up the elegant rooms which he occupied and live on the top of the house in a little garret; he had to black his own boots, and to mend them with a darning needle. None of his former friends came to see him, he lived so high up.

On one dark evening he could not even buy a candle. Then he remembered that there was a piece of candle in the tinder-box which he had fetched out of the hollow tree with the assistance of the witch. He took up the tinder-box and the little end of the candle, and was going to strike a light, when suddenly the door flew open, and the dog with a pair of eyes as large as tea cups, which he had seen under the tree, made his appearance and asked: "Your lordship's commands?"

"What is this?" asked the soldier. "That is a capital tinder-box if I can get through it what I wish for. Get me some money," he said to the dog. The dog was gone like lightning; but in a moment he returned again, holding a large bag of coppers in his mouth.

Thus the soldier learned what a wonderful tinder-box he had. If he struck once, the dog from the chest containing the copper appeared; two strokes made the dog who watched the silver come; and if he struck three times, the dog who sat on the chest containing the gold made his appearance. Now the soldier moved back into the elegant rooms, and appeared again well-dressed. All his former friends recognized him, and thought much of him.

One day the soldier thought: "It is very strange that nobody is allowed to see the princess. All agree in saying that she is so beautiful; but what is the use of her beauty if she is compelled to remain for ever in the big copper castle with its many towers? Is there no chance at all to see her?"

At this moment he thought of his tinder-box. He struck a light, and there the dog with a pair of eyes as large as teacups came.

"Although it is midnight," said the soldier, "I should very much like to see the princess for a moment."

No sooner had he pronounced his wish than the dog ran away, and returned in a few seconds with the princess. She was lying fast asleep on the dog's back; she was so lovely to look at, that nobody could help seeing at once that she was a princess. The soldier could not abstain from kissing her, for he was a true soldier.

Then the dog carried the princess back; but on the next morning, when she was at tea with the king and the queen, she told them that she had had a very strange dream of a dog and a soldier in the night; she had been riding on the dog and the soldier had kissed her.

"That would be a fine tale," said the queen.

Next night one of the Court ladies had to watch by the bed of the princess to see whether it was really a dream, or what else it could be.

The soldier felt a great longing to see the princess again, so he called the dog next night once more, who fetched her, running with her as fast as he could. But the old lady put on water-boots and followed him. When she saw that the dog disappeared with the princess in a large house, she took a piece of chalk and made a large white cross on the door, thinking that she would be able to recognize the house again. Then she returned home and went to bed.

The dog soon brought the princess back; and when he saw the white cross on the house where the soldier lived, he made white crosses on all the doors in the town, that the Court lady might not be able to find it.

Early on the next morning, the king, the queen, the lady, and many officers of the Court came to see where the princess had been.

"There is the house," said the king when he saw the first door with a white cross.

"No; there it is, my dear husband," said the queen, on seeing a second door with a white cross.

"But there is one, and there is another," said all, and wherever they looked they saw white crosses on the doors. Then they understood that it would be useless to search any more.

The queen was a very clever woman; she could do more than merely ride in a carriage. She took her large golden scissors, cut a piece of silk in squares and made a nice little bag of it. This bag she filled with ground buckwheat, then tied it to the princess's back, and cut a little hole into it, so that the buckwheat could run out all along the road the princess was taken.

At night the dog came again, took the princess on his back, and ran with her to the soldier, who was deeply in love with her, and wished nothing more than to be a prince, that he might marry her.

The dog did not notice how the buckwheat strewed all the way from the castle up to the soldier's house, where he climbed up the wall to enter the soldier's window. Next morning the king and the queen knew where their daughter had been taken to: the soldier was at once arrested and thrown into prison.

There he sat, and found it awfully dark and dull. He was told, "To-morrow you will be hanged." All this was very unpleasant, and the worst was that he had left his tinder-box at the inn.

On the next morning he could see through the iron bars how the people were hurrying out of the town in order to witness his execution. He heard the noise of the drums and saw the soldiers march past. In the crowd he noticed a shoemaker's apprentice with a leather apron and wooden slippers on, who ran so fast that one of his slippers came off and flew against the wall, quite close to the window at which the soldier sat behind the iron bars.

"You need not hurry so, boy," cried the soldier, "they can't do anything until I arrive. If you would run to the place where I used to live and fetch me my tinder-box, I will give you four shillings."

The boy, who was very anxious to have so much money, fetched the tinder-box and handed it to the soldier. Now, let us see what happened.

Outside the town they had erected a high gibbet; soldiers and many thousands of people stood around it. The king and the queen were sitting on a magnificent throne opposite the judges and counsel.

The soldier was already standing on the top of the ladder, and they were just going to put the rope round his neck, when he said he knew that it was a custom to grant a last request to a poor criminal before he suffered death, and he should very much like to smoke a pipe—the last he would ever have a chance of smoking in this world.

The king would not refuse this favor, and the soldier took up his tinder-box and struck—"One, two, three." And lo! there suddenly appeared the three dogs; the first with eyes as large as teacups, the second with eyes as large as mill-wheels, and the third having eyes as large as church-steeples.

"Help me now, that they cannot hang me," said the soldier.

Then the dogs rushed at the judges and the counsel, took the one up by the legs, the other by the nose, and threw them high up into the air, so that they fell down and were smashed to pieces.

"Leave me alone," said the king; but the largest of the dogs seized both him and the queen and threw them up after the others.

When the soldiers and all the people saw that, they had great fear, and cried: "Good soldier, you shall become our king and marry the beautiful princess."

They seated the soldier in the king's carriage, and the three dogs danced in front of it and cried "Hurrah!" The boys whistled on their fingers, and the soldiers presented arms. The princess came out of the copper castle and became queen, and she liked it very much.

The wedding festivities lasted eight days; the dogs sat at table and opened their eyes wide.

They seated the soldier in the king's carriage, and the three dogs danced in front of it and cried "Hurrah!"

There Is a Difference

It was in the month of May. The wind still blew cold, but bushes and trees, field and meadow, told that spring had come. Everything was covered with flowers, even to the blossoming hedges. Here spring was looking after his own business, and preaching down from a little apple-tree, from which hung a single branch, fresh and blooming, covered with delicate pink blossoms that were just about to open. The branch knew very well how beautiful it was, for that knowledge lies in the leaf as well as in the flesh; it was therefore not surprised when a nobleman's carriage stopped before it, and the young countess said that an apple-branch was the loveliest thing that could be seen, and that it was spring itself in its most beautiful form. The branch was broken off, and taking it in her delicate hand, she held it in the shadow of her silk parasol; then they drove to the castle, in which there were lofty halls and splendid rooms. Pure white curtains fluttered in front of the open windows, and beautiful flowers stood in shining transparent vases; in one of these, which looked as if it had been made of fresh-fallen snow, the apple-branch was placed between fresh light beech twigs. It was a pleasure to look at it.

Then the branch became proud, and that is quite human. People of different kinds came through the rooms, and according to their rank they were allowed to express their admiration. Some said nothing, others again too much, and the apple-branch soon understood that there was a difference between the different things that grew.

"Some are for ornament, and some for giving nourishment; there are even some one could do without altogether," thought the apple-branch; and as it stood just before the open window, whence it could see into the garden and across the field, it had flowers and plants enough to look at and think about, for there were rich ones and poor ones—some most miserable things too.

"Poor despised herbs!" said the apple-branch, "there is indeed a difference! How unhappy they must be; if that kind can feel like I and my equals do, there is indeed a difference, but that must be so, else they would all be alike."

And the apple-branch looked with a sort of pity upon a particular kind of flower which grew in great numbers in the fields and ditches. No one made nosegays of them, they were much too common; indeed they could be found even between the paving-stones. They sprang up like the worst kind of weeds, and had the ugly name of "dog-flower" or "dandelion."

"Poor despised plant," said the apple-branch. "It is not your fault that you were given the ugly name that you bear. But it is with plants as with men, there must be a difference!"

"Difference!" said the sunbeam, kissing the blossoming apple-branch, but also kissing the yellow dog-flower out in the fields; all the brothers of the sunbeam kissed them, the poor flowers as well as the rich.

The apple-branch had never thought about Heaven's boundless love for all that lives and is sustained by it, nor had it thought how many beautiful and good things may lie hidden though not forgotten; but that too was human.

The sunbeam, the ray of light, knew this better.

"You don't see far, you don't see clearly. What is the despised plant that you were just pitying?"

"The dog-flower!" said the apple-branch. "It is never made into a nosegay, and is trodden under foot; there are too many of them, and when they run to seed they fly like bits of wool along the roads and hang on to people's clothes. It is only a weed, but there must be weeds too. I am really very thankful that I was not made one of those flowers."

Across the fields there came a troop of children. The youngest of them was still so small that he was carried by the others. When he was placed among the yellow flowers in the ditch, he laughed aloud for joy, kicked his little legs about, and rolling over and over, plucked only the yellow flowers, kissing them in his sweet innocence. The elder children pulled the flowers from off the tall stalks, and bending the stalks round, stuck the ends into one another, so that, link by link, a chain was made. First one for their neck, then one to hang round their shoulders and waist, and then one to make fast on their breast and head—quite a wealth of green links and chains. But the eldest children of all carefully took the full-blown flowers by the stalks on which hung the feathery crown formed by the seeds; this loose airy wool-flower, which is a real work of art, looking as though made of the finest feathers, fleece, or down, they held to their mouths and tried to blow off with one breath. Their grandmother had told them that whoever could do that would get new clothes before the year was out. On such occasions the despised flower became quite a prophet.

"Do you see?" said the sunbeam. "Do you see its beauty? Do you see its power?"

"Yes, over children," answered the apple-branch.

An old woman then came into the field and, digging with the blunt blade of a knife round the roots of the plant, pulled them up. With some of them she was going to make tea for herself, and for the others she would get some money by selling them to the chemist.

"But beauty is something higher," said the apple-branch. "Only the chosen ones enter the kingdom of the beautiful. There is a difference between plants, just as there is a difference between human beings."

The sunbeam spoke of the boundless love of Heaven as revealed in creation, of all living beings, and of the equal distribution of all things in time and eternity.

"Yes, but that is only your opinion," said the apple-branch.

Some people now came into the room, and the beautiful young countess appeared—she who had placed the apple-branch in the transparent vase, where it was bathed in sunlight. She was carrying a flower, or whatever else the object might be that she had wrapped in three or four large leaves; these served as a shield, so that neither a draft nor gust of wind should injure it, and it was carried with such care as had never been bestowed upon an apple-branch. The large leaves were carefully removed, and the delicate feathery seed-crown of the despised yellow dandelion appeared. It was this that she had plucked so carefully, and carried with every precaution, so that not one of the loose, delicate feathery darts which make up its downy form should be blown away. She had brought it home uninjured, and admired its beautiful shape, its airy brightness, its own peculiar construction, and its beauty which was to be borne away by the wind.

"Do see how wonderfully sweet Heaven has formed it," she said. "I will paint it together with the apple-branch, which all think so extremely beautiful; but this poor flower has received quite as much from kind Providence in another way. However different they may be, they are still both children in the kingdom of beauty."

The sunbeam kissed the lowly flower and the blossoming apple-branch, the leaves of which seemed to blush at the act.

The Angel

Every time a good child dies, one of God's angels comes down to the earth, takes the dead child in his arms, spreads out his large white wings, flies over all the places the child has loved, and plucks a handful of flowers, which he takes up to God, that they may grow up there far more beautiful than on earth. God presses all the flowers to His heart, but the flower that pleases Him best He kisses, and then it receives a voice and can join in the great song of eternal bliss!

All this one of God's angels related while he carried a dead child up to Heaven, and the child heard it as if in a dream; and then they passed over the places at home where the little one had played, and they came through gardens with beautiful flowers.

"Which of them shall we now take with us and plant in Heaven?" asked the angel. There stood a slender, magnificent rose-tree, but a wicked hand had broken its stem, so that all its branches, full of large, half-open buds, hung round it withered.

"The poor rose-tree!" said the child. "Take it, that it may bloom up in Heaven!" And the angel took it and kissed the child, and the little one half opened his eyes. They plucked some of the gorgeous, rich colored flowers, but they also took the despised dandelion and the wild heartsease with them.

"Now we have flowers!" said the child, and the angel nodded, but he did not yet fly up to Heaven. It was night, and all was very quiet; but they still remained in the large town and hovered about in one of the narrow lanes, where heaps of straw, ashes, and dust were lying; it had been removal-day. There were fragments of plates, pieces of plaster-of-Paris, rags, and old hats—all things that did not look well. The angel pointed in this confusion to some fragments of a broken flower-pot, and to a lump of mold which was held together by the roots of a large withered field flower, which was good for nothing and had been thrown out in the street.

"This one we will take with us," said the angel; "I shall tell you why as we fly on."

"Down below in the narrow lane, in the low basement, lived a poor sick boy; from his infancy he had always been bedridden; at his best he could walk up and down the little room once or twice on crutches—that was all. On some days in the summer the sunbeams would penetrate as far as the floor of the basement for half an hour; and when the poor boy sat there and let the warm sun shine upon him, and saw the red blood in his delicate fingers, which he held before his face, then they said, "To-day he has been out!" He only knew the wood with its beautiful spring green from the fact that the neighbor's son had brought him the first beech branch; he held it over his head, and dreamed he was under the beeches where the sun shone and the birds sang. One day in spring the neighbor's boy also brought him some field flowers, and by chance there was one among them with a root; it was planted in a flower-pot and placed on the window-sill close to the bed. The flower had been planted by a lucky hand; it grew, threw out new shoots, and carried flowers every year. It became the sick boy's splendid flower garden, his little treasure here below. He watered it and nursed it, and took care that it received every sunbeam to the very last which glided through the low window; the flower itself grew into his dreams, for it bloomed for him, breathed forth fragrance and gladdened his eyes; towards it he turned in death, when the Lord called him. He has now been a year in Heaven; and the flower stood for a year on the window-sill; it was forgotten and withered, and therefore, on removing, it was thrown out into the street with the rubbish. And this is the flower, the poor withered flower that we have taken into our bunch; for this flower has caused more joy than the most beautiful flower in a queen's garden!"

"But how do you know all this?" asked the child which the angel was carrying up to Heaven.

"I know it," said the angel, "for I myself was the little sick boy who walked on crutches! I know my flower well!"

The child opened his eyes wide, and looked up into the angel's beautiful, joyous face, and at the same moment they were in God's kingdom, where there was peace and happiness. God pressed the dead child to His heart, and he received wings like the other angel, and flew about hand in hand with him. And God pressed all the flowers to His heart, but He kissed the poor withered field flower, and then it received a voice and sang with all the angels hovering round—some near, others farther away in large circles, farther and farther away into the infinite, but all equally happy. And all were singing, great and small, the good, blessed child and the poor field flower which had lain there withered, thrown among the dust, in the rubbish of removal day in the narrow dark lane.

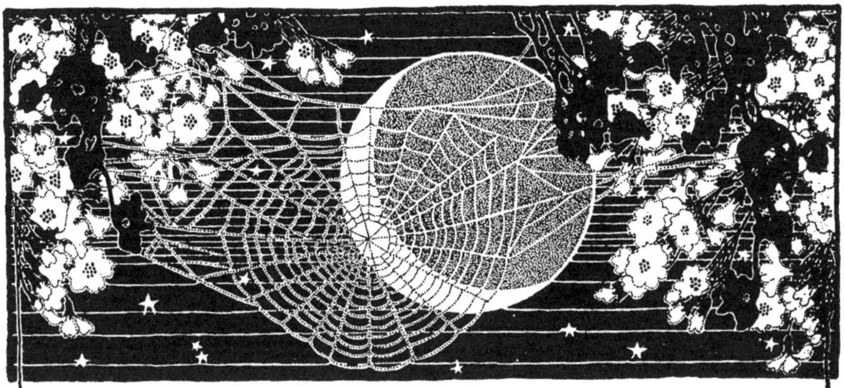

"What the Moon Saw"

(A Selection)

Whenever I feel most deeply impressed by something, strange to say, both my hands and my tongue seem tired. I am unable to give a correct description or an accurate picture of what fills my mind, although I am a painter; this is what my eye tells me, and my friends who have seen my sketches and designs are of the same opinion.

I am a poor lad, and live in one of the narrowest lanes in the town; I have plenty of light, for my room is at the top of the house, and from the window I have a wide outlook over the roofs of the neighboring houses. The first few days of my stay in town I felt depressed and lonely. In the place of the wood and green hills, which I was accustomed to see, I was surrounded by a wood of chimney-pots. I had no friends, nor did I see any face that was familiar to me.

When I was standing one evening at the window, very low-spirited, I opened it and looked out. What a joyful surprise awaited me! There was at last a face well known to me, the round, kindly face of a good friend whom I had known at home. It was the moon who was looking upon me. The dear old moon looked exactly as she had always done, when I used to see her shining through the willow-trees on the moor. I kissed my hand to her again and again, as she shone in at my window, and she promised me that every evening when she came out she would look in upon me for a short time. She has faithfully kept her promise. It is a great pity that each time she can only stay for such a little while, but whenever she comes she tells me something she has seen on the preceding night or on that very evening.

"Paint the scenes which I shall describe to you," she said to me, "and you will soon have a very fine collection of pictures." I have acted upon her advice for many a night. I have such a number of sketches that I could make up another "Thousand and One Nights," but this would be too much. Those I give here are arranged in the order as they were described to me. Some great painter, poet, or musician may do better with them if he likes; all I have done is to make some rough sketches, adding now and then some of my own ideas. The moon did not come out every evening, for sometimes a cloud hid her face from me.

First Evening

"Last night," I am quoting the moon's own words. "I was gliding over the cloudless sky of India. My face was reflected by the waters of the river Ganges, while I endeavored to penetrate the thick leafy branches of the banana trees, which formed arches, like the shell of a tortoise. A Hindoo girl, as lightfooted as a gazelle and as beautiful as Eve, came out of the thicket. Although she looked much like an apparition, her shadow stood sharply out from the surrounding objects. I could read in her face why she had come thither. In spite of the thorny creepers, which tore her sandals, she advanced very rapidly. The deer that had gone down to the river to drink, started up terrified, for the girl carried a burning lamp in her hand. I could see the blood through her delicate fingers, as she screened the wavering flame with them. She came down to the river, set her lamp on the water, and allowed it to drift away. The flame flickered, and was on the point of being extinguished every moment, but yet it continued to burn, while the girl's dark shining eyes, under their long silken lashes, followed it with trembling anxiety. If the lamp continued to burn as long as she could see it, her sweetheart was alive; but if it was extinguished before, then he was dead. The lamp continued to burn, and she knelt down and prayed, not minding a speckled snake which lay by her side in the grass. She only thought of Bramah and her sweetheart.

"He lives," she exclaimed with joy, "he lives," and the mountains echoed back to her, 'he lives.' "

Second Evening

"Last night," said the moon to me, "I was shining upon a small courtyard enclosed by houses on all sides. There was a hen with eleven chickens sitting there, and a nice little girl was running and playing around them. The hen in her fright clucked and covered her little brood with her wings. The little girl's father then came out and scolded her; I passed away, and forgot all about the matter. This evening, however, just a few minutes ago, I happened to look down into the same courtyard. While everything was perfectly quiet, I saw the little girl come out of the house and steal gently to the fowl-house; she unbolted the door, and slipped in to the hens and chickens; they cried out, fluttered down from their perches, and ran about frightened, the little girl following them. Looking in through a peephole in the wall of the fowl-house I saw all this; I was very angry at the naughty child, and was glad to see her father come out and scold her more than he had done the day before, seizing her by the arm. She cast her blue eyes, which were filled with tears, upon the ground.

"'What are you doing here?' he asked her.

"'I wanted to kiss the hen and beg her pardon for frightening her yesterday,' she said, crying bitterly, 'but I was afraid to tell you about it.'"

"The father gave the innocent child a kiss on the forehead, and I kissed her on the mouth and eyes."

Third Evening

"Yesterday," narrated the moon, "I was looking down upon gay and noisy Paris. I peeped into one of the many apartments of the Tuileries. An old woman, to judge from her poor apparel, belonging to the working class, was shown by one of the lower officials into the great lonely throne room—for this she was anxious to see, nay, she had made up her mind to see it. In order to realize her wish she had to make various sacrifices and say many an entreating word. She folded her thin hands, and her features expressed as much reverence as if she were entering a church."

"'Here it happened,' she said, 'in this very place,' approaching the throne from which hung the rich velvet fringed with gold lace. Then she knelt down and kissed the purple carpet. I think I saw tears in her eyes.

"'But,' said the official, 'it was not this same velvet,' and smiled.

"'Maybe, but it was this very place, and it must have looked just like this.'

"'It looked like this, and yet there was a great difference,' observed the man; 'the windows were broken, the doors were wrenched off their hinges, and the floor was covered with blood.'

"'Say what you like, but my grandson died upon the throne of France. Yes, he died,' repeated the old woman, with a trembling voice.

"I did not hear them say another word, and they soon left the room. The shadows grew longer, the light faded from the sky, and my rays lit up the throne of France, with its drapery of rich velvet.

"Who do you think this poor woman was? Listen—I will tell you.

"During the Revolution of July, on the night of one of the most eventful days, when every house was a fortress and every window a breastwork, the people stormed the Tuileries. There were even women and children in the crowd, which rushed into the halls and apartments of the palace. Among the rebels was a poor youth in a ragged blouse. Wounded to death by several bayonet thrusts, he sank down in the throne-room. They placed him upon the throne of France, and bound up his wounds with the costly velvet; his blood ran down upon the royal purple. That was a scene! The magnificent room filled with the fighting crowd. A tattered flag was lying on the floor, while the tricolor was floating above the bayonets. The unfortunate youth lay on the throne; his face was pale, his eyes were looking towards the sky, his limbs were twisting in agony. His breast was bare, but his poor coarse garments were partly covered with the rich velvet embroidered with fleur-de-lis. It had been predicted at the boy's cradle that he would die on the throne of France. This prediction had led the mother to imagine that he would one day be a second Napoleon.

"My rays have kissed the wreaths on his grave, and last night they kissed his old grandmother's forehead, while she saw in her dream the picture that you may draw—the poor boy on the throne of France."

Fourth Evening

It was dark; heavy clouds floated over the sky, and the moon did not come out. I stood in my little room looking up at the sky where she ought to have appeared, and feeling more lonely and low-spirited than ever. My thoughts traveled far up into the clouds where my good friend dwelled, who told me such interesting stories and showed me pictures every evening. What experience she has had! Her beams floated upon the waters of the flood; she smiled upon Noah's ark just as she has smiled upon me, bringing hope, and the promise of a new world which was to be formed from the old. She looked down sorrowfully upon the silent harps hanging upon the willow-trees, when the children of Israel sat weeping by the waters of Babylon. The round moon, half hidden by dark cypresses, hung in the clear air when Romeo scaled the balcony, and the promise of true love rose like a cherub towards Heaven. She saw the captive giant at St. Helena looking across the wide sea from his lonely rock, while his soul was filled with great thoughts. What histories the moon could relate! The lives of men are all like stories to her. This evening I shall not see you, old friend, nor can I draw a picture in memory of your visit. But as I looked pensively towards Heaven the sky became bright, and a passing ray of the moon shone in upon me. It was soon gone, and the dark clouds hurried past, but still it was a friendly good-night—a greeting from the moon.

Fifth Evening

"To-day I will give you a scene from Pompeii," said the moon. "I was in the Street of Tombs, as it is called, a little way out of the city. Beautiful monuments stood there, and here it was that youths, with wreaths of roses upon their heads, danced with the fair sisters of Laïs ages ago. The silence of death now reigns there, and German mercenaries in the Neapolitan service keep guard. They were playing cards and throwing dice when some strangers arrived from beyond the mountains; a soldier accompanied them. They wished to see the city that had risen from the grave by moonlight, and I showed them the wheel ruts in the streets, which were paved with broad slabs of lava, the names on the doors, the signs that still hung there, and the basins of the fountains, ornamented with shells, in the little courtyards, but no jet of water gushed forth, and no music sounded from the beautifully painted apartments where the bronze dog kept the door. It was the city of the dead; nothing stirred save Vesuvius, which thundered forth its everlasting hymn, each stanza of which men call an eruption.

"They went to the Temple of Venus, built of pure white marble, with its high altar standing before the broad steps, and the weeping willows bringing forth fresh shoots among the pillars. The air was blue and transparent, and black Vesuvius, with fire continually rising up from it, like the trunk of a fir-tree, formed the background. Above it rose the cloud of smoke, like the branches of the fir-tree; it was lit up by a blood-red reflection in the still night air.

"Among the strangers was a lady who was a great singer. I have seen the homage paid to her in the greatest cities of Europe. They all sat down on the amphitheater steps when they came to the tragic theater, and so a small part of the house was occupied by an audience as it had been hundreds of years ago. The stage was unaltered, with its walled side-scenes and the two arches in the background, through which one saw the same scene that had been used in olden times, a scene painted by Nature herself—the mountains between Sorrento and Amalfi. The lady gaily mounted the ancient platform and sang; the place inspired her, and she seemed to me like an Arabian steed that gallops onward like the wind, with distended nostrils and flowing mane; her song was so light and yet so firm; then it became so pathetic that I thought of the sorrowing mother beneath the cross at Golgotha. The sound of applause and delight now filled the theater just as it had done so long ago. 'What a wonderful gift such a voice is!' all the hearers exclaimed.

"In five minutes' time the platform was empty, the audience had disappeared, and no sound broke the stillness—it was over. But the ruins stood unaltered, as they will do when centuries have past. None will then know of the momentary applause and of the fair vocalist's triumph; all will be forgotten and gone—even for me this incident will be but a dream of bygone days."

Sixth Evening

"Near the path that leads through the wood are two small farm-houses," said the moon. "The doors are low, and some of the windows are quite high up, others close to the ground; they are surrounded by barberry and white-thorn bushes. The roofs of the two houses are covered with moss, yellow stonecrop, and houseleek. The only plants that grow in the garden are cabbages and potatoes, but near the hedge stands a large willow tree. Underneath this sat a little girl; she was gazing at the withered trunk of an old oak between the two houses. It had been sawn off at the top, and upon it a stork had built his nest; he stood in it clapping with his beak. A little boy came out and stood by the girl's side; they were brother and sister.

"'What do you see there?' he asked.

"'I am looking at the stork,' she answered. 'Our neighbor told me that he would bring us a little brother or sister to-day; let us stay here and see it come.'

"'The stork does not bring anything of the kind,' said the boy. Our neighbor said that to me also; she laughed when she said it, so I asked her if she could say, "upon my honor," and she could not, so I know now that the tale about the stork is not true; they only tell it to us children for fun.'

"'But where do the babies come from then?' asked the little maid.

"'An angel from Heaven brings them under his cloak, but no one can see him, and that is why we never know when he comes.'

"At this moment there was a rustling in the branches of the willow-tree; the children clasped their hands and looked at each other.

"It must certainly be the angel coming with the baby, they thought, and took each other's hands. Then the door of one of the houses opened and the neighbor appeared.

"'Come in you two,' she said, 'and see what the stork has brought; it is a little brother.'

"The children nodded gravely to one another; they already knew that the baby had come."

Seventh Evening

"I know a clown," said the moon, "whom the public loudly applaud whenever they catch sight of him. His movements are so comic that the house is thrown into roars of laughter, and yet there is no art in his acting—it is natural. When he was quite a little boy he was called Punch by his play-fellows. He had been intended for it by Nature, who had also provided him with a hump on his back and another on his breast; but on the other hand his inner man, his mind, was without any deformity. In depth of feeling or ready wit no one could surpass him. The theater was his ideal world, and if he had received a slender, well-proportioned figure, he might have become the first tragedian on any stage. His soul was filled with the great and heroic, and yet he became a clown. His very sorrow and melancholy only increased the comic dryness of his strongly marked features, and delighted the audience still more, who overwhelmed their favorite with applause. The pretty Columbine was always gentle and kind to him, but she preferred to marry the Harlequin. It would have been too absurd if such beauty and ugliness had been mated together.

"When Punchinello was sometimes very depressed, she was the only person who could make him smile—occasionally he even laughed. At first she would be melancholy with him, then quieter, and at last bright and cheerful. 'I know perfectly well what is the matter with you,' she said, 'you are in love!' Then he could not help laughing. 'I in love! That would look ridiculous. How the audience would shout!' 'To be sure, you are in love, and I,' she added with comic gravity, 'I am the person you are in love with!' Such things may be said when they are quite impossible. Punchinello laughed heartily, gave a leap in the air, and seemed to forget his sadness.

"But she had only spoken the truth. He did love and adore her as he loved all that was great and noble in art. On her wedding day he was the merriest among the guests, but at night, when all was quiet, he wept: if the audience had seen his distorted features, they would have applauded more than ever.

"Columbine died a few days ago. On the evening after her funeral Harlequin was not asked to appear on the stage; he was a sorrowing widower. The manager had to give a very lively piece so that the public might not miss the pretty Columbine and the clever Harlequin too much; so Punchinello had to be more amusing and entertaining than ever. He danced and strode about while grief filled his heart. The spectators whistled and shouted '*Bravo!*

bravissimo!' and Punchinello had to come before the curtain. People said no one could equal him.

"But at night the ugly little man stole out of the town quite by himself to the deserted church-yard. The wreath of flowers on Columbine's grave had already withered, and he sat down there. He might have served as a study for a painter as he sat with his chin on his hands looking up to me. He looked like a grotesque monument, a Punch on a grave! What an extraordinary sight. The people would have shouted once more, 'Bravo, Punchinello! *bravo, bravissimo!'* "

Eighth Evening

Listen to what the moon told me to-night. "I have seen a cadet putting on his smart uniform for the first time after he had been made an officer. I have gazed at a young bride in her wedding dress, and at the young princess just married happy in her splendid attire; but I have never seen any one so extremely joyful as the little four-years-old girl whom I watched this evening. Her parents had given her a new blue dress and a new pink hat; she had just donned these pretty garments, and every one was calling for a candle, as my rays, which shone in at the window, were not sufficiently bright for the occasion, and more light was necessary. The little girl stood stiff and upright like a doll, she held her arms out so as not to touch the dress, and her fingers were apart. Oh, that you could have seen the delight that shone out of her eyes and made her face beam! 'To-morrow,' said her mother to her, 'I will take you out in your new clothes'; the little girl looked first at her hat and at her frock and laughed with pleasure. 'Mother, dear,' she exclaimed, 'I wonder what the little dogs will think when they see me with these beautiful things on?' "

Ninth Evening

"I was at Rome," said the moon. "The ruins of the emperors' palace are to be seen in the center of the city upon one of the seven hills which it occupies. Wild fig-trees grow forth from the crevices in the walls, and cover their bareness with their broad leaves of a gray-green hue. The donkey, making its way over heaps of *débris,* treads on the green laurels, and enjoys the thistles. From this place, from which one day the eagles of Rome were carried abroad, whence they 'came, saw, and conquered,' a door leads into a miserable little cottage, erected of clay between two pillars; wild vines hang like mourning garlands over the crooked windows. There lives an old woman with her little granddaughter; they are now the masters in the palace of the Roman emperors, and

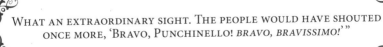

WHAT AN EXTRAORDINARY SIGHT. THE PEOPLE WOULD HAVE SHOUTED ONCE MORE, 'BRAVO, PUNCHINELLO! *BRAVO, BRAVISSIMO!*'"

show strangers what remains of its former glories. One bare stone wall is all that is left of the magnificent throne-room, while a cypress-tree overshadows the spot once occupied by the throne. The broken pavement is covered with dust lying several feet deep. The little girl often sits there when the evening bells ring. Through the keyhole in the door close by, which she calls her turret window, she can overlook half Rome, and see as far as the dome of St. Peter's.

One evening, when, as usual, all was perfectly calm round there, and my beams lit up the place, I saw the little granddaughter carrying water in an old-fashioned earthen pitcher. She was barefooted, her short skirt and her white sleeves were torn in many places. I kissed her lovely shoulders, her black eyes, and her shining black hair; she came up the steep steps, made of broken blocks of marble and of the capital of a destroyed pillar. The colored lizards, frightened, started at her footsteps, and glided away, but she was not afraid of them. She had already lifted her hand to ring the bell—a hare's foot attached to a string was the bell-handle at the palace of the Roman emperors—when she suddenly paused for a moment. What might have been passing through her mind? Did she perhaps think of the beautiful child Jesus, clad in gold and silver, below in the chapel, where the silver candlesticks glittered so brightly, and where her little friends sang psalms in which she could join? I cannot tell you. But when she moved again she stumbled and—the earthen pitcher fell down from her head and broke to pieces on the marble steps. The beautiful daughter of the palace of the Roman emperors cried over the vessel, and standing there, with her bare feet, she dared not pull the string, the bell-pull of the emperors' palace."

Tenth Evening

"My beams fell upon Tyrol," said the moon, "causing the black-looking fir-trees to throw long shadows upon the rocks. There pictures are painted upon the walls of the houses, enormous figures reaching from the ground to the roof. Among them I saw St. Christopher carrying the child Jesus, St. Florian in the act of pouring water on a burning house, and the Lord hung bleeding on the great cross by the side of the road. These pictures seem out of date to the present generation, but I saw them when they were put up, and noticed how one followed the other. High up on the mountain yonder, like a swallow's nest fixed on the gable of a house, stands a lonely convent. Two of the sisters were in the tower tolling the bell; both were young, and they looked from their high standpoint out into the wide world. Just then a coach passed below, and the postilion blew his horn. The two nuns threw a hasty and somewhat mournful glance at the carriage as it passed by; I saw a tear glittering in the eyes of the younger one. As the coach disappeared the sound of the horn grew fainter and fainter, and was drowned by the convent bell."

Eleventh Evening

"I saw a little girl in tears," said the moon; "she was crying over the wickedness of the world. A most beautiful doll had been given her as a present. Indeed it was a splendid doll, so fair and so fragile! Apparently it was not created to stand the rough wear and tear of this world. The brothers of the little girl, however, great mischievous boys, had fixed the doll high up in the branches of a tree and then run away. As the little girl could not reach her doll and take it down, she began to cry. Evidently the doll was crying too, for it stretched out its arms amidst the green leaves, and looked quite sad. Yes, yes, the little girl experienced some of the troubles of this world, which she had often heard her elders talk about. Poor doll! It was getting dark already, what would become of it if night set in completely? Was it to stay all night up in the tree quite alone? Never; the little girl could not think of such a thing. 'I shall stop with you,' she said tearfully, although this idea was not quite to her liking. She already imagined she saw distinctly little gnomes with high pointed caps sitting about in the bushes; in the background, in a long walk, she fancied she saw specters dancing about. They came nearer and nearer, stretching their hands towards the tree in which the doll was fixed; at the same time they laughed mockingly, and pointed at her with their fingers. The little girl was very frightened! Then she said to herself, 'I have often heard it said that evil spirits cannot hurt people who have done no wrong. I wonder if I have been naughty.' Then she remembered that she had laughed at a poor duck, which had a red rag tied round its leg and limped so funnily. 'Really I could not help laughing,' she said, 'but after all it's a sin to laugh at animals.' Looking up at the doll she asked it, 'Did you also laugh at the duck?' The doll seemed to shake its head."

Twelfth Evening

"Some years ago," said the moon, "I looked in at the window of a poorly furnished little room at Copenhagen. Father and mother were asleep, but a little son was still awake. The cretonne bed-hangings were moving, and I saw the child peep out. I thought first the boy was looking at the big clock brightly painted in red and green; at the top a cuckoo was sitting, heavy weights hung below it, while the pendulum with its polished brass disc was swinging to and fro—'tick—tick.' But he looked at his mother's spinning-wheel which was standing underneath the clock. Although the boy liked this best of all the furniture in the room, he dared not touch it, as he always got a tap on the fingers when he was caught meddling with it. Sometimes he would sit quietly for hours by his mother's side when she was spinning, and closely watch the rattling spindle and the turning wheel. Then many things passed through his mind, and often he wished that he might be allowed to turn the wheel himself. Now his father and mother were asleep, his eyes wandered from them to the spinning wheel; and all at once one little naked foot came out of the bed, and then the other, and his two little white legs followed. For a moment he stopped, to convince himself that father and mother were really still asleep, then he crept, noiselessly, in his little nightgown to the spinning-wheel, and began to work it. Soon the thread came off the wheel, which whirled round quicker and quicker. It was such a pretty sight! I kissed his golden hair and his blue eyes. Suddenly the mother awoke. I saw the curtain move and a head peep out; she fancied she saw a gnome, or some other kind of supernatural being. 'For heaven's sake!' she cried, and in her fright awoke her husband. He opened his eyes, rubbed them, and then looked at the little fellow: 'Why, that's our Bertel,' he said.

"But my eye glided away from the humble room, I have so many things to look at. I next saw the halls of the Vatican where the marble figures stand. My rays fell upon the group of Laocoon, the very stone seemed to sigh. I silently kissed the Muses; they all seemed to have life in them. But my rays dwelled longest on the Nile group with its colossal god. He lies there, thoughtfully resting himself against the Sphinx, as if he were meditating on the rolling centuries; little Cupids play with him and with the crocodiles. In the cornucopia little Cupid is sitting with folded arms and looking up at the great silent riven god. He is a faithful picture of the little boy at the spinning-wheel to the minutest detail. The little marble figure was beautiful and full of life, although the wheel had turned round more than a thousand times since it had been cut out of the stone. The little boy in the humble room turned the spinning-wheel as many times round as years passed, before an age could produce marble figures like those.

"Many years have elapsed since the events I have just described to you," continued the moon. "Yesterday I looked upon a bay on the eastern coast of Denmark. On that shore are splendid woods full of high trees; there you can see an old feudal castle, swans are majestically swimming in the lakes, and in the background lies, surrounded by lovely orchards, a little town and a church. Several boats, the inmates of which held burning torches in their hands, glided noiselessly over the water; the lights were not lit for catching fish, a festival was taking place—that one could see everywhere. There was music and singing, and in one of the boats stood upright a tall, broad-shouldered man, wrapped in a cloak, to whom the others paid homage. He had blue eyes, and his long hair was quite white. I recognized him at once, and thought of the Vatican, the group of the Nile, and the old marble statuary. I thought of the modest little room where I had seen Bertel in his nightgown working at the spinning-wheel. The wheel of time has turned round, and new statues have been carved out of the stone. The inmates of the boats shouted, 'Hurrah! hurrah! for Bertel Thorwaldsen.'"

Thirteenth Evening

"To-night," said the moon, "I will describe to you a scene from Frankfort. There is one house which particularly struck me; it is not the house where Goethe's cradle stood, nor the municipal building, through the great windows of which used to project the horns of the oxen which were roasted and given to the people on coronation days. No, it was a private house, with a humble outside, painted green, near the Jewish quarter. It was the house of the Rothschilds. I looked in at the open door; the hall was brilliantly lighted, and footmen, holding wax candles in solid silver candlesticks, were standing on either side and bowing to an elderly lady who was being carried downstairs in a chair. The master of the house stood bare-headed near the door, and kissed the old lady's hand; she was his mother. She nodded kindly to him and to the servants, and then they carried her back to a small house in a narrow gloomy lane where she dwelled. In this house all her children were born, and there the foundation-stone of their fortune was laid. She firmly believed that if she were to desert the little house in the miserable street, fortune would desert her children."

That is all the moon told me. I only saw her for a very short time. I could not help thinking of the old lady who lived in the despised street. One word, and she might have possessed a grand house on the banks of the Thames, or a villa at the Gulf of Naples.

"If I were to desert the humble house where the fortune of my sons was made, fortune would desert them!" It was a superstition, but of a kind that any one who knows the story, and saw this picture, would understand it, if there was nothing else written underneath it than the two words: "A mother."

Fourteenth Evening

"Yesterday morning at daybreak," related the moon, "when none of the many chimney-pots of the great city had begun to smoke, I was looking at them. All at once a little head peeped out of one of them, and then the upper part of a human body; the arms were resting on the rim of the chimney-pot. 'Hurrah!' exclaimed a voice. It belonged to a young sweep who had, for the first time in his life, climbed up in the chimney and put his head out at the top. 'Hurrah! hurrah!' Indeed it was very different to be up in the fresh air from creeping about in the black narrow chimneys! Here he could overlook the whole town and even see as far as the green wood. The sun, who was just rising, looking like a big fiery ball, illumined his face which, in spite of its being nicely blackened, beamed with joy.

"'Hurrah! hurrah!' he cried, swinging his brush, 'now the whole town can see me, and the moon and the sun too!'"

Fifteenth Evening

"I will give you another picture from Sweden," said the moon to me. "The little convent church of Wreta is beautifully situated amidst dark pine-woods, not far from the dreary banks of the river Stoxen. My rays penetrated through the railings into the spacious vaults, where kings sleep peacefully in their huge stone coffins. On the wall above each sarcophagus is fixed a royal crown, the symbol of their earthly dignity; it is, however, only made of wood, painted and gilded, hung up on a wooden peg let into the wall. Worms have eaten the gilded wood, spiders have spun their webs from the crowns down to the ground, like mourning banners, as frail and transient as the sorrowing of mortals. How peacefully they rest! I can very well remember them, I can still see their faces which so plainly expressed either grief or joy. The steamboats which pass over the lakes like magic snails often bring a stranger to the church; he also visits the vaults, and when he asks for the names of the kings, he hears names that have been long dead and forgotten. Smilingly he looks at the worm-eaten crowns; and if perchance he is a man who reflects, a certain melancholy mingles with his smiles. Sleep, ye dead ones! The moon remembers you, and at night sends her rays into your silent kingdom where the wooden crowns hang."

Sixteenth Evening

"What I am going to tell you to-night," said the moon, "occurred last year in a little provincial town; but that is of no importance. I saw the incident quite distinctly, but the account of it I read to-day in the papers is not half clear enough. A bear-leader was sitting over his supper in the public room of a little inn, while the bear was outside, tied to one of the logs of a pile of wood. Poor

Bruin had never hurt anybody, although he seemed quite capable of doing so. In the attic of the house three little children were playing by my light; the eldest might have been six years old, the youngest was certainly not more than two. 'Pit, pat—pit, pat'—there was somebody coming upstairs. Who could it be? The door was pushed open, and there was the big shaggy bear! When he was tired of waiting down in the courtyard he had broken away, and by chance found his way upstairs. I had witnessed it all," said the moon. "The children were terribly frightened at first when they saw the big shaggy beast, and tried to hide themselves in the corners of the room. The bear, however, found them and sniffed them, but did not harm them. Then the children, thinking he was a large dog, took courage and began to stroke the bear. When he laid himself down on the ground, the youngest boy mounted on his back, and putting his little head with the golden curls down, began to play at hide-and-seek in the animal's long fur. When, after a little while, the eldest boy took his drum and beat it, the bear rose on his hind legs and danced. It was a wonderful sight! Then the boys shouldered their guns and gave the bear one too; he carried it quite in the proper manner. They were quite delighted with their new play-mate, and just began marching—one-two, one-two—when the door opened, and the children's mother appeared. You ought to have seen her as she stood there horror-struck, as white as a sheet, her mouth half open, and her eyes dilated with terror. Her youngest boy nodded to her, and in his great delight exclaimed, 'Mother, we are playing at soldiers!'

"At this moment the bear-leader rushed into the room."

Seventeenth Evening

An icy wind was blowing, the clouds were sailing quickly; at intervals, and then only for a moment, I could catch sight of the moon. She said to me:

"I was looking down from the sky upon the restless clouds, and observed how their large shadows were chasing one another on the earth. I then saw a prison; a carriage stood before the door waiting to take a prisoner away. My rays penetrated through one of the iron-barred windows and fell upon the opposite wall, upon which a prisoner was engraving a few lines as a memento. What he wrote, however, were not words but notes of music, the outburst of his heart. The door opened, they came to lead him away, and he fixed his eyes upon my round disc; but clouds came between us as if they intended to prevent his looking upon my face. When he had entered the carriage, the door was locked, the horses were touched up with the whip, and they galloped into the dark forest, where my rays could not follow the prisoner. But I looked through the grating, my beams gliding over the notes, his farewell, scratched into the prison wall. Where words fail music can often speak! As, however, my rays could only illumine some of the notes, the greater part of his composition will always remain unknown to me. Was it a song of death that he wrote? Were these notes of joy? I wonder if he drove away to be executed, or to return into the arms of his beloved ones! My rays do not decipher all that is written by mortals."

Eighteenth Evening

"Last night I looked down upon a town in China," said the moon; "my beams illumined the long blank walls which border the streets. Here and there you certainly find a door, but it is always tightly shut, for what does the China-man care about the outside world. The windows of the houses behind the walls are closely covered with jalousies. The Temple was the only place whence the dim light shone through the windows. I looked in upon its gorgeous colors. The walls from floor to ceiling are covered with pictures in strong colors and rich gilding. They are representations of the labors of the gods here on earth. There is an image of a god in every niche, almost hidden by gorgeous draperies and floating banners. Before each of the gods—which are all made of tin—stands a little altar with holy water, flowers and burning wax tapers. At the upper end of the Temple stands Fu, the chief of all the gods; he is draped silk of the sacred yellow. At the foot of the altar sat a living being, a young priest. He seemed to be praying, but in the midst of his prayers to fall into a reverie; and no doubt that was a sin, for his cheeks burnt, and his head sank lower and lower. Poor Soui-houng! was he in his dreams seeing himself behind those dreary walls in a little garden of his own, working at the flower beds? Perhaps a labor much dearer to him than this of tending wax tapers in the Temple. Or was it his desire to sit at a richly spread table, wiping his lips between each course with tissue paper? Or, was his sin so great that, did he dare to express it, the heavenly powers would punish him death? Did his thoughts venture to stray with the barbarians' ships to their home in far-distant England. No, his thoughts did not fly so far afield, and yet they were as sinful as only the hot blood of youth can conceive them. Sinful, here in the Temple before the image of Fu and the other gods. I know whither his thoughts wandered.

"In the outskirts of the town, upon that flat flagged roof of a house where the parapet seemed to be made of porcelain, and among handsome vases full of large white bell-shaped flowers, sat the lovely Pé, with her narrow roguish eyes, full lips, and tiny feet. Her shoes pinched, but the pressure at her heart

Her thoughts wandered from her home
and sought the Temple, but not for the sake of God!
Poor Pé! Poor Soui-houng!

was far greater, and she wearily raised her delicately modeled arms in their rustling satin sleeves. In front of her stood a glass bowl with four goldfish in it; she slowly stirred the water with a little painted and lacquered stick—slowly, oh, very slowly, for she was musing. Was she thinking how richly the fish were clad in gold, and how securely they lived in their glass bowl with all their plentiful food, and yet, how much happier they would be if they had their freedom? Ah, yes, the fair Pé thoroughly comprehended that. Her thoughts wandered from her home and sought the Temple, but not for the sake of God! Poor Pé! Poor Soui-houng! their earthly thoughts met, but my cold beams fell between them like an angel's sword!"

Nineteenth Evening

"I am very fond of children," said the moon, "especially when they are quite small, because then they are so amusing. Sometimes I look into the rooms between the curtain and the window, when they do not know that I am there. I like to see them being dressed and undressed. The little round shoulders come first out of the frock, then the little white arms; or I see the stockings pulled off, and the plump little white legs appear with the tiny feet which one cannot help kissing, and I do kiss them.

"But I quite forget what I was going to tell you. To-night I was looking through a window before which there was no blind, for nobody lived opposite. There I saw a whole troop of little children, all brothers and sisters; there was one little girl among them, who, although she was only four years old, could say her prayers as well as the elder ones. Her mother sits beside her cot every evening and listens to her when she says her prayers; then she kisses her and stays until the little one falls asleep, which she generally does as soon as her head touches the pillow.

"To-night two of the elder children were somewhat noisy; one was hopping about on one leg in his long white nightshirt, while the other stood upon a chair where all the children's clothes were placed and said he was a Grecian statue. The third and fourth had folded their things and put them carefully into a box, as they had to do every evening; the mother sat by the side of the youngest and bade them all be quiet, as their little sister was going to say her prayers.

"I was shining over the lamp right into the little girl's bed, she was lying there under her snow-white counterpane, folding her hands, and there was a grave expression upon her little face. She was saying "The Lord's Prayer" aloud. Suddenly her mother interrupted her.

" 'How is it," she asked her, 'that after you have said, "Give us this day our daily bread," you always say something that I cannot understand? Tell me at once what it is.'

"The little girl was silent for a moment and looked at her mother in embarrassment.

" 'Will you tell me now what you say after "our daily bread"?' "

" 'Mother, dear, don't be angry with me, I only said, "and plenty of butter on it".' "

"I am very fond of children," said the moon, especially when they are quite small."

The Pigs

Since Charles Dickens has told us about a pig we are already good-humored when we hear one grunt. Holy Anthony has taken it under his patronage, and if one thinks of "the prodigal son" one is at once in one's mind in a pigsty; and it was before a pigsty that our carriage stopped over in Sweden. Towards the high-road, close by his house, a peasant had his pigsty, and indeed it was a pigsty without comparison. It had been one day an old state carriage; the seats were lifted out and the wheels taken off, and so it stood without any other alteration on the ground. There were four pigs in it; were these the first ones that were in it? Why, that was impossible to decide, but everything pointed out that it had been a state carriage, even the piece of red cloth that hung down from the ceiling—everything indicated that it had seen better days.

"Umph! umph!" sounded inside, and the old coach creaked and lamented; it had indeed a sad ending. "The beautiful is gone!" it sighed, or would have done so if it had been able to.

We came back in the autumn; the coach was still there, but the pigs were not. They were playing the masters in the wood; blossoms and leaves had fallen down from the trees, storm and rain were swaying the scepter, and let them have neither rest nor peace; the birds of passage were gone. "The beautiful is gone! Here the splendid green wood, the warm sunshine, the song of birds have all vanished!" So it sounded and cracked in the trunks of the lofty trees, and a sigh so deep, a sigh out of the heart of the wild rose-bush, from him who was sitting there—the rose king—was heard. Do you know him? He is beard all over—the most beautiful red-green beard—he is easily to be recognized. Go to the wild rose-hedges in the autumn, when all the leaves have fallen down, and only the red hips are left; you will often find among them a large red green mossy flower, that is the rose king; a small green leaf grew forth from his head, that is his feather; he is the only man of his kind on the rose-bush, and it was he who sighed.

"Gone, gone!—The beautiful is gone! The roses have gone, the leaves have dropped off! Here it's wet, here it's rough! The birds have become silent, and the pigs come to feed on acorns; they are the masters in the wood!"

There were cold nights and gloomy days, but the raven, nevertheless, sat on the branch and sang "brave, brave." Raven and crow sat on the high branch; they have a large family, and they all said "brave, brave!" and what the crowd says is always right.

Under the high trees on the road was a large pool, and here lay a herd of pigs, large and small; they found the place exceptionally beautiful; *oui,* they said, that was all the French they knew—that was at least something. They were so clever and so fat.

The old ones lay quietly and meditated; the young ones, on the other hand, were busy, and had no rest. A little pig had a curly tail, and this curl was the pride of the mother; she thought all the others only looked at the curl, and only thought of it, but this they did not do: they thought of themselves and of the useful, and for what purpose the wood was there.

They had always heard that the acorns which they ate grew at the roots of the trees, and therefore they rooted up the ground; but now came a little pig—for the youngest always find out new things—which declared that the acorns fell down from the branches; one had fallen on its own head, and gave rise to this idea, later on it had made observations, and now it was quite sure. The old ones put their heads together and said "Umph, umph! all the beauty is gone. The chirping of the birds is at an end, we want fruit! Everything that can be eaten is good, and we eat everything!"

"*Oui, oui,*" they all said.

But the old pig looked at her little one with the curly tail. "One must not overlook the beautiful," she said.

"Brave, brave," said the crow, and flew down from the tree in order to be appointed nightingale; there must needs be one there and the crow was at once appointed!

"Gone, gone," sighed the rose king; "the beautiful is gone!"

It was rough, gloomy, cold, and stormy, and the rain was sweeping in heavy showers over fields and wood.

Where are the birds which sang, where are the flowers on the meadow and the sweet berries of the wood? Gone, gone!

Then a light sparkled from the forester's cottage; it was lit like a star, and threw its long rays between the trees; a song sounded from the house; beautiful children were playing within round the grandfather; he sat holding the Bible on his knees and read of God and eternal life, and spoke of the spring which would come back, of the wood which would have fresh green, of the roses that bloom, of the nightingales that sing, and of the beautiful that would soon be master again!

But the rose king did not hear it; he was sitting in the wet cold weather and sighed, Gone, gone! The pigs were the masters in the wood, and the old sow looked at the little one with the curly tail. "There remains always some one who has eyes for the beautiful!" said the old sow.

"Delaying Is Not Forgetting"

There was an old mansion surrounded by a marshy ditch with a drawbridge which was but seldom let down: not all guests are good people. Under the roof were loopholes to shoot through, and to pour down boiling water or even molten lead on the enemy, should he approach. Inside the house the rooms were very high and had ceilings of beams, and that was very useful considering the great deal of smoke which rose up from the chimney fire where the large, damp logs of wood smoldered. On the walls hung pictures of knights in armor and proud ladies in gorgeous dresses; the most stately of all walked about alive. She was called Meta Mogens; she was the mistress of the house, to her belonged the castle.

Towards the evening robbers came; they killed three of her people and also the yard-dog, and attached Mrs. Meta to the kennel by the chain, while they themselves made good cheer in the hall and drank the wine and the good ale out of her cellar. Mrs. Meta was now on the chain, she could not even bark.

But, lo! the servant of one of the robbers secretly approached her; they must not see it, otherwise they would have killed him.

"Mrs. Meta Mogens," said the fellow, "do you still remember how my father, when your husband was still alive, had to ride on the wooden horse? You prayed for him, but it was no good, he was to ride until his limbs were paralyzed; but you stole down to him, as I steal now to you, you yourself put little stones under each of his feet that he might have support, nobody saw it, or they pretended not to see it, for you were then the young gracious mistress. My father has told me this, and I have not forgotten it! Now I will free you, Mrs. Meta Mogens!"

Then they pulled the horses out of the stable, and rode off in rain and wind to obtain the assistance of friends.

"Thus the small service done to the old man was richly rewarded!" said Meta Mogens.

"Delaying is not forgetting," said the fellow.

The robbers were hanged.

There was an old mansion, it is still there; it did not belong to Mrs. Meta Mogens, it belonged to another old noble family.

We are now in the present time. The sun is shining on the gilt knob of the tower, little wooded islands lie like bouquets on the water, and wild swans are swimming round them. In the garden grow roses; the mistress of the house is herself the finest rose petal, she beams with joy, the joy of good deeds: however, not done in the wide world, but in her heart, and what is preserved there is not forgotten. Delaying is not forgetting!

Now she goes from the mansion to a little peasant hut in the field. Therein lives a poor paralyzed girl; the window of her little room looks northward, the sun does not enter here. The girl can only see a small piece of field which is surrounded by a high fence. But to-day the sun shines here—the warm, beautiful sun of God is within the little room; it comes from the south through the new window, where formerly the wall was.

The paralyzed girl sits in the warm sunshine and can see the wood and the lake; the world has become so large, so beautiful, and only through a single word from the kind mistress of the mansion.

"The word was so easy, the deed so small," she said, "the joy it afforded me was infinitely great and sweet!"

And therefore she does many a good deed, thinks of all in the humble cottages and in the rich mansions, where there are also afflicted ones. It is concealed and hidden, but God does not forget it. Delayed is not forgotten!

An old house stood there; it was in the large town with its busy traffic. There are rooms and halls in it, but we do not enter them, we remain in the kitchen, where it is warm and light, clean and tidy; the copper utensils are shining, the table as if polished with beeswax; the sink looks like a freshly scoured meatboard. All this a single servant has done, and yet she has time to spare, as if she wished to go to church she wears a bow on her cap, a black bow, that signifies mourning. But she has no one to mourn, neither father nor mother, neither relations nor sweetheart. She is a poor girl. One day she was engaged to a poor fellow; they loved each other dearly.

One day he came to her and said:

"We have both nothing! The rich widow over the way in the basement has made advances to me; she will make me rich, but you are in my heart; what do you advise me to do?"

"I advise you to do what you think will turn out to your happiness," said the girl. "Be kind and good to her, but remember this; from the hour we part we shall never see each other again."

Years passed; then one day she met the old friend and sweetheart in the street; he looked ill and miserable, and she could not help asking him, "How are you?"

"Rich and prospering in every respect," he said; "the woman is brave and good, but you are in my heart. I have fought the battle, it will soon be ended; we shall not see each other again now until we meet before God!"

A week has passed; this morning his death was in the newspaper, that is the reason of the girl's mourning! Her old sweetheart is dead and has left a wife and three step-children, as the paper says; it sounds as if there is a crack, but the metal is pure.

The black bow signifies mourning, the girl's face points to the same in a still higher degree; it is preserved in the heart and will never be forgotten. Delaying is not forgetting!

These are three stories you see, three leaves on the same stalk. Do you wish for some more trefoil leaves? In the little heartbook are many more of them. Delaying is not forgetting!

Little Ida's Flowers

"My poor flowers are quite dead," said little Ida. "They were so beautiful last night, and now their leaves hang all withered on the stalks! Why do they do that?" she asked the student who was sitting on the sofa, and who liked her very much. He knew how to tell the most beautiful stories, and could cut the most amusing figures out of paper: hearts, with little ladies in them who danced, flowers, and large castles in which one could open the doors. He was a merry student. "Why do my flowers look so faded to-day?" she asked him again, and showed him the bunch, which was quite withered.

"Do you know what is the matter with them?" asked the student. "The flowers have been at a ball last night, and that is why they droop their heads so."

"My poor flowers are quite dead."

"But the flowers can't dance," said little Ida. "Certainly," said the student. "When it grows dark, and we are asleep, they jump merrily about; they have a ball almost every night."

"Cannot children go to this ball?"

"Oh, yes!" said the student; "the little daisies and the snowdrops."

"Where are the beautiful flowers dancing?" asked little Ida. "Have you not often been outside the town gate, near the large castle where the king lives in in the summer, where the beautiful garden is, with the many flowers? You have seen the swans which swim towards you when you give them bread-crumbs. Believe me, out there the great balls take place."

"I was out there in the garden yesterday with my mother," said Ida; "but all the leaves were off the trees, and there are no longer any flowers there. Where are they? In the summer I saw so many!"

"They are within the castle," said the student. "You must know that as soon as the king and his courtiers return to town the flowers immediately run into the castle and enjoy themselves. You ought to see that: the two most beautiful roses seat themselves on the throne, and then they are king and queen; all the red cockscombs come and place themselves on each side and bow—they are the chamberlains. Afterwards all the pretty flowers arrive, and a great ball takes place. The blue violets represent little naval cadets; they dance with hyacinths and crocuses, which they address as 'Miss'; the tulips and the large tiger-lilies are old ladies, who see that they all dance well, and behave themselves." "But," asked little Ida, "is nobody there who hurts the flowers because they dance in the king's castle?"

"The truth is, nobody knows about it," said the student. "Sometimes, of course, the old steward of the castle, who has to watch out there, comes during the night; he has a big bunch of keys, but as soon as the flowers hear the keys rattle they are quiet, and hide themselves behind the curtains, and only peep out with their heads. 'I smell that there are flowers here,' says the old steward, but he cannot see them."

"That's splendid!" said little Ida, and clapped her hands. "But should I not be able to see the flowers either?"

"Yes," said the student; "only remember, when you go out again to look through the window—then you will see them. I looked in to-day, and saw a large yellow lily resting on the sofa and stretching herself. She was a lady-in-waiting."

"Can the flowers from the Botanical Gardens also go there? Can they go such a long distance?"

"Yes, certainly," said the student; "if they wish it, they can fly. Have you not seen the beautiful red, yellow, and white butterflies? They almost look like flowers, and that they have been. They have flown off their stalks high into the air, and have beaten it with their petals as if they had little wings, and then they flew. And because they behaved themselves well they obtained permission to fly about in the daytime too, and had not to return home and sit still on their stalks; and thus the petals became in the end real wings. That you have seen yourself. It is, however, very probable that the flowers in the Botanical Gardens have never been at the king's castle, or do not know that there is such merriment out there at night. Therefore I will tell you how you can give a surprise to the Professor of Botany, who lives next door: you know him well, do you not? When you go into his garden you must tell one of the flowers that a large ball takes place at the castle every night; then the flower will tell all the others, and they will all fly away; and if the professor comes into the garden he will not find a single flower there, and he will be unable to understand what has become of them."

"But how can one flower tell the others? Flowers can't talk!"

"Of course they can't," said the student, "but then they make signs. Have you never seen that when the wind blows a little the flowers nod to one another and move all their green leaves? That they understand as well as us when we talk together."

"Can the professor understand their signs?" asked Ida.

"Certainly. One morning he came into the garden and saw a large stinging-nettle making signs with its leaves to a beautiful red carnation. It said: 'You are so pretty, and I love you with all my heart.' But the professor can't stand things of that sort, and beat the nettle at once on its leaves, which are its fingers; but then it stung him, and since that time he never dares touch a nettle again."

"That's amusing," said little Ida, laughing.

"How can one make a child believe such silly things!" said a tiresome actuary, who had come to pay a visit and was also sitting on the sofa. He could not bear the student, and always grumbled when he saw him cutting out the funny amusing figures: sometimes he cut out a man hanging on a gibbet and holding a heart in his hand, for he had been stealing hearts; sometimes an old witch, who was riding on a broomstick, and carrying her husband on her nose. But all this the old actuary could not stand, and then he generally said, as he did now: "How can one make a child believe such silly things? That is stupid fancy!"

But to little Ida what the student told her about the flowers seemed very amusing, and she thought a great deal of it.

The flowers hung their heads because they were tired and had danced all night; they were surely ill. Then she took them to her other toys, which were placed on a nice little table, and the whole drawer was full of beautiful things. In the doll's bed, her doll Sophy was sleeping, but little Ida said to her: "You must really get up now, Sophy, and be satisfied to lie in the drawer to-night. The poor flowers are ill, and they must rest in your bed; perhaps then they will recover!" And she took the doll out at once, but Sophy looked displeased and did not say a single word, for she was vexed that she could not keep her bed.

Then Ida placed the flowers in her doll's bed, pulled the little counterpane over them, and bade them lie quietly; she would make them some tea, so that they might get well again, and be able to get up in the morning. She drew the little curtains round the bed, lest the sun might shine into their eyes. She could not help thinking the whole evening about all the student had told her. And when she was going to bed herself, she first looked behind the curtains, which were hanging before the window, on which her mother's beautiful flowers stood, hyacinths and tulips, and she whispered in a low voice: "I know where you are going to-night—to the ball!" The flowers pretended not to understand her, and did not stir a leaf, but little Ida was convinced it was so.

When she had gone to bed she lay for a long time thinking how delightful it would be to see the beautiful flowers dancing on the king's castle. "I wonder if my flowers have really been there?" Then she fell asleep. In the night she woke up again; she had been dreaming of the flowers and of the student whom the actuary had blamed. It was quiet in the bedroom where Ida slept; the night lamp was burning on the table, and father and mother were asleep.

"I wonder if my flowers are still resting in Sophy's bed?" she thought, "how much I should like to know that!" She raised herself a little and looked towards the door, which was ajar; in the room to which it led were her flowers and all her toys. She listened, and it seemed to her as if she heard some one in the room playing the piano, but quite softly, and she had never heard any one play so well before. "I am sure all my flowers are dancing in there," she thought. "How much I should like to see them!" But she dared not get up for fear of waking her father and mother.

"Oh! I wish they would come in here," she thought. But the flowers did not come, and the music continued to sound sweetly; at last she could no longer bear it—it was too beautiful; she crept out of her little bed, went softly towards the door and peeped into the adjoining room. What a splendid sight she saw there! There was no night lamp burning, and yet it was quite bright—the moon was shining on the floor; it was almost as light as day. All the hyacinths and tulips stood in two long rows in the room; not a single one remained on the window-sill, where only the empty pots were left. On the floor all the flowers danced very gracefully round one another, made figures, and held each other by their long green leaves while swinging round. At the piano sat a large yellow lily, which little Ida was certain she had seen in the summer, for she remembered distinctly that the student had said: "How much this lily resembles Miss Lina!" But then they had all laughed at him; but now it seemed to little Ida as if the flower was really like the young lady: she had the same peculiar manners when she played—sometimes she bent her yellow smiling face to one side, sometimes to the other, and nodded in time to the sweet music! None of them noticed little Ida. Then she saw a large blue crocus jump on the table, walk straight to the doll's bed and draw away the curtains; there were the sick flowers, but they got up at once and nodded to the others, saying that they wished to dance with them. The old fumigator, in the shape of a man whose underlip was broken off, got up and bowed to the beautiful flowers; they looked by no means ill; they leapt down to the others and enjoyed themselves very much.

Then it seemed as if something fell from the table. Ida looked and saw the carnival birch-rod jump down, and it seemed as if it was one of the flowers. It looked very pretty, and a little wax doll with a broad-brimmed hat, such as the actuary usually wore, sat upon it. The carnival birch-rod hopped about among the flowers on its three red stilts, and stamped on the ground, for it was dancing a mazurka, a dance which the other flowers were unable to manage, as they were too light and could not stamp on the ground.

The wax doll on the carnival birch-rod suddenly grew up, and raising itself over the paper flowers which were on the rod, exclaimed: "How can one make a child believe such foolish things? That is stupid fancy!" And the wax doll looked exactly like the actuary—just as yellow and dissatisfied as he was. But the paper flowers beat against his thin legs, and then he shrank together again and became the little wax doll. All this was very amusing to see, and little Ida could not help laughing. The carnival birch-rod continued to dance, and the actuary had to dance too. There was no getting out of it, whether he made himself tall or long or remained the little yellow wax doll with the broad-brimmed black hat. Then the other flowers, especially those which had rested in the doll's bed, interceded in his favor, and the carnival birch-rod gave in. At the same moment a loud knock was heard in the drawer where Ida's doll Sophy lay with many other toys; the fumigator in the shape of a man walked up to the edge of the table, laid itself down at full length, and began to open the drawer a little way. Sophy rose and glanced with astonishment all round. "I suppose there is a ball here to-night," she said. "Why has nobody told me of it?"

"Will you dance with me?" asked the fumigator.

"You would be the right sort of fellow to dance with!" she said, and turned her back upon it.

Then she sat down on the edge of the drawer and thought that perhaps one of the flowers would ask her to dance, but none came. Then she coughed, "Hem, a-hem," but even in spite of this none appeared. Then the fumigator began to dance by itself—not so badly, after all! As none of the flowers seemed to notice Sophy, she let herself drop down from the drawer on the floor, to make a noise. All the flowers came running to her and inquired if she had hurt herself; they were all very polite to her, especially the flowers who had been in her bed. But she was not hurt, and Ida's flowers thanked her for the beautiful bed, and were very kind to her—took her into the center of the room, where the moon was shining, and danced with her, while all the other

. . . and danced with her, while all the other flowers stood in a circle round them.

flowers stood in a circle round them. Now Sophy was happy, and said they might keep her bed; she did not mind sleeping in the drawer.

But the flowers said: "You are very kind, but we cannot live any longer; we shall be dead by to-morrow. Tell little Ida to bury us in the garden, where she has buried the canary; then we shall wake up again next summer and be more beautiful than ever!"

"No, you must not die," said Sophy, and kissed them. Then the door flew open and many beautiful flowers came dancing in. Ida could not at all understand where they came from; surely they had come from the king's castle. Two beautiful roses with crowns on their heads walked in front; they were king and queen. Then came pretty stocks and carnations, bowing to all sides: they had brought music with them. Large poppies and peonies blew on pea-pods until they were quite red in the face. The blue hyacinths and the little white lilies of the valley tinkled as if they had bells. That was wonderful music! Then many other flowers came, and they all danced—blue violets, the red night daisies, and lilies of the valley. All the flowers kissed one another; it was very sweet to look at. At last the flowers said "Good-night" to one another, and then little Ida stole back into her bed again, and dreamed of all she had seen. When she got up in the morning she quickly went to the little table to see if her flowers were still there. She drew the curtains from the little bed, and there they lay, all withered—much more so than the day before. Sophy was lying in the drawer where she had placed her, but she looked very sleepy.

"Do you not remember what you have to tell me?" asked little Ida. But Sophy was dumb, and did not say a single word. "You are not good," said Ida; "have they not all danced with you?" Then she took a small paper box on which beautiful birds were painted, opened it, and placed the dead flowers inside. "This shall be your pretty coffin," she said, "and when my cousins come again they shall help me to bury you, out in the garden, that you may next summer grow again, and become more beautiful!"

The cousins were two bright boys called Jonas and Adolphe; their father had given them each a crossbow, which they had brought with them to show Ida. She told them about the poor flowers, and asked them to help her to bury them. The two boys walked in front with their crossbows on their shoulders, while little Ida followed, carrying the pretty box with the dead flowers. In the garden they dug a little grave. Ida first kissed the flowers and then laid them with the little box in the earth. Adolphe and Jonas shot with their crossbows over the grave, for they had neither guns nor cannons.

Then the door flew open and many beautiful flowers came dancing in.

The Ice Maiden

Little Rudy

Let us visit Switzerland and wander through that glorious mountain-land where the forests climb up the steep rocky walls; let us ascend to the dazzling snow-fields above, and descend again to the green valleys beneath, through which streams and rivulets rush along as hastily as if they could not reach the sea and disappear fast enough. The sun sends its scorching rays into the deep valley, and also falls upon the heavy masses of snow up above, so that in the course of years the latter melt into glimmering blocks of ice, and are formed into rolling avalanches and piled-up glaciers. Two such glaciers lie in the broad ravines below the "Schreckhorn" and the "Wetterhorn," near the little mountain town of Grindelwald; they are wonderful to behold, and for that reason they attract every summer many strangers from all parts of the world. They come across the high snow-covered mountains, and also through the deep valleys, and then they have to ascend for several hours; as they ascend, the valley sinks deeper and deeper, until, upon looking down into it, it appears as if viewed from a balloon. Above them the thick clouds often hang like a heavy veil around the mountain peaks, while down in the valley where numerous brown wooden houses lie scattered about, there may still be a stray sunbeam, bringing into brilliant relief a patch of green, as if it were transparent. Down below the waters go roaring along, dashing themselves into foam, while up above they ripple and purl, looking like silver ribbons streaming down the rocks.

On both sides of the way which leads up to the mountain there are wooden houses. Every house has its potato-garden, and this is indispensable, for there are many mouths to feed in the cottages, children, who are always ready for their meals, being plentiful. They pop up in all directions and crowd round the traveler, whether he is on foot or driving; the whole troop of children carry on a trade, offering for sale pretty little carved houses, models of those that are built here in the mountains. Whether there be rain or sunshine, the children are there with their wares.

Some twenty years ago there often stood here, but always at a little distance from the other children, a little boy who was also desirous of doing some business. He used to stand there looking very grave and holding his box of carved goods tightly with both hands as if he really had no wish to give it up; but it was this very gravity and the fact of his being such a very little fellow that led people to notice him, call him up to them, and buy most from him—he himself did not know why. An hour's walk higher up the mountain lived his grandfather who cut out the pretty little houses, and there in the old man's room stood a great cupboard crowded with all kinds of carved things, nut-crackers, knives and forks, boxes with leaf-work and leaping chamois—in fact, a haven of delight for any child. But the boy—Rudy was his name—looked with greater pleasure and longing at the old gun which hung down from one of the beams in the roof, and which his grandfather had promised him he should one day have, when he was tall and strong enough to use it.

Small as he was, the boy had to mind the goats, and if ever there was a good goatherd who knew how to climb, it was Rudy; he even clambered a little higher than the goats, for he loved to take the birds' nests from the treetops. He was bold and daring, but he was only seen to smile when he stood near a roaring waterfall, or heard the thunder of a rolling avalanche. He never played with the other children; he only came near them when his grandfather sent him down the mountain to sell things. And Rudy did not care particularly about selling; he preferred climbing about alone among the mountains, or sitting with his grandfather and hearing him tell of the olden days, and of the people in the village of Meiringen near by, where he had been born. The old man said that the race who lived had not always been there; that they were wanderers, and had come from the far north, where their ancestors had lived and had been called Swedes. Rudy was very proud of knowing this, but he also learned a good deal from other sources, such as those members of the family who belonged to the animal world.

There was a large dog, called Ajola, who had belonged to Rudy's father, and there was also a tom-cat. The tom-cat especially Rudy held in high honor, for he had learned climbing from him.

"Come out upon the roof with me!" the cat had said, very distinctly and intelligibly too; for young children, before they are able to speak, understand fowls and ducks very well. Cats and dogs then speak as intelligibly as our parents, but we have to be very young; at that age even grandfather's stick neighs and becomes a whole horse with head, legs, and tail. Some children keep this intelligence much longer than others, and of these it is said that they are very backward, and have remained children very long. That's what people say!

"Come out upon the roof with me, Rudy!" was about the first thing that the cat had said, and Rudy had understood. "All that people say about falling down is mere fancy; you will not fall unless you are afraid. Come on! Put one of your paws here, and the other there; then feel with your fore-paws. You must use your eyes and be active in your limbs. If you come to a hole, jump and hold tight; that's what I do!"

And so little Rudy did too; that is why he so often sat on the shelving roof with the tom-cat and up in the tree-tops, and even up on the high ledges of the rocks where the cat could not follow him.

"Higher up!" said trees and bushes. "Look how we climb, how high we reach, and how we hold fast even to the very narrowest ledges."

Rudy reached the mountain-tops even before the sun touched them, and there he drank his morning draft, the fresh invigorating mountain air—the draft that only the good God knows how to prepare, and of which mankind can only read the recipe, in which is included fresh fragrance from the mountain herbs, and from the mint and thyme of the valley. All that is heavy is absorbed by the lowering clouds, and these being diffused over the pine-tops by the wind, the spirit of the fragrance becomes air, light and ever fresh; this was Rudy's morning draft.

The sunbeams—those daughters of the sun who bring blessings with them—kissed his cheeks, while Giddiness stood on the watch without daring to approach fiim: the swallows from his-grandfather's house, upon which there were no less than seven nests, flew up to him and the goats, singing: "We and you! You and we!" They brought greetings from home, from his grandfather, and even from the two hens, the only birds in the house, with which, however, Rudy was never intimate.

Young as he was he had traveled, and no short journey either for such a little fellow. He was born in the Canton of Valais and had been carried across the mountains; he had recently walked as far as the "Staubbach," which flutters in the wind like a silver veil before the snow-clad dazzling white mountain of the Jungfrau. He had also been to the great glaciers at Grindelwald; but that was a sad story, for his mother had found her death there, and there, his grandfather used to say, little Rudy had lost all his childish merriment. "Before the boy was a year old, he laughed more than he cried," his mother had written, "but from the time that he fell into the crevasse in the ice, a great change had come over him." His grandfather seldom spoke about the matter, but it was known all over the mountain.

Rudy's father had been a postillion, and the great dog which was now in his grandfather's hut had always accompanied him in his journeys across the

Simplon down to the Lake of Geneva. Some relatives of Rudy on his father's side still lived in the Rhone valley, in the Canton Valais; his uncle was a famous chamois-hunter and a well-known Alpine guide. Rudy was only a year old when he lost his father, and his mother now longed to return with her child to her relatives in the Bernese Oberland. Her father lived a few hours' journey from Grindelwald; he was a wood-carver, and his trade enabled him to live comfortably.

In the month of June she set out homewards with her child, in the company of two chamois hunters, across the Gemmi to reach Grindelwald. They had already accomplished the greater part of the journey and had crossed the high ridges and come into the snow-field; already they perceived their native valley with all its well-known raftered houses, and had now only to cross one great glacier. The snow had recently fallen and hid a crevasse; not one of those, it is true, which reach down to the abyss below where the water rushed along, but still far deeper than a man's height. The young woman, who was carrying her child, slipped, sank down and disappeared; not a cry, not a groan was heard—nothing but the weeping of the babe.

More than an hour passed before her two companions obtained some ropes and poles from the nearest hut to aid them in their efforts, and after much exertion two dead bodies, as they appeared to be, were brought up out of the crevasse. Every means was employed to bring them back to life; with the child they were successful, but not with the mother, and so the old grandfather received into his house only his daughter's son—an orphan, the boy who laughed more than he cried. It seemed, however, as if the laughing had gone out of him, and the change must have taken place in the crevasse, in the cold unearthly ice-world, where the souls of the condemned are imprisoned until the Day of Judgment, as the Swiss peasant believes.

A rushing torrent, turned to ice and pressed as it were into blocks of green crystal, lies the glacier there, one great block of ice overtopping the other; and in the depths beneath the stream of melted ice and snow tears along where deep hollows and immense crevasses yawn. It is a marvelous palace of crystal, and in it lives the Ice Maiden, the queen of the glaciers. She, who slays and crushes, is half a child of the air, half the mighty ruler of the stream: therefore is she able to speed, with the swiftness of the chamois, to the highest peaks of the snow-clad mountains, where the bold climber has first to cut footsteps for himself in the ice. She sails upon a thin pine twig down the rushing stream, bounding from one rock to the other, with her long snow-white hair fluttering about her, and her bluish-green robe shining like the water in the deep Swiss lakes.

"To crush and to hold fast is in my power!" she cries. "A beautiful boy they stole from me—a boy whom I had kissed, but not kissed to death. He is again among the living; he tends the goats upon the mountain, climbing upwards, ever higher, away from others, but not from me. He is mine—I will have him!"

She gave the Spirit of Giddiness orders to act for her, for it was summer-time and too hot for the Ice Maiden in the green valley where the mint grows; so the Spirit—or rather, Spirits, for there were three of them—went up hill and down dale. This Spirit has many brothers, a whole troop of them, and the Ice Maiden chose the strongest among the many who exercise their power both within and without. They sit on the railings of steps and towers, they run like squirrels along the brink of the precipice, and jumping over parapets and bridges they tread the air as the swimmer does the water, luring their victims onwards and down into the abyss. The Spirit of Giddiness and the Ice Maiden both grasp after mankind as the polypus grasps after all that comes near it. The Spirit was to seize Rudy.

"Seize him, indeed!" said the Spirit; "I can't do it. That monster of a cat has taught him to climb. This boy has a power of his own that keeps me at a distance, and I am unable to get at him when he hangs from a branch over an abyss; however much I should like to tickle the soles of his feet, or send him flying head over heels through the air, I cannot manage it."

"We'll manage it some day," said the Ice Maiden. "You or I! I. I!"

"No, no!" rang out all around her, like a mountain echo of the pealing of the church bells; but it was the chant of a harmonious choir of other spirits of Nature—kind, loving spirits, the daughters of the rays of the sun. These encamp every evening in a circle around the mountain peaks, and spread out their rose-colored wings which, becoming redder and redder with the sinking sun, cast a glow over the lofty peaks, which is called by men the Alpine glow. When the sun has sunk they retire into the mountain tops, right into the white snow, where they slumber till the sun rises, when they again come forth. They are particularly fond of flowers, butterflies, and people, and among the latter they had taken a great fancy to Rudy.

"You shall not catch him! You shall not have him!" they said.

"I have caught bigger and stronger ones than he," said the Ice Maiden.

Then the daughters of the sun sang a song of the wanderer whose cloak the storm had torn away; the wind had taken the covering but not the man. "You can seize him, but you cannot hold him, you children of strength; he is stronger, more ethereal than even we. He ascends higher than our mother the sun; he possesses the magic word that binds winds and waters, and that compels them to serve and to obey him. You loosen the heavy oppressive weight, and he soars higher."

Glorious were the tones of the bell-like choir.

Every morning the sun's rays came through the one little window in the grandfather's hut, and shone upon the sleeping child. The daughters of the sun's rays kissed him, for they wished to thaw, melt, and dispel the icy kisses that the queenly maiden of the glaciers had given him as he lay in his dead mother's lap in the deep crevasse, and from which he had been saved as by a miracle.

The Journey to the New Home

Rudy was now eight years old. His uncle, who lived on the other side of the mountains, in the Rhone valley, wished to have the boy with him, so that he might learn something and get on better. His grandfather also thought this was for the best, and let him go.

So Rudy took his departure. Besides his grandfather there were several others to whom he had to bid farewell. First there was Ajola, the old dog.

"Your father was the postillion and I was the post-dog," said Ajola. "We used to travel backwards and forwards across the mountains, and I know both the men and the dogs on the other side. Talking was never much in my line, but now that we shall probably not be able to exchange a word for a long time, I will say a little more than usual. I will tell you a story that has been running in my head a long time and that I have ruminated upon at some length; I don't understand it, and you will not understand it either, but that doesn't matter. But this much I have made out of it: things are not dealt out quite equally in this world, either to dogs or to mankind. We are not all born to lie in people's laps or to drink milk. I have not been used to it; but I have seen a little dog traveling in a post-chaise and occupying the place of a human being. The lady who was his mistress, or whose master he was, carried a feeding-bottle full of milk with her, from which she fed the dog; she also gave him some sweets, but as he only sniffed at them and would not eat them, she gobbled them up herself. I was running along in the mud at the side of the carriage as hungry as a dog can be, and chewing the cud of my own thoughts, which seemed to tell me that things were not quite as they should be—but there is much that is not. Would you like to lie in laps and drive in carriages? I wish it you from the bottom of my heart. But you can't bring it about yourself; I have not been able to do so either by barking or whining."

These were Ajola's words, and Rudy threw his arms round his neck and kissed him heartily on his wet nose; then he took the cat in his arms, but lie struggled to be free.

"You are getting too strong for me, and I don't want to use my claws against you. Climb away over the mountains, for I have taught you how! But never imagine that it is possible to fall; in this way you will always have a sure footing."

With that the cat sprang away, for he did not want Rudy to read in his eyes how sorry he was.

The hens were strutting about in the hut; one of them had lost its tail, a traveler who pretended to be a sportsman, having shot it off, mistaking the poor fowl for a bird of prey.

"Rudy is going over the hills!" said one of them.

"He is in a great hurry, too," said the other, "and I'm not fond of saying good-bye"; and with that they both hopped away.

He also bade farewell to the goats, who bleated and wanted to follow him; it was very touching.

Two able guides of the district, who were going across the mountains near the Gemmi, took Rudy with them on foot. It was a stiff journey for such a little fellow, but he was very strong, and his courage did not sink.

The swallows flew a little way with them. "We and you! You and we!" they sang. The road led across the rushing Liitschine, which falls from the dark clefts of the Grindelwald glacier in numerous small streams. The trunks of fallen trees and blocks of stone serve here as bridges. Having reached the alderwood on the other side, they began to ascend the mountain where the glacier had loosened itself from the side of the rock, and now they marched along the glacier over blocks of ice and round them. Sometimes Rudy went on hands and knees, sometimes upright; his eyes sparkled with joy, and he trod so firmly in his iron-tipped mountain shoes that it seemed as if he wished to leave behind him the impression of each footstep. The black earth which the mountain stream had cast upon the glacier gave it the appearance of being somewhat thawed, but still the bluish-green glassy ice shone through. They had to go round the little pools which had formed themselves, dammed up by blocks of ice, and in making one of these circuits they came near a great boulder which lay rocking on the edge of a crevasse in the ice; the stone lost its balance and, rolling down, the echo of its fall thundered up out of the deep abyss of the glacier.

The way continued to lead uphill; the glacier itself extended upwards like a stream covered with blocks of ice heaped up one on the other, and wedged in between two steep walls of rock. Rudy thought for a moment how he had lain with his mother deep down in one of these heart-chilling crevasses, as he had been told; but such thoughts were soon banished, and the story left no more impression upon him than the many others he had been told. Now and then, when the men thought the way was somewhat too difficult for the lad, they lent him a hand, but he did not tire, and on the slippery ice he stood as firmly as a chamois. They now came to rocky ground, sometimes striding between bare cliffs, sometimes passing between fir trees and out again into the green meadows, always through ever-changing scenery. All around them towered the snow-clad mountains, whose names—the "Jungfrau," the "Monk," and the "Eiger"—were known not only to Rudy but to every child in the country. Rudy had never been up so high before, and had never trodden the wide-spreading sea of snow which now lay before him with its motionless billows, from which the wind occasionally carried away a snowflake as it blows along the foam from the waves of the sea. The glaciers stand here hand in hand, as it were; each of them is a palace of crystal for the Ice Maiden, whose power and will it is to seize and to bury. The sun shone warm and the snow glittered as if it had been strewn with sparkling bluish-white diamonds. Innumerable insects, especially butterflies and bees, lay dead in heaps upon the snow; they had ventured too high, or the wind had carried them up till they expired in the cold. Around the Wetterhorn there hung a threatening cloud, looking like a bundle of fleecy black wool, and sinking with the weight of what it contained within it—a "Föhn," one of the most violent storms when it breaks loose.

The impression of the whole journey, the night passed on the mountain, the remainder of the road, the deep crevasses where the water had worn away the rock during a period of time at the computation of which the brain reels—all this impressed itself indelibly upon Rudy's memory.

A deserted stone building on the other side of the sea of snow afforded shelter for the night. Here they found some charcoal and branches of pine-trees. A fire was soon kindled and a shakedown of some kind arranged; the men sat near the fire smoking their pipes and drinking the warm spiced beverage which they had themselves prepared, and of which Rudy also got his share. Tales were told of the mysterious state of the Alpine land, of the strange gigantic snakes in the deep lakes, of the spectral host that carry off sleepers at night through the air to the wonderful floating city of Venice, and of the wild shepherd who drives his black sheep over the pastures; if these had not been seen, the tinkling of their bells and the uncanny bleating of the flocks had undoubtedly been heard. Rudy listened with intense curiosity, but without any fear, for that he did not know; and while he listened he fancied he heard the weird bellowing of the spectral herd. It became more and more distinct, and the men hearing it too, sat listening to it in silence, telling Rudy not to go to sleep.

It was a "Föhn"—that violent hurricane that hurls itself from the mountains down into the valley, which snaps trees in its fury as if they were mere reeds, and which carries the wooden huts from one bank of a river to the other as we move men on a chess-board.

After the lapse of an hour they told Rudy that it was now all over, and that he might go to sleep; wearied by his long march, he slept as if it had been his bound duty to do so.

The next morning they again started on their way. The sun that day shone upon mountains, glaciers, and snow-fields that were all new to Rudy. They had entered the Canton Valais, and were upon that side of the range which is seen from Grindelwald, but still far distant from his new home. Other ravines, other pastures, woods, and rocky paths unfolded themselves, and other houses and other people were seen. But what kind of beings were these?

They were misshapen, uncanny wretches and podgy yellowish faces, their necks hanging down like bags with great ugly lumps of flesh. They were the cretins—dragging their miserable bodies along, and looking with stupid eyes at the strangers; the women were even more hideous than the men. Were these the people in his new home?

The Uncle

In his uncle's house, where Rudy now lived, the people were, thank God, such as he had been accustomed to see. There was only one cretin, a poor imbecile lad, one of those unfortunate creatures who in their destitute state are always traveling about in the Canton Valais from house to house, and who stay a few months in each family. Poor Saperli happened to be there when Rudy arrived.

Rudy's uncle was still a brave hunter, and could also earn his living as a cooper; his wife was a lively little woman with a face like a bird, eyes like an eagle, and a long neck covered all over with down.

Everything here was new to Rudy—dress, manners and customs, and even the language; but this his young ear would soon learn to understand. Things here looked quite prosperous compared to his former home with his grandfather. The room was larger; the walls were adorned with chamois horns and brightly polished guns; over the door hung a picture of the Virgin Mary, in front of which stood some fresh Alpine roses and a burning lamp.

His uncle was, as we have already mentioned, one of the ablest chamois-hunters of the whole district, and also one of the best guides. Rudy was now to become the pet of this household; it is true there was one already—an old dog who had formerly been used for hunting, but was now too blind and deaf to be of any use. But his good qualities of earlier days had not been forgotten, and he was therefore considered as one of the family and well taken care of. Rudy stroked the dog, who, however, did not take up easily with strangers, and such Rudy was at first. But he did not long remain so, and soon won his way to everybody's heart.

"It's not so bad in Canton Valais," said his uncle. "We have chamois here, which do not die off so fast as the wild goats, and things are much better than they used to be. Whatever they may say about the good old days, I think ours are better, and a hole having been made in the bag, we get a current of air now through our confined valley. Something better always turns up when worn-out things are done away with."

When his uncle became very communicative, he would relate stories of his youthful days, and even go back to the stirring times of his father, when Valais was still, as he expressed it, a closed bag, full of sick people, miserable cretins. "But the French soldiers came, and they were capital doctors, killing both the disease and the sufferers. The French were good at conquering in more ways than one, and even their girls were not behindhand at it." In saying this the uncle would nod at his wife, who was French by birth, and laugh. "The French had even tried their hand at conquering stones, and had succeeded well too. They had cut a road through the solid rock across the Simplon—such a road that I can say to a child of three years old, "Just go down to Italy; only mind you keep to the high road," and if it only keeps to the high road the child will come to Italy safe enough." Then the uncle would sing a French song, shout "Hurrah!" and "Long live Napoleon Buonaparte!"

Here Rudy for the first time heard of France and of Lyons, the great city on the Rhone, where his uncle had been. His uncle said that before many years had passed Rudy would become an able chamois-hunter, and that he had the right stuff in him for it; he taught him how to hold a gun, how to aim and fire. During the hunting season he took him to the mountains and made him drink the warm blood of the chamois, which prevents the hunter from becoming giddy; he also taught him to know the time when the avalanches are likely to roll down the different mountains—at noontide or in the evening, according as the sun's rays took effect. He taught him to observe the movements of the chamois when leaping, so that he might always come down firmly on his feet; he showed him how to hold himself up by his elbows, loins, and legs if there was no other support in the crevice of the rock, and how it was even possible, if necessary, to hang on by one's neck. He told him that the chamois were cunning and had outposts, but that the hunters must be more cunning than they, and put them off the scent

One day, when Rudy was out hunting with his uncle, the latter hung his coat and hat upon his Alpine staff, and the chamois mistook the coat for the man. The mountain path was very narrow, indeed; it was scarcely a path at all, but only a narrow shelf along the yawning abyss. The snow that lay here was half thawed; and as the earth crumbled away beneath one's tread, Rudy's uncle lay down and crept forward. Every fragment that detached itself from the rock fell bounding from one side of the chasm to the other till it found a resting-place at the bottom. Rudy stood about a hundred paces behind his uncle on a firm projecting point of rock; from this post he could see a great vulture circling in the air and remain hovering above his uncle, whom the bird wished to hurl into the abyss with a blow from its wing, in order to make him its prey. The hunter had only eyes for the chamois, which with its young was to be seen on the other side of the chasm; Rudy kept his gaze fixed on the bird, for he understood what it wanted, and therefore stood ready to discharge his gun. Suddenly the chamois made a spring and his uncle fired and struck the animal with the deadly bullet, but the young kid sprang away, as if for a long life it had been exercised in danger and flight. The great bird, frightened by the report of the gun, winged its way in another direction, and Rudy's uncle knew nothing of the danger through which he had passed till he was told of it by the lad.

As they were now wending their way homewards in the best of humors, the uncle whistling a song of his youthful days, they suddenly heard a peculiar noise very near them; they looked around them, and there, high up on the slope of the mountain, the covering of snow rose and fell in billows like the motion of a large sheet of linen when the wind plays under it. The crust of snow, only a little while before as smooth and firm as a marble slab, suddenly burst, resolving itself into a foaming cataract which rushed down with a roar like that of distant thunder. It was an avalanche rolling, not indeed over Rudy and his uncle, but near them—all too near!

"Hold fast, Rudy!" cried his uncle; "hold fast with all your might!"

Rudy threw his arms round the trunk of the nearest tree, his uncle climbing up above him and holding fast to the branches, while the avalanche rolled along a few feet distant from them. But the rush of air that swept along with it like the wings of the storm, snapped the trees and bushes all around as if they had been only dry reeds, hurling them far and wide. Rudy lay crouched upon the ground. The tree to which he held fast looked as though it had been sawn in two, and the upper part had been flung far off; there amidst the shattered branches lay his uncle with his head dashed to pieces. His hand was still warm, but his face was not recognizable. Rudy stood pale and trembling; it was the first shock of his life, the first terror he had ever experienced.

Late in the evening he reached home with the fatal tidings—that home which was now turned into a house of mourning. The wife could find no words nor tears: it was only when they brought the body home that her grief found utterance. The poor cretin crept into his bed, and was seen no more the whole of the next day; it was only towards evening that he came up to Rudy.

"Will you write a letter for me?" he asked. "Saperli can't write, but Saperli can take the letter to the post-office."

"A letter from you?" asked Rudy. "And to whom?"

"To our Lord Christ!"

"To whom do you say?"

And the idiot, as the cretin was called, looked with a touching expression at Rudy, folded his hands, and said solemnly and piously:

"Jesus Christ! Saperli wants to send Him letter; ask Him let Saperli lie dead and not master of the house here."

Rudy pressed his hand and said:

"The letter would not go, and cannot bring him back to us."

It was no easy task for Rudy to make Saperli understand how impossible it was.

"Now you are the support of the house," said his aunt and foster-mother, and such Rudy became.

Babette

Who is the best shot in the Canton Valais? That the chamois well knew.

"Beware of Rudy!" they might have said.

"Who is the handsomest hunter?"

"Why, Rudy!" said the girls; but they did not add:

"Beware of Rudy!"

Not even the sober mothers said that, for he nodded in quite as friendly a way to them as to the young girls. He was so brave and merry, his cheeks so brown, his teeth so white, and his black eyes so sparkling; he was altogether a handsome fellow, and twenty years old. He did not mind the coldest ice-water when he went swimming, and he would turn and twist about in it like a fish. He could climb better than any one else, sticking to the cliffs like a snail, and what kind of muscles and sinews he had was evident when he jumped, an art which he had first learned from the cat and afterwards from the chamois. Rudy was the best guide to whom one could trust oneself, and he could have made a good income by that calling. For the cooper's trade, which his uncle had also taught him, he had no inclination, his greatest pleasure being chamois-hunting, which brought in money too. Rudy would be a good match, it was said, if he only did not aspire beyond his station. He was such a dancer that the girls dreamed about him, and more than one carried him about in her waking thoughts too.

"He kissed me while we were dancing," said Annette, the schoolmaster's daughter, to her dearest friend; but she ought not to have told this even to her dearest friend. Such secrets are not easily kept; they are like sand in a sieve, they run through. It was soon known that Rudy, brave and good as he was, kissed when he danced, and yet it was not her he had kissed whom he would have liked to kiss most of all.

"O-ho!" said an old hunter; "he has kissed Annette. He has begun with A, and he'll kiss right through the alphabet."

A kiss while dancing was all that the busy tongues could find to say about him up to the present; he certainly had kissed Annette, and yet she was by no means the flower of his heart.

Down in the valley near Bex, amidst the great walnut-trees, by a small rushing mountain stream, lived the rich miller. The dwelling-house was a large three-storied building with small turrets; its roof was of thin wood covered with tin plates, which shone both in sunshine and moonshine. On the highest turret was a weather-cock—a glittering arrow piercing an apple—an allusion to Tell's feat. The mill looked very neat and prosperous, and would have looked pretty in a picture, or well in a description, but the miller's daughter would not have been so easy to paint or to describe—so at least Rudy would have said. And yet her image was engraved on his heart, and the eyes in this image blazed so that they kindled a fire there. It had burst out suddenly, like other fires; and the strangest part of it was that the miller's daughter, the pretty Babette, had no suspicion of it, for she and Rudy had never spoken a word to each other.

The miller was rich, and these riches placed Babette very high and made her a difficult catch. "But," thought Rudy, "nothing is so high that one may not reach it. All one has to do is to climb on, and one cannot fall if one doesn't think of it." This had been one of his earliest lessons.

It happened once that Rudy had some business to transact at Bex; it was a long journey, for in those days there was not yet any railway. From the Rhone glacier, along the foot of the Simplon, amidst the varying landscape presented by the numerous mountain heights, stretches the broad valley of Valais with its noble stream, the Rhone, which often overflows its banks, covering fields and roads and destroying everything in its course. Between the towns of Sion and St. Moritz the valley takes a turn, making a bend like an elbow, and becomes so narrow behind St. Moritz that there is only room for the bed of the river and the narrow carriage road. An old tower stands like a sentinel before the Canton Valais which ends here, and from it can be seen, across the stone bridge, the toll-house on the other side; it is the boundary of the Canton Vaud and the next town, not very distant in Bex. At every step can be seen an increasing luxuriance in the vegetation; it is as if we were in a garden of chestnut and walnut trees. Here and there cypress and pomegranate blossoms peep forth, and it is as sunny and warm here as if one were in Italy. Rudy arrived in Bex, and after having finished his business took a walk about the town, but not even a miller's boy, let alone Babette, could he see. This was not as it should be.

Evening came on, and the air was laden with the fragrance of wild thyme and the blossoming limes, while the wooded mountain slopes seemed to be covered with a shimmering sky-blue veil. Far and wide reigned a stillness, not as of sleep or death, but as if the whole of Nature were holding its breath, as if she were posing for her image to be photographed on the blue vault of Heaven. Here and there amidst the trees in the green fields stood the posts supporting the telegraph wires that ran through the silent valley. Against one of these leaned an object so motionless that it might have been mistaken for the trunk of a tree; it was Rudy, standing there as still as everything at that moment around him. He was not asleep, neither was he dead; but just as great events in the world, and matters of vital importance to individuals, often fly along the telegraph lines without the wires indicating it by the slightest quiver or sound, so were thoughts of mighty importance passing through Rudy's mind: the happiness of his life, the one thought that now constantly occupied him. His eyes were fixed on one point—a light that glimmered through the foliage from the parlor of the miller's house, where Babette lived. Rudy stood there so still that one would have thought he was taking aim at a chamois, but he himself was at that moment like the chamois, which will often stand as if hewn out of the rock, for minutes together, and then, when a stone rolls down, suddenly bound forward and rush away. And so it was with Rudy; an idea had just flashed through his mind.

"Never despair!" he cried. "A visit to the mill to say good evening to the miller and good evening to Babette. One can't fail as long as one has confidence. Babette must see me some time or other if I am to be her husband!"

Rudy laughed, for he was in a merry mood, and strode towards the mill; he knew what he wanted—he wanted Babette.

The stream flowed along over the yellow pebbles, and willows and lime-trees hung over the rolling waters, as Rudy went up the path leading to the miller's house. But as the children sing:

"There was no one at home but the cat!"

The cat standing on the steps put up its back and said "Mew." But Rudy had no mind for this kind of talk; he knocked, but no one heard him, no one opened the door for him. "Mew," said the cat again; and if Rudy had still been a child, he would have understood that language and known that the cat wanted to say, "There is no one at home here." But, as it was, he had to go across to the mill, and there he was told that the miller had gone to Interlaken, and taken Babette with him, to the great shooting festival which was to commence the following day, and which lasted a whole week. People from all the German cantons would be there. Poor Rudy! we may well say. He had not chosen a lucky day for his visit to Bex, and he might go back now. He did so, too, marching back through St. Moritz and Sion to his home in the valley; but he did not despair. When the sun rose the next morning, it found him in the best of spirits, for those, unlike the sun, had never sunk.

"Babette is in Interlaken," said Rudy to himself; "many days' journey from here. It is a long way if one follows the high road, but it is not so far if one cuts across the mountains, and that road just suits a chamois-hunter. I have been that way before, it leads to my home where I lived with my grandfather when I was a boy. And there is a shooting match at Interlaken! I'll go and try to get the first prize, and I'll be with Babette, when I've made her acquaintance."

With his light knapsack, containing his Sunday best, upon his back, and his gun and game-bag slung across his shoulder, Rudy started to take the shortest way across the mountains, which was no mean distance after all. But the festival was only to commence that day and lasted the whole week and more; and he had been told that during that time the miller and Babette would stay with their relatives in Interlaken. So Rudy crossed the Gemmi, intending to descend near Grindelwald. He strode merrily onwards in the fresh, light, invigorating mountain air. The valley sank lower and lower and the horizon extended; one after another the snowy peaks rose, and soon the whole Alpine range lay there in its dazzling purity. Rudy knew every mountain; he was now approaching the Schreckhorn, which stretches its white-powdered stone finger high up into the blue sky.

At last he had crossed the highest ridge, and now the pastures sloped down to the valley which had been his home. Both the air and his mind were light. Hill and dale were luxuriant in flowers and foliage, and his heart was full of those youthful feelings in which old age and death are out of the question: in which all is life, power, and enjoyment! He felt as free and as light as a bird. The swallows flew past him, and sang as they had sung in his childhood: "We and you! You and we!" All sang of flight and joy.

Beneath him lay the velvety green meadows, dotted with brown wooden cottages, while the murmuring Lutschine rolled along. He beheld the glacier with the green crystal edges and the soiled snow, and looking down into the deep crevasses saw both the upper and the lower glacier. The sound of the church bells came up to him as if they wished to ring him a welcome to his home; his heart beat faster, and became so filled with old memories that Babette was quite crowded out for a moment.

He once more strode along the road where, when a little boy, he had stood with the other children and sold carved toy-houses.

Yonder, behind the fir-trees, still stood his grandfather's house, but strangers lived in it now. Children came running up towards him and wanted him to buy; one offered him a mountain rose, which Rudy took as a good omen and thought of Babette. Soon he had crossed the bridge where the two streams unite; here the foliage was thicker, and the walnut trees afforded a pleasant shade. Soon he saw the waving flags bearing a white cross on a red ground, the standard both of the Swiss and the Danes; and before him lay Interlaken.

"It is indeed a splendid town and has no equal," thought Rudy. It was a little Swiss town in its Sunday dress. It was not like other towns, a somber heap of heavy stone houses, looking cold and stiff. No, here it looked as if the wooden houses had come down from the mountains into the green valley, and had ranged themselves side by side along the dear river which flows along swift as an arrow; they were a little irregular, but still formed a handsome street. The grandest of all the streets had certainly grown very much since Rudy had been here as a boy. It seemed to him as if it had been made up of all the pretty little houses which his grandfather had carved, and with which the cupboard at home had been filled, and that these had increased very much in size, like the old chestnut trees. Every house was called a hotel, and had a deal of carved wood work around the windows and balconies; the projecting roofs were gaily painted, and before each house was a flower garden leading on to the broad paved high road. This was lined by houses on one side only; otherwise the fresh green meadow in which the cows grazed, with the tinkling Alpine bells on their necks, would have been hidden. This meadow was encircled by high mountains which receded a little as if it were in the center, so that the snow-clad glittering peak of the Jungfrau, the most beautifully shaped of all Swiss mountains, could be distinctly seen.

What a number of finely dressed ladies and gentlemen from foreign parts, what a crowd of country-people from the different cantons there was! Every marksman wore his number in a band round his hat. There was music and singing of all kinds: hand-organs, trumpets, shouting and noise. The houses and bridges were adorned with emblems and verses. Flags and banners were waving, and shot upon shot was being fired. That was the sweetest music to Rudy's ears, and amidst all this turmoil he quite forgot Babette, on whose account only he had come.

The marksmen were crowding round the targets, and Rudy was soon among them. He proved himself the best shot, and was more fortunate than any of them; for he always hit the bull's eye.

"Who can the stranger be?" people asked. "He speaks the French of Canton Valais, and he also makes himself understood very well in our German," said some.

"He is said to have lived in the neighborhood of Grindelwald when he was a boy," said one of the sportsmen.

The young stranger was full of life, too; his eyes sparkled, and his aim and his arm were steady, therefore he always hit the mark. Good fortune brings courage, and courage Rudy always had. He soon had a circle of friends gathered round him; every one honored him and paid him homage. Babette had quite vanished from his thoughts. Suddenly a heavy hand was laid upon his shoulder, and a deep voice said to him in French: "Aren't you from the Canton Valais?"

Rudy turned round and saw a stout man with a ruddy, pleased face; it was the wealthy miller of Bex. His great body hid dainty little Babette, who, however, soon came to the fore with her bright dark eyes.

It had flattered the wealthy miller that it was a marksman from his own canton who had proved to be the best shot, and was honored by every one. Rudy was certainly born under a lucky star; those whom he had come all this way to see, but had forgotten when on the spot, now sought him out.

When people meet others from their part of the country far from home they always speak and make each other's acquaintance. Rudy, by his shooting, was the first man in the festival, just as the miller at home in Bex was first by reason of his money and his fine mill. So the two men shook hands, which they had never done before; Babette too held out her hand to Rudy frankly, and he pressed it, and looked at her so hard that she blushed deeply.

The miller spoke of the long way they had come, and of the many large towns they had seen; in his opinion they had performed quite a journey, having traveled by steamer, rail, and coach.

"I came the shorter way," said Rudy. "I came over the mountains. There is no road too high for a man to pass along."

"But he may break his neck!" said the miller; "and you look just the kind of man to break your neck some day, you are so daring."

"Oh! one does not fall as long as one does not think of it," said Rudy.

The miller's relations in Interlaken, with whom the miller and Babette were staying, invited Rudy to come and see them—for was he not of the same canton as the miller? This invitation was very acceptable to Rudy; good fortune favored him, as it always does those who depend upon their own efforts and remember that "Providence gives us the nuts, but does not crack them for us." Rudy was treated by the miller's relations as if he belonged to the family, and they drank to the health of the best shot; Babette clinked glasses with Rudy too, and he returned thanks for the toast.

In the evening they all went for a walk along the beautiful road past the stately hotels and under the old walnut-trees, and there were so many people and such crowding that Rudy was obliged to offer Babette his arm. He told her how happy he was to have met people from the Canton Vaud, for Vaud and Valais were good neighborly cantons. He expressed his pleasure so heartily that Babette could not resist squeezing his hand. They walked on side by side as if they had been old acquaintances, she chatting on, and Rudy thinking how admirably she commented upon the dress and walk of the foreign ladies. She said that she really did not want to make fun of them, for she knew that they might be good, upright people; she herself had a godmother who was a grand English lady. Eighteen years before, when Babette was christened, the lady was staying at Bex, and having acted as godmother to her had given her the costly brooch which she was now wearing. Her godmother had twice written to her, and this year they were to have met her and her daughter here in Interlaken; "the daughters were old maids—nearly thirty," said Babette, who was only eighteen.

The sweet little mouth was not still a moment, and everything that Babette said sounded in Rudy's ears as matters of the greatest importance, while he in his turn told her all he had to tell—how often he had been in Bex, how well he knew the mill, and how often he had seen Babette, while she had most probably never noticed him, and lastly how he had gone to the mill filled with thoughts he could not express, and found her and her father gone to a place far away—not so far, however, but that one could clamber over the wall to it by a short cut.

All this he said, and much more; he told her how fond he was of her, and that he had come here for her sake and not on account of the shooting.

Babette became silent when she heard all this; it seemed as if he were asking her to bear too much.

While they wandered on, the sun sank behind the great mountain wall.

The "Jungfrau" stood out in all her glory, encircled by the dark green wreath formed by the neighboring heights. Every one stood still to gaze at the beautiful sight; even Rudy and Babette enjoyed it too.

"Nowhere is it more beautiful than here!" said Babette.

"Nowhere!" said Rudy, looking at Babette.

"To-morrow I must return home!" he said, a few moments later.

"Come and see us at Bex!" whispered Babette, "my father will be very pleased."

On the Way Back

What a number of things Rudy had to carry when the following day he set out to cross the mountains on his way home! He had three silver cups, two fine guns, and a silver coffee-pot; the pot would be useful when he set up housekeeping. But all this was of minor importance; he carried, or rather was carried homewards across the mountains by something much weightier. The weather was raw, dark, and inclined to rain, and the clouds descended like a mourning veil upon the mountain heights, shrouding their glittering peaks. From the woods below came the sound of the ax, and down the mountain slope rolled the trunks of trees that looked from the heights like thin sticks, but which were nevertheless as stout as ship's masts. The Liitschine murmured monotonously, the wind whistled, and the clouds sailed along. Suddenly Rudy found a young maiden walking at his side; he had not noticed her till she was quite close to him. She was also about to ascend the mountain. The maiden's eyes had a peculiar power that compelled one to look into them; they were so strange, so clear, so deep and unfathomable.

"Have you a sweetheart?" asked Rudy; all his thoughts ran on love.

"I have none," answered the maiden, with a laugh, but she did not seem to be speaking the truth. "Don't let us go a long way round," she said. "We must keep more to the left; it is a shorter way."

"Oh, yes!" said Rudy, "and fall into a crevasse. You don't know the way better than that, and want to be the guide?

"I know the way well enough!" said the maiden, "and I have my thoughts collected. Yours are no doubt down in the valley. Up here one should think of the Ice Maiden; men say she bears their race no goodwill."

"I do not fear her," said Rudy, "she had to give me up when I was still a child, and I shall not give myself up to her now that I am older."

The darkness increased, the rain came down, snow fell, and the lightning was quite blinding.

"Give me your hand," said the maiden, "I will help you to mount," and he felt the touch of her icy fingers.

"You help me!" exclaimed Rudy, "I do not want a woman's help in climbing yet." And he strode on more quickly away from her.

The snow-flakes covered him as with a veil, the wind whistled, and behind him he heard the maiden laughing and singing; it sounded quite strangely.

"It must be a specter in the service of the Ice Maiden," thought Rudy, who had heard such things talked about when, still a boy, he had passed the night up here in his journey over the mountains.

The snow no longer fell so thickly, and the cloud lay beneath him; looking back, no one was to be seen, but he heard laughing and singing, and the sounds did not seem to proceed from a human throat.

When Rudy at last reached the top-most plateau, from which the path leads down into the Rhone valley, he saw two bright stars shining in the clear blue heavens in the direction of Chamouny; and he thought of Babette, of himself, and of his good fortune, and his heart glowed at the thought.

The Visit to the Mill

"What grand things you have brought home!" said his old foster-mother, and her strange eagle eyes sparkled as she wriggled and twisted her skinny neck more strangely and quickly than ever.

"You are a lucky fellow, Rudy! I must kiss you, my sweet boy."

And Rudy allowed her to kiss him, but it was written in his face that he forced himself to put up with these little home afflictions.

"How handsome you are, Rudy!" said the old woman.

"Don't talk such nonsense!" said Rudy, with a laugh, but he was pleased all the same.

"I must say it again," said the old woman; "you are a lucky fellow."

"Well, you may be right," said he, thinking of Babette. Never had he felt such a longing to get down into the deep valley.

"They must have come home!" he said to himself; "it is already two days over the time when they had intended to be back. I must go to Bex."

So Rudy walked over to Bex and found them at home in the mill. He was received very kindly, and they had brought him greetings from the family in Interlaken. Babette did not say much; she had become very silent, but her eyes spoke and that was quite sufficient for Rudy.

At other times the miller had always led the conversation, and was accustomed to hear people laugh at his jokes and sayings—for was he not the wealthy miller? But now he seemed to prefer listening to Rudy's adventures, as the latter told of the difficulties and dangers that the chamois-hunter has to endure on the lofty mountain peaks—how he has to creep along the flimsy ledges of snow which are only cemented as it were by wind and weather to the edge of the cliff, and across the frail bridge that the snowdrift has thrown over the deep ravines.

The eyes of the brave Rudy sparkled as he spoke of the life of a hunter, of the cunning of the chamois and of their bold leaps, of the powerful "Föhn" and the rolling avalanches. He noticed that at every fresh description the miller became more and more interested, and that he was especially moved by what he heard of the vulture and the royal eagle.

Not far off, in the Canton Valais, there was an eagle's nest, very skilfully built under a high projecting ledge of rock. In that nest was a young eagle, but it was impossible to get at it. An Englishman had a few days before offered Rudy a whole handful of gold if he brought him the young eagle alive. "But everything has its limits," said Rudy; "the eagle is not to be had, it would be madness to attempt it."

The wine flowed freely and the conversation too, but the evening seemed much too short for Rudy, although it was past midnight when he left the miller's after this his first visit.

The lights in the windows of the miller's house still shone for a short time through the green branches; out of the open skylight in the roof came the parlor cat, while along the water-pipe came the kitchen cat to meet her.

"Is there any news at the mill?" asked the parlor cat. "Here in the house there is a secret engagement. Father knows nothing of it yet. Rudy and Babette have been treading on each other's paws under the table all the evening; they trod on me twice, but I didn't mew, for that would have attracted attention.

"I should have mewed though," said the kitchen cat.

"What suits the kitchen would not suit the parlor," said the parlor cat. "But I am curious to know what the miller will say when he hears of the engagement."

Yes, what the miller would say—that Rudy would also have liked to know, but it was impossible for him to wait long to hear it. When a few days later the omnibus rattled over the Rhone bridge between the cantons of Valais and Vaud, Rudy was sitting in it in as good spirits as ever, indulging in pleasant thoughts of the favorable answer he expected to receive that evening.

And when evening came, and the omnibus was driving back along the same road, Rudy was again sitting inside, while the parlor cat was running about in the mill with the news.

"Have you heard it, you in the kitchen? The miller knows all now. It has come to a fine end. Rudy came here towards the evening; and there was a great deal of whispering and secret talk between him and Babette, as they stood in the passage before the miller's room. I was lying at their feet, but they had neither eyes nor thoughts for me. 'I will go to your father at once,' said Rudy, 'that is the most honorable way.' 'Shall I go with you?' asked Babette; 'it will give you courage.' 'I have courage enough,' said Rudy; 'but if you are there, he must be friendly, whether he will or not.' Upon that they went in, Rudy treading heavily on my tail. He's very clumsy; I mewed; but neither he nor Babette had ears to hear. They opened the door and entered together. I was in first and sprang upon the back of a chair, for I didn't know how Rudy would open the ball. However, the miller opened it with a mighty kick, and the other was out of the house and up the mountain to the chamois in a jiffy. Master Rudy will have to stick to those now, and give up aiming at our Babette."

"But do tell me what they said," said the kitchen cat.

"What they said? Why, everything that people say when they go a-wooing: 'I love her, and she loves me. And if there is milk enough in the can for one, there is enough for two.' 'But she is too far above you,' said the miller, 'she sits on heaps of grit—gold grit, as you know. You will never reach her.' 'There is nothing too high for a man to reach if he only has the will,' answered Rudy, for he is a bold fellow. 'But you yourself said a little while ago that you couldn't reach the young eagle; well, Babette is still higher than that nest.' 'I'll take them both,' said Rudy. 'I'll give you Babette if you bring me the young eagle alive,' said the miller, laughing till the tears stood in his eyes. 'But now I thank you for your visit, Rudy; come again tomorrow when there's no one at home. Good-bye, Rudy!' And Babette said good-bye too, but as mournfully as a little kitten that cannot see its mother yet. 'A man's word is his bond,' said Rudy. 'Don't cry, Babette; I shall bring the young eagle.' 'You'll break your neck, I hope,' said the miller, 'and we shall then be spared your company here." That's what I call a mighty kick. And now Rudy is gone and Babette sits and weeps, but the miller sings German songs that he learned on his last journey. I'm not going to pull a long face about the matter—that will not do any good."

"Still there's a chance left for all that," said the kitchen cat.

The Eagle's Nest

From the mountain path a voice trolled out some joyous and vigorous notes, giving proofs of good humor and undaunted courage. It was Rudy going to see his friend Vesinand.

"You must help me. I must take the young eagle out of the nest at the top of the cliff; we will take Nagli with us."

"Will you not have a try to reach the moon first? It would be just as easy," said Vesinand. "You seem to be in good spirits."

"Of course I am. I am thinking of marrying. But to be serious, I will tell you how matters stand."

And soon both Vesinand and Nagli knew Rudy's intentions.

"You are a bold fellow," they said. "It can't be done; you'll break your neck."

"I shall not fall as long as I don't think of it," said Rudy.

They set out about midnight, carrying with them poles, ladders, and ropes. The road lay through forest and underwood, over rolling stones, leading ever higher and higher in the dark night. Water foamed beneath them and trickled down from above, while damp clouds hung in the air. At last the hunters reached the edge of the precipice, where it was even darker, for the rocky walls almost met, and the sky could only be seen through the narrow crevice at the top; close beside them yawned the abyss with the foaming waters beneath. The three sat down on the stones to await the dawn, for when the parent eagle flew out they would have to shoot the old bird before they could think of obtaining possession of the young one. Rudy crouched down, as motionless as if he had been part of the stone on which he was sitting, holding his gun cocked ready to fire, and his gaze fixed steadily upon the highest point of the cliff, where the eagle's nest was hidden beneath the overhanging rock. The three hunters had a long time to wait. But now they heard a loud rustling high above them, and a great hovering object darkened the air. Two guns took aim as the black body of the eagle flew out of the nest. A shot was fired; for a moment only the wide-spreading wings moved, then the bird slowly sank, crushing the branches and bushes in its way. For a moment it seemed as if it would completely fill the chasm, and drag the hunters down in its fall by its bulk and its great outstretched pinions; but at last it lay in the abyss beneath.

Now the hunters moved themselves. Three of the longest ladders were bound together; it was thought that they would reach far enough. They were fixed on the ground as close to the edge of the precipice as safety would permit, but they did not reach far enough; and higher up, where the nest was protected by the projecting ledge, the cliff was as smooth as a wall. After consulting together, they determined to bind two ladders together, and by letting them down into the chasm from above, make them communicate with the three set up below. With great difficulty they dragged the two ladders up, binding them fast with ropes to the top; they were then let out over the projecting ledge, and hung swaying there over the abyss. Rudy was already seated on the lowest rung. It was a bitterly cold morning, and clouds of mist were rising up out of the dark ravine. Rudy sat there like a fly upon a piece of swinging straw which a bird, while making its nest, had dropped upon the edge of some tall factory chimney; but the fly can fly away if the straw gives way, while Rudy could only break his neck. The wind whistled round him, and beneath him in the abyss foamed the waters of the thawing glacier, the palace of the Ice Maiden.

He now made the ladder swing to and fro, like the spider swings its body when it wants to seize anything in its long wavy threads; and when Rudy for the fourth time touched the top of the ladders set up from below he had grasped it, bound them securely together with skilful hands—but they swayed and rattled as if they hung on worn-out hinges.

The five long ladders, which seemed to reach up to the nest, and which stood up perpendicularly against the cliff, looked like a waving reed; and now the most dangerous part of the work was to be accomplished. There was climbing to be done as only a cat can climb, but that was just what Rudy understood, for he had learned it from the cat; he did not even know the Spirit of Giddiness was in the air behind him, trying to grasp him with its polypus like arms.

When he at length stood upon the topmost rung of the ladder he saw that it did not reach high enough to enable him to look into the nest, and that he could only get up to it by using his hands.

He first tried the strength of the stout interwoven branches that formed the nethermost part of the nest; and having secured a firm hold on one of the strongest, he swung himself up from the ladder, and hanging on to the branch soon had his head and shoulders in the nest. He was met by a suffocating stench of carrion, for in the nest were sheep, chamois, and birds, all in a state of decomposition. The Spirit of Giddiness, who had little power over him, blew the poisonous vapors into his face, in order to make him dizzy and faint, while down in the black yawning gulf the Ice Maiden herself, with her long pale green hair, sat by the rushing waters staring at him with eyes as deadly as two gun-barrels.

"Now I'll have you," she was thinking.

In a corner of the nest he saw the eaglet, a great strong bird, but still unfledged. Rudy kept his gaze rivetted upon it, and holding on with all his might with one hand, he with the other threw a noose over the young eagle. It was caught—alive, its legs fixed in the tightly drawn cord.

Rudy slung the noose with the bird across his shoulder, so that the creature hung a good way beneath him while he held on to a rope flung out to help him, until his toes touched the topmost rung of the ladder.

"Hold tight! Don't think it possible to fall and you will not do so!" It was the old lesson; and Rudy acting on it, held tight, clambered down, and being convinced that he could not fall, of course did not.

Then arose loud and joyous hurrahs, as Rudy landed on the firm rock with his young eagle.

What News the Parlor Cat Had to Tell

"Here is what you asked for!" said Rudy, as he came into the miller's house at Bex, and placing a large basket on the floor, took off the cloth that covered it. Two yellow eyes set in black rings glared forth, flashing fire, and so wild that they seemed to wish to burn and penetrate everything they beheld; the short strong beak was opened to bite, and the neck was red and covered with young feathers.

"The young eagle," cried the miller. Babette shrieked and sprang back, but could not take her eyes either from Rudy or from the eagle.

"You are not easily frightened!" said the miller.

"And you are a man of your word," said Rudy. "We both have our characteristics."

"But how is it that you did not break your neck?" asked the miller.

"Because I held tight," replied Rudy. "And that I do still. Now I shall hold Babette tight."

"First see that you get her," said the miller, laughing; and Babette knew that was a good sign.

"We must get him out of the basket—it is terrible the way he glares. But how did you manage to get him?" Rudy had to describe the capture, and the miller opened his eyes wider and wider.

"With your courage and your good fortune you can support three wives!" said the miller.

"I thank you!" cried Rudy.

"It is true, you have not got Babette yet!" said the miller, slapping the young Alpine hunter good-humoredly on the shoulder.

"Do you know the latest news in the mill?" said the parlor cat to the kitchen cat. "Rudy has brought us the young eagle and takes Babette in exchange. They kissed each other, and the old man saw it. That's as good as an engagement. The old man was quite good-natured about it; he drew back his claws, took his afternoon nap, and left the two to sit and chatter. They have so much to talk about that they will not have finished by Christmas."

And they had not finished by Christmas either. The wind whisked away the yellow leaves, and the snow whirled through the valley as well as on the high mountains. The Ice Maiden sat in her stately castle, which increases in size in winter; the cliffs stood there covered with frost, and icicles, as thick as trees and as heavy as elephants, hung down, where in summer the water veil of the mountain streams flutters in the breeze; fantastic garlands of crystal ice hung glittering upon the snow-powdered pine trees. The Ice Maiden rode upon the howling wind away over the deepest valleys. The snow-blanket reached right down as far as Bex, and the Ice Maiden, coming down there, beheld Rudy sitting at the miller's; he sat indoors that winter much more than was his wont, for he was generally near Babette. The wedding was to take place the following summer; his ears often tingled, for friends spoke a good deal about it. In the mill all was sunshine, and there bloomed the loveliest Alpine rose, the merry, laughing Babette, beautiful as the coming spring—the spring which makes all the birds sing of summer-time and marriage.

"How those two are always sitting stuck together there," said the parlor cat. "I am tired of their mewing!"

The Ice Maiden

Spring had unfolded her fresh green garlands of walnut and chestnut-trees, and beautifully did they rear their stately heads along the banks of the Rhone from the bridge at St. Moritz as far as the Lake of Geneva. The river rushes along with wild speed from its source under the green glacier—the ice-palace, where the Ice Maiden dwells, whence she has herself borne up by the keen wind to the highest snow-field to bask in the warm sunshine on the snow-covered pools. Here she sat gazing fixedly down into the deep valleys where the people were busily moving about like ants on a sunlit stone.

"Beings of mental power, as the children of the sun call you," said the Ice Maiden, "you are only vermin. One rolling snowball—and you, your houses and cities, are crushed and wiped out." She raised her proud head higher and looked far and wide with her death-dealing eyes. From the valley beneath arose a rolling sound: rocks were being blasted—the work of men. Roads and tunnels for railways were being laid down.

"They are playing at being moles," she said; "they are digging passages under the earth: hence this noise, like the reports of a gun. When I move my castles, the noise is greater than the roar of thunder."

Out of the valley ascended a wreath of smoke moving forwards like a fluttering veil. It formed the waving plumes of the engine, which was dragging along the newly opened line the train that looked like a winding serpent with carriages for its joints. It shot past swift as an arrow.

"They pretend to be the masters down there, these mental powers," said the Ice Maiden. "But the powers of mighty Nature are still the ruling ones."

She laughed and sang, making the valley tremble.

"An avalanche is falling," cried the people.

But the children of the sun sang still louder of the ruling power of human thought which places a yoke upon the ocean, levels mountains and fills up valleys, and is lord over the powers of Nature.

Just at that moment a party of travelers came across the snow-field where the Ice Maiden sat; they had bound themselves fast to each other by ropes, so that they formed one large body as it were upon the slippery surface of the ice, at the edge of the deep abyss.

"Vermin!" said the Ice Maiden. "You lords of the powers of Nature!" and she turned her gaze from the party and looked scornfully down into the deep valley where the train was rushing along.

"There they sit, these thoughts! But they are in the power of Nature's forces. I can see them, one and all. One sits proudly alone, like a king, while the others are all heaped up together. Here again half of them are asleep, and when the steam-dragon stops, they get out and go their ways. The thoughts go out into the world!" And she laughed.

"There goes another avalanche!" said the people down in the valley.

"It will not reach us," said two who sat together on the back of the dragon—two souls but one mind—as they say. They were Rudy and Babette, and the miller was there too.

"Like baggage," he said; "I am there as a necessary encumbrance."

"There sit the two," said the Ice Maiden. "Many chamois have I crushed, millions of Alpine roses have I snapped and broken, and not even spared the roots. I will destroy them—these thoughts, these powers of mind."

And again she laughed.

"There goes another avalanche," said those down in the valley.

The Godmother

At Montreux, one of the nearest towns, which with Clarens, Vevey, and Crin encircle the north-east part of the Lake of Geneva, resided Babette's godmother, the grand English lady, with her daughters and a young gentleman, a relation of theirs. They had only lately arrived, but the miller had already visited them, announced Babette's engagement, and told them about Rudy and the young eagle and the visit to Interlaken—in short, the whole story. It had pleased them very much, and made them feel very kindly towards Rudy, Babette, and the miller too; they also insisted upon all three coming over to Montreux, and that is why they had come. Babette was to see her godmother, and her godmother was to see Babette.

At the little town of Villeneuve, at one end of the Lake of Geneva lay the steamer that made the journey to Vevey, below Montreux, in half an hour. These shores have often been celebrated in song; here, under the walnut-trees, by the deep blue lake, sat Byron, and wrote his melodious verses of the prisoner in the dark rocky castle of Chillon. Here, where Clarens with its weeping willows is reflected in the water, wandered Rousseau, dreaming of Heloise. The Rhone flows along at the foot of the high snow-capped mountains of Savoy, and here, not far from its mouth, lies a little island in the lake, so small that, seen from the shore, it looks like a ship upon the water. The island is a rock which about a hundred years ago a lady caused to be dammed up, and covered with earth; she also planted three acacia-trees which now overshadow the whole island. Babette was enchanted with this spot, which appeared to her the loveliest in the whole voyage; she would very much have liked to land there, it was so beautiful. But the steamer went on and did not stop till it reached Vevey. The small party walked slowly up from here between the white sun-lit walls that enclose the vineyards around the little mountain-town of Montreux, where the fig-trees overshadow the peasant's houses, and where laurels and cypresses grow in the gardens. Half-way up the mountain stood the hotel in which Babette's godmother resided.

The reception was very cordial. The godmother was a pleasant woman with a round, smiling countenance; as a child she must certainly have resembled one of Raphael's cherubs. Even at her age her head was still that of an angel, richly crowned with silver locks. Her daughters were fine, elegant girls, tall and slender. The young cousin whom they had brought with them was clad in white from head to foot; he had golden hair and golden whiskers, so large that they might have been divided among three gentlemen; he immediately paid Babette the greatest attention.

Richly bound books, music and drawings lay strewn about on the large table. The doors leading to the balcony stood open, affording a lovely view of the great lake, which lay so clear and still that the mountains of Savoy, with their towns, woods and snowy peaks were reflected in it.

Rudy, who was at other times so lively and gay, did not in the least feel himself at home; he moved about as if he were walking on peas over a slippery floor. The time seemed as long and tedious to him as if he were on a treadmill. And then they had to go out for a walk. That was just as slow and tedious; Rudy could have taken two steps forward and one backwards to keep pace with the others. They walked down to Chillon, the gloomy old castle on the rocky island, merely to see the instruments of torture, the dungeons in which people were buried alive, the rusty chains hanging from the walls of rock, the stone benches for those condemned to death, the trap doors through which the unfortunate creatures were hurled down and impaled upon iron spikes amidst the surge. They called looking at all this pleasure. It was a place of execution, made famous by Byron's lines. But Rudy could not forget its original use. He leaned out of one of the great stone windows and looked down into the deep blue water and across to the little island with the three acacias, wishing himself there away from the whole chattering party. Babette however was unusually lively; she had amused herself famously, she said, and thought the cousin perfection itself.

"Yes, a perfect fop!" said Rudy; it was the first time that Rudy had said anything that did not please Babette. The Englishman had given her a little book as a souvenir of Chillon; it was Byron's poem "The Prisoner of Chillon" translated into French so that she could read it.

"It may be a good book," said Rudy, "but I don't like the finely combed fellow who gave it you."

"He looked just like a flour-sack without any flour," said the miller, laughing at his own wit.

Rudy laughed too, and said that that was just what he was like.

The Cousin

When a few days later Rudy went to pay a visit to the mill, he found the young Englishman there. Babette was just placing a dish of boiled trout before him, which she had doubtless herself garnished with parsley to make it look nice and appetizing. But Rudy thought all this quite unnecessary. What did the

Englishman want there? What was his business there? To be treated and waited upon by Babette? Rudy was jealous, and that made Babette happy. It pleased her to study every corner of his heart—both the strong and the weak spots. Love was to her as yet only a game, and she played with Rudy's whole heart.

It must, however, be said that in him was centered all her happiness and all her life; he was her one thought, and her ideal of all that was good and noble in the world. Still, the darker his looks grew, the more her eyes laughed; she would even have kissed the fair Englishman with the golden whiskers if by doing so she could have enraged Rudy and sent him rushing away, for that would have proved how much he loved her. This was certainly not right in Babette, but then she was only nineteen years old. She did not reflect much on her conduct, and still less did she consider that it might be interpreted as flighty by the young Englishman, and as not at all becoming for the modest betrothed daughter of the miller.

Where the high road from Bex passes under the snow-clad rocky heights, which in the language of the country are called "Diablerets," stood the mill, not far from a rushing mountain stream, which lashed itself into a gray foam like soapsuds. It was not this stream, however, that turned the mill-wheel, but a smaller one, which came tumbling down the rocks on the other side of the river, and which, gaining a greater impetus and power by being dammed up with stones, ran out, through a wooden trough like a wide gutter, over the large stream. The trough was always so full of water that it overflowed and offered a wet slippery path to any one who took it into his head to get to the mill by this shorter road. The young Englishman, however, thought he would try it. Dressed in white like a miller's boy, he was climbing up the path one evening, guided by the light that streamed from Babette's bedroom window. But as he had never learned to climb, he nearly went head first into the stream, escaping with wet arms and bespattered trousers. All dripping and covered with slime, he arrived beneath Babette's window, and, clambering up the old lime-tree, he began to mimic the owl, that being the only bird he could imitate. Babette, hearing him, looked out through the thin curtains; but when she saw the man in white, and guessed who it was, her little heart beat with terror and also with anger. She quickly put out the light, and, after having assured herself that the window had been securely fastened, she left him to hoot and to screech as much as he liked.

What a terrible thing it would be if Rudy were now at the mill! But Rudy was not at the mill; no—what was worse still—he was standing right under the lime-tree. Loud angry words were spoken; there might be blows—perhaps even murder!

Babette, in great terror, opened her window, and calling Rudy's name, begged him to go away, adding that she could not allow him to stay there.

"You cannot allow me to stay here!" he cried. "Then this is an appointment. You are expecting some good friend whom you prefer to me. Shame on you, Babette!"

"You are unbearable," cried Babette. "I hate you!" she added, in tears. "Go—go!"

"This I have not deserved," said he, as he strode away, his cheeks and his heart burning like fire.

Babette threw herself on the bed weeping.

"I love you so dearly, Rudy! How can you think so ill of me?"

She worked herself into quite a passion, and that was a good thing for her; otherwise she would have been very grieved. As it was, she could fall asleep and enjoy the refreshing slumber that virtue brings.

Evil Powers

Rudy left Bex and took his way homewards, ascending the mountain path, with its fresh cool air, where amidst the snow the Ice Maiden reigns. The trees, with their thick foliage, were far beneath him, and looked like potato-tops; the pines and the bushes became smaller up there; the Alpine roses grew next to the snow, which lay in solitary patches, like linen put out to bleach. A blue gentian that grew in his path he crushed with the butt-end of his gun.

Higher up two chamois showed themselves; Rudy's eyes sparkled, and his thoughts took a new turn. But as he was not near enough for a sure aim, he mounted higher up, where only thick stubble grew from between the boulders; seeing the chamois calmly crossing the snow-field, he pressed on. Thick mists gathered round him, and suddenly he found himself on the brink of a steep precipice. The rain began to pour down in torrents.

He felt a burning thirst; his head was hot, while his limbs were shivering. He seized his hunting-flask, but it was empty; he had not thought of filling it when he rushed up the mountains. He had never been ill before, but now he had a feeling as if he were so; he was tired, and felt an inclination to lie down, a desire to sleep, but the rain was streaming down all around him. He tried to rouse himself, but every object danced and trembled strangely before his eyes.

Suddenly he perceived what he had never seen here before—a newly built low hut that leaned against the rock, and in the doorway stood a young girl. It almost seemed to him as if it were Annette, the schoolmaster's daughter, whom he had once kissed in the dance; but though it was not Annette, still he had seen the girl somewhere before, perhaps near Grindelwald the evening he was returning from the shooting-match at Interlaken.

"How did you come here?" he asked.

"This is my home. I am minding my flocks."

"Your flocks? Where do they graze? Here there is only snow and rocks."

"You know much about what is here!" said the girl, laughing. "Here behind us, a little way down, is a fine piece of pasture. That is where my goats go. I take great care of them. I never lose one; what is mine, remains mine."

"You're pretty sharp," said Rudy.

"So are you," replied the girl.

"If you have any milk in the house, give me some to drink; I am dreadfully thirsty."

"I have something better than the milk," said the girl, "and you shall have it. There were some travelers here yesterday with a guide and they left half a bottle of wine behind them, such as you have never tasted. They will not come back for it, and as I shall not drink it, you can have it."

And the girl brought the wine, poured it into a wooden goblet, and handed it to Rudy.

"That's excellent," he said. "I never tasted wine so warming and so fiery."

His eyes sparkled: he was filled with fresh life, and with a glow as if every care and vexation had vanished; the strongest feelings of a man's nature welled up within him.

"But surely you are Annette," he cried. "Give me a kiss."

"If you give me the pretty ring you have on your finger."

"My engagement ring?"

"Yes, that's it," said the girl, and re-filling the goblet with wine she held it to his lips, and he drank. The pleasure of life coursed through his veins; he felt as though the whole world belonged to him—then why torment himself? Everything was created for our enjoyment and our happiness. The stream of life is the stream of pleasure; to be carried, to be torn along by it, is happiness. He looked at the young girl. She was Annette, and yet not Annette; still less was she the phantom, the ghost, as he had called it, that he had met near Grindelwald. The girl up here on the mountain was fresh as the driven snow, blooming as an Alpine rose, and swift as a kid; but still formed from Adam's rib, like himself. He flung his arms around the beautiful creature and looked into her eyes, so strangely clear. A moment only did he gaze, but in that moment who shall express or describe it in words? Was it the life of the spirit, or the spirit of death that took possession of him? Was he carried on high, or was he sinking into the deep deadly crevasse, deeper, ever deeper?

He saw the walls of ice looking like blue-green glass; fathomless chasms yawned around him, and the water dripped down with a sound like the chime of bells—clear as a pearl, and lit up by bluish flames.

The Ice Maiden kissed him—a kiss that sent an icy shudder through his whole frame; a cry of pain escaped him and, tearing himself away, he staggered and all became dark to his eyes; but he opened them again. The evil powers had played their game.

Gone was the Alpine maiden, gone the sheltering hut; the water trickled down the naked rocks, and the snow lay all around. Rudy was shivering with cold, soaked through to the skin, and his ring—the engagement ring that Babette had given him—had disappeared. His gun lay in the snow beside him; taking it up he tried to discharge it, but it missed fire. Damp clouds filled the chasm like masses of snow, and up above sat the Spirit of Giddiness watching her powerless prey; while from the depths came a sound as if a mass of rock were falling, crushing and carrying away everything that obstructed its course.

At the miller's Babette sat and wept. Rudy had not been there for six days—he who was in the wrong, he who ought to ask her pardon, and whom she loved with all her heart.

In the Mill

"What a life these people do lead!" said the parlor cat to the kitchen cat. "Babette and Rudy have fallen out again. She sits and cries, and I suppose he thinks no more about her."

"I don't like that," said the kitchen cat.

"Neither do I," said the parlor cat, "but I shall not take it to heart. Babette can become engaged to the red-whiskered fellow. But he has not been here either since the time he wanted to get on the roof."

Evil powers carry on their game around us and in us. Rudy had found that out and thought a great deal about it. What was it that had gone on about and within him on the mountain? Was it a ghost that he had seen, or only the result of a feverish dream? He had never had fever, or any other illness, before. But while judging Babette he had examined the workings of his own heart, and there he had found traces of the wild course of the fierce storm that had raged there. Could he confess all to Babette, every thought that in the hour of temptation might have led to deeds? He had lost her ring, and by that very loss she had won him back. Would she be able to confess to him? It seemed as if his heart would burst when he thought of her; how many recollections rose within him! He saw her as if she were standing before him in the flesh, a laughing, saucy child. Many a loving word that she had uttered out of the fulness of her love came like a ray of sunshine to his heart, and soon it was filled with nothing but sunshine at the thought of Babette. Yes, she would undoubtedly be able to confess to him, and she should, too.

He went to the mill. There was a confession; it began with a kiss, and ended with Rudy remaining the sinner. It was all his fault in having doubted Babette's fidelity—it was abominable of him. Such mistrust, such violence, could only lead them both into unhappiness. That, indeed, they could! And therefore Babette read him a little sermon, which amused her greatly and which she delivered with a pretty little air. On one point she admitted that Rudy was right: her godmother's nephew was a fop. She would burn the book that he had given her, so that she should not possess the least thing that could remind her of him.

"Now it's all over," said the parlor cat. "Rudy has come back, and they are friends again, which they say is the greatest happiness of all."

"I heard the rats say last night," said the kitchen cat, "that the greatest happiness consists in eating tallow candles and having plenty of rancid bacon. Whom is one to believe—the rats, or the lovers?"

"Neither," said the parlor cat, "that is the safest."

The greatest happiness for Rudy and Babette, the happy day, as they called it, their wedding-day, was drawing near.

But the wedding was not to take place in the church at Bex, nor at the mill; Babette's godmother wished the marriage to be solemnized in the pretty little church at Montreux, and the festivities to be held at her house. The miller was very anxious that her wish should be acceded to; he alone knew what she had determined to do for the newly married couple. They were to receive a wedding present from her which was well worth some such concession to her will.

The day was fixed. They were to travel as far as Villeneuve on the previous evening to be in time to take the boat across to Montreux early the next morning, so that the godmother's daughters might dress the bride.

"I suppose there will be a wedding feast in this house too," said the parlor cat; "if not, I wouldn't give a mew for the whole thing."

"Of course there'll be a feast here," said the kitchen cat. "Ducks have been killed, pigeons plucked, and a whole roebuck is hanging on the wall. My mouth waters when I think of it. They start to-morrow!"

Yes, to-morrow! That evening Rudy and Babette for the last time sat together as an engaged couple in the miller's house. Outside the glow was on the Alps, the evening bells rang out and the daughter of the sun sang: "Let what is best, happen!"

Night Visions

The sun had gone down, and the clouds lay low in the Rhone valley between the mountain-peaks. The wind blew from the south across the high Alps It was the wind from Africa—a hurricane that scattered the clouds; and when it had passed, all was still for a moment. The rent clouds hung in fantastic forms between the wooded hills and over the rapid Rhone river. They hung in shapes like the sea-monsters of old, like the eagle hovering in the air, like the jumping frogs in the marsh; they lay low upon the rushing stream, and sailed down upon it, though floating in the air. The stream carried an up-rooted fir-tree down with it, making eddying circles all around it; the Spirits of Giddiness were there, more than one, circling on the foaming waters. The moon lit up the snow-clad mountain peaks, the dark woods, and the strange white clouds—those forms of night that are the spirits of Nature's powers. The mountain-dwellers saw them through the window-panes, sailing past in troops before the Ice Maiden as she came out of her glacier-castle, sitting on the frail bark formed by the uprooted fir; the glacier-water carried her down the stream to the open sea.

"The wedding-guests are coming," was whistled in the air and sung upon the waters.

There were visions without and visions within.

Babette was dreaming a strange dream.

She dreamed that she had been married to Rudy for many years. He was gone out chamois-hunting, but she was sitting at home, and the young Englishman with the golden whiskers was with her. His eyes were so eloquent, and his words possessed such power, that when he held out his hand to her, she was obliged to follow him. They strode away from the house by a path that led ever downwards. Babette felt as though a weight lay upon her heart, which continually grew heavier; she was sinning against Rudy and against God. Suddenly she found herself deserted, her clothes torn by thorns, and her hair turned gray; looking upwards in her grief, she saw Rudy standing on a cliff. She stretched her arms out towards him, but did not venture to call or beg him to come; besides, that would have been useless, for she soon discovered that it was not Rudy, but only his coat and hat which he had hung upon his alpenstock as the hunters do to deceive the chamois. In her boundless grief Babette exclaimed: "Oh! would that I had died on my wedding-day, the happiest day of my life! My God! that would have been a mercy and a blessing. That would have been the best that could have happened for Rudy and me. No one knows the future!" Then, in godless despair, she hurled herself into the deep ravine. A sound like the breaking of a harp-string and one plaintive note was heard, and then Babette awoke.

The dream was past and effaced; but she knew that she had dreamed something terrible about the young Englishman whom she had not seen nor thought of for several months. She wondered whether he was at Montreux, and whether she should see him at the wedding. A slight shadow passed over her pretty face, and her eyebrows contracted. But soon a smile played around her lips and her eyes sparkled with joy, for the sun was shining gloriously, and to-morrow she and Rudy were to be married.

Rudy was already in the parlor when she entered it, and soon they were off to Villeneuve. Both were exceedingly happy, and so was the miller; he laughed and proved himself in the best of humors. He was a kind father and an honest soul.

"Now we are the masters of the house," said the parlor cat.

Conclusion

Evening had not yet fallen when the three joyous companions reached Villeneuve and sat down to dinner. This over, the miller sat in an armchair, smoked his pipe and had a little nap. The young bridal pair walked through the town arm in arm, and along the high road, at the foot of the wooded rocks by the side of the deep blue lake. The gloomy castle of Chillon, with its gray walls and ponderous towers, was reflected in the clear waters; the little island with the acacias was still nearer, and looked like a bouquet lying on the lake.

"How charming it must be there!" said Babette. She again felt her former desire come over her to cross to the island; this wish could now be gratified, for on the shore lay a boat, and the rope by which it was moored could easily be loosened. Seeing no one whom they could ask for permission, they took the boat without more ado, Rudy knowing how to row very well. The oars moved through the pliant water like the fins of a fish—that water which is so yielding and yet so strong, which has a back for carrying and jaws for swallowing, which though mild and smiling when at peace can inspire such terror in its destroying moods. A white streak of foam followed in the wake of the boat, which in a few minutes took them both over to the island, where they landed. There was only just room enough for two to dance.

Rudy swung Babette round two or three times, and then they sat down, hand in hand, on the little bench under the drooping acacias, looking into each other's eyes, while all around was bathed in the splendor of the setting sun. The pine-woods on the mountains assumed a purplish red tint like that of the blooming heather, and where the rocks were no longer covered with trees, they glowed as if the hills were transparent. The clouds in the sky were brilliant with a crimson glow, and the whole lake was like a fresh blooming rose-leaf. Gradually the shadows crept up the snow-clad mountains of Savoy and lent them a dark-blue hue till only the topmost peak glowed like red lava. They thus represented a moment in the history of the creation of the mountains, when these masses had just arisen in full glow out of the bowels of the earth and had not yet cooled down. Rudy and Babette thought they had never beheld such an Alpine glow before. The snow-clad "Dent du Midi" shone like the disk of the full moon when it rises above the horizon.

"What beauty! what happiness!" both exclaimed.

"Earth can bestow no more on me," said Rudy. "An evening such as this is a whole life. How often have I felt my happiness, as I feel it now, and thought that if all were to come to a sudden end, what a happy life I should have lived, and how beautiful this world would have been for me. But the day passed, and a new one, more beautiful even than the other, dawned for me. How infinitely good God is, Babette."

"I am truly happy," said she.

"Earth can bestow no more on me," exclaimed Rudy. And the evening bells rang out from the hills of Savoy and the mountains of Switzerland, while in the west the dark-blue Jura stood out in golden splendor.

"God grant you all that is brightest and best!" said Babette.

"He will," said Rudy. "To-morrow I shall have it. Tomorrow you will be entirely mine. My own sweet wife!"

"The boat!" cried Babette suddenly.

The boat which was to carry them back had become unfastened and was floating away from the island.

"I'll bring it back," said Rudy; and taking off his coat and boots, he plunged into the lake and swam with vigorous strokes after the boat.

Cold and deep was the clear blue ice-water from the mountain glacier. Rudy looked down into it; he took only a single glance, yet he thought he saw a golden ring rolling, shining, and sparkling in the depths. He remembered his engagement ring, and the ring became larger, extending itself into a shining circle within which appeared the clear glacier; deep chasms yawned around it, and the water dropped tinkling like the sound of bells, and gleaming with pale blue flames. In a second he saw what it takes us many words to describe.

Young hunters and young girls, men and women who had once fallen into the crevasses of the glaciers stood, there alive with smiles upon their lips, and far beneath the church bells of buried towns were ringing. The congregation knelt under the vaulted roof; the organ-pipes were formed of icicles and the mountain torrent furnished the music. The Ice Maiden sat on the clear transparent ground, and raising herself up towards Rudy kissed his feet. There passed through his limbs an icy death-like chill, an electric shock—ice and fire: for it is impossible to distinguish one from the other in a brief touch.

"Mine, mine!" sounded around him and within him.

"I kissed you when you were a child, kissed you on your mouth. Now I kiss you on your toes and heels, and you are entirely mine."

And he disappeared in the clear blue waters.

All was still; the church bells ceased ringing, their last notes dying away with the glow on the red clouds above.

"You are mine," resounded in the depths; "you are mine," re-echoed from on high—from the infinite.

How glorious to pass from love to love, from earth to Heaven!

A sound like the breaking of a harp-string, and a plaintive note were heard—the icy kiss of death had conquered what is mortal. The prelude had ended so that the real drama of life might begin; discord had resolved itself into harmony.

Do you call this a sad story?

Poor Babette! For her it was unspeakable anguish.

The boat floated farther and farther away. No one on the shore knew that the bridal pair had crossed over to the little island. The clouds began to gather, and evening came on. Alone, despairing and wailing, she stood there. A storm burst over her; the vivid lightning lit up the Jura mountains and the heights of Switzerland and Savoy; from all sides followed flash upon flash, while the peals of thunder came one upon the other, each lasting several minutes. One moment the lightning would light up the sky, so that every single vine stem could be seen as though it were broad day, and the next everything would again be plunged into darkness. The flashes formed bands, circles, and zigzags of light, darting into the lake on all sides, while the roar of the thunder increased by its own echo. On land the boats were drawn up on the beach, and every living thing had sought a shelter. And now the rain poured down in torrents.

"Where can Rudy and Babette be in this terrible storm?" said the miller.

Babette sat with folded hands, her head in her lap, dumb with grief; she wept, she wailed no more.

"In the deep water," she said to herself. "He is deep down, as under a glacier."

Then came into her mind what Rudy had told her of his mother's death, and of his escape when brought up almost dead out of the crevasse. "The Ice Maiden has him again."

There came a flash of lightning as dazzling as the sun's rays on the white snow. Babette sprang up; the lake rose at that moment like a shining glacier, and there stood the Ice Maiden, majestic, and encircled by a pale blue light, while at her feet lay Rudy's corpse. "Mine," she said, and again all was darkness and rolling water.

"How horrible!" wailed Babette. "Why was he to die just as the day of our happiness dawned? Oh, God! enlighten my understanding, shed light into my heart. I do not understand Thy ways, nor the inscrutable decrees of Thy omnipotence and wisdom."

And God enlightened her heart. A thought, a merciful ray of understanding shot through her, reminding her of her vivid dream of the past night; and she remembered the words and the wish she had uttered concerning what might be best for Rudy and herself.

"Woe is me! Was that the germ of sin in my heart? Was my dream a glimpse of our future lives, one of which had to be thus violently taken to effect my salvation? Miserable wretch that I am!"

She sat there wailing in the dark night. Through the deep stillness she still seemed to hear Rudy's words, the last he had spoken here: "Earth can bestow no more on me!" They had been uttered in the fullness of joy, they re-echoed in the midst of deep sorrow.

Years have passed since then. The lake and its shores still smile, and the vines yield luscious grapes. Steamboats with waving flags shoot past; pleasure-boats with swelling sails fly swiftly over the water like white butterflies. The railway past Chillon is opened, leading far into the Rhone valley. At every station strangers get out, and, holding their red-bound guide-books in their hands, read what sights they have to see. They visit Chillon, they see out in the lake the little island with the three acacias, and they read in their guide-book of the bridal pair who one evening in the year 1856 sailed over to it. They read how the bridegroom met his death, and how it was only on the following morning that the despairing cries of the bride were heard from the shore.

But the guide-book does not speak of Babette's quiet life with her father, not at the mill—for strangers live there now—but in the fine house near the railway-station. Many an evening she sits at her window and looks out over the chestnut trees to the snowclad mountains which Rudy once climbed. She sees the evening Alpine glow as the children of the sun settle down upon the lofty peaks, repeating the song of the traveler whose cloak the whirlwind tore away—taking the covering, but not the man.

There is a rosy tint on the mountain snow, and a rosy gleam in every heart in which dwells the thought: "God's will is best!" But the truth of it is not always revealed to us, as it was revealed to Babette in her dream.

The Old Bachelor's Nightcap

In Copenhagen there is a street with a strange name—"Hysken Sträde." Where did this name come from, and what is its meaning? It is said to be German, but that is unjust to the Germans, as then it would have to be called "Hauschen"—not "Hysken." "Hauschen" means little house, and a few little houses stood here once long ago. They were very little more substantial than the wooden booths we see now in the market-places at fair-time. They were, perhaps, a little larger and had windows; but the panes consisted of horn or bladder, as glass was then too expensive to be used by every one.

But then, the time we are speaking of was long ago—so long ago that our grandfathers and great-grandfathers would speak of these days as "olden times"—it was in fact several centuries back.

The rich merchants in Bremen and Lubeck carried on trade with Copenhagen; they did not reside in the town themselves, but sent their clerks, who lived in the wooden booths in Hauschen Street, and sold beer and spices. The German beer was good, and there were many kinds of it; for instance, Bremen, Prussinger, and Sono beer, and even Brunswick mumm; and quantities of spices were sold—saffron, aniseed, ginger, and especially pepper. Yes, pepper was the chief article, and so it happened the German clerks got the nickname of "pepper gentry," and there was a condition made with them when they left Bremen and Lubeck that they would not marry in Copenhagen. Many of them became very old, and had to take care of themselves, look after their own comforts, and light their own fires when they had any; and some of them became very solitary old boys with eccentric ideas and habits. From this, all unmarried men who have passed a certain age are called in Denmark "pepper gentry," and this must be remembered by all who wish to understand this tale.

The "pepper gentleman" becomes a butt for ridicule, and is continually told that he ought to put on his nightcap, draw it over his eyes and go to sleep. The boys sing,

"Take your nightcap, go to rest,
Poor old bachelor so good;
Your warm bed you'll find the best
When you've finished chopping wood."

So they sing of the "pepper gentlemen," and make game of the poor bachelor and his nightcap, and turn them into ridicule, because they know very little of either. That sort of nightcap no one would wish to have! And why not? We shall hear.

In olden times Small House Street was not paved, and foot passengers stumbled out of one hole into another, as in a neglected byway, and it was also very narrow. The booths leaned side by side, and were so close together that often in the summer time a sail was stretched from one booth to its opposite neighbor, and at this time the smell of pepper, saffron, and ginger became doubly powerful. One seldom saw young men behind the counters: the clerks were generally old boys, but they did not look as we should be apt to picture them, with wigs, nightcaps, and velvet knee-breeches, and with coat and waistcoat buttoned up to the chin. No, our grandfathers' great-grandfathers may have looked like that in their portraits, but the "pepper gentlemen" had no money to spare and did not have their portraits painted, although it would indeed be interesting now to have a picture of one of them as he stood behind the counter or went to church on holy days. His hat was high crowned and broad brimmed, and sometimes one of the younger clerks would have a feather in his. The woollen shirt was concealed by a broad linen collar; the close jacket buttoned up to the chin, and a cloak hung loosely over it; the trousers were tucked into broad-toed shoes, for the clerks did not wear stockings. In their belt they usually had a table-knife and spoon; also a larger knife for the defense of the owner, and it was often very necessary.

Anthony, one of the oldest clerks, was dressed in this way on holidays and festivals, with the exception that instead of the high-crowned hat, he wore a low bonnet, and under it a knitted cap, a regular nightcap, and to which he had grown so accustomed that it was always on his head, and he had two, nightcaps I mean, not heads.

The old man would have made a good artist's model, for he was as thin as a lath, had many crows-feet round his eyes and mouth, long bony fingers, and bushy gray eyebrows. Over his left eye grew quite a tuft of hair, which was not beautiful, although it gave him a striking appearance. People knew that he came from Bremen, but this was not his native place, although his master lived there; his own home was in Thuringia, the town of Eisenach, near the Wartburg. Old Anthony did not speak of this often, but he thought of it a great deal. The old clerks of Small House Street very seldom met one another; each remained in his own booth, which was closed early in the evening, and then it looked very dark and melancholy out in the street; a faint glimmer of light forced its way through the little horn-pane on the roof, and the old clerk sat inside the booth, usually on his bed, his German hymn-book in his hand, singing an evening hymn in a low voice. Sometimes he went about in the booth until late at night, busy about all kinds of things.

Indeed it was not a very pleasant life; to be in a strange country is a hard lot; nobody takes any notice of you unless you happen to come in their way.

The place often looked very deserted and gloomy when it was dark outside with rain or snow falling. There were no lamps in the street, except one solitary light hanging before a picture of the Virgin which was fastened against the wall. One could distinctly hear the splash of waves against the breakwater at the castle wharf.

Evenings like this are long and dreary, unless people can find something to do; there are not always things to be packed or unpacked, nor can scales be polished nor paper bags be made continually. Failing these, one must invent some other employment, and Anthony did so; he mended his clothes and put pieces on his boots. When he at last went to bed he used from habit to keep his nightcap on; he drew it down a little farther over his face, but he soon pushed it up again to see if the light had been properly put out. He would touch it, press the wick together, and then lie down on the other side and pull his nightcap down again. But very often a doubt would arise in his mind as to whether every coal in the little firepan below had been properly put out—a little spark might remain burning, and might set fire to something and cause damage. Therefore he got up, crept down the ladder—it could hardly be called a staircase—and when he came to the firepan, not a spark was to be seen, so he might just as well go to bed again. Then sometimes when he got half-way back he would wonder if the shutters were securely fastened; then his thin legs would carry him downstairs again. When at last he crept into bed, he would be so cold that his teeth chattered; cold seems to be doubly severe when it knows it cannot stay much longer. He drew up the bed-covering and drew the nightcap lower over his face, and tried to think of something other than trade and the labors of the day.

But this was not always agreeable, for old memories would come sometimes and raise the curtain of the past, bringing such painful thoughts that they pierce the heart and fill the eyes with tears—and that often happened to Anthony; scalding tears like large pearls would fall from his eyes to the quilt or the floor, and it would sound as if one of his heart-strings had broken. Sometimes they seemed to rise up again in a flame, illuminating a picture of life which never faded from his heart. Then he dried his eyes with his nightcap; the tear and the picture were indeed crushed, but the source of the tears remained and would well up again in his heart. The pictures did not come before him in the order in which they had occurred; often the most painful would come together; then at another time the happiest would come, but these always had the deepest shadows on them.

Every one admits that the beechwoods of Denmark are very beautiful, but the woods of Thuringia were far more beautiful in Anthony's eyes. The old oaks around the old baronial castle, where the creeping plants hung down over the rocks, seemed grander and more venerable to him, and the apple-blossoms were sweeter there than in the Danish land.

He remembered all this very clearly; a glittering tear rolled over his cheek, and in this tear he could distinctly see two children at play—a boy and a girl. The boy had rosy cheeks, curly, golden hair, and clear blue eyes; he was the son of the merchant Anthony—it was he himself. The little girl had brown eyes and black hair, and had a bright intelligent expression. She was the burgomaster's daughter Molly. The two children were playing with an apple; they shook it, and heard the pips rattling inside. Then they cut it in two, and each of them took half; they even divided the pips and ate them all but one, which the little girl suggested they should put in the ground. "Then you shall see what will come out," she said. "It will be something you do not at all expect. A whole apple-tree will come out, but not at once."

She put the pip in a flower-pot, and they were both very busy and excited about it. The boy made a hole in the earth with his finger; the little girl dropped the pip into it, and they both covered it over with earth.

"Now you must not take it out to-morrow to see if it has taken root," said Molly. "That does not do at all. I did it with my flowers, but only twice; I wanted to see if they were growing—I did not know any better then—and they all died."

Anthony took the flower-pot away with him, and all through the winter he looked at it every morning, but nothing was to be seen except the black earth. At last, however, the spring came, the sun shone warmly again, and two little green leaves came up out of the pot.

"They represent Molly and myself," said the boy. "That's beautiful, that's wonderfully beautiful."

Soon a third leaf came. Whom did that represent? And another came, and yet another. Day after day and week after week it grew larger, until at last it began to look like a real tree.

All this was mirrored in a single tear which was wiped away, and disappeared; but it might come again from its source in old Anthony's heart.

There is a chain of stony mountains in the neighborhood of Eisenach. One of them has a rounded outline, and rises above the rest; it is quite bare and without tree, bush, or grass. It is called the Venus Mount, and in it dwells Venus, one of the old heathen deities. She is also called Lady Holle, and every child in the neighborhood of Eisenach has heard of her. It was she who enticed Tannhauser, the noble knight and minstrel, from the circle of the singers of the Wartburg into her mountain. Little Molly and Anthony often stood near this mountain, and one day Molly said, "Knock and say, Lady Holle, open the door—Tannhauser is here!"

But Anthony was not courageous enough. However, Molly did it, but she only said the words "Lady Holle, Lady Holle," aloud and distinctly; the rest she muttered so indistinctly that Anthony felt sure she really said nothing, yet she was as bold and saucy as possible; as saucy as she was sometimes when she came round him with other little girls in the garden, and they all tried to kiss him, because he did not like it and endeavored to send them away. Molly was the only one who took no notice of his resistance.

"*I* may kiss him!" she would say proudly; and Anthony put up with it and thought no more of it—it was only her vanity.

How charming Molly was, and what a dreadful tease! They said that Lady Holle was beautiful too, but that her beauty was tempting like that of an evil spirit. Saint Elizabeth possessed the greatest beauty and grace; she was the patron saint of the country, the pious princess of Thuringia, whose good deeds have been immortalized in so many lands by means of stories and legends. Her picture hung in the chapel surrounded by silver lamps, but it was not at all like Molly.

The apple-tree which the two children had planted grew year by year, and became larger and larger—so large that it had to be put out in the garden at last, in the fresh air where the dew fell and the sun shone. There it became so strong that it was able to stand the cold of the winter, and it seemed as if, when the severity of the winter was over, it put forth flowers in the spring for joy. It had two apples upon it in the autumn—one for Molly and one for Anthony. It could not very well do less.

So the tree grew very rapidly, and Molly grew with the tree. She looked as fresh as an apple-blossom; but Anthony was not to behold this flower for long. All things change; Molly's father left his old home, and Molly went far away with him. In our time the railways have made this a journey of a few hours only, but then it took a day and a night to go as far eastward from Eisenach to the city which is still called Weimar, at the farthest border of Thuringia. Molly and Anthony wept; but their tears united and had the sweet rosy hue of joy, for Molly told him that she loved him, loved him more than all the splendors of Weimar.

One, two, three years went by, and during this time he only received two letters: one came by the carrier, and a traveler brought the other. The way was long, difficult and circuitous, and passed through many towns and villages.

Molly and Anthony had often heard the story of Tristram and Isold, and the boy had applied it to himself and Molly, though the name Tristram was said to mean "born in tribulation," and that did not apply to Anthony, nor would he ever think, like Tristram, "She has forgotten me." But, indeed, Isold did not forget her faithful knight, and when they were both laid to rest in the earth, one on each side of the church, the lime-trees grew from their graves over the church roof and there mingled their blossoms and leaves together.

Anthony thought this a beautiful story, but sad—he was not afraid of anything sad happening to him or Molly—and he whistled a song composed by Walter of the Vogelweide, the old minnesinger:

> *"Under the lindens on the heath."*

One part of it he liked best of all:

> *"Through the wood and in the vale*
> *Sweetly trills the nightingale."*

This song was often upon his lips, and he sang and whistled it on the moonlight night when he rode along the deep hollow way, on the road to Weimar, to visit Molly. He wished to arrive unexpectedly, and he did so. He was welcomed with full goblets of wine, and introduced to many pleasant people; a pretty room and a good bed were provided for him. Yet his reception was not what he had imagined and hoped it would be; he could not understand himself, or the others, but *we* may understand why it was so. One may go into a house and associate with the family without becoming one of them;

one may talk together as people do in a stage-coach with a fellow-traveler, each inconveniencing the other, and wishing that either his good neighbor or himself were away. It was something of this kind that Anthony felt.

"I am a straightforward girl," said Molly, "and I will myself tell you how things stand. Much has changed since we were children together—both inwardly and outwardly. Habit and will cannot control our hearts. Anthony, now that I shall soon be far away from here, I should not like to make an enemy of you: I shall always think of you kindly, but I have never felt for you what I now feel for another man. You must reconcile yourself to this. Farewell, Anthony."

And Anthony bade her "good-bye" without a tear, but he felt he was no longer Molly's friend. Hot and cold iron both take the skin from our lips, and we have the same sensation when we kiss it; so his hatred sprang to life in a kiss just as his love had done.

Within twenty-four hours Anthony was back to Eisenach, but the horse he had ridden was ruined.

"What does it matter?" he said. "My life is ruined also—I will destroy everything that can remind me of her, or of Lady Holle—or Venus, the heathen woman! I will break down the apple-tree, and tear it up by the roots, so that it will never blossom or bear fruit again!"'

But the apple-tree was not broken down—he himself broke down, and was confined to his bed by a fever. But what raised him up again? A medicine that he was forced to take was given him—the bitterest medicine, which both body and spirit alike shrink from. Anthony's father was no longer a rich merchant. Hard days of trial came—misfortune came rolling into the house like the waves of the sea. Suffering and anxiety took away the father's strength, and Anthony had something else to think of beside nursing his love-sorrows and his anger against Molly. He had to take his father's place: to give orders, to help, to act with energy, and at last to go out into the world to earn his own living. He went to Bremen, and there learned what poverty and hardships meant; these sometimes make the heart callous, but at other times soften it too much.

How different the world and the people in it were to what he had imagined them to be in his boyhood! What were the minnesinger's songs to him now? An echo of something that had vanished long ago. Yes, so he thought at times: but once more the songs would sound in his soul, and his heart would become gentle again.

"God's will be done!" he would say then. "It is a good thing that I was not permitted to keep Molly's love—that she did not remain true to me. What misery might it not have brought about now fortune has turned away from me! She left me before she knew of this disaster, or what the future held in store for me. That is the mercy of Providence. Everything has happened for the best; she was not to blame—and yet I have been so hard and bitter towards her!"

Years rolled on—Anthony's father died, and strangers lived in the old house, but Anthony was destined to see it once more. His rich employer sent him journeys on business, and his way led through Eisenach, his native town. The old Wartburg stood unaltered, with "the monk and the nun" hewn out of stone. The old oaks made it look the same as in his childish days, and the Venus Mount stood gray and bare over the valley. He would have cried gladly:

"Lady Holle, Lady Holle, unlock the mountain; I will enter and remain in my native earth!"

But that was a sinful desire, and he crossed himself to drive it away. A little bird among the bushes sang sweetly, and the old minne-song was recalled to his memory:

"Through the wood and in the vale
Sweetly trills the nightingale."

Here, in the town of his childhood, which he saw again through tears, much came back into his remembrance—his father's house stood just as it had done in the old times, but the garden was altered. A path leading across the fields led through part of the old ground, and the apple-tree that he had not broken down stood there still, but it was outside the garden, on the further side of the path. But the sun threw his rays on the apple-tree as in former days, the dew fell gently upon it as it did then, and its branches were filled with such a load of fruit that they bent down towards the ground.

"How it thrives," he said; "the tree may well do so!"

One of its branches, however, was broken; mischievous hands had torn it down, as the tree stood near the high road.

"People break its blossoms off without an expression of thanks, they steal its fruit, and break its branches; one could say of the tree as it has been said of some people, it was not sung at its cradle that this should happen to it. Its story began so pleasantly, and to what has it come now? Forsaken and forgotten, a garden tree near a ditch in the field close by the high road. There it stands without protection, ransacked, and broken! It is not yet dead, but in time its blossoms will become fewer, and there will be no fruit at all—and then its story will be ended."

Thus thought Anthony while he stood under the tree, thus he thought during many a long night in the solitary chamber of the wooden house in the distant land—in Small House Street, Copenhagen, whither his rich master, the Bremen merchant, had sent him, on condition that he should never marry.

"Marry! Ha, ha," he laughed bitterly to himself.

Winter had come early, it was freezing hard. Outside a snowstorm was raging; every one who could, remained at home. Thus it happened that the people who lived opposite Anthony did not notice that his door had not been unlocked for two days, nor had he shown himself, for who would go out in such weather if he could help it? These were gray, gloomy days, and in the house, the windows of which were not made of glass, there was only alternately twilight and dark night. Old Anthony had not left his bed for these two days; he had not the strength to get up, already for a long time he had felt the effects of the weather in his limbs; forsaken by all, the bachelor lay there and could not help himself, he could hardly reach the water-jug which he had put by his bedside, and he had taken all to the last drop. It was not fever, nor illness, but old age that had laid him up. Where he lay it was as dark as if it were perpetual night. A little spider, which, however, he could not see, spun its web over him, busily and contentedly, as if it were weaving a band of crepe, which should wave over him when the old man closed his eyes.

Time was hanging heavily and painfully with him; he had no tears to shed, and he felt no pain. No thought of Molly entered his mind; he felt as if the world and its noise had no longer anything to do with him, as if he were lying outside the world, and nobody thought of him. For a moment he felt hungry or thirsty—yes, he felt both—but no one came to look after him. He thought of all who had suffered from want of food sometimes; of Saint Elizabeth when she wandered on earth, the saint of his native place, and of his childhood, the noble duchess of Thuringia, the kind-hearted lady who used to visit the humblest cottages administering food and comfort to its poor inmates. The thought of her pious deeds was as light to his soul. He remembered how she came to say words of consolation, dressing the wounds of the afflicted and feeding the hungry, although her severe husband had often scolded her for it. He remembered the legend about her, in which she is said to have carried a basket full of food and wine, and her husband who watched her, came and asked her angrily what she was carrying, and she answered, with fear and trembling, "Roses which I have picked in the garden"; how he had then torn the white cloth from the basket, and how a miracle had been performed for the good woman, as bread and wine, and everything in the basket, had been transformed into roses! Thus the memory of the saint filled Anthony's calm mind; she stood as if real, before his dim sight in his simple dwelling in the Danish land. He uncovered his head and looked into her mild eyes, and everything around him was bright and rosy—indeed the roses seemed to breathe forth fragrance—and a sweet strange smell of apples reached him; he saw an apple-tree in full bloom spreading its branches above him—it was the tree which he and Molly had planted together.

And the tree dropped its fragrant petals upon him, and cooled his hot brow; the petals fell upon his parched lips, and were like strengthening wine and bread; they also fell upon his breast, and he became calm and felt inclined to sleep.

"Now I shall sleep," he whispered to himself; "sleep will do me good. To-morrow I shall get up again and be strong and well. Wonderful, wonderful! The apple-tree planted in love I see now in magnificence!" And he slept.

The day after this—it was the third day that his booth remained locked—the snowstorm raged no longer; then a neighbor from the opposite house came to the booth where Anthony dwelled as he had not yet shown himself. He lay there stretched on his bed—dead—clutching his old cap tightly in both hands. They did not put it on when he was in his coffin; he had a clean white one on then.

Where now were the tears he had shed? What had become of the pearls? They remained in the nightcap—and the real ones do not come out in the wash—they were preserved in the nightcap, and in time forgotten; but the old thoughts and the old dreams, they still remained in the bachelor's nightcap. Don't wish for such a cap, it would make your forehead burn, your pulse beat quicker, and produce dreams which appear like reality.

The man who first wore the cap afterwards felt all this, though it was fifty years later, and he was the burgomaster himself who was tolerably wealthy, and had a wife and eleven children. He was immediately seized with dreams of unfortunate love, of bankruptcy and times of hardship.

"Good heavens! how the nightcap burns!" he cried, tearing it from his head; a pearl rolled out and then another, and another, and they sparkled and made a rattling sound.

"I must be suffering from gout," said the burgomaster; "something glitters before my eyes!"

They were tears, shed fifty years before by old Anthony of Eisenach.

Every one who put the nightcap on his head afterwards, had visions and dreams that excited him a great deal. His own life history was changed into that of Anthony and became a story—in fact many stories. But some one else must tell these; we have told the first one, and our parting word to you is—Don't wish for "the old bachelor's nightcap."

"Everything in the Right Place"

It is more than a hundred years ago! At the border of the wood, near a large lake, stood the old mansion: deep ditches surrounded it on every side, in which reeds and bulrushes grew. Close by the drawbridge, near the gate, there was an old willow-tree, which bent over the reeds. From the narrow pass came the sound of bugles and the trampling of horses' feet; therefore a little girl who was watching the geese hastened to drive them away from the bridge, before the whole hunting party came galloping up; they came, however, so quickly, that the girl, in order to avoid being run over, placed herself on one of the high corner-stones of the bridge. She was still half a child and very delicately built; she had bright blue eyes, and a gentle, sweet expression. But such things the baron did not notice; while he was riding past the little goose-girl, he reversed his hunting crop, and in rough play gave her such a push with it that she fell backward into the ditch.

"Everything in the right place!" he cried. "Into the ditch with you."

Then he burst out laughing, for that he called fun; the others joined in—the whole party shouted and cried, while the hounds barked.

While the poor girl was falling she happily caught one of the branches of the willow-tree, by the help of which she held herself over the water, and as soon as the baron with his company and the dogs had disappeared through the gate, the girl endeavored to scramble up, but the branch broke off, and she would have fallen backward among the rushes, had not a strong hand from above seized her at this moment. It was the hand of a peddler; he had witnessed what had happened from a short distance, and now hastened to assist her.

"Everything in the right place," he said, imitating the noble baron, and pulling the little maid up to the dry ground. He wished to put the branch back in the place it had been broken off, but it is not possible to put "everything in the right place"; therefore he stuck the branch into the soft ground.

"Grow and thrive if you can, and produce a good flute for them yonder at the mansion," he said; it would have given him great pleasure to see the noble baron and his companions well thrashed. Then he entered the castle—but not the banqueting hall; he was too humble for that. No; he went to the servants' hall. The menservants and maids looked over his stock of articles and bargained with him; loud crying and screaming were heard from the master's table above: they called it singing—indeed, they did their best. Laughter and the howls of dogs were heard through the open windows: there they were feasting and reveling; wine and strong old ale were foaming in the glasses and jugs; the favorite dogs ate with their masters; now and then the squires kissed one of these animals, after having wiped its mouth first with the tablecloth. They ordered the peddler to come up, but only to make fun of him. The wine had got into their heads, and reason had left them. They poured beer into a stocking that he could drink with them, but quick. That's what they called fun, and it made them laugh. Then meadows, peasants, and farmyards were staked on one card and lost.

"Everything in the right place!" the peddler said when he had at last safely got out of Sodom and Gomorrah, as he called it. "The open high road is my right place; up there I did not feel at ease."

The little maid, who was still watching the geese, nodded kindly to him as he passed through the gate.

Days and weeks passed, and it was seen that the broken willow-branch which the peddler had stuck into the ground near the ditch remained fresh and green—nay, it even put forth fresh twigs; the little goose-girl saw that the branch had taken root, and was very pleased; the tree, so she said, was now her tree. While the tree was advancing, everything else at the castle was going backward, through feasting and gambling, for these are two rollers upon which nobody stands safely. Less than six years afterwards the baron passed out of his castle-gate a poor beggar, while the baronial seat had been bought by a rich tradesman. He was the very peddler they had made fun of and poured beer into a stocking for him to drink; but honesty and industry bring one forward, and now the peddler was the possessor of the baronial estate. From that time forward no card-playing was permitted there.

"That's a bad pastime," he said; "when the devil saw the Bible for the first time he wanted to produce a caricature in opposition to it, and invented card-playing."

The new proprietor of the estate took a wife, and whom did he take?—The little goose-girl, who had always remained good and kind, and who looked as beautiful in her new clothes as if she had been a lady of high birth. And how did all this come about? That would be too long a tale to tell in our busy time, but it really happened, and the most important events have yet to be told.

It was pleasant and cheerful to live in the old place now: the mother superintended the household, and the father looked after things out-of-doors, and they were indeed very prosperous.

Where honesty leads the way, prosperity is sure to follow. The old mansion was repaired and painted, the ditches were cleaned and fruit-trees planted; all was homely and pleasant, and the floors were as white and shining as a pasteboard. In the long winter evenings the mistress and her maids sat at the spinning-wheel in the large hall; every Sunday the counselor—this title the peddler had obtained, although only in his old days—read aloud a portion from the Bible. The children (for they had children) all received the best education, but they were not all equally clever, as is the case in all families.

In the meantime the willow-tree near the drawbridge had grown up into a splendid tree, and stood there, free, and was never clipped. "It is our genealogical tree," said the old people to their children, "and therefore it must be honored."

A hundred years had elapsed. It was in our own days; the lake had been transformed into marsh land; the whole baronial seat had, as it were, disappeared. A pool of water near some ruined walls was the only remainder of the deep ditches; and here stood a magnificent old tree with overhanging branches—that was the genealogical tree. Here it stood, and showed how beautiful a willow can look if one does not interfere with it. The trunk, it is true, was cleft in the middle from the root to the crown; the storms had bent it a little, but it still stood there, and out of every crevice and cleft, in which wind and weather had carried mold, blades of grass and flowers sprang forth. Especially above, where the large boughs parted, there was quite a hanging garden, in which wild raspberries and hart's-tongue ferns thrived, and even a little mistletoe had taken root, and grew gracefully in the old willow-branches, which were reflected in the dark water beneath when the wind blew the chickweed into the corner of the pool. A footpath which led across the fields passed close by the old tree. High up, on the woody hillside, stood the new mansion. It had a splendid view, and was large and magnificent; its window-panes were so clear that one might have thought there were none there at all. The large flight of steps which led to the entrance looked like a bower covered with roses and broad-leaved plants. The lawn was as green as if each blade of grass was cleaned separately morning and evening. Inside, in the hall, valuable oil paintings were hanging on the walls. Here stood chairs and sofas covered with silk and velvet, which could be easily rolled about on casters; there were tables with polished marble tops, and books bound in morocco with gilt edges. Indeed, well-to-do and distinguished people lived here; it was the dwelling of the baron and his family. Each article was in keeping with its surroundings. "Everything in the right place" was the motto according to which they also acted here, and therefore all the paintings which had once been the honor and glory of the old mansion were now hung up in the passage which led to the servants' rooms. It was all old lumber, especially two portraits—one representing a man in a scarlet coat with a wig, and the other a lady with powdered and curled hair holding a rose in her hand, each of them being surrounded by a large wreath of willow-branches. Both portraits had many holes in them, because the baron's sons used the two old people as targets for their cross-bows. They represented the counselor and his wife, from whom the whole family descended. "But they did not properly belong to our family," said one of the boys; "he was a peddler and she kept the geese. They were not like papa and mamma." The portraits were old lumber, and "everything in its right place." That was why the great-grandparents had been hung up in the passage leading to the servants' rooms.

Two portraits—one representing a man in a scarlet coat with a wig, and the other a lady with powdered and curled hair holding a rose in her hand, each of them being surrounded by a large wreath of willow-branches

The son of the village pastor was tutor at the mansion. One day he went for a walk across the fields with his young pupils and their elder sister, who had lately been confirmed. They walked along the road which passed by the old willow-tree, and while they were on the road she picked a bunch of field-flowers. "Everything in the right place," and indeed the bunch looked very beautiful. At the same time she listened to all that was said, and she very much liked to hear the pastor's son speak about the elements and of the great men and women in history. She had a healthy mind, noble in thought and deed, and with a heart full of love for everything that God had created. They stopped at the old willow-tree, as the youngest of the baron's sons wished very much to have a flute from it, such as had been cut for him from other willow trees; the pastor's son broke a branch off. "Oh, pray do not do it!" said the young lady; but it was already done. "That is our famous old tree. I love it very much. They often laugh at me at home about it, but that does not matter. There is a story attached to this tree." And now she told him all that we already know about the tree—the old mansion, the peddler and the goose-girl who had met there for the first time, and had become the ancestors of the noble family to which the young lady belonged.

"They did not like to be knighted, the good old people," she said; "their motto was 'everything in the right place,' and it would not be right, they thought, to purchase a title for money. My grandfather, the first baron, was their son. They say he was a very learned man, a great favorite with the princes and princesses, and was invited to all court festivities. The others at home love him best; but, I do not know why, there seemed to me to be something about the old couple that attracts my heart! How homely, how patriarchal, it must have been in the old mansion, where the mistress sat at the spinning-wheel with her maids, while her husband read aloud out of the Bible!"

"They must have been excellent, sensible people," said the pastor's son. And with this the conversation turned naturally to noblemen and commoners; from the manner in which the tutor spoke about the significance of being noble, it seemed almost as if he did not belong to a commoner's family.

"It is good fortune to be of a family who have distinguished themselves, and to possess as it were a spur in oneself to advance to all that is good. It is a splendid thing to belong to a noble family, whose name serves as a card of admission to the highest circles. Nobility is a distinction; it is a gold coin that bears the stamp of its own value. It is the fallacy of the time, and many poets express it, to say that all that is noble is bad and stupid, and that, on the contrary, the lower one goes among the poor, the more brilliant virtues one finds. I do not share this opinion, for it is wrong. In the upper classes one sees many touchingly beautiful traits; my own mother has told me of such, and I could mention several. One day she was visiting a nobleman's house in town; my grandmother, I believe, had been the lady's nurse when she was a child. My mother and the nobleman were alone in the room, when he suddenly noticed an old woman on crutches come limping into the courtyard; she came every Sunday to carry a gift away with her.

"There is the poor old woman," said the nobleman; "it is so difficult for her to walk."

"My mother had hardly understood what he said before he disappeared from the room, and went downstairs, in order to save her the troublesome walk for the gift she came to fetch. Of course this is only a little incident, but it has its good sound like the poor widow's two mites in the Bible, the sound which echoes in the depth of every human heart; and this is what the poet ought to show and point out—more especially in our own time he ought to sing of this; it does good, it mitigates and reconciles! But when a man, simply because he is of noble birth and possesses a genealogy, stands on his hind legs and neighs in the street like an Arabian horse, and says when a commoner has been in a room: 'Some people from the street have been here,' there nobility is decaying; it has become a mask of the kind that Thespis created, and it is amusing when such a person is exposed in satire."

Such was the tutor's speech; it was a little long, but while he delivered it he had finished cutting the flute.

There was a large party at the mansion; many guests from the neighborhood and from the capital had arrived. There were ladies with tasteful and with tasteless dresses; the big hall was quite crowded with people. The clergymen stood humbly together in a corner, and looked as if they were preparing for a funeral, but it was a festival—only the amusement had not yet begun. A great concert was to take place, and that is why the baron's young son had brought his willow flute with him; but he could not make it sound, nor could his father, and therefore the flute was good for nothing.

There was music and songs of the kind which delight most those that perform them; otherwise quite charming!

"Are you an artist?" said a cavalier, the son of his father; "you play on the flute, you have made it yourself; it is genius that rules—the place of honor is due to you."

"Certainly not! I only advance with the time, and that of course one can't help."

"I hope you will delight us all with the little instrument—will you not?" Thus saying he handed to the tutor the flute which had been cut from the willow-tree by the pool; and then announced in a loud voice that the tutor wished to perform a solo on the flute. They wished to tease him—that was evident, and therefore the tutor declined to play, although he could do so very well. They urged and requested him, however, so long, that at last he took up the flute and placed it to his lips.

That was a marvelous flute! Its sound was as thrilling as the whistle of a steam engine; in fact it was much stronger, for it sounded and was heard in the yard, in the garden, in the wood, and many miles round in the country; at the same time a storm rose and roared: "Everything in the right place." And with this the baron, as if carried by the wind, flew out of the hall straight into the shepherd's cottage, and the shepherd flew—not into the hall, thither he could not come—but into the servants' hall, among the smart footmen who were striding about in silk stockings; these haughty menials looked horror-struck that such a person ventured to sit at table with them. But in the hall the baron's daughter flew to the place of honor at the end of the table—she was worthy to sit there; the pastor's son had the seat next to her; the two sat there as if they were a bridal pair. An old Count, belonging to one of the oldest families of the country, remained untouched in his place of honor; the flute was just, and it is one's duty to be so. The sharp-tongued cavalier who had caused the flute to be played, and who was the child of his parents, flew headlong into the fowl-house, but not he alone.

The flute was heard at the distance of a mile, and strange events took place. A rich banker's family, who were driving in a coach and four, were blown out of it, and could not even find room behind it with their footmen. Two rich farmers who had in our days shot up higher than their own corn-fields, were flung into the ditch; it was a dangerous flute. Fortunately it burst at the first sound, and that was a good thing, for then it was put back into its owner's pocket—"its right place."

The next day, nobody spoke a word about what had taken place; thus originated the phrase, "to pocket the flute." Everything was again in its usual order, except that the two old pictures of the peddler and the goose-girl were hanging in the banqueting hall. There they were on the wall as if blown up there; and as a real expert said that they were painted by a master's hand, they remained there and were restored. "Everything in the right place," and to this it will come. Eternity is long, much longer indeed than this story.

Anne Lisbeth

Anne Lisbeth was decidedly pretty. She had a beautiful pink and white complexion, gleaming white teeth, and bright eyes. Her step was light in the dance, and her mind was still lighter. But what was the good of it all? Her son was an ugly babe. Yes, he was not in the least pretty, so he was put out to be nursed by the laborer's wife. But Anne Lisbeth was taken into the count's castle, and sat there in the splendid apartments, clothed in silk and velvet; not a breath of air was allowed to blow upon her, for she was nurse to the count's child. He was as beautiful as an angel, as fair and delicate as a prince; and how much she loved him! Her own boy was provided for at the laborer's, where one's mouth watered more frequently than the pot boiled, and generally there was no one at home to look after the child. Then he cried; but what nobody knows, nobody troubles about. He would cry till he was tired, and then fall asleep, and in sleep one can neither feel hunger nor thirst. Sleep is a capital invention.

As the years passed on, Anne Lisbeth's child grew apace, like a weed, although they said his growth was stunted. He had become quite a member of the family in which he dwelled, for they had been paid to keep him altogether, so that his mother was rid of him for good. She had become a town lady, and had a comfortable home of her own, and when she went for a walk, she wore a bonnet, but she never walked so far as the laborer's cottage; that was too far from town, and indeed, there was no reason why she should go there. The boy belonged to these laboring people now, and she said he could eat, and must therefore do something to earn his bread, and consequently he kept Mad Jensen's red cow. He could already take care of cattle and make himself generally useful.

The big dog by the yard gate of a nobleman's house sits proudly outside his kennel when the sun shines, and barks at every one who goes by; but if it rains he creeps inside, and there he is warm and dry. Anne Lisbeth's boy also sat on the top of a fence in the sunshine, carving a pole-pin. In the spring, he knew of three strawberry plants that were in bloom and would be sure to bear fruit, and this was his greatest hope, but they did not come to anything.

He sat out in the rain in bad weather and got wet to the skin, and afterwards the cold wind dried the clothes on his back. Whenever he went to the farmyard belonging to the mansion he was hustled and knocked about, for the men-servants and maids said he was so dreadfully ugly; but he was used to that—nobody loved him.

This was how Anne Lisbeth's boy got on in the world; and how could one expect anything different? It was his destiny that no one should love him.

Until now he had been a "land crab," but the land at last threw him over. He went to sea in an unseaworthy vessel, and sat at the helm while the skipper sat over his grog. He was dirty and ugly, half starved and half frozen, looking as though he had never had enough to eat, and this was really so.

It was late in autumn, and the weather was rough, windy, and rainy. The cold penetrated the thickest clothing, especially at sea; and a wretched boat went out, with only two men on board, or, to speak more correctly, a man and a half, the skipper and his boy. It had been dull and overcast all day, and it soon became quite dark and bitterly cold, so the skipper took a dram to warm himself. The bottle was old and the glass too; it was whole at the top, but the foot had been broken off, and it therefore stood upon a little carved block of wood painted blue. "A dram is a great comfort, and two are still better," thought the skipper. The boy sat at the helm, which he held fast in his horny seamed hands; he was very ugly his hair was tangled, and he looked stunted and crippled. He was called the field laborer's boy, although he was entered in the church register as Anne Lisbeth's son.

The wind whistled in the rigging, and the boat darted over the sea. The sails were filled by the wind, and carried them along in mad career. It was rough and wet underfoot and overhead, and might soon be worse. But hold, what was that? what had struck the vessel? Was it a waterspout, or a heavy sea coming over them?

The boy at the helm cried out: "Heaven help us!"

The boat had struck upon a great rock standing out of the depths of the sea, and sank like an old shoe in a puddle, with "man and mouse," as the saying is. There were mice on board, but only one man and a half—that is to say, the skipper and the laborer boy. No one saw it but the seagulls flying overhead, or the fishes beneath; and even they did not see properly, for they started back, frightened when the boat filled with water and sank. It was lying scarcely a fathom below the water, and the skipper and his boy were buried and forgotten; they would never need anything more in this world. But the glass with its blue wooden foot did not sink, for the wood kept it afloat; the glass drifted away to be cast upon the beach and broken, but when and where is of no consequence. It had served its purpose, and had been loved, which Anne Lisbeth's boy had never been. But in Heaven no soul will be able to say "No one has ever loved me."

Anne Lisbeth had lived many years in the town: she was called "Madame," and felt very dignified in consequence, and she recollected the "noble" days when she had driven in the carriage, and had associated with countesses and baronesses. Her beautiful young count was the dearest angel and had the kindest heart, he had been so fond of her, and she had loved him in return; they had kissed and loved each other, and the boy had been her delight, her second existence. Now he was fourteen years old, tall, handsome, and clever; she had not seen him since she carried him in her arms; as it was such a long journey to the count's mansion she had not been there for many years.

"I must make an effort for once, and go," said Anne Lisbeth. "I must go and see my darling, my sweet young count; he also must long to see me, and he thinks of me, and loves me, as he did in those days when he flung his angel arms round my neck and cried 'Anne Liz!' It was like music to me. Yes, I must make an effort and see him again."

She drove across the country in a grazier's cart, and then got out and continued her journey on foot, and so reached the count's mansion. It was as great and magnificent as it had always been, and the grounds looked just the same as usual; but all the servants were strangers to her, not one of them knew Anne Lisbeth, or of what consequence she once was in the house; but she felt sure the countess would soon let them know it, and her darling boy too: how she longed to see him!

Now that she was at her journey's end, Anne Lisbeth was kept waiting a long time, and the time passes slowly for one who waits. But before the great people went in to dinner, she was called, and spoken to very graciously. She was to be sent for again after dinner, and then she was to see her sweet boy.

How slender and tall he had grown! But he still had his beautiful eyes and angelic mouth. He looked at her without saying a word; certainly he did not remember her. He turned and was about to leave the room, when she seized his hand and pressed it to her lips.

"Good, that is enough," he said; and with that he went out of the room—he who had filled her every thought, whom she loved better than any other creature, and who was her whole earthly pride!

Anne Lisbeth went out of the castle into the high road, feeling dejected and sad. He had been so cold and strange to her, he had not a word or thought for her, whom she had carried, day and night in her arms, and whom she still carried in her dreams.

A great black raven flew down in front of her on the high road and croaked again and again.

"Ah," she said, "what bird of ill omen are you?"

She passed the laborer's cottage before long; his wife stood at the door, and the two women spoke to one another.

"You look well," said the woman. "You are quite plump and stout; you're well off."

"Oh, yes," answered Anne Lisbeth.

"The boat went down with them," the woman went on. "Hans the skipper and the boy were both drowned, and there's an end of them. I always hoped the boy would be able to help me with a few shillings. He will never cost you anything more, Anne Lisbeth."

"So they have been drowned," repeated Anne Lisbeth, and then no more was said about it. She felt very low-spirited and miserable because the count's child had not felt inclined to talk to her, who loved him so much, and who had made such a long journey merely for the purpose of seeing him; and the journey had cost her something too, but she had derived no great pleasure from it. She would not relieve her heart by telling the laborer's wife all this, in case the latter should think she did not enjoy her former position at the castle. The raven screamed again, and flew over her once more.

"Black wretch!" said Anne Lisbeth, "he will end by giving me a fright to-day."

She had brought coffee and chicory with her, for she thought it would be a charity to give them to the poor woman to boil a cup of coffee, and then she also could have a cup.

The woman took the coffee, and while she was getting it ready, Anne Lisbeth sat down upon a chair and fell asleep. There she dreamed of something that had never occupied her thoughts before.

Her own child appeared to her in a vision, he who had wept and hungered in the laborer's cottage, who had been hustled about in the heat and cold, and was now lying, God knows where, in the depths of the sea. It seemed to her that she was still sitting in the hut, where the woman was busily preparing the coffee; she could smell the berries roasting.

But suddenly she fancied she saw a beautiful young form appear on the threshold, as beautiful as the count's child, and this apparition said:

"The world is passing away! Cling to me, for you are my mother after all. You have an angel in Heaven. Hold me fast!" And the angel child stretched out its hand to her, and there was a terrible rending noise, like the world crumbling to pieces; and the little angel was rising from the earth, and holding her so tightly by the sleeve that it seemed to her as if she was lifted from the ground; but also, it seemed as though something heavy clung to her feet and dragged her down. Hundreds of women were clinging to her, and cried:

"If you are to be saved, we must be saved too! Hold fast, hold fast!"

And then they all hung on to her; but there were too many of them, the sleeve gave way, and Anne Lisbeth fell down in horror, and awoke. And she was nearly falling over in reality with the chair on which she sat; she was so startled and frightened that she could not recollect what she had dreamed, only that it was something very terrible.

They had their coffee, and chatted together, and then Anne Lisbeth walked on towards the little town where she was to meet the carrier and drive back with him to her own home. But when she spoke to him, she found that he would not be ready to start before the evening of the next day. She began to think of the expense, and the length of the way; and when she considered that the route by the seashore was two miles shorter than the other, and that the moon shone brightly and the weather was good, she made up her mind to go the rest of the way on foot, and start at once that she might be home by the next morning.

The sun had set and the evening bells, tolled in the towers of the village churches, still sounded in the air, but no—it was only the frogs croaking in the marshes. Now they were silent, and everything was quiet; even the birds had all gone to rest, the owl also seemed to be at home: deep silence reigned on the margin of the forest and by the seashore. As Anne Lisbeth walked on, she could hear nothing but her own footsteps on the sand; there was no sound of the waves on the sea, everything out in the deep waters had sunk to silence. All were quiet, both living and inanimate creatures.

Anne Lisbeth walked on, "thinking of nothing at all," as the saying goes, or rather, her thoughts wandered, but thoughts had not gone far from her, for they are never absent, they only slumber. Thoughts that have not yet stirred within us, come forth at their proper season, and begin to move our hearts and brains, and seem sent to us from above. It is written that a good deed bears fruit in the form of blessings, and that the wages of sin is death. Much has been said and written that one has never heard of, or does not think of in general, and it was so with Anne Lisbeth; but it sometimes happens that a light arises in one's heart, and forgotten things are clearly seen.

All vices and virtues lie dormant in our hearts—in yours and mine too. They lie there like grains of seed, and then a ray of sunshine, or a breath of evil comes from outside, or you may turn the right-hand or left-hand corner, and that is decisive. Then perhaps, the little grain of seed is stirred; it swells and shoots up, and pours its sap into all your veins, influencing you either for good or evil.

Many tormenting thoughts may lie fermenting in the brain, and one does not notice them when one walks on with slumbering senses, but they are there all the same.

Anne Lisbeth walked on in this way, her senses only half awake, but thoughts were fermenting in her heart.

From one Shrove Tuesday to another much may happen that weighs heavily upon the mind—it is the reckoning of a whole year, and in that time much is forgotten—sins of thought and deed against Heaven, our neighbors, and our own conscience. We don't think of these things, and Anne Lisbeth did not think of them. She had committed no sin against the law of the land; she was an honorable and respected person and in a good position, she knew.

She continued to walk along the beach; she saw something lying there. What was it? Only an old hat—a man's hat. When might that have been washed overboard? She took a step nearer and stopped to look at the hat. Ha! what was lying yonder? She shuddered, yet it was nothing more than a heap of tangled seaweed flung across a stone, but it looked just like a corpse—only tangled seaweed, and yet it frightened her; and as she turned to walk on, much came into her mind that she had heard in her childhood, old superstitions about ghosts on the seashore, specters of drowned people who were unburied, and whose bodies had been washed up on the lonely and desolated beach. The corpse, she had heard, could do no harm to any one; but the spirit could pursue one, if alone, and attach itself to one, and demand to be carried to the church-yard, that it might rest in consecrated ground.

"Hold fast, hold fast!" the specter would then cry; and while Anne Lisbeth murmured these words to herself, her whole dream suddenly came before her, when the mothers clung to her and had repeated these words, when the world fell together with a crash, and her sleeve was torn, and she slipped out of the grasp of her own child, who wanted to support her in that dreadful hour. Her child, her own child, whom she had never loved, now lay buried in the sea, and might rise up like a specter from the waters and cry:

"Hold fast; carry me to consecrated ground."

When she thought of this, fear gave speed to her feet, so that she walked on faster and faster, terror came upon her like a cold clammy hand clutching her heart, and she almost fainted; and as she looked towards the sea, it grew darker and darker, a heavy mist was rising; it clung to bush and tree, distorting them into fantastic shapes; she turned round and looked up at the moon, which had risen behind her.

It looked like a pale rayless surface, and a heavy weight seemed to hang upon her limbs. "Hold fast," she thought, and turned to look at the moon a second time. Its white face seemed quite close to her, the mist hanging like a white garment from its shoulders "Hold, stop! carry me to consecrated earth!" sounded in her ears in strange, hollow tones. The sound did not come from the frogs or ravens; she saw no signs of any living creature. "A grave, dig me a grave!" was repeated quite distinctly. Yes, it was the ghost of her child, the child that lay in the deep waters, and whose spirit could have no rest until it was carried to the church-yard, until a grave had been dug for it in consecrated ground. She would go there at once, and dig; and as she went in the direction of the church the weight on her heart seemed to grow lighter, and even to vanish altogether, but when she turned to take the shorter way home it returned. "Stop, stop!"—the words were quite clear, although something like the croak of a frog or wail of a bird—"A grave! dig me a grave!"

The mist was damp and chilly, her face and hands were cold and clammy with horror, a heavy weight again clung to her, and seemed to drag her down; and in her mind a great space opened, for thoughts that were new to her.

In the North the beech-wood often buds in a single night, and appears in the morning sunlight in its full glory of young foliage; and thus in a single instant the conscience can realize a sin that has been committed in a thought, word, or deed of our past life.

It springs up and reveals itself in a moment, when once our conscience is awakened, and God wakens it when we least expect it.

Then we find no excuse for ourselves—the deed is there, and bears witness against us; our thoughts seem to become words, and to sound far out into the world. We are horrified to find what we have carried in our hearts, that we have not overcome the evil that we have sown in thoughtlessness and pride. The heart hides within itself all virtues and vices, and they grow even in the shallowest ground.

Anne Lisbeth now experienced the thoughts we have clothed in words. She was quite overpowered, and sank down, creeping along the sand for some distance on her hands and knees. "A grave! dig me a grave!" sounded again in her ears; she would gladly have buried herself, if oblivion and forgetfulness of every deed could have been found in the tomb.

It was the first hour of her awakening, full of anguish and horror. Superstition alternately made her shudder with cold and burn with the heat of fever. Many things of which she had feared even to speak came into her mind. Silently as the clouds pass over the moon, a ghostly apparition flitted by her; she had heard of it before. Four snorting horses galloped by quite close to her, with the fire spurting from their eyes and nostrils; they dragged a red-hot coach, and the wicked proprietor sat inside.

He had been lord of the manor a hundred years ago; and every night at twelve o'clock he drove into his castle-yard and out again, so the legend ran. See! he was not pale, as dead men are said to be, but as black as coal; he nodded to Anne Lisbeth, and beckoned to her. "Stop! stop! you may ride in a nobleman's carriage once more, and forget your own child!"

She pulled herself together, and hastened to the church-yard; but the black crosses and black ravens danced before her eyes, and she could not distinguish the one from the other.

The ravens croaked, as the raven had done that she saw in the daytime, but now she understood what they said.* "I am the raven-mother! I am the raven-mother!" each raven croaked; and Anne Lisbeth now understood that the name also applied to her, and she imagined she would be turned into a blackbird, and have to cry as they cried if she did not dig the grave.

She threw herself upon the hard ground, and dug with her hands in the earth, so that the blood ran from her fingers.

"A grave! dig me a grave!" still sounded in her ears; and she was afraid that the cock might crow and the first streak of dawn appear in the east before she had finished her task, and then all would be lost. And the cock crowed and the day dawned when the grave was only half dug. An icy hand passed over her head and face and down towards her heart "Only half a grave," a voice wailed and fled away. Yes, it fled away over the sea; it was the ocean specter—and Anne Lisbeth sank to the ground exhausted and overpowered, and her senses left her.

When she came to herself it was bright daylight, and two men were lifting her up; but she was not lying in the church-yard, but on the beach, where she had dug a deep hole in the sand, and cut her hand against a broken glass whose sharp stem was stuck in a little painted block of wood. Anne Lisbeth was in a fever. Conscience had awakened old superstitions, which so deeply impressed her mind that she fancied that she had only half a soul, and that her child had taken the other half down into the sea. Never more could she cling to the mercy of Heaven until she had got back this other half which was now held fast in the deep water.

After a time Anne Lisbeth returned to her home, but she was never again the woman she had been; her thoughts were confused like a tangled skein, and there was only one clear thought in her mind, namely, that she must carry the sea-ghost to the church-yard and dig a grave for him, and thus win back her soul. Many a night she was missed from home, and was always found on the beach, waiting for the ghost. Thus a whole year passed, and one night she

---

* All women who treat their children unkindly are called "raven mothers," as the raven is supposed to peck its little ones' eyes out.

disappeared again and could not be found. The whole of the following day was spent searching for her.

Towards evening, when the clerk went into the church to toll the bell for evening service, he saw Anne Lisbeth standing by the altar. She had spent the whole day there, and her strength was almost exhausted, but her eyes shone brightly and her cheeks were flushed. The last rays of the setting sun lit up the altar and gleamed upon the shining clasps of the great Bible, which lay open at the words of the prophet Joel, "Rend your hearts and not your garments, and turn unto the Lord."

"It was just a chance," people said; "many things happen by chance." Anne Lisbeth's face, illumined by the sun, shone with peace and happiness. She said she was happy now, for she had conquered. Last night the sea-ghost, her own child, had appeared to her and said: "Thou hast dug me only half a grave, but thou hast now for a year and a day buried me altogether in thy heart, and it is there a mother can best hide her child." Then he gave her back her lost soul, and brought her to the church. "Now I am in the house of God," she said, "and only there can one be happy."

When the sun set, Anne Lisbeth's soul had risen to that region where there is no more pain, and all her troubles were over.

"Beautiful!"

The sculptor Alfred—I suppose you know him? Everybody knows him: he won a gold medal, made a journey to Italy and then came home again; he was young at that time, he is still young, although he is ten years older than he was then.

When he had come home he paid a visit to one of the small towns of the island of Zealand. Everybody knew who the stranger was and whence he came, and one of the richest inhabitants gave a party in his honor, to which all who were of any consequence or had any property were invited; it was quite an event, and all knew of it, although it was not announced by beating of drums. Apprentice boys, the children of the lower class, and even some of their parents stood before the house and gazed upon the light that shone through the curtains; the watchman might have well imagined that he gave the party, such a number of people were in the street. It looked like a festival; and a festival took place in the house, for Mr. Alfred the sculptor was there. He talked and told anecdotes, and all listened to him with delight and with a kind of reverence; there was also an elderly widow of an official who seemed, as far as Mr. Alfred was concerned, to be like a piece of clean blotting paper; she took in all that was said and asked for more. She appreciated everything, and was terribly ignorant—a kind of feminine Caspar Hauser. Italy, of the purple hills, the blue Mediterranean, the azure sky of the south, the brightness and glory of which could only be surpassed in the north by a maiden's deep blue eyes. And this he said with a peculiar stress, but she whom he wished to understand his meaning looked quite unconcerned, and that was again charming.

"I should like to see Rome," she said. "It must be a charming city where so many strangers continually arrive. Do give me a description of Rome. What does the city look like when you enter its gate?"

"I am unable to exactly describe it," answered the sculptor. "A large open place, and in the center of it an obelisk a thousand years old."

"An organist!" exclaimed the lady, having never heard the word obelisk.

Some of the guests had difficulty in suppressing their laughter, and the sculptor also could hardly remain serious, but his smile vanished when he perceived close by the side of the inquisitive lady two dark-blue eyes—they belonged to her daughter, and a woman who had such a daughter could not be silly!

The mother was, as it were, a fountain of questions, while the daughter, who listened without saying a word, might have been taken for the beautiful naiad of the fountain. How beautiful she was! She was a study for the sculptor, to be contemplated but not to converse with, for she did not speak, or at any rate very little.

"Has the Pope a large family?" inquired the lady.

The young man considerately answered as if he had been asked a different question, "No, he does not come from a great family."

"That is not what I mean," persisted the widow; "I wish to know if he has a wife and children?"

"The Pope is not allowed to marry," said the sculptor.

"I don't like that," remarked the lady.

Indeed she might have asked more reasonable questions; but if she had not been allowed to speak in such a manner, would her daughter have been there, leaning so gracefully upon her shoulder, and looking straight in front of her with an almost sad smile on her face?

Then Mr. Alfred spoke again, and told of the glory of color in Italy, of the purple hills, the blue Mediterranean, the azure sky of the south, the brightness and glory of which could only be surpassed in the north by a maiden's deep blue eyes. And this he said with a peculiar stress, but she whom he wished to understand his meaning looked quite unconcerned, and that was again charming.

"Italy," sighed a few guests.

"Traveling," sighed others. "Charming, charming!"

"Yes, if I only win a hundred thousand dollars in the lottery," said the widow, "then we should travel, I and my daughter; and Mr. Alfred, you must be our guide. We three shall travel together and a couple of good friends with us." And she nodded in such a friendly way to the company that any one of them would have thought that he was to accompany them to Italy.

"Indeed we shall go to Italy! But we shall not go where robbers are; we shall keep to Rome, and to the high roads, where one is safe."

The daughter sighed very gently; and how much may a sigh mean, or how much can be attributed to it! The young man found it very significant. The two blue eyes, lit up this evening in his honor, must hide treasures—treasures of heart and mind—much richer than all the sights of Rome; and when he went home that night he had lost his heart, and was hopelessly in love with the young lady.

The widow's house was the one most frequently visited by the sculptor; and it was evident that his visits were not intended for the mother, although she was the person who conversed with him, but for the daughter. They called her Kala. Her real name, Karen Malene, was contracted into the one name, Kala. She was beautiful, but some people said she was rather dull, and remained in bed until late in the morning.

"She has been accustomed to that since her infancy," said her mother; "she is a beauty, and they are usually easily tired. She stays late in bed, but that is why her eyes are so clear."

What a power was in these bright, deep blue eyes! "Still waters run deep"; the young man felt the truth of this saying, and his heart had sunk into their depths. He talked and talked, and the mother was as simple and inquisitive in her questions as when they first met.

It was a pleasure to hear Alfred describe anything; he spoke of Naples, of excursions to Mount Vesuvius, and showed colored prints of several of the eruptions. The widow had never heard of them before, or given any thought to such things.

"Good gracious!" she exclaimed; "so that is a burning mountain. Is it not very dangerous to the people who live near it?"

"Whole cities have been destroyed," Alfred replied; "for instance, Pompeii and Herculanum."

"Oh, the poor people!—and you saw it all with your own eyes?"

"No, I did not see any of the eruptions depicted here, but I will show you a sketch of my own of an eruption I once saw."

He laid a pencil drawing on the table, and mamma, who had been absorbed in the contemplation of highly colored prints, looked at the pale drawing and exclaimed in astonishment. "Did you see it throw up white fire?"

Alfred's respect for Kala's mother suffered a severe shock for the moment; but, dazzled by the light which surrounded Kala, he soon found it quite natural that the old lady should have no eye for color. After all it was of very little consequence, for Kala's mother had the best of all possessions, namely, Kala herself.

Alfred and Kala were betrothed, which was natural enough, and the engagement was announced in the newspapers of the little town. The mother purchased thirty copies of the paper, that she might cut the paragraph out and send it to friends and acquaintances. The betrothed pair were happy, and the mother-in-law-elect was happy too, for she said it seemed like connecting herself with Thorwaldsen.

"You are a true successor of Thorwaldsen," she said to Alfred; and it seemed to him as if she had said a clever thing for once. Kala was silent, but her eyes sparkled, her lips smiled, and every movement was graceful; that cannot be repeated too often.

Alfred decided to take a bust of Kala, and also of her mother.

They sat to him accordingly, and saw how he molded and formed the soft clay with his fingers.

"I suppose it is only on our account that you perform this commonplace work yourself, instead of leaving it to your servant to do all that sticking together," said the old lady.

"No, it is necessary that I should mold the clay myself," he replied.

"Ah, yes, you are always so polite," she said with a smile; and Kala silently pressed his hand, all soiled as it was with the clay.

Then he unfolded to them both the beauties of Nature in all her works, pointing out how the inanimate matter was inferior to animate nature in the scale of creation; how the plant was above the mineral, the animal above the plant, and man above them all He strove to show them how beauty of mind is visible in the outward form, and how it is the sculptor's task to seize this charm of expression and reproduce it in his work.

Kala said nothing, but nodded approbation of what he said, while her mother made the following confession:

"It's difficult to follow all that, but I go hobbling after you with my thoughts, though what you say makes my head whirl round and round. Still I contrive to lay hold of some of it."

And Kala's beauty had a firm hold on Alfred, it filled his soul and held a mastery over him. Beauty gleamed from Kala's every feature—shone in her eyes, lurked in the corners of her mouth and in every movement of her fingers. Alfred, the sculptor, saw this: he spoke only to her, thought only of her, and the two became one, and so it might be said that she spoke much, for he and she were one, and he was always talking to her.

Such was the betrothal—now came the wedding, with bridesmaids and wedding presents, all duly mentioned in the wedding speech. The widow had set up Thorwaldsen's bust at the end of the table, attired in a dressing gown, for he was to be a guest; such was her whim. Songs were sung and cheers given, for it was a gay wedding, and they were a handsome pair.

"Pygmalion loved his Galathea," said one of the songs.

"Ah, that is one of your mythologies," said the old lady.

The next day the young couple started for Copenhagen, where they were to live. The mother accompanied them, "to look after the commonplace," as she said, meaning the domestic economy. Kala was like a doll in a doll's house, for everything was so bright and new and so fine. There they sat, all three of them, and as for Alfred, a proverb may describe his position—he was like a swan among the geese.

The enchanting form had taken him captive. He had looked at the casket without caring to inquire what it contained, and this omission often brings the greatest unhappiness into married life. The casket may be injured, the gilding may come off, and then the purchaser regrets his bargain. In a large party it is very disagreeable to find that one's buttons are giving way, and that there are no buckles to fall back upon; but it is worse still in a great company to be aware that your wife and mother-in-law are talking nonsense, and that you cannot depend upon yourself to produce a little ready wit to carry off the stupidity of the whole affair.

The young married couple often sat hand in hand, he speaking and she letting fall a word now and then, in the same melodious voice, the same bell-like tones. It was a mental relief when Sophy, one of her friends, came to visit them. Sophy was not pretty; she was certainly free from bodily deformity, though Kala always said she was a little crooked, but no eye but a friend's would have noticed it. She was a very sensible girl, yet it never occurred to her that she might be a dangerous person here. Her appearance was like a breath of fresh air in the doll's house, and a change of atmosphere was really necessary—they all owned that. They felt they needed a change, and so the young couple and the mother traveled to Italy.

"Thank Heaven, we are within our own four walls again!" mother and daughter both exclaimed when they came home a year afterwards.

"There is no real pleasure in traveling," said mamma; "to speak the truth, it is very tiring—I beg pardon for saying so. I soon got weary of it, although I had my children with me, and, besides, it is very expensive work traveling, very expensive. And all those galleries one is expected to see, and the quantity of things one is obliged to run after! It must be done for decency's sake, for you are sure to be asked, when you come back, if you have seen everything, and will be told most likely that you have left out the one thing that was worth seeing. I got tired at last of those endless Madonnas; I began to think I was turning into a Madonna myself."

"And then the living, mamma," said Kala.

"Yes," she replied, "no such thing as a respectable meat-soup; it is wretched stuff, their cookery."

The journey had also tired Kala; but she was always tired, that was the worst of it. So they sent for Sophy, and she was taken into the house to live with them; and her presence was a real advantage. Mamma-in-law acknowledged that Sophy was not only a clever housekeeper, but also well informed and accomplished, though the latter could hardly be expected from a person who was so badly off. She was a generous-hearted, faithful girl as well—they were able to see that while Kala lay sick, fading away. When the casket is everything, it should be strong, or else it is all over. And it was all over with the casket, for Kala died.

"She was beautiful," said her mother; "she was quite different from the beauties they call 'antiques,' for they are so damaged. A beauty should be perfect, and Kala was a perfect beauty."

Both Alfred and mamma shed tears and wore mourning. She wore mourning the longest, for black suited her, and she experienced another grief. Alfred married again, married Sophy, who was nothing at all to look at.

"He has gone to the very extreme," said mamma-in-law; "he has gone from the most beautiful to the ugliest, and he has forgotten his first wife. Men have no constancy. My husband was of a different stamp, but then he died before me.

"'Pygmalion loved his Galathea,' was a song they sang at my first wedding" said Alfred; "I once fell in love with a beautiful statue, which came to life in my arms; but the kindred soul, which is a gift from Heaven, the angel who can sympathize with and elevate us, I have not found and won till now. Sophy, you did not come in the glory of outward beauty; though you are fair, fairer than is necessary. But the chief thing is this: you came to teach the sculptor that his work is but dust and clay, a form made of material that decays, and that what we should seek for is the ethereal essence of mind and spirit. Poor Kala! ours was but a meeting by the wayside; in the next world, where we shall know each other by union of souls, we shall he almost strangers."

"That was not kindly said," replied Sophy, "nor spoken like a true Christian. In the next world, where there is no marrying, or giving in marriage, but where, as you say, souls will attract each other by sympathy, there everything beautiful is developed and raised to a higher state of existence. Her soul may acquire such completeness that it may harmonize with yours, even more than mine, and you will once more utter your first rapturous exclamation, 'Beautiful, most beautiful!' "

The Wind's Tale

When the wind sweeps over the meadows the long grass undulates like the water of a lake, but when it blows over a cornfield the ears move like the waves of the sea. This, people call the wind's dance; but the wind can do more than dance, it can tell stories. And how loudly it can sing deep bass notes! and what a variety of sounds it can produce when it shakes the tops of the trees in the forest, or when it blows through the clefts and cracks in the wall! Do you see how the wind chases the clouds up there, as if they were a frightened flock of sheep? Do you hear it sound through the valley, like a watchman blowing his horn? with peculiar tones it whistles and groans down the chimney right into the fireplace. The fire crackles and flares up, lighting up the room and making it warm and cozy. How pleasant it is to sit there and listen to the wind! But let the wind speak; it knows many tales and stories, far more, indeed, than any of us. Now listen to the story of the wind.

"On the shores of the great Belt, one of the straits by which the Cattegat is connected with the Baltic," relates the wind, "stands an old mansion with strong red brick walls. I know every one of its stones, I knew them when they still formed part of the castle of Marsk Stigs, on the promontory. The castle was razed to the ground, but the stones were used again in building up the walls of a new house in a different place, the baronial mansion of Borreby, which is still standing on the seashore.

"On the shores of the great Belt, one of the straits by which the Cattegat is connected with the Baltic . . . stands an old mansion with strong red brick walls."

"I knew many generations of noble lords and ladies that lived there, and now I will tell you about Waldemar Daa and his daughters. He was a very proud man, for royal blood ran in his veins, and he could do more than hunt the stag and empty the wine goblet. 'It shall be done,' he used to say.

"His wife, in garments embroidered with gold, proudly walked over the floors of polished marble. The walls were hung with magnificent tapestry, the furniture of the rooms was both costly and artistic. She had brought gold and silver plate with her when she came into the house, and the wine-cellars were well stocked. Black, fiery horses neighed in the stables. The house at Borreby, at that time, had a look of wealth and luxury about it

"They had three children, delicate girls—Ida, Johanna, and Anna Dorothea: I remember their names well. They were wealthy people of noble birth, and they lived in affluence."

The wind roared and then continued: "I did not see at Borreby, as in other nobleman's houses, the mistress sitting among her women in the hall at the spinning-wheel; she played upon the guitar, accompanying her songs; she did not always sing old Danish tunes, but sometimes also songs of a strange land. They led a life of merriment and pleasure here; there were always guests from far and near in the house, and sounds of music and clinking of glasses, and

I was unable to drown the noise," said the wind. "There was pride, splendor, display, and sovereignty, but not the fear of God.

"It was on the night of the first of May," continued the wind. "I had come from the west, where I had witnessed the ships being crushed by the waves, and thrown with all on board against the shores of Jutland. I had hastened over the moors and over Jutland's wooded east coast, and over the island of Fyen; now I passed with groans and sighs over the Great Belt, I lay down to rest on Zeeland's shore, not far from the mansion of Borreby, where then the beautiful oak forest was still standing. The young men of the neighborhood were gathering dry branches and brushwood under the oak-trees. They carried the largest and driest that were to be found into the village, piled them up in a heap, and set them on fire. Then the young men and girls were dancing and singing round the burning pile. While I lay quietly there," continued the wind, "I touched, noiselessly, one of the branches which one of the handsomest young men had brought; it flared up brightly, and the flames from it rose higher than those of all the others; he was elected chief, and was allowed before all the others to select a partner from the maids; and there was such joy and merriment as I had never before heard in the halls of the mansion. Just then the noble lady with her three daughters drove up to the mansion in a gilded carriage drawn by six horses. The daughters were young and handsome, three charming blossoms—a rose, a lily, and a white hyacinth. The mother resembled a proud tulip. She never acknowledged the obeisance of any of the men and maids, when they interrupted their game to honor her; the noble lady was evidently a flower with a rather stiff stalk. Rose, lily, and white hyacinth, indeed, I saw them all three! Whose lambkins will they become one day? thought I; their partner will be a gallant knight, perhaps a prince. The carriage drove by, and the young people continued their dance. That summer they drove through all the villages in the neighborhood. One night, however, when I blew again," said the wind, "the noble lady was lying there, never to rise again. What had happened to her happens to all, and there is nothing new in this. Waldemar Daa was standing silent and pensive awhile, a voice within him said: 'The most stately tree can be bowed without being broken.' His daughters cried, and all the people in the house wiped their eyes, but Lady Daa had driven away, and I drove away too," said the wind.

"I came back again; I frequently passed over the island of Fyen, and the shores of the Belt, and rested near Borreby in the magnificent oak-wood, where the heron had his nest, and where wood-pigeons, ravens, and even black storks dwelled. It was still spring; some of the birds were still sitting on their eggs, while others had already hatched their young. But they fluttered about and cried; the blows of the ax echoed through the wood, the trees were

"Just then the noble lady with her three daughters drove up to the mansion in a gilded carriage."

to be felled. Waldemar Daa intended to build a splendid ship, a man of-war, a three-decker, and was sure the king would buy it; that was why this wood, the landmark of the seamen, the refuge of the birds, had to come down. The hawk, startled, flew away; his nest was destroyed. The heron and all the other wood-birds had lost their homes, and were flying about in fear and anger. I could well feel with them. Crows and ravens scornfully croaked, while the trees and the nests fell one after another. In the midst of the wood, where the noisy woodcutters were at work, stood Waldemar Daa and his three daughters; they were laughing at the cries of the wild birds; only Anna Dorothea, the youngest, was grieved in her heart. When they made preparations to fell an almost dead tree, on the naked branches of which a black stork had built his nest, whence the young storks were stretching out their heads, she begged, with tears in her eyes, for mercy for the little ones. The tree, with the black stork's nest, was left standing, and it was, indeed, not worth much.

"There was a great deal of hammering and sawing going on; they were building the three-decker. The builder was of low descent, but very proud; his eyes and his forehead indicated intelligence; Waldemar Daa liked to listen to him, no less than his eldest daughter Ida, now fifteen years old. While he built the ship for the father, he was building for himself a castle in the air, where Ida and himself would live after their marriage. This might have come about if the castle had been of stone, with ramparts and moats. But with all his intelligence the builder remained a poor bird; and what business has a sparrow in a peacock's nest? I went away," said the wind, "and so did he, for he was not allowed to remain; little Ida very soon got over it, because she was compelled to get over it.

"The stately black horses in the stable were neighing; they were well worth looking at, and indeed they were looked at. The admiral sent by the king to inspect and measure the ship for the purpose of purchasing it, was full of praise and admiration for the beautiful horses. I heard all this," said the wind. "I went with the gentlemen through the open door and blew straws, like bars of gold, before their feet. Waldemar Daa desired gold; the admiral coveted the noble black horses, therefore he praised them so much. But what he hinted at was not carried out, and in consequence the ship was not purchased. It remained ashore, and was covered over with boards—a Noah's ark which never got on the water, and that was a great pity.

"In winter, when snow covered the fields and huge ice-blocks which I had blown towards the coast were floating on the water," related the wind, "flocks of crows and ravens came and perched on the deserted, solitary ship on the shore, and croaked aloud about the wood that no longer existed, about the many destroyed bird's nests and the homeless little ones, and all this had been done for the sake of that great piece of lumber, that stately ship, which was never to be afloat. I produced a snowstorm till the snow lay all around the ship and drifted over it; I let it hear my voice, so that it might know what a storm has to say. As far as I am concerned, I did all in my power to teach it seamanship. The winter passed away, summer and another winter passed away, and so they are doing now. I also pass away, the snow melts, the apple blossoms are scattered, the leaves drop, and men pass away too. But Waldemar Daa's daughters were still young; Ida was a rose, and still as beautiful as on the day when the shipbuilder saw her for the first time. I often played with her long brown hair when she stood in the garden near the apple-tree, not heeding when I strewed the blossoms upon it and disheveled it, while she was looking at the sun, or contemplating the sky through the thick underwood and the trees in the garden.

"Her sister Johanna was as beautiful and slender as a lily. She was tall and carried herself proudly, but like her mother she was rather stiff in the stalk. She liked very much to walk through the great hall where the portraits of her ancestors hung. The ladies were painted in dresses of silk and velvet, and little hats, embroidered with pearls, on their plaited hair. They were all handsome. The gentlemen were painted in steel armor, or in costly cloaks lined with ermine; they wore little ruffs round their necks, and had swords by their sides, but not buckled to their hips. Where would her portrait be placed on the wall one day? And what would he look like who was to be her lord and husband? Such were her thoughts, and of this she often spoke to herself in a low voice. I overheard it as I passed into the long hall and turned round to come out again.

"Anna Dorothea, the white hyacinth, now fourteen years old, was quiet and pensive; her large blue eyes had a dreamy look, but a happy smile of childhood was still around her lips; I was unable to blow it away, and did not wish to do so. I met her in the garden, in the lane, in the field, and on the meadow; she picked herbs and flowers, such as she knew would be useful to her father in preparing the drinks and drugs which he made himself. Although conceited and proud, Waldemar Daa had learned and knew a great deal. And people knew it too, and often expressed their opinion about his doings. There was a fire in his chimney even in the summer-time; he used to lock himself in his room, and the fire burnt for days. He did not talk much about his doings, for the forces of Nature had to be explored in quietude; and soon, so he hoped, he would discover the art of making the best of all things—gold. That is why smoke was always rising out of the chimney and the fire burnt so often. I was there too," said the wind. " 'Leave it alone,' I sang down the chimney, 'for it will but end in smoke, air, and ashes, and you will burn yourself! Leave it alone! leave it alone!'

"But Waldemar Daa did not leave it alone.

"What became of the stately black horses in the stable? What became of the old gold and silver plate, in chests and cupboards, of the cows in the fields, and of the house and home itself? Yes, they may easily be melted in the gold-making crucible and yet yield no gold.

"The barns, the store-rooms, the cellars, and the cupboards became empty. The number of servants was decreased, the mice multiplied. One window broke, and soon another, and there were openings for me to get in besides the door," said the wind. " 'Where the chimney smokes the meal is being cooked,' says the proverb. But at Borreby the smoking chimney devoured all the meals for the sake of obtaining gold.

"I blew through the gate like a watchman sounding his horn, but there was no watchman there. I turned the weather-cock on the tower round and round, till it creaked like the snoring of a warder, but instead of a warder there were only mice and rats. Poverty spread the tablecloth, want nestled in the wardrobe and in the larder; the door fell off its hinges, cracks and crevices became visible everywhere, and I went in and out through them as I pleased;

SHE PICKED HERBS AND FLOWERS, SUCH AS SHE KNEW WOULD BE USEFUL TO HER FATHER IN PREPARING THE DRINKS AND DRUGS WHICH HE MADE HIMSELF.

that's how I know all about it. While he was continually laboring amidst smoke and ashes, anxiety and long sleepless nights began to tell upon the hair and beard of the master of Borreby; deep wrinkles appeared on his forehead, and while his eyes still looked bright with the desire for gold, his skin became pale and yellow.

"I blew the smoke and ashes over his face and beard; instead of any profit, his labor resulted in debt. I howled through the broken windows and the crevices in the walls; I blew into his daughter's wardrobes, in which they kept the dresses that had become threadbare and faded by too much wear. All this had not been sung at the children's cradle. The life of affluence had turned into one of poverty. I alone rejoiced in that castle," said the wind. "I snowed them up, and they say snow keeps people warm. Wood they had none, for the forest, which might have provided them with it, did no longer exist. It was bitterly cold; I rushed through the openings into the passages, blew over the gables and roofs, and was very cutting. The three nobly born daughters were staying in bed, in order to protect themselves from the cold, and their father did the same. No food and no fuel in the house—that was a life for gentle-folks. 'Leave it alone, leave it alone,' I said, but Lord Daa could not make up his mind to do that.

"'After winter follows spring, after times of want come times of plenty. One must be patient and wait. Now my house and estates are mortgaged it is time that I should discover gold, perhaps at Easter!'

"While looking at a spider's web I heard him say one day:

"'You clever little weaver, you teach me how to persevere; if they tear your web you at once begin again and mend it. If they destroy it a second time you are not discouraged. That's what we ought to do, and perseverance must lead to success in the end.'

"It was on Easter morn. The bells of the village church were merrily pealing, and the sun shone brightly. Lord Daa had passed the night in feverish excitement, melting and cooling, distilling and mixing. He uttered sighs of despair; I heard him praying in a subdued voice. He did not perceive that the lamp had burned out. I blew the coal fire ablaze, and its red glow was reflected on his ghastly white face, making his sunken eyes appear prominent—they seemed to become larger and larger as if they were about to burst.

"'Look at the glass! There is something in the crucible that glows red-hot, it seems pure and heavy!'

"Holding it in his trembling hand he cried with a faltering voice:

"'Gold! gold!'

"He was quite bewildered; I could easily have blown him down," continued the wind; "but I only blew the glowing coals, and passed along with him through the door, to the room where his daughters sat shivering. His coat, his beard, and his matted hair were covered with ashes; standing upright, and holding up his priceless treasure in the fragile glass, he exclaimed:

"'I have found it! Gold! gold!' And he raised the glass again to let the sun shine upon its contents; it dropped out of his trembling hand with a crash to the ground, and was dashed into a thousand pieces. Thus the last bubble of his happiness burst," said the wind, "and I rushed away from the gold-maker's house.

"Late in autumn, when the days were growing short, and mists settle in large drops upon the berries and the denuded branches, I returned with new force; and rushing through the air I pushed the clouds along, and broke off the dry twigs; an easy task indeed, but it had to be done. Another kind of clearing out then took place at the mansion of Borreby. Waldemar Daa's enemy, Ove Ramel, of Basnœs, was there with the mortgage on the house and all it contained. I blew against the broken windows, shook the old rotten doors, and whistled through the holes and crevices. Mr. Ove Ramel did not much care to stay there. Ida and Anna Dorothea cried bitterly; Johanna stood pale and proud, and bit her lips till they bled, but what was the use of that? Ove Ramel was ready to let Waldemar Daa stay in the house till his death, but his offer was refused. I overheard all that was said; I saw how the ruined man proudly raised his head and shook it. I rushed with such force against the house and the lime-trees surrounding it, that one of the thickest, and still sound, branches broke down; it dropped just before the entrance, and there it remained, as if it were intended for a broom to sweep the place with; and there was a thorough clearing out indeed. It was difficult for any one to remain calm on that day, but the will of these people was as inflexible as their misfortune. Besides the clothes they had upon them they had nothing they could call their own; but hold, there was one thing more, a newly bought chemical glass filled with the fragments of the priceless treasure picked up from the ground, on which had been based so many hopes. Hiding the glass in his bosom, Waldemar Daa took his stick, and then the once wealthy lord walked with his daughters out of the mansion of Borreby. I cooled his heated cheeks, I smoothed his gray beard and long white hair, and sang as well as I could. Thus so much wealth and riches came to an end.

"Ida walked on one, Anna Dorothea on the other, side of the old man. At the gate Johanna turned round. Did she imagine Fate would alter its course because she turned? She looked at the walls, built with stones once belonging to the castle of Marsk Stigs; perhaps she thought of his daughters:

"'They went alone to a distant land.
The youngest holding her sister's hand.'

"But here there were three instead of two daughters, and their father was with them. They walked on the road where they had so often driven in their beautiful carriage; they were beggars now, and they walked with their father into the open fields to dwell in a little hut, rented at about four shillings and sixpence a year, their new home without furniture, and without food. The crows and magpies which flew above their heads cried, as if in mockery, 'Caw, caw, turned out of the nest—caw, caw,' as they had done when the wood of Borreby was being cut down.

"Lord Daa and his daughters could not avoid hearing it, but I blew about their ears, as I did not see what good it could do them to hear it. While they settled in the poor hut in the open field I went away over moors and meadows, through the leafless bushes and trees, to the open sea, and to the shores of other lands far away, year after year!"

And what became of Waldemar Daa and his daughters? The wind relates as follows:

"The one I saw last was the white hyacinth, Anna Dorothea; she was old and decrepit, for it was fifty years later; she survived them all, she knew all.

"On the heath, not far from the town of Viborg in Jutland, stood the canon's fine new house, built of red bricks with projecting gables, and clouds of smoke rose up from the chimneys. The canon's wife and her charming daughters sat in the bay-window, looking over the hawthorn hedge which surrounded the garden, towards the heath. What were they looking at? Their eyes were fixed upon a stork's nest on the other side and upon a tumbledown hut; the roof, that is to say what was left of it, was covered with moss and lichen; the greater part of it was taken up by the stork's nest, and that was in good order, for the stork kept it so.

"That was a hut," said the wind, "only to be looked at, not to be touched; I had to be careful with it. Although disfiguring the landscape, the hut had been suffered to remain on account of the stork's nest; they did not wish to drive the stork away, therefore the old hut was left standing there, and the poor woman who dwelled in it could stay too. She certainly owed this privilege to the bird of Egypt. Perhaps it was her reward for having one day interceded in favor of the nest of its black brother in the wood of Borreby!

"Then this poor woman was a young girl, a white hyacinth in the beautiful garden, she remembered all this well; for she was Anna Dorothea herself.

"She sighed deeply, indeed people can sigh like the moaning of the wind among the reeds and rushes.

"She sighed: 'No bell tolled at your burial, Waldemar Daa; not even did the boys from the charity school sing a psalm when you were laid to rest, but everything must end, even misery. My sister Ida married a peasant. Of all the misfortunes that came upon our father, the idea that his daughter should have married a serf whom he could have punished one day on the wooden horse, was the hardest. Probably he is also dead now. And what has become of you, Ida? Woe me, it is not yet ended. Oh! kind Heaven, let me die!'

"Such was the prayer which Anna Dorothea uttered in the miserable hut which had been left untouched on account of the stork. I took pity on the best of the sisters," said the wind. "She had the courage of a man, and disguised as a man she took service as a sailor on board a ship. She spoke very rarely, and looked gloomy, but she did her work. As, however, she did not know how to climb, I blew her into the sea, before any one had found out that she was a woman, and in this I think I have done well," said the wind.

"After many years, on an Easter morning much like the one on which Waldemar Daa had found what he believed to be real gold, I heard the sound of a psalm from the tumbledown hut under the stork's nest. It was Anna Dorothea's last song. Instead of a window, there was only a small hole in the wall of the hut, through which the sun, which looked that day like a mass of shining gold, peeped in. How brightly his glorious rays illumined the miserable dwelling! Anna Dorothea was breathing her last—she would have died that morning even if the sun had not shone. It was on account of the stork that she could stay in her hut until her death. I sung at her grave," said the wind, "I also sung at her father's grave. I know where he is buried; I know where her grave is, but no one else knows it.

"New times, changed times! Where the old high road was are now fields closed in with hedges; well-kept ditches run along the sides of the new road; soon the steam-engine with its row of carriages will come and rush over the graves of those whose names are long forgotten—hush!—gone!—passed away.

"This is the story of Waldemar Daa and his daughters. If anybody thinks he can tell it better, let him do so," said the wind. And thus saying he rushed away.

A Story from the Sand-Hills

This story is from the sand-dunes or sand-hills of Jutland, but it does not begin there in the north, but far away in the south, in Spain. The wide sea is the high road from nation to nation; journey in thought, then, to sunny Spain. It is warm and beautiful there; the fiery pomegranate flowers peep from among dark laurels; a cool refreshing breeze from the mountains blows over the orange gardens, over the Moorish halls with their golden cupolas and colored walls. Children go through the streets in procession with candles and waving banners, and the sky, lofty and clear with its glittering stars, rises above them. Sounds of singing and castanets can be heard, and youths and maidens dance under the flowering acacia trees, while even the beggar sits upon a block of marble, refreshing himself with a juicy melon, and dreamily enjoying life. It all seems like a beautiful dream.

Here dwelled a newly married couple who completely gave themselves up to the charm of life; indeed they possessed every good thing they could desire—health and happiness, riches and honor.

"We are as happy as human beings can be," said the young couple from the depths of their hearts. They had indeed only one step higher to mount on the ladder of happiness—they hoped that God would give them a child, a son like them in form and spirit. The happy little one was to be welcomed with rejoicing, to be cared for with love and tenderness, and enjoy every advantage of wealth and luxury that a rich and influential family can give. So the days went by like a joyous festival.

"Life is a gracious gift from God, almost too great a gift for us to appreciate!" said the young wife. "Yet they say that fullness of joy for ever and ever can only be found in the future life. I cannot realize it!"

"The thought arises, perhaps, from the arrogance of men," said the husband. "It seems a great pride to believe that we shall live for ever, that we shall be as gods! Were not these the words of the serpent, the father of lies?"

"Surely you do not doubt the existence of a future life?" exclaimed the young wife. It seemed as if one of the first shadows passed over her sunny thoughts.

"Faith realizes it, and the priests tell us so," replied her husband; "but amid all my happiness I feel that it is arrogant to demand a continuation of it—another life after this. Has not so much been given us in this world that we ought to be, we *must* be, contented with it?"

"Yes, it has been given to us," said the young wife, "but this life is nothing more than one long scene of trial and hardship to many thousands. How many have been cast into this world only to endure poverty, shame, illness, and misfortune? If there were no future life, everything here would be too unequally divided, and God would not be the personification of justice."

"The beggar there," said her husband, "has joys of his own which seem to him great, and cause him as much pleasure as a king would find in the magnificence of his palace. And then do you not think that the beast of burden, which suffers blows and hunger, and works itself to death, suffers just as much from its miserable fate? The dumb creature might demand a future life also, and declare the law unjust that excludes it from the advantages of the higher creation."

"Christ said: 'In my Father's house are many mansions,'" she answered. "Heaven is as boundless as the love of our Creator; the dumb animal is also His creature, and I firmly believe that no life will be lost, but each will receive as much happiness as he can enjoy, which will be sufficient for him."

"This world is sufficient for me," said the husband, throwing his arm round his beautiful, sweet-tempered wife. He sat by her side on the open balcony, smoking a cigarette in the cool air, which was loaded with the sweet scent of carnations and orange blossoms. Sounds of music and the clatter of castanets came from the road beneath, the stars shone above them, and two eyes full of affection—those of his wife—looked upon him with the expression of undying love. "Such a moment," he said, "makes it worth while to be born, to die, and to be annihilated!" He smiled—the young wife raised her hand in gentle reproof, and the shadow passed away from her mind, and they were happy—quite happy.

Everything seemed to work together for their good. They advanced in honor, in prosperity, and in happiness. A change came certainly, but it was only a change of place and not of circumstances.

The young man was sent by his Sovereign as ambassador to the Russian Court. This was an office of high dignity, but his birth and his acquirements entitled him to the honor. He possessed a large fortune, and his wife had brought him wealth equal to his own, for she was the daughter of a rich and respected merchant. One of this merchant's largest and finest ships was to be sent that year to Stockholm, and it was arranged that the dear young couple, the daughter and the son-in-law, should travel in it to St. Petersburg. All the arrangements on board were princely and silk and luxury on every side.

In an old war song, called "The King of England's Son," it says:

> *"Farewell, he said, and sailed away.*
> *And many recollect that day.*
> *The ropes were of silk, the anchor of gold.*
> *And everywhere riches and wealth untold."*

These words would aptly describe the vessel from. Spain, for here was the same luxury, and the same parting thought naturally arose:

> *"God grant that we once more may meet*
> *In sweet unclouded peace and joy."*

There was a favorable wind blowing as they left the Spanish coast, and it would be but a short journey, for they hoped to reach their destination in a few weeks; but when they came out upon the wide ocean the wind dropped, the sea became smooth and shining, and the stars shone brightly. Many festive evenings were spent on board. At last the travelers began to wish for wind, for a favorable breeze; but their wish was useless—not a breath of air stirred, or if it did arise it was contrary. Weeks passed by in this way, two whole months, and then at length a fair wind blew from the south-west. The ship sailed on the high seas between Scotland and Jutland; then the wind increased, just as it did in the old song of "The King of England's Son."

> *"'Mid storm and wind, and pelting hail.*
> *Their efforts were of no avail.*
> *The golden anchor forth they threw;*
> *Towards Denmark the west wind blew."*

This all happened a long time ago; King Christian VII, who sat on the Danish throne, was still a young man. Much has happened since then, much has altered or been changed. Sea and moorland have been turned into green meadows, stretches of heather have become arable land, and in the shelter of the peasant's cottages, apple-trees and rose-bushes grow, though they certainly require much care, as the sharp west wind blows upon them. In West Jutland one may go back in thought to old times, farther back than the days when Christian VII ruled. The purple heather still extends for miles, with its burrows and aerial spectacles, intersected with sandy uneven roads, just as it did then; towards the west, where broad streams run into the bays, are marshes and meadows encircled by lofty, sandy hills, which, like a chain of Alps, raise their pointed summits near the sea, they are only broken by high ridges of clay, from which the sea, year by year, bites out great mouthfuls, so that the overhanging banks fall down as if by the shock of an earthquake. Thus it is there today and thus it was long ago, when the happy pair were sailing in the beautiful ship.

It was a Sunday, towards the end of September; the sun was shining, and the chiming of the church bells in the Bay of Nissum was carried along by the breeze like a chain of sounds. The churches there are almost entirely built of hewn blocks of stone, each like a piece of rock. The North Sea might foam over them and they would not be disturbed. Nearly all of them are without steeples, and the bells are hung outside between two beams. The service was over, and the congregation passed out into the church-yard, where not a tree or bush was to be seen; no flowers were planted there, and they had not placed a single wreath upon any of the graves. It is just the same now. Rough mounds show where the dead have been buried, and rank grass, tossed by the wind, grows thickly over the whole church-yard; here and there a grave has a sort of monument, a block of half-decayed wood, rudely cut in the shape of a coffin; the blocks are brought from the forest of West Jutland, but the forest is the sea itself, and the inhabitants find beams, and planks, and fragments which the waves have cast upon the beach. One of these blocks had been placed by loving hands on a child's grave, and one of the women who had come out of the church walked up to it; she stood there, her eyes resting on the weather-beaten memorial, and a few moments afterwards her husband joined her. They were both silent, but he took her hand, and they walked together across the purple heath, over moor and meadow towards the sand-hills. For a long time they went on without speaking.

"It was a good sermon to-day," the man said at last. "If we had not God to trust in, we should have nothing."

"Yes," replied the woman, "He sends joy and sorrow, and He has a right to send them. To-morrow our little son would have been five years old if we had been permitted to keep him."

"It is no use fretting, wife," said the man. "The boy is well provided for. He is where we hope and pray to go to."

They said nothing more, but went on towards their house among the sand-hills. All at once, in front of one of the houses where the sea grass did not keep the sand down with its twining roots, what seemed to be a column of smoke rose up. A gust of wind rushed between the hills, hurling the particles of sand high into the air; another gust, and the strings of fish hung up to dry flapped and beat violently against the walls of the cottage; then everything was quiet once more, and the sun shone with renewed heat.

The man and his wife went into the cottage. They had soon taken off their Sunday clothes and come out again, hurrying over the dunes which stood there like great waves of sand suddenly arrested in their course, while the sand-weeds and dune grass with its bluish stalks spread a changing color over them. A few neighbors also came out, and helped each other to draw the boats higher up on the beach. The wind now blew more keenly, it was chilly and cold, and when they went back over the sand-hills, sand and little sharp stones blew into their faces. The waves rose high, crested with white foam, and the wind cut off their crests, scattering the foam far and wide.

Evening came; there was a swelling roar in the air, a wailing or moaning like the voices of despairing spirits, that sounded above the thunder of the waves. The fisherman's little cottage was on the very margin, and the sand rattled against the window panes; every now and then a violent gust of wind shook the house to its foundation. It was dark, but about midnight the moon would rise. Later on the air became clearer, but the storm swept over the perturbed sea with undiminished fury; the fisher folks had long since gone to bed, but in such weather there was no chance of closing an eye. Presently there was a tapping at the window; the door was opened, and a voice said:

"There's a large ship stranded on the farthest reef."

In a moment the fisher people sprung from their beds and hastily dressed themselves. The moon had risen, and it was light enough to make the surrounding objects visible to those who could open their eyes in the blinding clouds of sand; the violence of the wind was terrible, and it was only possible to pass among the sand-hills if one crept forward between the gusts; the salt spray flew up from the sea like down, and the ocean foamed like a roaring cataract towards the beach. Only a practiced eye could discern the vessel out in the offing; she was a fine brig, and the waves now lifted her over the reef, three or four cables' length out of the usual channel. She drove towards the shore, struck on the second reef, and remained fixed.

It was impossible to render assistance; the sea rushed in upon the vessel, making a clean breach over her. Those on shore thought they heard cries for help from those on board, and could plainly distinguish the busy but useless efforts made by the stranded sailors. Now a wave came rolling onward. It fell with enormous force on the bowsprit, tearing it from the vessel, and the stern was lifted high above the water. Two people were seen to embrace and plunge together into the sea, and the next moment one of the largest waves that rolled towards the sand-hills threw a body on the beach. It was a woman; the sailors said that she was quite dead, but the women thought they saw signs of life in her, so the stranger was carried across the sand-hills to the fisherman's cottage. How beautiful and fair she was! She must be a great lady, they said.

They laid her upon the humble bed; there was not a yard of linen on it, only a woollen coverlet to keep the occupant warm.

Life returned to her, but she was delirious, and knew nothing of what had happened or where she was; and it was better so, for everything she loved and valued lay buried in the sea. The same thing happened to her ship as to the one spoken of in the song about "The King of England's Son."

"Alas! how terrible to see
The gallant bark sink rapidly."

Fragments of the wreck and pieces of wood were washed ashore; they were all that remained of the vessel. The wind still blew violently on the coast.

For a few moments the strange lady seemed to rest; but she awoke in pain, and uttered cries of anguish and fear. She opened her wonderfully beautiful eyes, and spoke a few words, but nobody understood her. And lo! as a reward for the sorrow and suffering she had undergone, she held in her arms a new-born babe. The child that was to have rested upon a magnificent couch, draped with silken curtains, in a luxurious home; it was to have been welcomed with joy to a life rich in all the good things of this world; and now Heaven had ordained that it should be born in this humble retreat, that it should not even receive a kiss from its mother, for when the fisherman's wife laid the child upon the mother's bosom, it rested on a heart that beat no more—she was dead.

The child that was to have been reared amid wealth and luxury was cast into the world, washed by the sea among the sand-hills to share the fate and hardships of the poor.

Here we are reminded again of the song about "The King of England's Son," for in it mention is made of the custom prevalent at the time, when knights and squires plundered those who had been saved from shipwreck. The ship had stranded some distance south of Nissum Bay, and the cruel, inhuman days, when, as we have just said, the inhabitants of Jutland treated the shipwrecked people so cruelly were past, long ago. Affectionate sympathy and self-sacrifice for the unfortunate existed then, just as it does in our own time in many a bright example. The dying mother and the unfortunate child would have found kindness and help wherever they had been cast by the winds, but nowhere would it have been more sincere than in the cottage of the poor fisherman's wife, who had stood, only the day before, beside her child's grave, who would have been five years old that day if God had spared it to her.

No one knew who the dead stranger was, they could not even form a conjecture; the fragments of wreckage gave no clue to the matter.

No tidings reached Spain of the fate of the daughter and son-in-law. They did not arrive at their destination, and violent storms had raged during the past weeks. At last the verdict was given: "Foundered at sea—all lost." But in the fisherman's cottage among the sand-hills near Hunsby, there lived a little scion of the rich Spanish family.

Where Heaven sends food for two, a third can manage to find a meal, and in the depth of the sea there is many a dish of fish for the hungry.

They called the boy Jürgen.

"It must certainly be a Jewish child, its skin is so dark," the people said.

"It might be an Italian or a Spaniard," remarked the clergyman.

But to the fisherman's wife these nations seemed all the same, and she consoled herself with the thought that the child was baptized as a Christian.

The boy thrived; the noble blood in his veins was warm, and he became strong on his homely fare. He grew apace in the humble cottage, and the Danish dialect spoken by the West Jutes became his language. The pomegranate seed from Spain became a hardy plant on the coast of West Jutland. Thus may circumstances alter the course of a man's life! To this home he clung with deep-rooted affection; he was to experience cold and hunger, and the misfortunes and hardships that surround the poor; but he also tasted of their joys.

Childhood has bright days for every one, and the memory of them shines through the whole after-life. The boy had many sources of pleasure and enjoyment; the coast for miles and miles was full of playthings, for it was a mosaic of pebbles, some red as coral or yellow as amber, and others again white and rounded like birds' eggs and smoothed and prepared by the sea. Even the bleached fishes' skeletons, the water plants dried by the wind, and seaweed, white and shining long linen-like bands waving between the stones—all these seemed made to give pleasure and occupation for the boy's thoughts, and he had an intelligent mind; many great talents lay dormant in him. How readily he remembered stories and songs that he heard, and how dexterous he was with his fingers! With stones and mussel-shells he could put together pictures and ships with which one could decorate the room; and he could make wonderful things from a stick, his foster-mother said, although he was still so young and little. He had a sweet voice, and every melody seemed to flow naturally from his lips. And in his heart were hidden chords, which might have sounded far out into the world if he had been placed anywhere else than in the fisherman's hut by the North Sea.

One day another ship was wrecked on the coast, and among other things a chest filled with valuable flower bulbs was washed ashore. Some were put into saucepans and cooked, for they were thought to be fit to eat, and others lay and shriveled in the sand—they did not accomplish their purpose, or unfold their magnificent colors. Would Jürgen fare better? The flower bulbs had soon played their part, but he had years of apprenticeship before him. Neither he nor his friends noticed in what a monotonous, uniform way one day followed another, for there was always plenty to do and see. The ocean itself was a great lesson-book, and it unfolded a new leaf each day of calm or storm—the crested wave or the smooth surface.

The visits to the church were festive occasions, but among the festal visits in the fisherman's house one was especially looked forward to; this was, in fact, the visit of the brother of Jürgen's foster-mother, the eel-breeder from Fjaltring, near Bovbjerg. He came twice a year in a cart, painted red with blue and white tulips upon it, and full of eels; it was covered and locked like a box, two dun oxen drew it, and Jürgen was allowed to guide them.

The eel-breeder was a witty fellow, a merry guest, and brought a measure of brandy with him. They all received a small glassful or a cupful if there were not enough glasses; even Jürgen had about a thimbleful, that he might digest the fat eel, as the eel-breeder said; he always told one story over and over again, and if his hearers laughed he would immediately repeat it to them. Jürgen while still a boy, and also when he was older, used phrases from the eel-breeder's story on various occasions, so it will be as well for us to listen to it. It runs thus:

"The eels went into the bay, and the young ones begged leave to go a little farther out. 'Don't go too far,' said their mother: 'the ugly eel-spearer might come and snap you all up." But they went too far, and of eight daughters only three came back to the mother, and these wept and said, 'We only went a little way out, and the ugly eel-spearer came immediately and stabbed five of our sisters to death.' 'They'll come back again,' said the mother eel. 'Oh, no,' exclaimed the daughters, 'for he skinned them, cut them in two, and fried them.' 'Oh, they'll come back again,' the mother eel persisted. 'No,' replied the daughters, 'for he ate them up.' 'They'll come back again,' repeated the mother eel. 'But he drank brandy after them,' said the daughters. 'Ah, then they'll never come back,' said the mother, and she burst out crying, 'it's the brandy that buries the eels.'

"And therefore," said the eel-breeder in conclusion, "it is always the proper thing to drink brandy after eating eels."

This story was the tinsel thread, the most humorous recollection of Jürgen's life. He also wanted to go a little way farther out and up the bay—that is to say, out into the world in a ship—but his mother said, like the eel-breeder, "There are so many bad people—eel-spearers!" He wished to go a little way past the sand-hills, out into the dunes, and at last he did: four happy days, the brightest of his childhood, fell to his lot, and the whole beauty and splendor of Jutland, all the happiness and sunshine of his home, were concentrated in these. He went to a festival, but it was a burial feast.

A rich relation of the fisherman's family had died; the farm was situated far eastward in the country and a little towards the north. Jürgen's foster-parents went there, and he also went with them from the dunes, over heath and moor, where the Skjærumaa takes its course through green meadows and contains many eels; mother eels live there with their daughters, who are caught and eaten up by wicked people. But do not men sometimes act quite as cruelly towards their own fellow-men? Was not the knight Sir Bugge murdered by wicked people? And though he was well spoken of, did he not also wish to kill the architect who built the castle for him, with its thick walls and tower, at the point where the Skjærumaa falls into the bay? Jürgen and his parents now stood there; the wall and the ramparts still remained, and red crumbling fragments lay scattered around Here it was that Sir Bugge, after the architect had left him, said to one of his men, "Go after him and say, 'Master, the tower shakes.' If he turns round, kill him and take away the money I paid him, but if he does not turn round, let him go in peace." The man did as he was told; the architect did not turn round, but called back "The tower does not shake in the least, but one day a man will come from the west in a blue cloak—he will cause it to shake!" And so indeed it happened a hundred years later, for the North Sea broke in and cast down the tower; but Predbjörn Gyldenstjerne, the man who then possessed the castle, built a new castle higher up at the end of the meadow, and that one is standing to this day, and is called Nörre-Vosborg.

Jürgen and his foster parents went past this castle. They had told him its story during the long winter evenings, and now he saw the stately edifice, with its double moat, and trees and bushes; the wall, covered with ferns, rose within the moat, but the lofty lime-trees were the most beautiful of all; they grew up to the highest windows, and the air was full of their sweet fragrance. In a northwest corner of the garden stood a great bush full of blossom, like winter snow amid the summer's green; it was a juniper bush, the first that Jürgen had ever seen in bloom. He never forgot it, nor the lime-trees; the child's soul treasured up these memories of beauty and fragrance to gladden the old man.

From Nörre-Vosborg, where the juniper blossomed, the journey became more pleasant, for they met some other people who were also going to the funeral and were riding in wagons. Our travelers had to sit all together on a little box at the back of the wagon, but even this, they thought, was better than walking. So they continued their journey across the rugged heath. The oxen which drew the wagon stopped every now and then, where a patch of fresh grass appeared amid the heather. The sun shone with considerable heat, and it was wonderful to behold how in the far distance something like smoke seemed to be rising; yet this smoke was clearer than the air; it was transparent, and looked like rays of light rolling and dancing afar over the heath.

"That is Lokeman driving his sheep," said some one.

And this was enough to excite Jürgen's imagination. He felt as if they were now about to enter fairyland, though everything was still real. How quiet it was! The heath stretched far and wide around them like a beautiful carpet. The heather was in blossom, and the juniper-bushes and fresh oak saplings rose like bouquets from the earth. An inviting place for a frolic, if it had not been for the number of poisonous adders of which the travelers spoke; they also mentioned that the place had formerly been infested with wolves, and that the district was still called Wolfsborg for this reason. The old man who was driving the oxen told them that in the lifetime of his father the horses had many a hard battle with the wild beasts that were now exterminated. One morning, when he himself had gone out to bring in the horses, he found one of them standing with its forefeet on a wolf it had killed, but the savage animal had torn and lacerated the brave horse's legs.

The journey over the heath and the deep sand was only too quickly at an end. They stopped before the house of mourning, where they found plenty of guests within and without. Wagon after wagon stood side by side, while the horses and oxen had been turned out to graze on the scanty pasture. Great sand-hills like those at home by the North Sea rose behind the house and extended far and wide. How had they come here, so many miles inland? They were as large and high as those on the coast, and the wind had carried them there; there was also a legend attached to them.

Psalms were sung, and a few of the old people shed tears; with this exception, the guests were cheerful enough, it seemed to Jürgen, and there was plenty to eat and drink. There were eels of the fattest, requiring brandy to bury them, as the eel-breeder said; and certainly they did not forget to carry out his maxim here.

Jürgen went in and out the house; and on the third day he felt as much at home as he did in the fisherman's cottage among the sand-hills, where he had passed his early days. Here on the heath were riches unknown to him until now; for flowers, blackberries, and bilberries were to be found in profusion, so large and sweet that when they were crushed beneath the tread of passers-by the heather was stained with their red juice. Here was a barrow and yonder another. Then columns of smoke rose into the still air; it was a heath fire, they told him—how brightly it blazed in the dark evening!

The fourth day came, and the funeral festivities were at an end; they were to go back from the land-dunes to the sand-dunes.

"Ours are better," said the old fisherman, Jürgen's foster-father; "these have no strength."

And they spoke of the way in which the sand-dunes had come inland, and it seemed very easy to understand. This is how they explained it:

A dead body had been found on the coast, and the peasants buried it in the church-yard. From that time the sand began to fly about and the sea broke in with violence. A wise man in the district advised them to open the grave and see if the buried man was not lying sucking his thumb, for if so he must be a sailor, and the sea would not rest until it had got him back. The grave was opened, and he really was found with his thumb in his mouth. So they laid him upon a cart, and harnessed two oxen to it; and the oxen ran off with the sailor over heath and moor to the ocean, as if they had been stung by an adder. Then the sand ceased to fly inland, but the hills that had been piled up still remained.

All this Jürgen listened to and treasured up in his memory of the happiest days of his childhood—the days of the burial feast.

How delightful it was to see fresh places and to mix with strangers! And he was to go still farther, for he was not yet fourteen years old when he went out in a ship to see the world. He encountered bad weather, heavy seas, unkindness, and hard men—such were his experiences, for he became ship-boy. Cold nights, bad living, and blows had to be endured; then he felt his noble Spanish blood boil within him, and bitter, angry, words rose to his lips, but he gulped them down; it was better, although he felt as the eel must feel when it is skinned, cut up, and put into the frying-pan.

"I shall get over it," said a voice within him.

He saw the Spanish coast, the native land of his parents. He even saw the town where they had lived in joy and prosperity, but he knew nothing of his home or his relations, and his relations, knew just as little about him.

The poor ship boy was not permitted to land, but on the last day of their stay he managed to get ashore. There were several purchases to be made, and he was sent to carry them on board.

Jürgen stood there in his shabby clothes which looked as if they had been washed in the ditch and dried in the chimney; he, who had always dwelled among the sand-hills, now saw a great city for the first time. How lofty the houses seemed, and what a number of people there were in the streets! some pushing this way, some that—a perfect maelstrom of citizens and peasants, monks and soldiers—the jingling of bells on the trappings of asses and mules, the chiming of church bells, calling, shouting, hammering and knocking—all going on at once. Every trade was located in the basement of the houses or in the side thoroughfares; and the sun shone with such heat, and the air was so close, that one seemed to be in an oven full of beetles, cockchafers, bees and flies, all humming and buzzing together. Jürgen scarcely knew where he was or which way he went. Then he saw just in front of him the great doorway of a cathedral; the lights were gleaming in the dark aisles, and the fragrance of incense was wafted towards him. Even the poorest beggar ventured up the steps into the sanctuary. Jürgen followed the sailor he was with into the church, and stood in the sacred edifice. Colored pictures gleamed from their golden background, and on the altar stood the figure of the Virgin with the child Jesus, surrounded by lights and flowers; priests in festive robes were chanting, and choir boys in dazzling attire swung silver censers. What splendor and magnificence he saw there! It streamed in upon his soul and overpowered him: the church and the faith of his parents surrounded him, and touched a chord in his heart that caused his eyes to overflow with tears.

They went from the church to the market-place. Here a quantity of provisions were given him to carry. The way to the harbor was long; and weary and overcome with various emotions, he rested for a few moments before a splendid house, with marble pillars, statues, and broad steps. Here he rested his burden, against the wall. Then a porter in livery came out, lifted up a silver-headed cane, and drove him away—him, the grandson of that house. But no one knew that, and he just as little as any one. Then he went on board again, and once more encountered rough words and blows, much work and little sleep—such was his experience of life. They say it is good to suffer in one's young days, if age brings something to make up for it.

His period of service on board the ship came to an end, and the vessel lay once more at Ringkjöbing in Jutland. He came ashore, and went home to the sand-dunes near Hunsby; but his foster-mother had died during his absence.

A hard winter followed this summer. Snow-storms swept over land and sea, and there was difficulty in getting from one place to another. How unequally things are distributed in this world! Here there was bitter cold and snow-storms, while in Spain there was burning sunshine and oppressive heat. Yet, when a clear frosty day came, and Jürgen saw the swans flying in numbers from the sea towards the land, across to Nörre-Vosborg, it seemed to him that people could breathe more freely here; the summer also in this part of the world was splendid. In imagination he saw the heath blossom and become purple with rich juicy berries, and the elder-bushes and lime-trees at Nörre-Vosborg in flower. He made up his mind to go there again.

Spring came, and the fishing began. Jürgen was now an active helper in this, for he had grown during the last year, and was quick at work. He was full of life, and knew how to swim, to tread water, and to turn over and tumble in the strong tide. They often warned him to beware of the sharks, which seize the best swimmer, draw him down, and devour him; but such was not to be Jürgen's fate.

At a neighbor's house in the dunes there was a boy named Martin, with whom Jürgen was on very friendly terms, and they both took service in the same ship to Norway, and also went together to Holland. They never had a quarrel, but a person can be easily excited to quarrel when he is naturally hot-tempered, for he often shows it in many ways; and this is just what Jürgen did one day when they fell out about the merest trifle. They were sitting behind the cabin door, eating from a delf plate, which they had placed between them. Jürgen held his pocket-knife in his hand and raised it towards Martin, and at the same time became ashy pale, and his eyes had an ugly look. Martin only said, "Ah! ah! you are one of that sort, are you? Fond of using the knife!"

The words were scarcely spoken, when Jürgen's hand sank down. He did not answer a syllable, but went on eating, and afterwards returned to his work. When they were resting again he walked up to Martin and said:

"Hit me in the face! I deserve it. But sometimes I feel as if I had a pot in me that boils over."

"There, let the thing rest," replied Martin.

And after that they were almost better friends than ever; when afterwards they returned to the dunes and began telling their adventures, this was told among the rest. Martin said that Jürgen was certainly passionate, but a good fellow after all.

They were both young and healthy, well-grown and strong; but Jürgen was the cleverer of the two.

In Norway the peasants go into the mountains and take the cattle there to find pasture. On the west coast of Jutland huts have been erected among the sand-hills; they are built of pieces of wreck, and thatched with turf and heather; there are sleeping places round the walls, and here the fishermen live and sleep during the early spring. Every fisherman has a female helper, or manager as she is called, who baits his hooks, prepares warm beer for him when he comes ashore, and gets the dinner cooked and ready for him by the time he comes back to the hut tired and hungry. Besides this the managers bring up the fish from the boats, cut them open, prepare them, and have generally a great deal to do.

Jürgen, his father, and several other fishermen and their managers inhabited the same hut; Martin lived in the next one.

One of the girls, whose name was Else, had known Jürgen from childhood; they were glad to see each other, and were of the same opinion on many points, but in appearance they were entirely opposite; for he was dark, and she was pale,and fair, and had flaxn hair, and eyes as blue as the sea in sunshine.

As they were walking together one day, Jürgen held her hand very firmly in his, and she said to him:

"Jürgen, I have something I want to say to you; let me be your manager, for you are like a brother to me; but Martin, whose housekeeper I am—he is my lover—but you need not tell this to the others."

It seemed to Jürgen as if the loose sand was giving way under his feet. He did not speak a word, but nodded his head, and that meant "yes." It was all that was necessary; but he suddenly felt in his heart that he hated Martin, and the more he thought the more he felt convinced that Martin had stolen away from him the only being he ever loved, and that this was Else: he had never thought of Else in this way before, but now it all became plain to him.

When the sea is rather rough, and the fishermen are coming home in their great boats, it is wonderful to see how they cross the reefs. One of them stands upright in the bow of the boat, and the others watch him sitting with the oars in their hands. Outside the reef it looks as if the boat was not approaching land but going back to sea; then the man who is standing up gives them the signal that the great wave is coming which is to float them across the reef. The boat is lifted high into the air, so that the keel is seen from the shore; the next moment nothing can be seen, mast, keel, and people are all hidden—it seems as though the sea had devoured them; but in a few moments they emerge like a great sea animal climbing up the waves, and the oars move as if the creature had legs. The second and third reef are passed in the same manner; then the fishermen jump into the water and push the boat towards the shore—every wave helps them—and at length they have it drawn up, beyond the reach of the breakers.

A wrong order given in front of the reef—the slightest hesitation—and the boat would be lost.

"Then it would be all over with me and Martin too!"

This thought passed through Jürgen's mind one day while they were out at sea, where his foster-father had been taken suddenly ill. The fever had seized him. They were only a few oars' strokes from the reef, and Jürgen sprang from his seat and stood up in the bow.

"Father—let me come!" he said, and he glanced at Martin and across the waves; every oar bent with the exertions of the rowers as the great wave came towards them, and he saw his father's pale face, and dared not obey the evil impulse that had shot through his brain. The boat came safely across the reef to land; but the evil thought remained in his heart, and roused up every little fiber of bitterness which he remembered between himself and Martin since they had known each other. But he could not weave the fibers together, nor did he endeavor to do so. He felt that Martin had robbed him, and this was enough to make him hate his former friend. Several of the fishermen saw this, but Martin did not—he remained as obliging and talkative as ever, in fact he talked rather too much.

Jürgen's foster-father took to his bed, and it became his deathbed, for he died a week afterwards; and now Jürgen was heir to the little house behind the sand-hills. It was small, certainly, but still it was something, and Martin had nothing of the kind.

"You will not go to sea again, Jürgen, I suppose," observed one of the old fishermen. "You will always stay with us now."

But this was not Jürgen's intention; he wanted to see something of the world. The eel-breeder of Fjaltring had an uncle at Old Skjagen, who was a fisherman, but also a prosperous merchant with ships upon the sea; he was said to be a good old man, and it would not be a bad thing to enter his service. Old Skjagen lies in the extreme north of Jutland, as far away from the Hunsby dunes as one can travel in that country; and this is just what pleased Jürgen, for he did not want to remain till the wedding of Martin and Else, which would take place in a week or two.

The old fisherman said it was foolish to go away, for now that Jürgen had a home Else would very likely be inclined to take him instead of Martin.

Jürgen gave such a vague answer that it was not easy to make out what he meant—the old man brought Else to him, and she said:

"You have a home now; you ought to think of that."

And Jürgen thought of many things.

The sea has heavy waves, but there are heavier waves in the human heart. Many thoughts, strong and weak, rushed through Jürgen's brain, and he said to Else:

"If Martin had a house like mine, which of us would you rather have?"

"But Martin has no house and cannot get one."

"Suppose he had one?"

"Well, then I would certainly take Martin, for that is what my heart tells me; but one cannot live upon love."

Jürgen turned these things over in his mind all night. Something was working within him, he hardly knew what it was, but it was even stronger than his love for Else; and so he went to Martin's, and what he said and did there was well considered. He let the house to Martin on most liberal terms, saying that he wished to go to sea again, because he liked it. And Else kissed him when she heard of it, for she loved Martin best.

Jürgen proposed to start early in the morning, and on the evening before his departure, when it was already getting rather late, he felt a wish to visit Martin once more. He started, and among the dunes met the old fisherman, who was angry at his leaving the place. The old man made jokes about Martin, and declared there must be some magic about that fellow, of whom the girls were so fond.

Jürgen did not pay any attention to his remarks, but said good-bye to the old man and went on towards the house where Martin dwelled. He heard loud talking inside; Martin was not aione, and this made Jürgen waver in his determination, for he did not wish to see Else again. On second thoughts, he decided that it was better not to hear any more thanks from Martin, and so he turned back.

On the following morning, before the sun rose, he fastened his knapsack on his back, took his wooden provision box in his hand, and went away among the sand-hills towards the coast path. This way was more pleasant than the heavy sand road, and besides it was shorter; and he intended to go first to Fjaltring, near Bovbjerg, where the eel-breeder lived, to whom he had promised a visit.

The sea lay before him, clear and blue, and the mussel shells and pebbles, the playthings of his childhood, crunched under his feet. While he thus walked on his nose suddenly began to bleed; it was a trifling occurrence, but trifles sometimes are of great importance. A few large drops of blood fell upon one of his sleeves. He wiped them off and stopped the bleeding, and it seemed to him as if this had cleared and lightened his brain. The sea-cale bloomed here and there in the sand as he passed. He broke off a spray and stuck it in his hat; he determined to be merry and light-hearted, for he was going out into the wide world—"a little way out, beyond the bay," as the young eels had said. "Beware of bad people who will catch you, and skin you and put you in the frying-pan!" he repeated in his mind, and smiled, for he thought he should find his way through the world—good courage is a strong weapon!

The sun was high in the heavens when he approached the narrow entrance to Nissum Bay. He looked back and saw a couple of horsemen galloping a long distance behind him, and there were other people with them. But this did not concern him.

The ferry-boat was on the opposite side of the bay. Jürgen called to the ferry-man, and the latter came over with his boat. Jürgen stepped in; but before he had got half-way across, the men whom he had seen riding so hastily, came up, hailed the ferry-man, and commanded him to return in the name of the law. Jürgen did not understand the reason of this, but he thought it would be best to turn back, and therefore he himself took an oar and returned. As soon as the boat touched the shore, the men sprang on board, and before he was aware of it, they had bound his hands with a rope.

"This wicked deed will cost you your life," they said. "It is a good thing we have caught you."

He was accused of nothing less than murder. Martin had been found dead, with his throat cut. One of the fishermen, late on the previous evening, had met Jürgen going towards Martin's house; this was not the first time Jürgen had raised his knife against Martin, so they felt sure that he was the murderer. The prison was in a town at a great distance, and the wind was contrary for going there by sea; but it would not take half an hour to get across the bay, and another quarter of an hour would bring them to Nörre-Vosborg, the great castle with ramparts and moat. One of Jürgen's captors was a fisherman, a brother of the keeper of the castle, and he said it might be managed that Jürgen should be placed for the present in the dungeon at Vosborg, where Long Martha the gipsy had been shut up till her execution. They paid no attention to Jürgen's defense; the few drops of blood on his shirt-sleeve bore heavy witness against him. But he was conscious of his innocence, and as there was no chance of clearing himself at present he submitted to his fate.

The party landed just at the place where Sir Bugge's castle had stood, and where Jürgen had walked with his foster-parents after the burial feast, during the four happiest days of his childhood. He was led by the well-known path, over the meadow to Vosborg; once more the elders were in bloom and the lofty lime-trees gave forth sweet fragrance, and it seemed as if it were but yesterday that he had last seen the spot. In each of the two wings of the castle there was a staircase which led to a place below the entrance, from whence there is access to a low, vaulted cellar. In this dungeon Long Martha had been imprisoned, and from here she was led away to the scaffold. She had eaten the hearts of five children, and had imagined that if she could obtain two more she would be able to fly and make herself invisible. In the middle of the roof of the cellar there was a little narrow air-hole, but no window. The flowering lime trees could not breathe refreshing fragrance into that abode, where everything was dark and moldy.

There was only a rough bench in the cell; but a good conscience is a soft pillow, and therefore Jürgen could sleep well.

The thick oaken door was locked, and secured on the outside by an iron bar; but the goblin of superstition can creep through a keyhole into a baron's castle just as easily as it can into a fisherman's cottage, and why should he not creep in here, where Jürgen sat thinking of Long Martha and her wicked deeds? Her last thoughts on the night before her execution had filled this place; and the magic that tradition asserted to have been practiced here, in Sir Svanwedel's time, came into Jürgen's mind, and made him shudder; but a sunbeam, a refreshing thought from without, penetrated his heart even here—it was the remembrance of the flowering elder and the sweet smelling lime-trees.

He was not left there long. They took him away to the town of Ringkjöbing, where he was imprisoned with equal severity.

Those times were not like ours. The common people were treated harshly; and it was just after the days when farms were converted into knights' estates, when coachmen and servants were often made magistrates, and had power to sentence a poor man, for a small offense, to lose his property and to corporeal punishment. Judges of this kind were still to be found; and in Jutland, so far from the capital, and from the enlightened, well-meaning, head of the Government, the law was still very loosely administered sometimes—the smallest grievance Jürgen could expect was that his case should be delayed.

His dwelling was cold and comfortless; and how long would he be obliged to bear all this? It seemed his fate to suffer misfortune and sorrow innocently. He now had plenty of time to reflect on the difference of fortune on earth, and to wonder why this fate had been allotted to him; yet he felt sure that all would be made clear in the next life, the existence that awaits us when this life is over. His faith had grown strong in the poor fisherman's cottage; the light which had never shone into his father's mind, in all the richness and sunshine of Spain, was sent to him to be his comfort in poverty and distress, a sign of that mercy of God which never fails.

The spring storms began to blow. The rolling and moaning of the North Sea could be heard for miles inland when the wind was blowing, and then it sounded like the rushing of a thousand wagons over a hard road with a mine underneath. Jürgen heard these sounds in his prison, and it was a relief to him. No music could have touched his heart as did these sounds of the sea—the rolling sea, the boundless sea, on which a man can be borne across the world before the wind, carrying his own house with him wherever he goes, just as the snail carries its home even into a strange country.

He listened eagerly to its deep murmur and then the thought arose—"Free! free! How happy to be free, even barefooted and in ragged clothes!" Sometimes, when such thoughts crossed his mind, the fiery nature rose within him, and he beat the wall with his clenched fists.

Weeks, months, a whole year had gone by, when Niels the thief, called also a horse-dealer, was arrested; and now better times came, and it was seen that Jürgen had been wrongly accused.

On the afternoon before Jürgen's departure from home, and before the murder, Niels, the thief, had met Martin at a beerhouse in the neighborhood of Ringkjöbing. A few glasses were drank, not enough to cloud the brain, but enough to loosen Martin's tongue. He began to boast and to say that he had obtained a house and intended to marry, and when Niels asked him where he was going to get the money, he slapped his pocket proudly and said:

"The money is here, where it ought to be."

This boast cost him his life; for when he went home Niels followed him, and cut his throat, intending to rob the murdered man of the gold, which did not exist.

All this was circumstantially explained; but it is enough for us to know that Jürgen was set free. But what compensation did he get for having been imprisoned a whole year, and shut out from all communication with his fellow creatures? They told him he was fortunate in being proved innocent, and that he might go. The burgomaster gave him two dollars for traveling expenses, and many citizens offered him provisions and beer—there were still good people: they were not all hard and pitiless. But the best thing of all was that the merchant Brönne, of Skjagen, into whose service Jürgen had proposed entering the year before, was just at that time on business in the town of Ringkjöbing. Brönne heard the whole story; he was kind-hearted, and understood what Jürgen must have felt and suffered. Therefore he made up his mind to make it up to the poor lad, and convince him that there were still kind folks in the world.

So Jürgen went forth from prison as if to paradise, to find freedom, affection, and trust. He was to travel this path now, for no goblet of life is all bitterness; no good man would pour out such a draft for his fellow-man, and how should He do it, Who is love personified?

"Let everything be buried and forgotten," said Brönne, the merchant. "Let us draw a thick line through last year: we will even burn the almanac. In two days we will start for dear, friendly, peaceful Skjagen. People call it an out-of-the-way corner; but it is a good warm chimney-corner, and its windows open towards every part of the world."

What a journey that was. It was like taking fresh breath out of the cold dungeon air into the warm sunshine. The heather bloomed in pride and beauty, and the shepherd-boy sat on a barrow and blew his pipe, which he had carved for himself out of a sheep bone. Fata Morgana, the beautiful aerial phenomenon of the wilderness, appeared with hanging gardens and waving forests, and the wonderful cloud called "Lokeman driving his sheep" also was seen.

Up towards Skjagen they went, through the land of the Wendels, whence the men with long beards (the Longobardi or Lombards) had emigrated in the reign of King Snio, when all the children and old people were to have been killed, till the noble Dame Gambaruk proposed that the young people should emigrate. Jürgen knew all this, he had some little knowledge; and although he did not know the land of the Lombards beyond the lofty Alps, he had an idea that it must be there, for in his boyhood he had been in the south, in Spain. He thought of the plenteousness of the southern fruit, of the red pomegranate flowers, of the humming, buzzing, and toiling in the great beehive of a city he had seen; but home is the best place after all, and Jürgen's home was Denmark.

At last they arrived at "Vendilskaga," as Skjagen is called in old Norwegian and Icelandic writings. At that time Old Skjagen, with the eastern and western town, extended for miles, with sand-hills and arable land as far as the lighthouse near "Grenen." Then, as now, the houses were strewn among the wind-raised sand-hills—a wilderness in which the wind sports with the sand, and where the voice of the sea-gull and wild swan strikes harshly on the ear.

In the south-west, a mile from "Grenen," lies Old Skjagen; merchant Brönne dwelled here, and this was also to be Jürgen's home for the future. The dwelling-house was tarred, and all the small out-buildings had an overturned boat for a roof—even the pigsty had been put together from pieces of wreck. There was no fence, for indeed there was nothing to fence in except the long rows of fishes which were hung upon lines, one above the other, to dry in the wind. The entire coast was strewn with spoiled herrings, for there were so many of these fish that a net was scarcely thrown into the sea before it was filled. They were caught by cartloads, and many of them were either thrown back into the sea or left to lie on the beach.

The old man's wife and daughter and his servants also came to meet him with great rejoicing. There was a great squeezing of hands, and talking and questioning. And the daughter, what a sweet face and bright eyes she had!

The inside of the house was comfortable and roomy. Fritters, that a king would have looked upon as a dainty dish, were placed on the table, and there was wine from the Skjagen vineyard—that is, the sea; for there the grapes come ashore ready pressed and prepared in barrels and in bottles.

When the mother and daughter heard who Jürgen was, and how innocently he had suffered, they looked at him in a still more friendly way; and pretty Clara's eyes had a look of especial interest as she listened to his story. Jürgen found a happy home in Old Skjagen. It did his heart good, for it had been sorely tried. He had drunk the bitter goblet of love which softens or hardens the heart, according to circumstances Jürgen's heart was still soft—it was young, and therefore it was a good thing that Miss Clara was going in three weeks' time to Christiansand in Norway, in her father's ship, to visit an aunt and to stay there the whole winter.

On the Sunday before she went away they all went to church, to the Holy Communion. The church was large and handsome, and had been built centuries before by Scotchmen and Dutchmen; it stood some little way out of the town. It was rather ruinous certainly, and the road to it was heavy, through deep sand, but the people gladly surmounted these difficulties to get to the house of God, to sing psalms and to hear the sermon. The sand had heaped itself up round the walls of the church, but the graves were kept free from it.

It was the largest church north of the Limfjorden. The Virgin Mary, with a golden crown on her head and the child Jesus in her arms, stood lifelike on the altar; the holy Apostles had been carved in the choir, and on the walls there were portraits of the old burgomasters and councillors of Skjagen; the pulpit was of carved work. The sun shone brightly into the church, and its radiance fell on the polished brass chandelier and on the little ship that hung from the vaulted roof.

Jürgen felt overcome by a holy, childlike feeling, like that which possessed him, when, as a boy, he stood in the splendid Spanish cathedral. But here the feeling was different, for he felt conscious of being one of the congregation.

After the sermon followed Holy Communion. He partook of the bread and wine, and it so happened that he knelt by the side of Miss Clara; but his thoughts were so fixed upon Heaven and the Holy Sacrament that he did not notice his neighbor until he rose from his knees, and then he saw tears rolling down her cheeks.

She left Skjagen and went to Norway two days later. He remained behind, and made himself useful on the farm and at the fishery. He went out fishing, and in those days fish were more plentiful and larger than they are now. The shoals of the mackerel glittered in the dark nights, and indicated where they were swimming; the gurnards snarled, and the crabs gave forth pitiful yells when they were chased, for fish are not so mute as people say.

Every Sunday Jürgen went to church; and when his eyes rested on the picture of the Virgin Mary over the altar as he sat there, they often glided away to the spot where they had knelt side by side.

Autumn came, and brought rain and snow with it; the water rose up right into the town of Skjagen, the sand could not suck it all in, one had to wade through it or go by boat. The storms threw vessel after vessel on the fatal reefs; there were snowstorms and sand-storms; the sand flew up to the houses, blocking the entrances, so that people had to creep up through the chimneys; that was nothing at all remarkable here. It was pleasant and cheerful indoors, where peat fuel and fragments of wood from the wrecks blazed and crackled upon the hearth. Merchant Brönne read aloud, from an old chronicle, about Prince Hamlet of Denmark, who had come over from England, landed near Bovbjerg, and fought a battle; close by Ramme was his grave, only a few miles from the place where the eel-breeder lived; hundreds of barrow rose there from the heath, forming as it were an enormous church-yard. Merchant Brönne had himself been at Hamlet's grave; they spoke about old times, and about their neighbors, the English and the Scotch, and Jürgen sang the air of "The King of England's Son," and of his splendid ship and its outfit.

"In the hour of peril when most men fear,
He clasped the bride that he held so dear,
And proved himself the son of a King;
Of His courage and valor let us sing."

This verse Jürgen sang with so much feeling that his eyes beamed, and they were black and sparkling since his infancy.

There was wealth, comfort, and happiness even among the domestic animals, for they were all well cared for, and well kept. The kitchen looked bright with its copper and tin utensils, and white plates, and from the rafters hung hams, beef, and winter stores in plenty. This can still be seen in many rich farms on the west coast of Jutland: plenty to eat and drink, clean, prettily decorated rooms, active minds, cheerful tempers, and hospitality can be found there, as in an Arab's tent.

Jürgen had never spent such a happy time since the famous burial feast, and yet Miss Clara was absent, except in the thoughts and memory of all.

In April a ship was to start for Norway, and Jürgen was to sail in it. He was full of life and spirits, and looked so sturdy and well that Dame Brönne said it did her good to see him.

"And it does one good to look at you also, old wife," said the merchant. "Jürgen has brought fresh life into our winter evenings, and into you too, mother. You look younger than ever this year, and seem well and cheerful. But then you were once the prettiest girl in Viborg, and that is saying a great deal, for I have always found the Viborg girls the prettiest of any."

Jürgen said nothing, but he thought of a certain maiden of Skjagen, whom he was soon to visit. The ship set sail for Christiansand in Norway, and as the wind was favorable it soon arrived there.

One morning merchant Brönne went out to the lighthouse, which stands a little way out of Old Skjagen, not far from "Grenen." The light was out, and the sun was already high in the heavens, when he mounted the tower. The sand-banks extend a whole mile from the shore, beneath the water, outside these banks; many ships could be seen that day, and with the aid of his telescope the old man thought he descried his own ship, the *Karen Brönne*. Yes! certainly, there she was, sailing homewards with Clara and Jürgen on board.

Clara sat on deck, and saw the sand-hills gradually appearing in the distance; the church and lighthouse looked like a heron and a swan rising from the blue waters. If the wind held good they might reach home in about an hour. So near they were to home and all its joys—so near to death and all its terrors! A plank in the ship gave way, and the water rushed in; the crew flew to the pumps, and did their best to stop the leak. A signal of distress was hoisted, but they were still fully a mile from the shore. Some fishing boats were in sight, but they were too far off to be of any use. The wind blew towards the land, the tide was in their favor, but it was all useless; the ship could not be saved.

Jürgen threw his right arm round Clara, and pressed her to him. With what a look she gazed up into his face, as with a prayer to God for help he breasted the waves, which rushed over the sinking ship! She uttered a cry, but she felt safe and certain that he would not leave her to sink. And in this hour of terror and danger Jürgen felt as the king's son did, as told in the old song:

"In the hour of peril when most men fear.
He clasped the bride that he held so dear."

How glad he felt that hs was a good swimmer! He worked his way onward with his feet and one arm, while he held the young girl up firmly with the other. He rested on the waves, he trod the water—in fact, did everything he could think of, in order not to fatigue himself, and to reserve strength enough to reach land. He heard Clara sigh, and felt her shudder convulsively, and he pressed her more closely to him. Now and then a wave rolled over them, the current lifted them; the water, although deep, was so clear that for a moment he imagined he saw the shoals of mackerel glittering, or Leviathan himself ready to swallow them. Now the clouds cast a shadow over the water, then again came the playing sunbeams; flocks of loudly screaming birds passed over him, and the plump and lazy wild ducks which allow themselves to be drifted by the waves rose up terrified at the sight of the swimmer. He began to feel his strength decreasing, but he was only a few cable lengths' distance from the shore, and help was coming, for a boat was approaching him. At this moment he distinctly saw a white staring figure under the water—a wave lifted him up, and he came nearer to the figure—he felt a violent shock, and everything became dark around him.

On the sand reef lay the wreck of a ship, which was covered with water at high tide; the white figure head rested against the anchor, the sharp iron edge of which rose just above the surface. Jürgen had come in contact with this; the tide had driven him against it with great force. He sank down stunned with the blow, but the next wave lifted him and the young girl up again. Some fishermen, coming with a boat, seized them and dragged them into it. The blood streamed down over Jürgen's face; he seemed dead, but still held the young girl so tightly that they were obliged to take her from him by force. She was pale and lifeless; they laid her in the boat, and rowed as quickly as possible to the shore. They tried every means to restore Clara to life, but it was all of no avail. Jürgen had been swimming for some distance with a corpse in his arms, and had exhausted his strength for one who was dead.

Jürgen still breathed, so the fishermen carried him to the nearest house upon the sand-hills, where a smith and general dealer lived who knew something of surgery, and bound up Jürgen's wounds in a temporary way until a surgeon could be obtained from the nearest town the next day. The injured man's brain was affected, and in his delirium he uttered wild cries; but on the third day he lay quiet and weak upon his bed; his life seemed to hang by a thread, and the physician said it would be better for him if this thread broke. "Let us pray that God may take him," he said, "for he will never be the same man again."

But life did not depart from him—the thread would not break, but the thread of memory was severed; the thread of his mind had been cut through, and what was still more grievous, a body remained—a living healthy body that wandered about like a troubled spirit.

Jürgen remained in merchant Brönne's house. "He was hurt while endeavoring to save our child," said the old man, "and now he is our son."

People called Jürgen insane, but that was not exactly the correct term. He was like an instrument in which the strings are loose and will give no sound; only occasionally they regained their power for a few minutes, and then they sounded as they used to do. He would sing snatches of songs or old melodies, pictures of the past would rise before him, and then disappear in the mist, as it were, but as a general rule he sat staring into vacancy, without a thought. We may conjecture that he did not suffer, but his dark eyes lost their brightness, and looked like clouded glass.

"Poor mad Jürgen," said the people. And this was the end of a life whose infancy was to have been surrounded with wealth and splendor had his parents lived! All his great mental abilities had been lost, nothing but hardship, sorrow, and disappointment had been his fate. He was like a rare plant, torn from its native soil, and tossed upon the beach to wither there. And was this one of God's creatures, fashioned in His own likeness, to have no better fate? Was he to be only the plaything of fortune? No! the all-loving Creator would certainly repay him in the life to come for what hs had suffered and lost here. "The Lord is good to all; and His mercy is over all His works." The pious old wife of the merchant repeated these words from the Psalms of David in patience and hope, and the prayer of her heart was that Jürgen might soon be called away to enter into eternal life.

In the church-yard where the walls were surrounded with sand Clara lay buried. Jürgen did not seem to know this; it did not enter his mind, which could only retain fragments of the past. Every Sunday he went to church with the old people, and sat there silently, staring vacantly before him. One day, when the psalms were being sung, he sighed deeply, and his eyes became bright; they were fixed upon a place near the altar where he had knelt with his friend who was dead. He murmured her name, and became deadly pale, and tears rolled down his cheeks. They led him out of church; he told those standing round him that he was well, and had never been ill; he, who had been so grievously afflicted, the outcast, thrown upon the world, could not remember his sufferings. The Lord our Creator is wise and full of loving kindness—who can doubt it?

In Spain, where balmy breezes blow over the Moorish cupolas and gently stir the orange and myrtle groves, where singing and the sound of the castanets are always heard, the richest merchant in the place, a childless old man, sat in a luxurious house, while children marched in procession through the streets with waving flags and lighted tapers. If he had been able to press his children to his heart, his daughter, or her child, that had, perhaps never seen the light of day, far less the kingdom of Heaven, how much of his wealth would he not have given!" Poor child!" Yes, poor child—a child still, yet more than thirty years old, for Jürgen had arrived at this age in Old Skjagen.

The shifting sands had covered the graves in the church-yard, quite up to the church walls, but still, the dead must be buried among their relatives and the dear ones who had gone before them. Merchant Brönne and his wife now rested with their children under the white sand.

It was in the spring—the season of storms. The sand from the dunes was whirled up in clouds; the sea was rough, and flocks of birds flew like clouds in the storm, screaming across the sand-hills. Shipwreck followed upon shipwreck on the reefs between Old Skagen and the Hunsby dunes.

One evening Jürgen sat in his room alone; all at once his mind seemed to become clearer, and a restless feeling came over him, such as had often, in his younger days, driven him out to wander over the sand-hills or on the heath. "Home, home!" he cried. No one heard him. He went out and walked towards the dunes. Sand and stones blew into his face, and whirled round him; he went in the direction of the church. The sand was banked up the walls, half covering the windows, but it had been cleared away in front of the door, and the entrance was free and easy to open, so Jürgen went into the church.

The storm raged over the town of Skjagen; there had not been such a terrible tempest within the memory of the inhabitants, nor such a rough sea. But Jürgen was in the temple of God, and while the darkness of night reigned outside, a light arose in his soul that was never to depart from it; the heavy weight that pressed on his brain burst asunder. He fancied he heard the organ, but it was only the storm and the moaning of the sea. He sat down on one of the seats, and lo! the candles were lighted one by one, and there was brightness and grandeur such as he had only seen in the Spanish cathedral. The portraits of the old citizens became alive, stepped down from the walls against which they had hung for centuries, and took seats near the church door. The gates flew open, and all the dead people from the church-yard came in, and filled the church, while beautiful music sounded. Then the melody of the psalm burst forth, like the sound of the waters, and Jürgen saw that his foster-parents from the Hunsby dunes were there, also old merchant Brönne with his wife and their daughter Clara, who gave him her hand. They both went up to the altar where they had knelt before, and the priest joined their hands and united them for life. Then music was heard again; it was wonderfully sweet, like a child's voice, full of joy and expectation, swelling to the powerful tones of a full organ, sometimes soft and sweet, then like the sounds of a tempest, delightful and elevating to hear, yet strong enough to burst the stone tombs of the dead. Then the little ship that hung from the roof of the choir was let down and looked wonderfully large and beautiful with its silken sails and rigging:

> *"The ropes were of silk, the anchor of gold.*
> *And everywhere riches and pomp untold,"*

as the old song says.

The young couple went on board, accompanied by the whole congregation, for there was room and enjoyment for them all. Then the walls and arches of the church were covered with flowering junipers and lime trees breathing forth fragrance; the branches waved, creating a pleasant coolness; they bent and parted, and the ship sailed between them through the air and over the sea. Every candle in the church became a star, and the wind sang a hymn in which they all joined. "Through love to glory, no life is lost, the future is full of blessings and happiness. Hallelujah!" These were the last words Jürgen uttered in this world, for the thread that bound his immortal soul was severed, and nothing but a dead body lay in the dark church, while the storm raged outside, covering it with loose sand.

The next day was Sunday, and the congregation and their pastor went, to the church. The road had always been heavy, but now it was almost unfit for use, and when they at last arrived at the church, a great heap of sand lay piled up in front of them. The whole church was completely buried in sand. The clergyman offered a short prayer, and said that God had closed the door of His house here, and that the congregation must go and build a new one for Him somewhere else. So they sung a hymn in the open air, and went home again.

Jürgen could not be found anywhere in the town of Skjagen, nor on the dunes, though they searched for him everywhere. They came to the conclusion that one of the great waves, which had rolled far up on the beach had carried him away; but his body lay buried in a great sepulcher—the church itself. The Lord had thrown down a covering for his grave during the storm, and, the heavy mound of sand lies upon it to this day. The drifting sand had covered the vaulted roof of the church, the arched cloisters, and the stone aisles. The white thorn and the dog rose now blossom above the place where the church lies buried, but the spire, like an enormous monument over a grave, can be seen for miles round. No king has a more splendid memorial. Nothing disturbs the peaceful sleep of the dead. I was the first to hear this story, for the storm sung it to me among the sand-hills.

The Money-Pig

A lot of toys were lying about in the nursery, on the top of the wardrobe stood a money-box which was made of clay, and bought at the potter's; besides, it was shaped like a pig. It had, of course, a slit in its back, and this slit had been so enlarged with a knife, that half-a-crown, or even five-shilling pieces might slip in, and there were really two in the box, among a great number of pennies.

The money-pig was so crammed full that it could no longer rattle, and that is the highest state a money-pig can reach. There it stood on the top of the wardrobe, high and majestic, and looked down upon everything else in the room; it knew very well that all the other things in the room could be bought with the contents of its stomach, and that one calls having plenty of confidence in oneself.

This is what the others thought too, although they did not say so, for there were many other things to talk about. One of the drawers was half-pulled out, and there one could see a large handsome doll, although it was somewhat old and already riveted in the neck. It looked out and said: "Let us pretend to be human beings; that is always a game worth playing."

Now they all became very excited; even the framed pictures on the wall turned round and showed that they had a wrong side to them, but they did not do so in order to protest against the proposal.

It was in the middle of the night, and the moon shone through the window panes, and afforded the cheapest light. Now the game was to begin, and all, even the perambulator, which certainly belonged to the larger toys, were asked to join in it.

"Every one has his own peculiar value," said the perambulator. "We cannot all be of noble birth! There must be some to do the work, as the saying is."

On top of the wardrobe stood a money-box which was made of clay and... shaped like a pig."

The money-pig was the only one that received a written invitation; it stood too high, and they were of opinion that it would not accept an oral invitation; and it did not reply, nor did it say that it would come, and it did not come; if it was to take part in the game it must do so from its place—they could arrange accordingly, and that they did. The little doll's theater was so placed that the money-pig could look straight into it; they wished to begin with a comedy, which was to be followed by a tea-party and discussion; but they began with the latter at once. The rocking-horse spoke of training and thoroughbreds, the perambulator of railways and steam power—all this belongs to their calling, and therefore it was natural that they spoke about it. The timepiece spoke of politics—"tic—tic—!"—it knew what time had struck, although they whispered that it was not going right; the cane stood stiff and proud, thinking a great deal of its silver knob and its ferrule; on the sofa lay two embroidered cushions, beautiful and stupid.

Now the comedy began. All sat and looked at the play, it was requested that they should crack, clap and shout, just as they pleased. But the riding-whip said that it never cracked for old people—only for young ones who had no sweethearts yet. "I crack for everybody," said the cracker. Such were the thoughts that they had while they were looking at the comedy. The play was not at all good, but it was well performed; all the performers turned their painted side to the public, they were so made that one must only look at them from this side and not from the back; they all played wonderfully well, even beyond the footlights, for the wires were a little too long, that is why they came so much to the front. The mended doll was so delighted that its neck broke again in the place the rivet was put through, and the money-pig was in its own way so charmed that it made up its mind to do something for one of the artists, and to remember him in its last will, as the one who was to be buried with it in the family grave—that is, of course, when it had come to this. It was a real enjoyment, so that they gave up the tea and were satisfied with the discussion. That is what they called playing at human beings; and there was no harm in that, for they were only playing, and each one thought only of itself and of what the money-pig might think. The money-pig's thoughts traveled farthest, for it thought of its last will and burial. And when might this happen? Certainly much sooner than one should have expected. Crash! Smash! It fell from the wardrobe on the floor and broke to pieces. The coins danced and hopped about, so that it was a pleasure to see them; the smallest turned round like tops, while the big ones rolled off, particularly one of the five shilling pieces, which wished to get out into the world. And it did come out into the world, and so did all the others; the pieces of the money-pig were thrown into the dust-bin; but the next day a new clay money-pig stood on the wardrobe; there was not yet a farthing in its stomach, that was why it could not rattle, and in this point it resembled the other. This was at any rate a beginning, and with this we shall end.

Crash! Smash! It fell from the wardrobe on the floor and broke to pieces.

The Philosopher's Stone

In India, far away towards the east, the end of the world, stood the Tree of the Sun—a magnificent tree, such as we have never seen, and most likely will never see. The crown of this tree spread over many miles like an entire forest; each of its smaller boughs formed a complete tree; palms, beeches, pines, plane-trees, and many other varieties which are found in all parts of the world, were like little branches shooting forth from the enormous tree, while the larger branches, with their knots and curves, formed valleys and hills covered with soft green and many flowers. On all sides it was like a flowering meadow or a beautiful garden; here birds from all the quarters of the globe flocked together—from the primeval forests of America, from the rose gardens of Damascus, and from the deserts of Africa, where the elephant and the lion only have dominion. Birds from the polar regions also came here, and of course the stork and the swallow were there too. But besides the birds there were other living creatures: stags, squirrels, antelopes, and hundreds of other pretty light-footed animals took up their abode here. The summit of the tree formed a beautiful garden which spread far and wide, and in the center, where the green boughs made a kind of hill, stood a crystal castle, with a view towards every quarter of Heaven. Each cupola was built in the shape of a lily, and within the stem was a winding staircase, through which one could mount to the top and step out upon the leaves, which served as balconies. The cup of the flower formed a most beautiful, glittering, circular hall, above which the blue sky and the sun and stars were the only canopy. Just as much grandeur of a different kind was to be found in the spacious hall of the castle; the whole world was reflected on the wall—in fact everything that took place daily was visible here, so it was quite unnecessary to read the newspapers; indeed none were to be got in this place, as everything could be seen in the living pictures by any one who wished to know what was going on. But all would have been too much for even the wisest man, and this man lived here; his name is very difficult to pronounce: you would not be able to manage it, so we will leave it out. He knew everything that a man on earth can know or imagine; every invention in existence, or to be made in the future, was known to him, and much more, yet everything in this world has a limit. The wise King Solomon was not half as wise as this man; he could govern the powers of Nature, and ruled over powerful spirits, even Death himself had every morning to give him a list of those who were to die during the day. But King Solomon died at last, and this fact often occupied the great man's thoughts, who lived in the castle on the Tree of the Sun; he knew that he also, however high he might tower over other men in wisdom, must die one day; he knew that he and his children would fade like the leaves of the forest, and become dust. He saw mankind wither and fall like leaves from the tree; new men came to fill their places, but the leaves that fell off never became green again; they became dust, or were absorbed into other plants.

"What happens to man when touched by the angel of death?" the wise man asked himself. "What can death be? The body decays—and the soul? What is it, and whither does it go?"

"To eternal life," said the comforting voice of religion

"But what is the transition? Where and how shall we exist?"

"Above—in Heaven," answered the pious man; "it is there we go."

"Above!" repeated the wise man, fixing his eyes upon the moon and stars above him.

He saw that to this rolling globe above and below were constantly altering and changing according to the spot on which a man happened to be. He knew, also, that if he only ascended to the summit of the highest mountain in the world, the air, which seems to us clear and transparent, would be dark and heavy; the sun would have a coppery glow and send forth no rays, and our earth would lie beneath him, wrapped in an orange-colored mist. How narrow are the limits of our earthly vision, and how little can be seen by the eye of the soul! The wisest among us know next to nothing of that which is so important to us all.

In the most secret room in the castle was the greatest treasure in the world, the Book of Truth. The wise man had read it, page after page. Any man may read this book, but only in fragments: to many people the characters seem so mixed and confused that they cannot distinguish a single word. On certain pages the writing often seems so pale or so blurred that the page becomes a blank. The wiser a man is the more he can read, and those that are wisest can read the most.

The wise man knew how to blend the sunlight and moonlight with the light of reason and the hidden forces of Nature, and by means of this strong light many things in the pages were made visible to him. But in the portion of the book entitled "Life after Death," he could not see a single point plainly. This grieved him; should he never be able to obtain here on earth a light strong enough to make everything in the Book of Truth clear to him? Like King

Solomon the wise, he understood the language of animals and could interpret their talk and song, but that did not make him any wiser. He discovered the nature of plants and metals and their power in curing diseases and delaying death, but none to destroy death. In all created things within his reach he searched for the light that should shine upon the certainty of an eternal life, but he did not find it. The Book of Truth lay open before him, but its leaves were blank to him. Christianity gave him, in the Bible, a promise of eternal life, but he wished to read it in *his* book, and there he could see nothing.

He had five children—four sons, instructed as well as the children of such a wise father could be, and one daughter, who was beautiful, kind, and intelligent, but blind; yet this affliction did not seem of much consequence to her, for her father and brothers were her outward eyes, and a vivid imagination made everything clear to her mental vision.

The sons had never gone farther from the palace than the branches of the tree extended, and their sister had scarcely ever left home; they were happy children in the home of childhood, the sweet scented and beautiful Tree of the Sun. Like all other children they loved to hear stories related to them, and their father told them about many things that other children would not have understood; but they were as intelligent as grown-up people with us. He explained to them what they saw in the pictures of life on the castle walls—the achievements of men, and the progress of events in all the lands of the earth; and the sons often wished they could be present, and take part in these great deeds. Then their father told them that in the world there was nothing but toil and strife, and that everything was not as they saw it in their beautiful home; he spoke to them of the true, the beautiful, and the good, and that these three held together in the world, and in so doing became crystallized into a precious jewel, clearer than a diamond of the first water; a jewel that has value even in the sight of God before whose brightness all things are dim. This jewel was called the philosopher's stone. He told them that by search man could find the existence of God, and that it was in the power of every man to prove the certainty that such a jewel as the philosopher's stone really existed. This information would have been beyond the comprehension of other children, but these under stood, and others will learn to understand its meaning in due time. They asked their father questions about the true, the beautiful, and the good, and he explained it to them in various ways. He told them that God, when He made man from the dust of the earth, kissed His work five times, leaving five acute feelings, which we call the five senses. Through these the true, the beautiful, and the good are seen, understood and appreciated, and through these they are valued, protected, and encouraged. Five senses have been given, mentally and corporeally, inwardly and outwardly, to soul and body.

The children thought much upon all these things, and turned them over in their minds day and night. Then the eldest brother had a marvelous dream; strangely enough not only the second brother, but also the third and fourth, had exactly the same dream: this was that each went out into the world to find the philosopher's stone. Each one thought he found it, and that as he rode back again on his fleet horse at the break of day over the soft green meadows to his home in his father's castle, the stone gleamed from his forehead like a shining light, and threw such a brightness over the Book of Truth that every word which told of the life beyond the grave was illuminated. But the sister had no dream of going out into the wide world. Her world was her father's castle.

"I shall ride forth into the world," said the eldest brother. "I must see what life is like there, and mix with men; I will practice only the good and true, and with these I will protect the beautiful. Much will be altered for the better when I am there."

These thoughts were noble and courageous, as our thoughts usually are at home, before we have had contact with the world, and have felt its storms and tempests, its thorns and thistles.

The five senses were highly cultivated, both inwardly and outwardly, in him and in all his brothers, but each had one sense which in keenness and development surpassed the other four. With the eldest, the keenest sense was *sight,* which he hoped would be of great service to him. He had eyes for all times and all men—eyes that could discover hidden treasures in the depth of the earth, and look into people's hearts as through a pane of glass; he could see more than most people in the cheek that blushes or turns pale, or in the eye that looks down or smiles. Stags and antelopes followed him to the western boundary of his home, and there he found the wild swans. These he followed towards the north-west, far away from his native land, which extended eastward to the end of the earth. He opened his eyes with amazement! How many things were to be seen hero, and so different to the pictures he had seen in his father's castle At first he nearly lost his eyes in astonishment at all the flitter and worthless mockery brought forth to illustrate the beautiful, but he did not lose them, and they soon found full employment. He meant to go straightforwardly and thoroughly to work in his endeavors to find the true, the beautiful, and the good. But how were they represented in the world? He saw that the crown which belonged to the beautiful by right was often bestowed upon the ugly; that the good was frequently passed by unnoticed, while mediocrity was applauded when it should have been hissed; folks looked at the dress more than the wearer, and thought more of a name than of doing their duty; they trusted more to reputation than to real usefulness. Everywhere it was alike.

"I must make a vigorous protest against these things," he said, and accordingly did so. But while he was searching for the truth, the evil one, the father of lies, came to interrupt him; the demon would have plucked out the *Seer's* eyes gladly, but that would have been too direct a way for him to take, he went more cunningly to work. He permitted the young man to seek for and find the beautiful and the good; but while he was gazing upon them, the evil one blew one mote after another into each of his eyes, and this would, of course, injure the strongest sight. Then he blew upon the motes, and they became beams, so that the *Seer* was like a blind man in the world, and had no longer any faith in it; his clearness of vision was gone. He had lost his good opinion of the world as well as of himself, and when a man gives up the world and himself too, it is all over with him.

"All over," cried the wild swans, as they flew across the sea to the east. "All over," chirped the swallows, also skimming eastward to the Tree of the Sun. They did not bring home good news.

"The *Seer* has not had a good time of it, I fear," said the second brother, "but the *Hearer* may get on better."

This one possessed the sense of *hearing* to a very high degree; so keen was this sense that it was said he could hear the grass grow. He took an affectionate leave of them all at home, and rode off full of good intentions and provided with good abilities. The swallows went with him, and he followed the swans until he found himself out in the world and far away from home. But he soon perceived that one may have too much even of a good thing. His hearing was too sensitive; he not only heard the grass grow, but could hear every man's heart beat, in sorrow or in joy. The whole world to him was like an enormous clock factory, where all the clocks were going, "tick tick," and all the turret clocks striking, "ding, dong." It was unbearable; for a long time his ears endured it, but at last the hubbub and noise became too much for him to bear. Good-for-nothing boys of sixty years old—years alone do not make a man—raised a tumult which might have made the *Hearer* laugh but for the applause which followed, echoing through every street and house; it was even heard on the high road. Falsehood thrust itself forward, declaring it was the master, the bells on the fool's cap jingled and pretended to be church bells; at last the noise became so terrible for the *Hearer* that he thrust his fingers into his ears; still he could hear false notes and bad singing, gossip and idle words, scandal and slander, groaning and moaning, without and within. "Oh, Heaven, have pity!" He thrust his fingers farther and farther into his ears, till at last the drums burst! And so now he could hear nothing at all of the true, the beautiful, and the good, for his hearing was the means by which he hoped to succeed. He became silent and mistrustful, and at last had faith in no one, not even himself; and hoping no longer to bring home the precious jewel, he gave it up, and himself too, which was worse than all.

The birds flying towards the east carried the news, and after a time it reached the castle in the Tree of the Sun.

"*I* will try now," said the third brother. "I have a keen *nose.*" That was not a very elegant way of putting it, but it was his way, and we must make the best of it. He had a bright, happy temper, and was a real poet besides; he could make many things appear poetical by the way in which he spoke of them, and ideas struck him long before they occurred to the minds of others. "I can *smell fire*" he would say; and he attributed his ability to appreciate beauty to the keen sense of smell which he possessed in a remarkable degree. Every fragrant place in the world of the beautiful has its frequenters. One man feels at home in the atmosphere of the tavern, among flaring tallow candles, where the smell of spirits mingles with that of bad tobacco; another likes to sit amid an overpowering scent of jasmine, or perfume himself with scented olive oil. One man seeks the fresh sea air, while another climbs to the summit of a lofty mountain to look down upon the busy life in miniature beneath him.

When he spoke in this way it seemed as if he had already seen the world—as if he already knew, and associated with mankind. But this was intuitive—the poetic soul within him; a heavenly gift bestowed upon him at his birth. He took leave of his family in the Tree of the Sun, and journeyed on foot from the pleasant scenes around his home. When he reached the boundary he placed himself on an ostrich's back, for it can run faster than a horse, and when he met the wild swans he swung himself on the strongest of them, for he liked variety; and away he flew over the sea to distant lands, where there were great forests, deep lakes, lofty mountains, and imposing cities. Wherever he came it seemed as if sunshine traveled with him over the fields, for every bush and flower breathed forth new fragrance, as if they knew that a friend and protector was near; some one who understood them and appreciated their worth. The stunted rose-bush put forth new leaves, unfolded its petals, and bore the most beautiful roses; every one noticed it, even the black, slimy wood-snail saw how beautiful it was.

"I will give my seal to the flower," said the snail; "I will trail my slime over it, that is all I can do."

"Thus it always fares with the beautiful in this world," said the poet.

And he made a song upon it, and sung it after his own fashion, but nobody listened. Then he gave a drummer twopence and a peacock's feather, and composed a song for the drum, and the drummer beat it through the streets of the town, and when people heard it they said: "That is a capital song." The poet wrote many songs about the true, the beautiful, and the good; and his songs were listened to in the tavern, where the tallow candles flared, in the fresh clover field, in the forest, and on the high seas; and it seemed as if this brother would be more fortunate than the other two.

But the evil one was vexed to see this, so he set to work with soot and incense, which he can mix artfully enough to confuse an angel—how much more easily a poor poet! The fiend knows how to manage such people. He so completely surrounded the poet with incense that he lost his senses, forgot his mission and his home, and at last lost himself and vanished in smoke.

But when the little birds heard of it they were sad, and did not sing a single song for three days. The black wood-snail became still blacker, not for grief but for envy. "They should have offered me incense," he said, "for I gave him the idea of his most famous song—the drum song of 'The Way of the World,' and I spat at the rose—I can bring a witness to prove it."

But the news of this did not reach the poet's home in India. The birds were all silent for three days; and when their lime of mourning was over, their grief had been so deep that they had forgotten for whom they had mourned. This is the way of the world.

"Now I must journey forth into the world and vanish like the rest," said the fourth brother. He was as bright and happy tempered as the third, but was not a poet, although he was sometimes witty. The two eldest had filled the castle with happiness, and it seemed as if the last brightness was departing. Seeing and hearing have always been thought most of among men, and those which they wished to keep in practice; the other senses are considered of less consequence.

But the youngest brother thought differently; his *taste* had been highly trained, and taste is of great importance. It analyzes everything that enters the mouth, as well as all that presents itself to the mind. This brother undertook the tasting of everything stored away in bottles and jars—this he called his rough work. He looked upon every man's mind as a kind of stock-pot in which something was brewing, and every country was a kind of mental kitchen to him.

"There are no delicacies here," he said, and so wished to go out into the world to find something delicate to suit his taste. "Fortune may do more for me than for my brothers. I shall set out, but what mode of conveyance shall

I choose? Are balloons invented yet?" he asked his father, who knew of all inventions, past, present, and future. Balloons had not yet been invented, nor steamboats, nor railways.

"Very well," he said, "then I shall choose a balloon; my father knows how they are to be made and guided. Nobody has invented one yet, and the people will think I am a ghostly vision. When I have finished with the balloon I shall burn it, and for this purpose you must give another invention; I mean a few lucifer matches."

He received what he asked for, and flew away; the birds went farther with him than they had done with the other brothers, they were inquisitive to know how this flight would end. Many of them came flocking together; they thought it must be some kind of new bird, and he soon had a good company of followers. They came in clouds, till the air became darkened by the birds as it is by the clouds of locusts flying over Egypt. Now he was out in the wide world; the balloon descended over one of the greatest cities, and the aeronaut placed himself on the highest point—the church steeple. The balloon rose into the air again, which it ought not to have done—no one knows what became of it, nor does it matter, for balloons had not yet been invented.

He sat on the church steeple; the birds followed him no longer, they were tired of him, and he of them. All the city chimneys were smoking.

"These are altars erected to thy honor," said the wind, who wished to converse with him as he sat there boldly looking down upon the people in the street. One came walking along proud of his purse; another of the key he carried at his girdle, although he had nothing to lock up; one took pride in his moth-eaten coat; another in his worn-out body.

"Vanity! I must go down soon, and touch and taste; but I shall sit here a little longer, for the wind blows pleasantly upon me; I will remain as long as it continues to blow, and take a little rest. It is pleasant to sleep late in the morning when one has a great deal to do," said the lazy man, "so I shall stay here while the wind blows, for I like it."

He remained where he was; but as he sat upon the weather-cock of the steeple, which turned round and round with him, he thought the same wind still blew, and that he might just as well stay there.

But in the castle on the Tree of the Sun in India everything was lonely and quiet since the brothers had gone away one after another.

"Nothing goes well with them," said the father. "They will never bring home the sparkling gem, I shall not receive it; they are all dead and gone." So saying he bent over the Book of Truth, and gazed at the page on which life after death was spoken of, but for him it appeared blank.

His blind daughter was his consolation and joy; she clung to him with sincere affection, and she wished the precious jewel might be found and brought home for the sake of his happiness and peace of mind.

With tender longing she thought of her brothers. Where were they? Where did they dwell? She ardently wished she might dream of them; but strange to say, not even in dreams was she brought near to them. But at last one night she dreamed that she heard her brothers' voices calling to her from the far-off world, and that she could not resist going to them, and yet it seemed as if she did not leave her father's house. She could not see her brothers, but she *felt* a burning fire in her hand, which however did not hurt her, for it was the jewel she was bringing her father. When she awoke she fancied she still held the stone, but she only clutched the knob of her distaff. She had been spinning constantly during the long winter evenings, and threads, finer than those of a spider's web, were wound round the distaff; human eyes would not have been able to see these threads when separated from each other; she had moistened them with her tears, and the twist was as strong as a rope. She rose feeling sure that her dream was a reality, and made up her mind as to what she would do.

It was still night, and her father was asleep. She gently kissed his hand, then took her distaff and fastened the end of the thread to her father's house. As she was blind, she would never have been able to find her way back again without this aid; she must hold the thread fast, and not trust to others or even to herself. She plucked four leaves from the Tree of the Sun, which she gave up to the wind and weather, that they might be carried to her brothers as letters of greeting in case she did not meet them in the wide world.

Poor blind girl, what was to become of her in those countries so far away? But she had the invisible thread to which she could hold fast, and she possessed a gift which all the others had been without; this was thoroughness, and it made her feel as if she had eyes even at the tips of her fingers, and could hear from the depth of her heart. She journeyed quietly through the noisy, bustling, wonderful world, and wherever she went the sky grew brighter, and a rainbow above in the blue heavens seemed to encircle the dark earth. She felt the warm sunshine, she heard the birds sing, and she smelled the fragrance of the orange groves and apple orchards so strongly that she seemed to taste it. Gentle voices and sweet songs reached her ear, as well as discordant sounds and harsh words, and thoughts and opinions were in striking contrast to each other.

The echo of human thoughts and feelings penetrated the inmost recesses of her heart. She heard the following words sung mournfully:

"Our life on earth is a shadow vain.
A night of sorrow and bitter pain."

But then a brighter strain would follow:

"Our life on earth is a fragrant rose.
With its sunshine, joy, and sweet repose."

And if one stanza pained her:

"Each of us thinks of himself alone;
This truth, at least, is most clearly shown."

Then came the answer:

"God's love all through this world shall guide us,
Nor need we fear whate'er betide us."

She did indeed hear such words as these:

"On earth such petty strife is seen
That all seems paltry, vain, and mean."

But there were also words of comfort:

"Much is achieved and good is done
By many who live and die unknown."

Sometimes she heard a mocking voice:

"Shall we not join in the common cry,
And scorn all gifts from the throne on high?"

But in the blind girl's heart a much stronger voice sang:

"Trust thou in God, and falter never.
His holy will be done for ever!"

And whenever she came among human beings, men or women, young or old, the knowledge of the true, the beautiful, and the good entered their hearts; wherever she went, whether it was into the artist's studio, the spacious hall decorated for a festival, or the crowded factory with its whirring wheels, it seemed as if a ray of sunlight came shining in. Kind words were uttered, the flowers gave forth a sweeter fragrance, and a living dewdrop fell upon the exhausted heart.

But the evil one could not see this and remain happy. He is more cunning than ten thousand men, and soon found means to bring about what he wanted. He went to the marsh and collected a few little bubbles of stagnant water; then he muttered the echoes of untrue words over them that they might become strong. He blended hymns of praise with as many lying epitaphs as he could find, boiled them in tears shed by envy, and put upon them rouge which he had scraped from faded cheeks. From these he produced a maiden like the blind girl in form and appearance; men called her the angel of thoroughness. The evil spirit's stratagem succeeded; no one knew the true one from the imitation, and indeed how could they?

"Trust thou in God and falter never.
His holy will be done for ever!"

So sung the blind girl in full faith; she had given the four green leaves from the Tree of the Sun to the winds, as letters of greeting to her brothers, and she was quite sure that the leaves would reach them. She fully believed that the gem which out shines all the glories of the earth was to be found, and that it would gleam from a human forehead, even in her father's castle. "Even in my father's castle," she said. "Yes, this gem is to be found on earth, and I shall bring more than the mere promise of it with me. I feel it grow and strengthen in my closed hand; every grain of truth which the wind caught and brought towards me I have received and treasured; I allowed the fragrance of the beautiful, of which there is so much in this world, even for the blind, to blow upon it. I took the beatings of a heart engaged in a good action, and added them to my store. All I can bring is nothing more than dust, yet it is part of the gem we seek, and there is plenty, my hand is quite full of it."

She was soon at home again, carried there in a flight of thought; she had never ceased to hold the invisible thread she had fastened to her father's house. As she stretched out her hand to her father the powers of evil rushed over the Tree of the Sun with the violence of a whirlwind; a terrible blast dashed through the open doors into the sanctuary, where the Book of Truth lay.

"It will be blown to atoms by the wind," said the father, as he seized the hand she held towards him.

"No," she answered, with calm assurance, "it is indestructible. I feel its warmth in my very soul."

Then her father saw that a dazzling brightness shone from the white page upon which the glittering dust had fallen from her hand. It was there to prove the certainty of eternal life, and upon the page gleamed one shining word—only one—the word BELIEVE. The four brothers were also soon at home again with the father and daughter; when the green leaf from home had fallen upon the bosom of each a longing had seized them to return. They came, accompanied by the birds of passage, the stag, the antelope, and all the creatures of the forest, who wished to share their happiness.

One can often see, when a sunbeam enters a dusty room through a crack in the door, how a whirling column of dust seems to float round; but this was not ordinary, worthless, common dust, which the blind girl had brought—even the rainbow's hues are dim compared with the beauty which shone from the page on which she scattered it. The glowing word BELIEVE had the brightness of the true, the beautiful, and the good; it was brighter than the marvelous pillar of fire which led Moses and the children of Israel through the desert. From the word BELIEVE rose the bridge of hope, reaching even to the infinite love in the heavenly kingdom.

What the Old Man Does Is Always Right

I will tell you a story that I heard when I was still a little boy. Every time I thought of the story it seemed to me to become more and more beautiful, for it is with stories as it is with a great many people—they get more charming as they grow older.

I daresay you have all been into the country, and know what a very old farm-house with a thatched roof looks like. On such a roof moss and weeds generally grow wild, and there is always a stork's nest on the topmost gable—the stork is indispensable. The walls of the house are sloping, the windows low, and only one of the latter is made so that it can be opened. The oven makes the wall project like a fat little body. By the side of the fence and under the branches of the overhanging elder-tree is a pond with a few ducks. A dog, who barks at everybody and everything, is also lying there chained up.

Well, a farm-house just like that stood out in the country, and in it lived an old couple—a peasant and his wife. Although they possessed but little, there was one thing which they had that they could have done without—a horse, which grazed on what it found by the roadside. The old peasant rode to town on the horse, and it was often borrowed by the neighbors, who rendered the old people many a service in return. But still they thought it would be best if they sold the horse or exchanged it for something that might be of more use to them. But what was it to be? "That you know best, old man," said the wife. "It happens to be fair-day to-day, so ride to town and sell the horse, or make a good exchange. Whatever you do will be right. Go to the fair."

In it lived an old couple—a peasant and his wife.

She tied on his scarf for him, for she knew how to do that better than he. She tied it in a double bow, and it looked very pretty. She smoothed his hat with the palm of her hand, and kissed him on the lips.

Then he rode away on the horse which was to be sold or exchanged. Oh yes, the old man understood his business. The sun was scorching and there was not a cloud in the sky. The road was very dusty, and a great many people were going to the fair in carts, on horseback, or on foot. There was no shade anywhere from the burning sun.

Among the rest there was a man going along driving a cow to market. The cow was as beautiful as a cow could be. "She must give fine milk," thought the peasant. "That would be a good exchange: the cow for the horse."

"Hallo! You there with the cow!" he cried. Look here, I should think a horse is worth more than a cow; but that doesn't matter, a cow would be of more use to me. If you like, we'll change."

"All right—willingly," said the man with the cow; and so they changed.

So that was finished, and the peasant could very well have gone home again, for he had done what he had come out to do, but having once made up his mind to go to the fair, he thought he would go all the same, just to have a look at it, and so he went with his cow to the town.

Leading the cow he marched along briskly, and after a short time he overtook a man who was driving a sheep. It was a fine fat sheep, and well covered with good wool.

"I should like to have that," thought our peasant; "it would find plenty of grass by our fence, and in winter we could have it with us in the room. It would really be more suitable for us to have a sheep than a cow. Shall we change?"

The man with the sheep was ready at once, and the exchange took place. Our peasant continued his way along the high road with his sheep.

Soon he perceived another man who had reached the road from the fields, and who was carrying a large goose under his arm.

"That's a heavy bird that you have there; its feathers and fat are a pleasure to behold; it would look well in our pond at home with a string round its leg. It would be just the thing for my old woman; she could save all kinds of leavings for it. How often I have heard her wish that we had a goose! Now, perhaps, she can have one—and if it's possible, it shall be hers! Shall we change? I'll give you my sheep for your goose and thank you into the bargain."

The other had no objection to this, and so they changed. Our peasant received the goose.

By this time he had nearly reached the town, and the crowd on the high road kept continually increasing. People and cattle thronged together; they filled the road and overflowed on to the side-paths, and at the toll-gate they even went into the toll-keeper's potato field, where his only hen was strutting about tied to a string, lest it might be frightened at the crowd, go astray, and get lost. The feathers in its tail were very short, and it blinked one eye and looked very wise.

"Cluck, cluck!" said the hen. What it meant by that I don't know, but when our peasant caught sight of it, he immediately thought: "That is the finest hen I've ever seen—it's even finer than the parson's brood hen. By Jove! I should like to have that hen. A hen can always find a grain of corn, and can almost feed itself; I believe it would be a good exchange if I could get it for my goose."

"Shall we change?" he asked the toll-keeper.

"Change?" said the latter. "Well, that wouldn't be half bad!" And so they changed. The toll-keeper got the goose, the peasant the hen.

He had done a deal of business on his journey to town; it was hot too, and he was tired. A drop of spirits and something to eat was what he wanted, so he stopped at the next inn. He was just going in, when he met the ostler coming out of the door carrying a large sack.

"What have you got there?" asked the peasant.

"Rotten apples!" answered the man; "a whole sackful, enough for the pigs."

"But that's great waste! I wish my old woman at home could see that. Last year, the old tree by the turf-hole bore only one apple; but it was saved, and lay in the cupboard till it was quite spoiled and rotten. "It's something, after all," said my old woman; but here she could see a good deal, a whole sackful. I really wish she could see it!"

"What would you give me for the sackful?" asked the man.

"What would I give? I would give you my hen in exchange," and he gave the hen too, received the apples, and went with them into the inn. He stood the sack carefully against the stove and went up to the bar. But he had forgotten that there was a fire in the stove. There were a good many customers there: horse-dealers, drovers, and two Englishmen. The Englishmen were so rich that their pockets were stuffed out and almost bursting with gold; and they were betting too, as you shall hear.

Hiss-s-s! Hiss-s-s! What was that by the stove? The apples were beginning to roast.

"What's that?"

"Well, you see—" said our peasant; and then he told the whole story of the horse that he had exchanged for a cow, and so on right down to the apples.

"Well, your old woman will cuff you nicely when you get home; you'll come in for something!" said the Englishman.

"What! Cuff me?" said the old man; "she'll kiss me and say 'What the old man does is always right.' "

"I'll bet you she doesn't," said the Englishman. "I'll bet gold coin by the ton—a hundred pounds to the hundredweight."

"A bushelful will be enough," answered the peasant, "I can only lay a bushel of apples against it, and myself and the old woman into the bargain—that, I think, will be a piled up measure too!"

"Done!" cried the others, and the bet was made.

The landlord's cart was brought out and the Englishmen and the peasant got in; on they drove and soon stopped before the peasant's little house.

"Good evening, old woman!

"Good evening, old man!"

"I've made an exchange."

"Ah! you understand your business!" said his wife, embracing him, and looking neither at the sack, nor at the strangers.

"I changed the horse for a cow."

"That's glorious! What nice milk we shall have now, and butter and cheese on the table too! That was an excellent exchange."

"Yes! but I changed the cow afterwards for a sheep."

"Well, so much the better," replied his wife; "you think of everything. For a sheep we have pasture enough, and we can have milk and cheese from a sheep too, besides woolen stockings and jackets Those the cow does not give, she only loses her hair. How you think of everything!"

"But I changed the sheep after all for a goose!"

"Then we shall really have roast goose this year, my dear old man! You are always thinking of something to please me. How lovely that is! We can let the goose go about tied by a string and fatten it before we roast it."

"But I changed the goose for a hen!" said the man.

"A hen! That was a good exchange!" cried the woman. "The hen will lay eggs, and hatch them, we shall have little chickens and a whole poultry-yard. Why that was what I wished for most of all!"

"Yes, but I changed the fowl for a sackful of rotten apples!"

"What! Well, now I must really kiss you," said his wife. "My dear good husband! I'll tell you something. Do you know you were hardly gone this morning when I began to think how I could make you something very nice for to-night. Eggs and bacon with some chives, I thought. I had the eggs and the bacon too; all I wanted was the chives. So I went over to the schoolmasters'—they had some chives, I know—but the schoolmaster's wife is very mean, sweet as she looks. I asked her to lend me a handful of chives. "Lend!"

she answered; "nothing, absolutely nothing grows in our garden, not even a rotten apple; I couldn't even lend you one of those, my dear woman.' Now I can lend her ten, and even a whole sackful. I'm very glad of that—I shall die with laughter!" And then she gave him a good smacking kiss.

"Well, now I must really kiss you," said his wife.

"I like that!" cried both the Englishmen together. "Always going downhill, and yet always happy. Why, that alone is worth the money!"

So they paid a hundredweight of gold to the peasant who had not been cuffed but kissed.

Yes, it always pays when the wife sees, and always acknowledges that her husband is the cleverer of the two, and that what he does is right.

You see, that is my story. I heard it when I was still a child, and now you have heard it too, and know that "what the old man does is always right."

Grandmother

Grandmother is very old; she has many wrinkles, and her hair is quite white; but her eyes, which are as bright as two stars and still more beautiful, look at one in a kind and friendly way, and it does one good to gaze into them. Then, too, she can tell the most charming stories, and she has a gown with great big flowers worked upon it, and made of a good heavy silk that rustles. Grandmother knows a great deal, for she was born long before father and mother, that's quite certain. Grandmother has a hymn-book with great silver clasps, and very often reads out of it; in the middle of it lies a rose, quite flat and dry. It is not so beautiful as the roses she has standing in the glass, and yet she smiles at it more pleasantly than at the others, and it even makes tears come into her eyes. I wonder why grandmother looks at the faded flower in the old book like that! Do you know? Every time that grandmother's tears fall upon the flower the color becomes fresh again, the rose swells up and fills the whole room with its fragrance: the walls sink as if they were only mist, and all around her is the glorious greenwood, where the sun shines through the foliage of the trees; and grandmother—why, she is quite young, she is a charming girl with fair curls, with full rosy cheeks, pretty and graceful, and fresher than any rose; but the eyes, those gentle, happy eyes—yes, they still belong to grandmother. At her side sits a young man, tall and strong; he hands her the rose and she smiles—grandmother doesn't smile like that though—yes, she does! at this very minute. But he has vanished, and many thoughts, many forms float by: the handsome young man is gone, the rose lies in the hymn-book, and grandmother—well, she sits there again as an old woman, and gazes at the faded rose lying in the book.

Now grandmother is dead. She was sitting in her armchair telling a beautiful long long story; then she said that the story was ended, and that she was tired, so she leaned her head back to sleep a little. Her breathing could be heard as she slept; but it became lighter and lighter, and her countenance was full of happiness and peace. It seemed as if sunshine rested on her features; she smiled again, and then they said she was dead.

She was laid in the black coffin; there she lay shrouded in white linen, looking gentle and beautiful, though her eyes were closed; but every wrinkle had vanished, and she lay there with a smile upon her lips. Her hair was silver-white and venerable, and we were not afraid to look upon her who was still our dear, kind-hearted grandmother. And the hymn-book, was placed under her head, as she had herself wished, and the rose lay in the old book. Then they buried grandmother.

On the grave, close to the church wall, they planted a rose-tree. It was full of roses, and the nightingale flew singing over the flowers and the grave. On the organ inside the church were played the most beautiful psalms that were contained in the old book under the head of the dead. The moon shone down upon the grave, but the dead one was not there; every child could go there safely at night and pluck a rose from the church-yard wall. One who is dead knows more than all we living ones. The dead know what terror would come over us if such a strange thing were to happen as their appearance among us; the dead are better than all of us—they return no more. The earth has been heaped upon the coffin, and in the coffin there is earth too; the leaves of the hymn-book are dust, and into dust has crumbled the rose with all its recollections. But above there bloom fresh roses; there the nightingale sings and the organ peals, and there lives the remembrance of the old grandmother with the gentle, ever youthful eyes. Eyes can never die. Ours will one day behold grandmother again, young and beautiful, as when for the first time she kissed the fresh red rose that is now dust in the grave.

THE END
D·S·W·